DARK WITCH

Nora Roberts

BERKLEY
NEW YORK

BERKLEY
An imprint of Penguin Random House LLC
penguinrandomhouse.com

Library of Congress Cataloging-in-Publication Data

Roberts, Nora.
Dark witch / Nora Roberts.
pages cm
ISBN 978-0-425-25985-6
1. Americans—Ireland—Fiction. 2. Ireland—Fiction. 3. Man-woman relationships—Fiction. 4. Domestic fiction. I. Title.
PS3568.O243D375 2013
813'.54—dc23
2013006292

First Edition: October 2013

Printed in the United States of America
17th Printing

Book design by Kristin del Rosario

Nora Roberts

HOT ICE
SACRED SINS
BRAZEN VIRTUE
SWEET REVENGE
PUBLIC SECRETS
GENUINE LIES
CARNAL INNOCENCE
HONEST ILLUSIONS
DIVINE EVIL
PRIVATE SCANDALS
HIDDEN RICHES
TRUE BETRAYALS
MONTANA SKY
SANCTUARY
HOMEPORT
THE REEF
RIVER'S END
CAROLINA MOON
THE VILLA
MIDNIGHT BAYOU
THREE FATES
BIRTHRIGHT
NORTHERN LIGHTS
BLUE SMOKE
ANGELS FALL
HIGH NOON
TRIBUTE
BLACK HILLS
THE SEARCH
CHASING FIRE
THE WITNESS
WHISKEY BEACH
THE COLLECTOR
TONIGHT AND ALWAYS
THE LIAR
THE OBSESSION

DARK WITCH

From #1 *New York Times* bestselling author Nora Roberts comes a trilogy about the land we're drawn to, the family we learn to cherish, and the people we long to love. . . .

With indifferent parents, Iona Sheehan grew up craving devotion and acceptance. From her maternal grandmother, she learned where to find both: a land of lush forests, dazzling lakes, and centuries-old legends.

Ireland.

County Mayo, to be exact. Where her ancestors' blood and magic have flowed through generations—and where her destiny awaits.

Iona arrives in Ireland with nothing but her Nan's directions, an unfailingly optimistic attitude, and an innate talent with horses. Not far from the luxurious castle where she is spending a week, she finds her cousins, Branna and Connor O'Dwyer. And since family is family, they invite her into their home and their lives.

When Iona lands a job at the local stables, she meets the owner, Boyle McGrath. Cowboy, pirate, and wild tribal horseman, he's three of her biggest fantasy weaknesses all in one big, bold package.

Iona realizes that here she can make a home for herself—and live her life as she wants, even if that means falling head over heels for Boyle. But nothing is as it seems. An ancient evil has wound its way around Iona's family tree and must be defeated. Family and friends will fight with one another and for one another to keep the promise of hope—and love—alive. . . .

"When it comes to true romance, no one does it better than Nora."

—*Booklist* (starred review)

Series

Irish Born Trilogy
BORN IN FIRE
BORN IN ICE
BORN IN SHAME

Dream Trilogy
DARING TO DREAM
HOLDING THE DREAM
FINDING THE DREAM

Chesapeake Bay Saga
SEA SWEPT
RISING TIDES
INNER HARBOR
CHESAPEAKE BLUE

Gallaghers of Ardmore Trilogy
JEWELS OF THE SUN
TEARS OF THE MOON
HEART OF THE SEA

Three Sisters Island Trilogy
DANCE UPON THE AIR
HEAVEN AND EARTH
FACE THE FIRE

Key Trilogy
KEY OF LIGHT
KEY OF KNOWLEDGE
KEY OF VALOR

In the Garden Trilogy
BLUE DAHLIA
BLACK ROSE
RED LILY

Circle Trilogy
MORRIGAN'S CROSS
DANCE OF THE GODS
VALLEY OF SILENCE

Sign of Seven Trilogy
BLOOD BROTHERS
THE HOLLOW
THE PAGAN STONE

Bride Quartet
VISION IN WHITE
BED OF ROSES
SAVOR THE MOMENT
HAPPY EVER AFTER

The Inn BoonsBoro Trilogy
THE NEXT ALWAYS
THE LAST BOYFRIEND
THE PERFECT HOPE

The Cousins O'Dwyer Trilogy
DARK WITCH
SHADOW SPELL
BLOOD MAGICK

The Guardians Trilogy
STARS OF FORTUNE
BAY OF SIGHS
ISLAND OF GLASS

Ebooks by Nora Roberts

Cordina's Royal Family
AFFAIRE ROYALE
COMMAND PERFORMANCE
THE PLAYBOY PRINCE
CORDINA'S CROWN JEWEL

The Donovan Legacy
CAPTIVATED
ENTRANCED
CHARMED
ENCHANTED

The O'Hurleys
THE LAST HONEST WOMAN
DANCE TO THE PIPER
SKIN DEEP
WITHOUT A TRACE

Night Tales
NIGHT SHIFT
NIGHT SHADOW
NIGHTSHADE
NIGHT SMOKE
NIGHT SHIELD

The MacGregors
PLAYING THE ODDS
TEMPTING FATE
ALL THE POSSIBILITIES
ONE MAN'S ART
FOR NOW, FOREVER
REBELLION/IN FROM THE COLD
THE MACGREGOR BRIDES
THE WINNING HAND
THE MACGREGOR GROOMS
THE PERFECT NEIGHBOR

The Calhouns
COURTING CATHERINE
A MAN FOR AMANDA
FOR THE LOVE OF LILAH
SUZANNA'S SURRENDER
MEGAN'S MATE

Irish Legacy
IRISH THOROUGHBRED
IRISH ROSE
IRISH REBEL

LOVING JACK
BEST LAID PLANS
LAWLESS

BLITHE IMAGES
SONG OF THE WEST
SEARCH FOR LOVE
ISLAND OF FLOWERS
THE HEART'S VICTORY
FROM THIS DAY
HER MOTHER'S KEEPER
ONCE MORE WITH FEELING
REFLECTIONS
DANCE OF DREAMS
UNTAMED
THIS MAGIC MOMENT
ENDINGS AND BEGINNINGS
STORM WARNING
SULLIVAN'S WOMAN
FIRST IMPRESSIONS
A MATTER OF CHOICE

LESS OF A STRANGER
THE LAW IS A LADY
RULES OF THE GAME
OPPOSITES ATTRACT
THE RIGHT PATH
PARTNERS
BOUNDARY LINES
DUAL IMAGE
TEMPTATION
LOCAL HERO
THE NAME OF THE GAME
GABRIEL'S ANGEL
THE WELCOMING
TIME WAS
TIMES CHANGE
SUMMER LOVE
HOLIDAY WISHES

Nora Roberts & J. D. Robb

REMEMBER WHEN

J. D. Robb

NAKED IN DEATH
GLORY IN DEATH
IMMORTAL IN DEATH
RAPTURE IN DEATH
CEREMONY IN DEATH
VENGEANCE IN DEATH
HOLIDAY IN DEATH
CONSPIRACY IN DEATH
LOYALTY IN DEATH
WITNESS IN DEATH
JUDGMENT IN DEATH
BETRAYAL IN DEATH
SEDUCTION IN DEATH
REUNION IN DEATH
PURITY IN DEATH
PORTRAIT IN DEATH
IMITATION IN DEATH
DIVIDED IN DEATH
VISIONS IN DEATH
SURVIVOR IN DEATH
ORIGIN IN DEATH
MEMORY IN DEATH
BORN IN DEATH
INNOCENT IN DEATH
CREATION IN DEATH
STRANGERS IN DEATH
SALVATION IN DEATH
PROMISES IN DEATH
KINDRED IN DEATH
FANTASY IN DEATH
INDULGENCE IN DEATH
TREACHERY IN DEATH
NEW YORK TO DALLAS
CELEBRITY IN DEATH
DELUSION IN DEATH
CALCULATED IN DEATH
THANKLESS IN DEATH
CONCEALED IN DEATH
FESTIVE IN DEATH
OBSESSION IN DEATH
DEVOTED IN DEATH
BROTHERHOOD IN DEATH
APPRENTICE IN DEATH

Anthologies

FROM THE HEART
A LITTLE MAGIC
A LITTLE FATE

MOON SHADOWS
(with Jill Gregory, Ruth Ryan Langan, and Marianne Willman)

The Once Upon Series

(with Jill Gregory, Ruth Ryan Langan, and Marianne Willman)

ONCE UPON A CASTLE
ONCE UPON A STAR
ONCE UPON A DREAM
ONCE UPON A ROSE
ONCE UPON A KISS
ONCE UPON A MIDNIGHT

SILENT NIGHT
(with Susan Plunkett, Dee Holmes, and Claire Cross)

OUT OF THIS WORLD
(with Laurell K. Hamilton, Susan Krinard, and Maggie Shayne)

BUMP IN THE NIGHT
(with Mary Blayney, Ruth Ryan Langan, and Mary Kay McComas)

DEAD OF NIGHT
(with Mary Blayney, Ruth Ryan Langan, and Mary Kay McComas)

THREE IN DEATH

SUITE 606
(with Mary Blayney, Ruth Ryan Langan, and Mary Kay McComas)

IN DEATH

THE LOST
(with Patricia Gaffney, Mary Blayney, and Ruth Ryan Langan)

THE OTHER SIDE
(with Mary Blayney, Patricia Gaffney, Ruth Ryan Langan, and Mary Kay McComas)

TIME OF DEATH

THE UNQUIET
(with Mary Blayney, Patricia Gaffney, Ruth Ryan Langan, and Mary Kay McComas)

MIRROR, MIRROR
(with Mary Blayney, Elaine Fox, Mary Kay McComas, and R. C. Ryan)

DOWN THE RABBIT HOLE
(with Mary Blayney, Elaine Fox, Mary Kay McComas, and R. C. Ryan)

Also available . . .

THE OFFICIAL NORA ROBERTS COMPANION
(edited by Denise Little and Laura Hayden)

To the power of family,
those born, those made

When shall we three meet again?
In thunder, lightning, or in rain?
When the hurlyburly's done,
When the battle's lost and won.

—WILLIAM SHAKESPEARE, *Macbeth*

1

Winter 1263

NEAR THE SHADOW OF THE CASTLE, DEEP IN THE GREEN woods, Sorcha led her children through the gloom toward home. The two youngest rode the sturdy pony, with Teagan, barely three, nodding with every plod. Weary, Sorcha thought, after the excitement of Imbolg, the bonfires, and the feasting.

"Mind your sister, Eamon."

At five, Eamon's minding was a quick poke to wake up his baby sister before he went back to nibbling on the bannocks his mother had baked that morning.

"Home in your bed soon," Sorcha crooned when Teagan whined. "Home soon."

She'd tarried too long in the clearing, she thought now. And though Imbolg celebrated the first stirrings in the womb of the Earth Mother, night fell too fast and hard in winter.

A bitter one it had been, crackling with icy winds and blowing snow and ice-tipped rain. The fog had lived all winter, creeping, crawling, curtaining sun and moon. Too often in that wind, in that fog, she'd heard her name called—a beckoning she refused to answer. Too often in that world of white and gray, she'd seen the dark.

She refused to truck with it.

Her man had begged her to take the children and stay with his *fine* while he waged his battles over that endless winter.

As the wife of the *cennfine*, every door would open for her. And in her own right, for what and who she was, welcome would always be made.

But she needed her woods, her cabin, her place. She needed to be apart as much as she needed to breathe.

She would tend her own, always, her home and her hearth, her craft and her duties. And most of all, the precious children she and Daithi had made. She had no fear of the night.

She was known as the Dark Witch, and her power was great.

But just then she felt sorely a woman missing her man, yearning for the warmth of him, the fine, hard body pressed to hers in the cold and lonely dark.

What did she care for war? For the greed and ambitions of all the petty kings? She only wanted her man home safe and whole.

When he came home, they would make another baby, and she would feel that life inside her again. She mourned still the life she'd lost on a brutal black night when the first winter wind had blown through her woods like the sound of weeping.

How many had she healed? How many had she saved? And yet when the blood had poured from her, when that fragile life had flooded away, no magick, no offering, no bargain with the gods had saved it.

But then she knew, too well, healing others came more easily than healing self. And the gods as fickle as a giddy girl in May.

"Look! Look!" Brannaugh, her eldest at seven, danced off the hard path, with their big hound on her heels. "The blackthorn's blooming! It's a sign."

She saw it now, the hint of those creamy white blossoms among the black, tangled branches. Her first bitter thought was while Brighid, the fertility-bringing goddess, blessed the earth, her own womb lay empty inside her.

Then she watched her girl, her first pride, sharp-eyed, pink-cheeked, spinning through the snow. She'd been blessed, Sorcha reminded herself. Three times blessed.

"It's a sign, Ma." Dark hair flying with every spin, Brannaugh lifted her face to the dimming light. "Of coming spring."

"Aye, it's that. A good sign." As had been the gloomy day, as the old hag Cailleach couldn't find firewood without the bright sun. So spring would come early, so the legend went.

The blackthorn bloomed bright, tempting the flowers to follow.

She saw the hope in her child's eyes, as she'd seen it at the bonfire in other eyes, heard it in the voices. And Sorcha searched inside herself for that spark of hope.

But found only dread.

He would come again tonight—she could already sense him. Lurking, waiting, plotting. Inside, she thought, inside the cabin behind the bolted door, with her charms laid out to protect her babies. To protect herself.

She clucked to the pony to quicken his pace, whistled for the dog. "Come along now, Brannaugh, your sister's all but asleep already."

"Da comes home in the spring."

Though her heart stayed heavy, Sorcha smiled and took Brannaugh's hand. "He does that, home by Bealtaine, and we'll have a great feast."

"Can I see him tonight, with you? In the fire?"

"There's much to do. The animals need tending before bed."

"For a moment?" Brannaugh tipped her face back, her eyes, gray as smoke, pleading. "Just to see him for a moment, then I can dream he's home again."

As she would herself, Sorcha thought, and now her smile came from her heart. "For a moment, *m'inion*, when the work's done."

"And you take your medicine."

Sorcha lifted her brows. "Will I then? Do I look to you as if I'm in need of it?"

"You're still pale, Ma." Brannaugh kept her voice beneath the wind.

"Just a wee bit tired, and you're not to worry. Here now, hold on to your sister, Eamon! Alastar smells home, and she's likely to fall off."

"She rides better than Eamon, and me as well."

"Aye, well, the horse is her talisman, but she's near sleeping on his back."

The path turned; the pony's hooves rang on the frozen ground as he trotted toward the shed beside the cabin.

"Eamon, see to Alastar, an extra scoop of grain tonight. You had your fill, didn't you?" she said as her boy began to mutter.

He grinned at her, handsome as a summer morning, and though he could hop down as quick as a rabbit, he held out his arms.

He'd always been one for a cuddle, Sorcha thought, hugging him as she lifted him down.

She didn't have to tell Brannaugh to start her chores. The girl ran the house nearly as well as her mother. Sorcha took Teagan in her arms, murmuring, soothing, as she carried her into the cabin.

"It's dreaming time, my darling."

"I'm a pony, and I gallop all day."

"Oh aye, the prettiest of ponies, and the fastest of all."

The fire, down to embers after the hours away, barely held back the cold. As she carried the baby to bed, Sorcha held out a hand to the hearth. The flames leapt up, simmered over the ashes.

She tucked Teagan into the bunk, smoothed her hair—bright as sunlight like her father's—and waited until her eyes—deep and dark like her mother's—closed.

"Sweet dreams only," she murmured, touching the charm she'd hung over the beds of her babies. "Safe and sound through all the night. All you are and all you see hold you through dark into light."

She kissed the soft cheek, and as she straightened, winced at the pull in her belly. The ache came and went, but came more strongly as the winter held. So she would take her daughter's advice and make a potion.

"Brighid, on this your day, help me heal. I have three children who need me. I cannot leave them alone."

She left Teagan sleeping, and went to help the older children with the chores.

When night fell, too fast, too soon, she secured the door before repeating her nighttime ritual with Eamon.

"I'm not tired, not a bit," he claimed as his eyes drooped.

"Oh, I can see that. I see you're wide awake and raring. Will you fly again tonight, *mhic*?"

"I will, aye, high in the sky. Will you teach me more tomorrow? Can I take Roibeard out come morning?"

"That I will, and that you can. The hawk is yours, and you see him, you know him, and feel him. So rest now." She ruffled his bark brown hair, kissed his eyes—wild and blue as his father's—closed.

When she came down from the loft, she found Brannaugh already by the fire, with the hound that was hers.

Glowing, Sorcha thought, with health—thank the goddess—and with the power she didn't yet fully hold or understand. There was time for that, she prayed there was time yet for that.

"I made the tea," Brannaugh told her. "Just as you taught me. You'll feel better, I think, after you drink it."

"Do you tend me now, *mo chroi*?" Smiling, Sorcha picked up the tea, sniffed it, nodded. "You have the touch, that you do. Healing is a strong gift. With it, you'll be welcome, and needed, wherever you go."

"I don't want to go anywhere. I want to be here with you and Da, and Eamon and Teagan, always."

"One day you may look beyond our wood. And there will be a man."

Brannaugh snorted. "I don't want a man. What would I do with a man?"

"Ah well, that's a story for another day." She sat with her girl by the fire, wrapped a wide shawl around them both. And drank her tea. And when Brannaugh touched her hand, she turned hers over, linked fingers.

"All right then, but for only a moment. You need your bed."

"Can I do it? Can I bring the vision?"

"See what you have, then. Do what you will. See him, Brannaugh, the man you came from. It's love that brings him."

Sorcha watched the smoke swirl, the flames leap and then settle. Good, she thought, impressed. The girl learned so quickly.

The image tried to form, in the hollows and valleys of the flame. A fire within a fire. Silhouettes, movements, and, for a moment, the murmur of voices from so far away.

She saw the intensity on her daughter's face, the light sheen of sweat from the effort. Too much, she thought. Too much for one so young.

"Here now," she said quietly. "We'll do it together."

She pushed her power out, merged it with Brannaugh's.

A fast roar, a spin of smoke, a dance of sparks. Then clear.

And he was there, the man they both longed for.

Sitting at another fire, within a circle of stones. His bright hair braided to fall over the dark cape wrapped around his broad shoulders. The *dealg* of his rank pinned to it glittered in the light of the flames.

The brooch she'd forged for him in fire and magick—the hound, the horse, the hawk.

"He looks weary," Brannaugh said, and leaned her head against her mother's arm. "But so handsome. The most handsome of men."

"That he is. Handsome, and strong, and brave." And oh, she longed for him.

"Can you see when he comes home?"

"Not all can be seen. Perhaps when he's closer, I'll have a sign. But tonight, we see he's safe and well, and that's enough."

"He thinks of you." Brannaugh looked over, into her mother's face. "I can feel it. Can he feel us thinking of him?"

"He hasn't the gift, but he has the heart, the love. So perhaps he can. To bed now. I'll be up soon."

"The blackthorn is blooming, and the old hag did not see the sun today. He comes home soon." Rising, Brannaugh kissed her mother. The dog trotted up the ladder with her.

Alone, Sorcha watched her love in the fire. And alone, she wept.

Even as she dried her tears she heard it. The beckoning.

He would comfort her, he would warm her—such were his seductive lies. He would give her all she could want, and more. She had only to give herself to him.

"I will never be yours."

You will. You are. Come now, and know all the pleasures, all the glory. All the power.

"You will never have me, or what I hold inside me."

Now the image in the fire shifted. And he came into the flames. Cabhan, whose power and purpose were darker than the winter night. Who wanted her—her body, her soul, her magick.

The sorcerer desired her, for she felt his lust like sweaty hands on her skin. But more, more, she knew, he coveted her gift. His greed for it hung heavy in the air.

In the flames he smiled, so handsome, so ruthless.

I will have you, Sorcha the Dark. You and all you are. We are meant. We are the same.

No, she thought, we are not the same, but as day to night, light to dark, where the only merging comes in shadows.

So alone you are, and burdened. Your man leaves you a cold bed. Come warm yourself in mine; feel the heat. Make that heat with me. Together, we rule all the world.

Her spirits sagged, the ache and pull inside her twisted toward pain.

So she rose, let the warm wind come to blow through her hair. Let the power pour in until she shone with it. And saw, even in the flames, the lust and greed in Cabhan's face.

Here is what he wanted, she knew, the glory that rushed through her blood. And this was what he would never have.

"Know my mind and feel my power, then and now and every hour. You offer me your dark desire, come to me in smoke and fire. Betray my blood, my babes, my man, to rule o'er all, only take your hand. So my answer to thee comes through wind and sea, rise maiden, mother, hag in trinity. As I will, so mote it be."

She threw out her arms, released the fury, fully female, whirled in, flung it toward the beat of his heart.

An instant of pure, wild pleasure erupted inside her when she heard his cry of rage and pain, when she saw that rage and pain burst onto his face against the flames.

Then the fire was just a fire, simmering low for the night, bringing a bit of warmth against the bitter. Her cabin was just a cabin, quiet and dim. And she was just a woman alone with her children sleeping.

She slumped down in the chair, wrapping an arm around the tearing in her belly.

Cabhan was gone, for now. But her fear remained, of him, and that if no potion or prayer healed her body, she would leave her children motherless.

Defenseless.

SHE WOKE WITH HER YOUNGEST CURLED WITH HER, FOUND comfort even as she shifted to rise for the day.

"Ma, Ma, stay."

"There now, my sunbeam, I have work. And you should be in your own bed."

"The bad man came. He killed my ponies."

A fist of panic squeezed Sorcha's heart. Cabhan touching her children—their bodies, their minds, their souls? It brought her unspeakable fear, unspeakable rage.

"Just a dream, my baby." She cuddled Teagan close, rocked and soothed. "Just a dream."

But dreams had power and risks.

"My ponies screamed, and I couldn't save them. He set them afire, and they screamed. Alastar came and knocked the bad man down. I rode away on Alastar, but I couldn't save the ponies. I'm afraid of the bad man in the dream."

"He won't hurt you. I'll never let him hurt you. Only dream ponies." Eyes tightly closed, she kissed Teagan's bright, tousled hair, her cheeks. "We'll dream of more. Green ones, and blue ones."

"Green ponies!"

"Oh aye, green as the hills." Snuggling, Sorcha lifted a hand, circled her finger, twirled it, twirled it until ponies—blue ones, green ones, red ones, yellow ones—danced in the air above their heads. Listening to her youngest giggle, Sorcha stored up her fears, her anger, closed them in with determination.

He would never harm her children. She would see him dead, and herself with him, before she allowed it.

"All the ponies to their oats now. And you come with me then, and we'll break our fast as well."

"Is there honey?"

"Aye." The simple wish for a treat made Sorcha smile. "There'll be honey for good girls."

"I'm good!"

"You are the purest and sweetest of hearts."

Sorcha gathered up Teagan, and her baby held tight, whispered in her ear. "The bad man said he would take me first as I'm the youngest and weak."

"He'll never take you, I swear it, on my life." She eased Teagan back so her daughter could see the truth of it in her eyes. "I swear it to you. And, my darling, weak you're not, and never will be."

So she fed the fire, poured honey on the bread, and made the tea and oats. They'd all need their strength for what she would do that day. What she needed to do.

Her boy came down from the loft, his hair tousled and tangled from sleep. He rubbed his eyes, sniffed the air like a hound. "I fought the black sorcerer. I didn't run."

Inside her breast Sorcha's heart kicked to a gallop. "You dreamed. Tell me."

"I was at the turn of the river where we keep the boat, and he came, and I knew him for a sorcerer, a black one because his heart is black."

"His heart."

"I could see in his heart, though he smiled, friendly like, and offered me some honey cake. 'Here, lad,' says he, 'I've a fine treat for you.' But the cake was full of worms and black blood—inside it. I could tell it was poisoned."

"You saw inside his heart, and inside the cake, in the dream."

"I did, I promise."

"I believe you." So her little man had more than she'd known.

"I said to him, 'Eat the cake yourself, for it's death in your hand.' But he threw it aside, and the worms crawled out of it and burned to ashes. He thought he would drown me in the river, but I threw rocks at him. Then Roibeard came."

"Did you call the hawk in your dream?"

"I wished for him, and he came, and he flashed out with his talons. The black sorcerer went away, like smoke in the wind. And I waked in my bed."

Sorcha drew him close, stroked his hair.

She'd unleashed her fury at Cabhan, so he came after her children.

"You're brave and true, Eamon. Now, break your fast. We've the stock to tend."

Sorcha moved closer to Brannaugh, who stood at the base of the ladder. "And you as well."

"He came into my dream. He said he would make me his bride. He . . . tried to touch me. Here." Pale with the telling, she covered her chest with her hands. "And here." Then between her legs.

Shaking, she pressed her face to her mother when Sorcha embraced her. "I burned him. I don't know how, but I made his fingers burn. He cursed me, and made fists with his hands. Kathel came, leaping onto the bed, snarling, snapping. Then the man was gone. But he tried to touch me, and he said he'd make me his bride, but—"

Rage woke inside the fear. "He never will. My oath on it. He'll never put his hands on you. Eat now, and eat all. There's much work to do."

She sent them all out to feed and water the animals, clean the stalls, milk the fat cow.

Alone she prepared herself, gathered her tools. The bowl, the bells, the candles, the sacred knife, and the cauldron. She chose the herbs she'd grown and dried. And the three copper bracelets Daithi had bought her at a long-ago summer fair.

She went out, drew deep of the air, lifted her arms to stir the wind. And called the hawk.

He came on a cry that echoed over the trees and the hills beyond that, which caused servants in the castle by the river to cast their eyes up. His wings, spread wide, caught the glint of the winter sun. She lifted her arm so those wicked talons clutched on her leather glove.

Her eyes looked into his, and his into hers.

"Swift and wise, strong and fearless. You are Eamon's, but mine as well. You will serve what comes from me. Mine will serve what comes from you. I have need of you, and ask this for my son, for your master and your servant."

She showed him the knife, and his eyes never wavered.

"Roibeard, I ask of thee, a drop of blood from your breast times three. A single feather from your great wing, and for these gifts your praises I sing. To guard my son, this is done."

She pricked him, held the small flask for the three drops. Plucked a single feather.

"My thanks," she whispered. "Stay close."

He lifted from her hand, but soared only to the branch of a tree. And closing his wings, watched.

She whistled for the dog. Kathel watched her with love, with trust. "You are Brannaugh's, but mine as well," she began, and repeated the ritual, gathering the three drops of blood, and a bit of fur from his flank.

Last, she moved into the shed, into the sound of her children laughing as they worked. She took strength from that. And stroked her hand down the pony's face.

Teagan raced over when she saw the knife. "Don't!"

"I do him no harm. He is yours, but mine as well. He will serve what comes from me, and you, as you will serve what comes from him. I have need of you, Alastar, and ask this for my daughter, for your mistress and your servant."

"Don't cut him. Please!"

"Only a prick, only a scratch, and only if he consents. Alastar, I ask of thee, a drop of blood from your breast times three. A bit of hair from your pretty mane, and for these gifts, I praise your name. To guard my little one, this is done.

"Just three drops," Sorcha said quietly as she pricked with the tip of the knife. "Just a bit of his mane. And here now." Though Alastar stood quiet, his eyes wise and calm, Sorcha laid her hands on the small, shallow cut, pushed her magick into it to heal. For her daughter's tender heart.

"Come with me now, all of you." She lifted Teagan onto her hip, led the way back into the house. "You know what I am. I have never hidden it. You know you carry the gift, each of you. I have always told you. Your magick is young and innocent. One day it will be strong and quick. You must honor it. You must use it to harm none, for the harm you do will come back on you threefold. Magick is a weapon, aye, but not one to be used against the innocent, the weak, the guiltless. It is a gift and a burden, and you will all carry both. You will all pass both to those who come from you. Today you learn more. Heed me and what I do. Watch, listen, know."

She moved to Brannaugh first. "Your blood, and mine, with the blood of the hound. Blood is life. Its loss is death. Three drops from thee, three drops from me, and with the hound's, the charm is bound."

Brannaugh placed her hand in her mother's without hesitation, held steady as Sorcha pricked her with the knife.

"My boy," she said to Eamon. "Three drops from thee, three drops from me, and from the hawk's heart, to seal three parts."

Though his lips trembled, Eamon held out his hand.

"And my baby. Don't fear."

Her eyes shone with tears, but Teagan watched her mother solemnly as she held out her hand.

"Three drops from thee, three drops from me, with the horse as your guide, the magicks ride."

She mixed the blood, kissed Teagan's little hand. "There now, that's done."

She lifted the cauldron, slid the vials into the pouch at her waist. "Bring the rest. This is best done outside."

She chose her spot, on the hard ground with snow lumped in the cool shadows of the trees.

"Should we get firewood?" Eamon asked her.

"Not for this. Stand here, together." She moved beyond them, called on the goddess, on the earth, the wind, the water, and the fire. And cast the circle. The low flame bubbled over the ground, rounded until end met end. And inside, warmth rose like spring.

"This is protection and respect. Evil cannot come within, dark cannot defeat the light. And what is done within the circle is done for good, is done for love.

"First the water, of sea, of sky." She cupped her hands, opened them over the cauldron, water blue as a sun-kissed lake poured out, poured in. "And the earth, our land, our hearts."

She flicked one hand, then the other, and rich brown earth spilled into the cauldron. "And the air, song of the wind, breath of body." She opened her arms, and blew. And like music, the air swept in with earth and water.

"Now the fire, flame and heat, the beginning, the ending."

She glowed, the air around her simmering, her eyes burning blue as she threw her arms up, cast her hands down.

Fire erupted in the cauldron, shooting flame, dancing sparks.

"These your father gave to me. They are a sign of his love, a sign of mine. You are, all three, of that love."

She cast the three copper bracelets into the flame, and circling it, added fur and hair and feather, added blood.

"The goddess gifts to me the power so I stand in this place, in this hour. I cast the charm, protect from harm my children three and all that comes from them, from me. The horse, the hawk, the hound, by blood they are ever bound to shield to serve from life to life in joy, in sorrow, in health, in strife.

"In earth, in air, in flame, in sea. As I will, so mote it be."

Sorcha lifted her arms high, turned her face to the sky.

The fire shot up in a tower, red and gold, wild blue in its core as it spun and twisted into the cold winter sky.

The earth shook. The icy water in the stream went to roaring. And the wind howled like a wolf on the hunt.

Then it stilled, it died, and there were just three children, hand gripping hand, watching their mother—pale as snow now—sway.

Sorcha shook her head as Brannaugh started toward her. "Not yet. Magick is work. It gives, and it takes. It must be finished." She reached in the cauldron, drew out three copper amulets. "To Brannaugh the hound, to Eamon the hawk, to Teagan the horse." She slipped an amulet over each child's head. "These are your signs and your shields. They protect you. You must keep them with you always. Always. He cannot touch what you are if you have your shield, if you believe its power, believe in mine and your own. One day you will pass this to one who comes from you. You'll know which. You'll tell your children the story and sing the old songs. You'll take the gift, and give the gift."

Teagan admired hers, smiled as she turned the small oval in the sunlight. "It's pretty. It looks like Alastar."

"It's of him, and of you, and of me and your father, of your brother and your sister. And why shouldn't it be pretty?" She lowered to kiss Teagan's cheek. "I have such pretty children."

She could barely stand, and had to bite back a moan as Brannaugh helped her to her feet. "I must close the circle. We must take everything inside now."

"We'll help you," Eamon said, and took his mother's hand.

With her children, she closed the circle, let them carry the tools into the house.

"You need to rest, sit by the fire." Brannaugh pulled her mother to the chair. "I'll fix you a potion."

"Aye, and a strong one. Show your brother and sister how it's done."

She smiled when Teagan wrapped a shawl around her shoulders, when Eamon spread a blanket over her lap. But when she started to reach for the cup Brannaugh brought, her daughter held it back. Then squeezed at the flesh around the cut on her hand until three drops of blood plopped into the cup.

"Blood is life."

Sorcha sighed. "It is, aye. It is. Thank you."

She drank the potion, and slept.

2

FOR A WEEK, THEN TWO, SHE WAS STRONG, AND HER power held. Cabhan battered at it, he pushed, he slithered, but she held him back.

The blackthorn bloomed, and the snowdrops, and the light turned more toward spring than winter.

Each night Sorcha watched for Daithi in the fire. When she could, she spoke to him, risked sending her spirit to him to bring back his scent, his voice, his touch—and to leave hers with him.

So to strengthen them both.

She told him nothing of Cabhan. The magicks were her world. His sword, his fist, even his warrior's heart could not defeat such as Cabhan. The cabin, hers before she'd taken Daithi as her man, was hers to defend. The children they'd made together, hers to protect.

And still she counted down the days to Bealtaine, to the day she would see him riding home again.

Her children thrived, and they learned. Some voice in her head urged her to teach them all she could as quickly as she could. She didn't question it.

She spent hours at night in the light of the tallow and the fire writing out her spells, her recipes, even her thoughts. And when she heard the howl of the wolf or the beat of the wind, she ignored it.

Twice she was called to the castle for a healing, and took her children so they could play with the other youths, so to keep them close, and to let them see the respect afforded the Dark Witch.

For the name and all it held would be their legacy.

But each time they journeyed home, she needed a potion to revive the strength sapped from the healing magicks she dispensed to those in need.

Though she yearned for her man, and for the health she feared would never be fully hers again, she schooled her children daily in the craft. She stood back when Eamon called to Roibeard—more his than hers now, as it should be. Watched with pride as her baby rode Alastar, as fierce as any warrior.

And knew, with both pride and sorrow, how often Brannaugh and her faithful Kathel patrolled the woods.

The gift was there, but so was childhood. She made certain there was music, and games, and as much innocence as she could preserve.

They had visitors, those who came for charms, for salves, who sought answers to questions, who hoped for love or fortune. She helped those she could, took their offerings. And watched the road, always watched the road—though she knew her love was still weeks from home.

She took them out on the river in the little boat their father had built on a day of easy winds when the sky held more blue than gray.

"They say witches can't travel over water," Eamon announced.

"Is that what they say then?" Sorcha laughed, lifted her face to the breeze. "Yet here we are, sailing fine and true."

"It's Donal who says it—from the castle."

"Saying it, even believing it, doesn't make it truth."

"Eamon made a frog fly for Donal. It was like boasting."

Eamon gave his younger sister a dark look, would've added a poke or pinch if his mother hadn't been watching.

"Flying frogs might be fun, but it isn't wise to spend your magick for amusements."

"It was practice."

"You might practice catching us some fish for supper. Not that way," Sorcha warned as her son lifted his hands over the water. "Magick isn't every answer. A body must know how to fend for himself without it as well. A gift should never be squandered on what you can do with your wit and your hands or your back."

"I like to fish."

"I don't." Brannaugh brooded as the little boat plied the river. "You sit and sit and wait and wait. I'd rather hunt. Then you have the woods, and we could have rabbit for dinner."

"Tomorrow's as good as today for that. We'll look for fish tonight if your brother has luck and skill. And perhaps a potato pie."

Bored, Brannaugh handed her line to her sister, and gazed out over the water to the castle with its great stone walls.

"Did you not want to live there, Ma? I heard the women talking. They said we were all welcome."

"We have our home, and though it was just a hut once, it's stood longer than those walls. It stood when the O'Connors ruled, before the House of Burke. Kings and princes come and go, *m'inion*, but home is always."

"I like the look of it, so grand and tall, but I like our woods better." She leaned her head on her mother's arm a moment. "Could the Burkes have taken our home?"

"They could have tried, but they were wise to respect magick. We have no fight with them, nor they with us."

"If they did, Da would fight them. And so would I." She slid her gaze toward her mother. "Dervla from the castle told me Cabhan was banished."

"That you knew already."

"Aye, but she said he comes back, and he lies with women. He whispers in their ear and they think he's their lawful husband. But in the morning, they know. They weep. She said you gave the women charms to keep him away, but . . . he lured one of the kitchen maids away, into the bog. No one can find her."

She knew of it, just as she knew the kitchen maid would never be found. "He toys with them, and preys on the weak to feed himself. His power is black and cold. The light and the fire will always defeat him."

"But he comes back. He scratches at the windows and doors."

"He can't enter." But she felt a chill through her blood.

Just then Eamon let out a shout, and when he yanked up his line, a fish flashed silver in the sunlight.

"Luck and skill," Sorcha said with a laugh as she grabbed the net.

"I want to catch one." Teagan leaned eagerly over the water as if searching for a likely fish.

"We'll hope you do, as we'll need more than one, even such a fine one. It's good work, Eamon."

They caught three more, and if she helped her baby a bit, the magick was for love.

She rowed them back with the sun sparkling, the breeze dancing, and the air full of her children's voices.

A good, fine day, she thought, and spring so close she could almost taste it.

"Run on home then, Eamon, and clean those fish. You can get the potatoes started, Brannaugh, and I'll see to the boat."

"I'll stay with you." Teagan snuck her hand into her mother's. "I can help."

"That you can, as we'll need to fetch some water from the stream."

"Do fish like us to catch and eat them?"

"I can't say they do, but it's their purpose."

"Why?"

And *why*, Sorcha thought as she secured the boat, had been Teagan's first word. "Didn't the powers put the fish in the water, and give us the wit to make the nets and lines?"

"But they must like swimming more than the fire."

"I expect so. So we should be mindful and grateful when we eat."

"What if we didn't catch and eat them?"

"We'd be hungry more often than not."

"Do they talk under the water?"

"Well now, I've never had a conversation with a fish. Here now." Sorcha pulled Teagan's cloak more closely around her. "It's getting cold." She glanced up, saw the clouds rolling over the sun. "We may have a storm tonight. Best get home."

As she straightened, came the fog. Gray and dirty, it slunk like a snake over the ground and smothered the sparkle of the day.

Not a storm coming, Sorcha realized. The threat was here already.

She pushed Teagan behind her as Cabhan rose out of the fog.

He wore black picked through with silver like stars against a midnight sky. His hair waved to his shoulders, an ebony frame for his hard and beautiful face. His eyes, dark as a gypsy's heart, held both power and pleasure as he scraped them over Sorcha.

She felt them, like bold hands on her skin.

Around his neck he wore a large silver pendant shaped like a sun with a fat jewel—a glinting red eye—in its center. And this was new, she thought, and sensed its black power.

"My lady," he said, and bowed to her.

"You have no welcome here."

"I walk where I will. And what do I see but a woman and her small, pretty child alone. Treats for brigands and wolves. You have no man to see you safe, Sorcha the Dark. I will escort you."

"I see myself safe. Begone, Cabhan. You waste your time and powers here. I will never submit to such as you."

"But you will submit. Joining with me is your destiny. I've seen it in the glass."

"You see lies and desires, not truth or destiny."

He only smiled, and like his voice, his smile held seduction. "Together we'll rule this land, and any others we wish. You will wear fine cloth in bright colors and drape your skin in jewels."

He swirled his hands. Teagan gasped when she saw her mother wearing the rich red of royalty, the sparkle of jewels, and a gold crown studded with them.

Just as quickly, Sorcha flicked a wrist and was once again draped in her simple black wool. "I have no need, no wish for your colors and shine. Leave me and mine, or you will feel my wrath."

But he laughed, the sound rolling from him in smooth and terrible delight. "Is it a wonder, my heart, that I want none but you? Your fire, your beauty, your power, all meant to be mine."

"I am Daithi's woman, and will ever be."

With a grunt of disgust, Cabhan flicked his fingers. "Daithi cares more for his raids, his games, his petty little wars than for you or the whelps you bore him. How many times has the moon waxed and waned since he last shared your bed? You grow cold in the night, Sorcha. I feel it. I will show you pleasures you've never known. And I will make you more than you are. I will make you a goddess."

Fear tried to crawl into her like the fog crawled over the ground. "I would die by my own hand before being bedded by you. You only crave more power."

"And you're a fool not to. Together we will crush all who stand against us, live as gods, be as gods. And for this I will give you what your heart most desires."

"You don't know my heart."

"A babe in your belly to replace the loss. My son, born of you. More powerful than any has known before or will again."

Grief for the loss struck, and fear, a terrible fear for the tiny seed of want in her for what he offered. A life growing in her, strong and real.

Sensing that fear, Cabhan stepped closer. "A son," he murmured. "Bright in your womb. Thriving there, born strong and glorious, like no other. Give me your hand, Sorcha, and I will give you your heart's desire."

She trembled for a moment, a moment only, as oh, by all the gods, she craved that life.

And as she trembled, Teagan leaped out from behind her skirts. She hurled a rock, striking Cabhan on the temple. A thin line of blood, dark, dark red, trickled down his pale skin.

His eyes went fierce as he swung out. Before the blow could land, Sorcha shoved him back with sheer force of will.

She pulled Teagan up, into her arms.

Wind whipped around her now, one born of her own fury. "I will kill you a thousand times, I will give you agony for ten thousand years if you lay hands on my child. I swear this on all I am."

"You threaten me? You and your runt?" He fixed his eyes on Teagan's face, and his smile spread like death. "Pretty little runt. Bright as a fish in the water. Shall I catch and eat you?"

Though she clung to Sorcha, though she shivered, Teagan didn't cower. "Go away!"

In fury and fear, her young, untried power slapped out, struck as true as the stone. Now blood ran from Cabhan's mouth, and his smile became a snarl.

"First you, then your brother. Your sister . . . a bit of ripening first for she, too, will bear me sons." With a fingertip, he smeared the blood on his face, crossed it over the amulet. "I would have spared them for you," he told Sorcha. "Now you will see their deaths."

Sorcha pressed her lips to Teagan's ear. "He can't hurt you," she began in a whisper, then watched in horror as Cabhan changed.

His body shifted, twisted like the fog. The amulet glowed, the gem spun until his eyes sparked as red as the stone.

Black hair covered his body. Claws sprang from his fingers. And as he seemed to spill over onto the ground, he threw back his head. He howled.

Slowly, carefully, Sorcha set Teagan down again behind her. "He can't hurt you." She prayed it was true, that the magick she'd imbued into the copper sign would hold even against this form.

For surely he'd bartered his soul for this dark art.

The wolf bared its teeth, and sprang.

She pushed back—thrusting out her hands, drawing up her strength so that pure white light shot from her palms. When it struck the wolf it screamed, almost like a man. But it came again, and again, leaping, snapping, its eyes feral and horribly human.

The claws lashed out, caught Sorcha's skirts, tore them. Then it was Teagan's scream that sliced the air.

"Go away, go away!" She pelted the wolf with rocks, rocks that turned to balls of fire as they struck, so the fog smelled of burning flesh and fur.

The wolf lunged again, howling still. Teagan tumbled back as Sorcha slashed down at it. The little girl's cloak fell open. From the copper sign she wore burst a blue flame, straight and sharp as an arrow. It struck the wolf's flank, scored a mark shaped like a pentagram.

On an agonized cry, the wolf flew back. As it pawed and snapped at the air, Sorcha gathered all she had, hurled her light, her hope, her power.

The world went white, blinding her. Desperate, she groped for Teagan's hand as she fell to her knees.

The fog vanished. All that remained of the wolf was scorched earth in its shape.

Weeping, Teagan clutched at her mother, burrowed into her—just a child now, frightened of monsters all too real.

"There now, it's gone. You're safe. We need to go home. We need to be home, my baby."

But she lacked the strength even to stand. She could have wept herself to be brought so low. Once she could have summoned the power to fly through the woods with her child in her arms. Now her limbs trembled, her breath burned, and her heart beat so fast and hard it pounded her temples.

If Cabhan gathered himself, came back . . .

"Run home. You know the way. Run home. I'll follow."

"I stay with you."

"Teagan, do as I say."

"No. No." Knuckling her eyes, Teagan stubbornly shook her head. "You come. You come."

Gritting her teeth, Sorcha managed to get to her feet. But after two steps, she simply sank to her knees again. "I can't do it, my baby. My legs won't carry me."

"Alastar can. I'll call him, and he'll carry us home."

"Can you call him, from all this way?"

"He'll come very fast."

Teagan rose on her sturdy legs, lifted her arms.

"Alastar, Alastar, brave and free, heed my call and come to me. Run swift, run true to find the one who needs you."

Teagan bit her lip, turned to her mother. "Brannaugh helped me with the words. Are they good?"

"They're very good." Young, Sorcha thought. Simple and pure. "Say it twice more. Three is strong magick."

Teagan obeyed, then came back to stroke her mother's hair. "You'll be well again when we're home. Brannaugh will make you tea."

"Aye, that's what she'll do. I'll be fine again when I'm home." She thought it was the first time she'd lied to her child. "Find me a good, strong stick. I think I could lean on it and walk a ways."

"Alastar will come."

Though she doubted it, Sorcha nodded. "We'll meet him. Find me a sturdy stick, Teagan. We have to be home before dark."

Even as Teagan scrambled up, they heard the hoofbeats.

"He's coming! Alastar! We're here, we're here!"

She'd called her guide, Sorcha thought, and a sharp stab of pride pierced her fatigue. As Teagan ran forward to meet the horse, Sorcha gathered herself again, pushed painfully to her feet.

"There you are, a prince of horses." Grateful, Sorcha pressed her face to Alastar as he nuzzled her. "Can you help me mount?" she asked Teagan.

"He will. I taught him a trick. I was saving it for when Da comes home. Kneel, Alastar! Kneel." Giggling now, Teagan swept a hand down.

The horse bowed his head, then bent his forelegs, and knelt.

"Oh, my clever, clever girl."

"It's a good trick?"

"A fine trick. A fine one, indeed." Grasping the mane, Sorcha pulled herself onto the horse. Nimble as a cricket, Teagan leapt on in front of her.

"You hold on to me, Ma! Alastar and I will get us home."

Sorcha gripped the little girl's waist, put her trust in the child and the horse. Every stride of the gallop brought pain, but every stride brought them closer to home.

When they neared the clearing she saw her older children, Brannaugh dragging her grandfather's sword, Eamon holding a dagger, racing toward them.

So brave, too brave.

"Back to the house, back now! Run back!"

"The bad one came," Teagan shouted. "And he made himself into a wolf. I threw rocks at him, Eamon, like you did."

The children's voices—the questions, the excitement, the licks of fear—circled like echoes in Sorcha's head. Sweat soaked her. Once again she grasped Alastar's mane, lowered herself to the ground. Swayed as the world went gray.

"Ma's sick. She needs her tea."

"Inside," Sorcha managed. "Bolt the door."

She heard Brannaugh giving orders, clipping them out like a chieftain—"fetch water, stir the fire"—and felt as if she floated inside, into her chair, where her body collapsed.

A cool cloth on her head. Warm, potent liquid easing down her throat. A quieting of the pain, a clearing of the mists.

"Rest now." Brannaugh stroked her hair.

"I'm better. You have a strong gift for healing."

"Teagan said the wolf burned up."

"No. We hurt him, aye, we hurt him, but it lives. He lives."

"We'll kill it. We'll set a trap and kill it."

"It may come to that, when I'm stronger. He has more than he did, this shifting of shapes. I can't say what price he paid for the power, but it would be dear. Your sister marked him. Here." Sorcha clutched a hand on her left shoulder. "The shape of a pentagram. Watch for this, be wary of this, and any who bear that mark."

"We will. You don't be fretting now. We'll make the supper, and you'll feel stronger for eating, and resting."

"You'll make a charm for me. Exactly as I say. Make the charm, and bring it to me. Supper can wait until that's done."

"Will it make you stronger?"

"Aye."

Brannaugh made the charm, and Sorcha hung it around her neck, next to her heart. She sipped more potion, and though her appetite was small, forced herself to eat.

She slept, and dreamed, and woke to find Brannaugh keeping watch.

"Off to bed now. It's late."

"We won't leave you. I can help you to bed."

"I'll sit here, by the fire."

"Then I'll sit with you. We're taking turns. I'll wake Eamon when it's his, and Teagan will bring you morning tea."

Too weary to argue, too proud to scold, Sorcha only smiled. "Is that the way of it?"

"Until you're all well again."

"I'm better, I promise you. His magick was so strong, so black. It took all I had in me, and more, to stop it. Our Teagan, you'd be proud. So fierce and bright she was. And you, running toward us with your grandda's sword."

"It's very heavy."

The laugh felt good. "He was a big man with a red beard as long as your arm." On a sigh, she ran her hand over Brannaugh's head. "If you won't go to your bed, make a pallet there on the floor. We'll both sleep awhile."

When her child slept, Sorcha added a charm to make Brannaugh's dreams good and sweet.

And she turned to the fire. It was time, long past, to call Daithi home. She needed his sword, she needed his strength. She needed him.

So she opened her mind to the fire, opened her heart to her love.

Her spirit traveled over the hills and fields, through the night, through woods, over water where the moon swam. She flew across all the miles that separated them to the camp of their *clann*.

He slept near the fire with the moonlight like a blanket over him.

When she settled down beside him, his lips curved, and his arm curled around her.

"You smell of home fires and wooded glades."

"It's home you must come."

"Soon, *aghra*. Two weeks, no more."

"Tomorrow you must ride with all haste. My heart, my warrior." She cupped his face. "We have need of you."

"And I of you." He rolled over onto the vision of her, lowered his mouth to hers.

"Not for the bed, though oh, I ache for you. Every day, every night. I need your sword, I need you by my side. Cabhan attacked today."

Daithi sprang up, his hand on the hilt of his sword. "Are you hurt? The children?"

"No, no. But nearly. He grows stronger, and I weaker. I fear I can't hold him."

"There is none stronger than you. He will never touch the Dark Witch."

Her heart broke at his faith in her, for she could no longer earn it. "I'm not well."

"What is this?"

"I didn't wish to burden you, and . . . no, my pride. I valued it too much, but now I cast it away. I fear what comes, Daithi. I fear him. I cannot hold him without you. For our children, for our lives, come home."

"I will ride tonight. I will bring men with me, and ride for home."

"At first light. Wait for the light, for the dark is his. And be swift."

"Two days. I will be home with you in two days. And Cabhan will know the bite of my sword. I swear it."

"I will watch for you, and wait for you. I am yours in this life and all that come."

"Heal, my witch." He brought her hands to his lips. "It's all I will ever ask of you."

"Come home, and I will heal."

"Two days."

"Two days." She kissed him, holding tight and close. And carried the kiss with her as she flew back over the mirror of the moon and the green hills.

She came back into her body, tired, so tired, but stronger as well. The magick between them flowed rich, flowed true.

Two days, she thought, and closed her eyes. While he rode to her she would rest, she would let the magick build again. Keep the children close, draw in the light.

She slept again; she dreamed again.

And saw in her dream he didn't wait for the light. He mounted in the moonlight, under the cold stars. His face was fierce as his horse danced over the hard ground.

His horse lunged forward, far outpacing the mounts of the three men who rode with him.

Using the moonlight and the stars, Daithi rode for home, for his family, for his woman. For the Dark Witch he loved more than his life.

When the wolf leaped out of the dark, he barely had time to clear his sword from its sheath. Daithi struck out, but cut through only air as the horse reared. Fog rose like gray walls, trapping him, blocking his men.

He fought, but the wolf sprang over the blade, time after time, snapping out with its jaws, swiping viciously with claws only to vanish into the fog. Only to charge out from it again.

She flew to reach him, soaring over those hills again, across the water.

She knew when those jaws tore, knew when the blood spilled from his heart—from hers. Her tears fell like rain, washing away the fog. Crying his name, she dropped to the ground beside him.

She tried her strongest spell, her most powerful charm, but his heart would not beat again.

As she clasped Daithi's hand in hers, cried to the goddess for mercy, she heard the wolf laugh in the dark.

BRANNAUGH SHIVERED IN SLEEP. DREAMS STALKED HER, FULL of blood and snarls and death. She struggled to outpace them, to break free. She wanted her mother, wanted her father, wanted the sun and warmth of spring.

But clouds and cold covered her. The wolf stepped out of the fog and into her path. And its fangs dripped red and wet.

On a muffled cry she shoved up on her pallet and clutched her amulet. Curling her knees up, she hugged them hard, swiped her teary face against her thighs to dry them. She wasn't a babe to weep over bad dreams.

It was past time to wake Eamon, and then hope to sleep more calmly in her own cot.

She turned her head first to check on her mother, and saw the chair empty. Knuckling her eyes, she called softly for her mother as she started to rise.

And she saw Sorcha lying on the floor between the fire and the loft ladder, still as death.

"Ma! Ma!" Terror seized her as she sprang over to drop at her mother's side. Hands shaking, she turned Sorcha over to cradle her mother's head in her lap. Saying her name over and over like a chant.

Too white, too still, too cold. Rocking, Brannaugh acted without thought or plan. When the heat surged through her, she poured it into her mother. Those shaking hands pressed hard, hard on Sorcha's heart as her own head fell back, as her eyes glazed and fixed. The black smoke of them pulled for the light and shot arrows of it into her mother.

The heat poured out, the cold poured in, until shuddering, she slumped forward. Sky and sea revolved; light and dark swirled. Pain such as she'd never known sliced through her belly, stabbed into her heart.

Then was gone, leaving only exhaustion.

From somewhere far away, she heard her hound baying.

"No more, no more." Sorcha's voice croaked out, harsh and weak. "Stop. Brannaugh, you must stop."

"You need more. I will find more."

"No. Do as I say. Quiet breaths, quiet mind, quiet heart. Breath, mind, heart."

"What's wrong? What happened?" Eamon came flying down the ladder. "Ma!"

"I found her. Help me, help me get her to bed."

"No, not bed. No time for it," Sorcha said. "Eamon, let Kathel in, and wake Teagan."

"She's waked, she's here."

"Ah, there's my baby. Not to fret."

"There's blood. Your hands have blood."

"Aye." Burying her grief, Sorcha stared at her hands. "'Tisn't mine."

"Fetch a cloth, Teagan, and we'll wash her."

"No, not a cloth. The cauldron. Fetch my candles, and book, and the salt. All the salt we have. Build up the fire, Eamon, and Brannaugh make my tea—make it strong."

"I will."

"Teagan, be a good girl now and pack up what food we have."

"Are we going on a journey?"

"A journey, aye. Feed the stock, Eamon—aye, it's early yet, but feed them and well, pack all the oats you can for Alastar."

She took the cup from Brannaugh, drank deep, drank all. "Now, go pack your things, your clothes, blankets. You'll take the sword, the dagger, all the coin, the jewels my granny left me. All that she left me. All, Brannaugh. Leave nothing of value. Pack it all, and be quick. Quick!" she snapped, and had Brannaugh dashing away.

Time, the Dark Witch thought, it came, it went. And now she had so little left. But enough. She would make it enough.

She sat quiet while her children did her bidding. And built her strength, amassed her power.

When Brannaugh came down, Sorcha stood straight and tall. Her skin held warmth and color, her eyes focus and energy.

"You're well!"

"No, my darling, well I'm not, nor will be again." She held up a hand before Brannaugh could speak. "But strong is what I am, for this time and for this need. I will do what I must, and so will you." She looked to her son, her baby girl. "So will all of you. Before the sun rises, you will go. You will keep to the woods, go south. Do not use the road until you are well away. Find my cousin Ailish, the Clann O'Dwyer, and tell her the tale. She will do what she can."

"We will all go."

"No, Eamon. I will bide here. You must be strong and brave, protect your sisters, and they protect you. I would not survive the journey."

"I will make you well," Brannaugh insisted.

"'Tis beyond you. 'Tis meant. But I do not leave you alone or helpless. What I am, what I have will live in you. One day you will come back, for this is home, and home is the source. I cannot give you your innocence, but I will give you power.

"Stand with me, for you are my heart and soul, my blood and bone. You are my all. And now I cast the circle, and no dark shall enter."

Flame circled the floor and, at the flick of her hand, leapt under the cauldron. Looking down at her hands again, she sighed once, then stepped forward.

"This is your father's blood." She opened her hands over the cauldron, and the blood poured. "And these are my tears, and yours. He rode to protect us, rode home as I asked him. A trap, set by Cabhan, using my fear, my weakness. He took your father's life, as he will take mine. The life, but not the spirit, not the power."

She knelt, enfolded her weeping children. "I would comfort you in every moment I have left, but there is no time for grieving. Remember him who made you, who loved you, and know I go to be with him, and watch over you."

"Don't send us away." Teagan sobbed on her mother's shoulder. "I want to stay with you. I want Da."

"You'll take the light in me with you. I will always be with you." With hands now clean and white, Sorcha brushed tears from her daughter's cheek. "You, my bright light, my hope. You, my brave son." She kissed Eamon's fingers. "My heart. And you, my steady, searching one." She cupped Brannaugh's face. "My strength. Carry me with you. And now, we work this spell together. Stand with me! Say as I say, do as I do."

She held out her hands.

"With blood and tears we spill our fears." She waved a hand over the cauldron, and the liquid within began to stir. "A pinch of salt times four to close and bolt the door. Weeds to bind, berries to blind. My children he will not see, and they will live safe and free. Pretty petals tinged with hate, scented sweet and so to bait. Boil it all in fire and smoke, and on this potion Cabhan chokes. When I call he comes to me, as I will, so mote it be."

The light flashed so all in the circle burned with it.

She called on Hecate, on Brighid, on Morrigan and Babd Catha, summoning the strength and power of the goddesses. The air quaked, seemed to split and crack. It rang with voices as Sorcha stood, arms high in both prayer and demand.

The smoke turned red as blood, fogged the room. Then, as if in a whirlpool, sucked back into the cauldron.

Eyes bright, Sorcha poured the potion into a vessel, sealed it, slid it into her pocket.

"Mother," Brannaugh breathed.

"I am, and will be. Don't fear me, or what I give you now. My baby." She took Teagan's hands. "It will grow in you, as you grow. You will ever be kind, ever ask why. You will ever stand for those who cannot stand. Take this."

"It's hot," Teagan said as her hands glowed in her mother's.

"It will cool again, until you need it. My son. You will fly, and you will fight. You will ever be loyal and true. Take this."

"I would take you. I would guard you."

"Guard your sisters. Brannaugh, my first. So much to ask of you. Your gift is strong already, and now I give you more. More than Teagan and Eamon, as I must. You will build and you will make. When you love, you will never stop. You will ever be the one they look to first, and will ever bear the burden. Forgive me, and take this."

Brannaugh gasped. "It burns!"

"Only for a moment." And in that moment Sorcha grieved a thousand years. "Open. Take. Live."

She kept only enough, just enough, then let herself slide to the floor when it was done. She was the Dark Witch no more.

"You are the Dark Witch, one by three. This is my gift, and my curse. Each of you is strong, and stronger together. One day you'll return. Go now, and quickly. Day comes. Know my heart goes with you."

But Teagan clung to her, kicked, cried when Eamon pulled her away.

"Take her outside, onto Alastar," Brannaugh said quietly.

But first Eamon knelt to his mother. "I will avenge my father, and you, my mother. I will protect my sisters with my life. I swear this."

"I am proud of my son. I will see you again. My baby," she said to Teagan. "You will return. I promise you."

Brannaugh turned to her sister, passed a hand over her head. And Teagan nodded to sleep.

"Take her, Eamon, and the packs you can carry. I'll bring the rest."

"I'll help you. I'm strong enough," Sorcha insisted. And she didn't intend to allow Cabhan into her house.

As they loaded the horse, Brannaugh looked into her mother's eyes. "I understand."

"I know."

"I'll let no harm come to them. If you cannot destroy Cabhan, your blood will. If it takes a thousand years, your blood will."

"Night's fleeting, go quickly. Alastar will carry the three of you far enough into day." Sorcha's lips trembled before she found the will to firm them. "She is tender of heart, our baby."

"I will always care for her. I promise you."

"Then that's enough. Go, go, or all is for naught."

Brannaugh pulled herself up behind her brother and her spell-struck sister. "If I am your strength, Mother, you are mine. All that come from us will know of Sorcha. All will honor the Dark Witch."

Through the blur of tears, she looked ahead, and kicked the horse into a gallop.

Sorcha watched them, kept them in her mind's eye as they rode through the dark of the woods, away from her. Toward life.

And as day broke, she took the potion from her pocket, drank. Waited for the dark one to come.

He brought the fog, but came as a man, drawn to her scent, to the shimmer of her skin. To her power, false now, but potent.

"My man is dead," she said flatly.

"Your man stands before you."

"But you are not a man like other men."

"More than others. You called me, Sorcha the Dark."

"I am not a woman like other women, but more. Needs must be met. Power calls to power. Will you make me a goddess, Cabhan?"

Greed and lust darkened his eyes and, Sorcha thought, blinded him.

"I will show you more than you can imagine. Together we will have all, be all. You have only to join with me."

"What of my children?"

"What of them?" His gaze shifted to the house. "Where are they?" he demanded, and would have pushed by her.

"They sleep. I am their mother, and I would have your word on their safety. You cannot enter until it's given. I cannot join with you until you swear your oath."

"They will come to no harm from me." He smiled again. "So I swear to you."

Liar, she thought. I can still see your mind, and the dark pit of your heart.

"Then come and kiss me. Make me yours as I make you mine."

He pulled her hard against him, twisted her hair cruelly in his hand to drag her head back. And crushed his lips to hers.

She opened those lips, and with death in her heart allowed his tongue to sweep into her mouth. Allowed the poison to do its work.

He stumbled back, clutching at his throat. "What have you done?"

"I have beaten you. I have destroyed you. And with my last breaths, I curse you. On this day and in this hour, I call upon what holds of my power. You will burn and die in pain, and know the Dark Witch has you slain. So my blood curses your blood for all eternity. As I will, so mote it be."

He threw his power at her, even as his skin began to smoke, to blacken. She fell, in blood, in agony, but clung to life. Clung only to watch his death.

"All that come from you be damned," she managed as flames burst from him, as his screams tore the world.

"My death for his," she whispered when the black ashes of the sorcerer smoldered on the ground. "It is right. It is just. It is done."

She let go, released her spirit and left her body by the cabin in the deep green woods.

And as the fog swirled, something shifted in the black ashes.

3

County Mayo, 2013

THE COLD CARVED BONE DEEP, FUELED BY THE LASH OF the wind, iced by the drowning rain gushing from a bruised, bloated sky.

Such was Iona Sheehan's welcome to Ireland.

She loved it.

How could she not? she asked herself as she hugged her arms to her chest and drank in the wild, soggy view from her window. She was standing in a castle. She'd sleep in a castle that night. An honest-to-God Irish castle in the heart of the west.

Some of her ancestors had worked there, probably slept there. Everything she knew verified that her people, on her mother's side in any case, had sprung from this gorgeous part of the world, this magical part of this magical country.

She'd gambled, well, pretty much everything to come here, to find her roots, to—she hoped—connect with them. And most of all, to finally understand them.

Burnt bridges, left them smoldering behind her in the hopes of building new ones, stronger ones. Ones that led somewhere she wanted to go.

She'd left her mother mildly annoyed. But then her mother never rose to serious anger, or sorrow, or joy or passion. How difficult had it been to find herself saddled with a daughter who rode emotions like a wild stallion? Her father had just patted her head in his absent way, and wished her luck as casually as he might some passing acquaintance.

She suspected she'd never been any more than that to him. Her paternal grandparents considered the trip a grand adventure, and had given her the very welcome gift of a check.

She was grateful, even knowing they belonged to the out-of-sight-out-of-mind school and probably wouldn't give her another thought.

But her maternal grandmother, her treasured Nan, had given her a gift with so many questions.

She was here in this lovely corner of Mayo, ringed by water, shadowed by ancient trees, to find the answers.

She should wait until tomorrow, settle in, take a nap, as she'd barely slept on the flight from Baltimore. At least she should unpack. She had a week in Ashford Castle, a foolish expense on the practical scale. But she wanted, so wanted that connection, that once-in-a-lifetime treat.

She opened her bags, began to take out clothes.

She was a woman who'd once wished she'd grow taller than her scant five three, and curvier than the slim, teenage boy body the fates had granted her. Then she'd stopped wishing and compensated by using bright colors in her wardrobe, and wearing high, high heels whenever she could manage it.

Illusion, Nan would say, was as good as reality.

She'd once wished she could be beautiful, like her mother, but worked with what she had—cute. The only time she'd seen her mother close to genuinely horrified had been just the week before when Iona had chopped off her long blond hair to a pixie cap.

Far from used to it herself, she raked her fingers through it. It suited her, didn't it? Didn't it bring out her cheekbones a little?

It didn't matter if she regretted the impulse; she'd regretted others. Trying new things, taking new risks—those were her current goals. No more wait-and-see, the mantra of her parents as long as she could remember. Now was now.

And with that in mind, she thought, the hell with unpacking, the hell with waiting until tomorrow. What if she died in her sleep?

She dug out boots, a scarf, the new raincoat—candy pink—she'd bought for Ireland. She dragged a pink-and-white-striped cap over her hair, slung her oversized purse on cross-body.

Don't think, just do, she told herself, and left her warm, pretty room.

She made a wrong turn almost immediately, but it only gave her time to wander the corridors. She'd asked for a room in the oldest section when she'd booked, and liked to imagine servants scurrying with fresh rushes, or ladies sitting at their spindles. Or warriors in bloody mail returning from battle.

She had days to explore the castle, the grounds, the nearby village of Cong, and she meant to make use of all of it.

But her primary goal remained to seek out and make contact with the Dark Witch.

When she stepped outside into the whistling wind and drenching rain, she told herself it was a perfect day for witches.

The little map Nan had drawn was in her bag, but she'd etched it on her memory. She turned away from the great stone walls, took the path toward the deep woods. Passed winter-quiet gardens, spreads of soaked green. Belatedly she remembered the umbrella in her bag, dragged it out, pushing her way forward into the evocative gloom of the rain-struck woods.

She hadn't imagined the trees so big, with their wide, wide trunks, crazily gnarled branches. A storybook wood, she thought, thrilled with it even as the rain splashed over her boots.

Through its drumming she heard the wind sigh and moan, then the rumble of what must be the river.

Paths speared, forked, but she kept the map in her head.

She thought she heard something cry overhead, and for a moment imagined she saw the sweep of wings. Then despite the drumming, the rumbling, the sighs and the moans, everything suddenly seemed still. As the path narrowed, roughened, her heartbeat pounded in her ears, too quick, too loud.

To the right an upended tree exposed a base taller than a man, wider than her arm span. Vines thick as her wrist tangled together like a wall. She found herself drawn toward them, struck by the urge to pull at them, to fight her way through them to see what lay beyond. The concept of getting lost flitted through her mind, then out again.

She just wanted to see.

She took a step forward, then another. She smelled smoke and horses, and both pulled her closer to that tangled wall. Even as she reached out, something burst through. The massive black blur had her stumbling back. She thought, instinctively: Bear!

Since the umbrella had flown out of her hand, she looked around frantically for a weapon—a stick, a rock—then saw as it eyed her, the biggest dog ever to stand on four massive paws.

Not a bear, she thought, but as potentially deadly if he wasn't somebody's cheerful pet.

"Hello . . . doggie."

He continued to watch her out of eyes more gold than brown. He stepped forward to sniff her, which she hoped wasn't the prelude to taking a good, hard bite. Then let out two cannon-shot barks before loping away.

"Okay." She bent over from the waist until she caught her breath. "All right."

Exploring would definitely wait for a bright, sunny day. Or at least a brighter, dryer one. She picked up her soaked and muddy umbrella and pressed on.

She should've waited on the whole thing, she told herself. Now she was wet and flustered and, she realized, more travel weary than she'd expected. She should be napping in her warm hotel bed, snuggled in listening to the rain instead of trudging through it.

And now—perfect—fog rolled in, surfing over the ground like waves on the shore. Mists thickened like those vines, and the rain sounded like voices muttering.

Or there were voices muttering, she thought. In a language she shouldn't understand, but almost did. She quickened her pace, as anxious to get out of the woods as she'd been to get into them.

The cold turned brutal until she saw her breath hazing out. Now the voices sounded in her head: Turn back. Turn back.

It was stubbornness as much as anxiety that had her pushing ahead until she nearly ran along the slippery path.

And like the dog, burst into the clear.

The rain was just the rain, the wind just the wind. The path opened into a road, with a few houses, smoke puffing out of chimneys. And beyond, the beauty of the mist-shrouded hills.

"Too much imagination, not enough sleep," she told herself.

She saw dooryard gardens resting their bright blooms for spring, cars parked on the roadside or in short drives.

Not far now, according to Nan's map, so she walked along the road, counting houses.

It sat farther off the road than the others, farther apart as if it needed breathing room. The pretty thatched-roofed cottage with its deep blue walls and bright red door transmitted that same storybook vibe—yet a shiny silver Mini sat in the little driveway. The cottage itself jogged into an L, fronted by curved glass. Even in the winter, pots of bright pansies sat on the stoops, their exotic faces turned upward to drink in the rain.

A sign of aged wood hung above the curve of glass. Its deeply carved letters read:

THE DARK WITCH

"I found her." For a moment Iona just stood in the rain, closed her eyes. Every decision she'd made in the last six weeks—perhaps every one she'd made in her life—had led to this.

She wasn't sure whether to go to the L—the workshop, Nan had told her—or the cottage entrance. But as she walked closer she saw the gleam of light on the glass. And closer still, the shelves holding bottles full of color—bright or soft—hanks of hanging herbs. Mortars and pestles, bowls and . . . cauldrons?

Steam puffed from one on a stove top, and a woman stood at a work counter, grinding something.

Iona's first thought was how unfair it seemed that some women could look like that even without fussing. The dark hair bundled up, sexily messy, the rosy flush from the work and the steam. The fine bones that said beauty from birth to death, and the deeply sculpted mouth just slightly curved in a contented smile.

Was it genes or magick? she wondered. But then, for some, one was the same as the other.

She gathered her courage and, setting her umbrella aside, reached for the door handle.

She barely touched it when the woman looked up, over. The smile deepened, polite welcome, so Iona opened the door, stepped in.

And the smile faded. Eyes of smoke gray held so intensely on her face that Iona stopped where she was, just over the threshold.

"Can I come in?"

"It's in you are."

"I . . . I guess I am. I should've knocked. I'm sorry, I . . . God, it smells amazing in here. Rosemary and basil and lavender, and . . . everything. I'm sorry," she said again. "Are you Branna O'Dwyer?"

"I am, yes." As she answered, she took a towel from under the counter, crossed to Iona. "You're soaked through."

"Oh, sorry. I'm dripping on the floor. I walked over from the castle. From the hotel. I'm staying at Ashford Castle."

"Lucky you, it's a grand place."

"It's like a dream, at least what I've seen of it. I just got here. I mean, a couple hours ago, and I wanted to come to see you right away. I came to meet you."

"Why?"

"Oh, I'm sorry, I—"

"You're sorry for a lot it seems, in such a short time."

"Ha." Iona twisted the towel in her hands. "Yeah, it sounds like it. I'm Iona. Iona Sheehan. We're cousins. I mean, my grandmother Mary Kate O'Connor is cousins with your grandmother Ailish, um . . . Ailish Flannery. So that makes us . . . I get confused if it's fourth or third or whatever."

"A cousin's a cousin for all that. Well then, take off those muddy boots, and we'll have some tea."

"Thanks. I know I should've written or called or something. But I was afraid you'd tell me not to come."

"Were you?" Branna murmured as she set the kettle on.

"It's just once I'd decided to come, I needed to push through with it." She left her muddy boots by the door, hung her coat on the peg. "I always wanted to visit Ireland—that roots thing—but it was always eventually. Then . . . well, it was now. Right now."

"Go have a seat at the table back there, by the fire. It's a cold wind today."

"God, tell me! I swear it got colder the deeper I went into the woods, then . . . Oh Jesus, it's the bear!"

She stopped as the massive dog lifted his head from his place at the little hearth, and gave her the same steady stare he had in the woods. "I mean the dog. I thought he was a bear for a minute when he came bursting through the woods. But he's a really big dog. He's your dog."

"He's mine, yes, and I'm his. He's Kathel, and he won't harm you. Have you a fear of dogs, cousin?"

"No. But he's *huge*. What is he?"

"Breeding, you mean. His father is an Irish wolfhound, and his mother a mix of Irish Dane and Scottish deerhound."

"He looks fierce and dignified at the same time. Can I pet him?"

"That would be up to you and him," Branna said as she brought tea and sugar biscuits to the table. She said nothing more as Iona crouched, held out the back of her hand for the dog to sniff, then stroked it gently over his head.

"Hello, Kathel. I didn't have time to introduce myself before. You scared the crap out of me."

She rose, smiled at Branna. "I'm so happy to meet you, to be here. Everything's been so crazy, and it's all running around in my head. I can hardly believe I'm standing here."

"Sit then, and have your tea."

"I barely knew about you," Iona began as she sat, warmed her chilled hands on the cup. "I mean, Nan had told me about the cousins. You and your brother."

"Connor."

"Yes, Connor, and the others who live in Galway or Clare. She wanted to bring me over years ago, but it didn't work out. My parents—well, mostly my mother—didn't really want it, and she and my father split up, and then, well, you're just bouncing around between them. Then they both remarried, and that was weird because my mother insisted on an annulment. They say how that doesn't really make you a bastard, but it sure feels like it."

Branna barely lifted her eyebrows. "I imagine it does, yes."

"Then there was school and work, and I was involved with someone for a while. One day I looked at him and thought, Why? I mean, we didn't have anything for each other but habit and convenience, and people need more, don't they?"

"I'd say they do."

"I want more, sometime anyway. Mostly, I never felt like I fit. Where I was, something always felt a little skewed, not quite right. Then I started having the dreams—or I started remembering them, and I went to visit Nan. Everything she told me should've sounded crazy. It shouldn't have made sense, but it did. It made everything make sense.

"I'm babbling. I'm so nervous." She picked up a cookie, stuffed it in her mouth. "These are good. I'm—"

"Don't be saying you're sorry again. It's coming on pitiful. Tell me about the dreams."

"He wants to kill me."

"Who?"

"I don't know. Or I didn't. Nan says his name is—was—is Cabhan, and he's a sorcerer. Evil. Centuries ago our ancestor, the first dark witch, destroyed him. Except some part of him survived it. He still wants to kill me. Us. I know that sounds insane."

Placidly, Branna sipped her tea. "Do I look shocked by all this?"

"No. You look really calm. I wish I could be really calm. And you're beautiful. I always wanted to be beautiful, too. And taller. You're taller. Babbling. Can't stop it."

Rising, Branna opened a cupboard, took out a bottle of whiskey. "It's a good day for a little whiskey in your tea. So you heard this story about Cabhan and Sorcha, the first dark witch, and decided to come to Ireland to meet me."

"Basically. I quit my job, I sold my stuff."

"You . . ." For the first time Branna looked genuinely surprised. "You sold your things?"

"Including twenty-eight pairs of designer shoes—bought at discount, but still. That stung some, but I wanted the break clean. And I needed the money to come here. To stay here. I have a work visa. I'll get a job, find a place to live."

She picked up another cookie, hoping it would stop the flood of words, but they just kept pouring out. "I know it's crazy spending so much to stay at Ashford, but I just wanted it. I've got nothing back there but Nan, not really. And she'll come if I ask her. I feel like I might fit here. Like things might balance here. I'm tired of not knowing why I don't belong."

"What was your work?"

"I was a riding instructor. Trail guide, stable hand. I'd hoped to be a jockey once, but I love them too much, and didn't have the passion for racing and training."

Watching her, Branna only nodded. "It's horses, of course."

"Yeah, I'm good with them."

"I've no doubt of that. I know one of the owners of the stables here, the hotel uses them for guests. They do trail rides, and riding lessons and the like. I think Boyle might find a place for you."

"You're kidding? I never figured to get stable work right off. I figured waitress, shop clerk. It would be fabulous if I could work there."

Some would say too good to be true, but Iona had never believed that. Good should be true.

"Look, I'll muck out stalls, groom. Whatever he needs or wants."

"I'll have a word with him."

"I can't thank you enough," Iona said, reaching for Branna's hand. As they touched, gripped, heat and light flashed.

Though Iona's hand trembled, she didn't pull away, didn't look away.

"What does it mean?"

"It means it may be time at last. Did cousin Mary Kate give you a gift?"

"Yes. When I went to see her, when she told me." With her free hand, Iona reached for the chain under her sweater, took out the copper amulet with the sign of the horse.

"It was made by Sorcha for her youngest child, her daughter—"

"Teagan," Iona supplied. "To shield her from Cabhan. For Branaugh it was the hound—I should have realized that when I saw the dog. And for Eamon, the hawk. She told me the stories as long as I can remember, but I thought they were stories. My mother insisted they were. And she didn't like Nan telling them to me. So I stopped telling her—my mother—about them. My mother prefers to just sort of glide along."

"That's why it is the amulet wasn't passed to her, but to you. She wasn't the one. You are. Cousin Mary Kate would come, but we knew she wasn't the one, but like a guardian for the amulet, for the legacy. It was passed to her by others who guarded and waited. Now it comes to you."

And you, Branna thought, have come to me.

"Did she tell you what you are?" Branna asked.

"She said . . ." Iona let out a long breath. "She said I'm the Dark Witch. But you—"

"There are three. Three is good magick. So now we're three. You and I, and Connor. But each must accept the whole, and themselves, and the legacy. Do you?"

Hoping for calm, Iona took a gulp of whiskey-laced tea. "I'm working on it."

"What can you do? She wouldn't have passed this to you unless she was sure. Show me what you can do."

"What?" Iona wiped suddenly damp palms on her jeans. "Like an audition?"

"I've practiced all my life; you haven't. But you are the blood." Branna tilted her head, her beautiful face skeptical. "Have you no skills as yet?"

"I've got some skills. It's just I've never . . . except with Nan." Annoyed, uneasy, Iona drew the candle on the table closer. "Now I'm nervous," she muttered. "I feel like I'm trying out for the school play. I bombed that one."

"Clear your mind. Let it come."

She breathed again, slow and steady, put her focus, her energy on the candlewick. Felt the warmth rise in her, and light seep through. And she blew gently.

The flame flickered, swayed, then burned true.

"It's so cool," Iona whispered. "I'll never get used to it. I'm just . . . magick."

"It's power. It must be trained, disciplined, and respected. And honored."

"You sound like Nan. She showed me when I was little, and I believed. Then I thought they were just magick tricks, because my parents said they were. And I think—I know—my mother told her to stop or she wouldn't let her see me."

"Your mother's mind is closed. She's like a lot of others. You shouldn't be angry with her."

"She kept me from this. From what I am."

"Now you know. Can you do more?"

"A few things. I can levitate things—not big things, and it's fifty-fifty. Horses. I understand what they're feeling. I always have. I tried a glamour, but that was a terrible bust. My eyes went purple—even the whites, and my teeth glowed like neon. I had to call in sick for two days before it wore off."

Amused, Branna added more tea and whiskey to the cups.

"What can you do?" Iona demanded. "I showed mine. You show yours."

"Fair enough then." Branna flicked out a hand, and held a ball of white fire in her palm.

"Holy shit. That's . . ." Warily Iona reached out, brought her fingertips close enough to feel the heat. "I want to do that."

"Then you'll practice, and you'll learn."

"You'll teach me?"

"I'll guide you. It's already in you, but needs the route, the signs, the . . . finesse. I'll give you some books to read and study. Take your week at the castle, and think about what you want, Iona Sheehan. Think carefully, for once it begins, you can't go back."

"I don't want to go back."

"I don't mean to America, or your life there. I mean from the path we'll walk." She flicked her hand again and, with it empty, picked up her tea. "Cabhan, what is left of him, may be worse than what was. And what is left wants what you have, what we have. And he wants our blood. Your power and your life, you'll risk both, so think carefully, for it's not a game we'd be playing."

"Nan said it had to be a choice, my choice. She told me he—Cabhan—would want what I have, what I am, and do whatever he could to get it. She cried when I said I was going to come, but she was proud, too. As soon as I got here, I knew it was the right choice. I don't want to ignore what I am. I just want to understand it."

"Staying is still a choice. And if you decide to stay, you'll stay here, with me and Connor."

"Here?"

"It's best we stay together. There's room enough."

Nothing had prepared her for this. Nothing in her life measured as amazing a gift. "You'd let me live here, with you?"

"We're cousins, after all. Take your week. Connor and I have committed, have taken an oath if the third came, we'd accept. But you haven't had a lifetime, so think it through, and be sure. The decision has to be yours."

Whatever it was, Branna thought, would change all.

4

THE RAIN SOAKED HER AGAIN ON HER TREK BACK, BUT it didn't dampen her mood. After warming her bones in the shower, Iona dug out flannel pants, a thermal T-shirt, then, dumping her suitcase on the floor—she'd unpack properly later—she crawled into bed.

And slept like the dead for four solid hours.

She woke in the dark, completely disoriented and starving.

Though her thoroughly disorganized possessions taunted her, she rooted through for jeans, a sweater, warm socks, boots. Armed with her guidebook and one of the books Branna had lent her, she took herself off to the hotel's cottage restaurant for the food, the company.

A fire snapped in the hearth while she dug into a bowl of roasted vegetable soup and pored over her books. She liked the comfort of the mix of voices around her, Irish, American, German—and, she thought, possibly Swedish. She dined on fish and chips, and since it was her first night, treated herself to a glass of champagne.

The waitress had a smile as brilliant as her bright red hair, and gifted Iona with it as she refilled the water glass. "Are you enjoying your meal then?"

"It's wonderful." Drawing her shoulders up and in, in a self-hug, Iona beamed a smile back. "Everything's just wonderful."

"Would it be your first time at Ashford?"

"Yes. It's amazing. It still feels like a dream."

"Well, they say we should have better weather tomorrow if you're after rambling about."

"I'd like to." Should she rent a car? Iona wondered. Try her luck on the roads? Maybe just a walk to the village, for now. "Actually, I took a walk through the grounds, the woods this afternoon."

"In all that drench?"

"I couldn't resist. I wanted to see my cousin. She lives nearby."

"Is that the truth? Sure it's nice to have family while you're visiting. Who is she, if you don't mind me asking?"

"They, really, though I only met Branna today. Branna O'Dwyer."

The girl's smile didn't dim, but her eyes showed new focus. "A cousin to the O'Dwyers, are you now?"

"Yes. Do you know them?"

"Everyone knows Branna and Connor O'Dwyer. He's a falconer. The hotel will book hawk walks through the falconry school, and that Connor manages. It's a very popular activity with the guests here. And Branna . . . she has a shop in Cong. She makes soaps and lotions and tonics and the like. The Dark Witch, it's called, after a local legend."

"I saw her workshop today. I'll have to check out the shop and the falconry school."

"Both are pleasant walks right from the hotel. Well then, enjoy your meal."

The waitress left her to it, but Iona noticed she stopped by another server for a quick word. And both of them glanced back to Iona's table.

So, she thought, the O'Dwyers were local interests. Hardly

surprising. But it was weird sitting there eating her fish and chips knowing she'd become an object of speculation.

Did they all know Branna wasn't merely the owner of the Dark Witch, but was one?

And so am I, Iona thought. Now I have to learn just what that means. Determined to do just that, she opened another book, and read her way through the rest of the meal.

The rain eased, but the night wind blew fierce, urging her to hurry back to the main hotel rather than strolling along the river Cong as she'd hoped.

She got "good evenings" and "welcome backs" from the staff as she stepped in, crossed through the lobby. Curious, she took brochures on the falconry school and the stables, then—what the hell, she was sort of on vacation—asked for tea to be sent to her room.

Once inside, she made herself set the brochures and books aside to deal, finally, with the unpacking.

After the brutal purge of her wardrobe, the selling of whatever she'd put aside, she still had more than enough. And she'd brought all she thought she'd need for her new life.

By the time she'd filled the wardrobe, the drawers, repacked items she decided could wait, the tea arrived, along with a plate of pretty cookies. Satisfied she'd done her chores, she changed back into her sleep pants, piled up the pillows and, sitting in bed, composed the email on her notebook to let her grandmother know she'd arrived safe, had met with Branna.

> Ireland's all you said and more, even just the little I've seen. So is Branna. It's so generous of her to let me stay with her. The castle's just awesome, and I'm going to enjoy every minute I'm here, but I'm already looking forward to moving in with Branna—and Connor. I hope I

meet him soon. If I get the job at the stables, it'll just be perfect. So think good thoughts.

Nan, I'm sitting in this wonderful bed in a castle in Ireland, drinking tea and thinking of all that's yet to come. I know you said it could be a hard road, hard choices, and Branna sure as hell made that clear. But I'm so excited, I'm so happy.

I think, maybe, I've finally found where I fit.

Tomorrow I'll check out the stables, the falconry school, the village—and Branna's shop. I'll let you know how it all goes. I love you!

Iona

She sent dutiful emails to her mother, her father. A few cheerful ones to friends and coworkers. And reminded herself to take some pictures to send next time.

She set the notebook aside to charge, retrieved the books, the brochures. This time she got into the bed, wiggled her shoulders back against the pillows.

Blissfully happy, she scanned the brochures, studied the photos. The school sounded absolutely fascinating. And the stables perfect. One of her mother's favorite warnings was: Don't get your hopes up.

But Iona's were, high, high up.

She slipped the stable brochure under her pillow. She'd sleep on it for luck. Then she opened Branna's book again.

Within twenty minutes, with the lights on, the tea tray still on the bed beside her, she'd dropped back into sleep.

And this time dreamed of hawks and horses, of the black hound. Of the deep green woods where a stone cabin nestled with fog crawling at its feet.

After dismounting a horse as gray as the fog, she walked through the mists, the hood of her cloak drawn up to cover her hair. She carried roses, for love, to the stone polished smooth and carved deep by magick and grief. There she laid the roses, white as the innocence she'd lost.

"I am home, Mother. We are home." Dabbing the tears on her cheeks with her fingers, she traced the name.

SORCHA
The Dark Witch

And the words bled against the stone.

I am waiting for you.

Not her mother's voice, but his. With all that had been done, all that had been sacrificed, he survived.

She had known it. They had all known it. And hadn't she come here, alone, for this as much as to visit her mother's grave?

"You will wait longer yet. You will wait a day, a moon, a thousand years, but you will never have what you covet."

You come alone, in the starlight. You look for love. I would give it to you.

"I am not alone." She spun around. Her hood fell back and her bright hair caught the light. "I am never alone."

The fog swirled, spun up, spun out, coalesced into the form of a man. Or what had been a man.

She'd faced him before, as a child. But she had more than rocks now.

A shadow he was, she thought. A shadow to haunt dreams and smother light.

Such a pretty thing. A woman now, ripe for plucking. Do you still throw stones?

Even as she stared into his eyes, she watched the red stone he wore around his neck gleam.

"My aim is as true as it was ever."

He laughed, weaved closer. She caught his scent, the hint of sulphur. Only a devil's bargain could have given him the power to exist.

Your mother is gone, no skirts to hide behind now. I defeated her, took her life, rent her power with my hands.

"You lie. Do you think we cannot see? Do you think we do not know?" His amulet pulsed red—his heart, she thought. His center, his power. She meant to take it, at any cost. "With a kiss she burned you. And I marked you. You bear it still."

She held up her hands, fingers curled toward him so the mark on his shoulder burned like a flame.

On his scream she leapt forward, snatching at the stone he wore. But he lashed out, fingers going to claws, and scored their grooves in the back of her hand.

Damned to you and all your blood. I will crush you in my fists, wring what you are out into a silver cup. And drink.

"My blood will send you to hell." She struck out with her bleeding hand, driving her power through it.

But the fog collapsed so she struck only air. The red stone pulsed, pulsed, then vanished.

"My blood will send you to hell," she repeated.

And in the dream he seemed to stare at Iona, into her eyes. Into her spirit.

"It is not for me, in this time, in this place. But for you in yours. Remember."

And cradling her wounded hand, called to her horse.

She mounted. She turned once to look at the stone, the flowers, the home she'd once known.

"On my oath, on my love, we will not fail though it takes a thousand lifetimes." She laid her hand on her belly, on the gentle bulge. "There is already another coming."

She rode away, through the woods, toward the castle where she and her family were housed.

Iona woke trembling. Her right hand throbbing with pain, she groped for the light with her left. In its flash she saw the raw gashes, the run of blood. On a shocked cry, she scrambled up, dashed toward the bath, snatching a towel as she lurched toward the sink.

Before she could wrap the wound, it began to change. She watched in fascinated horror as the gashes in her skin closed, the blood dried, then faded, like the pain. Within seconds she examined her unmarked hand.

A dream, but not, she thought. A vision? One where she'd been an observer, and somehow a participant.

She'd *felt* the pain—and the rage, the grief. She'd felt the power, more than she'd ever experienced, more than she'd ever known.

Teagan's power?

Lifting her gaze, Iona studied herself in the mirror, called back the images from the dream. But it *had* been her face . . . hadn't it? Her build, her coloring.

But not, she thought now, her voice. Not even her language, though she'd understood every word. Old Gaelic, she assumed.

She needed to know more, to learn more. To find a way to understand how events that had happened hundreds of years before could draw her in so absolutely that she actually felt genuine pain.

Leaning over the sink, she splashed cold water on her face, caught the time on her watch. Still shy of four A.M., but she was done with sleep. Her body clock would adjust eventually, and for now she might as well just go with it. Maybe she'd read until sunrise.

She walked back into the bedroom, started to lift the tea tray she'd ended up sleeping with. And she saw on the lovely white sheets three drops of red. Of blood. Hers, she realized.

The dream—vision—experience—hadn't just given her pain. She'd bled in it.

What kind of power could drag her into her own dreams and cause her to bleed from an ancestor's wound?

Leaving the tray where it was, she sat on the side of the bed, brushed her fingers over her throat.

What if those claws had struck there, slashed her jugular? Would she have died? Could dreams kill?

No, she didn't want books, she decided. She wanted answers, and she knew who had them.

By six, fueled with coffee, she headed out once again past the fountains and flowers and green lawns to the thick woods. This time the light held soft and luminous to drip palely through branches as the wide path narrowed. And this time she saw the signposts for the falconry school, the stables.

Later that morning, she promised herself, she'd visit both, then top it off with a hike to Cong. But she wouldn't be put off with a stack of books and a bit of tabletop magick.

The dream stayed with her so closely she caught herself checking her hand for claw marks.

A long, high note had her head snapping up, her gaze shooting skyward. The hawk soared across the pale blue, a gorgeous golden brown sweep that circled, then swooped. She swore she heard the wind of its wings as it danced through the trees, and landed on a branch overhead.

"Oh my God, look at you! You're just gorgeous."

He stared down at her, golden eyes steady, unblinking, his wings regally folded. She wondered fancifully if he'd left his crown at home.

Slowly, she dug into her back pocket for her phone, holding her breath as she hit camera mode. "I hope you don't mind. It's not every day a woman meets a hawk. Or a falcon. I'm not sure which you are. Just let me . . ." She framed him in, took the shot, then a second.

"Are you hunting, or just out for your version of a morning stroll? I guess you're from the school, but—"

She stopped when the hawk turned its head. She thought she caught it, too, a faint whistle. In response, the hawk lifted off the branch, swooped and dodged its way through the trees and was gone.

"I'm definitely booking a falcon walk," she decided, and checked her photos before she stuffed the phone away to hike on.

She reached the upended tree, the wall of vines. Though the pull returned, she pushed it back. Not now, not today when the emotion of the dreams swam so close to the surface.

Answers first.

The dog waited at the edge of the woods as if he'd been expecting her. He swished his tail by way of greeting, accepted the stroke on his head.

"Good morning. It's nice to know I'm not the only one out and about early. I hope Branna's not pissed when I come knocking, but I really need to talk to her."

Kathel led the way to the pretty blue cottage, straight to the bright red door. "Here goes." She used the knocker shaped like a trinity knot, considered how best to approach her cousin.

But the one she hadn't yet met answered the door.

He looked like some rumpled, sleepy warrior prince with his mass of waving hair, a burnished brown that spilled around a face as elegantly boned as his sister's. Eyes green as the hills blinked at her.

He stood tall and lean in gray flannel pants and a white pullover unraveling at the hem.

"I'm sorry," she began, and thought those words appeared to be her default when she came to this house.

"Good morning to you. You must be cousin Iona from the States."

"Yes, I—"

"Welcome home."

She found herself enfolded in a big, hard hug that lifted her up to the toes of her boots. The cheerful gesture made her eyes sting, and her nerves vanish.

"I'd be Connor, if you're wondering. Did Kathel find you and bring you 'round?"

"No, that is, yes. I was already coming here, but he found me."

"Well then, come in out of the cold. Winter's still got its teeth in us."

"Thanks. I know it's early."

"That it is. The day will insist on starting that way." In a gesture she found both casual and miraculous, he flicked a hand at the living room hearth. Flames leaped up to curl around the stacked peat. "We'll have some breakfast," he continued, "and you can tell me everything there is to know about Iona Sheehan."

"That won't take long."

"Oh, I'll wager there's plenty to tell." He grabbed her hand and pulled her through the house.

She had a quick impression of color and jumble and light, the scents of vanilla and smoke. And space, more of it than she'd expected.

Then they were in the kitchen with a pretty stone hearth, long counters the color of slate, walls of lake blue. Pots of herbs thrived on wide windowsills, copper pots hung over a center island. Cabinets of dark gray showed colorful glassware, dishes behind their glass fronts. In a jut ringed with windows stood a beautiful old table and charmingly mismatched chairs.

The combination of farmhouse casual and the modern efficiency of glossy white appliances worked like magick.

"This is really beautiful. Like something out of a really smart magazine."

"Is it? Well, it's Branna who has very definite ideas, and this is one of them." Tilting his head in study, he gave her another quick, charming smile. "Can you cook?"

"Ah . . . sort of. I mean, I can, I just suck at it."

"Well now, that's a real pity. I'm on duty then. Will it be coffee or tea for you?"

"Oh, coffee, thanks. You don't have to cook."

"I do if I want to eat, and I do. In general, around here Branna's the cook and I'm the bottle washer, but I can manage breakfast well enough."

He punched controls on a very intimidating-looking coffeemaker as he spoke, pulled a basket of eggs, a hunk of butter, a pack of bacon from the fridge.

"Take off your coat and be at home," he told her. "Branna says you're living the life at Ashford for a few days before you're coming here. How are you finding Ashford?"

"Like a dream. I slept too much of the day away yesterday. Obviously, I'm making up for it. You don't mind me moving in?"

"Why would I? We'll be taking turns as bottle washers, so that's one for me."

He got down a skillet, set it on the stove top. "Cups up there, and fresh cream if you're wanting it, and sugar as well." He gestured here and there before he tossed bacon into the skillet.

All of it, and all of him, she thought, seemed as casual and miraculous as his wrist-flick fire-starting.

"I hear you're after working at the stables."

"I'm hoping."

"Branna had a word with Boyle. He'll be talking to you about that today."

"Really?" Her heart actually leapt at the prospect. "That's great. That's fantastic. A lot of people thought I'd lost my mind, just packing up, coming here without a serious plan, without a ready job or a place to stay."

"What's an adventure if you know all the steps before you take them?"

"I know!" She grinned at him. "Now I've got a job interview, and family to live with. And this morning—certainly it wasn't my plan last night to walk over at six A.M.—I saw a hawk in the woods. It flew right down, sat on a branch and watched me. I took pictures."

She dug out her phone to show him. "I guess you'd know what kind of hawk—falcon—he is."

As he lifted the bacon out of the skillet, Connor angled his head to study the image. "A Harris's hawk—the same we use for our hawk walks. That's Fin's Merlin, and a fine bird he is. Finbar Burke," he added. "He owns the stables with Boyle, and he started the falconry school here at Ashford. He owns quite a bit of this and that, does Fin."

"Will I interview with him, too?"

"Oh, he'd likely leave that to Boyle. Plenty of cream and two sugars in my coffee, if you will."

"Same as me."

"Branna, she's one for just a dollop of the cream. Go ahead and fix her up. She's on her way down, and she'll need it."

"She is? How do you . . . Oh."

He only smiled. "She sends out fierce vibrations of a morning before her coffee, and it's a bit on the early side for her so she may bite."

Iona grabbed another cup, hurriedly poured the coffee. She was stirring in that dollop of cream when Branna walked in, dark hair tumbled nearly to her waist, eyes blurry and annoyed.

She took the cup Iona held out, took two deep swallows as she watched Iona over the rim. "All right then, what happened?"

"Ah now, don't poke at her," Connor said. "She's had a rough go. Give her a chance to get some food into her."

"I doubt she's come here at dawn for breakfast. You're going to overcook those eggs, Connor, as always."

"I'm not. Slice up some bread for toasting why don't you, and she'll tell us once she's settled."

"She's standing right here," Iona reminded them.

"At half-six in the bloody morning," Branna finished, but she picked up a bread knife, took a cloth off a loaf on a cutting board on the counter.

"I'm sorry, but—"

"Every second sentence she utters starts with those two words." Branna sliced bread, tossed it into the toaster.

"Jesus, finish your coffee before your black mood ruins my appetite. Let's have some plates, Iona, there's a girl." His tone shifted from sharp to gentle as his sister leaned back against the counter and sulkily drank her coffee.

Saying nothing, Iona got down plates and, at his direction, located the flatware, set the table.

She sat with her cousins, looked at the platter heaped with bacon and eggs, the plate of toasted bread, listened to the two of them bicker about how the eggs were cooked, whose turn it was to go to the market and why the laundry hadn't been folded.

"My coming here like this put you at odds, so you're fighting, but I—"

"We're not fighting." Connor scooped up a forkful of eggs. "Are we fighting, Branna?"

"We're not. We're communicating." Then she laughed, tossed her magnificent hair, and bit into her toast. "If we were fighting, more than these eggs would be scorched."

"They're not scorched," Connor insisted. "They're . . . firm."

"They're good."

Branna rolled her eyes at Iona. "You'd have eaten better at the hotel, be sure of it. The chef there is brilliant."

"I wasn't thinking about food this morning. I can't just read books, and stumble around trying to . . . I don't know what to do unless I *know*."

"She's a bit of food in her now," Branna said to Connor. "So, what happened?"

"I had a dream, that wasn't a dream."

She told all of it, every detail she could remember as carefully as she could manage.

"Let me see your hand," Branna interrupted. "The one that bled."

She took it, held it fast while she traced fingertips over the back. The skin split, filled with blood. "Be still!" Branna snapped when Iona gasped and tried to pull free. "It's but a memory now. There's no pain. This is just the mirror of what was."

"It was real. It hurt, burned. And there was blood on the sheet."

"Then, yes, it was real. This is only a reflection." She traced her fingertips over it again, and the wound vanished.

"I was pregnant. I mean, she was pregnant. In the vision, or dream. He didn't know. He couldn't see it, or feel it? I don't know which." Agitated, Iona shoved at her hair with both hands. "I have to know, Branna. You said I needed to think carefully, but how can I when I don't have all the information?"

"It's twined close," Branna said, and got Connor's nod. "And you're more open than I understood. I'll give you something to filter the visions; it may help you keep yourself a step back we'll say. We'll guide you, Connor and I, best that we can. But we can't tell you what we don't know. If Teagan went alone back to the cabin, back to the woods, was confronted, you're the one telling us."

"We know pieces, Branna and I, and now you'll know more. We've both gone back, had glimpses, felt as you feel now."

"But we were only two," Branna added. "There must be three."

"He was bolder with you, as you're more vulnerable. You won't stay that way," Connor assured her.

It sounded ridiculous, but she had to say aloud what churned through her mind. "Can he kill me? If I go back, when I sleep, could he kill me?"

"He could try and likely will try." Branna answered the ridiculous with bald simplicity. "You'll stop him."

"How?"

"With your will, with your power. With the amulet you wear, and must always wear, and with what I'll give you."

Branna stopped pushing her eggs around her plate, picked up her coffee. And once again watched Iona over the rim.

"But understand, if you stay, if you mean to be with us, and be what you are, he will come for you. You must stay freely, and knowing that, or go and live your life."

It was all too fantastic. And yet. She'd lived that dream. She'd felt the pain.

And she knew the draw and pull of what lived inside her.

Bridges burned, Iona reminded herself, for the chance to build new ones. Wherever they led—and they'd already brought her closer to what and who she was than any of the ones before.

"I'm not leaving."

"You've had little time to think or understand," Branna began, but Iona only shook her head.

"I *know* I've never belonged anywhere before. And I think I understand this is why. Because I belong here. I come from her, from Teagan. I understand, too, she wanted me to see she hurt him that night, and he was afraid. Doesn't that— Couldn't that mean I can hurt him?"

"If it's here you belong, and I believe it is, then here you are. But don't rush your fences," Connor warned her, and patted her hand. "You've only begun."

"I'm an excellent rider with a damn good seat. And I'll learn. Teach me." She leaned closer as the urgency rose in her. "Show me."

Branna sat back. "You haven't much patience."

"It depends. No," Iona admitted. "Not a lot."

"You'll need to find some, but we'll take some steps. Small ones."

"Tell me about the cabin. They lived there, Sorcha died there. Is it still there? There's a big tree, uprooted, and these thick vines, and—"

"Don't go there," Branna said quickly. "Not yet and not alone."

"She's right. You have to wait for that. You have to promise not to go through on your own." Connor gripped her hand, and she felt the heat pump against her palm. "Your word on it, and I'll know if you mean to keep it."

"All right. I promise. But you'll take me."

"Not today," Branna told her. "I have things I have to do, and Connor needs to go to work. And you need to go see Boyle."

"Now?"

"After breakfast's soon enough, and after you've washed up as payment for getting me out of my bed at this ungodly hour. Come back later. I should be done and ready by about three."

"I'll be here." Settled, confident again, Iona helped herself to another piece of toast.

5

AS SHE FOLLOWED THE PATH, IONA TRIED WORKING ON her interview skills. What to say, how to say it. She hoped she'd dressed appropriately, as she hadn't expected an immediate job interview when she'd left her hotel room that morning in jeans and her favorite red sweater. Still, she was aiming for a stable job, so she'd hardly need a business suit and a briefcase.

Neither of which she had anyway, she mused, or had ever wanted.

What she did have was the resume she'd put together, the recommendation by her previous employers, all the references from her students or their parents.

She didn't care what they paid her, not to start. She just needed a riding boot in the door. Then she could, and would, prove herself. And while she proved herself she'd not only have work, she'd have the work she loved.

Her stomach knotted, as it did when she wanted something too much, so she ordered herself not to babble when she met the man who could hire her or just send her on her way.

The minute she turned into the clearing, saw the building, the nerves dropped away. Here was the familiar, a kind of home. The shape of the stables and its weather-faded red paint, the two horses with their heads poking out of the half doors, the trucks, the trailers scattered around the graveled lot.

The scents of hay, horses, manure, leather, oil, grain caught at her heart. It all flooded over her as her boots crunched on the gravel.

She couldn't help herself. She went straight to the horses.

The chestnut held her gaze steadily, watching her approach. He snorted at her, shifted his weight. He bent his head when she stroked his cheek, then gave her an easy push with his nose.

"It's nice to meet you, too. Look how handsome you are."

Clear eyes, clean, glossy coat, well-brushed mane, and a look of the easygoer about him, she noted. Healthy, well-tended horses boosted the as-yet-unmet Boyle McGrath and Finbar Burke in her estimation.

"I'm hoping we'll be seeing a lot of each other. And who's your friend?" She turned to the second horse, a sturdy-looking bay who rubbed his neck on the window frame as if he wasn't the least bit interested in her.

When she stepped toward him, he laid his ears back. Iona just angled her head, sent him soothing thoughts until they perked up again. "That's better. No need to be nervous. I'm just here to say hello."

She gave him a quick rub.

"That's Caesar taking your measure there."

Iona turned, saw the Amazon in riding boots behind her. The woman's curvy body filled out snug riding pants and a rough plaid jacket. Her hair, worn in a long, messy braid, reminded Iona of her grandmother's prized mink coat—rich and luxurious brown. Though

Ireland sang in her voice, her golden skin and deep brown eyes spoke of sunny climes and gypsy campfires.

"He generally likes to act fierce on first acquaintance. And can be shy about being touched—usually," she added when Iona continued to stroke him.

"He's just careful around strangers. Are they both trail horses?"

"We save Caesar for experienced riders, but they both have a job here, yes."

"I'm hoping I will, too. I'm Iona Sheehan. I've come to talk to Boyle McGrath."

"Ah, you'd be the Yank, a cousin of Connor's and Branna's. I'm Meara Quinn." She stepped forward, shook Iona's hand firmly, gave her a quick, no-nonsense appraisal. "You've come early today."

"I'm still adjusting to the time change. I can come back if it's not a good time."

"Oh, one time's as good as another. Boyle's not here, but will be soon enough. I can show you about if you'd like."

"I would, thanks." Like Caesar's, Iona's nerves dropped away. "Have you worked here long?"

"Oh, about eight years. Closer to nine, I'm thinking. Well, who's counting, yeah?"

She led the way in, long strides on long legs that had Iona quickening her pace to keep up. Iona saw a room off to the side, jumbled and crowded with riding hats, leg protectors, some boots. A lean tabby sidled out, gave Iona a look as measuring as Meara's had been, then strolled outside.

"That was Darby, who graces us with his presence. A fierce mouser is Darby, so we put up with his sullen moods. He earns his kibble, and comes and goes as he pleases."

"Nice work if you can get it."

Meara grinned. "That's the truth. And so, we take bookings for rides, guide the customers between the Lough Corrib and Mask.

Usually an hour, but we'll do longer if they ask and pay for it. And we have the training ring here."

Iona walked in to watch a woman in her thirties on the back of a compact chestnut, and the fireplug of a man in work jeans putting horse and rider through the paces.

"That's our Mick. A jockey he was in his youth, and has unlimited stories to tell about those days."

"I'd like to hear them."

"Be sure you will if you're here above five minutes." Meara set her hands on her hips, watched Mick a moment, letting Iona do the same. "Took a bad fall, Mick did, in a race at Roscommon, and so ended that portion of his career. Now he teaches and trains, and his students collect blue ribbons."

"Sounds like you're lucky to have him."

"That we are. We've another area at the big stables, not far from here, for jumping practice and instruction. We cater to locals as well for lessons, and the occasional guided ride. We tend to run a bit slow this time of year, but there's plenty needs doing. We've twenty-two horses between what we keep here and what's at the other stable. The tack room's this way."

She glanced over at Iona. "We ride English, so if you're used to a Western saddle, you'd have to adjust."

"I ride both."

"That's handy for you. Boyle's fierce about keeping the tack in good order," she continued as she gestured Iona into the room. "Those of us who work here do whatever comes to hand. Deal with the tack, take bookings, muck out, groom, feed—there's a board with each horse's feed schedule and diet hung outside their stalls. Have you done any guided rides?"

"Back home, sure."

"Then you know it's more than plodding along with the clients. You need to judge how they handle the ride, the mount, and most who book here want some color, if you understand me, some talk of the area, the history, even flora and fauna."

"I'll study up. Actually, I've already done some. I like knowing where I am."

"Hard to know where you're going unless you do."

"I'm open to surprises there."

Familiar scents surrounded her—leather and saddle soap. To most eyes, she imagined, the tack room would strike as cluttered and disorganized, but she saw the basic pattern, the day-to-day use, repair, maintain.

Bridles hung on one wall, the saddles on their racks on another. Harness racks on the third, with hooks and racks for bits and saddle pads, shelves for this and that, rags and brushes and saddle soaps and oils. And a kind of alcove for brooms, pitchforks, the curry combs, hoof picks, hooks again for buckets. She spotted an old refrigerator.

"Medicine's in there," Meara told her. "Close and handy when there's need. We do what we can to keep it all reasonably tidy, and a time or two a year when we're slow, we put some elbow grease into it. Would you have your own gear?"

"I sold it." That had been painful. "Except for my riding boots, my muck boots, riding helmet. I didn't know if I'd have any place to keep it, or even if I'd be able to use it, at least for a while. Do I need my own?"

"You don't, no. Well then, you'll want to see the horses we have here. We board as well, but at the big stable. Here we keep the riding hacks, and switch them out between here and there as needed."

Meara walked and talked, more long strides in battered boots as she led Iona through to the stalls.

"We've a booking for four later this morning, and two more this afternoon, a party of two and another of six. Lessons booked through the day so we've a full house here."

She stopped to rub the head of a sturdy chestnut with a white blaze. "This is Maggie, as sweet as they come. She's good with children or the skittish. She's patient, is Maggie, and likes the quiet life. Don't you, darling?"

The mare nuzzled at Meara's shoulder, then dipped her head at Iona.

"Such a pretty face." After a rub and a scratch, Maggie bumped at Iona's pocket, made her laugh. "I don't have any with me today. I'll be sure to bring along an apple next time. She's . . ." Iona trailed off as she caught Meara's questioning look. "What?"

"Odd, is all. Maggie has a particular fondness for apples." Leaving it at that, Meara gestured. "And that's our Jack. He's a big boy, and likes his naps, and will try to graze his way through the ride if he's able. Needs a firm hand."

"Like to eat and sleep, do you? Who doesn't? I bet a big, strong boy like you can carry three hundred without blinking an eye."

"He will that. And here we have Spud. He's young and feisty but goes well."

"A dark horse." Iona moved over to run a hand down his black mane. "With a weakness for potatoes." She caught the look again, used a smile. "His name. Spud."

"We'll use that one if you like. And here's Queen Bee, as she thinks she is. She bosses the others every opportunity, but she likes a good ride."

"I wouldn't mind one myself. She's had some trouble with her right foreleg?"

"A bit of a strain a week or so back. Healed up nicely. If she told you different, she's just looking for sympathy."

Unsure, Iona took a step back, slid her hands into her pockets.

"I'm not likely to get the jitters if someone shares a communion with horses," Meara commented. "Especially someone blood kin to the O'Dwyers."

"I'm good with them. Horses," Iona qualified as she stroked the regal-eyed Queen Bee. "I'm hoping to work on getting good with the O'Dwyers."

"Connor's an easygoer, with a weakness for a pretty face. You've got one. Branna's fair, and that's enough."

"You're friends."

"We are, and have been since we were in nappies, so I know Branna, being fair, wouldn't have sent you to us if you weren't suited."

"I'm good at this. It's what I'm good at." All, she thought, she was certain she was good at.

"You'll need to be. All my life," Meara said at Iona's questioning look. "So I know it's the one who communes with horses who makes the three."

Iona thought of the looks from the waitstaff over dinner the night before. "Does everyone know?"

"What people know, what they believe, what they accept? Those are all different matters, aren't they? Well then, since Boyle's running behind, we can—" She broke off, pulled out her phone when it jingled in her pocket, checked the text. "Ah, good, he's on his way. We'll just go out, if that's good for you, and meet him."

Her potential new boss, Iona thought. "Any tips?"

"You could remember Boyle's fair as well, though he's often short on words and temper."

Meara gestured Iona along as she shoved her phone away again. "He's riding Fin's latest acquisition over. Fin's Boyle's partner, and travels about when he's a mind to buying horses and hawks or whatever strikes his fancy."

"But Boyle—Mr. McGrath—runs the stables."

"He does—or they both do, but it's Boyle who deals more with the day-to-day. Fin found this stallion in Donegal, and had him sent, as Fin himself's still rambling. He plans to stud him out later in the year, and Boyle's just as determined to teach him manners."

"Fin or the stallion?"

Meara let out a big, brassy laugh as they stepped back outside.

"That's a question, and it may be both, though I'd wager he'll have better luck with the horse than Finbar Burke."

She nodded toward the end of the road. "He's a fine-looking bastard for all that, with a devil's temper."

Iona turned. She couldn't say if Meara spoke of the horse or the man astride him. Her first impression was of magnificence and hotheads on both counts.

The horse, big and beautiful at easily sixteen hands, tested his rider with the occasional buck and dance, and even with the distance, she could see the fierce gleam in his eyes. His smoke gray coat showed some sweat, though the morning stayed cool—and his ears stayed stubbornly back.

But the man, big and beautiful as well, had his measure. Iona heard his voice, the challenge in it if not the words, as he kept the horse at a trot.

And something in her, just at the sound of his voice, stirred. Nerves, excitement, she told herself, because the man held her happiness in his hands.

But as they drew closer, the stir grew to a flutter. Attraction struck her double blows—heart and belly as, oh, he really was as magnificent as the horse. And every single bit as appealing to her.

His hair, a kind of rich caramel that wasn't altogether brown, wasn't quite red, blew everywhere in the breeze. He wore a rough jacket, faded jeans, scarred boots, all suiting the tough, rawboned face. The strong jaw and a mouth that struck her as stubborn as the horse he rode just echoed the hard lines of temper barely leashed when the horse bucked again.

A thin scar, like a lightning bolt, cut through his left eyebrow. For reasons she couldn't quite comprehend, it stirred up a delicious little storm of lust inside her.

Cowboy, pirate, wild tribal horseman. How could he be three of her biggest fantasy weaknesses all rolled into one big, bold package?

Boyle McGrath. She said his name in her head, and thought: You could be trouble for me, and I'm so *interested* when it comes to trouble.

"Oh, he's in a mood, our Boyle is. Well, you'd best get used to it if you come to work here, for God knows he has them."

Meara stepped forward, raised her voice. "Giving you a run for it, is he then?"

"Tried to take a chunk out of me. Twice. The right bastard. Tries it again I may geld him myself with a bleeding butter knife."

When Boyle pulled up, the horse shook, pranced, tried to rear.

Big hands, scarred at the knuckles like the eyebrow, the boots, fought the horse down. "I may murder Fin for this one."

As if daring his rider, the horse tried to rear yet again. Instinctively Iona stepped up, gripped the bridle.

"Stay back there," Boyle snapped. "He bites."

"I've been bitten before." She spoke directly to the horse, her eyes on his. "But I'd rather not be again, so just stop it. You're gorgeous," she crooned. "And so pissed off. But you might as well cut it out and see what happens next."

She flicked a glance up at Boyle. He wouldn't bite, she thought, but suspected he had other ways to take a chunk out of a foe.

"I bet you'd get testy, too, if somebody packed you up and took you away from home, then dumped you with a bunch of strangers."

"Testy? He kicked a stable hand and bit a groom, and that was just this morning."

"Stop it," Iona repeated when the horse tried to jerk his head free. "Nobody likes a bully." Using her free hand, she stroked his neck. "Even beautiful ones like you. He's pissed off, that's all, and making sure we all know it," she said to Boyle.

"Oh, is that all? Well then, no harm done." He dismounted, shortened the reins. "You'd be the American cousin then, the one Branna sent."

"Iona Sheehan, and I'm probably as inconvenient to you as this stallion. But I know horses, and this one didn't like being taken away from all he knew. Everything's different here. I know what that's like," she said to the horse. "What's his name?"

"Fin's calling him Alastar."

"Alastar. You'll make your place here." She released the bridle, and the horse flicked his ears. But if he considered trying for a nip, he changed his mind, looked carelessly away.

"I brought my resume," Iona began. Business, business, business, she reminded herself. And stay out of trouble. And pulled out the flash drive she'd stuck in her pocket that morning.

"I've ridden since I was three, and worked with horses—grooming, mucking, trail and guided rides. I've given instruction, private and group. I know horses," she repeated. "And I'm willing to do whatever you need for a chance to work here."

"I've shown her around and about," Meara began, then took the flash drive from Iona. "I'll put this on your desk."

Boyle kept the reins firm in his hand, and his eyes, a burnished gold with hints of green, direct on Iona. "Resumes are just words on paper, aren't they? They're not doing. I can give you work, mucking out. We'll see if you know your way around a horse for grooming before I set you on that. But there's always tack to clean."

Riding boot in the door, she reminded herself. "Then I'll muck and clean."

"You'd make more walking over to the castle and seeing about work there. Waitresses, housekeeping, clerking."

"It's not about making more. It's about doing what I love, and what I'm meant to do. That's here. I'm fine with mucking out."

"Then Meara can get you started on it." He took the flash drive from Meara, stuck it in his own pocket. "I'll see to the paperwork once I get this one settled."

"You're going to put him in a stall?"

"I'm not after checking him into the hotel."

"He'd like . . . Couldn't he use a little more exercise? He's gotten warmed up."

Boyle arched his brows, drawing her gaze to the scarred one—the sexy one. "He's given me near an hour's fight already this morning."

"He's used to being the alpha, aren't you, Alastar? Now you come along and you're . . . a challenge. You said a resume's not doing. Let me do. I can take him around your paddock."

"What are you? Seven stones soaking wet?"

He was giving her a job, she reminded herself. And compared to him—even compared to Meara—she probably did come off as small and weak. "I don't know how much seven stones is, but I'm strong, and I'm experienced."

"He'd rip your arms out, and that's before he tossed you off his back like a bad mood."

"I don't think so. But then, if he did, you'd be right." She glanced back at the horse. "Think about that," she told Alastar.

Boyle considered it. The pretty little faerie queen had something to prove, so he'd let her try. And she could nurse her sore arse—or head, depending on which hit the ground first.

"Once around the ring. Inside," Boyle said, pointing. "If you manage to stay on him that long. Get her a helmet, will you, Meara. It might help her from breaking her head when she lands on it."

"He's not the only one who's pissed off." Confident now, Iona offered Boyle a smile. "I need to shorten the stirrups."

"Inside," he repeated, and led the horse in. "I hope you know how to fall."

"I do. But I won't."

She shortened the stirrups quickly, competently. She knew Boyle watched her, and that was fine, that was good. She *would* settle, and gratefully, for a job doing no more than mucking out stalls and cleaning tack.

But God, she wanted to ride again. And she wanted, keenly, to ride this horse. To feel him under her, to share that power.

"Thanks." She strapped on the helmet Meara brought her, and since Meara had carried one over, Iona used the mounting block.

Alastar quivered under her. She tightened her knees, held out a hand for the reins.

Now he reconsidered—she could see it in those tawny eyes.

"Branna won't be pleased with me if you end up in the hospital."

"You're not afraid of Branna."

She took the reins. Maybe she'd never been sure where she belonged, but she'd always, from the first moment, felt at home in the saddle.

Leaning forward, Iona whispered in Alastar's ear. "Don't make a fool out of me, okay? Let's show off, and show him up."

He walked cooperatively for four steps. Then kicked up his hind legs, dropped down, reared up.

Stop it. We can play that game another time.

She circled him, changed leads, circled back, changed again before nudging him into a trot.

When the horse danced to the side, tried another kick, she laughed.

"I may not weigh as much as the big guy, but I'm sticking."

She took him up to a pretty canter—God, he had beautiful lines—back to a trot.

And felt alive.

"She's more than words on paper," Meara murmured.

"Maybe so. Good seat, good hands—and for some reason that devil seems to like her."

He thought she looked as if she'd been born on a horse, as if she could ride through wind and wood and all but fly over the hills.

Then he shifted his feet, annoyed with his own fanciful thoughts.

"You can take her out with you—*not* on that devil—see how she does on a guide."

"He'll breed well, you know. Fin's got the right of that."

"Fin's rarely wrong. But when he is, it's massive. Still, she'll do. Until she doesn't. Have her put Alastar in the paddock. We'll see if he stays there."

"And you?"

"I'll see to her paperwork."

"When do you want her to start?"

Boyle watched her slide into a fluid lope. "I'm thinking she already has."

SHE DIDN'T GET TO THE VILLAGE. HER PLANS CHANGED IN the best possible way as she spent the rest of her morning mucking out, grooming, signing papers, learning the basics of the rules and rhythms from Meara.

And best of all, she tagged along on a guided ride. The pace might have been easy to the point of lazy, but it was still a ride on the cheerful Spud. She tried to remember landmarks as they rode placidly along the hard path, through the deep green woods, along the dark hum of the river.

An old shed, a scarred pine, a tumble of rocks.

She listened to the rise and fall of Meara's voice as she entertained the clients—a German couple on a brief getaway—and enjoyed the mix of accents.

Here she was, Iona Sheehan, riding through the forests of Mayo (employed!), listening to German and Irish, feeling the cool, damp breeze on her cheeks and watching the fitful sunlight sprinkle through clouds and trees.

She was here. It was real. And she realized with a sudden, utter certainty she was never going back.

From this day forward, she thought, this was home. One she'd make herself, for herself. This was her life, one she'd live as she wanted.

If that wasn't magick, what was?

She heard other voices, a quick rolling laugh so appealing it made her smile.

"That would be Connor," Meara told her. "Out on a falcon walk."

When they came around a curve she saw him down the path, standing with another couple. A hawk perched on the woman's gloved arm while the man with her snapped pictures.

"Oh, that's amazing!" Dazzling, Iona thought. And somehow out of time. "Isn't it amazing?"

"Otto and I have booked for tomorrow," the German woman told her. "I look forward, very much."

"You'll have so much fun. I have to try it. That's my cousin," she added, unabashedly proud. "The falconer."

"He's very handsome. You have your cousin, but you have not done a falcon walk?"

"I just got here yesterday." She beamed as Connor lifted a hand, sent her or Meara, probably both, a cheeky wink.

"'Tis a Harris's hawk you see there," Meara said. "As you've booked a walk for tomorrow, you should be sure to take the time to tour the school. I'm wagering the falcon walk will be one of the highlights of your visit to Ashford, and it's more complete if you see the other hawks and falcons, and learn a bit about them."

The hawk took wing, glided up to a branch. The two groups gave room to each other.

"Good day to you, Connor," Meara said as they passed.

"And to you. Out for a ride, cousin?"

"I'm working."

"Well, that's brilliant, and you can buy me a pint to celebrate later."

"You're on."

And now, Iona thought, she'd have a beer with her cousin after work. It really *was* magick.

"I'm sorry. My English is sometimes not good."

"It's excellent," Iona disagreed as she shifted to look at the woman rider.

"This is your cousin. But you're not Irish."

"American, Irish descent. I've just moved here. Literally."

"You came only yesterday? Not before?"

"No, never before. I'm actually staying at the castle for a few days."

"Ah, so you are visiting."

"No, I live here now. I came yesterday, got this job today, and I'm moving in with my cousins next week. It's all kind of wonderful."

"You just came, from America to live here? I think you're very brave."

"I think I'm more lucky. It's beautiful here, isn't it?"

"Very beautiful. We live in Berlin, and work there. It's very busy. This is quiet and . . . not busy. A good holiday."

"Yes." And an even better home, Iona thought. Her home.

BY THE TIME SHE'D RUBBED DOWN SPUD, PUT AWAY HER TACK, met the other staff on duty that day—Mick with his ready grin, whose oldest daughter turned out to be the waitress who'd served her dinner the night before—and helped feed and water the horses, Iona deemed it too late to visit Cong or the falconry school.

She approached Meara.

"I'm not really sure what my hours are."

"Oh well." Meara took a long drink from a bottle of orange Fanta. "I expect you didn't plan to be working a full day, which you nearly have. Are you up for working tomorrow?"

"Sure. Absolutely."

"I'd say eight's good enough, but you'd best be checking with Boyle to be certain, as he may have put a schedule together. I'd think you could go on now, as Mick and Patty have things handled here, and I've got a private over at the big stables."

"I'll find him and see. Thanks, Meara, for everything."

Going with the joy of the day, she wrapped her arms around Meara in a hug.

"I'm sure you're welcome but I didn't do anything, less than usual as it happens, as you did most of my sweaty work."

"It felt good. It feels good here. I'll see you tomorrow."

"Have a good one, and my best to Branna and Connor when you see them."

Iona checked the ring, then what Boyle called his office, backtracked, circled, and found him outside in the paddock having a stare-down with Alastar.

"He doesn't think you like him."

Boyle glanced back. "Then he's an intuitive bastard."

"But you do." She boosted herself up to sit on the fence. "You like his looks and his spirit, and wonder how you can smooth his temper without breaking that spirit."

She smiled when Boyle walked toward her. "You're a horseman. There's not a horseman alive who wouldn't look at that magnificent animal and think just what I said. You irritate each other, but that's because you're both big and gorgeous and strong-willed."

Feet planted, Boyle hooked his thumbs in his front pockets. "And that's your conclusion after this brief acquaintance, is it?"

"Yeah." The sheer joy of her day sat on her like sunlight. She thought she could sit there for hours, in the cool, damp air, with the man and the horse. "You challenge each other, so there's respect—and strategies brewing on both sides to work out how to come out on top."

"As I'll be riding him rather than the other way around, that's already a conclusion."

"Not altogether." She sighed as she studied Alastar. "When I was little, I used to dream about having a horse like that—a big, bold stallion all of my own, one only I could ride. I guess most girls go through that equine fantasy stage. I never grew out of mine."

"You ride well."

"Thanks." She glanced down at him, and realized it was a good thing she sat on the fence or she might have given him a hug as she had Meara. "It got me a job."

"It did that."

He said nothing as Alastar wandered over, oh so casually, and ignoring him, went all but nose to nose with Iona. The horse, Boyle thought, looked at the woman as if she knew every answer.

"We had a good day, didn't we?" She stroked the smooth cheek, down the strong line of throat. "It's a good place here. Just takes some getting used to."

Then, the horse, who only that morning had left a welt the size of a man's fist on his veteran groom's biceps, seemed to sigh as well. And stepped in, all but laying his head on Iona's shoulder so she could glide her hands over his long neck.

I'll look out for you, she told him. *And you'll look out for me.*

"Sure, you're one of them," Boyle murmured. "An O'Dwyer, through and through."

Caught up with the horse, Iona answered absently. "My grandmother, mother's side."

"It's not a matter of sides, but blood and bone. I should've figured it the way you handled this one, first time up."

He leaned back against the fence to give Iona a long, careful study. "You don't have the look of them, of Branna or Connor, being a bright-haired little thing, but it's blood and bone."

Because she thought she understood him, nerves came back. "I hope they think so, since they're giving me a place to live. And because Branna helped me land this job so I don't have to scramble to find one I'd probably be terrible at. Anyway, I—"

"Legend has it the younger daughter of the first dark witch talked to horses, and they to her. And even as a babe could ride the fiercest of warhorses. And some nights, in the dark of the moon, when the mood was on her, she took one to flying over the trees and hills."

"I . . . should probably study up on the local legends, for the guided rides."

"Oh sure, I'm thinking you know that one well enough. The one of Cabhan, who lusted for and craved Sorcha, for her beauty and her power. And the three who came from her, and took the power she passed to them, and all the burdens with it. Blood and bone," he said again.

It made her throat dry, the way he looked at her, as if he could see something in her she'd yet to fully comprehend. Sensing her distress, Alastar quivered, laid his ears back as he turned his head to Boyle.

Cautious, Iona slid her fingers under the bridle to calm him.

My own fault, she told Alastar. *I don't know what to say, how to react yet.*

"My grandmother told me a lot of stories." Evading, she knew, but until she knew *him*, that seemed best all around. "Anyway, unless you need me to do something else, I should go. I'm supposed to meet Branna, and I'm late. Meara said I should be clear for the day, and come in tomorrow at eight?"

"That's fine then."

"Thanks for the job." She gave Alastar a last stroke before getting off the fence. "I'll work hard."

"Oh, I'll see that you do, be sure of it."

"Well." Now her hands felt sweaty enough to rub against her jeans. "I'll see you tomorrow."

"My best to your cousins."

"Okay."

He watched her walk away, moving fast, as if getting clear of something boggy in the ground.

Pretty thing, he thought, though he'd be wise to ignore that. Pretty and sunny and a bloody faerie goddess astride a horse.

Ignore all that for certain. Harder, he figured, to ignore the fact that he'd just hired a witch.

"A dark one, the last of the three. All here together now, with hound and hawk, and by God horse." He gave Alastar a scowl. "You'd be Fin's doing then, no doubt of it. And what in hell's name will that mean?"

He wondered, too, what Fin—friend, partner, next to brother—had in his mind, in his heart.

As if expressing his opinion on Fin, and Boyle for that matter, Alastar raised his tail and shat.

Boyle managed to jump aside before the opinion hit his boots. Then, after one fulminating stare, he threw back his head and laughed.

6

SURE OF HER WAY, IONA HURRIED THROUGH THE WOODS. She saw a young couple, strolling along, hand in hand, and thought hotel guests, maybe honeymooners. Tourists, taking advantage of a dry day and patchy sunlight.

She'd be a guest of the hotel for a few more days, but no longer qualified as a tourist. She was an expat.

It sounded strange and glamorous even if she smelled of horses, and maybe just a slight whiff of manure. But as she was already a little late, she didn't want to take the time to go back to her room, shower, and change.

She'd have to work out some sort of loose schedule, she thought, which included that visit to the falconry school and a trip to Cong. Maybe she could work the visit into her break tomorrow, assuming she had one. If Connor was up for it, she'd buy him that pint in the village after her lesson with Branna, maybe have dinner.

And she could hardly wait to email Nan, tell her about the job, about her day, about whatever she learned from Branna. Her life, so scattered and unsatisfying only days before, now brimmed with possibilities.

This was her walk now, to work, to home. No more commuting in traffic to and from her tiny apartment. No more wishing for just a little adventure because now she was living one.

No more wondering what she lacked that made it so easy for people to walk away from her. This time she'd done the walking. No, she corrected, she'd done the arriving. That mattered so much more.

Now it was up to her to make it all matter.

As she came to the downed tree she felt that pull, that yearning, and heard the seductive whisper of her name. Pausing, she looked around, saw no one.

And yet, it came again, that soft, almost sweet whisper of her name.

She hesitated—was there a light, faint, and distant flickering through that wall of vines? Like a light in a window, a welcoming home?

Though she reminded herself she was late, that Branna had told her not to linger there, to explore there, she took a step closer.

It would only take a minute, just to look.

Another step, and it all became so dreamy. The light growing stronger, the whispers deeper, and a sleepy warmth, creeping out, creeping into her.

Home, she thought again. She'd wanted one for so long. And this . . .

As her fingers touched the vines, the air pulsed like a heartbeat; the light dimmed softly to twilight.

Behind her, the dog barked sharply, jolting her back.

She trembled, like a woman teetering on a cliff, and took several steps back until she stood with the dog, one hand braced on his handsome head.

Her own breath sounded so loudly in her ears she barely heard her thoughts through it.

"I was going through. It felt like I had to, and wanted it more than anything else. I almost broke my word, and I never do. What is this place?" She rubbed her chilled hands together, gave one last shudder. "I'm glad you came, and I bet it wasn't just happenstance. We'll go. I imagine she's waiting for both of us."

The wind lifted as they walked away. Before she came to the edge of the woods, rain pattered down, from a single cloud as far as Iona could tell, as the sun continued to send out pearly light.

She and Kathel quickened their pace. Though she'd aimed for the cottage door, she caught a glimpse of Branna in the workshop, and changed course.

As before, the workshop smelled glorious—smoke and herbs and candle wax. Branna stood, her hair bundled up, a sweater the color of plums skimming her hips. She set a white flowerpot on the work counter, arranging it with a white bowl, a fat white candle and a white feather.

"I'm late. I'm sorry, but—"

"You said you might be on the message you left on my phone. It's not a matter." She studied Iona as Kathel walked over to rub against her leg. "Congratulations to you. Your first day went well?"

"Amazing. Fabulous. Thank you. Thank you so much." As she spoke, Iona rushed across the room to throw her arms around Branna in a hard hug.

"All right then." Branna gave Iona a little pat on the back. "Still it's Boyle who did the hiring."

"You got my foot in the door." After another squeeze Iona stepped back. "It's everything I could want. It felt . . . right from the first second. Do you know what I mean? Everything just clicked. And Meara—you know Meara."

"I do indeed." In her smooth way, Branna turned to put the kettle on. "She's a good friend to me, and one you can count on."

"I liked her right away, another click, I guess. She showed me around before Boyle got there, and I met Mick—you probably know him, too."

"I do, yes."

"He's so funny and full of stories. I already have a little crush on him."

"He's a wife and four children, with the first grandbaby on the way."

"Oh, I didn't mean . . . You're teasing. Anyway, it was great, just so great. Even though Boyle was in a bad mood."

"He's known to have them." Branna put cookies on a plate, chocolate ones today.

"He came riding in, like something out of a movie, him on that magnificent horse. Both of them so pissy and handsome and, well, tough. And he's cursing the horse. I'm pretty sure the horse was cursing him right back. His partner—Fin, right?—bought him, and had him sent to Boyle. And he's just spectacular."

"The horse, you're meaning."

"Yeah. Well, Boyle's not too shabby. In fact, I had a couple minutes of . . ." She drummed her hand against her heart. "Just looking at him. Too bad about the moods, because, really." She grinned, rolled her eyes, fanned her hand. Then her eyes widened. "Oh God, you aren't— You and Boyle aren't a thing?"

"Romantically? No." With an easy laugh Branna began to brew the tea. "He and Connor have been mates since boyhood, and for that matter, we've been friends longer than I can remember. He's a fine man with a hot temper, but like Meara, one you can count on, thick and thin."

"Good to know, and I guess he had reason for the mood today. Alastar was giving him a bad time, and he'd bitten one of the stable hands. Kicked one, too, I think, and—"

"Wait." Branna gripped Iona's arm to stop the flood of words. "You said Alastar? The horse is Alastar?"

"Yes. What is it? What's wrong?"

"And Fin, he bought the horse, had it sent?"

"Yes. Meara said Fin was still traveling, but sent the horse ahead a couple days ago."

"So." She took a long breath, laid her hands on the counter for a moment. "He knows."

"Who, and what? You're freaking me out, Branna."

"Fin. He knows you're here. Or he knows the three are here, together. That it's to begin. Alastar, it's said, was the name of Teagan's horse. He was her first guide."

"Alastar. I didn't know, but . . . it was like we recognized each other. There was something there, but I thought, I guess I thought it was just he needed me, needed someone who understood him. Alastar. Teagan's horse. You don't think it's coincidence."

"That you would come, and so would this horse? And Boyle all but bringing him to you this morning? I bloody well don't, and add in Finbar Burke and there's no mistaking it."

"How would he know about me, or the name of Teagan's horse?"

Branna set teacups down with a clatter. "He has power."

"He's like us? Fin?"

"He's like no one but himself, but he comes from the blood, as we do. He springs from Cabhan, the black sorcerer."

"Wait a minute. Wait." She tried to take it in, even pressed her hands to the sides of her head as if to hold it all in. "The evil guy, the one that Sorcha killed—or mostly killed? This Fin is descended from him?"

"He is." Eyes flashing, face grim, Branna shoved impatiently at a loosened pin in her hair. "He bears the mark, and it was Teagan who marked Cabhan. He has power, and the blood."

"He's evil?"

In an impatient gesture, Branna waved a hand in the air, then poured the tea. "Sure there's no simple answer to a question like that. He's harmed no one, and I would know. But he's of Cabhan, and the time's coming 'round. He sent the horse so we'd know."

"But isn't having Alastar an advantage, for me? For us? For our side of this?"

"We'll see what we see."

"I don't understand." Because they were there, Iona took a cookie, gestured with it. "He's Boyle's partner, and his friend, I got that. I don't see how he could be dangerous if—"

"An easier question to answer. Dangerous Fin is, and always has been."

"But if Boyle's such a stand-up guy, how can they be friends?"

"Life's a puzzle."

"One thing, it explains how Boyle knew I was . . . you know."

On a sigh, Branna lifted her teacup. "*Witch* isn't a bad word, Iona. It's who and what you are."

"It hasn't exactly been cocktail-party conversation in my life. I'm getting used to it, a little. I should've told you before, right away. He knew. I didn't tell him—why would I?—but he knew. He didn't seem very weirded out by it, but since he's friends with a sorcerer—"

"Fin's a witch, just as we are."

"Right. It just sounds a little girly."

"You've much to learn, cousin." She handed Iona her tea.

"I should tell you something else first. I don't break my word. It's important. But today, walking back from the stables, I started to go through those vines. I didn't mean to, but I thought I saw a light, and I heard my name, over and over. It was almost like the dream I had. I felt out of myself, pulled in. Like I needed to go through, to whatever waited. Kathel stopped me—again. I don't break promises, Branna. I don't lie."

"Ever?" Branna sipped her own tea.

"Ever. I'm crap at it anyway, so why bother? But I'd have gone back there if Kathel hadn't come. I couldn't have stopped myself."

"He's testing you."

"Who?"

"Cabhan, or what remains of him. You'll have to be stronger, and smarter. Once you're both, Connor and I will take you back, as we promised. Well then, let's see what we have to work with."

Too delighted to drink, Iona set the tea aside. "Are you going to teach me a spell?"

On another laugh, Branna shook her head. "Did you gallop the first time you sat a horse?"

"I wanted to."

"Today you walk, and on a lead. Tell me what your granny said was the most important thing about your power, about the craft?"

"To harm no one."

"Good. An it harm none. What you have is as much a part of you as the color of your eyes, the shape of your mouth. What you do with it is a choice. Choose well."

"I made the choice to come here, to you."

"And I'm hoping you won't regret it. Now then, the elements are four." She gestured to the worktable. "Earth, air, water, fire. We call on them, use them, with respect. It's not our power over them, but the merging of our power with theirs. Fire, almost always the first learned."

"And the last lost," Iona put in. "Nan said."

"True enough. Light the candle."

Pleased to have something to show, Iona stepped forward. She schooled her breathing, focused her mind, imagined drawing up the power in her, then releasing it on a long, quiet breath.

The candlewick sparked, then burned.

"Very good. Water. We need it to live. It runs through our physical bodies, it dominates the world we live in."

She gestured to the white bowl, filled with water. "Clear and calm now. Still. But it moves, like the sea, rises like a geyser, spills like a fountain. Its power, and mine."

Iona watched the water stir, form little waves inside the bowl that lapped at the side. She let out a muffled gasp when it shot up to the ceiling, rippled, a liquid spear, then opened almost like a flower, and spilled back into the bowl without a drop lost.

"That was beautiful."

"A pretty bit of magick, but an important skill. Stir the water, Iona. Feel it, see it, ask it."

Like the candle flame, she thought. It would be focus, and that drawing up. She steadied her breath again, tried to do the same with her mind, her pulse. She stared at the water, tried to form an image of those little waves rocking its quiet surface.

And didn't manage a ripple.

"I'm doing something wrong."

"No. You lack patience."

"It's a problem. Okay, again."

She stared at the water, pushed herself at it until her eyes ached.

"It takes longer for some. Where is your center of power. Where do you feel it rise?" Branna asked.

"Here." Iona pressed a hand on her belly.

"For Connor it's here." Branna tapped her heart. "Pull it up, send it out. Use your hand for a guide. Up, out. Imagine, focus, ask."

"Okay. Okay." She loosened her shoulders, shoved at her hair, took a new stance. She wanted to move the damn water, she thought. She wanted to learn how to send it up like a spear. Maybe she'd been too timid. So . . .

She drew in a breath, pulled, drawing her hand up from her belly, flinging it out toward the bowl.

And barely choked back the scream when the water flew up toward the ceiling.

"Holy shit! I just—oops!"

It fell again, like a small flood. Stopped, went still just above the counter.

"I'd prefer to avoid the mess," Branna said, and with a flick of her finger, had the water spilling back into the bowl.

"Oh, you did it. I thought I had."

"You sent it up, lost your focus. I spared you the mopping."

"I did that?" Thrilled, she did a quick dance in place. "Go me. Wow, it's just so cool. Not respectful," she said with a wince.

"No reason there can't be joy and wonder. It's magick after all. Do it again. But slow. Smooth. Control, always."

"Like riding a horse," Iona murmured.

She took it up, only inches this time, and imagining a small fountain, created it. Slowly, slowly, she turned the fountain so it circled just above the bowl. The dance of the water filled her with that joy and with that wonder.

"You have a lot sleeping inside you," Branna told her.

Delighted, proud, dazzled at herself, Iona let the water slide back into the bowl. "Let's wake it up."

WHEN CONNOR WALKED IN, SHE FLOATED A FEATHER. NOT in the graceful dance Branna demonstrated, but it floated.

He sent her a wink, then, twirling a finger, had the feather spinning up to tickle her under the chin.

"Show-off," she said, but laughed, and did a twirl of her own. "I'm in witch kindergarten. I've made flame, moved water, floated the feather, and I did that."

She gestured toward the white flowerpot, and the pretty painted daisy blooming in it.

"That's well done." Impressed, he walked to the worktable.

"I did that," she corrected, showing him the little seedling beside the bloom. "Branna did the flower."

"Still well done. It's quite the day you've had, cousin." He draped an arm around her shoulders for a quick hug. "And I'm here to collect on my pint. School's out, don't you think, Branna? It's half-six, and I'm next to starving."

"The magick's in his heart, but our Connor thinks with his belly. Or what's just below it."

"And shamed I am of neither. Let's go to the pub. Iona buys my pint, I buy the meal. That's a good deal on any table."

"Why not?" Branna decided. "We've things to talk about, and I could do with a pint and some food while we're doing it."

She pulled the clips from her hair, shook it, and had Iona sighing with envy. "Come on, Kathel. I'll be five minutes," she said.

"She'll be twenty," Connor corrected. "We'll meet you there," he called out, and reached for Iona's hand.

"I don't mind waiting."

"She's going to decide to change her clothes, then having done that, to fuss with her face. I could have my pint by the time she's finished, and you can be telling me about your day."

"Possibly the best day ever. It'll take a while."

"I've nothing but time—as long as we're heading for that pint and my supper."

MAYBE IT WAS THE RESIDUAL ENERGY FROM THE POWER she'd practiced, combined with the excitement of a new job, but Iona felt she could have sprinted all the way to the village.

Connor had other ideas and set a meandering pace on the winding road. She knew she chattered, but he'd asked, after all. And he listened, laughed, tossed in comments.

When she told him of Alastar, Connor lifted his eyebrows, angled his head. His eyes, so full of fun, seemed to sharpen with a quick, canny focus.

"Well now, that's an interesting sort of development, isn't it then?"

"It upset Branna."

"Well, Fin tends to most days of the week, and him sending back this particular horse? That's a message from him, to her particularly."

"A warning?"

He gave Iona a quiet smile. "She might take it as one."

"It doesn't upset you."

"It's coming, isn't it—whatever it will be. We knew that when you showed up on the doorstep."

He looked away, toward the woods, and his eyes, she thought, looked beyond anything she could see.

"This is just the next of it," he told her, "and I'd say having a good horse is a positive thing."

"But he's Fin's, and if Fin's part of the—I don't know—opposing force—"

"He's not."

"But . . . Branna said—"

"Blood ties, curses, and devil's marks." Connor shrugged them off like an old jacket.

"Is he Cabhan's descendant?"

"That he is. I'd like to know who doesn't have a twisted branch on his family tree. Coming from something doesn't make it what you are. You've choices, don't you? You've made your own. Fin makes his own, that's God's truth, as does our Branna. She's my sister, and as important to me as my next breath. And Fin's my friend, as he's been all of my life. So I walk that line, and it's fortunate I've good balance."

"You don't think he's evil."

Connor paused long enough to draw her to his side, brush his lips on the top of her head with an easy affection that warmed her to the bone. "I think evil comes in too many forms to count. Fin's not one of them. As for Alastar being his? Buying something doesn't make it yours as you can keep it, lose it, give it away. It's you who connected with the horse, isn't it?"

"I guess that's true. You trust him, I can see that. But Branna doesn't."

"She's conflicted, you could say, which she is on little else. He'll be back when he's a mind to, then you can decide for yourself where you stand on it."

"You were boys together? You and Fin and Boyle."

"Still are."

She laughed, but felt a little pang with it. "I don't have any lifelong friends. We moved when I was about six, then my parents split up when I was ten, so another move, and a lot of back and forth, and other moves when each of them remarried. It's nice, I think, to have friends you grew up with."

"Friends are friends whenever you make them."

"You're right. I like that."

He took her hand again, gestured with the other as they came into the village. "There you have the ruins of Cong Abbey. It's a fine ruin for all that, and the tourists come to wander around it, though most come to Cong for the Quiet Man."

"Nan loves that movie. I watched it again myself before I came."

"We've a festival in September to commemorate the film. It's grand. Maureen O'Hara herself came two years back. She's still a rare beauty. Regal and real all at once."

"Did you get to meet her?"

"For a moment I did. Sure it was a fine moment. You didn't get your village tour today?"

"No, but there's plenty of time. I feel like I've been here. From everything Nan's told me," she explained. "And her photos, the guide-book. It's just like I imagined."

The pretty shops and pubs and restaurants, the little hotel, the flowers in pots and window boxes tipped down the road in the shadow of the ruined abbey. Though the shops were closed, the pubs were open, and a scatter of people strolled along the narrow sidewalks.

"Where's Branna's shop?"

"Around the corner, there, down a bit next to the tea shop. She'll be closed now, but I've a key if you want to see it."

"That's all right. I'll have a day off, I assume."

"Sure you'll have your day off. Boyle, he'll work you hard enough, but not to the bone."

They walked down, against the rise of the road, and she lifted her face, happy to feel the cool air on her skin. "Is that . . . Is it peat I smell?"

"Sure it is. Nothing like a peat fire on an evening, and a pint to go with it. And here, we'll have both."

He opened a door, nudged her in.

The yeasty smell of beer pouring from the tap, the earthy scent of peat simmering in the hearth—yes, Iona thought, there was nothing like it. People claimed stools at the hub of the bar, or sat at tables already into their meal. Their voices hummed over the clink of glassware.

A half dozen patrons hailed Connor the minute he stepped in the door. He called out greetings, sent out a wave, and steered Iona to the bar.

"Good evening to you, Sean. This is my cousin Iona Sheehan, from America. She's granddaughter to Mary Kate O'Connor."

"Welcome." He had a shock of white hair shaggy around a ruddy face, and sent her a quick beam out of cheerful blue eyes. "And how's Mary Kate faring?"

"She's very well, thanks."

"Iona's working for Boyle at the stables. Had her first day."

"Is that a fact? A horsewoman are you then?"

"I am."

"She's buying me a pint to celebrate. I'll have a Guinness. What's your pleasure, Iona?"

"Make it two."

"Branna's on her way, so it's to be three. We'll just find us a table. Well, it's Franny." Connor gave a pretty blonde a peck on the cheek. "Meet my cousin Iona from America."

So it began. Iona calculated she met more people in ten minutes within feet of the bar than she normally did in a month. By the time they moved away she carried a blur of faces and names in her head.

"Do you know everybody?"

"Hereabouts, most. And there's two you know yourself."

She spotted Boyle and Meara at a table crowded with pints and plates. Connor snagged one beside them. "How's it all going then?"

"Well enough. Taking in the local nightlife are you, Iona?" Meara asked her.

"Celebrating my new job. Thanks again," she said to Boyle.

"It happens we're working out schedules," Meara told her, "and you've Thursday off if you've a mind to make plans."

"I'm nothing but plans right now."

"Iona tells me Fin sent you a new horse. Alastar, is it—and temperamental."

"My arse." Boyle hefted what was left of his pint. "Tried making a meal out of Kevin Leery's arm this morning after he kicked the shit out of Mooney."

"Take any piece of you?"

"Not yet, and not for lack of trying. Behaved like a gentleman for your cousin."

Iona smiled into her beer. "He's just misunderstood."

"I understand him fine."

"We wonder what Fin's about with this one." Meara spooned up some soup, kept her eyes on Connor. "Alastar's no riding hack, that's for certain. It may be he'll breed well, but he never said he was after acquiring a stallion for that when off he went."

Connor gave his easy shrug. "No one knows what's in Fin's mind save Fin, and plenty's the time he doesn't know either. And speaking of that, there's our Branna."

He lifted a hand, caught her eye.

"Well now, it's a party," she said when she walked to the table. Her hand lowered to rub on Meara's shoulder as she sent Boyle a smile. "Are you working my girl then, right through her supper?"

"More the other way around," Boyle claimed. "She's relentless. I was coming to see you tomorrow. The salve you made for us is about gone."

"I've more on hand. I'll send it along with Iona in the morning." She sat, picked up her beer. "So, here's to Iona and her new position, and to you for having the good sense to hire her."

She felt nearly giddy, sitting there. Cousins, boss, coworker—and ordering, at Connor's suggestion, the beef and barley stew.

As her first working day in Ireland, it couldn't get better.

And then it did.

Connor slid away from the table. He came back a few moments later with a violin.

"Connor," Branna began.

"I'm buying, so the least you can do is play for your supper."

"You play the violin?"

Branna glanced at Iona, gave a shrug much like her brother's. "When the mood comes."

"I always wanted to play something, but I'm hopeless. Please, won't you?"

"How can you say no?" Connor handed his sister the violin and bow. "Give us a song, Meara darling. Something cheerful to match the mood."

"You didn't pay for my supper."

He sent her a wink, both cheeky and wicked. "There's always a sweet to come, if you've the appetite."

"One." Branna tested the bow. He'd rosined it, she noted, confident he'd coax her into it. "You know he won't leave off till we do."

She angled her chair, tested again, tweaked the tuning. Voices around them quieted as Branna smiled, tapped her foot in time.

Music danced out, cheerful as Connor had asked, lively and quick. Branna's gaze laughed toward Meara, and Iona saw the friendship, the ease and depth of it even as Meara laughed and nodded.

"I'll tell me ma when I go home, the boys won't leave the girls alone."

More magick, Iona thought. The bright, happy music, Meara's rich, flirtatious voice, the humor on Branna's face as she played. Her heart, already high, lifted as she imprinted everything—the sound, the look, even the air on her memory.

She'd never forget this moment, and how it made her feel.

She caught Boyle watching her, a bemused smile on his face. She imagined she looked like a starstruck idiot, and didn't care.

When applause rang out, she found herself bouncing on her seat. "Oh, that was great! You're both amazing."

"Won us a prize once, didn't we, Branna?"

"That we did. First prize, Hannigan's Talent Show. A short-lived enterprise to match our short-lived career."

"You were grand, both of you, then and now, but we're grateful Meara didn't run off to be a singing star." Boyle gave her hand a pat. "We need her at the stables."

"I'd rather sing for the fun than my supper."

"Don't you want to have more fun?" Iona gave Meara a poke on the arm. "Give us another."

"Look what you started," Branna said to her brother.

"You don't play for fun often enough. I always wish you would." And when he laid a hand on Branna's cheek, she sighed.

"You have a way, you do, and you know it."

"Iona's not the only Yank in here tonight. I've spotted a few others.

Give them 'Wild Rover,' and send them back with the memory of the two beauties in the pub in Cong."

"Such a way, you do," she said and laughed. And shaking her hair back, lifted the fiddle.

Iona saw the smile fade, all the humor fade out of the smoky eyes. Something else came into them, so quick there, then gone, she couldn't be sure. Longing? Temper? Some combination of both.

But she lowered the instrument again.

"Your partner's back," Branna said to Boyle.

EVERYTHING ABOUT HIM WAS SHARP. THE CHEEKBONES, the jaw, even the bold green of his eyes—and the glint in them.

He'd come in on a kick of wind that had the simmering peat fire giving a quick snap.

As they had with Connor, several people hailed him. But Connor had been greeted with easy and affectionate warmth. Finbar Burke's welcome was edged with respect and, Iona thought, a little caution and wariness.

He wore a black leather coat that skimmed to his knees. Rain, which must have started while she'd been cozy and warm, beaded on it, and on his sweep of black hair.

Cautious herself, Iona skimmed her gaze toward Branna. Nothing showed on her cousin's face now, as if that momentary swirl of emotion had been nothing more than illusion.

Fin wound through the crowd and, as Branna had with Meara, laid a hand on Boyle's shoulder, and on Connor's. But his gaze, Iona noted, fixed on Branna.

"Don't let me interrupt."

"And there he is, home from the wars at last." Connor sent him a cheeky grin. "And just in time to stand the next round."

"Some of us have to work tomorrow," Branna reminded her brother.

"Sure it's fortunate my boss is an understanding and generous sort of man. Unlike yours," Connor added with a wink for Branna, "who's a tyrant for certain."

"I'll stand the round," Fin said. "Good evening to you, Meara, and how's your mother faring? I got word she was feeling poorly," he said when she blinked at him.

"She's better, thanks. Just a bout of bronchitis that lingered awhile. The doctor dosed her with medicine, and Branna with soup, so she's well again."

"It's good to hear it."

"You brought the rain," Boyle commented.

"Apparently. And Branna. You look more than well."

"I'm well enough. You cut your travels short then?"

"Six weeks was long enough. Did you miss me?"

"No. Not a bit."

He smiled at her, quick and again sharp, then turned those vivid eyes on Iona. "You'd be the American cousin. Iona, is it?"

"Yes."

"Fin Burke," he said and extended a hand over the table. "As this lot doesn't have the manners for introductions."

She took his hand automatically, and felt the heat, a quick zip of power. Still smiling, he cocked an eyebrow as if to say: What were you expecting?

"Another Guinness for you?" he asked.

"Oh, no. Despite understanding and generous bosses, this is my limit. Thanks anyway."

"I wouldn't mind some tea before I head out in the rain," Meara said. "Thanks, Fin."

"Tea then. Another pint, Boyle?"

"I'm in my truck, so this will have to do me."

"I'm on my feet," Connor said, "so I'll have another."

"Sure I'll join you." Fin had barely glanced around when their waitress hurried up. "Hello there, Clare. The ladies, they'll have tea. Connor and I will have a pint. Guinness tonight."

He found a chair, pulled it up. "We won't bring business into the party," he said to Boyle. "We'll talk later in that area, though I think we've kept each other up to date. And you as well, Connor."

"Suits me. I took Merlin out a few times while you were rambling, as did Meara," Connor told him. "And he took himself out when he wanted. Will you be coming by the school tomorrow?"

"I'll make a point of it, and the stables."

"Make sure you have a kind word for Kevin and Mooney." Boyle lifted his beer. "As your newest acquisition battered both of them."

"Got spirit, he does, and an iron will. Has he battered you as well?"

"Not for lack of trying. He likes this one." Boyle nodded toward Iona.

Locking eyes with Iona again, Fin tapped his fingers on the table as if to an inner tune. "Does he now."

"After doing his damnedest to buck me across to Galway, the Yank here mounts him and takes him around the ring like a show horse."

Fin smiled slowly. "Is that a fact? Are you a horsewoman then, Iona?"

"It is, and she is," Boyle answered. "She's now in our employ, which I'm keeping you up to date with in person."

"Happy to have you. A working holiday for you, is it?"

"I . . . I'm going to live here. That is, I'm living here now."

"Well then, welcome home. Your grandmother's well, I hope. Mrs. O'Connor?"

"Very. Thanks." To keep them still, Iona clutched her hands together under the table. "I needed a job, so Branna asked Boyle to meet with me. I worked at Laurel Riding Academy in Maryland. I have references, and my resume. That is, Boyle has them now, if you need to see them."

Shut up, shut up, she ordered herself, but nerves overwhelmed her. "You have a wonderful operation. Meara showed me around. And you're right. Alastar has spirit, and a strong will, but he's not mean. Not innately. He's just mad and unsettled, finding himself in a strange place, with people and horses he's not used to. Now he has something to prove, especially to Boyle.

"Thank God," she breathed when the tea arrived. She could use it to stop her mouth.

"You make her nervous." Amused now, Branna spoke to Fin. "She tends to chatter on when she's nervous."

"I do. Sorry."

"And apologizes continually. That really has to stop, Iona."

"It does. Why did you buy him—Alastar?" she began. Then held up a hand. "Sorry. None of my business. Plus you said you didn't want to talk business."

"He's beautiful. I have a weakness for beauty, and strength, and . . . power."

"He's all that," Meara agreed. "And anyone who knows bloody anything about horses knows he's not meant to plod around with tourists on his back every day."

"No, he's meant for other things." He looked at Branna. "Needed for other things."

"What are you about?" she murmured.

"He spoke to me. You understand me," he said to Iona.

"Yes. Yes."

"So, he's here, and on her way is the prettiest filly in the West Counties. Spirited, too, a two-year-old, fine as a princess. She's Aine, for the faerie queen. We'll be playing matchmaker there, Boyle, when she's mature enough. Until she is, she'll do well on the jump course, even, I think, with novices."

"You've more than breeding on your mind." Branna nudged her tea aside.

"Ah, darling, breeding's ever on it."

"You knew she'd come, and what it would mean. It's already begun."

"We'll talk about it." Fin laid a hand over Branna's on the table. "But not in the pub."

"No, not in the pub." She drew her hand from under his. "You know more than you say, and I'll want the truth of it."

Irritation simmered in his eyes. "I've never lied to you, *mo chroi*. Not in all our lives, and you know it. Even when a lie could have given me what I wanted most."

"Leaving gaps is no different from a bold lie." She pushed to her feet. "I've work yet. Boyle, use your truck to see Iona back to the hotel, would you? I won't have her walking through the wood at night."

"Oh, but—"

"I'll see to it." Boyle interrupted Iona's protest smoothly. "Not to worry."

"I'll get that salve to you in the morning. And see you, Iona, tomorrow, after work. We've much more to do."

"Well and hell." Connor sighed, started to rise as Branna left.

"No, stay and finish your pint." Meara rubbed at Connor's arm as if to soothe even as she pushed back her chair. "I'll go with her. It's time I started home anyway. Thanks for the tea, Fin, and welcome back. I expect I'll see the lot of you tomorrow."

Grabbing her jacket, Meara dragged it on as she hurried out of the pub.

Connor patted Iona's arm. "You'll need to get used to that."

"That's God's truth," Fin muttered, then very deliberately eased back, smiled. "I tend to put our Branna in difficult moods. So tell us, Iona from America, what is it you've seen and done in Ireland?"

"I . . ." How could they just pick up the small talk when the air actively pulsed with temper and heartbreak? "Ah . . . not very much. And a lot, I guess. I came to meet Branna and Connor, and to find a place, to find work. Now I have. But I haven't had time, yet, to see anything but here. It's so beautiful, it's enough."

"We'll have to get you out and about more than that. You say you found a place, to live you mean? That's quick work."

"I'm staying at Ashford for a few more days."

"Now there's a rare treat."

"It really is. Then I'm going to live with Branna and Connor." She saw his eyes flicker, narrow, shift quickly to Connor. "Is that a problem?"

In answer, Fin leaned over the table, kept those eyes focused on her face. "She knew you. She reaches out to many, but holds precious few. Home is sanctuary. If hers is yours, she knew you. Have a care with them," he murmured to Connor. "By all the gods."

"Don't doubt it."

"Speaking of gaps." Frustrated, Iona looked from one man to the other, and to Boyle who sat, saying nothing at all. She'd get nothing out of any of them, not there and then. "I should go. Thanks for dinner, Connor, and for the tea, Fin. You don't have to drive me back to the hotel, Boyle."

"She'll skin my arse if I don't, and it could be literal. I'll see you back at home," he said to Fin.

"I'll be coming along shortly."

Stuck, Iona walked to the door. She took one glance back, caught a glimpse of Fin brooding into his pint, and Connor leaning over the table, talking quick and low.

She stepped out into windy rain, and found herself grateful after all for the ride.

"You and Fin live together?"

"I keep my place over the garage, and make use of his house when I've a mind to, as he's out as much as in. It's handy for both of us, living there near the big stables."

He opened the door of an old truck with faded red paint, and reaching in, shoved at the clutter on the seat. "Sorry about that. I wasn't expecting a passenger."

"Don't worry about it. It's a relief to see someone's as messy as I am."

"If that's the way of it, take a warning. Hide and confine your debris. Branna's orderly, and she'll hound you like a dog if you leave things flung about."

"So noted."

She boosted up, slid in among clipboards, wrappers, an old towel, rags, and a shallow cardboard box holding hoof picks, bridle rings, a couple of batteries, and a screwdriver.

He got in the opposite door, shoved a key in the ignition.

"You didn't say much in there."

"Being friends with all parties, I find it best to stay out of it altogether."

The truck rattled, the rain pattered, and Iona settled back.

"They're a thing."

"Who's a thing?"

"Branna and Fin. They either are, or were, involved. The sexual buzz was so loud my ears are still ringing."

He shifted, frowned out at the road. "I'm not after gossiping about friends."

"It's not gossip. It's an observation. It must be complicated, for both of them. And it's clear I need to know what's going on. You know more about any of it than I do, and I'm in it."

"Put yourself there from what I can see."

"Maybe I did. So what? How did you know I'm like them?"

"I've known them most of my life, been a part of theirs. I saw it in you, with the horse."

Brows knit, she shifted to face him. "Most people wouldn't be so casual about it. Why are you?"

"I've known them most of my life," he repeated.

"I don't see how it can be that simple. I can do this." She held out her palm and, focusing hard, managed to flick a small flame in its center.

It was pitiful compared to Branna, but she'd been working on it off and on.

He barely glanced her way. "Convenient if you're backpacking and misplace the matches."

"You're a cool customer." She had to admire it. "If I'd pulled that on the guy I'd been dating, he'd have gone through the door, leaving a cartoon-guy hole in it."

"Must not have been much for backpacking."

She started to laugh, then caught her breath when fog rose up on the road ahead like a wall. Her hands balled into fists as the truck punched through it, tightened as the fog blanketed over them.

"Do you hear that? Can you hear that?"

"Hear what?"

"My name. He keeps saying my name."

Though he was forced to slow to a crawl, Boyle kept his hands steady on the wheel. "Who's saying your name?"

"Cabhan. He's in the fog. Maybe he *is* the fog. Can't you hear him?"

"I can't." And so far, never had. He wouldn't mind keeping it that way. "I'm thinking you'll work with Meara again tomorrow."

"What? What?"

"I'll want her go-ahead before you take any guests out on your own." He spoke easily, drove slowly. He could navigate this road blindfolded, and thought he damn nearly was. "And I'll want to see how you handle instruction. We'll have you work with Mick there, or with me from time to time. Do you do any jumping?"

He knew she did, and had the blue ribbons and trophies to prove it, the certification to teach it. He'd read her resume.

"Yes. Competitively since I was eight. I wanted to try for the Olympic team, but . . ."

"Too much commitment?"

"No. I mean, yes. In a way. You need a lot of family support for that kind of training. And the financial backing." While her eyes tracked right and left, she rubbed a hand from between her breasts up to her throat, back again. "Did you hear that? God, can't you hear that?"

"That I did." The wild howl shot cold fingers up his spine. And that, he thought, was new, at least to him. "I expect he doesn't like us talking over him."

"Why aren't you afraid?"

"I'm riding with a witch, aren't I? What have I got to worry about?"

She choked out a laugh, struggled to steady her pulse. "I learned to levitate a feather today. I don't think that's going to do a lot of good."

And he thought he had his two fists, and the utility knife in his pocket, if needed. "It's more than I can do. See now, the fog's thinning, and there's Ashford up ahead."

So it was, the glamorous fairy-tale spread of it, windows lighted pale gold.

"They went there. The first three. They came back, years after their mother sent them away to save them. They stayed in the castle, walked the woods. I dreamed of the youngest coming back, riding back as she'd ridden away as a child. On a horse named Alastar."

"Ah, well then. I didn't know the name of the horse. That explains it, doesn't it?"

"I don't know what it explains. I don't know what I'm supposed to do."

"What you must."

"What I must," she murmured as he stopped at the hotel's entrance. "Okay. Okay. Thanks for the ride, and for talking me through the weird."

"Not a problem. I'll see you in."

She started to object. She was only steps from the door. And thinking of the voice in the fog, changed her mind. It was just fine to have a big, strong man walk her in. No shame in it.

With him she walked into the warmth, into the rich colors, the flowers. And the smile of the woman on duty at the lobby table.

"Good evening to you, Ms. Sheehan. And Boyle, it's good seeing you."

"Working late, Bridget?"

"I am. A good night for it, as it's gone wet again. I've your key right here, miss. I hope you enjoyed your day."

"I did, very much. Thanks again, Boyle."

"I'll see you to your door."

"Oh, but—"

He just took the key from her, glanced at the number. "This is in the old part, isn't it?" So saying, he took Iona's arm, pulled her along and down the corridor.

"It's that way now." Iona made the turn.

"The place is a rambling maze."

"Part of its charm." She tried not to worry about the desk clerk likely thinking she and Boyle were a thing.

He stopped at the door, unlocked it. After pushing the door open, he took a long, careful look.

"Well, you are messy."

"As advertised." Her eyes widened when he walked right in. He couldn't possibly think—

He picked up the hotel pen on the nightstand, scrawled something on the pad.

"That's my mobile. If you get nervous, ring me up. Better you ring Branna, but I'm just minutes away if it comes to that."

"That's . . . That's so kind."

"Don't get watery about it. I've just hired you, haven't I, and done the bloody paperwork. I can't have you running back to America. Lock the door and go to bed. Switch on the telly if you need the noise."

He walked to the door, opened it. "And remember," he said, looking back at her. "You can hold a flame of your own making in the palm of your hand."

He shut the door. Even as she started to smile, he rapped hard enough to make her jump.

"Lock the bloody door!"

She dashed to it, locked it. And listened to his boot steps fading away.

SHE MADE A BARGAIN WITH HERSELF. AT WORK, SHE'D FOCUS on work. She couldn't and wouldn't let whatever she might have to face interfere with making a living.

When work was done, she'd take whatever time Branna was willing to give. She'd learn, she'd practice, she'd study.

But she would also demand and get answers.

So she mucked, cleaned, brushed, hauled, fed, and watered. And did her best to stay out of Boyle's way. Remembering the ride home, and her panic, left a thin layer of embarrassment. *She* was the one with power, however unrefined, and she'd gone weak and trembly, and let him look after her.

Worse, for just a second—maybe two or three seconds—when he'd come into her room, she'd been the one with the wrong idea. A sad fact she'd been forced to admit when she'd pulled out of a dream. Not of evil sorcerers and shadows, she thought as she brushed Spud's mane.

But of a sex dream, and a damn good one, involving her and Boyle and a *Wizard of Oz* field of poppies.

But it sure as hell hadn't put them to sleep.

That subconscious revelation added a lot of thicker layers to the embarrassment.

Meara poked her head in the stall. She wore a kelly green cap today, with her hair streaming through the back opening in a long tail. "You braided Queen Bee's mane."

"Oh, yeah. I just . . . I'll take it out."

"No, indeed. It looks charming, and she's fairly preening with her new do. Just don't do the fancy work with any of the geldings. Boyle'll huff about, say we're making them into dandies when they're good plain hacks. He's such a man, is Boyle."

"I noticed. You're good together."

"Well, I should hope. It's going clear, so the ride's on for the afternoon. They shifted to three, hoping for better weather, and it looks like we may get it. It's a party of four—two couples, friends from America, so that should be nice for you. Boyle's sent off for Rufus, he's a big, playful gelding. One of our guests is near to two meters tall."

"Which is what?"

"Oh, in Yank?" With a frown, she pushed at her cap, scratched her head. "About six and a half feet, I'm thinking. Otherwise, we'll saddle up Spud there, and Bee, and Jack. You can take your pick from the rest."

"Maybe Caesar, unless you want him."

"Go ahead." Meara made a little note on her clipboard. "They asked for ninety minutes, so you'll see more than yesterday."

"I want to see it all. And, Meara?" The guilt over the dream wouldn't allow her to just let it go. "I just wanted to say thanks for lending me Boyle last night for the ride home."

"I'm not in the habit of lending him, but you're welcome to keep him if you like."

"Oh, did you have a fight?"

"About what?" The puzzled frown gave way to wide eyes, then a roll of wicked laughter. "Oh! You're thinking me and Boyle are tangled. No, no, no! I love the man to distraction, but I don't want him in my bed. It would be like shagging my brother. And that thought's just put me off my lunch."

"You're not . . ." Embarrassment kicked up several notches. "I just assumed."

"Look like lovebirds, do we?"

"There's just something, I guess, intimate, between you, so I thought you were together. That way."

"We're family."

"Got it. Good. I guess it's good. Maybe it's a problem."

Now Meara leaned on the side of the stall opening. "You're a fascination to me, Iona. A problem?"

"It's just that when I assumed, I had a good reason to ignore the . . ." She wiggled her fingers over her stomach.

"You've got"—Meara mimicked the gesture—"for Boyle."

"He looks really good, on a horse and off. The first minute I saw him, I just . . . whew." She laid one hand on her heart, the other on her belly, patted both.

"Is that the truth?"

"He's all tough and cranky. Then there's the big hands, the scar," she said, tapping her eyebrow. "And those liony eyes."

"Liony." Meara tried out the words. "Well now, I suppose they are. Boyle McGrath, King of the Beasts." She let out another of her barroom laughs.

"That's just looks, but they're really impressive. On top of it, he was really kind to me. Then there was the sex. Dream," Iona said quickly when Meara's mouth fell open. "Sex dream. I had one last night, and I felt so guilty because I really like you. And you don't want to hear any of this."

"You're mistaken, entirely. I want to hear all of this, in the greatest of detail."

On a laughing moan, Iona covered her face with her hands. "You're Boyle's friend. If you tell him the Yank's got this slow simmer going on, he'll either laugh himself into a coma or fire me."

"He'd do neither, but why would I tell him any such thing? There's a sisterhood that covers such matters. That's a universal sort of thing to my mind."

"Of course there is. Anyway, I think I'm just jet-lagged, and turned around, and coming to grips. It's nothing. It'll pass."

"Maybe you should take him on a ride before you—"

She broke off at the sound of raised voices. "Ah, Christ."

Turning on her heel, Meara strode out, and as the voices—male, extremely pissed—escalated, Iona followed her.

Boyle faced off with a hard-packed bull of a man in a red cap and plaid jacket. The bull, his face nearly as red as his cap, jabbed out with a finger. "I come here being reasonable, though you're a cheat and a liar for all that."

"And I'm telling you, Riley, what business we had is done and over. Get off my property, and keep clear of it."

"I'll get off your bleeding property when you give me back the horse you next to stole from me, or hand over fair payment. You think you can steal from me. Bloody thief." He shoved Boyle back two steps.

"Oh Jesus," Meara muttered. "Now he's done it."

"Don't put your hands on me again," Boyle warned, very quietly.

"Oh, I'll put more than my hands on you, you fucking shite."

Riley threw a punch. Boyle shifted his weight, angled his head, and the fist breezed by his ear.

"We should call the police. The guard, whatever it's called."

Meara barely glanced at Iona. "No need."

"You get one more." With his arms still down by his sides, Boyle spread his hands. "Take it, if you've a mind to, and know you won't be walking away from this if you do."

"I'll beat ya bloody." Riley charged, fists up, head down.

Dancing to the side, Boyle turned, jabbed two short punches.

Kidney punches? Iona wondered as her eyes went wide. Oh God!

Riley stumbled, but stayed on his feet, punched out again. The blow grazed Boyle's shoulder as Boyle slapped it away with a forearm.

Then he followed up. A right to the jaw, left to the nose. Jab, uppercut—Iona thought—a left cross. Two punches to the middle.

Fast, so fast. Light and quick on his feet, barely showing a reaction when Riley managed to land a blow. Bare knuckles slapped and crunched into flesh and bone. Riley, his nose pouring blood, his mouth dripping it, made a staggering charge. On a pivot, Boyle swept up his fist—definitely an uppercut—hitting the jaw like an arrow in a bull's-eye.

He started to follow up, pulled back. "Fuck it," she heard him mutter as he simply put a boot on Riley's ass and shoved him facedown on the ground.

"Oh God. My God."

"There now." Meara patted her shoulder. "It's just a bit of a dustup."

"No. It's . . ." She fluttered her fingers over her belly.

Meara snorted out a laugh. "Aye, a fascination to me you are."

A few feet away, Fin sat astride a restless Alastar. "Again?" he said mildly.

"Fucker wouldn't walk away." Boyle sucked at his raw knuckles. "And I gave him every chance."

"I saw you giving him those chances as I rode up, and how could he be walking away with your fist in his face?"

Boyle only grinned. "That was after the chances."

"Well, let's make sure you haven't killed him, as I've no desire to help you hide a body this morning." As he dismounted, he crooked a finger at Iona. "Yes, you. Be a darling and tie Alastar to the post. Don't unsaddle him."

When he held out the reins, she hurried over to take them.

Using his boot again, Boyle rolled Riley onto his back. "Broke his nose, that's for certain, and loosened some teeth, but he'll live through it."

Fin stood, hands in his pockets as they both studied the unconscious Riley. "This goes back to that horse you won off him, I take it."

"It does."

"Bloody git."

Whistling cheerfully through his teeth, Mick strolled out carrying a bucket of water. "Thought you could be using this."

Fin took it. "Stand clear then," he advised, then tossed the water in Riley's face.

The man sputtered, coughed. His eyes opened and rolled in his head.

"Good enough." Boyle crouched down, took one arm. On a sigh, Fin took the other.

Absently stroking Alastar, Iona watched them haul the man to his truck, shove him up and in. She couldn't hear what words were exchanged, but in moments, the truck drove away, weaving a bit.

As she did, the men watched it. Then Fin said something that had Boyle letting out a laugh before he slung an arm around Fin's shoulders and turned to walk back.

She saw it then, the ease between them. More than partners, she realized. More still than friends. Brothers.

"Performance is over for the day," Boyle called out. "There's work needs doing."

At his words, the staff that had gathered, scattered.

Iona cleared her throat. "You should put something on those knuckles."

Boyle merely glanced at them, sucked at them again. And shrugging, continued inside. Fin stopped by Iona.

"He's a brawler, is Boyle."

"The other guy started it."

Now Fin laughed. "No doubt. Maturity's given Boyle the sense to wait until he's well provoked, and rare is it for him to throw the first punch. Otherwise, he'd have given Riley the hammering he deserved weeks ago instead of making the wager."

She should mind her own business. She should . . . "What was the wager?"

"Riley's a horse trader of the lowest sort. He had in his possession a mare he'd neglected. I'm told she was skin and bones and sick and lame. He planned to sell her off for dog food."

Eyes fired, lips peeled back in a snarl. "I'd like to punch him myself."

"You don't have the hands for it." Fin watched Alastar nuzzle at Iona's shoulder, and the way she leaned her head to his. "Best to use your feet for such matters, and aim for the balls."

"I'd be happy to, in this case."

"I'll tell you, as Boyle likely won't, as he's a man of few words—or none at all if he can manage it. He offered Riley what he'd have gotten for selling her off, and more besides, but Riley doesn't care much for Boyle, or for me, and he demanded double that. So being a cannier businessman than you might think, Boyle wagered him on who could drink the most whiskey and stay on his feet. If Riley won, Boyle would pay the asking price. If Boyle won, Riley turned over the mare for what was offered. The publican wrote it in the book, and considerable money changed hands, I'm told."

As he spoke, Fin unlooped the reins from the post. "And at the end of the long night, it was Boyle still on his feet. Though I'd wager he had the devil's own head the next morning, he had the mare as well."

"A drinking bet."

"As I said, our Boyle's matured. Now then." Fin handed the reins to Iona, made a hammock with his hands. "Up you go."

Her mind full of questions, impressions, she put her boot in Fin's hands, mounted Alastar smoothly. "Where do you want him?"

"I want both of you in the ring. Let's see what you can do."

8

AT THE END OF THE WORKDAY, SHE LET HERSELF THINK of magick. What would Branna teach her today? What new wonder would she see, feel, do? She said good-bye to the horses, to her coworkers before starting out.

And saw Boyle in his little office, all beetled brow and swollen knuckles as he hacked away at paperwork.

Definitely a flutter going on, she thought. Not that she intended to flirt with her boss. Plus, for all she knew, he had a parade of girlfriends. Or maybe even more daunting, didn't find her attractive.

Besides, she wasn't looking for a relationship, or an entanglement. She needed to get her feet firmly planted in her new life, learn more about her awakening powers—and hone them if she intended to be a real help to her cousins.

When a woman planned to go up against ancient evil, she shouldn't allow herself to become distracted by sexy eyebrows or broad shoulders or—

"In or out," Boyle ordered, and kept pecking at his keyboard. "Stop the bleeding hovering."

"Sorry. I, ah, wasn't sure if . . . I'm finished for the day," she told him.

He glanced up, held her eyes for a beat. Grunted and looked back down at his work.

His hands had to hurt, she thought. She could practically see them throbbing. "You really should ice down those knuckles."

"They'll be all right. I've had worse."

"Probably, but if they're swollen and stiff—or worse, get infected—you won't be much good around here."

"Don't need a nurse, thanks."

Stubborn, she thought. But so was she. She went back in, got the first-aid kit, a couple of ice packs. Marched back to his office.

"Some would say you're being stoic and manly," she began as she dragged over a chair. "But my take is sulky baby because your hands hurt."

"I enjoyed the getting of them, so I'm not sulky. Put that away."

"When I'm done with it." She got out the antiseptic, gripped his wrist. "This is going to sting."

"Don't be— Shit! Bloody fucking hell."

"Baby," she said with some satisfaction, but blew on the sting. "If you're going to punch somebody in the face with bare knuckles, you're going to pay the price."

"If you disapprove of fighting, you're in the wrong place. Likely the wrong country."

"I don't—that is situationally, and that jerk deserved it. Just let this lie while I clean this one up." She set the ice pack on one hand while she doctored the other. "You knew what you were doing. Did you box in college?"

"In a manner of speaking." Resigned—and in any case the ice pack felt just grand—he sat back a little. "Are you trying to set my hand on fire to purify it?"

"It'll only sting for a minute. What manner of speaking?"

The look he gave her could only be described as a glower. She'd always wondered what a glower actually looked like.

"You're full of questions."

"It's only one," she pointed out. "And talking will distract you. What manner of speaking?"

"Jesus. I worked my way through university fighting. Bare-knuckle matches, so this current situation isn't new to me. I know how to tend to myself."

"Then you should have done it. That's a hard way to earn tuition."

"Not if you like it, and not if you win."

"And you did both."

"I liked it better when I won, and I won my share."

"Good for you. Is that how you got that scar through your eyebrow?"

"That's another question. A different kind of fight—pub fight, and a broken bottle. As I'd been drinking myself, my reflexes were a bit slow."

"You're lucky you have the eye."

Surprised by her response, and the matter-of-fact tone, he cocked that scarred brow. "Not that slow."

She only smiled. "Switch hands."

He had big ones, she thought. Strong, with blunt fingers and wide palms. The rough hands of a man who worked with them, and she respected that.

"Fin told me about the mare, and the bet."

He didn't glower this time, but shifted a little on the chair. "Fin loves a story, and the telling of one."

"I'd like to meet her."

"We keep her at the big stables. She's skittish around strangers yet, and needs more time and pampering."

"What do you call her?"

He shifted again, as she knew now he did when uncomfortable or mildly embarrassed. "She's Darling. It fits her. Haven't you done with that yet?"

"Nearly. I like that you drank him under the table for the horse that needed you. And I like that you knocked the crap out of him today. I probably shouldn't. My parents tried to raise me to be someone who wouldn't. But they failed."

She glanced up to find his eyes on her again. "You can't be what you aren't."

"No, you really can't. I'm a mild disappointment to them, which is worse somehow than being a serious disappointment. So I'm working hard not to be any kind of disappointment to myself."

She eased back. "There." And took his hands gently by the fingers to examine the knuckles. "Better."

Oh yeah, she thought as their eyes met yet again. Flutters and tingles, and a quick churning to top it off. She'd be in serious trouble if she didn't watch herself.

But it was Boyle who drew away. "Thanks. You'd better get on. You'll have things to do."

"I do." She started to reach for the kit, but he brushed her away.

"I'll deal with it. Eight tomorrow."

"I'll be here."

When she left, he brooded down at his hands. He could still feel her touch on them. A different kind of sting. He looked up when Fin eased into the doorway, leaned on the jamb. Smiled.

"Don't start with me."

"She's a pretty thing. Bright, eager. And if she'd been flirting any harder, I'd have been forced to shut the door for privacy."

"She was doing no such thing. She'd had it stuck in her head to tend to my hands, that's all."

"Not nearly all, and I know you, *mo dearthair.* You think of her, even as you tell yourself you shouldn't think of her."

Sure if he had, he was human, wasn't he? But he was also not a stupid, irrational sort of man.

"She's Connor's cousin, and she works for us. I've no business thinking of her beyond that."

"Bollocks. She's a pretty woman, and smart and strong enough to make her choices—as she's already proved. The power now, that worries you some."

Now Boyle sat back, gave a slow nod with his eyes on Fin's. "What it means, and what all of you, and me besides, as I'm with you, may be doing concerns me. And should be your priority as well. It's no time for flirtations."

"If not now, when? For this could be the end of all of us and I'd sooner die after bedding a woman than before."

"I'd rather live, and bed the woman after the battle's won."

Fin's mood lightened with his smile. "Eat your pudding first. You can always have seconds. I'll be taking Alastar for a ride, see how he does."

"Toward Branna's?"

"Not yet, no. She's not ready. I'm not either."

Alone, Boyle went back to brooding. They needed to get ready, he thought, remembering the howl in the fog. Every blessed one of them.

AT THE END OF THE WEEK, IONA SAT IN BED AT JUST BEFORE six in the morning. She'd spent her last night in the castle. She wanted so much to make her home with her cousins, but to do that, she had to leave this indulgent dream.

No more cheerful maids to tidy her room and bring her tea and biscuits. No more dazzling breakfast buffets. No more snuggling in at night, listening to the wind or the rain or both and imagining herself in the thirteenth century.

But she was trading all that for family. A much better deal.

She'd done most of the packing the night before, but rose now to finish, to calculate the tip for housekeeping. To take her last castle shower.

With a half hour to spare before Connor—at his insistence—picked her up, she practiced her craft.

The feathers seemed safest, considering. Branna had refused to teach her anything new until she'd mastered the four elements. And mastered them to Branna's high watermark.

No amount of wheedling, bribery, cajoling had moved her cousin one inch.

So master them, she would.

At least she'd progressed to a small pile of feathers rather than a single one.

In the dim light she quieted her mind, reached down for the power. Reaching out her hands, she thought of air lifting, warm gentle breeze, a stir, a whisper.

Fluttering, the white feathers rose, separated, swayed, and turned in the air. She sent them higher, little climbs, gentle tumbles. Easy, easy, she told herself. A light touch.

She held her arms high, circled herself, watched them circle with her. And joyful, quickened just a bit.

A turn, a twirl, pretty white feathers mirroring her moves. Up, down, lazy swirls, perfect rings, then a slim white tower.

"I feel it," she murmured. "I do. And it's lovely."

On a laugh, she spun, again, again. Spread her arms so feathers followed each one, formed two whirling circles. Serpentine, figure eights, then again into one downy cloud.

"A plus. Even Branna has to give me the mastery check mark on this one."

At the hard and rapid knock on the door, she let out a yelp. The feathers fell, tumbling over her.

"Damn it!"

She brushed them off her shoulders. Blew them out of her face as she walked to the door.

"You broke my hold," she began. "I was just— Oh. Boyle."

"There's feathers everywhere. Did you rip the pillow?"

"No. They're my feathers. What are you doing here?" Irritation cleared into worry. "Is something wrong? Is someone hurt?"

"Nothing's wrong. No one's hurt. Connor got called in to the falconry school. A plumbing thing, and he's the handy one. I'm drafted to fetch you. Are you packed?"

"Yes. I'm sorry. I could've gotten someone from the hotel to take me."

"I'm here, so let's get your things."

"All right. Thanks. I've just got to clean this up. The feathers."

"Hmm." He reached out, surprising her with the skim of his fingers over her hair. "Here's a couple more," he said, and handed them to her.

"Oh. Okay." She got on her hands and knees, started scooping feathers.

"Are they valuable feathers you have scattered everywhere?"

"They're just feathers."

"Well then, leave them. The housekeeper will deal with them. It'll take you an hour to pluck them off the floor."

"I'm not leaving this mess for Sinead." She plucked a few more, then sat back on her heels. "I'm an idiot."

"I'll not comment on that."

"Wait. Just wait." She got to her feet, took a breath. Quiet the mind first, she reminded herself.

And floated the feathers up. On a pleased little laugh, she gathered them, then cupped her hands, let them fall into her palms.

"Did you see that?" Glowing, she held her cupped hands out. "Did you see?"

"I've eyes, don't I?"

"It's just so wonderful. It's feels so *right*. Watch this."

She threw her hands up, sent the feathers flying, sent them swirling again, dipping, rising, then once again cupped her hands to gather them.

"It's so pretty. I've been practicing for days, and I've finally got it. Really got it."

Still beaming, she looked up at him. Stopped. Everything stopped.

He looked at her, in that straight way he had—dead eye to eye. It wasn't wonder she saw there, or amusement, or irritation.

It was heat.

"Oh." She sighed it, and following her heart, leaned toward him.

He stepped back, a quick and complete evasion. "You've got your feathers." Moving past her, he dragged the two suitcases off the bed. "Grab something. If there's more, I'll come back for it."

"Just my jacket, and my laptop. I'll get them. I'm sorry." Mortified, she dumped the feathers in their bag, secured it. "I guess I was caught up, and I misread. I thought you . . . but obviously not."

"Get a move on, will you?" The words snapped out of him; she felt them like hard finger flicks on her cheeks. "We've all of us got work."

He carried the cases as if they weighed nothing, and breezed right by her.

"Fine. Fine! I get it. And again, I'm an idiot. You're not attracted to me, message received. But you don't have to be rude about it."

She shoved the bag of feathers in her laptop case. "I've been rejected before, and somehow I survived. Believe me, I'm not planning on jumping you, so you don't have to add the slap and kick. I'm a big girl," she added, snatching up her jacket and scarf. "And I'm responsible for my own—"

He dropped the cases with a bang that made her jump. "You talk too bloody much." With that, he gave her a yank. Off guard, she plowed into him, and managed no more than a quick *oof* before he shoved her chin up. And took her mouth like a man starving for it.

Rough and hard, the kind of kiss that gave her no choice but to hang on. Blasts and booms of that heat assaulted her. She'd have staggered from them if he hadn't hauled her right off her feet.

Dazzled, done for, she wrapped her arms around his neck and rode that high, hot wave.

And seconds later he dropped her unceremoniously back on her feet.

"That shut you up at least."

"Ah—"

He hefted the cases again. "You want the ride, get yourself moving."

"What?" She shoved her hands through her hair. "What *was* that?"

"You are an idiot. Of course I'm attracted to you. Any man with blood in him would be. That's not the issue."

"It's not the issue. What is?"

"I'm not interested in doing anything about it. And if you ask one more question, I'm dumping these bags, and you can find your own way to Branna's."

"All I did was move in a little," she said as she dragged on her jacket. "You're the one who did the grabbing." She snatched up her laptop case, and sailed out of the room.

"That I did," he muttered. "And that's made me an idiot as well."

She kept her mouth firmly shut on the short drive. She wouldn't say a word. It took bitter willpower, as she had plenty to say, but she refused to give him the satisfaction.

Better to ignore him. More mature to say nothing.

No, she decided, more *powerful* to keep silent.

Even as she thought it, the truck jolted, as if it hit an invisible bump on the smooth road.

Boyle spared her one brief, hot look.

Had she done that? Iona gripped her hands together, fighting against a leap of glee. Had she actually lifted an entire truck? Unintentionally, but still a big jump from a pile of feathers.

She considered trying it again, just to see, but fortunately for all involved Boyle pulled up at Branna's cottage.

She shoved out of the truck, started around to the bed to drag out her suitcases. Then thought the hell with it. He'd carted them out, so he could cart them in. She reversed, strode straight for the cottage door.

A sleepy-eyed Branna opened it before she knocked. "You're timely."

"He was early. Thanks again for letting me stay."

"See if you're thanking me after a week or two. Good morning to you, Boyle. If you're after hauling those all the way, it's the second on the left. I'll show you your room," Branna continued, and led the way up the narrow stairs. "Mine's at the back, and Connor's the front. I've my own bath, as when we added on, that was priority. Sharing a bath with him was a trial, and one you'll now experience for yourself."

"I don't mind, not at all."

"And if you're saying the same after that week or two, you're a liar. But that's how it has to be."

The bed with its simple headboard of iron slats painted creamy white faced a window where the view of the woods was framed in lace. The ceiling followed the slant of the roof and formed a cozy nook for a little desk and chair with a needlepointed seat.

The dresser, small scale again, bloomed with painted flowers against the same creamy white as the headboard. A little pot of shamrocks with their pretty white bells blooming sat on the dresser. The same rich green covered the walls and served as a backdrop for colorful prints of the hills, of the woods and gardens.

"Oh, Branna, it's wonderful. It's so pretty." Iona brushed her fingers over the cloud-soft throw, an energetic pop of plums and purples and lavenders, folded at the foot of the bed. "I love it. I'm so grateful."

This time Branna was a bit more prepared for the enthusiasm of the embrace, if not the quick bounce.

"You're very welcome of course, and if you've a mind to change anything—"

"I wouldn't change a thing. It's perfect."

"Where do you want these?" Boyle demanded from the doorway in a tone that took no trouble to hide aggravation.

Iona turned, and eyes that had gone misty dried cool. "Anywhere. Thank you."

Taking her at her word, he dropped them just over the threshold, and kept the toes of his boots firmly on the other side. "Well, I'll be off then."

"You've time yet, don't you?" Branna's mind might have leapt with questions at the temper, the hot and cold of it, running in the room like open taps, but she kept her smile and tone easy. "I'll fix you breakfast for your trouble."

"Thanks for that, but I've things to do. Nine's soon enough to come in this morning. Take time to settle."

He left quickly, and with a clomp of boots on the stairs.

"So, what's all this about?" Branna wondered, then noting the fire in Iona's eyes, held up a hand. "Hold that in until we're down in the kitchen. I've a feeling I'll be wanting more coffee for this."

She led the way, then poured two mugs. "Go on then, cut it loose."

"He comes banging on the door. I'd been floating feathers. I've got it, Branna. I'll show you. But he broke my focus, and there's feathers everywhere, but I pulled it back, and I showed him. I was excited and happy, who wouldn't be? But I'm not blind or stupid."

She stomped around the kitchen as she spoke, one hand gesturing wildly. Branna kept her eye on the coffee in the mug in case it threatened to lap over.

"I know when a man's thinking about making a move. I know that look. You know that look," she said, pointing at Branna.

"I do indeed, and it's a fine one under most circumstances."

"Exactly, and since it felt fine, I went with it, or would have. I mean, for God's sake, all I did was lean in a little, and he pulls back like I'd jabbed him with a burning stick."

"Hmm," Branna said and got down a skillet.

"I felt like an idiot. You know how that kind of thing makes you feel. Well, you probably don't," Iona reconsidered. "What man would pull back from you? But I felt hot, not in the good way. Embarrassed. So I apologized. Just read it wrong, that's all, sorry about that. Okay, so maybe I babbled a little, but I felt awful and stupid, and completely flustered because I'd thought he and Meara were a thing, but she said no, so I let myself open that door, which I hadn't because of Meara, and you don't poach. Besides, he's the boss, and you don't want to step in it. And then I did, so it was worse. And I'm apologizing and trying to make it like no big thing, and he *grabs* me."

Branna paused for a moment in her task of frying bacon and eggs. "Is that the truth of it?"

"He yanked me in, and kissed me until my brains leaked out of my ears and the top of my head blew clean off." She made an exploding noise, threw her hands up, fountained them down. "And in like five seconds he just drops me, and makes some nasty comment about shutting me up, and says let's get going."

"A poet Boyle McGrath will never be."

"Screw poetry. He didn't have to slap me down that way."

"He didn't, no." Sympathy twined around amusement. "He's brusque, is Boyle, and sometimes that can be taken for unkindness, but he's not unkind as a rule."

"I guess he broke the rule with me."

"I'd say he did, by kissing the brains from your ears. You work for him, so it's an awkward sort of situation. He'd take that to heart, Boyle would."

"But I—"

"Here, have this at the table." She offered Iona a plate with the bacon and egg on a thick piece of toasted bread. "Morning drama stirs my appetite." Branna carried her own, and her coffee, took a seat. "I'll tell you, he's a man of rules. You don't cheat, steal, or lie. You don't misuse animals or take advantage of those weaker than you. You don't spoil for a fight—which is a rule come to be in the last few years—but you don't walk away from one. You stand for your friends and for your round in the pub. You never touch a woman who belongs to another, and you don't give your word unless you intend to keep it."

"I wasn't spoiling for a fight, and I don't belong to anyone. I'm not weaker than he is. Physically, sure, but I have something more. I think I lifted his truck—lorry—just a little, like a good-sized bump in the road. On the way over here."

More amused now, Branna enjoyed her breakfast. "Temper can spark power. You'll want to learn how to control that. You said yourself, he's your boss. He'd think of that, Iona. It would count with him, and yes, even though you could say you made the first move. So if he kissed the brains out of your ears, you can be sure he wanted to enough. It—like the bump of the lorry—wasn't controlled."

Thoughtfully now, Iona cut into the open-faced sandwich. "You don't think he did it to teach me a lesson?"

"Oh no, not Boyle. No, he'd not think of such a thing. I'm saying—and it's just my thought hearing only from you—he said what he did after only because he was mad at his own self. He gave you a look or two the other night at the pub."

"He . . . Really?"

"Ah, what a position this is. My cousin and dark sister on one hand, and the man I've been friends with most of my life."

"You're right. I shouldn't put you in the middle."

"Don't be daft. Sisters weigh the scale. I'd say he's had a thought about it, decided it's against the rules. And now he's pissed and frustrated, as he's muddied the waters more than they were."

"Good." Iona cut another bite, decisively. "Then we can both be pissed and frustrated. But I feel better, talking to you. I know I throw most everything out there, and you . . . well, you don't. But I want to say if you ever need to talk to anyone, I know when to shut up and listen."

"We'll have plenty to talk about. Now that you're living here, we'll need to put our time to good use. You've much yet to learn, and I don't know how long you have to learn it. I can't see it, and that worries me not a little."

"I know it's a small thing, but I floated all the feathers at once. I could direct them, change the speed, turn them. And it was like I didn't have to think how once I understood. I just felt it."

"It's not a small thing. You've done well so far. If it was only a matter of bringing out what's in you, we could take all the time, and there'd be more joy in it for both of us." Branna looked out the windows toward the hills. "But I don't know how or when he'll come. I don't know how it's possible he can, as he was burned to ash by powerful magicks. But he will, cousin, when he believes he's strong enough to defeat us all. We have to make certain he's wrong."

"There are four of us, so—"

"Three," Branna said sharply. "We're three. Fin isn't part of the circle."

"All right." Dark territory, Iona thought. She'd try to steer clear of that until she had more light. "We're three, he's one. That's a big advantage."

"He can and will bring harm to all and any to win. We're bound by our blood, by our art, by everything we are to harm none. He may not understand it, but he knows it."

She rose, went to the back door. When she opened it, the dog padded in. Iona hadn't heard a thing. "Kathel will walk with you to the stables when you're ready."

"My guard dog?"

"He enjoys the ramble. Cabhan will pay more mind to you as your power lights, so be aware of it."

"I will. When will you take me to the place in the woods?"

"Soon enough. I need to get ready. I've work. Go on and get unpacked before you head out."

"I'll clear up here. You don't have to make me breakfast."

"Be sure I won't unless I'm in the mood to," Branna said in such an easy way it made Iona feel only more welcome. "And you'll not clear today, but you and Connor will work that out between you from tonight. If I do the cooking, one or both of you does the clearing."

"More than fair."

"There's a little washer and dryer—though in good weather, we hang out the wash—right in there. And we'll be working out the marketing and the other chores. Come the spring, there'll be gardening, and you won't touch a blade of grass until I'm sure you know what you're about."

"Nan taught me. I'm pretty good."

"We'll see. You'll want to go hawking with Connor."

"I'd love to."

"You'll enjoy it, but it's for more than that. We each of us have our guide, but we're stronger when we connect with each, and they with all of us."

"All right. Will you come see Alastar?"

"I will, soon enough. This is your home now, and ever will be."

"You've always known where you belong. I don't know if you can understand what it means to me to finally feel that."

"Then go, put your things away. And when you come home, we'll work. And for you." Branna lifted a hand, closed it into a fist, then opened it again. A silver key lay in her palm. "We don't always lock the doors, but in case, this will open them for you."

"You have to show me how to do that," Iona murmured, and took the key, still warm from Branna's magick. "Thank you."

"Sure, you're welcome. I'll be in my workshop when you're done at the stables for the day. Come there, and come ready to learn."

"I will." Thrilled at the prospect, Iona all but danced out and up the stairs.

Her home now, Branna thought again. She'd tend to it, work for it, and one day, she'd have no choice but to fight for it.

9

IONA LED HER FIRST GROUP SOLO, MOUNTED ON ALASTAR. She couldn't be sure if she'd earned the responsibility, or if Boyle had tossed it at her to get her out of the way.

It didn't matter.

She enjoyed the hour with the horse, and though she knew he'd have preferred a good gallop, sensed his pleasure in her companionship. Just as she gained pleasure from the easy conversation with the couple from Maine, and the pride of being confident on the paths, the directions, and most of the answers.

We're earning our keep, she thought, giving Alastar a pat on the neck.

When she returned, Meara came out to greet her and her group. "I'll take it from here, if you don't mind. Iona's needed at the big stables."

"I am?"

"And Alastar. Can you find your way?"

"Sure. You showed me, and I marked it on the map. But—"

"Fin's orders, so you'd best go on. And how was your ride?" she asked the couple.

At a loss, Iona turned her mount, headed back the way she'd come.

Had Boyle complained about her? Was she about to be fired?

Her unsettled thoughts had Alastar turning his head to stare at her.

"I'm being stupid. Just overreacting, that's all. Boyle's pissy, but not petty." Plus, she thought Fin liked her, at least a little.

She'd know when she got there. And thinking that, gave herself the pleasure of letting Alastar have his head.

"Let's go," she decided, and even before she could give him a light kick with heels, he flew. "Oh God, yes!" On a laugh, she lifted her face to the sky as Alastar thundered down the path.

Her thrill, his thrill—the same. Glorious and entwined. Power, she realized, his and hers, spurred them both so that for an instant, just an instant more, she felt them both lift above the ground. Flying truly now, the wind whipping her hair, his mane.

As she laughed, Alastar bugled in triumph.

He'd been born for this, she realized. So had she.

"Easy," she murmured. "We should stick to the ground. For now."

The moment of flight, and now the joy of the gallop with a gorgeous horse under her blew away any worries. She let him set the speed—the stallion could *move*—turned with the river, then away, down a narrow path through the thick trees, and into the clearing where the stables spread behind a big jumping paddock.

Slowed him now—easy, easy—so she could catch her breath and look.

The house rose, gray stone with two fanciful turrets and many glinting windows. A pretty stone courtyard backed by a garden wall separated it from the garage and the rooms—Boyle's—over it.

A second paddock cocked to the right. A trio of horses stood at the fence, gazing toward the trees as if in deep contemplation.

She saw men, trailers, trucks—lorries, damn it—a husky black four-wheeler.

It all looked, she thought, prosperous, practical, and fanciful at the same time. Slowing Alastar to a dignified trot, she aimed for the stables, then him pulled up when she heard her name called.

She spotted Fin—jeans, boots, that enviable leather jacket—wave her over toward the jumping paddock as he walked to it himself.

He opened the gate, gestured her in.

"Meara said you wanted to see me."

"That I do." He cocked his head, studied her with those sharp green eyes. "You've had some fun."

"I . . . What?"

"You're glowing a bit, as is our boy here."

"Oh. Well. We had a good gallop over."

"I'll wager you did, and likely more, but in any case," he continued before she could think how to respond, "I want to see how you and Alastar handle the course here."

Little could have surprised her more. "You want me to take him over the course?"

"As I said." He shut the gate, slid his hands into his pockets. "Take it as you please."

She sat for a moment, studying the course. She'd have called the current layout intermediate. A couple of doubles, nothing tricky, and plenty of room for the approach.

"You're the boss." She nudged Alastar forward, circled him around, kicked him up to an easy lope.

She never doubted him—after all, they'd flown together. She felt him gather for the first jump. They sailed over it, approached the next, glided up and over.

"What are you about?" Boyle muttered to Fin as he came out. His hands were in his pockets as well, but his fingers curled.

Fin barely glanced over as Boyle stepped up behind him. "I told you I wanted to see what she's about. I need to know. Reverse it, take him around again," he called out.

He skimmed his gaze toward the woods. No shadows now but trees, but that would change. So he needed to know.

"You don't need me here for this," Boyle began.

"I've business over in Galway, as you know. One of us has to stay with her until we're sure she can handle the lesson."

"No need to use her for it."

"No need not to, is there? Jesus, they're silk, the pair of them. That horse is already hers. I find I'm jealous of that. He likes me well enough, but he'll never love me as he does her. Sure, another crack for my heart."

He gave Boyle a slap on the shoulder. "Meet me at the pub, I should be well done and back by eight. We'll have a pint and a meal, and you'll tell me how she fared. And we'll have a second pint where your tongue might loosen enough for you to tell me what happened between you and the blond witch to put that brood in your eyes."

"Two pints doesn't loosen my tongue, mate."

"We'll go for three then. Well done, Iona. You're a picture, the pair of you."

"He was born for it." She rubbed Alastar's neck as she walked him over. "I'm just ballast."

"You're a unit. We've a new student due in a few minutes. She's eleven, and she's a steady rider, but she's decided she wants to learn to jump. You'll take her."

"Take her where?"

"On. As instructor. You'll earn part of the fee for the lesson. If it works well for both of you. Boyle will stay on to supervise this first lesson out, as I've business elsewhere."

Fin watched her eyes track over to Boyle, then flick away again. "All right. What's her name, and what mount do you want for her?"

"She's Sarah Hannigan, and her mother will be along as well—that's Molly. They'll be saddling up Winifred, Winnie we call her.

She's a veteran. It's thirty minutes today, the lesson. We'll see how she likes it. If it's on, you'll work out times and days among you."

"Sounds good. This is fine for now, but I'd prefer a jumping saddle next time I instruct."

"Sure, we'll fix you up. I'm off then. At the pub, Boyle."

As Fin strode off, Iona glanced down at Boyle, watched him shift his weight. "So?"

"I'll see Winnie's saddled."

When he turned toward the stables, Alastar butted Boyle hard with his head.

"Alastar! Sorry," she said immediately, and bit down hard on the gurgle of laughter that wanted to escape. "Don't be rude," she told the horse, and leaning over to his ear added, "even if it's funny."

She dismounted, looped the reins around the fence. "Wait here. Can I see your Darling?" she asked Boyle.

"My what?"

"The horse, Darling. The one you got from that asshole."

"Ah." He scowled a moment, then shrugged. "She's inside."

"You can just point the way. I should take a look at Winnie, to see what I'm working with."

"All right then."

He strode off, and after rolling her eyes at Alastar, she followed. With her mouth firmly shut.

He didn't introduce her to the stable hands, or the black-and-white mutt with the wagging tail, so she introduced herself. And, ignoring Boyle's obvious impatience, she shook hands with Kevin and Mooney, and scratched Bugs (because he ate them) between the ears.

She judged the operation to be at least half again the size of the other stable, but the smells, the sounds, the look felt the same.

He paused outside a stall and the good-looking bay mare. "This is Winnie."

"She's clever, isn't she? You're a smart girl, aren't you, Winnie?"

Compact, Iona judged as she stroked Winnie's cheek. A good size for a young girl, and the steady look in her eyes boded well for a novice on the jump course.

"I can saddle her for the lesson if you show me the tack room."

"Kevin will handle it. Kevin! We've young Sarah coming in for her first jumps. It's Winnie for her."

"I'll get her ready then."

Iona turned. And saw the white filly.

"Oh my God, look at you."

Nearly pure white, sleek, regal—young, Iona thought as she approached—the filly watched her with eyes of gilded brown.

"That's—"

"Aine," Iona finished. "Fin's faerie queen. Still a princess yet, but one day." When Iona lifted a hand, Aine bent her head as if granting a great favor.

"She's astonishingly beautiful, and knows it very well. She's proud, and only waiting for her time to come. And it will."

"We'll wait, another year, I think, before breeding her."

Not that time to come, Iona thought, but only nodded.

You'll fly, she thought. And you'll love.

"Fin knows his horses," Iona commented as she stepped back.

"He does."

She paused to greet other horses on the walk down the sloped concrete. Good, healthy animals, she judged, and some real beauties—though none reached the level of Alastar and Aine—housed in clean, roomy stalls. Then she came to the roan mare with the big, poignant eyes, the long white blaze down her nose, and knew without being told.

"You're Darling, and that's just what you are."

Even before Boyle stepped up beside her, the mare turned her head, big eyes warming, body quivering. Not in fear, Iona thought, but simple delight.

She'd smelled him, sensed him, before he came into view. And it was love twined with utter devotion that had the mare stretching her neck so her head could bump his shoulder, light as a kiss.

"That's the girl." He all but crooned it, and Darling whickered, turned her head for his hand.

He opened the stall door, eased in. "I'll just check the foreleg while I'm here."

"It's better," Iona said. "But she remembers how much it hurt. She remembers being hungry. Being afraid. Until you."

Saying nothing, he crouched to run his hands up the foreleg, down again as Darling nibbled playfully at his hair.

"Do you have an apple in your coat pocket? She's pretty sure you do."

It was . . . disconcerting, to have his horse's thoughts translated to him, but he rose again, slid his hands along Darling's flank.

Iona thought if a horse could purr, she would have.

While Aine had astonished her, so much beauty and grace, Darling tugged her heart with her simple, unabashed devotion.

They knew, she and Darling, what it was to yearn for love, or at least genuine understanding and acceptance. To wish so hard and deep for a place, for a purpose.

It seemed they'd both gotten that wish.

Then Boyle reached in his pocket for the apple, into another for his pocketknife. Iona felt Darling's pleasure in the treat, and more, that it would be offered.

"You're filling out well, my girl, but what's a bit of an apple, after all?" She took it neatly, eyed the second half as she ate.

"This one's for Winnie, if she behaves with her student."

"You saved her." Iona waited while he stepped out, closed the stall door. "She'll never be anything but yours."

Iona reached up to stroke; Darling stretched out her neck again.

"She's not skittish with you," Boyle noted. "That's progress. She's still a bit nervy with strangers."

"We understand each other."

When Darling angled her head so her cheek pressed to Boyle's, and when he took the half apple out of his pocket, and fed it to her, Iona knew she was done.

"I'll get another for Winnie. You haven't had enough of them in your life."

"That's done it," Iona muttered. "I'm good at getting mad, mostly when it's justified. At least I think so. But I suck at staying mad. I just can't hold on to it, it's so heavy. Then add in me standing here watching this mutual love affair, and I can't do it. So I'm finished being mad at you, if that matters."

Boyle eyed her with some cautious speculation. "The day and the work go easier without having the mad weighing it down."

"Agreed. So." She held out a hand. "Peace?"

He frowned at her hand a moment, but he took it. He meant to let it go, right away. But he didn't.

"You work for me."

Iona nodded. "That's true."

"You're cousin to one of my closest mates."

Her pulse skipped lightly, but she nodded again. "I am."

"And it's barely a week since I first set eyes on you."

"I can't argue."

"And what you are is . . . a matter."

Now she frowned. "A matter of what?"

"A matter of, well, fact. And something you yourself are just getting acquainted with."

"Okay. Is it the fact that's a problem for you?"

"I wasn't saying it was a problem."

"Are you a witch bigot?"

Insult flew across his face so the green shimmered deeper over the tawny gold of his eyes. "That's a softheaded thing to say, seeing as I'm friends with three of them, and one of those stands as my partner as well."

"Then why did you bring it up as one of the reasons you're not or shouldn't be—I'm not sure which—interested in me?"

"Because it's there. It is. And I'd like to know one single bloody man," he continued with some heat, "who wouldn't give it some considerable thought."

"Maybe I should get mad again." She mulled it over. "But it's hard to work that up when Darling's standing there watching you with adoring eyes. Plus, everything you said is true, can't be denied. And if all of that is an issue for you, it is. None of it's an issue for me."

"But you're not standing where I'm standing."

"No, I'm not. Peace holds." And so, if you factored in her hand, did he. "Are we good?"

"Some of it should be an issue for you."

"Why? People get involved with bosses and employees all the time, and it's fine—from my point of view—as long as the power structure isn't used as a lever. People date friends' relatives all the time, too. And I can't, and wouldn't, change what I am."

"Being logical doesn't change a thing."

She had to laugh. "Being illogical does?"

"It's not— Bloody hell."

He gave her his second yank of the day, as frustrated as the first. And since she was still laughing, he put the stop to it by crushing his mouth to hers.

She tasted as he imagined light would, warm and bright with a snap of energy. It pulled at him, that taste, made him want more of it, and more still. She befuddled him, that's all it was, all that warm and bright there in the dim, closed in by the familiar scent of horses. His world, and now she was in it.

And she wrapped her arms around him as if she always would be.

If that didn't jolt a man, what would?

He jerked back. "This isn't wise."

"I wasn't thinking about wise or unwise. Kiss me again and I will."

She had to boost up on her toes, pull his head down, but she met his mouth with hers. She thought it was like clinging to a volcano just before it erupted, or flying on a cloud about to swirl into a tornado.

What would it be like when the fire spewed and the storm broke?

She wanted, very much, to find out.

But again, he drew back. "You're not thinking."

"You're right, I forgot. Let's try it again."

He laughed himself, and though there was a little pain in it, he might have taken her up on it. Except for the exaggerated throat-clearing behind him.

"Begging your pardon, but Sarah and her mother are here." Kevin gave a wide smile. "Winnie's saddled and ready—that is, whenever you are."

"I'm on my way." She looked at Boyle. "Is there paperwork?"

"Just a form for her mother to sign. I'll take care of that."

"All right. I'll go get her started."

As Iona strode out, Darling gave another whicker that might have been an equine chuckle. Kevin slid his hands in his pockets, whistled a tune.

"Not a bloody word," Boyle muttered. "From either of you."

PLEASED WITH HER DAY ON EVERY LEVEL, IONA WALKED home through the green shadows. It felt good to step into her instructor's boots again, and with such a promising student. Maybe, with that door cracked, Fin or Boyle would trust her with another student or two.

And speaking of doors cracking, the unexpected and thoroughly satisfying interlude in the stables gave both her ego and her mood a big, lofty boost.

Plus, she could see some very interesting possibilities through that crack.

Boyle McGrath, she thought. Tough, taciturn, temperamental. And a marshmallow when it came to the pretty, traumatized mare who adored him. She really wanted to get to know him better, to find out if all this fluttering and stirring equaled basic physical attraction, or something more.

She'd hoped for something more most of her life.

Plus, it boosted everything higher because he was reluctant, conflicted, and a little pissed off. He just couldn't help himself, and that was so sexy.

Maybe she should ask him out, just something casual. A drink at the pub? A movie? First she'd have to find out where people went to movies around here.

If she could cook, she'd invite herself to his place to make him dinner. But there lay disaster waiting to happen. Maybe instead, she could . . .

She paused, baffled as she glanced around. She hadn't veered from the path, had she? Maybe she hadn't paid strict attention, but after taking this walk back and forth for days, it was instinct.

Yet, something was wrong, the direction seemed off.

She did a circle, rubbing arms that had gone suddenly cold.

And watched the fog crawl across the ground.

"Uh-oh."

Iona took a step back, struggled to orient herself. On impulse she turned right, started down the narrow track at a jog. It took only seconds to realize she'd chosen wrong, and was moving deeper into the woods.

When she turned around to backtrack, trees wide as her arm span blocked the way. Fog oozed between their rugged trunks.

She ran. Better to run in any direction than become trapped. But to the right, trees pushed out of the ground, crackling, snapping as they broke through the turf. And forcing her to angle away.

The light changed, going gray like the fog. Wind, ice-edged, whistled through limbs as they knotted and tangled together to close out the sun.

Air, she thought frantically, trees through the earth, water in the form of fog.

He used the elements against her.

She forced herself to stop, pulled for power though fear rose with it. Throwing out her hands, she held twin balls of fire.

The chuckle sounded low, pricked over her skin like the legs of a spider. She shivered at the whisper of her name. Then every muscle quivered at the rustle, at the growl.

"Kathel."

But what stepped out of the gray light was the wolf of her nightmare.

Not a dream this time. As real as her terror, as the wild beat of her heart.

As he padded closer, slinking toward her, she caught a glimpse of the jewel glowing red at his throat.

"Keep back," she warned, and the wolf showed his fangs.

She'd never outrun it, she thought even as she took a step back. And the look in its glinting eyes told her it knew.

She hurled the fire, one ball, then the other, only to watch them burst into smoke inches from the wolf that stalked her. Desperate, she struggled to conjure another, but her hands shook, and her mind clogged with terror.

Quiet mind, she ordered, but it wanted to scream.

All real, she thought. It had all seemed so fanciful, so otherworldly—sorcerers, curses, fighting an evil that lived in shadows.

But it was all very, very real. And it meant to kill her.

She saw the wolf poised, ready to spring. Then on a feral scream, the hawk dived out of the sky. Its talons scored the wolf's flank, drawing blood as black as the hide before the hawk soared up again.

A moment's hot relief doused when a second growl sounded behind her. When she whirled, relief poured back. Kathel stood snarling. Iona sidestepped to him, laid a hand on his head, and felt a ribbon of calm wind through her fear even as Connor, then Branna, stepped through the fog.

Connor lifted one gloved arm so the hawk glided down to land, wings outstretched.

"Take my hand," he told Iona, keeping his eyes calm and cold on the wolf.

"And mine."

Connor and Branna flanked her, and when hands joined it wasn't calm she felt, but the hot rise of power filling her like life.

"Will you test us here?" Branna challenged. "Will you try it here and now?" A bolt of light, jagged as lightning, flew from her outstretched hand, arrowed into the ground a bare whisper from the wolf's forelegs. It retreated. The red jewel glowed, fiercely red; its snarl sounded like thunder, but it retreated.

Fog gathered in on itself, boiled into a smaller and smaller mass. Connor lifted Iona's hand with his. Light glowed from it, spread and strengthened until the fog tore and vanished.

And with it, the wolf was gone.

"I . . . God, I was just—"

"Not here," Branna snapped out at Iona. "We'll not be talking here."

"Take her back to the cottage. Roibeard and I will have a look around, then we'll be home."

Branna nodded at Connor. "Have a care."

"I always do. Go on now with Branna." He gave Iona's hand a steadying squeeze. "You'll have a tot of whiskey, and you'll do fine enough."

With Iona's hand clasped in hers, that power still humming at the edges, Branna strode briskly through the woods. Wanting nothing more than to get inside, Iona let herself be pulled along despite her shaking knees.

"I couldn't—"

"Not until we're inside. Not a bloody word about it."

The dog led the way, always in sight. As she saw the cottage through the trees—at last—Iona watched the hawk circle through the heavy sky.

The minute they were inside, Iona's teeth began to chatter. As gray teased the edges of her vision, she pressed her hands to her knees, lowered her head between them.

"Sorry. Dizzy."

"Hold your guts a moment." Though her voice rang with impatience, the hand Branna laid on the back of Iona's head stayed gentle, and the dizziness passed as quickly as it had come.

"Sit," she ordered, giving Iona a shove into the living room, flicking her fingers toward the smoldering fire to have the flames leap up and spread more heat. "You're having a bit of shock, that's all. So sit, breathe."

Briskly she walked to a decanter, poured two fingers of whiskey in a short glass. "And drink."

Iona drank, hissed a little, drank again. "Just a little . . ." She sighed. "Scared shitless."

"Why were you off the path, and so deep?"

"I don't know. It just happened. I didn't turn off, or don't remember turning off. I was just walking home, and thinking about stuff. Boyle," she admitted. "We made up."

"Oh well, that's fine then." With two jerks, Branna pulled pins from her hair, tossed them on the table as it tumbled free. "All's well."

"I didn't go off the path, not knowingly. And when I realized I wasn't where I was supposed to be, should've been, I started back. But . . . the fog came first."

Iona looked down at the empty glass, set it down. "I knew what it meant."

"And didn't call us, or your guide? Called to none of us."

"It all happened so fast. The trees—they moved, the fog closed in. Then the wolf was there. How did you come? How did you know?"

"Connor was out with Roibeard, and the hawk saw, from above. You can thank him for calling Connor, and me."

"I will. I do. Branna—" She broke off as the door opened and Connor walked in.

"There's nothing now. He's gone to whatever hole he uses." He walked to the whiskey, poured his own. "And how are you doing now, cousin?"

"Okay. All right. Thank you. I'm sorry I—"

"I don't want apologies," Branna snapped. "I want sense. Where's your amulet?"

"I—" Iona reached for it, then remembered. "I left it in my room this morning. I forgot—"

"Don't forget, and don't take it off."

"Ease back a bit there." Connor touched Branna's arm as he walked over to Iona. "You gave us all a fright." Now his hand stroked Iona's arm, and the calm seeped into her. "It's not your fault. It's not her fault," he said to Branna before she could snap back. "She's barely a week under her feet. We've a lifetime."

"She won't have time or opportunity for more if she doesn't have the good sense to wear what protection she has, and to call out for her guide and for us when she needs more."

"And who's been educating her if not you?" Connor tossed back.

"Oh, so it's my fault now she's no more sense than a babe in a pram."

"Don't fight about me, and don't talk over me. It was my fault." Steadier, Iona rose to go stand nearer the fire, and the warmth. "I took off the amulet, and I wasn't paying attention. Neither will happen again. I'm sorry I—"

"By all that's holy, I swear I'll sew your lips shut a week on the next apology."

Iona just threw up her hands at Branna's threat. "I don't know what else to say."

"Just tell us what happened, in detail, before we got to you," Branna told her. "No, back in the kitchen. I'll make the tea."

Iona followed her back, then crouched to pet Kathel, to thank him. "I was walking home, from the big stables."

"Why were you there?"

"Oh, Fin sent for me. They gave me a student, for jumping instruction. I rode over on Alastar. We flew a little."

"Sweet Brighid."

"I didn't mean to, exactly, and I stopped. Then Fin had to leave, but Boyle stayed to supervise, to make sure I didn't screw it up, I'd say. I asked to meet Darling, but first I met Aine, and oh my God, she's miraculous."

"I'm not interested in a report on the horses," Branna reminded her.

"I know, but I'm trying to explain. Then I met Darling, and watched her and Boyle, and I couldn't stay mad at him. Then one thing led to another because I wasn't mad at him."

"Why were you?" Connor wondered.

"Oh, we had kind of a thing this morning when he picked me up."

"He kissed the brains out of her ears," Branna supplied, and Connor's grin broke out.

"Boyle? Did he indeed?"

"Then he was rude and nasty, and that pissed me off. But then, watching him and Darling, I just couldn't stay mad, so I told him I wasn't mad anymore, and then it was the one thing leading to another and he just grabbed me and did it again. I've probably lost at least twenty percent of my brain cells now. And the lesson went really well, it felt so good to have a student again, so I was feeling good, and distracted," she admitted, "and thinking that maybe I should ask Boyle out—for a drink or the movies, or something. It was such a good day, after a rocky start, and I was just full of all of it. Then I wasn't where I should've been."

She told them the details she remembered.

"You didn't focus," Branna said. "If you're to use fire as defense or offense, you have to *mean* it."

"She's never used it against anything or anyone," Connor pointed out. "But she had the wit and the power to bring the fire. Next time she'll burn his arse. Won't you, Iona darling?"

"Damn right." Because she'd never feel that helpless and terrorized again. "I was going to try again, and okay, I was terrified. Then Roibeard dived out of the sky. He's the most beautiful thing I've ever seen."

"He makes a picture," Connor said with a smile.

"Then Kathel was there, then both of you. I did freeze," she admitted. "It was like being caught in a dream. The fog, the black wolf, the red gem glowing at its throat."

"Feeding his power. The stone," Branna explained, "and your fear. We'll work harder. You'll wear the amulet. Connor will walk you to the stables in the mornings, and we'll see someone brings you home at the end of the day."

"Oh, but—"

"Branna's right. A week and he's come at you in dreams, and in the here and now. We'll be more careful, is all. Until we decide what's to be done. Go get the amulet now, and we'll get to work."

Iona rose. "Thanks for being there."

"You're ours," Connor said simply. "We're yours."

The words, and the quiet loyalty in them, made Iona's eyes sting as she hurried through the back toward the kitchen and the cottage.

"She's taken on a great deal in no time at all," Connor began.

"I know it. I know it perfectly well."

"And you were sharp with her, as you were frightened for her."

Branna said nothing a moment, just went about the soothing process of making the tea. "I'm the one who's teaching her."

"It's not your fault any more than it's hers. And this was, for all of us, a lesson learned. He's grown bold since she's come here."

"With the three of us together, he knows, as we do, the time's coming. If he can harm her, or turn her—"

"She won't turn."

"She won't, no, not willingly. She's got your loyalty, I think, and far too much gratitude for too little given."

"When you've had less than little in some things, you're grateful for even a spoonful of more. We've always had each other. And we've always been loved. She wants love, the giving and the having of it. I didn't pry," he added. "It's so much a part of her, I can't not see it."

"I see it myself. Well, she has us now, like it or not."

Connor took the tea his sister gave him. "So, it's Boyle, is it? Grabbing our cousin and kissing her stupid from the sounds of it. She's barely landed on our doorstep, and my mate's jumping her like a rabbit."

"Oh, leave off being such a child."

He laughed, drank tea. "Why would I leave off, when it's such a grand time?"

10

FOCUS. BRANNA HARPED ON IT RELENTLESSLY. IONA struggled to find it, then hold it. She'd improved—Branna gave her frustratingly faint praise for that—but she'd yet to reach the skill her exacting mentor judged strong enough.

She wondered how the hell anyone could focus soaking wet and half frozen.

Rain poured out of thick gray skies as it had, without pause, for two solid days and nights. That equaled, for the most part, inside work for both her job and her craft. She didn't mind it, not really. She enjoyed reorganizing the tack room with Meara, and working with Mick on instructing one young rider, and one feisty octogenarian in the ring.

She loved having extra time to groom and bond with the horses. She'd braided the manes of all the mares, delighted by the way they preened at the added attention. And though she sensed the geldings would have liked that style and attention just as much, she knew Boyle would object. So she'd worked a small, single braid into each, to please the horse and satisfy the boss.

And she learned. Inside Branna's workshop with the fire simmering, the scents of herbs and candle wax sweetening the air, she'd learned to expand her own understanding, embrace her power, and begin to polish those raw edges. At night, she read, she studied while the wind blew that steady rain against the windowpanes.

But how the hell was she supposed to think, much less focus, with rain splatting on her head, and the raw chill of it shivering straight to her bones.

Worse, Branna stood there, absolutely dry, her hair a gorgeous black sweep, and her eyes merciless.

"It's water," Branna reminded her. She stood in the quiet sunlight she'd created, smiling coolly through the curtain of rain that fell outside her boundary.

"I know it's water," Iona muttered. "It's running down the back of my neck, into my eyes."

"Control it. Do you think you'll be warm and dry and happy every time you need what you are, what you have? Will Cabhan wait for fine, fair weather to come for you?"

"All right, all right, all right!" Flickers of fire sizzled from Iona's fingertips, and a stream of rain went to steam.

"Not that way. You're not after changing it, though well done enough there. Move it." Smoothly, effortlessly, Branna widened her sunny spot a few inches.

"Show-off," Iona muttered.

"It's in you as much as me. Slide the rain away from you."

She liked the feel of the fire snapping through her, from her, but drew it back. And used the frustration and annoyance that helped her call it to nudge, to slide, to open.

An inch, then two—and she saw it, felt it. It *was* just water. Like the water in the bowl. Thrilled, she pushed, and pushed hard enough to have that streaming rain leap away, gather. And splat with some force against Branna's borders.

"I didn't mean to— I mean I wasn't trying to splash you. Exactly."

"It wouldn't have hurt your feelings if you'd managed to," Branna said easily. "So well done as well there. You'll work on subtlety, and finesse—and absolute control—but you managed it, and that's a start."

Iona blinked, swiped at her wet face, and saw she'd opened a narrow but effective swath of dry. No pretty pale gold sunlight in her little corner, but no rain either.

"Woo to the hoo!"

"Don't lose it. Don't spread it. It's only for you."

"The rest of the county would probably appreciate some dry, but I get it. Stop rain here, maybe cause a flood there."

"We can't know, so we don't risk it. Move with it," Branna demonstrated, walking in a wide circle, always within the dry.

On her attempt, the edges of Iona's circle turned soggy, but she kept control.

"Well done. As it's Ireland, you'll have no lack of rain to practice on as we go, but well done for today. We'll go inside, have a go at a simple potion."

As Branna headed back toward the workshop, Iona struggled to keep up—and maintain her dry area. "I could help on the bottling and packaging of your stock, for your shop. I'd like to help somewhere," she continued. "You do almost all the cooking, and you're spending a lot of your time—Connor, too—teaching me. I'm pretty good at following directions."

"You are."

Branna had always preferred the solitude of her workshop. It was one matter to hire clerks and such for the shop in Cong, to have them deal with customers, shipping, and so on. But her workshop was her quiet place. Usually.

And still, she thought, the lessons, and the need for them, did cut into her time.

"It would be a help," she decided. "We'll see about it."

Branna stepped into the workshop, and Iona nipped in behind her dripping on the floor.

"I was about to leave you a note," Meara said from behind the work counter. "The both of you."

"Now you'll have some tea, and a visit. I've missed seeing you. Iona, don't track up the floor."

"Easy for you to say. You're dry, I'm soaked. I must look like a wet cat."

"More a drowned one," Meara commented.

Branna walked straight to the kettle. "Do a glamour."

Saying nothing, Iona glanced at Meara.

"Meara knows all there's to know, and likely more besides. Fix yourself up."

"I'm no good at glamours. I told you I tried one once, and it was a disaster."

"Sure it's why it's called practice. For usual, it's my thinking glamours or drying your clothes instead of changing them is lazy and vain, but for now, it's good practice. If you end up with warts or boils, I'll fix it for you." With a wicked smile, Branna glanced back. "Eventually."

"You did one for me, do you remember, Branna, when we were fifteen, I think, and I desperately wanted to go blond, as Seamus Lattimer, my heart's desire at that time, preferred them."

At home, Meara took off her jacket, hung it on a peg, unwrapped her scarf to do the same, then her cap. "I was about to do the deed—had the hair product I'd saved two weeks to buy, and Branna came along, did the glamour, and changed it for me."

Considering, Iona studied Meara. "I can't picture you as a blonde, not with your coloring."

"It was a rare disaster. I looked as if I'd developed the jaundice."

"And you were too stubborn to admit it," Branna reminded her.

"Oh, I was, so I lived with it near to a week before I begged her to turn it back. Do you remember what you said to me?"

"Something about changing for yourself was one matter, changing for a man was weak and foolish."

"Wise, even so young," Meara said with her bawdy laugh. "And Seamus spent his time snogging with Catherine Kelly, as blond as a daffodil. But I lived through the disappointment."

"A lesson learned, of some sort," Branna said. "But in this case, we're considering it practice. Fix yourself up there, Iona, and we'll have some tea."

"Okay. Here goes." She released a breath, sincerely hoping she didn't set herself on fire as she concentrated on her jacket, sweater, and jeans first.

Steam puffed, but no flames snapped. She began to feel her toes thaw out, her skin warm, and, smiling, ran a hand over the dry sleeve of her jacket.

"It worked."

"Think of the time I'd save on laundry if I had a trick like that," Meara commented.

Grinning, Iona ran a hand over her wet, dripping hair, turned it to a sunny, dry cap. On a quick laugh, she covered her face with her hands, closed her eyes briefly. When she lowered them, her face glowed, the color of her lips deepened to a rosy pink, her eyelashes darkened, lengthened.

"How do I look?"

"Ready to head to the pub and flirt with all the handsome men," Meara told her.

"Really?" Delighted, Iona rushed to the mirror. "I look good! I really do."

"Smoothly done, and with a bit of finesse as well. You've come along well."

"Stick around," Iona said to Meara. "She never says things like that to me."

"So when I do, you know I mean them. I've shortbread biscuits, Meara, and the jasmine tea you're fond of."

"I won't say no to either." She made herself at home at the table, taking a moment to rub Kathel when he laid his big head in her lap. "The weather's dampening our business, and they're saying we're in for more of the same tomorrow. Boyle's arranged for classes from the school to come in, see the horses. We'll give the young ones rides on leads around the ring."

"That's a good idea."

"Oh, he has them, our Boyle does." Meara smiled at Iona as she helped herself to a cookie. "And as for you, I had a thought for my sister's birthday next month. Maureen. She lives down in Kerry, as she and her husband work there," she added for Iona. "You know the sets you do—the soap, the candle, the lotion, and such—the special ones you make with that particular person's traits and personality in mind."

"I do. You'd like one done for Maureen?"

"I would, yes. She's the oldest of us, as you know, and about to turn thirty-five. For some reason, she's gone half mad over it, as if her youth is done and over, and she's nothing but the miseries of age left to her."

"Bless her, Maureen was always one for drama."

"Oh, that she is. She married her Sean when she was just nineteen, so she's had sixteen years of his plodding. He's a sweet man under it," she continued, "but a plodder for all that. She's two teenagers driving her to the edge of insanity, or beyond it, and another coming up behind them. She's taken to texting me, our other sister, or our ma all day and half the night to keep us abreast of her trials and tribulations.

I'm thinking the gift, being it's created for her, and it speaks to pampering and female things, might perk her up enough to have her leave off hounding me until I want to thrash her."

"So it's about you," Branna said with a laugh.

"I'm saving her life, and that makes me a fine sister."

"I'll have it for you next week."

"I always wanted a sister," Iona mused.

"Would you like one of mine? Either of them's up for the grabbing. I'll keep my brothers, as they're not gits most of the time."

"Being an only child is lonely and you never get to bitch about your siblings."

"I would miss the bitching," Meara admitted. "It makes me feel so superior and smart."

"I had imaginary siblings."

Amused, Meara sat back with her tea. "Did you now? What did you call them?"

"Katie, Alice, and Brian. Katie was the oldest, and patient, smart, comforting. Alice was the baby, and always made us laugh. Brian and I were the closest in age. He was always getting into trouble, and I was always trying to get him out of it. Sometimes I could see them, as clear as I see you."

"The power of your wishes," Branna told her. Lonely child, she thought. So not tended, so not understood or cherished.

"I guess. I didn't understand that kind of thing, not really, but they were more real to me, a lot of the time, than anyone else. Between them and horses, I kept pretty busy."

She stopped, laughed. "Am I the only one who had imaginary people in her life?"

"Connor was more than enough for me."

"He's more than enough, indeed," Meara echoed.

"And we both knew, Connor and I, much younger than you, what we were about."

"And even with that, you both forged other really strong things. Your work here, the shop, his falconry—and his handy hands. And you, Meara. You're not one of the owners, but you're an essential element in the business."

"I like to think so."

"It's clear you are. Both Boyle and Fin respect your skills and your opinion, and depend on both. I don't think either of them give that sort of thing lightly. It's what I want. To forge something, and to earn respect, to have people who matter know they can depend on me. Do either of you want more than that?"

"It's good to have what you say," Meara considered. "I wouldn't mind a pot of money to go with it."

"What would you do with it?"

"Well now, that's a thought. I think first a fine house. Doesn't need the fancy, just a good house, with a bit of land and a little barn so I could have my own horse or two."

"No man?"

"For what?" Meara laughed. "For the keeping or for the fun?"

"Either or both."

"I'd take the fun, there's been a lack of that sort of amusement in my life in recent months. Keeping though, that's not what I'm after. Men come and go," she added as she settled back with her fragrant tea. "Except for sweet and plodding Sean, as far as I've seen. Best not to expect or want them to stay, then it's less fraught."

"But fraught means you're living," Iona said. "And I want one to keep, one who wants me just as much. I want wild, crazy love, the sort that never goes away. And kids—not just one—a dog, a horse, a house. A big, sloppy family. What about you?" she asked Branna.

"What do I want? To live my life. To end this curse that hangs over all of us, and crush what remains of Cabhan."

"That's not just for you. Just you, Branna," Iona insisted. "Money, travel, sex? Home, family?"

"Enough money to travel to exotic places and have reckless sex with exotic men." She smiled as she poured more tea. "That should cover the lot."

"I'll travel with you." Meara laid a hand over Branna's. "We'll break hearts the world over. You're welcome to join us," she told Iona. "We'll see all the wonders, and take our pleasures where we find them. Then you can come back, pick the one you'll keep, and make the babies. I'll build my house and barn, and Branna will live her life exactly as she pleases, curse-free."

"Agreed." Branna lifted her teacup to toast. "We've only to vanquish ancient evil and earn great wealth, and the rest is but details."

"Both of you could have all that exotic sex now," Iona protested. "It's not hard to have your pick of men when you look like Celtic goddesses."

"We're keeping her," Meara told Branna. "She's a wonder for my ego."

"It's true. Branna looks like something out of a fairy tale without even trying, and you're this image of a warrior princess. Men should be falling at your feet."

The door opened, bringing in the rain, along with Connor, Boyle, and Fin.

"Not all of them," Meara murmured.

"Look what I've dragged in." Connor shook rain from his hair like a dog as Kathel bounded over to greet the newcomers. "It was haul them in or build a bleeding ark. Have you tea and biscuits to spare?"

"Of course. Don't track up my floor. Has the business world shut its doors then?"

"For the day," Boyle told Branna. "We were nudging Fin along to buy us dinner, but damn near drowned considering the where."

"And here's better." Connor walked over to hold his hands out to the fire. "Especially if someone could be cajoled into making a vat of soup."

"Someone?"

Connor merely smiled at Branna. "And I thought of my own darling sister."

"You think of me in the kitchen entirely too often."

"But you're brilliant in it." He leaned down to kiss her.

"I'll peel and chop whatever you need." It was, Iona calculated, sort of like asking Boyle to dinner. "You can peel and chop, can't you, Boyle?"

"I can, especially if it gets me dinner."

"I'm willing to be a kitchen slave for a hot meal on a night like this," Meara added. "What of you, Fin?"

He continued to unwind the scarf from around his neck. "Whatever Branna needs or wants tonight."

"Then I'd best go see what there is to put together for this famous vat of soup." She rose, and moved through the rear doorway. The dog left Fin's side to follow her.

"She'd be easier if I went on," Fin said.

"You'll not." A rare edge of anger laced Connor's voice. "It can't be that way, and she knows it as well as you do. We need you. I've told Fin and Boyle what happened a few days ago," he told Iona.

"What happened?" Meara demanded.

"I'll tell you as well, in a moment. But it stands, Fin. We need you, and she understands that. In the end she won't let what's tangled between you get in the way of it."

"Maybe someone should tell me about the tangle." Iona shoved her tea away. "It might help to know all the details instead of trying to figure everything out with pieces of them."

Fin walked over to the table, then tugged down the neck of his sweater. "This is his mark, the mark your blood put on mine. I bear it, and Branna won't see past it to what she is to me or what I am to her."

Iona rose to study it closely. A pentagram, as the legend claimed, and as clear and defined as a tattoo. "It doesn't look like a birthmark, but more like a scar or a tattoo. Were you born with it?"

"No. It . . . manifested much later than that. I was more than eighteen."

"Did you always know?"

"Not where the power had come from, no, but only that I had it." He adjusted his sweater. "You're a steady one, Iona."

"Not really, or not enough. Yet."

"I think you're wrong there." He tipped her head up with a hand on her chin. "You'll hold when it counts most, I think. She'll need that steadiness from you, and that open mind."

"Connor says we need you, and I trust him. I'm going to go help Branna get started."

"I'm with you." Meara rose. "Give her a few minutes to settle into it, but don't gorge on the biscuits. She'll do whatever needs be, Fin, whatever the cost."

"As will I."

Iona went with Meara through the back, in and out of the storeroom, and into the house.

"Wait, before we go into Branna." Iona stopped. "What happened between Fin and Branna? I'm not asking you to gossip, or betray the sisterhood, and one that's so obviously close and intimate between you and Branna. I think you know that. I hope you know that."

"I do, and still it's not easy to say to you what she hasn't. I'll tell you they were in love. Young and wild for each other. Happy in it, though they scraped and squabbled. She was going onto seventeen when they came together the first time. It was after they'd been together the mark came on him. He didn't tell her. I don't know whether to blame him for that, but he didn't tell her. And when she found out, she was angry, but more, she was devastated. He was defensive and the same. So it's been an open wound between them ever since. A dozen years of wanting and turmoil and too much distrust."

"They still love each other."

"Love hasn't been enough, for either of them."

It should be, Iona thought. She'd always believed it would be. But she went with Meara toward the kitchen to do what she could to help.

IT MIGHT HAVE BEEN AN ORDINARY GATHERING OF FRIENDS and family on a rainy night. The little fire simmering in the kitchen hearth, with the big dog snoring in front of it. The wine Connor pulled out, uncorked, and poured generously into glasses. Volunteers dutifully peeling and chopping small mountains of potatoes and carrots, mincing garlic and onions while the hostess busied herself dredging chunks of beef in flour, browning it in a big, sturdy pot on the stove. The scents rising up, teasing of what was to come, and the mix of voices all talking to or over one another.

It might have been just a gathering, Iona thought while she chopped carrots, and the parts that were warmed her, gave her so much of what she'd come to understand she'd yearned for her whole life. But it wasn't just a friendly gathering, and the undercurrents tugging and pulling beneath the surface were deadly.

Still, she didn't want to spoil the moment, send ripples over that surface. After all, she stood hip to hip with Boyle—who unquestionably had a more competent hand than she with the kitchen knife—and he seemed more relaxed here than when they worked together at the stables.

And he smelled wonderful, of rain and horses.

Better to say nothing, she decided, than say the wrong thing. So she watched and listened instead. She watched Connor reach over to flick a tear from Meara's cheek as she minced onions, and caught the easy flirtation in the gesture in his eyes.

"If you were mine, Meara my love," he said, "I'd ban onions from the house so you'd never shed a tear."

"If I were yours," she shot back, "I'd be shedding them over more than onions."

He laughed, but Iona wondered. Just as she wondered when Fin topped off Branna's wineglass and, at her request, handed her oil for a skillet. Their polite tone remained as stiff as their body language, but under it—oh yeah, undercurrents everywhere—there boiled such passions, such wild emotion she'd have had to have been both blind and heartless not to feel it.

It was Connor, she thought, who kept it all going, tossing out comments, questions, knitting the group together with relentless cheer and encompassing affection.

The man struck her as next to irresistible. So why did Meara—

"You study everything and everyone," Boyle put in, "as if there's to be an exam within the hour. And your brain's full of questions and conclusions."

"It feels like family." She spoke the first thought that popped from the tangle of them in her mind. "It's something I always wanted to feel, be part of."

"Sure it is family," Connor told her. "And yours."

"You're generous with people. It's your nature. Not everyone is, or at least they're more cautious before opening the door. I'm the newest here, on a lot of levels. Observing gives me a better sense of that family. Even just observing Boyle peel and chop a lot faster and better than I do."

"Well now, he's no Branna O'Dwyer," Fin told her, "but he's a passable cook. It's just one reason Connor and I tolerate him."

"If a man can't toss a few things in a pan, he's too often hungry. Here, put the palm of your hand on the tip, fingers up, out of range." Boyle took Iona's hand, to show her. "And the other on the hilt so you can use that to steer the blade."

She let him guide her hands to produce nice, neat rounds of carrot, and appreciated the light press of his body to hers.

"I'll have to practice," she decided. "And figure out what to do with them after I chop them. It's probably just as well I didn't get the chance to ask you to dinner."

She glanced up and around at him, caught the surprise on his face, and the hint of embarrassment as the room went quiet.

"You're better off with Branna doing the cooking," Iona continued. "I'll have to figure out some other way to get you on a date."

When Connor failed to disguise a chuckle with a cough, she shrugged.

"Family," she said again. "And more, family with the kind of problem and mutual goal that means we could all get our asses kicked, or worse, tomorrow or anytime after. So I figure there's not a bunch of time to waste or circle around what might make us happy. Speaking as someone who's lived her life with half the happy, I'd like to finish it out—especially considering potential ass kickings—with a great big armload of it."

From where he stood, leaning against the counter, Fin smiled at her. "I believe I'm already half in love with you myself."

"You don't have half to spare." Then she sighed. "Now, let's see. Who else can I embarrass?"

"You haven't me," Fin told her. "And as for love, *deirfiúr bheag*, there are no limits to it."

"I've always hoped that. What does that mean, what you called me?"

"Little sister."

"I like it. I should learn Irish. Do all of you speak it?"

"Branna, Connor, and Fin." Finished with her mincing, Meara walked over to rinse her hands. "Boyle and I have enough to get by, wouldn't you say, Boyle?"

"Enough."

"Is magick more powerful, do you think, with it? Sorry," Iona said immediately. "I shouldn't keep bringing that up and screwing with the mood. And I shouldn't have put you on the spot like that," she said to Boyle.

"You just disconcerted him, as he wouldn't be accustomed to a woman who speaks her mind and feelings right out, without filtering. Connor," Branna continued, "I need a Guinness for the pot, and I'd say another bottle of wine for the rest of us. And you're right as well, Iona, to speak of the rest of it. We can't know if we've a day or a year before we'll face what's coming, but logic says a day's the closer to it. And all that said, I'm damned if any one of us will have our ass kicked. So we'll get this stew on the simmer, have more wine, and we'll talk of it."

She turned, face flushed from the steam, eyes glittering with a determination so fierce Iona couldn't believe it could be defeated.

"Well then, let's have those vegetables. They won't cook themselves."

11

IT STILL MIGHT HAVE BEEN ANY GATHERING OF FRIENDS and family—all crowded around the kitchen table with glasses of wine, and the dog still sprawled at the hearth.

But Iona recognized it for what it truly was.

A power summit.

"I'd like to say something first," Branna began, "to Meara and to Boyle. 'Tisn't your blood mixed into this, and you've neither power of your own as weapon or shield."

"To begin with insulting us doesn't make a strong first step," Boyle told her.

"Sure it's not meant like that, but to acknowledge what it means to the rest of us to know you're with us. In truth, I don't know how Connor or myself would have fared without you. You're the truest friends I've ever had, or ever will. I don't know if, as Fin claims, love has no limits, but I know I've yet to reach the limit of mine for either of you. And there, that's said."

"We don't have power, but we're not helpless. Far from it." Meara looked to Boyle, got his nod.

"We have our brains, our fists. He's never shown interest in us, and that's his mistake."

"That may be, and we should find a way to use it. But he's taken a strong interest in Iona." Connor gestured toward her. "Branna and I agree he's hoped to do her harm—and worse—and by doing that, take her power, increase his own. It cost him, we think, to set the trap for her a few days ago, then fail."

"What trap?" Boyle demanded. "Were you hurt?" he grabbed Iona's arm. "Why didn't you tell me?"

"It isn't easy to talk about this kind of thing at the stables. And I wasn't hurt. Branna and Connor saw to that."

Fin spoke quietly. "What happened? Be specific. Iona, you tend to be just that. Tell the rest of us."

"It was the day I gave Sarah her first lesson. When I was walking home."

She told them, specifically, and didn't gloss over her fear.

As she spoke, Fin rose, strode to the window looking out over the back gardens. On the table, Boyle's hands balled into fists.

"You'll not walk to work or home alone from now on."

Iona gaped at Boyle. "That's ridiculous. I have to—"

"You'll not. And that's the end of it."

Before Iona could speak again, she caught Meara's eye, and her friend's subtle shake of the head.

"Connor can walk with her to the stables." Branna spoke smoothly. "They go the same way, and you and Fin have only to see their schedules mesh close enough."

"It's done," Boyle said definitely. "And I'll see her home. It's done," he repeated.

"I appreciate the concern. Is someone going to be with me every time I take a step out of the house, or want to go into the village? And you'd better start sleeping with me, too," she told Boyle. "Because he's poking around in my dreams. I'm allowed to be afraid, but I'm not allowed to be helpless. And no one else is allowed to think I am."

"Far from helpless," Connor soothed. "But precious. And necessary. We need you, so a few precautions, at least for now, will ease our minds."

"Precious. Necessary." Fin turned, his face cool. "I agree with that. And yet you didn't call me when the precious and necessary was threatened."

"It was quick," Connor told him. "And in truth I only thought to get to Iona, and to bring Branna as fast as we both could. So you're right, the fault's mine there."

"Could you have done more?" Branna asked Fin.

"We can't know, can we? But you have to decide, all of you, if I'm to be a part of this, or if you'll hold me outside."

Rather than answer, Branna changed angles. "Can you read him? Sense his thoughts?"

"I can't, no. He's blocked me out. He knows I've chosen my side. Sure he believes I can be turned still, and he'll pull at me. In dreams, and in waking ones."

"You don't block him."

Fin bit off a curse. "I've a life to live, don't I? Other thoughts in my head. He's got only the one purpose for his whole existence, and I've more than that. And if I block him altogether, if I could, there's no chance then, is there, none at all that I might learn something that could help us end this. If you don't believe I want that, to end it, to see even the thought of him destroyed, I've nothing left to convince you."

"I don't doubt that. I don't." Branna rose to go over, stir the soup. "She needs the horse. Iona needs her guide."

Sheer frustration flicked over Fin's face. "He's been hers since the first I saw him. You've no place to keep Alastar here, so he's with Boyle and me. If you don't trust that, I'll sign his papers over to her tomorrow."

"No!" Appalled, Iona pushed to her feet. "That's not right."

"Nor is it what I was saying or meaning. It's you who have to tell her he's hers. You and Boyle, as you brought him here, and you're keeping him for her. I only meant that."

"Even without any magick to it, the horse was hers the minute they set eyes on each other." Boyle lifted his hands, let them fall. "And Fin's the right of it. You've no place here to keep him as he needs to be. We spoke of it the very night Fin came home again."

"I'm grateful to you, both." Branna's tone softened. "And I'm sorry, truly, if it seemed I wasn't."

"I've never wanted your gratitude or your apologies," Fin told her.

"You have them, wanted or not, and can do what you please with them." Setting the spoon aside, Branna came back to the table.

Iona, like Fin, remained standing.

"Thank you."

"You're entirely welcome," Fin told her.

"And thank you," she said to Boyle. "Since he's mine, I'll pay for his food and lodging. And that's the end of it," she said as Boyle opened his mouth in obvious protest. "I haven't had much that was mine that mattered, but I take care of what belongs to me."

"Fine then. We'll work it out."

"Good. I also know what it's like to be held outside. There's no colder place than right outside the warmth. None of you know what that's like but me, and Fin. All of you have always been a part of something, even the center of it," she added, looking at Branna. "So you don't know what it is to feel you're not wanted or accepted or understood. I think what's between you and Fin, and what stands between you is personal. But there's a lot more here to consider. You said I'm part of this, that this is family and it's mine. So I want to say that Fin's my family, too."

On impulse she picked up the wine, and though he'd barely

touched his, added a few drops to his glass. "You should come sit down," she told him.

He murmured something in Irish before he came back, took his seat. And lifted his wine to drink.

"He said his heart and hand are yours," Branna told her.

"Oh. Back at you, and that's why we'll win."

"You've shamed me in my own house."

"Oh, oh, Branna, I didn't mean to—"

"And it's good you did. I earned it, and it seems needed, the same sort of unfiltered thoughts and feelings you gave Boyle. We're a circle or we're not, and a circle with chinks in it is easily breached. So a circle we are, from here till it's done." She lifted her glass, held it toward Fin. After a moment, he tapped his to it.

"*Sláinte.*" Connor tapped his own to Fin's, then his sister's, then around the table. "Or better yet, may all the gods who ever were bless us, and help us send the bloody bastard to hell."

"I'm good with that." A little exhausted from the emotion, Iona sat again. Under the table Boyle took her hand in his. Surprised, she looked at him, met his quiet, steady gaze.

She all but felt something spill into her heart, something full of warmth and light, and hope.

"Well," Meara said from across the table, "now that we've settled all that, what the hell do we do next?"

Plenty of ideas shot around the table with arguments for and against. At some point Meara got up and, obviously at home, put together a plate of crackers and cheese and olives to keep hunger at bay as the stew simmered.

"We're not ready to confront." Connor popped an olive as he ticked off reasons against Boyle's push for a frontal attack. "We don't have a solid plan, with the contingencies we'd surely need as yet, and more, Iona isn't as well armed as she needs to be."

"I'm not going to be responsible for holding anyone back."

"Then study and practice more," Branna ordered.

"Nag, nag. Didn't I stop the rain?"

Brows lifted, Boyle pointed to the window where it lashed in wet whips.

"Temporarily and in a limited location. I'm better with fire."

"It controls you more than you controlling it," Branna corrected.

"Harsh, but true. Still, I'm better. And . . ." She focused, managed to levitate the table a few inches, then cautiously set it down again. "Getting air pretty well, and I've done the flowers in the workshop, so earth's coming along. If I could try a couple spells . . ."

"You've not worked with her on spells?" Fin asked.

"She's barely getting her grip on the elements."

"Caution has its place, Branna, but as you've said yourself, we don't know how much time we have."

"Push me," Iona begged. "At least a little."

"You might regret the asking of it, but that's what I'll do."

"I think if there's any of this prodding into dreams, you should all write them down." Meara spread a cracker with cheese, handed it to Branna. "They stay clearer that way, and you could compare them. There might be something there."

"That's a sensible thing," Connor agreed.

"What about the place in the woods?" Iona asked. "Where the first dark witch lived. When can I see it?"

In the beat of silence that followed, Iona felt tension, fury, grief. Once again, Boyle took her hand under the table.

"You're not ready," Branna said simply. "You need to trust me there."

"If I'm not ready to go there, why can't you tell me why?"

"It's a place between." Fin spoke slowly, frowning at his wine. "Sometimes it's simply a place with the ruins of an old cabin, and the echoes of the life lived there, the power wielded there. A gravestone where that power lies under the earth. It's the trees and the quiet."

"And other times," Connor said, "it slips away, and it's alone. It's not tightly bound to the world, to the here. Without the knowing, a person might be caught there, in that other, that alone. And it's there he might come, stronger for it, and take what you are."

"But you go there, have gone there. I have to know how to go, and how to stay."

"It'll come," Branna promised.

"He took me there in a dream."

"Not him, I think, but her. Teagan. To show you, and still keep you safe. Be patient here, Iona."

"He marked me there."

Silence fell again after Fin's words. "I knew of him, but not that I'd come from him. And there, in a place that had been a kind of sanctuary, at a time when there was joy and promise, he laid his mark on me, and the burn of it seemed to sear down to my bones. He slipped the bounds, took it all adrift, and marked me. And he came in the form of a man, and I could see myself in this man. He told me he would give me more power than I could imagine, that I would have all and more anyone could dream of. I was his blood, and all this I would have. I had only to do one thing for it."

"What?"

"Only to kill Branna as she slept beside me. Just that."

A shudder wanted to rise out of her, but Iona fought it back, kept her gaze on Fin's, quiet and steady. "But you didn't."

"It's him I'd've killed had I known how. One day I will, know how and get it done and finished. Or die trying. So it's best you wait a bit longer before we take you there. And all of us will take her when that time comes. That's a firm line, Branna. I'll not be shut out of it."

"When the time comes," she agreed. "For now, we wait and watch. We learn, and we plan."

"And talk more than we have," Connor added. "We'll be stronger for that."

"You're right. We close no one out." Branna touched a hand, briefly, to Fin's arm. "I was wrong. Will we say Fin and Connor will use their hawks to patrol—if that's the word—the woods? We've Meara and Iona leading the guided rides most days, and keeping their eyes and ears open there. Boyle's seeing Iona home, so I'll make a charm for you, Boyle, for protection."

"I'll see to it," Fin told her.

"Fair enough. I'll work with Iona, and there I may call on all of you from time to time for help. If we dream, we write it down, all the details of it."

"There'll come a time it'll take more than protecting ourselves," Boyle said.

"I know it. What I don't know is what it will take, and how to get it."

"It's time to find it."

Branna nodded. "We can hope with six of us looking, we will. Now, as has been said, we've lives to live. We can start that by setting the table while I see to the stew."

"And I say we live it well." Connor pulled his sister up, kissed her. "For that's surely a boot up his fucking arse."

"All right then, well it is. Put on some music, Connor, and we'll start living well right now."

They set the dark aside, for the moment, with Connor and Meara arguing over the music until Connor tapped in some sort of fast jig with lots of fiddles and drums, and pulled her into a dance.

"Wow," was Iona's reaction. "They're really good."

"They've both of them wings on their feet." Boyle took the bowls Iona held, set them around the table. "Always have."

"Can you do that?"

"I haven't got the wings, but I don't have lead either."

"Ask the lady to dance then, you git." Fin dropped napkins on the table.

Iona only shook her head. "I don't know how to do that."

"Then it's past time you learned," Connor proclaimed and, snatching her hand, pulled her in.

"You're slow, brother," Fin murmured to Boyle.

"I move at the pace that suits me."

"Slow," Fin repeated. "As a snail on a turtle's back."

But Boyle shrugged it off. He liked watching Iona try to keep up with Connor's fast and clever feet. More, he liked the way she laughed as she spun around.

And who could argue with the laughter, he thought when Fin twirled Meara in three fast circles, and at the stove Branna clapped her hands in time.

The light and the laughter felt good, felt needed. So he'd take it.

Neither he nor any of the others in the bright kitchen with the warm smells, the quick music, the rolling laughter saw the shadow outside the rain-splashed window that watched. That hated.

WITH THE MEAL BEHIND THEM, THE KITCHEN PUT TO RIGHTS, and the hour growing late, Boyle readied to go.

"We'll see you home, Meara. I've my lorry. Branna, I meant to ask if you've any of the tonic you make for head colds. Mick's been blowing and sneezing for the last two days, and I've a mind to pour some of it down his throat."

"I do, of course." She started to rise.

"I'll get it for him," Iona said. "In the blue bottle, right, on the shelves nearest the front window."

"That's the one. You can settle up with me here or at the shop, Boyle, at the end of the month."

"I'll do that, and thanks for dinner. I'll meet you and Meara out front," he told Fin.

He walked back with Iona, made the turn into the workshop. She hit the lights.

"I've been trying to get a good sense of her stock and what she keeps here, what she sells in the village. She won't let me make anything yet—not unsupervised—but at least I'm learning some of what goes into what."

She reached for the bottle, clearly marked with Branna's Dark Witch label. "I hope this helps Mick. He's been miserable the last couple days."

"Less if he'd taken his medicine sooner."

"I guess swallowing witch potions makes some people nervous."

"He'll swallow this, if I have to personally hold his nose." Boyle slipped the bottle in his pocket. "I wanted to say, while there's a moment, it meant something before, the way you stood up for Fin."

"Being excluded hurts, just like being blamed for what you are hurts. I can understand Branna's feelings, but my instincts are to trust him, and I get tripped up when I go against my instincts. Sometimes when I go with them, too."

"Speaking out as you did, it mattered. So . . ." He shifted his feet. "We'll go have dinner sometime."

"Oh?" Her heart grinned like an idiot, but she did her best to keep her smile polite. "All right."

"I prefer doing the asking. Whether or not that's old-fashioned, it's how it is."

"Good to know. My social calendar's pretty clear."

"Then we'll book something. I'll see you in the morning."

He started out, got halfway to the door, turned back.

This time Iona was ready for the grab, and grabbed him back.

She loved the way he hauled her to her toes. It didn't make her feel small. It made her feel wanted. The reluctance in it only added a sexy edge. Everything about the kiss, the heat of his lips, the strong grip of his hands made her feel irresistible.

And that was a heady sensation, a powerful thrill.

He kept meaning to take it slow with her, if at all. He'd taught himself control, learned—for the most part—to balance heat and temper with cool-headed thinking and logical steps.

Yet here he was again, wrapped around her, wrapped up in her. And it was God's own truth, he just wanted to sink there, be there, and draw all that natural sweetness, that cheerful energy in.

And with it, he wanted his hands on all those pretty curves and dips, his mouth on that smooth skin. That surprisingly tough little body moving, moving, moving under his.

She clung another moment when he would've pulled back, and nearly undid him.

"Well then," he managed, and ordered his hands back down by his sides. Then, safer yet, into his pockets.

She just stood there, her pretty eyes heavy, her lips curved and so soft. So soft he wanted to—

"You could come back, after you take Meara home. You could drop Fin off and come back. Then you could take me to work in the morning."

"I . . ." The idea of it, a night with her, had every need inside him threatening to boil over. "I'm thinking with Branna and Connor in the house that would be awkward at best. And there's the matter of rushing the fences."

"You want dinner first." Her smile perked up when she clearly saw he didn't get the joke. "That's fine. I think it's simpler to be clear, from my side, that when it's not awkward or rushed, I want to be with you. It's not that I take sex lightly, it's that I don't."

"You're a puzzle, Iona. I'd like to figure more of you out."

"That's nice. I don't think I've ever been a puzzle to anyone before. I think I like it." She rose on her toes again, brushed his lips lightly with hers. "I'll help you fit some of those pieces together if I can."

"I'll work on it in my own time. In the morning then."

"Okay. Good night."

She locked up behind him, watched through the rain as he strode to his truck. And did a little dance in place as she watched the lights sweep, then move away through the dark.

She puzzled him, and wasn't that wonderful? Iona heart-on-her-sleeve Sheehan, the girl who too often blurted out her thoughts before they'd fully formed, puzzled Boyle McGrath.

Talk about power. Talk about wonder.

The delight of it carried her out of the workshop and into the kitchen, where she threw her arms around Branna for a spin.

"Well then, I see groping with Boyle's given you a fine burst of energy."

"It was really good groping. He asked me out, in his Boyle way. 'We'll go have dinner sometime.'"

"Christ Jesus!" Eyes wide, hand flying to her heart, Branna goggled. "It's all but a proposal of marriage."

Too happy to be dampened, Iona laughed. "It's a big step up from grunting at me. He thinks I'm a puzzle, can you imagine? I mean, seriously, who couldn't figure me out? I'm as simple as they come."

"Do you think so?"

"I sure don't run deep. I'm going to have some tea. Do you want tea? God, I'm crazy about him."

"It's early days for crazy, isn't it?"

"I don't get that, never have." Iona put the kettle on, contemplated Branna's collection of homemade teas. "Don't you know when you know? Five minutes, five years—how does that change what you know? I wanted to know with the man I was with before. I tried to know. I liked him, and I was comfortable with him. I told myself, give it more time. But time didn't change anything. Not for either of us as it turned out."

Branna thought of what Connor had said. "You want to give love, and to be given it."

"It's what I've always wanted most. I'm going for your lavender blend, not only because it smells wonderful, but it's for relaxation." She glanced back. "For a restful night's sleep. I'm so up I need to come down some to get one. Right?"

"It's a good choice, and yes, you're learning. Which brings me to this. It's a bit late, but I think we've both got another hour in us. We'll work a spell. Something very, very simple," she said as Iona's face burst with joy. "A toe in the water."

"I'm a jump-in-feet-first fan, but I'll take the toe. Thanks, Branna."

"Thank me in an hour, and if you've managed to master the spell. Here."

"A broom. Am I going to fly on it?"

"You are not. You'll learn a protection spell, and with this, you'll learn to sweep away the negative energies, the films and dusts of dark forces and lay in the strong, the positive. Our home is always to be protected. It's the first you should learn, and I should've taught you before this."

Iona took the broom. "Teach me now."

SHE SLEPT DEEP AND DREAMLESS, AND FACED THE DAY—RAIN, but slower and thinner—with enthusiasm. As she beat both her cousins to the kitchen, she put on the coffee and considered trying her hand at breakfast for three. Her talents there might be limited, but she thought she could handle scrambled eggs. And if she cooked ham and cheese in them, they'd be a sort of lazy-woman's omelet.

Organization, she told herself. Line up ingredients and tools first. She got down a skillet, a mixing bowl and whisk, a grater for the cheese, a knife and board for the ham.

So far so good.

Eggs, ham, cheese from the fridge—oh, and butter for the skillet. Break eggs in bowl, she instructed herself, then open the cupboard under the sink to toss the shells in the bin Branna used for compost waste. She noted then in the confusion of cleanup the night before they'd neglected to take out the trash.

Determined to be organized, she pulled out the filled liner, tied it, and hauled it to the door to take out to the big bin.

Inches beyond the little stoop lay a pile of dead rats. Black as midnight, coated with blood and gore, they lay in a circle of scorched earth.

The bag slipped out of her hand, hit the stoop with a hard splat. Revulsion urged her to step back in, close and bolt the door. Indeed her hand shook as she groped back for the knob to do just that.

Can't run, she reminded herself. Can't hide. There would be a shovel in the garden shed, she thought. She only had to get it, dig a hole, bury the ugliness. Sprinkle the ground with salt.

She started to step out, around the horrible circle.

"What's it then, in or out?"

Connor's sleepy voice behind her had Iona jumping back, barely muffling a scream.

"Didn't mean to give you a start. Is this breakfast to be? Here, I'll take that out when we leave for work, then—"

He stepped over, reached for the bag. Stopped when he saw the rats.

"So, he's sent us a gift." The sleepy cheer in his voice turned to flint on the words. "Here now." And still his hand as he took Iona's arm to draw her back held warmth, comfort. "I'll deal with it."

"I was going to. Get a shovel from the shed."

"That's what big, strong cousins are for." He touched his lips to her forehead.

"And just what are they for other than waking a body up singing in the shower like he's on the bleeding *X Factor*?" The annoyance Branna led with faded as she got a clear look at Iona's face, then her brother's. "What is it?"

"See for yourself." He moved back to the door, opened it.

"He's bold," she said coldly, as she looked out. "Leaving such a thing on our doorstep."

"I didn't do the spell right. Last night, the protection spell. I—"

"Is that ugly mess *in* the house?" Branna demanded. "Are they living and scampering about in here?"

"No."

"Then you did it fine and well. Do you think he wanted them dead, and outside if he could've had them in and swarming over us?"

The image had Iona shuddering. "No. Good point." She let out a long breath as at least the guilt she felt fell away. "I was going to bury them."

"No, it's not burying we do with them, not at first. We burn them." Branna turned to Iona. "All of us, but the first fire is yours. Strong, white, and hot."

She took Iona's hand, stepped outside, with Connor behind them.

"Say the words I say, then send the fire.

"White to dark, power I call. On evil's stench my fire will fall. Destroy this threat to mine and me. As I will, so mote it be.

"Say it," Branna demanded. "Feel it. Do it."

Iona repeated the words, her voice growing stronger, her rage keener. And her power at the end of them full and white.

Flames snapped, shot to the center of the circle, spread.

"Again," Branna told her, as she and Connor joined her on the words.

Fire, white as lightning, burned. When it banked, only black ash remained.

"We bury the ash?" Iona's body tingled, as if from an electric shock. Even her blood felt hot.

"We do."

"And salt the earth."

"I've better than that, but that would do as well. Fetch the dustpan and broom," she told Iona, "and Connor the shovel. I've the spot for this."

She waited a moment as they moved off to obey. "Oh aye, just the spot for this."

She led them around, to the far front corner of the workshop.

"Here?" Iona stared at her. "So close to the house, to where you work. I don't—"

"She's a plan, make no mistake." And trusting it, Connor shoved the blade of the shovel into the rain-softened ground. "Just what I wanted to be about this morning. Digging a hole for rat ashes in the bleeding rain."

"I can help with that." Calling on her lesson from the day before, Iona slid the rain back so the three of them stood in the warm, the dry.

"Very well done." Branna shook back her damp hair, laid her hands on her hips as Connor dug. "That'll do well enough. Dump them in, Iona. We've all three taken part in this, and the work's stronger for it."

"Then you can shovel the dirt back over them," Connor suggested when Iona dumped the black ashes into the hole.

"You're doing such a fine job, and I've my own to do when you're done with it."

"He's watching," Connor said quietly as he tossed dirt back into the hole. "I can just feel it."

"I thought he might be. So much the better. Now this is mine."

In her flannel pants, bare feet, her hair wet from the rain, Branna lifted her hands, palms up.

"Fire of white to purify, power of light to beautify. From Cabhan's dark grasp I set you free. As I will, so mote it be."

From the freshly turned earth flowers burst, bloomed, spread. A deep rainbow of colors shimmered in the gloom of morning, pretty shapes dancing in the light wind.

"It's beautiful. It's brilliant." Iona clasped her hands together as the defiant palette glowed. "You're brilliant."

With a satisfied nod, Branna tucked her hair back. “I can’t say I disagree.”

“And there’s a fragrant stick up the arse for him.” Connor set the shovel on his shoulder. “I’m hungry.”

Beaming happy, Iona hooked arms with her cousins. “I’m cooking breakfast.”

“God help us, but I’m hungry enough myself I’ll risk it.”

Branna walked back with them, glancing back once. Right up the arse, she thought.

12

SHE ENJOYED THE NEW ROUTINE, WALKING WITH CONnor in the mornings, riding Alastar on the guideds, juggling in a few students, then having Boyle walk or drive her home again.

Late afternoons meant work and practice, and an additional hour at night for refining her skills.

The sun came out again, so the river sparkled with it. The loughs went to gleaming mirrors, and the green of the fields and hills only deepened under its shine through the puffs and layers of clouds streaming across the sky.

She could forget—almost—all that lay on the line, all yet to be faced. After all, she was having a romance.

Not one that included poetry and flowers, and her romantic sensibilities would have relished just that. But when your heart aimed toward a man like Boyle, you had to learn to find poetry in brief words and long silences, and flowers in an unexpected mug of tea pushed into your hands or a quick nod of approval.

And who needed flowers when the man could kiss the breath out of her? Which he did in the green shadows of the woods, or in the disordered cab of his lorry.

Romance, a home, a steady paycheck, a magnificent horse she could call her own, and the new and brilliant understanding of her craft. If she just eliminated the threat of ancient evil, her life struck the top of the bell.

She finished her lesson with Sarah, both of them pleased with the progress.

"Your form's really improving. We're going to work more on changing leads, smoothing that out."

"But when can we add another bar? I'm ready, Iona, I know it."

"We'll see how it goes next lesson." Looking up into Sarah's pleading eyes, Iona patted her mount's neck. And remembered herself at that age. "I'll tell you what. One bar up, one jump before you take Winnie in and tend to her."

"You mean it! Oh, thanks! Thanks! This is brilliant."

"One bar, one jump," Iona repeated, and glanced at Sarah's mother as she started to the bars. She hefted one, maneuvered it in place.

Just three feet, she thought, and believed her student could handle it. If not, the horse would know.

She looked back at the horse now.

She wants to fly, wants to feel you fly with her. Keep it steady.

Iona stepped back, noted Sarah's mother twisted the ends of the scarf she wore around her neck.

"All right, Sarah. It's only one bar, but you have to let Winnie know you're in it together. Trust her, and let her know she can trust you. Eyes open, let's have a good, steady pace, and remember your form."

Her heart was pounding, Iona knew. With such excitement, and some nerves. Still a beginner's course, even with the single additional bar, but a new challenge, a new hope.

"Good, that's good," she called out, circling as Sarah took Winnie around the course. "Posture, Sarah, light hands. You both know what to do."

Set, she thought, steady and smooth. Gather. And go.

She flew a little herself as she watched her student soar cleanly over the bar, land well, adjust. Then wave one hand over her head in triumph.

"Oh, it's like magick, it is! Can't I do it again, Iona? Just once more?"

"Once more around, then Winnie needs her rubdown."

She watched now with a critical eye, noting little things they'd work on.

"I feel I could do it forever, and jump twice as high."

"One bar at a time," Iona told her.

"Did you see, Ma! Did you see me?"

"I did. You were beautiful. Go on now, see to your horse, and we'll go home and tell your da. Could I have a word?" she said to Iona.

"Sure. I'll be right in, Sarah. And tell Mooney Winnie earned an apple."

"I nearly made you stop," Mrs. Hannigan told her. "I nearly called out to you, no, not yet. All I could see in my mind's eye was Sarah flying off, lying on the ground with something broken."

"It's hard to let her push new boundaries."

"Oh, it is indeed, and you'll know yourself one day when you've children. But I knew, under it, you wouldn't let her do something she wasn't ready for. She's doing so well with you, is so happy with you. I wanted you to know that."

"She's a joy to teach."

"I think it shows in both of you. I took a picture with my phone when she did the jump." She pulled the phone out, turned the screen to Iona. "My hand shook, I'm afraid, so it's a bit blurry, but I knew I'd want to have that moment."

Iona studied the screen, the flight—the young girl on the back of the sturdy horse, and the bar and air under them. She gave the slightest push, then turned the screen back.

"It's a wonderful shot, and it's clear and sharp. You can see the joy and the concentration on her face."

Lips pursed, Mrs. Hannigan studied the photo again, then those lips curved. "Oh, it is good. It must've been my eyes blurry when I first looked at it."

"You stay for every lesson." Her mother hadn't, Iona remembered. "I think it makes her strive to do better, knowing you're here for her, that you support her."

"Well of course I do. I'm her ma. I'm going to call her father right now, and tell him to pick up some strawberry ice cream. It's her favorite. We'll have a little celebration after dinner. I won't keep you, but I wanted to thank you for building her confidence, and my own. They're lucky to have you here."

Iona wasn't sure her boots touched the ground all the way into the stables. She stopped when her eyes adjusted to the change of light and she spotted Boyle.

"I didn't know you were here."

"Only just, and I've gotten an earful from Sarah. She's floating three feet off the ground."

"We both are. I wish you could've seen her. I should make sure she's tending Winnie."

"She is, and well, as she's now fully in love. And Mooney's keeping an eye. I thought you might want to take Alastar out. I'm going to give Darling a try, just see how she goes. He'd be good company for her. And you for me," he added after a moment.

"I'd love it, but I've still got about a half hour on the clock."

"You'll be helping exercise the horses, so you can consider it a job if it eases your conscience."

"Works for me."

In fact she couldn't think of a better way to end her workday than with a ride with the man who made her heart flutter.

She watched Darling as Boyle mounted, caught the quiver along her flanks, the expression in her eyes.

"She's nervous."

"I can feel that for myself." To soothe, he bent over, murmuring and stroking.

"Do you know why?"

"She's more weight on her than she's used to, and hasn't had a rider on her back in weeks."

"That's not it." Iona turned Alastar so Boyle and Darling fell into step beside her. "She trusts you, and loves you. She's nervous she won't do well, and you won't want to ride her again."

"Then she's foolish. It's a fine day for a ride. We'll head to the lough, and around a bit if it's all right with you."

"More than all right."

"You'll tell me if she hurts, and I don't notice."

"I will, but she's feeling very sound. She likes the look of Alastar," she added, sotto voce. "Thinks he's very handsome."

"He is that."

"He's pretending not to notice her, but he's peacocking a little."

"Now you're hunting up a romance for the horses?"

"I know he's for Aine, but a stallion like Alastar's meant to sire foals, and she's made for breeding. Plus, I don't have to hunt up anything. I just have to pay attention to say they like the look of each other."

"I hadn't thought of breeding her."

"Aine will make the regal and the magnificent," Iona said. "Darling? She'll make the sweet and the dependable. In my opinion," she added.

"Well, Alastar's yours, so you'll have a say in it."

"I think he has the most to say, as do the ladies. It's almost spring." She lifted her face, looked at the sky through the boughs. "You can feel it coming."

"Still cold as February."

"That may be, but it's coming. The air's softer."

"That would be the rain moving in tonight."

She only laughed. "And I saw a pair of magpies flirting out by Branna's feeder this morning."

"Just how does a magpie flirt?"

"They fly to and away, to and away, then chatter at each other and do it again. I asked Connor why the hawks don't go after them, and he said they have an arrangement. I like that."

They moved into single file when the path narrowed, and wound by the river where the water thrashed under a broken rope bridge.

"Will they ever fix that?" she wondered.

"I'm doubting it, as people would be foolish enough to walk on it, and end up falling in. You'd be one of them."

"Who says I'd fall in? And if I did, I'm a strong swimmer." Because she enjoyed flirting, she sent him a long, under-the-lashes look. "Are you?"

"I live on an isthmus on an island. I'd be a bleeding git not to swim and well."

"We'll have to take a dip sometime." She glanced back again, and remembered her first sight of him, and how striking, how compelling he'd looked—the big, tough man on the big, tough horse.

But she realized he only looked more striking now, seated on the mare he'd brought back to health, his hands light on the reins, her eyes glowing with pride.

"She's not nervous anymore."

"I know it. She's doing fine and well." He moved up beside Iona as the path allowed.

"I talked to my grandmother last night," she began. "I couldn't settle for email anymore, just wanted to hear her voice. She sends you her best."

"And mine goes back to her."

"She's planning to come for a few weeks either this summer or fall. I want her to, but at the same time . . ."

"You worry if we've still battles to fight. You want her safe."

"She's everything to me. I thought when . . . I talk too much."

"No doubt of it, but you might as well speak your mind."

"I was just going to say how Sarah's mother's always there for her lessons and her father's come by twice to watch her. My mother would just drop me off, or more often I'd catch a ride to and from with one of the other students. My father never came. Never once. Rarely to a competition either. But Nan did, whenever she could. She'd drive to wherever they were, whenever she could. Sometimes she'd just be there, and I wouldn't know she'd planned to come. She paid for the lessons, and the entry fees. I didn't know that until I was staying with her once, and heard a message on her machine about renewing the contract with the stables."

"She gave you what you loved."

"I want her to be proud of me. I guess it's a lot like Darling. I want to do well, so she can see she didn't waste the time and effort."

"Then you're foolish as well."

"I know. Can't seem to help it."

She looked out over the lake, away to the elegant rise of the castle, its gardens still caught in the last of winter's bite. People strolled around, here to see and do and experience from wherever they'd traveled.

She understood it was like the photo of Sarah, a moment she wanted to have. So as they walked the horses along the water, she let everything else go, and took a page from Boyle's book.

She embraced the silence.

"We should start back," he said at length. "I don't want to overwork her."

"No, and Branna will be expecting me for *my* lesson."

"Going well enough then?"

"Yes. Branna might have some quibbles, but I think it's going just . . . grand."

She glanced to him with a grin, saw him looking past her with a frown. "What's wrong?"

"Nothing's wrong. I was . . . noticing the cottage there. They've a fine menu. Maybe after your lesson, you'd like to have some dinner there."

She lifted her eyebrows. "With you?"

His frown only deepened. "Well, of course, with me. Who else?"

"There's no one else," she said simply. "I'd love to. I could be ready by seven or seven thirty."

"Half-seven's good. I'll book it, and fetch you."

"That sounds grand, too."

As they slipped into the woods, into the dimmer light, she began a mental inventory of her wardrobe. What should she wear? Nothing too fancy, but not jeans or trousers. Maybe Branna could help her out there, as her options were limited.

Something simple, but pretty. Heels, not boots. Her legs were damn good if she said so herself. She'd like to dazzle him, at least a little, so—

Alastar shied; Darling reared.

And the wolf stepped across the path.

Her thoughts centered on the safety of the horses, Iona didn't think, just acted. She streamed a line of fire across the path between them.

"It won't hurt you. I won't let it hurt you."

Boyle drew a knife from a sheath on his belt she hadn't noticed. "He bloody well won't."

"Don't dismount!" Iona shouted, anticipating. "She's terrified. She'll bolt, and it might get to her. You have to hold her, Boyle."

"Take her reins, talk her down, and get them safe. I'll hold it off."

"Separating us makes us easier prey." It's what it wanted, hoped for—she could *feel* it. "Trust me, please. Please."

And struggling to focus, she murmured, her voice quiet, steady, an incantation she learned from the books. One still untried.

The wolf lunged at the line of fire, looking for an opening. With its fierce charge the flames dimmed, lowered.

Gripping the reins in one hand, Iona lifted the other high.

"From north and south, from east and west, bring on the wind for this contest. Strike up the power, bring on the fire until the tower whirls higher and higher. Blow strong, blow fierce, blow wild and free. As I will, so mote it be.

"You think I don't have it," she said between her teeth. "You're wrong."

Above, the sky churned, and with her lifted hand she balled a fist, as if pulling the flame-edged whirlwind that formed into her fingers.

She flung out her arm, sent a raging funnel of wind through the fire.

It lifted the wolf off its feet, threw it up as it screamed in rage. And she hoped, in fear. It spun, claws lashing air as it bore him up and away.

Iona fought to control what she'd conjured, felt it building beyond her. A tree snapped, collapsed into jagged splinters.

"Take it down." Boyle's voice came steady in her ear. "It's more than you need, and too much. Take it down again now, Iona, as only you can. Let it calm. Let it go."

A line of sweat beaded down her back as she fought to do just that. The roar of the wind began to fade, the impossible swirl of it to slow.

"All the way down now, Iona."

"I'm trying. It's so strong."

"It's you who made it. It's you who's strong."

She'd made it, she thought. She'd control it. She'd end it.

"Still now," she said. "And soft. Calm and sweet. Disperse."

The wolf dropped like a stone in the light breeze. Then sprang up, fangs dripping. Did the red jewel seem dimmer? she wondered.

Then it leapt into the woods, pulsing out a curtain of smoky fog. After one distant howl, silence fell again.

"It could come back." All calm deserted her as her hands shook, as her voice jumped. "It could come back. We need to get the horses in. I need to make sure the stables are safe. It—"

"That's what we'll do. Breathe a minute. You've gone dead pale."

"I'm all right." Under her Alastar pawed the ground. He'd pursue, she realized—longed to. To calm him, she had to calm herself. "We've done enough," she said softly. "It's enough for now. I need to tell Branna, Connor. But the horses—"

"We're going now, easy."

"Easy." She took those breaths, then laid her hand on Alastar's neck, and over on Darling's. "Easy," she repeated. "It won't hurt you. I . . . didn't know you had a knife. A really big knife."

"A pity I didn't get to use it." Those gilded eyes hard, he sheathed the blade again. "But worth it for the show I suppose. And you need more lessons on this business."

"Absolutely. That one wasn't even on the lesson plan."

"What do you mean?"

"I read it in a book. I guess you could say I added a bar to the jump. It seemed like the time."

"In a book. She read it in a book. Christ Jesus."

"I could really use a drink."

"You're not alone there."

She didn't say more, needed to steady herself. Needed to tell her cousins, she thought again. Needed, really, to sit down on something that didn't move.

They were nearly back to the stables before she could think clearly, or almost clearly again. "Darling was so scared. For herself, but for you, too. My fire scared her, too. I wish I'd thought of something else."

"She did just fine. Wanted to bolt, but didn't. You may not know it, but that one? He was a rock under you. He never, from that first start, flinched a muscle. I'm thinking he would have done whatever you asked, even up to charging through the fire and taking the beast by the scruff."

"I didn't have to think. I didn't have to tell him. He just knew. I need to call Branna."

"I'll see to that."

When they reached the stables, he dismounted, then stepped over to her. "Come on down then."

"I'm not sure I can."

"That's what these are for." He lifted his hands, took hold of her, helped her down. "Go sit on the bench there for a minute or two."

"The horses."

"They'll be seen to, and well, what do you think?" The sizzle of impatience had her obeying. And her shaky legs carried her to the bench, almost wept with gratitude as she sat.

When Boyle came out, she managed to get to her feet. "I need to do a protection spell, for the stables."

"Do you think Fin hasn't already seen to that?" Boyle simply took her arm, pulled her along. "He's not due home for a few hours, but I think he knows what he's about in these matters. Branna knows where you are. She'll tell Connor."

"Where am I going?"

"Up to mine, where you'll have that drink and sit a bit more."

"I could really use both."

She climbed the stairs with him. Not exactly the circumstances she'd imagined for her first invitation into his place, but she'd take it.

He opened the door off a narrow porch. "Company wasn't expected."

She peeked in first, then smiled. "Thank God it's not all neat and tidy or I'd feel intimidated. But it's nice." She stepped in, looked around.

It smelled like him—horses, leather, man. The room, a kind of combination living/sitting/kitchen, let in the early evening light. A mug sat next to the sink, a newspaper lay spread on the short counter that separated the kitchen from the rest.

A couple of books and some magazines were scattered around—mystery novels, she noted, and horsey magazines. A tumble of boots in a wooden box, a clutter of old jackets on pegs. A sofa with a little sag in the middle, two big chairs, and, to her surprise, a big flat screen on the wall.

He noticed her speculative look. "I like it for watching matches and such. You'll have some whiskey."

"I absolutely will, and a chair. I get shaky after it's all done."

"You were steady enough while it counted."

"I almost lost it." She spoke as he went to the kitchen, opened cupboards. "You helped me hold on."

Since she was here, and safe, and it was done, he could speak of it. Or try. "You were glowing like a flame. Your eyes so deep it seemed like worlds could be swallowed up by them. You reached up, and you pulled a storm from the sky with your hand. I've seen things."

He poured whiskey for both of them, brought the glasses back to where she sat, dwarfed in one of the big chairs. "I've run tame with Fin most of my life, and Connor, and Branna. I've seen things. But never have I seen the like of that."

"I've never felt anything like it. A storm in my hand." She looked down at it now, turned it, amazed to recognize it, to find it so ordinary. "And a storm inside me. I don't know how to explain it, but it was inside me, so *huge* and full. And absolutely right.

"I broke a tree, didn't I?"

He'd watched it shatter like brittle glass, into shards and splinters. "It could've been worse, entirely."

"Yeah, it could've been. But I need more lessons, more practice." More control, she thought, and more of the famous focus Branna continually harped on.

Then she looked at Boyle. The hard, handsome face, the scarred eyebrow, the tawny eyes with temper still simmering in them.

"You were going to fight it with a knife, with your hands."

"It bleeds, doesn't it?"

"I think so. Yes." She let out one more cleansing breath. "It bleeds. It wasn't expecting what I did, or could do. Neither was I."

"I think neither of you will underestimate that again. Drink your whiskey. You're pale yet."

"Right." She sipped at it.

"I think it's not the night for dinner out with people."

"Maybe not. But I'm starving. I think it's something to do with expending all that energy."

"I'll throw you together something. I've a couple of chops, I think, and I'll fry up some chips."

"Are you taking care of me?"

"You could use it at the moment. Drink your whiskey," he said again, then walked back to the kitchen.

Rattling pans, a thwack of a knife on wood, the sizzle of oil. Something about the sounds eased her frayed nerves. She sipped more whiskey, rose, and walked back to where he stood at the stove, frying pork chops in one skillet, chipped potatoes in another.

She wasn't sure she'd ever had a fried chop, but wasn't complaining.

"I can help. Keep my hands and head busy."

"I've a couple of tomatoes in there Mick's wife gave me from her little greenhouse. You could slice them up."

So she worked beside him, and felt better for that, too.

He made some sort of thin gravy from the drippings, tossed some herbs in it, then poured it over the chops.

Seated at the counter, Iona sampled a bite. "It's good."

"What were you expecting?"

"I didn't have a clue, but it's good. And, God, I'm seriously starving."

Her color came up well as she ate, he noted, and that slightly dazed look faded from her eyes.

She'd gone from glowing and fierce to pale and shaky in the blink of an eye. And now, it relieved him to see her slide back to just normal. Just Iona.

"He didn't use the fog," she said abruptly. "I just realized, he just—it just walked out of the trees. I don't know what that means, but I have to remember to tell Branna and Connor—and Fin. And the jewel, the red jewel around its neck. It wasn't as bright at the end. I don't think. Was it?"

"I couldn't say. I was more about its teeth, and the way you'd gone so white. I wondered if you'd slide right out of the saddle."

"Never going to happen." She laughed a little, closed her hand over his. And stilled when his turned under hers, gripped hard.

"You scared the life out of me. The fucking life."

"I'm sorry."

"What in hell are you apologizing for? It's an irritating habit."

"I'm . . . working on it."

"One minute we're riding along, easy as you please, and I'm thinking, well then, we'll have dinner and see how that goes. The next, you're reaping a bloody whirlwind."

He shoved up, snatched his plate and hers. Which was too bad, she thought, as she'd had a couple more chips, and would've eaten them.

"If you don't want me to apologize, don't yell at me."

"I'm not yelling at you."

"Who then?"

"No one. I'm just yelling. A man can express himself as he pleases in his own house."

"Nobody ever yelled in my house."

"What?" He looked genuinely astonished. "Were you reared in a church?"

She laughed again. "I think, maybe—if I go by your gauge—nobody cared enough to yell. Do you care, Boyle?"

"I care you're not lying on the ground out there with your throat torn out." He cursed himself as her color slid away. "Now I'm sorry. Truly. I've the devil's own tongue when I'm in a temper. I'm sorry," he repeated, and put his hands gently on her face to cup it. "You were so fierce. I don't know what turned me more around. The wolf or you."

"We came through it. That means a lot." She put her hands over his. "And you made me dinner, you let me settle before you let it rip. That means a lot, too."

"Then we're all right, all right enough for now."

He touched his lips to hers, gentle this time. And her hands slid to his wrists, tightened.

"I should take you home now." He eased back, but she kept her hands on his wrists.

"I don't want you to take me home. I want to stay with you."

"You're still turned around."

"Do I look turned around?"

He managed to step back, a foot away. "Maybe I'm turned around."

"I don't mind that." She rose. "I might even like it. We won a battle, Boyle, together. I want to be with you, to hold on to you, to go to bed with you."

"I think . . . the sensible thing is to take some time, to talk about that before . . . that."

"I thought I was the one who talked too much." She took a step toward him, then another.

"You do, Jesus, you do. But I think, under the circumstances . . . We'll talk later," he said, and grabbed her.

"Perfect," she said, and grabbed him back.

13

Her feet left the floor again, a giddy sensation with her mouth pressed to his. He had a hand fisted on the back of her sweater as if he might rip it away at any second, which would have suited her just fine. If she could have managed it, she'd have wiggled right out of the sweater—and everything else.

"We need to—" Whatever he'd meant to say slid away as her mouth came back, avidly, to his.

"Where's the bedroom?" It had to be close, and if not, the saggy couch looked more than adequate.

"It's . . ." He tried to think through the hot haze in his brain, then just gripped her ass, gave her a boost. She hooked her legs around his waist as her arms chained around his neck.

Everything tilted and sizzled. She had a vague impression of a dimly lit room, some clutter, some of which he kicked away as he carted her to a bed with dark wooden spindles and cool white sheets.

Then she might have been anywhere—the forest, the ocean, a city sidewalk, a country meadow. There was nothing but him, the weight of him pressed down on her, the big hands roaming, the urgent mouth seeking, taking. Nothing but those cool white sheets growing warmer, warmer as he tugged the sweater over her head, tossed it aside.

Everything about her was so small and exquisite. The breasts that fit so perfectly into his palms, the hands that dived under his shirt to glide over his skin. He wasn't a clumsy man, but feared he would be with her, and tried to slow his pace, smooth out his rhythm.

But her hips arched up, her fingers dug into bunched muscles, urging him on.

He wanted her naked, as simple and basic as that. He wanted that pretty little body uncovered for him, stripped bare for his hands, for his mouth.

He reached down, tugged at the buckle of her belt. She spoke, the words muffled against his lips.

"What? What?" If she'd said stop, he'd kill himself.

"Boots." Her lips roamed over his face, then her teeth nipped at his jaw. "Boots first."

"Boots. Right. Right." Already winded, and a bit disconcerted by it, he slid down, knelt at the foot of the bed, yanked at her right boot. He tossed it; it landed with an abrupt thump. As he tugged on the left, she levered up, got a grip on his hair and yanked his head back to hers.

"You look— It's all shadowy, and I can just hear the rain starting, and my heart's pounding so hard." She punctuated the words with wild kisses. This time when he threw the boot, something crashed and shattered.

"Yours, let me get yours." She wiggled back for his boot. "They have to go, have to go because I have to get you naked or I'll go out of my mind."

"I was thinking the same of you."

"Good, good." Her laugh, shaky with nerves and excitement, raced up his spine. "Same page, same station." She shoved the first boot to the floor. "Put your hands on me, would you? Anywhere, everywhere. I've almost got this."

She couldn't know it, but she'd gotten her wish. She'd dazzled him. "Will it shut you up?"

"Maybe. Probably. There!" She pried off the boot, dropped it.

And flew at him.

She nearly upended them both off the bed, but he managed to wrap around her and roll. Even as he sank into the next kiss, her hands got busy on his shirt. "You've got such great shoulders. I just want to—" She dragged it off, pulled the thermal beneath it up and away.

She made a sound like a woman licking melted chocolate from a spoon as her hands ran over his pecs, up to his shoulders, down to squeeze his biceps.

"You're so strong."

"I won't hurt you."

She laughed again, no nerves this time. "I'm not going to promise the same."

Agile and quick, she reached back, unclipped the clasp of her bra. "Made it easy for you."

"I'm up for difficult work." He drew the bra aside. "Now be quiet, so I can concentrate on it."

In a moment she couldn't think, much less speak. So many sensations rushed over her like his hands that thrilled, that took, that tortured. Those rough, workingman palms, the prickly stubble of a daylong beard—thrill over thrill on her quivering skin.

Boys, she realized. Every one who'd ever touched her had been a boy compared to him. All too smooth, too easy, too practiced. Now she had a man who wanted her.

He wasted no time peeling her out of the jeans, exploring her body, feasting on it.

She'd brought the whirlwind in the woods. Now he stirred one inside her just as reckless and wild.

She gave to him, with no hint of restraint or shyness—a bounty of delights and demands that aroused him beyond reason. Her gasp or groan fired more needs, her willful hands sparked nerves over and under his skin. And her mouth, restless and hungry, stirred in his blood like a drug.

Mad for her, he took her hands, drew her arms back until they both gripped the spindles.

When he drove into her, he thought, for a moment, the world exploded. It shook him, the force of it, blinded him, the brilliance of it. Left him, for that breath of time, utterly weak.

Then she rose up to him, taking him deeper on the sigh of his name.

And he was strong as a god, randy as a stallion, mad as a hatter.

He thrust into her, again, again, again, crazed for all that heat, all that softness. She matched his frantic pace, her fingers twining with his, her hips slick pistons—driving and driven.

He felt himself flying—an arrow from a bow—the helpless glory of it. Heard her, dimly, let out a sobbing cry as she flew with him.

He collapsed, mindless of his weight on her. His mind still whirled; his lungs still labored. And something in his speeding heart pulsed like an ache.

She quivered beneath him, trembling limbs, pinging muscles. She wanted, badly, to wrap around him, to stroke and nuzzle. But she didn't have the strength.

He'd just hulled her out.

She could only lie there, washed in heat, listening to his rapid breathing and the slow patter of rain.

"I'm smothering you."

"Maybe."

His own muscles shook as he pushed himself off, then just flopped over on his back. He'd never been so . . . caught up, he decided.

What did it mean?

She took a couple of deep drinks of air, then curled over to nestle her head on his chest. There was a simple sweetness in that he couldn't resist, and he found himself drawing her in a bit closer.

"Are you cold then?"

"Are you kidding? We generated enough heat to melt the Arctic. I feel amazing."

"You're stronger than you look."

She tipped her head up to smile at him. "Small but mighty."

"I can't argue."

It would be easy, he realized, to just stay as they were, to just drift off into sleep awhile. Then take each other again. And what did it mean that he was thinking about it again when he'd barely gotten his breath back?

It meant, perhaps, easy was a mistake.

"I should take you home."

She didn't speak for a moment, and the hand lazily stroking his chest stilled.

"Branna'd be waiting, I'd think."

"Oh." He felt her breath go in, go out. "You're right. She'll want to know exactly what happened before. I forgot about all that for a minute. It seems like something outside all this. It's a good thing one of us is practical."

Turning her head, she brushed her lips over his skin, then sat up.

When he looked at her in that shadowed light, a glow against the coming dark, he wanted to draw her close again, close, and just hold on.

"We'd better get dressed," she said.

BRANNA WAS WAITING, AND TRYING NOT TO PACE AND FRET. She *hated* only having bits and pieces. Though Boyle had assured her no one was hurt, and he'd look after Iona until she was well settled again, it had been two hours now.

More, she realized.

Worse, Connor had told her not to be such a mother hen, and had taken himself off to the pub rather than—in his words—have his brain assaulted with all her fussing.

Fine for him, she thought with some bitterness. Off he goes to flirt with available women, have a pint or two, and she was left to brood alone.

If Iona didn't walk in the door within another ten minutes, she'd—

"At last," she muttered when she heard the front door open. Striding out, half a lecture already in mind, she stopped both her forward progress and her nagging words the minute she saw both of them.

A woman didn't have to be a witch to realize how the pair of them had spent a portion of the last two hours.

"So." She laid her hands on her hips as Kathel padded over to greet them both. "We'll have some tea, and you'll tell me what happened. You as well," she said to Boyle, anticipating him. "I want to hear it all, so don't think about scooting out the door again."

"Is Connor about?"

"He's not, no. Took himself off to the pub to flirt with whoever's about, so you've no cover there. Have you had anything to eat?" she asked as she walked into the kitchen.

"Boyle fixed dinner," Iona told her.

"Did he now?" Brow lifted, Branna sent him a sidelong look as she put the kettle on.

"I was starving after. I was hungry after the spell with the rats, but this was like eat or pass out."

"It won't always be so keen. You're new at it. And you're looking fit and fine and more than well tended to now. Oh, stop shuffling about, Boyle. A blind monkey could see the two of you have been at each other. I've no problem with that except instead of a good shag, I've been twiddling about waiting for you to come talk to me."

"I should've come home sooner, instead of worrying you."

Branna shrugged, then softened. "If I'd had a man willing to make me dinner and give me a good roll after a fright like that, I'd have taken it as well. I trust he did a good job with both."

Iona grinned. "Exceptional."

Heat rose up Boyle's back like a fever. "Would you mind not batting around my sex life, at least while I'm sitting here?"

"We'll bat it around when you're not then." Branna poured his tea, kissed the top of his head.

"Have you eaten?" Iona asked her.

"Not yet. I will once I hear what you have to say. From the start, Iona. And if she leaves anything out, Boyle, however slight, you fill it in."

Iona began, trying to speak in full detail, and with calm.

Branna gripped her hand. "You're saying you called a whirlwind? How did you know the way?"

"It's in the books. I know it's advanced, and it's risky, but it was . . . I don't know why or how, but I knew it was what I needed to do. I knew I could."

"Why didn't you call me, or Connor? Both?"

"It was so fast. When I play it back, it's like it was hours, stage by stage, but it was so fast. I don't think it was more than a couple minutes."

"If that," Boyle confirmed.

"All right, but it's best if you call for me and Connor."

"Or Fin," Boyle put in.

"I'm not shutting him out." Or only a little, Branna admitted. "But blood calls to blood, Boyle. We've the same blood, Connor, Iona, and I. And this is blood magicks at work. You weren't so afraid. Connor would have sensed that, as he did before. You weren't so afraid as before, in the woods alone."

"A little, but no, not like before, maybe because I wasn't alone. I could only think he'd hurt Boyle and the horses, to get to me. It helped me focus, I think."

Branna nodded, but pushed at her hair. "I'm jumping you around. You said he didn't bring the fog."

"No."

"More to catch you off guard than to rattle your nerves then. And it may be he pulls some power from the fog as well, and wasn't as strong."

"Didn't think he'd need to be?" Boyle nodded. "He learned different. She turned a tree to toothpicks."

"I had some trouble with control."

"Calling a whirlwind with no practice? I'm not surprised, and it's a wonder if a tree's all the damage done."

"All that I saw," Boyle said. "Unless you count the bastard spinning around in the air."

"If I could've held it, focused it better, I might have destroyed it."

Branna dismissed that with a shrug. "If it was that easy, I'd have done it myself before this. You did well. Finish it out now."

Listening, nodding, Branna didn't interrupt again.

"Yes, you did well indeed. I'd tell you it was a big risk, but I can't question your instincts. They told you this was the way, and you followed them. You're safe and well. I think you took Cabhan off guard, and you cost him. It may be you hurt him a bit as well, if his power source—the jewel is that, I think—lessened. How did it feel?"

"Enormous. Like I could feel every cell in my body burning. Like nothing could stop me."

At that, Branna's brows drew together. "There's the danger as true as the wolf."

"I think I know. Part of feeling that invincibility was why I couldn't control it, or started to lose it, and let it control me."

"It's a vital lesson learned. It's that being engulfed by the power, the thirst for more of it that made Cabhan."

Iona thought she understood how that could be, how the temptation, the seduction of such great power could overwhelm. "Boyle talked me down. He helped me hold it, calm it, and finally stop it."

Now those eyebrows rose. "Is that the way of it? That's no small feat, to rein in a witch who's not only reaping a whirlwind but riding one. Otherwise, the pair of you would be roaming about Oz looking for ruby slippers."

"But I'd be the good witch."

"Hmm. I'm relieved you weren't hurt, either of you. And I'm thinking we might have a space of time, before he makes another lunge at us, to smooth out more rough edges. I'm proud of you," she added, then rose.

Simple words, simply spoken, but they poured into Iona like fine wine. "Thanks."

"I've a thing or two to see to in the workshop now that my head's clear," Branna continued. "I'll tell Connor all of this, and as he came at you when you were with Boyle, it's best if we tell Meara the whole of it as well. And Fin," she added before Boyle could. "We'll meet again, would you say, in a day or two, once I've—once we've all had time to think it all through."

"I think that's the right thing," Iona said. "We're stronger together, right, than separately?"

"I'll hope. See you at breakfast, Boyle," Branna said with a wink, then left them.

"Oh well, I don't know as I should—"

"You should." Now Iona got to her feet, held out a hand. "You really should. Come upstairs with me, Boyle."

The wanting was so steep he couldn't climb out of it. He stood, took her hand, and went upstairs with her.

UNDER STRICT ORDERS TO REPORT TO BRANNA'S WORKSHOP directly from the stables, and with Boyle busy in a meeting with Fin, Iona tapped Meara for a ride home.

"I have to get a car." She frowned at the winding, narrow road

Meara zoomed along as if it were a six-lane highway. “A cheap car. A cheap, reliable car.”

“I can put the word out on that.”

“Yeah, that’d be good. Then I have to learn how to drive on the wrong side of the road.”

“It’s you Yanks who drive on the wrong side, and can put the fear of God into a person just driving out to do the weekly marketing.”

“I bet. But why do you guys drive on the left? I read it was about having the right hand free for the sword, but it’s been a really long time since people needed to battle it out on horseback with swords.”

“You never know, do you? Most don’t battle it out on horseback with whirlwinds as a rule.”

“You got me there. Maybe I can talk Boyle into letting me drive some tomorrow. He’s going to take me around to some sites. I’ve been so buried in work and lessons I haven’t seen anything outside of that, and the village. Not really.”

“A day off’s good for the soul. But it’ll take considerable talk of the very sweetest of nature, and very likely promises of exotic sexual favors to convince Boyle to let anyone behind the wheel but himself.”

“I’m a good driver,” she insisted. “Or was when the steering wheel was on this side. And does everyone know I’m in the position to offer Boyle sex?”

“Anyone with eyes. If there’d been more opportunity today, I’d’ve pulled more out of you about the whirlwind business, and the sex. But we had too many people about for it.”

“You could come in,” Iona said as Meara pulled up at the workshop. “Then Branna couldn’t dump me right into more work, and I could give you lots and lots of details.”

“Why is it so entertaining to have a window into others’ sexual adventures? Maybe so we don’t have to deal with the upheaval of them in our own lives. In any case,” Meara continued before Iona could think of an answer, “I’d be all ears, that’s for certain. But I’ve errands need doing. Now, I could meet you at the pub later, with my ears, unless you're already planning more adventures with Boyle."

"I could squeeze in time for a drink with a friend. Do you believe in reincarnation?"

"Sure that's a question." Meara shoved back her cap. "Where did it come from?"

"I was wondering why some connections seem so easy, so natural, as if they'd already been made and are just getting picked up again. It's the way it worked for me with you, with Branna and Connor. With Boyle. Even Fin."

"I guess I don't discount anything. You don't when your best friend in the world's a witch. But I think a big part of that is you're open to those connections. You reach for them, you do. It's hard not to reach back, even when you're not the reaching type in general."

"You're not?"

"Not as a rule, no. I keep my circle tight. Less upheavals, so to speak."

"Then I'm glad you widened it for me. See you at the pub? A couple hours?"

"That'll do fine."

"Thanks for the lift." Iona jumped out, shot back a wave. She liked the idea of being open to connections, and the prospect of meeting a friend for a drink. Maybe she could talk Branna into joining them—a kind of impulsive girls' night out.

Then maybe she'd get lucky and top it off with a little adventure with Boyle.

Pleased with the plan, she swung through the door.

"Let the lesson begin, then we can— Oh, sorry. I didn't see you had company—a customer."

She hesitated at the doorway, not quite sure if she should go in or out, then recognized the woman standing at the work counter with her cousin.

"Oh, hi. I met you my first night at Ashford, at the Cottage. You're Mick's daughter. Iona," she added when the woman simply stood there, flushed and staring.

"I remember, yes. My father speaks well of you."

"He's terrific. Just one more reason I love my job. Sorry to interrupt. I'll just go—"

"No, no, it's not a problem a'tall. I've just finished. And thanks, Branna, I'll be on my way then. Best to Connor."

She hurried out, pushing a little bottle into her coat pocket.

"Sorry. I know you do some business here, even though most of it's through the shop in the village."

"A bit here, a bit there." Branna tucked some euros into a drawer. "Those who come here are often looking for what I don't sell in the village."

"Oh."

"I'm not a doctor, but I'm discreet. Still, in this case I'll tell you, as it's hardly the secret Kayleen thinks it is, and there may come a time you'll be asked for the same."

She lifted a ladle, poured a pale gold cream from bowl to bottle through a funnel, and touched the air with the scent of honey and almonds.

"There's a fine-looking Italian come over to work at his uncle's restaurant in Galway City. Our Kayleen met him a few weeks ago at a party, and they've been seeing each other a bit. I met him myself when they came into the shop, and he's charming as a prince and twice as handsome." She continued to work as she spoke, filling her bottles, then wiping them clean before sealing them with the stoppers.

"Kayleen's mad in lust for him, and who could blame her for it? I'd have a go at him myself if I was in the market. Others feel the same, and it appears he's fine with that situation. And who could blame him?" she added, tying a thin gold ribbon around the bottle's neck.

"But Kayleen doesn't want to share, and feels the handsome Italian only requires a bit of a boost to pledge to her alone. She had in mind I'd give her the boost."

"I'm not following."

Branna set the finished bottle in a box for transporting. "A love spell was her request, and she was willing to pay a hundred hard-earned for it."

"A love spell? Can you do that?"

"Can and will are different matters entirely. There are ways, of course. There are always ways, and there's nothing more dangerous or filled with pain and regret as spells that involve the heart."

"You told her no. Because it's taking someone's choice away. And because you're not supposed to use magick for gain."

Hands quick and clever, Branna tied the next ribbon. "Every spell's for gain, one way or the other. You want something or believe in something, want to protect or block or vanquish. This cream here, it'll make the skin smooth and fragrant, and it can lift the ego of the one wearing it, as well as draw a response from the one catching its scent. I create it, someone buys it, and I'm paid. That's gain as well."

"I guess that's a way to think about it."

"It is. As for choice, there are times we do that as well, however well-intentioned. And so we have to be willing to pay the price, for magick's not free." She looked up then, met Iona's eyes with her smoky ones. "Not for us, not for any."

"Then why did you say no?"

"Emotions are magick of their own, aren't they? Love and hate the strongest and most powerful. It's my philosophy that you don't tamper with feelings, don't push them in one direction or the other, not with power. The risk is great. What if the love is already there, about to bloom? You push it along, maybe it opens to obsession. Or the one who paid for the spell has a change of mind or heart. Or there's another who loves and would be loved and is now shunted aside by magickal means. So many ors and ifs there. I don't play with love spells or their kin. You'll make up your own mind where you stand on it, but it's, to me, an unethical and risky line to cross."

"Unethical, yes. And even more it just wouldn't be fair." For Iona, that was even more important. "And yeah, I get what you're saying. A lot of magick isn't fair. But love should be, I don't know, sacred. People have to be able to love who they love."

"And not love when they don't. So I said no, and always will."

"What did you sell her instead?"

"Truth. She'll decide if she makes use of it. If she does, they'll both be able to say what they feel, and want and expect. If not, she can go along enjoying what is for as long as it lasts. I think she won't use it. She has a fear of magick, and she's not ready for truth."

"If she loved him, she'd want the truth."

Branna smiled, slipped the next bottle into the box. "Ah, and there you have it. She's a bit besotted and wildly in lust, but not anywhere near the borders of love. She only wishes to be. Love doesn't break under the truth, even when you want it to."

The door opened. Kathel trotted in, and Fin followed.

"Ladies." He pushed back his wind-tossed hair. "I heard we had a bit of trouble. You're all right, darling?" he said to Iona.

"Yes. Fine."

"I'm glad of it. And still, I'd like the details of it all, and what's being planned in the certainty there'll be another attack."

"Boyle didn't come with you?"

"He's dealing with the farrier, and Connor's out on a hawk walk, so it's left to the two of you to deal with me on this."

"Boyle was there as well." Branna carried the box to a shelf in the back. "He'll have as many details as Iona."

"He sees it from his eyes. I want hers."

"We've work, Fin. She needs more knowledge, more practice."

"Then I'll help you with it." As if it was already accepted, he shrugged out of his coat.

"We have different . . . techniques, you and I."

"So we do, and Iona would only benefit from seeing, and trying the differences."

"This habit of talking about me in the third person when I'm right here is getting really old," Iona decided.

"And rude," Fin said with a nod. "You're right. I'd like to help, and once we're done with the work, I'd very much like if you'd tell me exactly what happened, and how you left it—from your eyes, Iona. If you will."

"I . . . I'm supposed to meet Meara later. But . . ." Iona glanced back at Branna, watched her cousin sigh, shrug. "We could ask her to come here, and Boyle, too. It would be smart, I think, to have us all here, go through it once and for all, and talk about what comes next."

"All right then. I can have dinner brought in. You've no need to cook for a horde again, Branna."

"I've sauce I put on an hour ago for pasta. It'll stretch easily enough."

"I'll ring up the others then." He drew out his phone. "Then we'll get started."

14

IT FELT GOOD, AND IT FELT RIGHT TO HAVE EVERYONE together again. Everyone tucked into the roomy kitchen with good cooking smells, voices carrying over voices, the dog sprawled at the hearth.

It made the normal, to Iona's mind, despite the dark and light of the paranormal.

She tossed a big salad, kind of her specialty. She did pretty well in the kitchen as long as it didn't involve actually cooking.

So she felt good and right and, with the increased push on her lessons with Branna, strong. Even the recounting of the altercation with the wolf, once again, reminded her of the power in the blood, at her fingertips. And made her feel confident.

"It's bold, isn't it?" Meara commented as she slathered herbed butter over thick slices of baguette. "To come at the pair of you that way, in the daylight and so close to Ashford."

"I'm thinking it wasn't planned." Connor nipped a slice of bread from the baking tray before Meara could slide it in the oven to toast. "But more he saw an opportunity and took it, without the planning."

"Maybe to frighten more than harm," Fin suggested. "To harm certainly if that opportunity opened. You were having a nice, easy ride, relaxed."

"And not on guard." Boyle nodded. "A mistake we won't be making again."

"It's a kind of terrorism, isn't it?" Fin carried the big bowl of salad to the table. "The constant threat, the not knowing when or where it may come. And the disruption of the normal rhythm of things."

"Sure he's the one who bore the brunt of it." Branna dumped drained pasta in a cheerful blue-and-white bowl. "And got his arse kicked by a witch barely out of the cupboard."

"Satisfying."

But as Fin spoke, Iona caught the quick look he shared with Branna.

"But? But what?"

"He's come after you twice. Here, sit now, get started," Branna ordered. "And both times he's been sent off with his tail between his legs."

"He underestimated her," Boyle said as he took his seat.

"No doubt of that, and little that he'll do so again." Branna handed the salad set to Meara. "Dish it up. I'll turn the bread."

She could follow the dots, Iona thought, especially when they were so clearly marked. "You think he'll come after me again? Specifically?"

"It's you coming here that's set things in motion that held for hundreds of years. There's apples in here," Connor discovered as he sampled the salad. "It's nice."

"So if he scares her off—at least—and back to America?" Meara frowned. "What does that do?"

"I'm not sure it matters now. She's the third." Branna brought the bread to the table, sat to have her salad. "And he knows it, as we do now. Her power has opened, and wider and faster than he—or I for that matter—had anticipated. The cork's not going back in that bottle."

While she appreciated the compliment, Iona continued to follow the dots, into a very uneasy place. "But if he kills me, or either of you?"

"Pain's better." Connor ate with obvious enjoyment, and spoke with something kin to cheer. "Or seduction. Those lead to turning, and by turning any of us, he gains more power. Killing outright, he'd get some, but far from all. Still he might try it out of frustration or spite."

"There's a happy thought," Meara muttered.

"If that's true, why hasn't he gone for either of you long before I got here?"

"Oh, he's made a few swipes from time to time, but no scars." As soon as the words were out of his mouth, Connor winced. "I'm sorry for that, Fin."

"It's no matter. He couldn't know, as none of us could know, the three of you *were* the three. Not until you came, Iona, and the links clicked together."

"And the amulets help to shield," Branna added. "And if he did away with me or Connor, there'd be another. There's O'Dwyers a plenty."

"Not like you." Boyle spoke quietly. "Nor like Connor. Or you," he said to Iona. "You knew, Fin, it would be this three and this time."

"Only for certain when I saw the horse. I saw you on him," Fin said to Iona. "Astride the stallion under a moon so full and white it seemed to pulse against the black sky like a bright heart. I saw fire in your hands, and power in your eyes."

"You said nothing of this before."

Fin glanced at Branna. "I bought the horse because I knew it was hers. I didn't know when you'd come, not for certain," he said to Iona. "Only that you would, and you'd have need of Alastar. And he of you."

"What else have you seen?" Branna demanded.

His face shuttered. "Too much, and not enough."

"I'm not looking for riddles, Finbar."

"You're looking for answers, as always you do, and I don't have them. I've seen the fog spread, as you have, seen him watching from the shadows, a shadow himself. I've seen you under that same bright moon, glowing like a thousand stars. With the wind flying through your hair, and blood on your hands. I've wondered if it was mine."

Saying nothing, Branna rose to go to the stove, to pour the simmering sauce in a bowl.

"I don't know what it means," Fin continued, "or how much is real and true, how much is wondering."

"When the time comes, it'll be his blood spilled." The cheer left Connor's voice. Now there was only a hard edge, a lick of temper.

"Brother. I am his blood."

"He doesn't own you." With her shoulders very straight, her eyes very direct, Iona looked at Fin. "And feeling sorry for yourself isn't helping. He's been around, waiting for hundreds of years," she continued in a practical tone as Branna shot her a quietly approving look over her shoulder. "What the hell has he been doing for centuries?"

"Fin thinks he goes back and forth, when he's a mind to, between times, or worlds. Or both," Boyle added.

"How does he— Oh, the cabin, the ruins. The place behind the vines. If he can do that, why doesn't he kill Sorcha before she burns him to ashes?"

"He can't change what was. Her magick was as powerful as his, maybe more," Fin speculated, "before she took ill, before he killed her man. It's her, I think, who spellbound the place, protects it still. What was, was, and can't be altered. I've tried myself."

"Well now, you're full of secrets, aren't you then." Branna dropped the bowls on the table, snatched up the salad to put it aside.

"If I could've finished what she started, and ended him, it would be done."

"But so would you," Iona pointed out. "Maybe. I think. Time paradoxes are . . . paradoxical."

"In any case, I couldn't change it. My power was there, I felt it, but it made no matter. And I couldn't hold my place, if you take my meaning. It all wavered, and brought me back where I'd started."

"You could've been lost," Connor reminded him. "Taken somewhere, or some time else entirely."

"I wasn't. I think it's like a string of wire, from then to now, and there's no veering off from the wire."

"But there's a lot of years on the wire," Iona mused. "Maybe it's a matter of finding the right spot."

"Change one thing that was, it all changes. And you should know better," Branna said to Fin.

"I was young, and foolish." He sent Iona a quick smile. "And feeling sorry for myself. Now that I'm older and wiser, I see it's not any one of us who'll end him or the curse he carries, but all of us."

"What if we all went back?"

Connor paused in ladling sauce over his pasta to study Boyle. "All of us, together?"

"Maybe it would change things, but we don't know when he'll try to harm any one of us, or what else he might do. I don't know why you can't change what was, or why you shouldn't try when what was is something evil."

"It's a slippery hill to climb, Boyle." Branna twirled pasta, untwirled, twirled it again. "Some ask if you had the way and means, wouldn't you go back and kill Hitler? Oh, the thousands of lives saved, and so many innocent. But one of those lives saved might be worse and more powerful than Hitler ever dreamed."

"But don't you try all the same? A lot of years on the wire, as Iona said. Can't we find the time, the place, take the battle to him? A time and place we know won't wink Fin out of existence."

"Thanks for that."

"I'm used to you," Boyle shot back to Fin. "And have no desire to run the businesses on my own. Is there not some magick the four of you can devise to give us the best chance of it?"

"We may not come back to the world we left, if we come back at all," Branna insisted.

"Maybe we'd come back to better. He's a shadow in this time, as Fin said."

"Shadows fade in the light." Meara lifted her wine. "That's something to consider. I may not be able to conjure a spell, but I know basic physics. Is it physics? Ah, well, action, reaction, yes? And I know it's always better to take the enemy by surprise, on ground of your choosing."

"You'd go?" Iona asked. "I mean if we could, and would."

"Well now, unless I had a hot date lined up."

"It's not a joke, Meara."

Meara reached over, rubbed a hand on Branna's arm. "You've carried the weight long enough. Time to spread it around. Saying we're a circle and really meaning it are different matters, Branna. You can't protect us all, so let's protect each other."

"We could think on it. On how to find that time and place, and block him from knowing it. And how to make the time and place here and now—or here and when we've found the answer to destroying him once and for good."

"SHE'LL STUDY AND THINK AND WORK," IONA SAID QUIETLY to Boyle as they cleared the table. "And worry. I wonder sometimes if there'd be less work and worry all around if I hadn't come."

"It's been an axe dangling over their heads long before that. And you did come. I don't think much about what's meant, but it seems you were meant to come. It needs to end sometime, doesn't it? Why not now? And with us?"

"I'm not a big fan of procrastination." She thought it over as she wiped the table clean, kept her voice down under the clatter of dishes being loaded into the washer. “I just like plowing through to whatever’s next. But I think I could happily push all this into a box in a corner for a couple hundred years.”

“Someone’s got to shovel the shit.”

“And we’ve got the shovels. Yeah,” Iona conceded. “Might as well put our backs into it. I’m looking forward to tomorrow, and not just to get out and see the world beyond a two-mile radius of Ashford.”

“It’s kilometers here.”

“I’ve a feeling I’ll master Irish easier than the metric system. I think getting a better sense of the area beyond our little core of it might be helpful. Plus, I have an exceptional guide.”

“We’ll be seeing about that.”

Take the moments, she thought. Every moment of normal, of happiness and ease. “I want ruins and old cemeteries and green hills. And sheep.”

“You don’t have to ramble far for any of that.”

“But I’ll be rambling with you.” Turning, she wrapped her arms around his waist.

She felt him shift, that subtle move of embarrassment, though the clatter and chatter continued around them. And because she found it endearing, she added to it by raising to her toes and giving him a quick kiss. “I could drive for a while. Practice the on-the-left thing before I buy a car.”

“I think no, most firmly.”

“I know how to drive a truck.”

“You know how to drive a truck on the right when you’re counting the miles. But you don’t know how to drive a lorry on the left when you’re clicking off kilometers.”

He had her there. “That’s the point. You could teach me.”

“Best you try that with someone less . . . volatile,” Branna suggested.

"She means someone less likely to shout blue murder if you clip a hedgerow or veer off the wrong direction on a roundabout," Meara explained. "You're better off with Connor, as he's long on patience."

"I'd need be no longer than a thumbnail to have more patience than Boyle. I'll take you out on the road, cousin, first chance we have for it."

"Thanks."

"And if you're after buying a car, I've a friend in Hollymount in the trade who'd make you a fair deal."

"Connor's friends everywhere."

He merely smiled at Meara. "Sure I'm a friendly sort."

"And all the girls attest to it. I should be off. You'll text me if you devise some grand scheme," she said to Branna.

"I've some thoughts to put together. I'll let you know when I have them sorted out."

"Have a care." Meara added a hug.

"I could use a care as well."

Lifting her eyebrows at Connor, Meara tapped his cheek. "Enjoy your rambling, Iona, and you and Boyle have a care as well. And you, Fin."

"I'll walk out with you. I've some thoughts of my own to put together," he said to Branna. "We might consider Litha."

She nodded. "I am."

"Isn't that—yes, that's the summer solstice," Iona remembered. "Not till June?"

"A bit of time yet. Light smothers dark—and it's the longest day, which we may use to our advantage. I've to think about it."

"Would you rather I stay here tomorrow? Work with you?"

"No, go rambling. You're right that it's good for you to have a better sense of the world around this core of it. And I need that time to think."

"Why don't we give you some peace then," Boyle suggested. "I'll come fetch you, Iona, about nine."

"You could. Or I could go with you now, and we can leave from your place whenever you're ready." She smiled at him. He didn't shift, but she sensed he wanted to. "They all know we're sleeping together."

"Is that a fact?" Connor feigned surprise. "And here I thought you've been having a chess tournament and discussing world events."

"You're a rare one," Boyle muttered. "We can leave from my house if you'd rather. Just don't take half the night getting together what you need, as we'll just be tramping around rubble and gravestones."

"I packed a bag already, just in case. Call me," she told Branna, "if you need me for anything."

"Just have a good time of it." She moved them along, friends and family, up to waving them away from the front door of the cottage.

And stood there a moment longer in the chilly dark.

"All right then, it's just you and me as you wanted." Connor laid a hand on her shoulder. "What is it?"

He wouldn't look, Branna thought. Though she knew how to block him, he wouldn't draw on her heart or mind. He'd consider it an intrusion.

"I don't mean to cut Iona out, and she's proven herself, God knows."

"But you're still getting used to her—and used to the others, all being part of it. Makes you feel tight in your skin, doesn't it, all these people crowding you?"

How he knew her, she thought, and thank all the gods for it, and him. "It does, yes. How we ever came from the same parents is a wonder. Nothing suits you more than a crowd, and nothing suits me less."

"Keeps us balanced."

"Seems it does, and I'm thinking balance might be the thing."

"Ostara, the equinox, the balance of day to night? Rather than the solstice?"

"I've thought of it—as obviously you have as well—but the time's just too short to prepare it all, as it's nearly on us."

"I didn't think her ready, our Iona," he admitted, "but I wonder if I was wrong about that."

"She needs more seasoning, to my mind. And deserves it as well. The solstice is close enough, and that's a kind of balance as well. That tipping point of the year. It may be a chance. If you'd work with me a bit now. Just putting our heads together."

He touched his forehead to hers. "A ritual, a spell of balancing—and banishing at the moment day holds longest—then slides into its ebbing."

"There, you see. I don't have to explain to you, so it goes easier."

"What you're thinking won't come within a league of easy, but it might work. We'll see what we can put together. Just us two for now, and the rest soon enough."

They went to the workshop together, with Branna trying not to feel guilty over the relief that it was just the two of them, at least for now.

"I EMBARRASSED YOU," IONA SAID WHILE THEY MADE THE short drive to Boyle's.

"What? No. I'm not embarrassed."

"A little. I probably should've said something about staying with you tonight when there weren't other people around. I never think about things like that. And it occurred to me too late to consider you might not have wanted company."

"You've stopped being company."

What did it say about her that she found the careless comment romantic? Oh well.

"Then it occurred to me you'd have had no problem saying no, and you'd pick me up in the morning."

"Do I look thickheaded to you?"

"Not a bit."

"I'd have to be not to want to spend the night with you, wouldn't I?"

More romance, she thought, Boyle McGrath–style. "But I shouldn't have announced it like the minutes of the next meeting. If we took minutes."

"It's a private thing."

"I get that, and it would be. Or I'd try harder there. But it seems to me, the way things are, privacy's not really on the table. That's harder for you than it is for me."

"It may be, but you're right. There are more immediate things to worry about."

He pulled in right behind Fin, jiggled his keys as he got out.

"Good night then," Fin called out, "and enjoy tomorrow."

"I'll have my mobile if there's a need."

Iona bumped against Boyle as they climbed the stairs to his rooms. "It *is* harder on you. But Fin's got to be used to you bringing a date back with you now and then, and you with him doing the same."

"I don't bring women here. As a rule," he said after a moment.

"Oh." Privacy, she thought, and more. "If you go to their place, you can leave when you want."

"There's that." He stepped inside.

"You need to tell me when you want me to go. I'd rather be told than tolerated."

"I don't tolerate much." He tossed his keys in a bowl. "I'm not tolerating you."

It made her smile. "Good. Don't. It's miserable to be tolerated."

He set her little bag on a chair. "If I didn't want you here, you'd be somewhere else. Do you want something to drink?"

"I thought I wasn't company anymore."

"You're right."

He grabbed her the way she liked, pulled her through to the bedroom. "You can get your own drink after."

"I'll get you one, too." She yanked his jacket off his shoulders and away. "Boots," she said and made him laugh.

"I'm aware of the order of things."

And still they dived toward the bed. Pulling, tugging, then tossing boots.

"We broke something last time," she remembered as she rushed to unbutton his shirt. "What was it?"

"My grandmother's crystal vase."

Her fingers stilled, her eyes widened in distress. Then he grinned.

"Oh! Liar!" She threw a leg over him, shoved him onto his back. "You're going to pay for that." Crossing her arms, she grabbed the hem of her sweater, pulled it over her head, winged it over her shoulder.

"I'll pay more," he told her. He slid his hands up her sides, over her breasts as she fought open the last buttons.

"You bet you will, buddy." She lowered her head, catching his mouth in a crushing kiss before scraping her teeth over his bottom lip, ending with a nip.

He retaliated by flipping her over, doing the same.

They wrestled off clothes, wrestled each other in a rush of give-and-take.

So much the same, she thought, wonderfully the same, but now she *knew* what they could bring to each other. All heat and demand and speed, like flying through fire—simmers and flashes and bursts.

She reveled in the thrill of skin sliding against skin—his to hers, hers to his—the heady friction of it. His mouth, dark with hunger, his hands, rough with greed, raced over her.

How had she lived without knowing what it was to be wanted so completely, so urgently, so thoroughly?

She needed to give him the same, to show him how the want for him flooded through her.

He couldn't get enough of her. Whatever he took only sparked a bright hot need for more. When he had her like this, moving, moving in the dark, he couldn't think, could only feel.

And she made him feel drunk, half-mad with it. Made him feel strong as a god, reckless as a cornered wolf.

The world outside dissolved; time spun away.

Just her body, the shape of her, those sleek muscles under smooth skin. The sound of her—breath and sigh and soft, soft moan. And her taste, so hot and sweet.

She struggled up, fast hands, quick legs, to straddle him, and starlight caught in the crown of her hair like diamonds.

She took him in, fast and deep, her hands pressed to her own breasts as the first wave of ecstasy swamped her.

Then she rode, free and wild, starlight on her skin, dark triumph in her eyes.

He gripped her hips, clinging to her and some last thread of sanity.

And she lifted her arms high, crying out in that same dark triumph.

Flames shimmered at her fingertips, tiny pinpoints of light that flashed, bright and blinding as the sun. Stunned by them, bewitched by her, he held on—and he let go.

IN THE DARK, IN THE DREAM, SHE REACHED FOR HIM.

"Do you hear that? Do you hear that?"

"It's just the wind."

"No." The woods were so thick, the night so black. Where was the moon? Why was there no moon, no stars?

And with a shudder, she understood. "It's *in* the wind."

Her name, the seductive pull of the whisper. A stroke of silk on bare skin.

"You need to sleep."

"But I am. Aren't I?"

When she shivered again, he rubbed her chilled hands between his. "We should have a fire."

"It's so dark. It's too dark, too cold."

"I know the way home. Don't fret now."

He began to guide her, through the trees, away from the little licks of fog that flicked, sly as the tongue of a snake, along the ground.

"Don't let go," she said as the whisper slid and stroked over her skin.

"The way's blocked, do you see?" He gestured to the thick branches blocking the path. "I'll need to move them before we can get through."

"No!" On a spur of panic, she gripped his hand tighter. "It's what he wants. Just like before, to separate us. We have to stay together. We have to hold on."

"The way's blocked, Iona." He turned her now, looked into her eyes. His were dark gold, intense, unwavering. "We should have a fire."

"The fog's closer. Can you hear it?"

The wolf now, just the faintest growl through the black, through the fog.

"I hear it. Fire, Iona. It's what we need."

Fire, she thought. Against the dark, against the cold.

Fire. Of course.

She threw her arms out, out, lifted her face up. And called it.

Strong, bright, with a whip-snap that lashed through the creeping fog, made it boil, made it steam and die to thin black ash.

"To the dark I bring the light. Against the black I forge the white. From my blood I call the fire to burn, to flame high and higher. Awake or in dreams, my power runs free. As I will, so mote it be."

A curl of fog snuck out, slithered close. Boyle lunged in front of Iona, threw out a fist.

He felt a quick pain across his knuckles. Then both fog and ash vanished, and there was only fire and light.

She saw blood well up across Boyle's hand.

And woke with a jolt.

Morning, she saw now, the pearly promise of it glowing against the window.

A dream, just a dream, and she took a breath to steady herself. When Boyle sat up beside her, she reached for his hand.

And saw the blood.

"Oh God."

"In the woods, together." His fingers curled tight over hers. "Is that how it was?"

She nodded. "It's a kind of astral projection, I think. We're here, but we were there. I must have pulled you in with me. You . . . You hit out at the fog."

"It worked, and felt fine as well, though your fire did more."

"No, yes. I don't know. You struck out, and it was like you punched a hole, for a moment. I . . . But you're bleeding."

"Sure it's but a scratch."

"No, it's from him. I don't know if it's just a scratch." She could call on Connor or Branna, but she *felt*, somehow, this was for her to do.

"I need to fix it."

"Just needs a quick wash, and ointment if you're going to fuss about it."

"Not that way." Her heart beat so fast now, faster, she realized, than it had, even through the fear of the dream.

He bled, and it was Cabhan who'd drawn that blood.

"It's an unnatural wound. I've studied it, if you'll trust me."

She laid her hand over the shallow gash, closed her eyes. She saw his hand—strong, broad, the fascinating scarred knuckles from his boxing days. The blood, and deeper, looking deeper, the thin black line of Cabhan's poison.

Just as she'd feared.

Draw it out, she told herself. Out and away. White against black again. Light against dark. Out and away before it sank deeper, before it could spread.

She felt it go, little by little, felt it burn away. She knew by the way his hand stiffened, it caused him pain. But now the wound ran clean. Slowly, carefully, she set to the healing of the shallow gash. Now the pain—small, sharp stings were hers. But they faded, faded.

Just a scratch, as he'd said, once the poison had been drawn out.

She opened her eyes, found his on her.

"You've gone pale."

"It took some doing. My first try at this kind of thing." Her head spun a little, and her stomach did a couple of slow rolls.

But the wound was clean, and it was closed. She studied his hand, satisfied. "He used poison. I don't know if it would've done anything, but it might have spread. It wasn't much, but it's gone now. You could have Connor take a look."

Boyle continued to study her as he flexed his fingers. "I'd say you did well enough."

"I don't know if he expected me to pull you with me. And I don't know how I did. But you told me what needed to be done. The fire. You told me, and it worked."

"Burned him to ashes."

"Well, wouldn't be the first time, and I really don't think it's the last."

"No, not the last of it."

"I'd say I'm sorry I dragged you into that, but I'm awfully glad you were with me."

"It was an experience for certain."

One that left him shaken, and more, puzzled him. During it he'd felt such calm, and such absolute faith she would do what needed to be done.

"It seemed like a dream," he continued, "the way your mind can be a bit slow, and you don't question the oddities."

"I'll do a charm for the bed, or better, have Branna do one. It should help."

"I hurt him." Again, Boyle flexed his fingers. "He wasn't expecting a punch, I'm thinking. I know when one lands well, and it did. I'm thinking as well, the poison was for you. Could I have pulled you back out, as you did me? Do you know that? And if I did that, could I have gotten you to Connor in time to deal with the poison, if I'd thought to?"

"You knew what to do." Instinctively, she lifted her hands to rub at his shoulders, found them knotted. "You knew we needed fire, and you stayed so calm. I needed you to stay calm. I'm going to believe you'd know what to do if and when he comes at us again."

She let out a long breath. "I'm starving. I'll go fix breakfast."

"I'll do it. You're a terrible cook."

"That's so entirely true. Fine, you cook. I'll give Branna a call, tell her, just in case. Are we still on for that rambling?"

"I don't see what this changes about it."

"Great. I'll grab a shower, then call Branna. It's early, and she'll be less cranky with another fifteen minutes' sleep."

"I'll put the kettle on."

But he picked up his phone first and, while she ran the shower, punched in Fin's number. He'd sooner know what Fin had to say before he fried up the bacon.

15

IT WAS THE COUNTRY OF HER BLOOD, AND AS SHE WATCHED it rise and fall and spread outside the truck window, Iona understood it was the country of her heart.

It settled into her like a sip of whiskey on a cold night, warm and comforting. Green hills rolled under a sky layered with clouds, stacked like sheets of linen. The sun shimmered through them, making intermittent swirls of blue luminous as opals. Fat cows and woolly sheep dotted emerald fields bisected with rough hedgerows or silvery gray rock walls.

Farmhouses, barns, pretty little cottages scattered over the land with postcard charm as the road twisted and curved. Dooryard gardens reached for spring, with brave blooms opening in wild blues, sassy oranges, delicate whites, topped here and there by the heralding trumpets of daffodils.

She would have spring in Ireland, Iona thought, the first of a lifetime. And like those brave flowers, she determined to bloom.

The road might turn, curve out like a tunnel with high, high hedgerows of wild fuchsia hugging the sides of the twists, the turns with their blooms dripping like drops of blood. Then the world opened again to the hills, the fields, and, thrillingly, the shadows of mountains.

"How do you stand it?" Iona wondered. "Doesn't it constantly dazzle your eyes, take your breath, make your heart ache?"

"It's home," Boyle said simply. "There's nowhere I'd rather be. It suits me."

"Oh, me, too." And finally, she thought, she felt she suited it.

The wind kicked, and a splatter of rain struck the windshield. Then the sun ran behind it to turn the drops into tiny rainbows.

Magick, Iona thought, simple and mysterious.

As was Ballintubber Abbey.

Its clean lines lent a quiet dignity to the old gray stone. It made its home on pretty grounds backed with fields of sheep spread before the green hills, the loom of mountains.

Simple grandeur, she thought, finding the oxymoron the perfect description of the ancient and the life going quietly on around it. She climbed out of the truck to study the pathways, the gardens defying winter's last shivers, and smiled as the breeze carried the baaing of sheep.

She thought she could sit on the grass and spend an entire day happily just looking, just listening.

"I suppose you'll be wanting the history of the place."

She'd read some of it in her guide, but enjoyed the idea of Boyle giving her his take.

"I wouldn't mind."

"Well, it was Conchobair who built it—Cathal Mor of the wine-red hand, of the O'Connor clan, so he'd be one of yours."

"Oh. Of course." How deep her blood ran here, she thought. And how marvelous was that? "Like Ashford, before the Burkes won it."

"There you are. Back in 1216 it was. I know the date, as they're after restoring the east wing, I think it is, for its eight-hundred-year celebration. And so the legend—or one of them—says while Cathal was the son of King Turloch, he was forced to flee from Turloch's queen, and spend some time laboring and in hiding before he took the throne. And there was a man who treated him kindly, and Cathal, now king, asked him what he could do to repay him. It was a church that the man, now old, wanted, in Ballintubber, and so Cathal ordered it built."

They walked the path as he told the tale, with his voice rising and falling on the words, the sheep baaing their chorus. Ridiculously happy, Iona took Boyle's hand to link them, to seal the moments.

"After some years, the king saw the old man again, and was scolded for not keeping his word. It seems the church had been built right enough, but in Roscommon."

Laughing, Iona looked up at him. "Oops."

"So you could say. But Cathal ordered another church built, and it came to be Ballintubber Abbey."

"A man of his word."

"So it's said."

"I like knowing I have a grateful and honest king in my ancestry."

"And it's a lasting legacy, as it's said to be the only church in Ireland founded by an Irish king and still in use."

"I think that's wonderful. People too often knock down the old for the new instead of understanding that legacy."

"What comes before now matters," he said simply. "Pierce Brosnan was married here a few years back, and that's been a newer claim to fame. Older it's the start of Tórchar Phádraig."

"The pilgrimage route to Saint Patrick's mountain. I've read about that."

"It's also said Seán na Sagart, who was a nefarious priest hunter, is buried in the cemetery here. There." Boyle lifted his hand to point to a large tree. "So it's said."

"It's a good place. Clean, powerful. And I feel this recognition somewhere deep, this connection. Is that weird?"

He only shrugged. "Your blood built it."

"So you made it our first stop." Smiling, she leaned her head against his arm. "Thanks." She glanced down at an old, pitted stone and its carving. "The Crowning?"

"Oh well, they've more than the abbey, and the graves and such. That's part of the Stations. They've added that, a Rosary Walk, and over there, a little cave that's fashioned as a stable, for the Nativity. It's a bit odd."

"It's wonderful." Tugging his hand she followed the path, finding other stones and markers among the trim and pretty gardens. "It's so abstract, so contemporary, and a really creative contrast against the antiquity."

She paused at a little stream, its bank blanketed with low, spreading bushes as it rose to rough stones. Three crosses topped it to represent the Crucifixion.

"It should be sad, and I know it should be reverent. It is, but it's more . . . compelling. And then this." She stepped into the cave to look over the statues of Mary, Joseph, the Baby Jesus. "It's wonderful, too—sweet and a little kitschy. I think Cathal would like what's been done."

"He's made no objections that I know of."

They went inside, and there she found hushed reverence.

"The Cromwellians set fire to the place," Boyle told her. "You can see from the ruins outside the monastery that the quarters and such fell. But the church stood, and still does. The baptismal area there, they say, is a thousand years old."

"It's comforting, isn't it, to know the things we build can survive. It's beautiful. The stained glass, the stone."

The way her footsteps echoed in the quiet only added to the atmosphere.

"You know a lot about it," she commented. "Did you study up?"

"Didn't have to. I had an uncle worked here on some of the repairs and improvements."

"So my blood built it, and yours helped keep it. That's another connection."

"True enough. And I've had two cousins and a couple of mates married here, so I've been around and about it a few times."

"It's a good place for a wedding. The continuity, the care, the respect. And the romance—tales of kings and priest hunters, Cromwellians and James Bond."

He laughed at that, but she only smiled. She felt something here. A kinship, a recognition, and now a kind of knowing.

She'd come here before, she realized, or her blood had come.

To sit, perhaps, in that quiet reverence.

"Candles and flowers, light and scent. And music. Women in pretty dresses and handsome men." She wandered again, painting it in her mind. "A fretful baby being soothed, a shuffle of feet. Joy, anticipation, and love making a promise. Yes, it's a good place for a wedding."

She wanted it for hers, this place of age and contrast and endurance.

She went back to him, took his hand again. "Promises made here would matter, and they'd hold, if the ones making them believed it."

Back outside she wandered the ruins, brushing her fingers over old stone, moved through the cemetery where the long dead rested.

She took pictures to mark the day and, though he grumbled about it, persuaded Boyle to pose with her as she took a self-portrait with her cell phone.

"I'll send it to my Nan," she told him. "She'll get a kick out of seeing . . ."

"What is it?"

"I . . . The light. Do you see it?" She held out the phone to him.

On the screen they posed with her head tipped to his shoulder. She smiled, easy, and Boyle more soberly.

And light, white as candle wax, surrounded them.

"The angle maybe. A flash from the sun."

"You know it's not."

"It's not, no," he admitted.

"It's this place," she murmured. "Founded by my blood, kept by yours—that's part of it. It's a good place, a strong place. A safe one. I think they came here, the three. And others that came from them. Now me. I feel . . . welcome here. It's a good light, Boyle. It's good magick."

She took his hand, studying the back of it where dark magick had spilled blood.

"Connor said it was clean," he reminded her.

"Yeah. Light banishes shadows. Meara was right about that." Still holding his hand, she looked into his eyes. "But like promises made, the light has to believe it."

"And do you?"

"I do." She lifted her free hand to his face, rose on her toes to brush her lips to his.

She believed it. Deep down in her belly she carried faith and resolve. And her heart came to accept what she understood as she'd walked with him along the paths and tidy gardens that opened for spring, among the spirits and the legends, into the promise kept by one of hers.

She loved. At last. Loved as she'd always hoped. He was her once in a lifetime. And with him she had to learn patience, and hold only to that faith as well. The faith that he would love as she loved.

She put on her best smile. "What's next?"

"Well there's the Ross Abbey. Actually, it's a friary. Ross Errilly. It's not far, and you'd probably like to poke about in it."

"Bring it on."

She glanced around as they walked to the truck, and knew she'd come back. Maybe to walk the Stations or just stand in the breeze and look out at the fields.

She'd come back, as her blood had come.

But now, as he drove away, she looked forward.

She saw it from the road, the foreboding mass of it, its peaks and tower and rambling walls. Under the thick sky it looked like something out of an old movie where creatures who shuffled in the dark hid and plotted.

She couldn't wait to get a closer look.

The truck bumped down a skinny track with pretty little houses on one side, laced with gardens with blooms testing the chill. The other side of the track spread with fields loaded with cows and sheep.

Ahead, beyond the tidy and pastoral, loomed the ruins.

"I didn't study up," he told her. "But I know it's old, of course—not as old as the abbey, but old for all that."

She walked toward it, heard the whistle of the wind through the peaks and jut of stone, and the flapping of wings from birds, the lowing of cattle.

The central tower speared up above the roofless walls.

She stepped inside a doorway, and now her feet crunched on gravel.

Vaults for the dead, or stones for them fixed flat into the ground.

"I think the Brits kicked out the monks, as they were wont, then, as *they* were wont, the Cromwellians did the rest and sacked the place. Pillaged and burned."

"It's massive." She stepped through an arch, looking up at the tower and the black birds that circled it.

The air felt heavy—rain to come, she decided. Wind blew through the arched windows, whistled down the narrow curve of stone steps.

"This must've been the kitchen." She didn't like the way her voice echoed, but moved closer to look down in what seemed to be some sort of dry well. "Stand over there." She gestured to the ox-roasting fireplace.

He shuffled his feet, gave her a pained look. "I'm not much for pictures."

"Indulge me. It's a big fireplace. You're a big guy."

She snapped her pictures. "They'd butcher their own meat, grow their own vegetables, mill flour. Keep fish in the well there. The Franciscans." She wandered out, even at her height ducking under archways, to an open area.

A line of archways, gravestones, grass. "The cloister. Quiet thoughts, robes, and folded hands. They looked so pious, but some had humor, others ambition. Envy, greed, lust, even here."

"Iona."

But she moved on, stopped at the base of steps where a Christ figure had been carved in the arch. "Symbols are important. The Christians followed the pagans there, carving and painting their one God as the old ones carved and painted the many. Neither understand that the one is part of the many, the many part of the one."

Wind fluttered through her hair as she stepped out on a narrow balustrade. Boyle took her arm in a firm grip.

"I died here, or my blood did. It feels the same. Breaking the journey home, too old, too ill to continue on. Some would burn the witch, such is the time, but her power's gone quiet, and they take her in. She wears the symbol, but they don't know what it means. The copper horse."

Iona's hand closed over her amulet. "But he knows. He smells her weakness. He waits, but must come to her. She can't finish the journey. And she feels him nearing, greedy for what she has left. He has less than he did, but enough. Still enough. She has no choice now. it can't be done in the place of her power, at the source. He's whispering. Can you hear him?"

"Come away now."

She turned. Her eyes had gone nearly black. "It's not done, and it must be done. She has her granddaughter—such love between them, and the power simmers in the young. She passes what she has, as the first did, as her own father had done with her, and with the power, she passes on the symbol. A burden, a stone in the heart. It's always been that for her, never with joy to balance it. So she passes power and symbol with grief.

"And the rooks flap their wings. The wolf howls on the hill. The fog creeps along the ground. She speaks her last words."

Iona's voice rose, carried over the wind—in Irish. Above the layered clouds something rumbled that might have been thunder, might have been power waking. The circling birds swooped away with frightened calls, leaving only sky and stone.

"The bells tolled as if they knew," she continued. "Though the girl wept, she felt the power rise up—hot and white. Strong, young, vital, and fierce. So he was denied what he craved yet again. And again, and again, he waits."

Iona's eyes rolled back. When she swayed, Boyle dragged her in close.

"I have to leave here," she said weakly.

"Bloody right." He plucked her off her feet, carried her down the narrow, curving stairs, through archways where he nearly bent double to pass through, and out again into the air and the patter of rain.

The wet felt like heaven on her cheeks. "I'm okay. Just a little dizzy. I don't know what happened."

"A vision. I've seen Connor caught in one."

"I could see them, the old woman, the girl, bathing her grandmother's face. Fever, she was so hot, like she was burning from the inside out. I could hear them, and him. I could hear him trying to get to her, trying to draw her out. I felt her pain, physical and emotional. She wished, so much, she could spare the girl she loved from the risk and responsibility. But there wasn't a choice, and there wasn't time."

He shifted her to open the truck door, maneuvered her inside, amazed his hands didn't shake to mimic his heart.

"You spoke in Irish."

"I did?" Iona shoved at her hair. "I can't remember, not exactly. What did I say?"

"I'm not sure of it all. 'You're the one, but there must be three.' And I think . . ." He struggled with the translation. "'It ends here for me, begins for you.' Something like that, and more I couldn't understand. Your eyes went black as a raven's, and your skin pale as death."

"My eyes."

"They're back," he assured her, stroked her cheek. "Blue as summer."

"I need more training. It's like trying to compete in the Olympics when you're still learning how to change leads and gaits. And that's a potent place, full of energy and power."

He'd been there before, felt nothing but some curiosity. But this time, with her . . .

"It hooked to you," he decided. "Or you to it."

"Or she did, the old woman. She's buried in there. One day we should come back, one day when this is finished, and leave flowers on her grave."

At the moment he wasn't inclined to bring her back ever. But as he walked around to get in the truck, the rain stopped.

"Look." She took his hand, pointed with the other at the rainbow that glimmered behind the ruins. "Light wins."

She smiled and meant it and, thinking rainbows, leaned over to kiss him.

"I'm starving."

He didn't think at all, but pulled her in again to kiss her until the image of her swaying on the ledge faded away. "I know a place not far that does a fine fish and chips. And Christ knows I could do with a pint."

"That's what I'm talking about. Thanks," she added.

"For what?"

"For showing me two amazing places, and for catching me before I fell."

She looked back at the friary, at the black birds, at the rainbow. Her life had forever changed, she thought. But unlike her ancestor, she considered it a gift.

IN THE COZY KITCHEN WITH THE HOUND AT HER FEET AND a fire in the hearth, Iona told her cousins everything.

"A busy day for you," Connor commented.

"And then some."

"That would be three events, we'll call them, in a single day."

Branna, her hair still bundled up from her workday, contemplated her tea. "But only the first involving Cabhan."

"The last one, too," Iona reminded her. "She felt him coming."

"A vision of the past. Whether yours or another's, still the past. I doubt he'd venture so far now." Branna looked at Connor.

"Not now, no, and why should he? Tell me what you were feeling—before, during, after the vision came on you."

"Before I'm not sure. I felt I'd been there before, like the abbey, but not . . . bright, not happy like that. It was dark and, well, sorrowful. I knew the layout, what things were, but I realize now it was her, our ancestor. I was thinking her thoughts, and some were pretty damn bitter. She knew she was dying, but more than death she hated passing the amulet, the power, the responsibility on to her granddaughter.

"I don't remember going up the steps. It seemed I was just there. The old woman in bed, gray hair streaked with white. Her face gray, too, and shiny with fever. And the girl sitting beside her, bathing her face. Long red hair. Eimear—I think she called the young girl Eimear."

"You don't remember the Irish you spoke," Connor prompted her.

"No, just what Boyle thought it meant, or what he understood of it. I remember sorrow and fear, then the light just bursting into the room. For an instant, a sense of power—just wild, huge. Like a, well, like a really excellent orgasm. Then it all went gray, and spinning. Dizzy, weak, disoriented, and when that passed, hungry."

"The dizziness will ease after a time," Connor told her. "It's good you weren't alone when you had your first. You weren't expecting this then?" he asked Branna.

"Not yet, no. Not yet. I want to say she's—you're," she corrected, and addressed Iona directly, "accelerating. I think it's where you are, and who you're with. We're three together, so what you have is coming ripe more quickly than it might otherwise. It's a good thing, this. You'll be stronger, less vulnerable."

"Should I expect any more surprises?"

"You'll take them as they come."

"Let's backtrack a minute. The dream. Did Boyle and I share the dream because we were together?"

"The sex." Connor leaned back, shot his legs out. "It's a powerful link. Or can be."

"So if I have sex with Boyle he can get dragged in with me? But it hurt him. His hand. The poison."

"Which you tended to well. That's good instinct."

"But the next time it could be worse."

"You take it as it comes," Branna reminded her. "Cabhan hurt him, but Boyle hurt Cabhan as well. Cabhan felt the blow—a human blow and in a dream—and that's interesting to me."

"It was black, mixed in Boyle's blood. I could see it. If it had spread before—"

"It didn't," Branna said briskly. "We deal with what is. You can't cloud what is with what-if, and the emotions."

"She loves him." Connor rubbed a hand over Iona's when she jolted. "Love clouds everything and shines through it as well."

"I never said I . . . How do you know what I just figured out?"

"It's coming through you so strong I can't avoid seeing it." He gave her hand another rub. "I don't mean to peek through the door, but it's wide open."

"I haven't said anything to him." Couldn't and shouldn't, she thought, reminding herself of her vow to be patient. "I'm just sort of savoring it. I've wanted to feel this way for so long, tried to feel this way. And with Boyle I didn't have to want or try. I just did."

"That's all well and good, and sure he's one of the best men I know. But you can't let what you have filter through the haze of love," Branna warned.

"We have different ways of thinking on that," Connor put in. "I think love only adds to the power. Where she is, yes," he said to Branna. "And being with us. But I'm thinking what she feels is another reason she's gaining so fast. How she knew the poison was in Boyle, and how she drew it out so clean, when she'd never done the like before."

"I won't argue. It's different for everyone, isn't it? Love, magick, and how we see and deal. And in each, the choices we make. I'll only say you've had but a short time here, and with him, to think of love and the choices that go with it."

"I knew the minute I saw him. Maybe that was a kind of vision. I don't know. But I felt this flutter." She pressed a hand to her belly. "And this rising." Slid her hand to her heart. "Attraction, I told myself, because he looked so amazing riding in on Alastar. But it was more. I told myself I couldn't go there because, well, at first I thought he was with Meara."

She lifted her eyebrows when Connor let out a laughing snort.

"I don't know why that's so funny. They're gorgeous together. Tall and fit and stunning. And they have this connection—it was clear from the start."

"Sure like Branna and me, for they're as close as brother and sister, and never been otherwise. But you thought they were more, so you pushed aside what you felt or might have felt. That's to your credit. Not all would do the same. I'm wondering if I would myself."

"Love at first sight's a fairy tale," Branna said, firmly.

"I love fairy tales." With a laugh, Iona propped her elbows on the table, her face on her fists. "I decided it was just attraction, and okay once Meara set me straight. I decided I just wanted to sleep with him, but I've never felt what I feel for him. And I know what it is, and I know it started when I saw him riding up on Alastar, both of them so fierce and furious. I fell for both of them right then and there. I'm trying to be patient, which isn't my nature at all. Alastar figured out he loved me. Now I just have to wait for Boyle to figure it out."

"You're confident he will?" Branna asked her.

"You can't just hope for happy endings. You have to believe in them. Then do the work, take the risks. Slay the dragon—though I really think dragons get a bad rap—kiss the princess, or the frog, defeat the bad witch."

"Well defeating the bad witch is happy ending enough for me."

It shouldn't be, Iona thought, but Connor gave her hand a little squeeze before she said it.

"I've things to see to, but later on, after dinner," Branna continued, "we'll practice again. Connor can help you with the visions, the healing. The solstice comes closer every day, and there's still work to be done."

"You have an idea what to do?"

"You said Boyle hurt him, in a dream, and with only a fist. We can do better than a fist."

"I've got to go back to the school, check on some hatchlings. But I'll be home within the hour."

"I'll walk with you," Iona told Connor. "I'd like to give Alastar some exercise, even if it's just around the jumps course."

"Then I'll come back by, walk home with you."

"I can probably get a ride, but if not, I'll text you."

"Fine then, go off with both of you, give me some thinking time." Branna pushed back from the table. "You said Fin was to do a protection charm for Boyle's bed. Make sure he has before the two of you make use of it again."

"Okay."

"The next time you, or any of us, go into a dream, I want it to be a choice, and us doing the pulling in."

16

IONA CHANGED INTO RIDING BOOTS, AND TOOK TEN SECONDS to put on some lip gloss in case she ran into Boyle. They both had obligations that evening—his paperwork, her spell casting—but she hoped to talk him into a ride after work the next day, maybe a casual dinner out, then a cozy night in, at his place.

Outside, she hooked her arm through Connor's. The air might have blown cool and damp, but spring rode with it and nudged the blackthorn into bloom.

"Have you ever been in love?" she asked him.

"Sure countless times, and never the way you mean. Though my heart's been bruised and bumped, never has it been broken."

"I had the bumps, too, and some bruises. When I was in high school, I actively wished for actual heartache, just to know what it felt like. I always wanted those big feelings, you know? The rush and the fall. What I got was mostly even ground. Settling for someone I knew was settling for me. It makes you feel forever mediocre."

"And now?"

"Now I feel powerful, purposeful." She circled her fingers, made tiny lights dance. "Joyful."

"And all look good on you."

"Do you want to? Fall in love?"

"Sure one day. She'll walk into the room, beautiful and brilliant, a sexual goddess with the mind of a scholar and an angel's temperament. She'll cook like my aunt Fiona, who can't be equaled in the kitchen, match me pint for pint at the pub, and like little better than to go hawking with me."

"You don't ask much."

His eyes, green as the moss, twinkled at her. "Why not ask for all, as you never know what life's going to hand you?"

"Good point," she said, and made another dance of lights.

IN THE STABLES BOYLE BRUSHED DARLING AS MUCH TO soothe himself as to groom her. He'd sent his stable hands home a bit early, as he'd coveted a little time alone. Now, with the sweet mare for company in the quiet stables, he could roll through all the things crowding his mind.

There were bills to pay and orders to make, and he'd get to all that, wouldn't he? He had all evening for that, as he needed.

Wanted, he corrected.

A man needed time and space of his own without a woman expecting his attention.

So he shouldn't be thinking about going by and scooping her up so she'd be in his time and space.

If anything, once the paperwork was seen to, he should take some of that time to think about all that had happened that day.

He'd have to tell Fin the whole of it, of course, and would whenever Fin got back. They'd talk it out over a pint, so there was no room for Iona, even if he was inclined for her.

Which he was, all the damn time.

What the hell did it mean when a man couldn't keep a woman out of his space, much less his mind?

Bewitched is what he was, by blue eyes and an easy laugh, and a pretty body he couldn't keep his bloody hands off of. And that utter faith in the good and the happy that lived inside her, though he understood, more and more, how little of either she'd had.

Finding himself wanting to give her the good and the happy troubled him more than a little. Hadn't he planned out the entire day with the goal of giving her just that? Not that it had worked out in all cases, considering dark visions and a scare that had near stopped his heart. But he'd planned it all, with her in mind.

Always in his mind, she was.

It was time to remind himself that what a man needed, when it came down to it, was room, work, a good horse, and a pint at the end of a hard day.

"That's it, isn't it, Darling? We've got what counts right here."

In the next stall Alastar snorted and blew.

"I'm not after talking to you, am I? Bad-tempered beast."

"And you'd know about that," Fin said from behind him. "What are you brooding about, brother?"

The man could sneak up on a body, Boyle thought, like smoke from a flue. "Who says I'm brooding?"

"I do." Fin reached out, stroked Darling's neck. "Sent the men off early, did you?"

"A bit. Everything's done needs doing today."

"I thought you'd be out rambling still with Iona."

"We did enough, maybe more than."

"Trouble then? Of a personal sort or a magickal sort?"

"Both, I'm thinking. It started early this morning, as you know, when I shared a dream with her and came to blows with that cursed bastard."

"You had more trouble from that?"

When Fin gripped his shoulder, Boyle just kept brushing the horse. "Nothing serious or lasting. So I'll tell you the rest."

And he did, from the beginning, right on through to when he carried Iona out of the friary. Only grunted when Fin grabbed his hand.

"I told you she fixed it, and Connor had a look as well."

"I'll look for myself now." Once he did, Fin nodded, let Boyle's hand go. "You said you hurt him. You're sure of it now that some time's passed and you've thought it through?"

Boyle curled his hand into a fist. "I know when I land a blow, mate."

"Aye, you would." Fin paced away and back again. "I've given it some thought, and we'll use that; I'll think on it more, but use it we will. And I've a protection charm for you before you turn in for the night. Is she coming by?"

"She's not, no. I need a night to myself, don't I? I've work, and I've thinking of my own to do without being crowded."

Fin lifted an eyebrow at the tone. "Had a row?"

"We did not. After I carted her out of the cursed friary, she packed away fish and chips like a starving woman. I took her around to Clew Bay, as she wanted to see the water, then she spotted more ruins, another graveyard, so she wandered about, but there was nothing for her there like the other places. And that was a relief."

"She handles it well, for someone coming into it later than most."

"I suppose she does, and it's a lot on her plate for all her appetite. And it makes me wonder."

Fin gestured an opening. "Wonder away."

"I want her here, even when I don't. Or I think I don't, then I do." The words sounded mad to his own ears, but he couldn't stop them now that he'd started. "And I never have much liked women in my place, as they tend to fuss or leave things behind, or bring little bits over, look to change the order of things."

"Hmm. And does she?"

"She doesn't, and that's suspect, isn't it?" Boyle jabbed a finger in the air as if his point had been made.

"So if she does those things, she's encroaching. If she doesn't, she's suspect? *Mo dearthair*, you're acting the gom."

"I'm not." Insulted, Boyle rounded on Fin. "It's not being a fool to wonder if she'd got some plan under there. She talked of weddings, mind you. Of a wedding at Ballintubber Abbey."

"Which it's famed for. Did she propose to you then, along the Stations? I'm seeing no ring on your finger or through your nose."

"Smirk if you must, but I'm wondering. I think about her too much. 'Tisn't comfortable. When I have her in bed it's like nothing else ever was. No one else. So I end up staying, or having her stay, and then there's breakfast, and on to work. I have to work, don't I? And she's pushed into my mind even then. It's fucking annoying now that I say it out loud."

"I can see that. It has to be a trial to you, having a woman as pretty as a spring morning, and as fresh and sweet, taking up your time and attention."

"I've a life to live, don't I?" Boyle snapped back, as every word Fin spoke made him, well, feel as if he acted the gom. "And a right to like that life just as it is—was—before."

"Sure as I'm standing here I'd trade places with you if I could, to have a woman in my mind and heart who was pleased and willing to have me in hers. But you have, of course, every right to live your life without a sweet and fresh and pretty woman in it."

"She's more than that, as well you know. I've never seen the like of her, and I've seen you, Branna, Connor. But when it's on her, I've never seen the like. It takes my breath. I don't know why that is."

"I've a speculation on it."

Boyle mimicked Fin's gesture. "Speculate away."

"You sound like a man in love to me."

"Oh sure and that's helpful." Boyle resisted throwing the brush only because it would startle Darling. "I'm telling you, she's pushed herself into my mind, my life, my bed so I've barely a minute to myself. I took a day off work, which I don't do, as you know, to drive her all around Mayo and Galway. I can't get away from her even when I'm sleeping.

"I think she's bewitched me."

"Oh Christ Jesus, Boyle."

But Boyle had the bit between his teeth now. "She's come into it late, as you said, and she's full of the power of it. So she's done a love spell to wrap me up this way."

"Bollocks. Even if she were inclined, and I don't see it, Branna would never allow it."

"Branna doesn't know everything," Boyle muttered, and glanced over darkly as Alastar kicked the wall of the stall. "She's new to it, Iona is, testing her footing so to speak. She's testing it on me so I'm tangled up taking walks and rides and drives and fixing her breakfast after a night of her sleeping wrapped around me like a vine. So if she's put a love spell on me, you need to break it."

"Is that what you think?" Very quietly, Iona stepped up to the stall. "I'm sorry but you were too busy shouting to hear me come in. What a lot you think of yourself, Boyle, and how little you think of me."

"Iona—"

She stepped back, chin jerking up. "Do you really think I'm so weak, so sad, so pitiful that I'd want someone who didn't want me of their own free will? That I'd use magick to enchant you into spending time with me, having feelings for me?"

"No. I'm only trying to work it out."

"Work." Her eyes filled, killing him, but the tears didn't come. "Yeah, I know it's so much work to care about me. So I'll make it easy for you. There's no need, and there's no spell. I have too much respect for what I am to use it in such a small, selfish way. And I love you too much to ever use you at all."

Every word came as a jab to his heart. "Come upstairs now, we'll talk this through."

"There's nothing else for me to say, and I really don't want to talk to you now." Deliberately, she turned away from him. "Fin, could you give me a ride home?"

"I'll take you myself—" Boyle began.

"You won't. No, you won't. I don't want to be with you. I can call Connor if you can't take me, Fin."

"Of course I can."

"You're not just walking away after—"

"Watch me." She shot him a look so full of both devastation and fury, he said nothing more when she turned and walked away.

"Let it be for now," Fin said quietly, "and use some of this famous time and space to learn how to do a proper grovel."

"Ah, fuck me."

"And so you have." He hurried out after Iona, reached down to open the car door for her.

"He's never felt like this for anyone," he began.

"Don't try to smooth it over, please. If you could do me one favor, just don't say anything. Anything at all. I just want to go home."

He did exactly as she asked, kept his silence on the short drive. He could feel her pain. It seemed to pulse from her, sharpen the air in the car so keenly he thought it a wonder it didn't draw blood.

Love, as he knew too well, could slice you to pieces and leave no visible scar.

He pulled up at the cottage, smoke curling from the chimney, an amazing array of colorful flowers twinkling in the evening gloom. And somewhere inside, Branna, as distant as the moon.

"Should I come in with you?"

"No. Thanks for bringing me home."

When she started to get out, he simply touched her hand. "You're not hard to love, *deirfiúr bheag*, but for some, loving is strange and boggy ground."

"He can be careful where he steps." Though her lips quivered, she managed an even tone. "But he can't blame someone else for where he ends up."

"You'd be right. I'm sorry you heard what was—"

"Don't apologize. It's better to see and know you're a fool than to keep your eyes shut and keep acting like one."

She got out quickly. He waited until she'd gone in the house before driving away. He half wished he was in love with her himself, and could show her what it was to be cherished.

But as that wasn't an option, and it likely wasn't wise to go home and pound on Boyle's rock-hard head with a hammer, he'd go by and fetch Connor. They'd sit down with a bottle of whiskey, the three of them, and as good mates would, get Boyle drunk instead.

Iona went straight in. She had no intention of crying on Branna's or anyone else's shoulder. She had no intention of crying at all. What she intended to do was hang on to the anger, and that would see her through the worst of it.

So she went straight in, and straight back to the kitchen where Branna sat at the table with her enormous spell book with its carved and well-tended brown leather binding, an iPad, a notebook, and several keenly sharpened pencils.

Branna glanced up, cocked her head in question. "What, did you just go, turn around and come back?"

"Yep. I'm having a really big glass of wine," she said as she walked to the cabinet. "Do you want one?"

Now Branna's eyebrows drew together. "I wouldn't say no. What happened? Did you have another encounter with Cabhan?"

"Not everything is about Cabhan and ancient fricking evil." True to her word, she poured an enormous glass of wine, then a more sedate one for her cousin.

"Well now, here's a mood that's come on in under twenty minutes. Wasn't your horse happy to see you then?"

"I never got to Alastar, which is just one more thing I can be pissed about. I never saw my horse, never got my ride." She handed Branna the glass, tapped her own to it. "Bloody *sláinte*."

When Iona flopped down at the table, Branna took a sip of wine, studied her cousin over the rim. Anger, yes, but hurt besides. Deliberately she kept her voice breezy.

"Not Cabhan or the horse, so what does that leave? Let me see, could it be Boyle?"

"Could be and is. I walked into the stables when he was ranting to Fin about how inconvenient it is for him to have me around all the time, in his space. In his way, in his bed. Wrapped around him like a vine in his words."

"He's an idiot, and I hope you gave him a solid boot for it. Men can be loathsome creatures, especially when they put their heads together."

"Oh, there's more, as if that wasn't bad enough. He's decided since I've managed to push my way into his life, his head, his bed, I've put a love spell on him."

"Bollocks to that!" The sympathy Branna tried to keep mild erupted in stunned insult. "He must've been joking, just having it on with Fin who likely teased him a bit."

"He wasn't joking, Branna. He was furious, shouting. He didn't even hear me come in. When I did he was saying—loudly—that he barely has any time to himself the way I've pushed myself on him, and I'd put a love spell on him. I'm new at all this, and testing the waters, and decided to test them on him with a love spell. He told Fin to break it."

"What a pair of right gobdaws."

"I don't know what that means, but it sounds insulting, so good. Except not Fin. He said bollocks to that, too."

"I'm pleased to hear that at least. Now we won't be turning him into a slug and drowning him in beer."

Iona tried to laugh, but it kept catching. "It's a good word *bollocks*, I'm going to start using it a lot. Bollocks, bollocks, bollocks."

Her eyes filled, her throat burned. So she shook her head, gulped wine. "No, no, no. I am *not* going to cry. I have to stay mad so I won't."

"Did you speak to Boyle, or just turn his penis into a warty little stub?"

"I spoke with him." Iona swiped at the single tear that got through. "I let him know I had too much respect for myself to use magick to get someone to want me. To love me. He tried to make excuses, but bollocks to that, right? I asked Fin to bring me back, and he did. He was kind."

He could be, Branna thought, enormously kind. To some. "Then I'm glad he was there. I won't make excuses for Boyle. What he said was a harsh and unwarranted insult to those like you and me. And more, it's hurtful because you have such strong feelings for him. I'll only say that while he's got a black temper at times, and is in the way of being, well, gruff's a simple word for it, at other times, I've never known him to hurt anyone like this. It's my thinking he's taken considerably aback by his feelings for you."

"He doesn't want them. I'm not going to cry over someone who doesn't want feelings for me. I may get a little drunk, but I'm not going to cry about it."

"A sensible attitude." Branna's phone jingled. "It's Connor. Give me a moment. And where are you?" she said into the phone by way of greeting. "Right here, yes. No, we could do without you, you being a man for all that. That's best, that's fine. And when I want your fine advice, I'll be asking for it. Go on, be jackasses together, and you can tell Boyle he can count his luck I don't make that literal."

She clicked off. "Fin went by the school for Connor. I've told him, as you gathered, to go on, as men can just jam things up. I've a mind to ring up Meara, unless you'd rather I didn't. We can sit around, drink more wine, and say all the rude and truthful things about men without any of them around."

"That'd be great. Really. But you're working."

"I'll get back to it."

"You feel sorry for me."

"A poor sort I'd be if I didn't. But I'm pissed right along with you, for you, myself, and every other self-respecting witch, and every self-respecting woman. Love spell, my arse."

WHEN CONNOR AND FIN WALKED INTO FIN'S HOUSE, BOYLE paced the living room.

"What took you so bloody long," he began, then spotted Connor. "Ah, well. Before you jump up my arse I never knew she was there, and was just having a bit of a rant. I'm entitled to have a bit of a rant in my own stables."

"One question, before we go any further on the matter." Connor held up a single finger. "Are you saying Iona used magick to trap you—a love spell?"

"I said it, as you bloody well know, but I'm not saying it. I was blowing off, is all. Or mostly all."

"Do you think she used magick on you?"

"No, not when I—"

"No's enough for now," Connor told him. "No means I'm not obliged to plant my fist in your face, the result of which would be you kicking the living shit out of me, and I'd rather have a beer. Bugger it, Boyle, you know what we're about, and what's over a line for us. You should know the same of Iona."

"I do. But it's . . . Well, fuck it, have a swing. I won't hit back as I earned it."

"There's no satisfaction in punching under those conditions."

"I'll do it," Fin volunteered.

"You're not her cousin," Boyle shot back, then threw up his hands. Jutted out his chin. "Go on then, have a go."

Fin only smiled. "I'll save that offer, and have that go when you least expect it."

"Why didn't I think of that?" Connor shrugged out of his jacket. "I want the beer, then you can tell me how you plan to fix this up with Iona."

"If she'd just be reasonable—"

"That's not the way, mate." Connor dropped down on the big leather couch. "Any crisps to go with the beer?"

"I'll take care of it. There's steaks, and Boyle can do the cooking in a bit," Fin decided. "To practice being humble and apologetic."

"Look here." Boyle sat down, leaned forward. "You asked if I meant it, right? I said I didn't, and that's that. Reasonable."

"And you expect her to be the same?"

"I was blowing off," Boyle insisted. "When she's calmed herself I'll tell her I was just, what do you call it, venting, and didn't mean anything by it. That's all."

Connor said nothing for a moment, then glanced over as Fin came back with bottles of Smithwick's and a bag of potato chips.

"I know he's been around and with women before," Connor said conversationally. "I've seen that for myself, and met some of them as well. But if I didn't know better I'd swear an oath the man had just crawled out of a cave full grown without having any female contact whatsoever."

"Ah, feck off."

"Groveling." Fin tossed the beers, one to Connor, one to Boyle, dropped down on the sofa, propped his feet on the oversized coffee table he'd found on his travels.

"I'm not doing that."

"*Mo dearthair*, I wager you will before it's done. I've a hundred I'll put on it. He's mad for her," he said to Connor.

"Sure that's one more reason he'll make a complete bags of it."

"I should go talk to her now, get it done and finished."

"I wouldn't advise it." Connor grabbed a handful of chips. "She's with Branna, and my sister isn't too pleased with you at the moment. I reckon she'll pull Meara in, so that'll be all the three of them sending hard thoughts, at the least of it, your way."

"Well, Jesus, I can't go about fixing anything if she won't talk to me, and she's being guarded by a witch and a woman with a tongue as sharp as a razor."

"Resign yourself to stewing in it tonight, and maybe a day or two more," Fin advised. "After that . . . I'm thinking flowers won't do the trick here."

Connor washed down the chips with beer. "She's a romantic soul, our Iona, but flowers are paltry considering the insult."

"I didn't insult her," Boyle began, then swore bitterly before gulping down beer. "All right then, I did. I admit it. Admitting a wrong and apologizing ought to be enough."

Fin slid down to a slouch. "I'm forced to agree with you, Connor, though it pains me, about the cave. She's not a man, brother, and you don't handle her as one with a sorry, mate. I'll stand you a round. Flowers, as she's romantic, and something with some shine to it to show you understand the depth of your mistake."

Astonished, Boyle shot straight up in his chair. "Now I'm buying her jewelry just for blowing off when she wasn't even meant to be there? I'll not do it." A man had his pride, and his spine, didn't he? "It's nothing but a bribe."

"Think of it more as an investment," Fin suggested. "Christ Jesus, man, have you never put your foot in it with a woman and had to find the way to pull it out again?"

Boyle set his jaw. "If I'm wrong, I say I'm wrong. If that's not enough, well, that's that. I've never gone around with a woman who matters, so . . ."

"And she does. Matter," Connor finished.

"It should be apparent enough." He brooded into his beer. "I'm not going around buying flowers and baubles to put a patch on it. I'll apologize, for I couldn't be sorrier to have put that look on her face. The mad, that's fine. You shout it out and it's finished. But I hurt her, and I'm sorry for it."

He pushed up. "I'll see about the steaks."

"Mad for her," Fin said when Boyle left the room.

"And panicked with it, which would be good fun if this hadn't happened. She'll forgive him, for she's tenderhearted and just as mad for him. But she won't shine again until he gives her back what she's so willing to give him."

"What would that be?"

"Love, given freely and without conditions. The flowers, the bauble will make her smile, when she's ready. But he'll have to give over himself before she shines again."

"It's what makes us all shine," Fin observed.

IN THE LIVING ROOM OF THE COTTAGE WITH THE FIRE SIMmering and candles lit, Iona snuggled into the corner of the couch. Meara had not only come, but with provisions of pizza and ice cream.

"Pizza, cookie dough ice cream, wine, and girls." Iona lifted her glass in toast. "The best there is."

"I keep the pizza and ice cream in the freezer for just such emergencies."

"It's perfect. We should all be lesbians."

"You'll have to speak for yourself there." Amused, Meara took a second slice.

"I think the Amazons were probably lesbians. Or some of them anyway. That's what I thought of you when I first saw you."

Choking on her bite of pizza, Meara downed some wine. "You took a look at me and thought: Why, there's a lesbian?"

"Amazon. I hadn't thought about your sexual orientation, then I saw you and Boyle together and figured you were together, but that was wrong. Amazon," Iona repeated. "Tall and gorgeous and built. I'm a little bit drunk." She smiled at Branna. "Thanks."

"Oh, anytime a'tall."

"We can all be Amazons."

"You're a bit short for it," Meara pointed out.

"There had to be some runts in the litter."

"Word is she's small but mighty," Branna added.

"Damn right! See what I can do?" She popped a jittery ball of flame into her hand.

"Best not to play with fire, or magick, when you're a little bit drunk," Branna advised.

"Right." She winked it out. "But I can do it, that's the point. I can take care of myself. I'm going to buy a car, then when I want to drive around, I'll drive my own damn self. I've got power and purpose. I don't need a man."

"If we're to be Amazons, we'll just use them for sex or whatever else comes to mind, then cast them out or kill them."

Iona nodded at Meara. "Let's do that. Not the killing, it's a little extreme. But the sex and whatever. I really like sex."

"Here's to it." Meara lifted her glass, drank, then glanced at Branna. "Aren't you drinking to sex?"

"I'll drink to it, as that's the closest I've come to it in some time."

Iona sighed, a little bit drunkenly. "You could have sex with anybody. You're so gorgeous."

"Thanks very much, but anybody doesn't appeal to me at this time."

"She's particular about the matter," Meara added.

"Me, too, or I have been. I think I'll stop doing that. Sex with Boyle was spectacular."

"Do tell," Meara commented. "And I mean do. I've all the time in the world."

With a laugh, Iona sipped more wine. "Hot and wild and sweaty. Like the world was going to end any minute and you *had* to have each other first."

"Ah well, I haven't come close to that particular brand in some time myself."

"Done now." Iona swiped a hand through the air. "It's time for a good dose of cynicism because love sucks. Who needs it when you've got pizza and ice cream and girls, and lots of wine?"

"I've always figured it was the frosting."

Now Iona stabbed a finger toward Meara. "Frosting's fattening and gives you cavities."

"There's the risk of that to be sure, but . . . Well, you've got to bake the cake, don't you? Bake it well so it satisfies yourself. And maybe you decide to add frosting, maybe you don't."

"Love as a choice?" No, Iona thought. No. Love just picked you up and tossed you in. "But how do you choose? You've baked your cake, and there it is, and you're thinking that's a pretty good cake, that's good enough for me. Then you blink and all this wonderful frosting just plops down on it out of nowhere."

Meara shrugged. "You could scrape it off."

"You can," Branna agreed. "But it takes some of the cake with it, and you never get all the frosting gone."

"That's sad. It sounds true," Iona murmured, "and sad. We can't be sad. I refuse it. We need music," she decided. "Would you play, Branna? I love to hear you play."

"Why not?" Branna stood. "I'm in the mood to play. I'll get my fiddle, and Meara, you tune up your pipes."

Iona got up to stir the fire when Branna went out. "I know Branna's answer because I've seen her and Fin, and heard the story. But have you ever been in love?"

"Well, sticking with the theme, I've dipped my finger in the bowl of frosting and had a small sample or two, but nothing more." From her own corner of the couch, Meara shifted. "I want to say, Boyle can be a idjit."

"Branna called him a gobdaw."

"And that as well, as can most men. And I'm sorry to say our side as well has moments of grand stupidity. I want to say as well, I've known him a good long time, and I've never seen him look at another woman the way he looks at you."

She believed that. She'd felt that. But. "I wish it could be enough. My problem is I always want more."

"Why is that a problem?"

"It's a problem when you don't get it."

She plopped down again as Branna came back with her violin case. "He's out there," Branna said.

"Boyle?" And damn it, Iona felt her heart jump.

"No. Cabhan."

This time her nerves jumped even as she and Meara pushed off the couch.

"There's fog all around the house, pressed right up to the windows like a Peeping Tom."

"What should we do?" Iona saw it now, the gray curtain of it as she stepped to the glass with her friends. "We should do something."

"We will. We'll have music. He can't go past my shield on this place," Branna said as she calmly took out the fiddle, the bow. "So we'll have more wine, and we'll have music. And we'll shove the sound of it right up his arse."

"Something lively then." Meara shot her middle finger at the window before she turned. "Something for dancing. I'll see if I can teach Iona a few steps."

"I'm a fast learner," she said, as much to what lurked outside as to Meara.

17

THE HANGOVER WOKE HER, THE STEADY THROB, THROB, throb in her temples that picked up the beat from the bang, bang, bang in the center of her skull.

She'd had worse, Iona thought, but not by much.

She considered pulling the covers over her head and trying to sleep it off, but she couldn't—wouldn't—miss work. Cautiously she opened her eyes, then squinted at the living room window.

Not in bed, she realized, but on the couch with a pretty throw in melting shades of purple tucked around her. She remembered now. She'd stretched out on the couch after dancing herself breathless and after joining her friends in a song or two.

She didn't have their quality of voice, but she knew the words thanks to Nan, and could pull off some decent harmony.

Plus it was fun, she thought. And defiant, making song as the fog curled outside.

She'd drunk, eaten, talked, laughed, then sung and danced her way through that first awful punch of pain. And now she had a hangover to distract her, and that was all to the good.

She hadn't cried—or not enough to count—and that was even better.

She'd down a gallon of water, a bottle or two of aspirin, make herself eat something. Then shower for a few days. All better.

And she'd work through the rest.

Sometime between the first glass of wine and the last, she determined she'd go to the stables as usual. She wouldn't crawl off and quit a job she loved because her boss—her lover—had broken her all-too-fragile heart.

If he wanted her gone, he'd have to fire her.

She got up, shuffled her way to the kitchen. She'd gulped down water, some aspirin, and was contemplating trying some dry toast when Meara walked in looking annoyingly bright-eyed and rosy.

"Got a bit of a head this morning, do you?"

Iona gave Meara as close to the stink eye as she could manage. "Why don't you?"

"Oh, I've a head like a rock and a stomach like iron." She spoke cheerfully as she put on coffee. "Can't remember ever being the worse for wear after a drinking night."

"I hate you."

"And who's to blame you? We left you where you dropped last night, as it seemed best. Since I'd brought a change with me in case we made a night of it, I slept in your room. You'll want the coffee and some food in your system. Oatmeal, I'm thinking."

Iona winced. "Really?"

"Good and healthy. I'll make it up, as Branna won't be stirring as yet."

"Does she have a head like a rock and a stomach like iron, too?"

"I'd say she does, yes. But then she's careful how much she drinks. She's one to keep her wits about her, always. Here now." Meara poured the coffee. "When she's up, ask her to fix you a potion for the head. She has one that's renowned."

"Good to know. I'd like a clear head when I get to work."

"So you're sticking with it then?" Meara gave her a light shoulder punch of approval. "Good for you."

"I'm not going to deprive myself of work I love, or mope in a corner. I need the job, so we'll figure out how to work together, unless he fires me."

"He never would. He's not so hard, Iona."

"No, he's not. Besides, the sun may be out now, but there's always a chance of fog. With that to deal with, we have to put the rest aside. No chinks in the circle, right?"

"You've got spine." This time Meara gave her a quick rub on the shoulder.

"If you're really making oatmeal, I'll go up, soak some of this hangover away in the shower, and get dressed for work." She hesitated, then wrapped her arms around Meara in a hug. "You and Branna got me through a tough night."

"Ah, well now, what else are friends for if not that?"

By the time she got out of the shower, the throbbing and banging had clicked down a couple levels. But a sober study of her face in the mirror told her more help was needed. Instead of her usual workday slap-and-dash-on makeup, she took some time, some care. She didn't want Boyle to think the pale cheeks and smudged eyes were due to him, though indirectly they were, since she'd overindulged to buffer the hurt.

Satisfied she'd done the best with what she had to work with, she dressed and went back down to face oatmeal.

She found Branna, sleepy-eyed in her pajamas, drinking coffee as Meara hummed a tune while she slapped butter on toasted bread.

"And there's herself now, and looking only half dragged out."

"That bad?"

"Not bad at all," Meara said staunchly, and dished out oatmeal.

"Sure we can do better." Branna crooked a finger. "Lean down here, since you won't do it for yourself." She glided her hands gently over Iona's face. "Just a touch, as we don't want him to think you fussed for him either."

That brought on a smile. "You read my mind."

"It's sensible, so a little glamour adds just the right touch. We women, and witches, stick together. Meara says you've a bit of a head."

"It's better."

"Drink that." She tapped her finger on a glass filled with pale green liquid.

"What is it?"

"Good for what ails you. Herbs and such, and a touch of more. No point going in as you are, feeling less than well, or looking it. You're showing backbone by dealing with what is, so you'll have a reward."

"And oatmeal." Meara set three bowls on the table, went back for the toast, then sat.

"Here goes." Considering it medicine, Iona drank the potion—but found it had a cool, fresh flavor with a faint hint of mint. "It's nice."

"Good for what ails you doesn't have to be unpleasant. Eat as well, it adds to it."

"You're both taking care of me. I want to say if either of you get the crap kicked out of you by love, I'll be there for you."

"That's reassuring." Meara dug into the oatmeal.

The hangover slid away, like raindrops sliding down a window pane—a kind of slow, soft, liquid fading that left Iona feeling refreshed and rested.

"You could make a fortune off that single potion," she told Branna as she pulled on her jacket. "It's a miracle."

"Not quite that, and making fortunes isn't all it's thought to be. We work tonight, cousin, and twice as hard for the night off."

"I'll be ready. I know you're not much for hugs," she added as she gave Branna a squeeze. "But I am." She stepped outside with Meara. "I don't think Cabhan liked the music."

"I hope it rings in his ears still. I'll speak with you later," Meara said to Branna, and strode to her truck. "I hate I'm saying this," she continued when Iona sat beside her. "But don't be too awful hard on him. Oh, he deserves it with no doubt, the donkey's arse, but men can be such fumblers."

"I don't want to be hard on him. I just want to get through."

"Then you will."

HE DIDN'T EXPECT HER TO COME TO WORK, AND IT CHAFED at him that he couldn't blame her. Before the mucking and feeding, watering and daily morning medications began, he huddled down with the weekly schedule. In a relatively short time, he realized, he'd assigned Iona to so many tasks, students, duties he'd need to do a bit of scrambling to fill in her spots.

Pain in the arse, and really when you thought about it all in a rational way there was no reason she'd get herself in such a state so she'd toss the work in the trash bin along with the rest.

And if he could just have a rational word or two with her, he'd surely climb out of the bin himself.

If women were more like men, life would run along smoother, without a doubt.

He stewed, and finagled the schedule, brooded and shifted hours and students. As he pushed away to pull out his mobile and begin to make the necessary calls, he heard Meara's truck drive up. Hers ran with a cougar's purr rather than Mick's aging lion with bronchitis.

He strolled out, determined to pass the calls to her, and to, very casual-like, pump her for information on Iona, as word was she'd stayed over at Branna's.

So it threw him off stride when Iona hopped out of the passenger's door, dressed for the workday.

"Morning then," Meara said with a kind of fierce cheer, and walked right by him into the stables.

He led with: "Ah . . ."

"I'm here to work." In a clipped voice he'd never heard her use, Iona stopped a foot away to speak to him. "And that's all. I need the work, I like the work, I'm good at the work. If you intend to fire me—"

"Fire you?" Shocked, and once again off stride, he gaped at her. "Of course I'm not after firing you. Why—"

"Good. Then that's that."

"Well now, wait a minute there, we need to talk about—"

"We don't." She cut him off in that same tone, cool and dismissive. "I know what you feel and think, and on some level I understand it. You're entitled to feel what you feel, and I'm responsible for my own feelings. So it's just work, Boyle, and you have to respect that."

She turned her back on him, walked to the stables. He could stop her, just pluck her up and haul her off somewhere private where she'd have to talk it out and over. He thought of doing just that for a moment, then let her go.

He stuffed his hands in his pockets, stood in the cool morning air, and wished he'd gotten the damn flowers.

He tried it her way. As he was the one who'd fucked up, he was obliged to give her the room she asked for.

She went about her work, but not all brisk business as he'd expected. Oh no, she had plenty to say to Meara, to Mick and the others, a laugh to share, a question to ask. But not a bloody word did she speak to him unless given no choice.

She managed to be cordial and distant at once.

It pissed him off, then when the mad faded, the guilt piled in.

"You're driving him mad." Meara watched Iona saddle Spud for a guided ride.

"I'm just doing my job, and leaving the personal out of it."

"Exactly what's driving him mad. He'd say, being male, and being especially Boyle, the logical thing to do in such situations is separate the business from the personal, but you doing just that's squeezing his balls. He doesn't know whether to yelp or drop."

"I'm getting through." After tightening the cinch, Iona put on her riding helmet. "That's what counts. But I can't say I'm sorry it's giving his balls a good squeeze."

She led the group out—a couple and two teenage girls from America taking advantage of spring break—letting them chatter among themselves. But she did glance back, once, and couldn't deny a quick twist of satisfaction at catching Boyle watching her ride away.

As they turned into the woods, she brushed her fingers over the amulet she wore, then tapped them to her pocket where she'd put a protection charm that morning.

She wouldn't fear the woods, she told herself. She wouldn't fear what came. And she wouldn't fear living her life alone if that's what destiny handed her.

Putting her guide's smile on, she shifted in the saddle, glanced back at the family. "So, how are you enjoying your visit so far?"

A BUSY DAY MOVED QUICKLY, AND FOR THAT SHE WAS GRATEful. Knowing she did just exactly what she needed to do didn't make it any easier to do it. She wanted to smile at Boyle, and see him flash her a grin in return. Wanted to feel entitled to touch him, just a hand to his, a hand on his arm, and have him feel entitled to do the same.

She wanted to be easy with him again. Even if they couldn't be lovers, even if she had to find a way to snuff out the light of the love she felt for him, she wanted him in her life.

Needed him, she corrected as she cleaned up at the big stables after her lesson with Sarah. Until Cabhan was defeated, until what Sorcha had begun so long ago was finished, they all needed one another.

What they faced was so much bigger than a bruised heart and some scarred pride.

They'd find a way. If Branna and Fin could work together, she could certainly work with Boyle. It might take some time to find the right way, to smooth out the bumps—and they'd have to talk it out, she admitted.

But not yet. Too tender yet.

She hugged Alastar's neck, pleased when he nuzzled her. "I've got you, don't I? My guide, my friend, my partner. I've got family who cares about me, and understands me. And I've got a home, a place I belong. It's more than I ever had before."

She drew back, kissed his nose. "So no complaints, no pity parties. I'll see you tomorrow."

She walked out, noted she timed it well when she spotted Connor strolling toward the stables, his whistled tune leading the way.

The perfect Irish picture, she thought, a good-looking man, all lanky limbs and wicked angel face, hands in the pockets of his rough work pants, and the brown path and green, green woods behind him.

"All done for the day then?" he called out.

"Just now. You?"

"Ready to walk my pretty cousin home, and see if our Branna baked any fresh biscuits today. I've a yen for some, and since according to our Branna we're working tonight, I deserve them as well."

"I'm ready for magick." She wiggled her fingers. "And to learn something new."

"New, is it?"

"Astral projection. I'm doing it in dreams, either on my own or manipulated by Cabhan, I don't know for sure. But I don't control it. I want to."

"It's a good arrow for your quiver. And so . . . how did it all go with Boyle today?"

"Maybe a little awkward and tense here and there, but we got through it. It should be easier going forward."

"He's feeling a right shit about the whole business."

She would not feel pleased (maybe just a little). She would not feel sorry, or she'd ignore the sorry.

"He feels what he feels, that's why we're here. He's your friend." She gave Connor's arm a quick rub. "He feels bad he hurt me. You feel bad that he feels bad. We all just have to get past it and not lose sight of what we have to do."

"And you can do that?"

"I've had a disappointed heart before." She said it lightly, had to, as it went so deep. "I think some of us are just destined not to connect that way."

"But you don't." He took her hand in his, gave it a bolstering squeeze. "You don't think that at all."

"I think," she said more carefully, "there's something about me that makes it difficult for others to forge an intimate connection to."

"Bollocks," he began, but she shook her head.

"My own parents couldn't. Is that them, or is it me? Who knows, but if they can't, and there's been no one until Boyle I wanted, deep down, to make that connection to, I can't blame him. If it's me, I have to work on me. And I have been. I'm a classic work-in-progress."

"You're wrong, about the connection, or anything about it being you. You're as easy to love as a summer morning. If we weren't cousins, I'd marry you myself."

She laughed at that, touched. Then sent him a sultry, sidelong stare. "We're distant cousins."

"Cousins all the same." He slung an arm around her shoulders. "And it's too odd and tangled for that."

"Too bad, because you're so pretty."

"I'll say the same right back to you."

He opened the door to the workshop, gave his arm an exaggerated sweep to usher her in. Then sniffed the air.

"Ginger biscuits, and what a fine welcome home."

"Have some and your tea, as we've work to make up."

At the counter Branna poured white liquid wax into a clear jar, already weighted with a long white wick. Iona wondered how Connor scented the ginger over the summer fragrance of hydrangea.

"How did it all go then?" Branna asked as she tipped up the pan, moved down to the next jar.

"First day down, and not too bad."

"She thinks she's unlovable." Connor spoke over a mouthful of cookie.

"Oh bollocks."

"I didn't say that, don't think that. I meant—never mind." She grabbed a cookie for herself. "Do you need help with those?"

"I'm about done, but you can help me with the labels and wick trimming later on. I've made dozens as we were running low, and the tourists come thicker in spring than in winter. Have your tea. We'll work twice as much today for working not at all yesterday."

"I'm ready."

"She's after astral projection," Connor put in.

"Astral projection, is it?" Pursing her lips, Branna studied Iona. "It wasn't what I had in mind, but well, why not? It's a fine skill to have."

With the last jar filled, she left them cooling on the rack, pulled off the white bib apron she'd worn to protect her poppy red sweater from drips and spills.

"It's not the same as the active dreaming you've done, but not so very different. Have you been practicing your meditating?"

Iona winced. "Probably not as much as I should. My mind always wants to go somewhere."

"Training your mind's part of it. Training it, quieting it, and as

I've said, focusing it. Here, bring your tea to the fire. You should be relaxed in body and mind and spirit."

Iona obeyed, and Kathel stirred from his nap to lay a paw on her foot in hello.

"Just watch the fire, have your tea. You like the taste of it, and the biscuit. Quiet breathing. Inhale, pause, exhale, pause. You can smell the peat fire, and the candles just poured, the herbs hanging to dry."

"Rosemary especially."

"Sure it's a favorite. You hear your breath go in and out, and Kathel's tail swishing against the floor, the crackle of the fire, and the sound of my voice. It's soothing, all soothing. The touch of my hand, and Kathel's paw. Soothing all, so you can drift a bit, float a bit. Quiet and peaceful."

"But I—"

"Trust me. I'll be with you this first time, take you this first time. See where you want most to go, see it in the fire, see it in your mind."

"Nan's kitchen," Iona realized all at once. "I miss her. She's never done anything but love me, believe in me. She's been the only one who has for so long. I'm what I am because of Nan."

Branna glanced at Connor as he came over to sit on Iona's other side. "A long trip for a first," she murmured.

"Her heart takes her there."

"And so will we. Do you see it, Nan's kitchen, in the fire, in your mind?"

"It's like yours. I mean feels like yours, not looks like. It's smaller, and there's no hearth. I see the walls, they're like a warm peach and the cabinets are dark, dark brown. There's an old butcher block table. When I sat with her there, I could tell her anything. She told me what I am, told me about the first dark witch while we sat at that table having tea and cookies—biscuits. Just like now. She keeps herbs on the windowsill, and the blue and green pottery bowl I gave her for her birthday years ago on the table. There were red apples in it the day she told me everything, not just pieces, but all. Shining red apples in the green and blue bowl. Her eyes are like mine, the same color, the same shape. And when they look at me, I believe."

"Focus on the bowl, the colors of that, the shape of that. Let yourself lift, let yourself go where you want to go. Quiet breaths, quiet mind, quiet purpose. Lift. Float. Fly."

She lifted, floated as if weightless. The air, the light all pulsed blue—quiet, soothing. And as she felt the first stirring of its power, of hers, she flew.

Fast, free, soaring over green hills misted by blue, over water—blue under blue.

Branna's voice sounded in her mind. *Breathe. Keep your focus.*

"It's amazing! It's beautiful." She threw her arms out to the side, laughed with the sheer joy of it.

Hold on now. Nan's kitchen. See it.

She saw it in her mind, and then, she was simply there. Standing by the old butcher block table, with the blue and green bowl. Lemons and limes today, Iona thought, a bit dizzy.

And there was Nan, stepping in the back door, toeing out of her gardening shoes, taking off the wide-brimmed straw hat.

Small statured, small framed, as Iona was. Trim and pretty in her jeans and light jacket. Her hair, maintained a soft golden red, formed a stylish wedge around her face. Light, discreet makeup. Nan wouldn't even garden before taking care of the basics.

She started to walk to the fridge, stopped. Then very slowly turned.

Her hand went to her heart, and eyes wide, she let out one short gasp. "Iona! You're here. Oh, oh, Branna and Connor as well. Oh, look at you, my baby girl. How much you've learned already."

"You can see me."

"Sure I can see you, you're standing right there, aren't you? And so pretty. Sit, sit, all of you, and tell me everything."

"Can we sit?" Iona wondered.

"There's enough power in this room to light the next fifty kilometers." Branna pulled out a chair, sat. "Of course we can sit."

On a little cry, Iona rushed forward, grabbed Nan in a hug. "I can touch you. I can feel you. I've missed you."

"As I've missed you."

"We can't stay long this time, cousin." Branna smiled at them. "It's a long distance for her first time."

"The first?" With a laugh, a beam of amazement in her eyes, Nan hugged again. "Oh no, not long then. But long enough to say how proud and happy I am."

"Will you come? You said you'd come to Ireland."

"And so I will, when it's time. I'll know. You're happy, but . . . there's something unhappy."

"She's had a . . . disagreement," Connor decided. "With Boyle."

"Ah, I see. I'm sorry for it, as I'm well fond of him. If it's right, it'll mend."

"He doesn't trust me. It's not important."

"Of course it is."

"I mean right this minute. I want to know how you are."

"Fit and fine, as you see. Planting pansies today, as they'll take the cool, and it's been cool this spring. And cabbage, of course, and a bit of this and that. You're teaching her well, Branna, as she tells me. And you, Connor."

"She learns well. And she's needed." Branna reached out a hand, took Nan's. "I want to say to you, you were right to send her, right to give her the amulet. I'm grateful to you."

"No need for that. It's ours to do. It's our blood."

"It is, and it will be. He's stronger now that the three are together, but we're stronger yet. I'm sorry we can't have a proper visit." Branna rose. "But she's only begun on this skill."

"Even a moment is a great treat. You take care, my girl. And keep your heart and your mind open, Iona. That's when the best come into them."

"I remember." She kissed Nan's cheek, hugged her hard. "I'll come back if I can." On impulse, she took a lemon from the bowl. She felt its skin against her palm and, lifting it, caught its scent. "I know it's silly, but can I take this with me? Is that possible?"

"Let's find out." Branna took her hand, and when Iona pushed the lemon in her pocket, Connor the other.

"We've missed you back home, Cousin Mary Kate," Connor told her.

"And I you. You'll take me hawking one day soon, won't you, Connor?"

"It'll be a pleasure to me."

"Tell your mother, and hers, when you see them, I look forward to a good gossip in person."

"Come to the Dark Witch," Branna told Nan. "There'll be a fire burning for you, and the kettle on the boil."

"I will, and thanks. My love goes with all of you, and every hope with it."

"Bye, Nan. I love you."

And again, she lifted, floated. Flew.

18

SHE FELT AMAZING, AND STILL BRANNA PUSHED A POTION on her.

"Your first time. It's best if you level it out a bit now."

"Can I do it again?"

Branna quirked her eyebrows while Connor grabbed two more cookies. "Now?"

"No, not this minute. I mean can I do it? Am I capable? On my own?"

"Connor and I were just along for the ride, you could say." She stepped over to check her candles. "Helping you prepare, then going along to see you through."

"Like being on a learner's permit?"

"Sorry?"

"Learning to drive a car—I really have to deal with getting a car. It always gets pushed back, but . . . I am a little buzzed," she admitted, and drank the potion.

"Learning to drive." Connor considered, nodded. "Like that in a sense, yes. Where you need supervision until you can handle it on your own."

"At least one of us should go with you when you try again."

"You sort of hypnotized me."

"I helped you find the right meditative state, is all. You've a very active mind, and need practice quieting it."

"It meant a lot to me to see her. Really see her." Reaching in her pocket, Iona pulled out the lemon she'd taken from the blue and green bowl, brought it to her face to inhale the scent.

"Family's the root, and the heart. Now, see what you can do with this." She opened a drawer, took out a printed list.

"A wand tipped with a rose quartz crystal," Iona read. "An athame, decorated with a Celtic trinity knot, a silver cup of the Fire Goddess, Belisma, a copper pentagram amulet."

Frowning, Iona looked up. "The four elemental tools?"

"Very good, the wand for air, the knife for fire, and so on. Read on."

"Okay, a sword with a bloodstone in the hilt, and its sheath; a spear with a sharpened tip of hematite; a shield decorated with a pentagram and hematite, amethyst, sunstone, and red jasper; and a cauldron with the symbol of fire. The four corresponding weapons."

"You've studied. Now you'll do a seeking spell, and find them."

"Like a scavenger hunt?"

"In a way, yes, like that."

"Well, I like a good game."

"'Tisn't one," Connor told her. "But practice, and important. We'll need to seek him out when we're ready to take him on for once and done."

"We'll have an advantage if we know when and how he comes," Branna added.

"Why don't we seek him now? He's got to have a lair of some kind. We could—"

"We're not ready, and if we seek, he may know. He has power, and if we can't block him, he'll see. But when we're ready, we'll want him to see—what we want him to see. When the time comes," Branna continued, "the three of us will seek and find, combining our power, as the three."

"And Fin?"

"I . . ."

"It's Fin who should seek, and find." Connor turned to his sister, held her gaze with a quiet look. "He's of the blood, and that would be for him."

"You trust so much."

"And you too little. It's for him, Branna. You know it as I do."

"All right, we'll come to that when we do. But now let's deal with this. This is for you to do, Iona. Do the spell, each one in turn, find what you seek, and bring each one in turn, here."

"Okay." She glanced at the list again, folded it into her pocket. Then closed her eyes and tried to visualize the wand. "What I see within my mind, I will seek and I will find. Bring it now before my eyes and I will go to where it lies. Slim and strong it calls to me. As I will, so mote it be."

She saw it clearly, catching the late light of the sun on the little table by the window in the music room. "Be right back."

Connor leaned on the counter where Branna began to meticulously label her cooled candle jars.

"It pains you, I know." His voice stayed as quiet as his eyes. "But if you don't accept what Fin is, what he truly is, and believe in him, in his loyalty, it limits us all."

"I'm trying. I can get past the hurt, or can most days. Trust is a harder thing."

"He'd die for you."

"Don't say it," she snapped. "Do you think I'd want that? I only want to do what must be done, and I will. I will. You're right that he should be the one to seek, to find. You're right. Leave it at that for now."

"All right, we'll leave it there." Then he smiled a little, to soothe her. "Want to time her?"

"No hurry." Branna shrugged, relieved he could leave it, that he would, for her sake. "Some of them are easy to build her confidence. Others will take more."

"Well then, I'm ready for a pint. Want one?"

"Hmm. A glass of wine might be nice. And don't fool with the pork roast I have in the oven."

"Pork roast?"

"Leave it be, and what's in with it. I've got a timing spell on the lot as I didn't know how long this would take. Bring the bottle, why don't you, and a glass for Iona. She can have it when she's done."

Iona rushed in, flushed with victory, brandishing the wand. "Got it."

"Nicely done. Set it down there, and find the next."

"Okay. You're labeling. I was going to help you."

"There'll be plenty more. The athame."

"Right." On a deep breath, Iona began again.

Connor had his pint and played a little tug-the-rope with the dog while Branna finished the first round of candles. Iona traveled back and forth, bringing in the listed items.

"Jesus, this spear." Iona hefted it, miming a warrior as she strode back in. "Took me as long to find as everything else so far combined."

Not quite, Branna thought, but long enough.

"I could *see* it, and the tree you had it leaning against outside, but I couldn't tell which tree. So I did a secondary spell for that after I'd wandered around out there for a while."

"A good choice. We'll work a bit more so you'll narrow it as we go."

Iona gave a nod to the items she'd spread on a counter. "They're all so cool. Anyway, just two more."

The shield eluded her so long she nearly switched to the cauldron, but Branna had instructed each in turn, so she cleared her mind—a challenge, as it was so damn full—then refreshed the spell.

She found the shield—and oh my God, a work of art it was, hanging in the earthy, herby-smelling greenhouse.

"She's done well," Connor commented, rubbing the dog with his foot as the game had played out. "Under difficult circumstances."

"She has, and they are. She'll be better yet, as the circumstances will worsen."

"Always a happy note in you, Branna."

"Always a realistic one." With the candles she'd finished boxed for transport to her shop, she began to set the ones she'd culled out on shelves.

"Found it." Iona hauled in the cauldron. "In the little attic over your room, Branna—that I didn't even know was there."

"It's not used for much. And so you've found all."

"Each in its turn." Iona set the cauldron by the rest. "Every one of them is beautiful, and unique."

"So they are. Tools they may be, but I don't see why a tool shouldn't be beautiful as well as practical and useful. So they're yours."

"Sorry, what?" Because her mind was full again, Iona simply stared at Branna.

"They're yours now." Branna poured her a glass of wine, passed it to her. "Connor and I chose them for you, from what has been given to us, or what we collected, or what we found elsewhere since you came to us."

"But—" Overwhelmed, she couldn't come up with the words that so often rolled out of her mind and straight off her tongue.

"Every witch needs her own tools," Branna continued. "And these are the most important of them. You'll find and choose others for yourself along the way."

"Fire comes easiest to you." Connor rose to join them. "So the symbols are yours. And on the athame, the trinity knot for the three in you, and the three of us."

"The rose quartz on the wand, for it seems your power comes from your instincts—the belly—and then passes through the heart. Bloodstone on the sword for strength."

"Stones of protection—physical and psychic—for the shield. Hematite for your spear tip, for confidence in your air." Connor tapped a finger on it. "And the pentacle of copper, Sorcha's chosen medium."

"I don't know what to say to you."

"The sword and shield have been passed down, blood to blood," Branna told her. "The cup I found in a shop I favor, as Connor found the pentacle in another. So there's a mix here of old and new."

Tears she'd denied herself the night before wanted to rush up now, from her heart. In sheer gratitude. "Thank you, more than I can say. It seems like so much, too much."

"It's not," Branna corrected. "You must be armed for what's coming."

"I know. A sword." Carefully, she drew it from its sheath. "I don't know how to use it."

"You will. Some will come through it to you."

"Some," Connor agreed. "And Fin can work with you, and Meara as well. She's bloody good with a sword. Either Branna or I can help with the spear, but I think you'll find the tool itself will fit your hand."

"Once you've cleansed them, and recharged them," Branna added. "That's not for us to do. I think we'll have dinner now. We can all use the break and the food. Then you'll tend to them."

"I'll treasure them. Thank you. Thank you," she repeated, taking Branna's hand, then Connor's, linking the three. "You've opened up my life in so many ways."

"You're part of ours. Come then, we'll eat. I've prepared a special meal anticipating your success here. Bring your wine, as you've yet to drink it."

"One day I'll pay you back for all you've done."

"It's not a matter of payment, and can't be."

"You're right. That was the wrong term. Balance. One day I'll find the balance."

She started on it by setting the table, and telling Connor he was banned from kitchen cleanup. He didn't argue. Her mood, lifted from seeing Nan, from the gifts, went rising higher when she sampled the little feast Branna had prepared.

"God, this is so good! I know I'm hungry, but this is just amazing. I swear you could open your own restaurant."

"That's something I won't be doing now, or ever. Cooking, like tools, is necessary. No reason it shouldn't be good."

"I wish mine was. I really have to learn."

"Plenty of time for it, and more important things to learn now. Connor, Frannie at the shop tells me Fergus Ryan got drunk as two penny whores on holiday and walked into Sheila Dougherty's house, thinking it was his own, stripped down to the skin and passed out on the living room sofa. Where a none-too-pleased Sheila Dougherty—she who's about seventy-eight and mean as a rattlesnake—found him in the morning. What do you know of that?"

"I know of the black eye Fergus is sporting, and the knot raised on the back of his head from the whack of Mrs. Dougherty's cane. And how he managed to grab only his boots and his aching head while trying to defend himself, and ran straight out with the old woman chasing him and flinging curses and whatever else came to hand."

"I thought you would." Branna picked up her wine. "Tell all."

So the conversation turned to local gossip, business, stories. The kind of meal, Iona would think as she dealt with dishes and pots, she'd had only rarely growing up, and had craved all the more from the lack.

So, like the gift of her tools, she'd treasure it, and all those that came.

For now, she tried to embrace the quiet, as Branna and Connor were upstairs or about somewhere on their own devices. She had work yet. The cleansing for tonight. And tomorrow she'd imbue and recharge what was now hers.

A good day, she congratulated herself. She'd gone to work, had her first face-to-face with Boyle, and gotten through it without humiliating herself.

Major points.

And she'd flown to Nan's kitchen, a personal high point.

She'd worked seeking spells, and had the priceless reward from it.

To cap it, she'd had a meal with her cousins full of talk and laughter.

And tomorrow, she'd do whatever tomorrow brought her way.

To start on that balance, she cleaned the kitchen to a sparkle. The next time Branna walked in, she thought, giving it all a narrowed eye, it would damn near blind her.

Satisfied, she started to walk through to the workshop to begin her last task of the day, when the knock on the front door stopped her.

Normally, the prospect of company would have pleased her, but she really wanted to get started on her tools. Probably one of Connor's mates or prospective lady friends, she thought. She'd yet to meet anyone who didn't love Connor, or seek him out when they wanted a good time, or needed a shoulder for a bad one.

When she opened the door, her greeting smile faded, as there was Boyle standing there with a big, bright spring bouquet.

She managed an "Oh."

He looked so sexy, so appealing, big, scarred hand around stems, his face just a bit flushed, his eyes full of embarrassed determination.

And he shifted his weight and nearly did her in.

"I'm sorry. I need to tell you I'm sorry. These are for you."

"They're beautiful." Better, she thought, so much better for herself if she just sent him on his way. But she couldn't do it, not when he'd brought her flowers and a sincere apology. "Thank you," she said instead, and took the flowers. "They're really beautiful."

"Will they get me in the door, for a minute or two?"

"All right. Sure. I want to go back and put these in water." She led the way back to the kitchen, using every trick she'd learned to keep her mind, her heart, quiet and steady.

"It shines in here," he commented.

"I've been balancing some scales." She found a large, pretty vase of mossy green, Branna's kitchen flower scissors, and the flower food her cousin made herself. And set to work.

"I'm sorry, Iona, for upsetting you, for hurting you. I never would have meant to."

"I know that." The flowers, so lovely, the scents, so poignant, helped her with her own balance. "I'm not angry with you, Boyle. Not anymore."

"You should be. I earned it."

"Maybe. But you weren't completely wrong in what you said to Fin. I did push, and I did get in your way."

"I'm not one to be pushed if I'm not wanting to be. Iona—"

"You were attracted to me. I used that. I never used magick."

"I know it. I know it." Trying to find the words, he raked his fingers though his hair. "I'm not used to all this going on inside me. I lost my seat, and you happened to come in before I'd righted it again. Give me a chance, will you, to make it up?"

"It's not that, or not only that."

Balance, she thought again. She wouldn't find it without being honest with herself, and with him.

"Everything about you came on me so fast, and I just went with it. Grabbed for it, and I think, held on too tight. I didn't want it all to slip away. I always wanted to feel all this going on inside me. I've craved it like breath. So I got in your way, I got in your bed, and I didn't let myself think what could go wrong."

"It doesn't have to be wrong. It's not wrong," he said, and took her shoulders.

"It's not right either." Cautious, she stepped to the side so he no longer touched her. "Do you want a beer? I didn't even ask if you—"

"I don't want a bloody beer. It's you I want."

Her eyes, blue and beautiful even touched with sadness, lifted to his. "But you don't want to want me. That's still true. And I can't keep accepting that, keep settling for that just because I always have. It goes all the way back, Boyle. My parents never really noticed when I wasn't there, or cared much when I was or I wasn't. And more awful yet, didn't notice that I knew."

"I'm sorry to say it, as they're your ma and da, but it strikes me, Iona, your parents are right shits."

She laughed a little. "I guess they sort of are. I think they love me, as much as they can, because they're supposed to, but not because they want to. The boys and men I've tried to fall in love with? They'd want me back for a while, but they never wanted me enough, or wanted to want me enough, so it went away. And then I'm left wondering, what's wrong with me? Why can't someone love me without reservations, without all the buffers? Or worse, that I'm a kind of placeholder till someone better comes along."

Had he done that? he wondered. Had he added to that? "There's nothing wrong with you, and it's nothing of the kind."

"I'm working on believing that, and I can't unless I stop accepting less. And that's *my* problem, *my* issue. Maybe I didn't really, all the way, realize that until you punched me in the face with it. Metaphorically," she added with an easier smile than she'd expected to pull off.

Because he could see her face still, as she'd stood there in the stables, he felt as though he'd struck her. "Oh Christ, Iona. I'd give anything to take the words back, to stuff them down my own throat and choke on them."

"No. No." She took his hands a moment and squeezed. "Because it knocked me down, I had to get up. And this time deal all the way. Because before that, Boyle, I'd have taken anything you'd given. I'd have wrapped my own gauzy layers around it and convinced myself that it was right. But it would never have been right. I can't be happy, not really down-to-the-bone happy, with less than I need. And if I'm not happy, I can't make someone else happy."

"Tell me what you need, and I'll give it to you."

"It doesn't work like that." And God, she loved him more that he would try, that he'd be willing to try. "Maybe it is magick after all. What makes us love and need and want one person, over everyone else. Love and need and want them absolutely. I want the magick. I'm not settling for less. You're why. So in a strange way I'm grateful."

"Oh yeah, thank me now and put a fine, foamy head on it."

"You showed me that I'm worth more than I thought, or let myself think. And that's a lot to be grateful for. I'm the one who rushed in, so I'm the one responsible for the fallout. It was all too fast, too intense. It's no wonder you felt cornered."

"I never felt . . . I don't know what I was talking about."

"You'll figure it out. Meanwhile, the flowers are beautiful, and so was your apology." She carried them over, put them on the table. "On second thought, I can tell you some things I need."

"Anything."

"I need to go on working for you and Fin, not only because I need to make a living, but because I'm good at it. And because I love it, and I want to do what I love."

"There's no question about that. I told you."

"And I need to be friends with you, so we're not awkward or uncomfortable around each other. It's important. I couldn't handle working for you or with you if we held on to resentment or difficult feelings. I'd end up walking away from the job to spare us both, and then I'd just be pissed off and sad."

"There's no resentment from me. I can't promise no difficult feelings, for that's what they are. They're all tangled for me, and slippery with it. If you'd just—"

"Not this time." Not with you, she thought, because with him, she'd never get up again whole. "I don't just. I'm responsible for my feelings, and you for yours. You'll figure it out," she repeated. "But we both have good work that matters to us, good friends in common. And more important than anything, right here, right now, we have a common enemy and purpose. We can't do all we have to do if we're not on solid footing."

"When did you get so bloody logical?" he muttered.

"Maybe I'm borrowing a little from Branna. She's taught me a lot, shown me more than I ever imagined I'd see. I have a legacy, and I'm going to be true to it. I'm going to fight for it. And I'm going to be true to myself."

"So it's work together, fight together, and be friends? And that's the lot of it?"

She offered another smile. "That's a lot for most people. And I'm not holding back sex as a punishment."

"I wasn't meaning . . . Though now that you say it, it has that effect. It wasn't just sex, Iona. Don't think it."

"No, it wasn't. But I pushed there, too. Jumping in, as I tend to, well, boots first."

"I like the way you jump in. But if it's what you need, it's friends." For now, he thought.

"Good. Want that beer now?"

He nearly said yes, to buy more time, and maybe to soften the line she'd drawn between them. But she'd told him what she needed from him, and he'd give it.

"I'd best be on. I've all that untangling to do, after all."

"Might as well get started."

"I'll let myself out, and see you in the morning." He started to go, turned for a moment just to look at her. So bright, so pretty, with all the flowers beside her. "You deserve all, Iona, and not a bit less."

She closed her eyes when she heard the front door close behind him. It was so hard to stand firm, to do and say what she knew was right when her heart ached. When her heart yearned to take less, and make do.

"Not with him," she murmured. "Maybe with anyone else, but not with him. Because . . . there's only him."

She'd leave the flowers on the table, for everyone to enjoy. But before she went back to the workshop to cleanse her tools, she found a tall, slim vase, chose three flowers—a magick number—and, sliding them in, took them to her room where she'd see them before sleep. Where she'd see them when she waked in the morning.

19

As spring spread over Mayo, through the green forests, over the lush hills, rains came soft and steady. Wildflowers rose and opened to drink, gardens burst to glorious life. In the fields lambs bleated, ducks plied the lough, while the forest filled with birdsong.

Iona planted flowers and vegetables and herbs with her cousins, scraped mud off her boots, put in long hours at the stables, long hours with the craft.

Bealtaine with its maypoles and songs came and went, and brought the solstice closer.

As the days lengthened, she often rose before dawn and worked well into the night, using the energy that fueled her to push harder.

And in the rain and the mud, she learned how to handle a sword.

Though she couldn't imagine herself in an actual sword fight, she liked the way it felt in her hand. Liked the heft of it, and the fact that—small but mighty—she could strike and block.

She'd never be in Meara's league. Her friend resembled an Amazon warrior even more with her hair braided back and a sword in her hand. But she learned—angles, footwork, maneuvers.

Within the thin veil Branna conjured she sliced and parried while Meara, relentless, drove her back. While the swords sang and Meara shouted insults or instructions, Branna sat on a garden bench like some exotic housewife, calmly peeling potatoes for dinner.

"Put your shoulder into it!"

"I am!" Winded, and seriously starting to ache, Iona shifted her weight, tried to advance.

"Come *at* me, for feck's sake. I could slice off your limbs like you were Monty Python's Black Knight."

"It's only a flesh wound." Giggles caught her, distracted her, and Meara moved in like a demon.

"Mind the . . ." Branna sighed hugely as Iona lost her footing and fell backward into a massive spread of wild blue lobelia.

"Ah well."

"Ouch. Sorry."

"You've got the basics well enough." Sheathing her sword, Meara held a hand down to help pull Iona to her feet. "And you take your lumps like a woman. You've good speed and agility, and endurance enough. But you've no killer in the blood, and so you'll always be bested."

Iona rubbed her butt. "I never planned on killing anyone."

"Plans change," Branna pointed out. "Fix those flowers now, as it's your rump that crushed them."

"Oh yeah." Iona turned back to them, considered.

"No." Branna snapped her fingers. "Don't stop and think, just do."

"I'm just catching my breath."

"You may not have time for that. Sword, magick, a blend of both. And wit to tie them together. Just do."

So she held out her hands in instinct rather than plan. The crushed blue flowers plumped.

"I gave them a little boost while I was at it."

"So I see." With a faint smile, Branna plied her paring knife.

"I could use a shower and a beer. No, beer first."

"We'll go again, then a beer," Meara told her. "Don't hold back this time. Didn't Branna tell you she'd charmed the blades as dull as our first form science teacher? Remember her, Branna?"

"To my sorrow, I do. Miss Kenny, who could out-sister the sisters for the hard eye and bore your brain to liquid between your ears."

"I heard she moved to Donegal and married a fishmonger."

"I pity him." Branna rose with her bowl of potatoes, her compost bucket of peels. "I'll put these on and fetch the beer while the two of you hack at each other."

Stalling, as she really did need to catch her breath, Iona studied her sword. "You don't really think we'll use these, this way, against Cabhan."

"There's no telling, is there? And as I don't have what you do, this may be what I'll use and need should the time come."

"Why don't you sound scared?"

"I've known of the legend all my life, and the hard fact of it since I've known Branna, which seems forever. That's the one part. And on the other . . ." Meara looked around her, the new plantings, those from past years spreading and spearing, the woods beyond in their rainy evening gloom.

"It doesn't seem real, does it? That come the solstice we'll try to end all this by whatever means we can. Blood and magick, blade and fang. It's not life, but a story. And yet it is. I'm caught up in that, I think. Above that, when it comes, I'll be with people I trust more than any others. So, the fear's not there. Yet."

"I wish it were now. Some nights I think, let it be tomorrow, so it can be over. Then in the morning, I think, thank God it's not today, so I have another day. Not just to practice, to learn, but—"

"To live."

"To live, to be here. To be a part of all this. To ride Alastar, to work, to see my cousins, and you and . . ."

"Boyle."

Iona shrugged, almost managed casual. "I like seeing him. I think we've been dealing with everything really well. Being friends was the right answer."

"Oh bollocks. You're friends right enough, but that'll never be all. The pair of you send out so much haze that's sex and lust and emotion I don't know how any of us see straight."

"I'm not sending out anything. Am I?"

"Sure you are. I don't suppose a woman in love can help it. But plenty's coming from his direction." Meara threw up her hands at the thought of so many she cared about refusing to reach for what they wanted most. "Iona, the man brought you flowers, and I'm thinking the only woman he's carried bouquets to might be his ma or his granny. And aren't the drinks you like stocked in the little fridge?"

"Ah, now that you mention it—"

"Who do you think's seen to that? And who brought you a toasted sandwich when you couldn't stop for lunch just yesterday?"

"He'd do the same for anyone."

Meara could only roll her eyes skyward. "He did it for you. And didn't I hear him with my own ears tell you only days ago that the blue sweater you wore to the pub looked fine on you? And who made sure you sat out of the draft of the door while we were there?"

"I . . . didn't notice."

"Because you're trying so hard not to notice. You're putting everything you can into your work, your practice so you don't have much left to think of him, because it's hard for you. At the same time you've blinded yourself to the wondrous fact that the man's besotted. He's wooing you."

"He is not." The heart she'd worked so hard to steady stumbled a little. "He is?"

"Try to notice," Meara advised. "Now come at me like you mean it." She drew her sword. "And earn that beer."

SHE LET HERSELF NOTICE, A LITTLE, THE NEXT DAY. SHE KNEW she had a habit of letting hope overrule everything else. All logic, all sense and self-preservation could, and usually did, fizzle under the bright light of hope.

Not this time, she warned herself. Too much at stake. But she could notice, a little, if there was something to notice.

He brought Alastar to her, and that was hard not to notice. Boyle rode him over rather than drive the horse in the trailer Alastar detested.

"I thought you might want him today, as you've three guideds on your slate."

"I always want him." She cupped Alastar's face, rubbed cheeks with him. And sent Boyle a sidelong glance. "Thanks for thinking of it."

"Oh well, it's no trouble, and he's needing the exercise. I've a mind to switch out two of the horses for tomorrow, so I'll be riding Caesar over to the stables tonight if you're wanting to ride this one back. I'll drive you home from there if it suits you."

"Sounds good."

Nothing in his tone, she thought, but friendship, as agreed. And yet . . . "I'll put him in the paddock until I've checked in the first group."

She took the reins, rolled her aching right shoulder, gave it an absent rub.

"Are you hurt?"

"What? No. Just sore. Sword arm," she said, a little cocky, brandishing her arm. "Meara's a brute."

"She's a fierce one. Why haven't you fixed it? Or had Connor do it?"

"Because it serves to remind me not to drop my guard."

She led the horse away, determined not to look back. But she *felt* his eyes on her. And wasn't that interesting enough to let just a little hope eke through?

He didn't stint on the work he assigned. As a result, she stayed busy—body and mind—until midafternoon when he shifted her balance again by bringing her a bottle of the Coke she preferred.

"Thanks."

"It seemed you should wet the throat you must've worked dry calling out corrections to the student you had in the ring."

"She's really young." Grateful, Iona took a long sip. "And she likes the idea of riding. She just doesn't put much into learning how. I think she mostly likes the outfits she gets to wear, and how she looks on a horse."

"Her parents are divorcing it seems."

"Oh, that's rough. She's only eight."

"It's been coming on awhile, from what I hear. And it seems their way of compensating is to indulge her and her brother. Her with the fancy boots and riding pants and such and him with video games and sports jerseys."

"It won't work."

"Likely not, no. I wonder if you have a minute to take a look at our Spud. He's been off his feed today. I thought before I call the vet you could take a pass at him."

"I'll go right now. I haven't worked with him today," she said as she hurried out of the ring. "Barely saw him this morning."

She worked her way down the stalls, Boyle beside her, and stopped at Spud's.

The horse just gave her a sorrowful look as he moved restlessly in the stall.

"Don't feel good today, do you?" She murmured it as she opened the stall door. "Let's have a look."

In answer he kicked at his belly.

"That's where it hurts, huh?" Gently, gently, she ran her hands over him, down and around his belly.

And closing her eyes, calming her mind, she let herself see, let herself feel.

"It's not colic, so that's lucky. And not an ulcer. But it's uncomfortable, isn't it, baby? And you can't do what you like best. Eat."

"I couldn't even tempt him with a potato, his favorite."

"He's not sweating," she added. "Has he been rolling around on the floor?"

"No. Just barely touched his feed."

"Indigestion." Which, it occurred to her, Boyle would've thought of himself. But now there they were, the two of them in the stall together, close, arms brushing now and then as they stroked the horse.

"I think I can take care of it, if you trust me to."

"I would, and more, he would. He's not fond of the vet for all that. And if indigestion it is, we can always dose him. But he's not in favor of that overly either."

"Let's see if we can avoid it. Would you hold his head?"

As Boyle moved to do so, she crouched down, hands sliding, gliding over Spud's belly. "It aches," she said quietly. "So hard to understand the hurt. You've been eating too fast, that's all. Slow down and enjoy it more. Quiet now, quiet."

Her stomach burned a moment as she drew the pain away, but she felt Spud's relax under her touch. Heard his snort of relief.

"Better now, that's better. And I bet you're already starting to think about eating again."

She rose, saw Boyle staring at her.

"You go to gleaming," he told her. "It's a dazzle."

"It's odd because it feels so calm now to do it. And with little hits like that I'm not immediately thinking about food myself. It wouldn't hurt to put some of that homeopathic potion in his feed, just to cover the tracks."

"Sure I'll do that, and thanks for this. He's a favorite around here as you know." He continued to stand at Spud's head, blocking the stable door. "So, are you faring well, Iona?"

"Yeah. Fine. You?"

"Oh, well and fine. Busier as you know with spring."

"And summer follows."

"And summer follows. We're to meet again in another two days, to talk of that. I wondered if there was anything I could do for you in the meantime? If you wanted some time off so you could . . . do what you do at home, have more time to put into that."

"Working here keeps me sane, I think. And balanced. The routine of it, and knowing I want that routine when this is over."

"If ever you did need the time, you've only to tell me."

"I will."

"I could buy you a pint for the vet service after work—in a friendly way," he added. "After the workday if you've a mind for it."

He'd do the same for anyone, she reminded herself. But . . .

"I would, but Branna's expecting me. She's a brute just like Meara. We haven't much time left before the solstice."

"No, there's not much left. It's weighing on you."

"Not being sure what I'll need to do, what I'm meant to do weighs. Both Branna and Connor have blocked any thought of me going to the cabin ruins before the solstice. They seem to think I'll pull more from it the very first time, and that may help."

"You'd tell me if you . . . had more dreams or any encounter with him?"

"It's been quiet. That weighs, too. He's watching, you can feel it. But not too close." She shuddered, rubbed her arms.

"I don't mean to upset you talking of it."

"It's not the talking. It's the waiting."

"Waiting," he said with a slow nod. "It's never easy. Iona, I want to—" Mick hailed him, and came down the stalls with quick boot clicks.

"There you are. I wanted to ask if . . ." With his gaze shifting from Iona to Boyle, Mick flushed. "Beg pardon. I'm interrupting."

"No, that's fine." Boyle shuffled his feet, turned. "We're just finished with Spud here."

"I'll dose him, chart it," Iona offered.

"Thanks for that."

Alone, Iona leaned against the horse. "He's been starting conversations," she realized. "He never does that, but he has been, ever since . . . And he bought me Cokes." She stepped out, picked up the bottle she'd set outside the stable door, took a long pull.

"Hell, Spud, I think maybe I am being wooed. And I have absolutely no idea how to handle it. Nobody ever really tried before."

With a sigh, she studied the bottle in her hand, wondered what it said about her that her heart was so easy it could be touched by a damn soft drink.

Just . . . see what happens, she warned herself, then went to get Spud's medicine.

NOTHING HAPPENED REALLY—CONVERSATIONS, SMALL ATtentions, casual offers of help. But he made no move toward more. A good thing, Iona reminded herself as she helped Branna prepare the group dinner. She'd meant everything she'd said to him when he'd brought the flowers to her, the apology to her.

For once in her life she intended to be sensible, to be safe, to look—both ways—before she leaped.

"Your thoughts are so loud they're giving me a headache," Branna complained.

"Sorry, sorry. I can't seem to stop the loop. Okay, we'll put it on pause. I've never made scalloped potatoes before. Not even out of a box."

"Don't talk of potatoes in a box in this kitchen."

"Only as an insult. Am I doing it right?"

"Just keep doing the layers as I showed you." At the stove, Branna stirred the glaze she intended to use on the ham she had baking.

"Fancy meal for a strategy meeting."

"I was in the mood. And now we'll have cold ham for days if I'm not in the mood again."

Conscientiously, Iona sprinkled flour over the next layer of sliced potatoes. "I was thinking about Boyle."

"Is that a fact? Never would I have guessed."

Rolling her eyes at Branna's back, Iona added the salt and pepper, started the butter. "How do you know? I can't figure out how you know, sensibly, and that's what I'm working on. Is he just missing the sex, maybe even the companionship on some level? Is he feeling guilty because he hurt me, trying to be nice to make up for it, to be friendly because that's what I asked? Or, does he, maybe, care more than he thought?"

"I'm the wrong one to ask about matters of the heart. Some say I barely have one."

"No one who knows you says that."

Some did, and there were times she wished they had the right of it.

"I don't know about men, Iona. Whenever I think I do, think I've got it all in a box, just as it is, it all scrambles out when I'm not looking. When I get it all back in, it's something else than it was.

"I know my brother, but a brother's a different thing."

"Love shouldn't be hard."

"There I think you're wrong. I think it should be the hardest thing there is, then it's not so easily given away, or taken away, or just lost."

Stepping away from the stove, she moved over to check Iona's progress. "Well, it's taking you long enough as you've all but placed each slice of potato like an explosive, so careful and precise. But you've got that done. Take it over and pour that hot milk right over it."

"Just pour it over it?"

"Yes, and not drop by drop. Dump it on, put on the cover, stick it in the oven. Timed this first part, for thirty minutes."

"Okay, got it." And as if it might explode, Iona let out a breath of relief when she had it inside the oven with the ham.

"You know they shouldn't both fit in there."

"They fit as I want them to. Now I think we'll do a side of the green beans I blanched and froze from the garden last year, then we'll . . . There's someone coming now," she said as she heard the sound of cars. "Let's just see who it is, and how we can put them to use in here."

"I'm all for it. You know," Iona continued as they walked to the front of the cottage, "I think my goal should be to be able to put one really good meal together—figure out what that is, make it my thing. Oh, Iona's making her brisket. I'm not even sure what brisket is, but it could be mine."

"A fine goal indeed."

Branna opened the door. Outside Meara stood beside her truck, Fin climbed out of his, and both Connor and Boyle shoehorned their way out of a bright red Mini.

"Isn't that the cutest thing?" With a laugh, Iona stepped closer. "How did you guys fit in there?"

"It wasn't a simple matter," Connor told her. "Nor was driving it, as Boyle's knees sat at his ears the whole way. But she cleaned up well, and runs fine enough. Seems a better fit for you."

"Get in and see," Meara suggested.

Obliging, Iona slid in, put her hands on the wheel. "Much more my size. Is this from the friend you told me about?" she asked Connor. "It's great. It's really adorable, but I don't think I can afford adorable at this point."

"But you like it," he prompted. "The look of it, the color and feel and so on."

"What's not to like?" In fact, she could already picture herself driving around like a little red rocket. "It's just perfect. Do you think he'd consider holding it, letting me pay some now, some later?"

"Well, he might, but it's already sold." Connor glanced at Branna, got her nod. "Happy birthday."

"What?"

"It's Connor and Boyle who found the car, and we all put in a share to buy it. For your birthday," Branna added. "Do you think we didn't know it's your birthday?"

"I didn't— I thought with everything that's going on it was better to— But you can't just . . . A car? You can't."

"Already have," Connor pointed out. "And whatever else there is, a birthday's a thing to remember. We're your circle, Iona. We wouldn't be forgetting yours."

"But it's a *car.*"

"One that's over ten years old, and truth be told, wheezes like an asthmatic on damp mornings. Which is nearly daily," Fin commented. "But she'll do for you."

She began to laugh, and to weep. On a combination of both, she scooted out to throw her arms around Connor as he stood closest. Then she spun to each one in turn.

When her body pressed to Boyle's, her arms squeezed hard around him, he struggled not to make it more. To just let it be.

"I don't know what to say. Don't know how to say it. It's amazing! Beyond amazing. Thank you so much. All of you."

"There'll be a bit of paperwork to see to," Fin put in, "but you can see to it later. Now you should try it out, shouldn't you?"

"I should drive it. I should *drive* it." On another laugh, Iona spun in a circle. "Someone has to go with me on my first voyage. Who wants to go?"

Every man stepped back as one.

"Cowards," Meara said in disgust. "What do you say, Branna? We could squeeze in."

"I expect we could, but I've dinner on."

Meara only let out a snort. "Well, I'm not afraid. I'm with you, Iona."

She jumped in, waited while Iona slid behind the wheel.

Iona started the car, bounced on the seat, wiggled into it. She lurched forward three times. Fit, start, fit, start, fit, start, then zipped down the road weaving like the cloth loop on a potholder loom.

"Ah God," was all Boyle managed.

"I told you I put a little charm for safety on it," Connor reminded him. "She just needs a bit of practice as she's a Yank after all. So Fin here's contributed bottles of champagne to the birthday feast, and being Fin, it's fancy and French. I say we have the first bottle waiting for her."

"We've important business to discuss as well," Branna reminded him. "And should be doing that with clear heads rather than French bubbles."

"It's her birthday."

"Ah well." On a sigh, Branna relented. "One bottle among us shouldn't hurt anything."

"I SHOULD'VE BEEN AFRAID," MEARA MUTTERED TO CONNOR on the return as Fin popped the first cork. "She's a right terrible driver."

"Only needs practice."

"Please the gods and be right on that as I thought she'd do us both in the first kilometer. Still, it's worth it. She never expected such a thing. Not just the gift, but the whole of it. And I think for all my family is fucked, I've never given a thought but there'd be a bit of a fuss for my birthday."

"We've cake as well."

"I never doubted it." In the mood, Meara gave him a quick and affectionate one-armed hug.

He linked his arm around her before she could pull away, did a quick step. Laughing, she mimicked the footwork, then reached for the glass Fin held out. "I'll take that for certain."

"I'm going to make a toast," Iona decided. "Because I've thought of what I want to say. In addition to thank you, which just doesn't cover it. All of you, you're mine, and that's a gift I'll always treasure. Every one of you is a gift to me, a blend of friends and family that's stronger and truer and brighter than anything I ever imagined having. So, to all of us, together."

She sipped. "Oh God, that's really good!"

"A fine toast, and fine champagne." Branna opened a cupboard, took a wrapped gift off a shelf. "And from your grandmother. I put it aside for her as she asked me."

"Oh, Nan." Delighted, Iona set the glass aside to open the gift, took out a sweater in dreamy blues. "She'd have made it," Iona murmured, rubbing it to her cheek. "It's so soft. She'd have made it for me."

She took out the card, opened that.

For my Iona. There's love and charms and hope in every stitch. Wear it when you want to feel most confident and strong. With wishes for your happiness today, and all days.

Love, Nan

"She never forgets."

"Put it on," Meara urged her. "I've never seen a lovelier jumper."

"Good idea. I'll be right back."

"When you're back, we'll begin," Branna said. "We've time before the food's done to talk of the solstice, and what we'll do. We do it well and right," she added, "and on Iona's next birthday, we'll have nothing but friends and food and wine. And that's a gift for all of us."

"Well said," Fin murmured. "Put on your gift, as it brings your grandmother close. Branna and I will shroud the house. No eye, no ear, no mind but ours will know what we do here, say here, think here tonight."

20

THEY USED LIGHT, NOT DARK, TO CLOAK THE COTTAGE and all in it. If Cabhan looked, as shadow, as man, as wolf, he would see only the light, the colors, hear only music, laughter.

It would, Branna explained, bore him, or annoy him. And he would think they simply played while he plotted.

"At moonrise, on the longest day, we form the circle on the ground where Sorcha lived, and where she died."

Candles flickered throughout the kitchen where Branna spoke. The scents of cooking, the simmering hum of the fire, the steady breaths of the dog who slept under the table all spoke of ordinary things while they talked of the extraordinary.

And that, Iona realized, was the point.

"It's for Fin to seek him, to lure him. Blood to blood."

"You still doubt me."

Branna shook her head. "I don't. Or only a little," she admitted.

"Not enough to stop doing what has to be done. What I understand is this can't be done without you, and shouldn't be. Isn't that enough?"

"It'll have to be, won't it?"

Their eyes held, a long, long moment. In it Iona felt thousands of words, scores of impossible feelings passed between them. Only them.

"I'll get him there," Fin said, and broke that moment.

"Meara and Boyle must stay inside the circle—at all costs. Not just to protect yourselves." Branna turned to them. "But to hold it strong. And Fin as well must stay within it."

"Damned to that."

"Fin, you must," Branna insisted. "Within the circle he can't use what runs in you against you, or against us. And what you have will hold it without chink."

"Four of us outside it, against him, are stronger than three."

Facing him, Branna lifted her hands, palms up. And the flames of every candle burned brighter. "We are the three. We are the blood, and we must be the way."

"Within the circle I'll stay," Fin told her. "Until or unless I feel we've more chance ending him with me outside of it. It's the best bargain I can give you."

"We'll take it." Connor spoke up, shifted his gaze from Fin to Branna, left it coolly on her. "And done."

Branna started to speak, sighed instead. "And done then."

"We have to take our guides," Iona realized.

"We do, yes." Branna drew her amulet from under her sweater, ran a thumb over the carved head that so resembled Kathel's. "Horse, hound, hawk. And weapons and tools. I have a spell I've worked on for some time, and I think it's an answer, but only if we draw him to the right place, the right time. And then we'll need his blood to seal it."

"What spell is this?" Fin demanded.

"One I've worked on," Branna repeated. "I've used bits of Sorcha's spells, others that have come down, something of my own."

"And practiced it?"

Irritation flickered over her face. "It's too risky. If he learns of it, he can and will block against it. It must be done the first time on Sorcha's ground. You need to trust I know what I'm about."

"You must be trusted," Fin repeated.

"Bloody hell." Branna started to shove back from the table, but Iona raised a hand.

"Just wait. What kind of spell? I mean, a banishing, a drawing, a vanquishing spell? What?"

"A vanquishing, a light spell, a fire spell. All of them in one, sealed with blood magick."

"Light defeats the dark. Fire purifies. And blood is at the heart of all."

Branna smiled. "You learn well. But it may come to nothing if not done at the right time, at the right place. It will come to nothing if we all, each one, don't agree and stand together, in that time and place."

"Then we will." Iona lifted her hands as she looked from face to face. "We all know we will. You'd do anything you could to destroy him," she said to Fin. "For Branna, for yourself, for the rest of us. In that order. And Branna would do anything to sever whatever link he might have with you, so you'd be free of it. Connor and Meara would stand for love and friendship, for what's right and good whatever the risk or cost. Boyle would fight because that's how he works. You just have to say when and where, and he'd be with you. And because, whatever's changed between him and me, he'd never want anything to happen to me. And I would never want anything to happen to him.

"For love and friendship, for family and friends, we'll stand together in the right time, in the right place and fight with each other. Fight for each other."

After a moment's silence, Fin picked up the champagne he'd ignored, lifted the glass toward Iona. "All right, *deirfiúr bheag*. We'll be your happy few." He shifted toward Branna. "Trust," he said, waited.

"Trust." She lifted her own glass, touched it to his. In that quiet clink a spark of light flashed, then softened away.

"With that settled, let's get down to the nitty of it then." Connor leaned forward. "Step-by-step."

Boyle said nothing as Branna walked them through her plan, as that plan was revised, questioned, adjusted. He said nothing because looking at Iona as she'd spoken had given him all and every answer.

He'd hold on to them until it was time to give them back to her.

SHE COUNTED DOWN THE DAYS AS MAY DRIFTED INTO JUNE, and let herself cling to each one for itself. She could prize the blue skies when she had them, welcome the rain when it fell. She came to believe that whatever happened on the longest day, she'd had these weeks, these months, and these people in her life, and so her life, even for that short time, had been richer than ever before.

She'd been given a gift and learned how to use it, how to trust and respect it.

She was, and ever would be, of the three. She was, and ever would be, a dark witch of Mayo, charged with power and with light.

She believed they would triumph, her nature demanded she believe. But that gift she'd been given demanded the respect of caution and care.

As the solstice approached, she wrote a long letter to her grandmother—pen and paper, she thought. Old-school, but it was important, felt important, to take the time, make the effort. In it she spoke of love, for her grandmother, her cousins, her friends. For Boyle, and the mistakes she'd made.

She spoke of finding herself, her place, her time, and what it meant to her to have come to Ireland. And to have become there.

She asked only one thing. If something happened, her grandmother would find the amulet, take it and Alastar, and pass them both to the next.

There would be a next if she failed. That, too, she believed absolutely.

However long it took, light would beat back the dark.

ON THE MORNING BEFORE THE SOLSTICE SHE WENT DOWN early, the letter in her back pocket. She tried her hand at cooking a full breakfast fry, and though she thought she'd never be more than a half-decent cook, it didn't mean not making the effort.

Connor walked in, sniffing the air.

"And what's all this then?"

"We'll be busy tomorrow, so I thought I'd take the opportunity to do it up right and spare Branna the time. She was up late again, wasn't she?"

"Barely sleeping the past week or so, and no amount of cajoling or arguing changes it."

"I hear her music, like last night, and it smooths me right out. She does it on purpose."

"Claims she thinks clearer when the two of us aren't thinking." He snagged a sausage from the plate. "You're worried."

"I guess I am, now that it's down to hours instead of days. Why aren't you?"

"We're meant to do what we're doing. If something's meant, what's the point in worrying over it?"

For comfort, she leaned against him a moment. "You smooth me out as much as Branna's music."

"I have every faith. In you." He wrapped an arm around her waist for a squeeze. "In Branna, in myself. And in all the others as well, and as much. We'll do what's meant, and do our best. And that's all anyone can ever do."

"You're right, on all of it." She eased away to pile a plate full for him. "I feel him lurking, don't you? I feel him around the edges of my dreams trying to get in. He nearly does, and part of me realizes I'm allowing it. Then there's Branna's music, and the next I know it's morning."

Iona got down another plate, arranged about half as much on it as she had for Connor. "I'm going to leave this warming in the oven for Branna."

When she turned around, Connor just wrapped his arms around her. He had, Iona thought, the most comforting way.

"There now, stop the fretting. He's never faced the like of us three, or the three with us."

"You're right again. So let's eat, then I'm going to drive to work, taking the long way for practice."

"You'd be there in half the time if I walked you."

"True, but I wouldn't practice." Or be able to stop off at the hotel, ask if they'd post her letter the next day.

She kept her eyes peeled for any trace of fog, of the black wolf, of anything that alarmed her instincts or senses. She made it to Ashford Castle without incident or accident. Really, she thought she handled the Mini, the roads, the left-hand drive very well, whatever Meara said to the contrary.

Just as she believed she handled the throbbing nerves of the waiting, of the silence, very well.

Maybe her pulse jittered every time she looked out a window of the cottage to scan forest, road, hills. Maybe she recognized the ache of stress in her back and shoulders every time she prepared to lead a group through the green shadows and thick woods.

But she continued to look from the window, continued to guide groups. And that, Iona told herself as she pulled up to the stables, counted most.

As she was the first to arrive, she opened the doors, shifted to flip on the lights.

And there in the center of the ring stood the wolf.

The doors slammed behind her; the lights flashed off. For one shocked moment, all she could see were three red glows. The wolf's eyes, and its power stone.

They blurred when it charged.

She threw up a hand—a block, a shield. The wolf struck it with such force she felt the ground tremble. Just as she felt the cracks zig across her block like shattering glass.

She watched the shadow of its shape bunch to charge again.

She heard the cries of the horses, full of fear. And that decided her course.

As the wolf charged, she vanished the shield, jumped to the left. The momentum carried it through so it struck the doors with the force of a cannonball. When they burst open, it was Iona's turn to charge.

She rushed out, threw the shield behind her this time. It wouldn't get through, wouldn't harm the horses. Bracing her feet, she prepared to protect even as the wolf circled back. Even as it rose up on two legs and became a man.

"You're a quick one, and clever enough." As in the dreams, his voice was like cold hands gliding over the skin. And still, somehow seductive. "But young, in years and in power."

"Old enough in both."

He smiled at her. Something in her spirit repelled even as something in her body stirred.

"I could kill you with a look."

"Not so far."

"Your death isn't my wish, Iona the Bright. Only give me what has come so late to you, what is still so young, so fresh in you." Dark, dark eyes holding hers, he edged closer as he spoke in that silky voice. "I want only the power you don't yet understand, and I'll spare you. I'll spare all of you."

Her heart pounded, too hard, too fast. But her power stirred, in the belly, and would rise. She would make it rise.

"Is that all? Really? Ah . . . no." She heard the cry of the hawk overhead, and now she smiled. "Company's coming."

"You'll be the death of them. Their blood will stain your hands. Look. See. Know."

She glanced down at her hands, at the blood staining them, dripping from them to pool on the ground. The sight of it, the warmth of it, sliced true fear through her belly, through her heart.

When she looked up Cabhan was gone. And Boyle rode like a madman on Alastar up the dirt path.

"I'm fine," she called out, but her voice sounded tinny, and her knees wanted to buckle. "Everything's fine."

The hound streaked to her side as Boyle leapt from Alastar's back. "What happened?"

When he started to grab her hands, she instinctively pulled them back. Then saw, both shocked and relieved, they were clean.

"He was here, but he's gone." She leaned against the horse, as much to soothe him as for his support. The hawk landed as lightly, as neatly on Alastar's saddle as he might on a tree branch. And Kathel sat quiet at her side.

All of them here, she thought. Horse, hawk, hound.

And Boyle.

"How are you here?"

"I'd just saddled Alastar to ride him over when he let out a bloody war cry and bolted for the fence. I barely had time to jump on his back before we went over it. Let me look at you." He grabbed her, spun her around. "You're not hurt? You're sure of it?"

"No. I mean yes, I'm sure. Alastar heard me." She laid a hand on the horse's neck. "They all heard me," she murmured as the hawk watched her, as Kathel's tail gave one quick thump. And her cousins pulled up in Connor's truck, spewing dirt and gravel with the slam of brakes.

"They . . ." She paused as Fin's truck, then Meara's sped into the stable yard. "They all heard me. He couldn't stop that. It couldn't stop that from getting through."

"What the bloody, buggering hell happened?" Boyle demanded.

"I'll tell you. All of you," she said, speaking to the group. "But we need to check the horses. He didn't hurt them. I'd know if he did. But they're afraid."

She brought Alastar with her, felt the need to keep him close as she went back inside.

They would purify the ring, she thought. Branna would see to it.

She soothed the horses, one by one, and so doing soothed herself. By the time the stable hands arrived to see to the morning routine, she huddled with the rest, crowded in Boyle's little office, and told the tale.

"There's a sexuality, on the most elemental level," she added. "He uses it like a weapon. It's powerful, and it pulls. But more, he was stronger this time. Maybe he's been storing it up somehow. I don't know the answer, but I know when he hit the shield, it cracked. It wouldn't hold him back."

"So you removed it, took him straight out the doors. Clever," Fin told her.

"That's what he said. Right before he promised to spare all our lives if I gave him my power."

"He's a liar," Branna reminded her.

"I know it. I know. But the blood on my hands." Fighting a fresh shudder, she pressed her palms together. "It felt real, and it felt like yours. He knows I'm still the weak spot."

"He's wrong, and so are you if you believe it." With the lack of space, Boyle couldn't pace off the anger, so he just balled his fists into his pockets. "There's nothing weak in you."

"He wanted to scare me, and tempt me. He managed both."

"And what did you do about it?"

She nodded. "I like to think I would have, could have kept doing it if all of you hadn't come so quickly. But the point is I'm still his focus. Take what's mine, and he believes he can take the rest."

"So we'll use that. We will," Fin said before Boyle could object. "The slightest adjustment to the plan, and he'll see her as vulnerable, see it as the time and place to close in, and have it done."

"It's more complicated," Branna began.

"And since when have a few complications buggered you up?"

"More dangerous," Connor added.

"If we're in it, we're in it." Meara shrugged. "Today proves Iona can't even come to work in the morning without a risk. Why should she live that way? Or any of us?"

"The next time he might hurt the horses," Iona added. "To damage me, to distract me. I won't have that. I couldn't live with that. What adjustments?"

"He thinks you'll go alone tomorrow, to the ruins."

Iona stared at Boyle, saw the fury behind his eyes. "I'm bait. But bait with knowledge and power. And a very strong circle."

Before Boyle could curse, Branna laid a hand on his arm. "She's never alone, never will be. You've my word, and the word of all of us here."

She gave his arm a rub, then considered. "It could be done. I think it could be done well enough."

"You'll work with me on just that today then?"

Branna looked at Fin, fought her nasty internal war. "I will, for Iona. For the circle."

"We'll get started. Keep in the company of others," Fin added, tracing a finger over Iona's cheek. "For the day, keep others close, will you, little sister?"

"No problem."

It was easy enough, especially since Boyle or Meara hovered.

Boyle took her off guided rides for the day—a frustration to her—and stuck her on stable duties.

She groomed, fed, cleaned stalls, repaired tack, polished boots.

And the day dragged.

She rode Alastar to the big stables—Boyle on Spud beside her—to deal with the lesson she had scheduled for the end of the day.

This time tomorrow, she thought, she'd make the final preparations. And she'd take the next steps toward her destiny.

"We're going to win this," she said to Boyle.

"Cocksure's a foolish thing."

"It's not cocksure, or not cocky." She remembered Connor's words, and her feeling with him, in the morning kitchen. "It's faith, and faith's a strong, positive thing."

"I don't care for you being the tip of the spear in this."

"I sure didn't plan to be, but because I am, he's the one who'll be cocksure and foolish. Think about that."

"I've been thinking of it, and considerable else."

At the stables he dismounted, waited for her to do the same. "I've something to show you."

He started into the stables. Before one of the hands could speak, Boyle signaled him away, jerked a thumb and sent him out. Then led the way to the tack room with its scent of leather and oil.

"It's that."

She followed the gesture, hummed in pleasure at the gleam of the saddle sitting on its stand.

"That's new, isn't it?" She stepped to it, ran a hand over the curve, over the smooth black leather. "Beautifully made, and just look at the stirrups shine! It's hand-tooled, isn't it? It's—"

"It's yours."

"What? Mine?"

"It's made for you, specifically, and for Alastar. For the pair of you."

"But—"

"Well, I didn't know, did I, the others would be after buying the car for you, and this was meant for your birthday."

If he'd offered her a pirate's chest of gold and jewels she'd have been less stunned. "You . . . You had this made for me, for my birthday?"

His brows drew together, just short of a glower. "A horsewoman of your caliber should have her own saddle, and a fine one."

When she said nothing, he lifted the saddle, turned it over. "See, it's your name there."

Gently, she brushed her fingers over her name. Just Iona, she thought. Just her first name, and a symbol of flames beside it—Alastar's name, and a trinity knot, across from it.

"I know a man who does the work," Boyle continued, flustered when the silence dragged out. "The leather work, and the . . . ah, well, it seemed fitting to me."

"It's beautiful. It's the most beautiful gift."

"You'd sold your own."

"That's right." She looked at him then, just looked. "To come here."

"So . . . sure now you have another. And if we're to do this tomorrow, you should have it. You and Alastar should use it." He started to turn it over again, secure it. Iona put a hand over his.

"It's much more than another saddle. Much more to me." She rose on her toes, brushed her lips over one of his cheeks, the other, then lightly over his lips. "Thank you."

"You're welcome, of course, and happy birthday again. I've things to see to now. Fin'll be keeping an eye out, as he let me know he and Branna are done for today."

"All right. Thank you, Boyle."

"As you've said."

She let him go. She had a lesson to prepare for. And decisions to make.

SHE WALKED OVER TO FIN WHEN HER STUDENT LEFT. GAVE a short sigh. "I didn't give her my best today."

"I wager she'd disagree. And if you're a bit distracted today, there's cause enough."

"I guess." She glanced toward the rooms over the garage. "And you and Branna?"

"Did what we set out to do, with little drama. That's a blessing in itself. I'll take you back to the stables if you're wanting your car, then follow you home to be safe and sure."

"Oh, thanks, but . . . I want to— I need to . . . I have to talk to Boyle. About something. He can take me home, I think."

"All right then." With an easy smile rather than the laugh in his heart, Fin took Alastar's reins. "I'll just see to our boy here."

"You don't have to—"

"I'll enjoy it. And I'll say he and I have things to discuss as well."

"You do talk to him, and the other horses. The way I can."

"I do, yes."

"And the hawks—your own, Connor's, the others. Kathel, our hound. Even Bugs. All of them."

Fin moved his shoulders, a kind of half shrug that managed to be elegant and a little sad. "They're all mine, and none of them mine. There's no guide for me, as there is for you. No connection that intimate. But, well, we understand each other. Go on now, say what you need to say to Boyle."

"Tomorrow . . ."

"You'll shine, brighter than you ever have." He cupped her chin a moment, tapped a finger on her jaw. "I believe it. Go see Boyle. I'll be around and about if you need me."

She took two steps, turned. "She loves you."

Fin just stroked a hand over Alastar's neck. "I know it."

"It's harder, isn't it, knowing someone loves you and can't let it just be love?"

"It is. Harder than anything else."

With a nod, she walked over, then climbed the steps to Boyle's room. Straightened her shoulders, knocked.

When he answered the door, she had her smile ready. "Hi. Can I talk to you a minute?"

"Of course. Is something wrong?"

"No. Maybe. It depends. I need to . . ." She closed her eyes, held her hands out to the side, palms out.

He saw something shimmer, caught the faintest change of the light, of the air.

"He's focused on me," Iona said. "So he might find ways to hear, to listen, to see, even when we're inside. I don't want him to hear what we talk about."

"All right. Ah, do you want tea? Or a beer?"

"Actually, I wouldn't mind some whiskey."

"That's easily done." He crossed over to take a bottle down from a cupboard, then two short glasses. "This is about tomorrow."

"In a way. I meant what I said before. I believe we'll win. I believe we have to, that we're meant to. And I know what blood feels like on my hands. I know, or I believe, the good, the light, defeats evil, the dark. But not without cost. Not without price, and sometimes the price is very high."

"If you weren't afraid, you'd be stupid."

She took the glass he offered. "I'm not stupid," she said, and tossed the whiskey back. "We can't know what will happen tomorrow, or what the price may be. I think it's important, tonight, to grab what good we have, what light we have, and hold on to it. I want to be with you tonight."

He took a careful step back. "Iona."

"It's a lot to ask, considering I asked you exactly the opposite not so very long ago. You gave your word, and you kept it. Now I'm asking you to give me tonight. I want to be touched, to be held. I want to feel before tomorrow comes. I need you tonight. I hope you need me."

"I never stopped wanting to touch you." He set his whiskey aside. "I never stopped wishing to be with you."

"We'd both have tonight, whatever comes. I think we'd be stronger for it. It's not breaking a promise if I ask you to throw it away. Will you take me to bed? Will you let me stay till morning?"

There were things he wanted to say, yearned to say. But would she believe them, even with her shining faith, if he said them here and now?

The words would wait, he told himself, until the dawn after the longest day. Then she'd believe what he'd come to know.

Instead of speaking he simply stepped to her. Though they felt big, clumsy, he cupped her face with his hands, then lowered his mouth to hers.

She leaned into him, her arms wrapping, her lips heating.

"Thank God! Thank God you didn't send me away. I've—"

"Quiet," he murmured, and kissed her—soft, soft, tender as a bud just opened.

They had till morning, he thought. All those long hours, only that finite time. He would do what he'd never thought to do. He would take each minute, make it precious. Show her, somehow, she was precious.

"Come with me now." Taking her hand, he led her to the bedroom. Then crossed over to pull the blinds down on the windows. The light went dim and dusky.

"I'll be a moment," he told her, left her there.

He had candles. For emergencies rather than atmosphere, but a candle was a candle, wasn't it?

He might not be a romantic sort of man, but he knew what romance was.

He unearthed three candles, brought them in, set them around. Then remembered matches. He patted his pockets. "I'll just find the matches, then . . ."

She trailed a finger through the air, and the candles flamed.

"Or we could do that."

"I'm not sure what we're doing, but you're making me nervous."

"Good." He went back to her, ran his hands down, shoulder to wrist and back again. "I wouldn't mind that. I'd like feeling you tremble," he murmured, opening the buttons of her shirt. "I'd like looking in your eyes and seeing you can't help yourself. That nervous or not, you want me to go on touching you."

"I do." She reached up, managed to open a button on his shirt before he stopped her.

"I want you to take what I give you tonight. Just take, just let me give. I've missed seeing the shape of you," he continued, and drew her shirt off her shoulders. "Missed the feel of your skin under my hands."

He circled her nipples with his thumbs, then gently brushed the pads over them, over them until the tremble came.

He took his hands over her, took her mouth with his—everything slow, everything dreamy, even the thick thud of her heart against him.

"Take what I give." He backed her to the bed, brushing, stroking, eased her onto it. Watched her in the candlelight as he drew off her boots, set them down.

"Come lie with me."

"Oh, I will. In time."

He unbuttoned her jeans, drew the zipper down. Slow. Followed its path with his lips.

What was he doing to her? She found herself clutching at the bed covers one minute, going limp as water the next. He undressed her so slowly, inch-by-inch torture. And yet the pleasure was sumptuous, a banquet of exotic delicacies. The heat of it enervated. The weight of it left her arms too heavy to lift.

She knew nothing but the feel of his hands, his lips, the sound of his voice, his scent. Him. Him. Him.

Once, twice, a third time he guided her to the shuddering edge, held her there, poised, desperate for the leap, only to ease her back again until her breath sobbed with need, with the speechless desire for the next.

Then with lips, tongue, ruthlessly patient hands he slid her over that edge.

Not a leap, but a fall—breathless, endless, a tumble of senses and sensations. And the world revolved.

"Oh God. God. Please."

"What do you please?"

"Don't stop."

His mouth, on her breast, her belly, her thigh. Then his tongue, sliding over her, into her until she fell yet again, then mindlessly craved the next climb.

He hadn't known he'd wanted her helpless, or what it would do to him to know he'd made her so. But to see her alight—she couldn't know she glimmered like one of the candles—to feel her body rise up to take what he offered, to feel it fall again as she grasped that pleasure. It was more than he'd known, more than he'd imagined.

And the wanting of her filled every part of him—mind, body, spirit.

"Look at me now, Iona. Would you look at me now?"

She opened her eyes, saw his in the candle glow. Saw nothing else.

"I'm with you," he said as he slipped into her. "I'm with you."

They climbed again, eyes and bodies locked. Climbed until she swore the air thinned. And when her eyes gleamed with tears, they fell together.

21

TODAY, BOYLE THOUGHT AS HE DRANK BRUTALLY STRONG coffee at his kitchen window.

He couldn't stop it, or her. And in some part of himself he knew, even accepted that he, that she, that all of them had prepared for this day all of their lives.

Hard enough, it had always been hard enough to understand what his closest friends in the world might face one day—today—but with Iona it was only harder.

Whatever he could do he would to see her safely through it, to help her and the rest end it.

And then?

Once this day was done there would be a great deal more to do, if only he could figure out the hows of it all.

Sure how could he figure out anything when the day was to be filled with magick and violence, struggle and destinies? And very likely life and death.

His life, he thought, would've been easier by far if she'd never come into it.

Then he sensed her, turned, saw her standing outside his bedroom door, that short halo of hair still damp from her shower, her eyes deep and a bit sleepy yet before her coffee.

And he knew without a shadow, easier wasn't what he wanted.

"Should we talk?" she asked him.

"Probably so, but it's a strange day for all that."

"It is, yeah. Later's better."

He nodded. "After, yes. There's a lot to be said after this day." Get busy, he told himself. Get moving. "You'll have coffee, won't you?"

"Absolutely." But she didn't move to pour it for herself as she'd done before.

He'd done that, he knew, made her feel a guest again. Words wanted to be said, but he held them back, and would until this long, strange day was done.

So he got down a mug, poured it for her.

"Thanks. I'm going to go down, spend some time with Alastar. Do you have any problem with me riding him home today, keeping him there until it's time?"

"I don't, no. He's yours after all. I'll ride with you."

"Actually, I think Fin will. He and Branna need to refine any details of the magicks with Connor and me."

"All right, but you don't ride alone." Carefully, he touched a hand to her shoulder. "Are you afraid?"

"No. Not afraid. I thought I'd be revved, pumped, with some good, healthy fear mixed in. I'm just not, and not sure why. I feel almost unreasonably calm. Today's what I've been working for, training for, learning for. And that was ordained, I guess is the word for it, on the night Sorcha sacrificed herself.

"We finish what she started. And then . . ."

When he said nothing, she sipped at her coffee. "And then," she continued, "we do good work, we lead good lives. That's enough for anyone."

"Your work and your life are here."

"Yes." On that, at least, she had no doubts. "My place is here."

"I'll fix us up some breakfast."

"Thanks, but I feel like I ought to be a little hungry, and . . . light for now. I'll be down with Alastar until it's time to go back home." She set her coffee, barely touched, aside. "I needed you last night, and you were there. I won't forget it." She walked quickly to the door. "I'll see you, an hour before moonrise."

She slipped out the door and left him wondering over her.

SHE GROOMED ALASTAR CAREFULLY, THOROUGHLY SO HIS coat gleamed like pewter. Her calm remained as she brushed even the threat of tangles out of his mane, his tail.

Today he was a warhorse, and she believed that he, too, had prepared for this day all of his life.

"We won't fail." She circled around to his head, laid her hands on either side of his face and looked into his deep, dark eyes. "We won't fail," she repeated. "And we'll keep each other safe as we do what we're meant to do."

She chose a saddle blanket—red for battle, for blood, then retrieved the saddle Boyle had given her.

She felt Alastar's pleasure, his pride when she put the saddle on him. And she felt his courage, drew some of it for herself.

"There's magick in a gift, and this was given to both of us. He thought of us when he had it made, so there's more magick there. And last, it bears our names."

She'd braid charms into his mane, she decided. When they got home she would choose ones for strength, for courage, for protection.

And she would carry the same with her, under the sweater her grandmother had made. Another gift.

"Time to go."

She allowed herself one moment to wonder if she'd ever be back in this stall, then set any doubt aside and led her horse out.

She found Fin waiting outside, and the sleek black he called Baru saddled.

"I've kept you waiting."

"Not at all. There's time enough. Odds are Branna's just getting her wits about her by now in any case. I see Boyle gave you the saddle."

"It's wonderful. You knew?"

"When you live and work so close with another, secrets are hard to keep." Fin linked his hands into a basket to help her mount.

"You look a picture, the pair of you," he said when she sat the horse.

"We're ready for what's coming."

"It shows." He mounted Baru, turned so they could walk down the narrow road together.

IN THE WORKSHOP, CLOSED, LOCKED, SHIELDED FOR THE DAY, Iona listened to the plan—its step-by-step progression—to the spell she was charged to make, the words to be said, the actions to take.

"You're quiet," Fin commented. "Have you no questions?"

"The answers are on Sorcha's ground. I'm ready to go there, and to do what I'm meant to do."

"It's a complicated spell," Branna began. "Each piece has to fit."

"I can handle it. And as you've said, I won't be alone. You'll be there, and so will Boyle and Meara. If I pull this off, on my own, he won't know that, won't see that. Advantage us. Then you come in from here, here, here," she said, tapping the map Branna had drawn. "That distracts him, throws him off balance, and takes the heat off me. All non-witches inside the circle, and Fin, too. They'll need you to keep the protective circle strong," Iona said as temper flashed into Fin's eyes. "So will we. We'll need that time when he tries to get to you for the three of us to finish it. Finish him."

"You're bloody calm about it," Connor muttered.

"I know. It's odd. Why worry when it's meant, right? And still I should be jumping out of my skin, but I just feel . . . right. Maybe I'm saving the jumping for when it's done. Then I'll probably babble like an idiot until you want to knock me unconscious. But right now, I'm ready."

"If you're so ready, tell me all the steps, from the beginning," Branna ordered.

"All right. We gather here, an hour before moonrise."

Iona walked her way through it as she spoke, envisioned it, every step, every motion, every word.

"And when Cabhan is ash," she concluded, "we perform the final ritual and consecrate the ground. Then comes the happy dance and drinks on the house."

Gauging her cousin's expression, Iona reached for Branna's hand. "I'm taking it very seriously. I know what I have to do. I'm focused. I trust you, all of you. Now you have to trust me."

"I'd wish for more time, that's all."

"Time's up." To demonstrate, Iona rose. "I want to change, and get everything I need from my room. I'll be ready."

When she walked away, Connor rose as well. "I'd take some of her calm just now, but I'll have to make do with too much energy. I'm going to check on the hawks, yours and mine, Fin, and the horses as well."

As the door closed behind him, Branna got up to put the kettle back on. Though she doubted a vat of tea would drown the anxiety.

"You think we're asking too much of her?" Fin asked.

"I can't know, and that's the worry." One that ate at her, night and day. "If I try to see, and he catches even a glimmer, all could be lost. So I don't look. I don't like putting the beginnings of it all in her hands, even knowing it's the right choice."

"She asked for trust. We'll give her that."

"You don't think it's too much for her?"

"I can't know," he said in an echo of her words, "and that's the worry."

She busied herself making tea for both of them. "You care for her a great deal."

"I do, yes. For herself, as she's charming and full of light, and such . . . clarity of heart. And again, as my friend loves her, even if he buggered it up."

"He did that. And still she went to him last night."

"She forgives, easier than others." Fin rose to walk toward her, to stand near her. "There are things for us, Branna. Words to be said. Will you forgive me, at last, when this is done?"

"I can't think about that now. I'm doing what I have to do. Do you think it's easy for me, being with you, working beside you, seeing you day after day?"

"It could be. All those things used to make you happy."

"We used to be children."

"What we had, what we've been to each other wasn't childish."

"You ask for too much." Made her remember, far too clearly, the simple joy of love. "Ask for more than I can give."

"I won't ask. I'm done with asking. You don't reach for happiness, or even look for it."

"Maybe I don't."

"What then?"

"Fulfillment. I think fulfillment contents me."

"You wanted more than contentment once. You ran toward happiness."

She had, she knew. Recklessly. "And the wanting, the running hurt me more than I can bear, even now. Put it away, Finbar, for it only brings more hurt to both of us. We've important work to do tonight. There's nothing else but that."

"You'll never be all you are if you believe that. And it's a sorrow to me."

He walked away, walked out. And that, Branna told herself, was what she needed.

He was wrong, she told herself. She'd never be all she was, never really be free, as long as she loved him.

And that was her sorrow.

AT AN HOUR BEFORE MOONRISE THEY GATHERED. BRANNA lit the ritual candles, tossed ground crystals into the fire so its smoke rose pale and pure blue.

She took up a silver cup that had come down to her, stepped into the circle they formed.

"This we drink, one cup for six, from hand to hand and mouth to mouth to fix with wine our unity. Six hearts, six minds as one tonight as we prepare to wage this fight. Sip one, sip all, and show each one here answers the call."

The cup passed hand to hand three times before Branna placed it in the center of the circle.

"Power of light, strong and bright, bless us this night, shield us from sight."

Light erupted in the cup, burned like white flame.

"Now his eyes be blind until this magick I unwind. Not heart nor mind nor form will he see. As we will, so mote it be."

She lowered the arms she'd lifted. "While it burns we're the shadows. Only you, Iona, when you break this vial. Wait," she added as she pressed it into Iona's hand. "Wait until you're on Sorcha's ground."

"I will. Don't worry." She slid the vial into her pocket. "Find him," she said to Fin.

"So I will. Find, seek, lure."

He took a crystal, round as a ball, clear as water, from his own pocket, cupped it in the palm of his hand.

As he spoke in Irish, the ball began to glow, to lift an inch above his hand. And to revolve, slower, then faster, faster until it blurred with speed.

"He seeks, blood to blood, mark to mark," Branna told Iona quietly. "He uses what he is, what they share, to see, to stir. He . . ."

Fin's eyes began to gleam, to glow, as unearthly a light as the crystal.

"Not so deep! He can't—"

Connor caught Branna's arm before she lurched forward. "He knows what he's about."

But for a moment, something dark lived behind the light in Fin's eyes. Then it was gone.

"I have him." His face a mask, Fin closed his fingers over the crystal. "He'll come."

"Where is he?" Boyle demanded.

"Not far. I gave him your scent," he told Iona. "He'll follow it, and you."

"Then I'll take him where we want him."

"We're behind you." Meara grasped Iona's arms. "Every one of us."

"I know." She breathed slow, kept her calm. "I believe."

She touched her fingers to the hilt of the sword at her side, looked from one to the other, and thought what a wonder it was to have them all, to have what was inside her, to have such a purpose.

"I won't let you down," she said and started for the door.

"Bloody hell." In two strides Boyle caught her, whirled her around, crushed his mouth to hers with everything that lived inside him.

"Take that with you," he demanded, and set her aside.

"I will." And she smiled before she walked out into the soft light of the longest day.

Alastar waited, pawed the ground at her approach.

Yeah, she thought, we're ready, you and I.

She gripped his mane, hurled herself into the saddle. She closed a hand briefly around her amulet, felt heat pulse from it.

Ready, she thought again, and let Alastar have his head.

Faster was better. The others would come as quickly as they could, but the faster she reached her ground, the less time Cabhan could plot, plan, question.

Wind rushed by her ears. The ground thundered. And they flew.

When she reached the downed tree, the wall of vines, she drew her sword.

"I am Iona. I am the Dark Witch. I am the blood. I am one of three, and this is my right."

She slashed out. The vines fell with a sound like glass shattering, and she rode through.

Like the dream she'd had that night at Ashford, she thought. Riding alone through the deep forest, through air so much stiller than it had a right to be, where the light went dim though the sun showered down.

She saw the ruins ahead, vine- and brush-covered as if it grew out of the trees. She walked the horse toward it, and toward the stone that bore Sorcha's name.

Now her skin vibrated. Not nerves, she realized, but power. Energy. Alastar quivered under her, let out a bugle that sounded of triumph.

"Yes, we've been here before. The place of our blood. The place where our power was born." She dismounted, looped the reins, knowing Alastar would stay with her, stay close.

She took the vial from her pocket, crushed it under her boot.

So it would begin.

From the bag she'd secured to the saddle, she took the flowers first. Simple wood violets, then a small flask holding bloodred wine.

"For the mother of my mother and hers, and all who lived and died, who bore the gift with its joys and sorrow, back to Teagan who is mine, and the Dark Witch who bore her."

She laid the flowers by the stone, poured wine over the ground in tribute.

Speaking the words of the spell only in her mind, pulling power up from her belly, she took the four white candles from the bag, set them on the ground at the compass points. Next, the crystals, between each point.

As she laid them, Alastar let out a warning chuff. She saw fingers of fog crawling over the ground.

We're with you. Connor's voice sounded in her ear. *Finish the circle.*

She drew her athame, pointed north. Flame sparked on the first candle.

"You think that can stop me?" Cabhan spoke with amusement. "You come here, where I rule, and play your pitiful white magick."

"You don't rule here."

The second candle flamed.

"See." He threw his arms high. The stone around his neck flamed with light both dark and blinding. "Know."

Something changed. The ground tipped under her feet as she struggled to finish the ritual. The air turned, turned until her head spun with it. The third candle flamed, but she fell to her knees, fighting the terrible sensation of dropping from a cliff.

The vines drew back from the ruin. The walls began to climb, stone by stone.

Night fell like a curtain dropped.

"My world. My time." The shadows seemed to lift from him. The stone pulsed, a dark heart over his. "And here, you are mine."

"I'm not." She got painfully to her feet, laid a hand on Alastar's flank as he reared. "I'm Sorcha's."

"She sought my end, gained her own. It's she who sleeps in the dark. It's I who live in it. Give me what you have, what weighs on you, what it demands from you, what it takes from you. Give me the power that fits you so ill. Or I take it, and your soul with it."

She lit the last candle. If they could come, they would come, she thought. But she couldn't hear them through the rush in her ears, or sense them through the stench of the fog.

No retreat, she told herself. And never surrender.

She drew her sword. "You want it? Come and get it."

He laughed, and the sheer delight on his face added a terrible beauty. "A sword won't stop me."

"You bleed, so let's find out." She punched power into the sword until it flamed. "And I bet you'll burn."

He swept an arm out, and from feet away, threw her back, knocked her to the ground. Winded, she tried to push to her feet. Alastar reared again, screaming in rage as his hooves lashed out.

She saw Cabhan's face register pain, and shock with it. Then he hunched, dropped to all fours, and became the wolf.

It leapt at Alastar, scoring the horse's side.

"No!" Like lightning, Iona surged to her feet, charged.

Her sword whistled through the air, but the wolf streaked to the side, then barreled into her with a force that propelled her, had her skidding on her back, and her sword flying away.

The wolf straddled her, jaws snapping. And became a man again.

"I'll burn him to cinders," Cabhan warned. "Hold him back or I set him on fire."

"Stop! Alastar, stop!"

She felt his rage even as he obeyed. And felt the amulet she wore vibrate between her and Cabhan.

His gaze lowered to it; his lips peeled back in a snarl.

Then he smiled again, terrifyingly, into her eyes.

"Sorcha betrayed me with a kiss. I'll draw what's in you into me the same way."

"I won't give it to you."

"But you will."

Pain exploded, unspeakably. She screamed, unable to stop. Red everywhere, as if the world caught fire. She heard Alastar's screams join hers. Ordered him to *run, run, run*. If she couldn't save herself, she prayed she could save him.

Above all, she would never give up. She would never give her light to the dark.

"A kiss. You've only to give me one kiss, and the pain will vanish, the burden will drop."

Somewhere in her frantic mind she realized he couldn't take it. He could kill her, but he couldn't take what she was. She had to surrender it.

Instead she groped, found her athame with a shuddering hand.

She wept, couldn't stop that either, but through the screams and sobs she managed one word. "Bleed."

And plunged the knife into his side.

He roared, more fury than pain, and, leaping up, dragged her with him, holding her a foot above the ground by a hand clamped around her throat.

"You're nothing! Pale and weak and human. I'll crush the life out of you, and your power with it."

She kicked, tried to call for fire, wind, a flood, but her vision grayed, her lungs burned.

She heard another roar, and flew, hitting the ground hard enough to shock her bones and clear her vision.

She saw Boyle, his face a mask of vengeance, pummeling his fists into Cabhan's face.

With each hit, flames leapt.

"Stop." She couldn't get the word out, no more than a croak, even as Boyle's hands burned.

She managed to gain her knees, swayed as she fought to find her center.

The man dropped away. The wolf slipped out of Boyle's hold and bunched for attack.

The hound streaked into the clearing, snarling, snapping. Hawks dove, talons slicing at the wolf's back.

An arm circled her waist, lifted her to her feet. Hands linked with hers.

"Can you do it?" Branna shouted.

"Yes." Even the single word cut her throat like shards of glass.

The fog thickened, or her vision grayed. But all she could see through it were vague shapes, the flash of fire.

"We are the three, dark witches we, and stand this ground in unity. Before the longest day departs, we forge all light against the dark. On this ground, in this hour, we join our hands, we join our power. Blood to blood, we call on all who came before, flame to flame, their fires restore. Match with us, your forces free. As we will, so mote it be."

Light, blinding, heat churning, and the wind that whirled it all into a maelstrom.

"Again!" Branna called out.

Three times three. And as she cast the spell, her hands caught tight with her cousins', Iona felt she *was* the fire. Made of heat and flame, and a cold, cold rage that burned in its core.

Even as she pushed to finish, the fog vanished. She saw blood, smoke, both Fin and Meara at the edge of—not in—the circle, swords in hand. And Boyle, kneeling on the ground, pale as death, his hands raw and blistered.

Alastar, blood seeping from his wounds, nudged his head against Boyle's side, while the hound guarded him. Two hawks perched in branches beside the stone cabin.

"Boyle." Iona stumbled forward, fell to her knees beside him. "Your hands. Your hands."

"They'll be all right. You're bleeding. And your throat."

"Your hands," she said again. "Connor, help me."

"I'll see to it. Here now, this isn't for you. You're hurt, and I'll do better without you."

"Here, little sister, let me help you." Fin crouched down as if to lift Iona into his arms.

"I'll tend her." Briskly, Branna took Iona's arm. "Help Connor with Boyle as he's taken the worst of it."

"His hands were on fire." When her head spun, Iona simply slid to the ground. "His hands."

"Connor and Fin will fix him right up, you'll see. Quiet now, cousin. Meara, I want his blood. Find something to put it in. The blood, the ash. Look at me now, darling. Look at me, Iona. It'll hurt a little."

"You, too."

"Just a little."

It did, a little more than a little, then relief, cool and soothing on her throat. Warm, healing down her sides where the bruising ran deep.

"It's better. It's all right. Boyle."

"Shh. Hush now. That'll take a bit longer, but he's fine, he's doing fine. Look and see while I finish."

Through streaming tears, Iona looked over, saw Boyle's hands. Still raw, but no longer blackened and blistered. Still, he'd gone gray with the treatment, and the pain.

"Can't I help?"

"They've got him. I've just your ankle left here. It's not broken, but it's badly wrenched."

"I wasn't strong enough."

"Hush."

"Alastar. He hurt Alastar. He said he'd burn him alive."

"He's cut a bit, that's all. Why don't you see to that? See to your horse."

"Yes. Yes. He needs me."

She gained her feet, walked, a bit drunkenly, to the horse. "You're so brave. I'm so sorry."

Swallowing tears, she laid her hands on the first gash, and began to heal it.

"I've used two of the vials from your bag." Meara handed them to Branna. "One for the blood, the other for the ash. I felt a bit like one of those forensic types." Then she let out a shuddering breath. "Oh God, Branna."

"We won't talk of it here. We need to get home."

"Can we?"

"I got us here. I'll get us back."

"Where did he go, bloody bastard?"

"I don't know. We hurt him, and he lost blood—plenty of it—but it's not finished. I saw him slide away, using the fog, into the fog. Our fire scorched, and well, but didn't take him. It was not finished tonight, for all we thought it would be. I'm taking us back," she called out. "Are you ready?"

"Christ, yes." Fin put an arm around Boyle, helped him stand.

"I'm fine now, I'm fine. Help her get us home, the both of you."

Nudging the other men aside, Boyle walked to Iona. "Let me see you."

"I'm okay. Branna took care of it. Alastar. I can't heal this scar. He's scarred."

Boyle studied the slash of white over the gray flank. "A battle scar, worn with pride. We're going home now, all of us. Up you go. And none of that," he added as the tears rolled. "Stop that now."

"Not yet." She leaned forward, wrapped her arms around the horse's neck as the ground tilted, as the air turned and turned.

And kept her silence as they left the clearing, and the ruins.

EPILOGUE

IONA ACCEPTED THE WHISKEY, WITH GRATITUDE, AND curled into the corner of the living room sofa. The fire snapped, but brought comfort instead of fear and pain.

"I'm sorry. I wasn't strong enough. I wasn't good enough. He rolled right over me."

"Bollocks to that." Connor tipped more whiskey in his own glass. "Bloody, buggering bollocks to that."

"Well said," Branna agreed. "'Tis I who's sorry. Every step in place, every detail. But one. I never thought of him slipping through time like that, not on command. I didn't know he could so quickly, and with us so close."

"No." Fin shook his head when she glanced at him. "I never saw it coming. He's too clever by half, changing the ground to one where his power burned stronger than we knew."

"And where we couldn't get to Iona. Where she was alone, after all." Boyle reached over, took her hand, held it firmly in his.

"But you came, all of you."

"Not as fast as I would like. It's not enough to know where, but when. We might not have found you, but you called so strong. You believed, just as you said, and you called. You finished the circle, even with all that, you finished the circle, opened the power, and we could find you. And nearly took him."

For a moment, Branna closed her eyes. "Nearly, I swear it was close."

"It's no fault of yours," Connor told Iona, "or anyone's come to that. It's true enough we didn't finish him, but we gave him a hell of a fight, and we hurt him. He won't forget the pain we gave him this night."

"And he'll be more prepared for next time." Meara lifted her hands. "It's true, and needs to be said, so we don't walk into that kind of trap again."

"That's fine, but . . . you're burned."

Meara glanced at her wrists, the backs of her hands, and the scatter of burns. "Blowback, mostly. What about you?"

"Fin and I took care of each other. Why didn't you say something? Stubborn arse." Connor rose, gripped her hands.

"I've worse cooking breakfast."

"There's no need for pain. Are you burned as well?" he asked his sister.

"Not a fucking mark. We have his blood, and the ash his torn flesh turned to. We'll use it against him. We'll figure out just how, and we'll use it against him when next we come at him. And it won't be his ground the next time. We'll be sure of it."

Iona didn't ask how. Sitting there, with those she loved, with her hand in Boyle's, she felt her faith come back.

"He couldn't take it," she said slowly, and touched her free hand to her amulet. "Even when I was helpless, or as close to helpless as I've ever been, even when he hurt me, he couldn't take it from me.

He needed me to give it to him. He could kill me, but he couldn't take what's in me. That pissed him off."

"Good."

Iona smiled. "Damn good. I stabbed him with my athame."

"Did you now?" Fin rose, walked over, and, bending down, kissed her hard on the lips. "That's our girl. A weapon of light against the dark. It may be why there was so much blood left for us."

"We'll use that as well. I'm putting a meal together. I can't promise what it might be, but we'll eat well tonight. And there's a bottle yet of that French champagne. We didn't finish it, but I'd say the first battle is ours, and we'll celebrate that. You lot can give me a hand. Not the two of you," Branna said to Iona and Boyle. "You took the worst of it, so you'll sit there and drink your whiskey by the fire a bit."

"I've not finished with the stubborn arse yet."

Meara punched Connor's shoulder. "Mind your own arse."

"Why when yours is not only stubborn but shapely as well?"

"In the kitchen, I said." And this time Branna rolled her eyes at Connor to give him a clue.

"Fine, fine, I'm half starved anyway."

He trooped out, dragging Meara with him.

"I'll take a look at the horses. So you can rest your mind there."

Iona smiled at Fin. "Thanks. They're fine, but it never hurts."

Then she leaned her head back, closed her eyes. "I was fire," she said softly. "Not just making it, being it. It was terrifying and glorious."

"It was, looking at you with Connor and Branna, burning like a torch, all white and heat. It was terrifying, and glorious."

"And still, it wasn't enough. I wanted it to be over, now. Tonight."

"Some things don't happen as fast as you like." Boyle turned her hand over in his, then gave in and pressed it to his cheek. "It doesn't mean they won't happen."

"That's right. And Branna's right. When we weigh it all, we tipped the scales on this one. The way you flew through the fog. You and Alastar, you're my heroes."

"Since I know what store you put by the horse, I'm in fine company."

"When I close my eyes and see your hands. See them on fire."

"Look at them here. See that? Same as ever."

Big, scarred. Precious.

"I didn't think we'd get to you." He spoke slowly, and with great care. "I didn't think we'd get to you in time if at all, and that I might never see you again. I didn't have your faith. I want you to know I have it now. So, you can say you're my hero as well."

She tipped her head to his shoulder a moment.

"And I think, all things considered . . ."

She took a sip of whiskey. "What things?"

"I'm saying, I think considering all of it, and the fact we're done for now, and don't know as yet what might be next. Considering all that, and all the rest, I think it would be best all around if you married me."

She lowered the glass to stare at him. "I'm sorry, what?"

"I know all you said after I was, well, just a raving git, and I've done what you wanted, or tried my best to. But I think it's time we were past that now, and considering it all, we'll get married and put all that away."

"Married." Had the battle, the bruisings, the flaming addled her brain? "As in married?"

"It's the sensible thing. We're good for each other, as you've said yourself. And . . . we have horses in common."

"Can't forget the horses."

"It matters," he muttered. "You love me. You said you did, and you're a woman honest about her feelings."

"That's true."

"So, we're good for each other, and have the horses. You love me and it's the same for me, so we'll just get married."

She decided her brain was working just fine, thank you. "What's the same for you?"

"Jesus." He had to stand for a moment, circle around the room. Stall by tossing more peat on the fire. "I never said it to a woman not my mother or related in some fashion. I don't toss such things about as if they're nothing."

His hair, caught between brown and red, was a tumbled mess. She hadn't noticed before, she realized. Or the blood on his shirt, the way his jaw set, so stubborn.

But she could see, very clearly, the intensity in his eyes.

"I believe you."

"Some words matter more than others, and it's one of those."

"What's one of those, exactly?"

"Love is. I know what love is, damn it, because you put it in me, and you've given it to me. And I'll never be the same again. I'll never feel it for anyone else."

"It."

"I love you, all right then?" He punched the words out like an argument waiting to happen, and she was totally, utterly done for.

"I'm saying it clear enough." His brows drew together in that half scowl as he threw up his hands. "I love you. I . . . want to as well. I want all that I feel for you, as I'd only be half alive without it. And I want to marry you, and live with you, and have a family with you some time or other. But for now, I want you to stop making me run around it all, and just say it's all right with you."

She only stared at him a moment, as she wanted it all, every tiny detail of it, etched forever in her memory. "This is the most romantic thing that's ever happened to me."

"Oh bugger it. You want fancy words? Maybe I could pull some Yeats out or something."

"No, no, no." Laughing, she got to her feet, and felt stronger and surer than she'd ever felt before. "I meant it. This is romance, for me, from you. If you could say it just one more time. The three words, the word that matters more than others."

"I love you. Iona Sheehan, I love you. Give me a bloody answer."

"It was yes as soon as you opened your mouth. I just wanted to hear it all. It was yes the minute you asked."

He blinked at her slowly, then narrowed his eyes. "It was yes? It's yes?"

"I love you. There's nothing I want more than to marry you."

"Yes?"

"Yes."

"Well good. Grand. God." He lunged at her, and she met him halfway. "God, thank God. I don't know how much longer I could've done without you."

"Now you'll never have to know." She gave herself over to the kiss, and all the promises in it. "You'll never have to do without me." She held on, tight, tight. "We did win tonight, in so many ways. In ways he'll never understand. We have love. He doesn't know what it means. We have love."

"I'm marrying a witch." Hauling her off her feet, he circled with her. "I'm a lucky man."

"Oh, you really, really are. When?"

"When?"

"When are we getting married?"

"Tomorrow would do me."

Delighted, she laughed. "Not that soon. Talk about boots-first. I need a fabulous dress, and I need Nan to be here. And I haven't met your family."

"A lot of them are right in this house."

"That's true. We won't wait too long, but long enough to do it right."

"I have to buy you a ring. The boys were right, after all. I need to get you something shiny."

"Absolutely."

"And you're right, too, it has to wait a little bit of time. At least long enough to get a booking at Ballintubber Abbey."

"At . . ." Joy all but drowned her. "You'd marry me there?"

"It's what you want, isn't it? And by God, it seems it's what I want as well. There, in the ancient and holy place. It's what's meant for us."

He grabbed her hands, yanked them to his lips, then laughed down at her. "You'll be mine, and I'll be yours. That's what I want."

She laid her cheek on his heart. Love, she thought, given freely, taken willingly.

There was no stronger magick.

"It's what I want," she murmured, then smiled when she heard Alastar bugle. "He knows I'm happy." She tipped her head back. "Let's go tell everybody else, and pop that champagne."

With wine and music and light, she thought. They'd come through the fire, beaten back the dark for another day.

And now, on the longest day, when the light refused to surrender, she was loved. At last.

DEEP IN THE WOODS, IN ANOTHER TIME, THE WOLF WHIMpered. The man inside it cursed. And with arts as black as midnight, slowly began to heal.

Carefully, began to plan.

Keep reading for an excerpt from
the two hundredth novel
by Nora Roberts

THE WITNESS

Now available from Berkley

June 2000

ELIZABETH FITCH'S SHORT-LIVED TEENAGE REBELLION began with L'Oréal Pure Black, a pair of scissors and a fake ID. It ended in blood.

For nearly the whole of her sixteen years, eight months and twenty-one days she'd dutifully followed her mother's directives. Dr. Susan L. Fitch issued *directives,* not orders. Elizabeth had adhered to the schedules her mother created, ate the meals designed by her mother's nutritionist and prepared by her mother's cook, wore the clothes selected by her mother's personal shopper.

Dr. Susan L. Fitch dressed conservatively, as suited—in her opinion—her position as chief of surgery of Chicago's Silva Memorial Hospital. She expected, and directed, her daughter to do the same.

Elizabeth studied diligently, accepting and excelling in the academic programs her mother outlined. In the fall, she'd return to Harvard in pursuit of her medical degree. So she could become a doctor, like her mother—a surgeon, like her mother.

Elizabeth—never Liz or Lizzie or Beth—spoke fluent Spanish, French, Italian, passable Russian and rudimentary Japanese. She played both piano and violin. She'd traveled to Europe, to Africa. She could name all the bones, nerves and muscles in the human body and play Chopin's Piano Concerto—both Nos. 1 and 2—by rote.

She'd never been on a date or kissed a boy. She'd never roamed the mall with a pack of girls, attended a slumber party or giggled with friends over pizza or hot fudge sundaes.

She was, at sixteen years, eight months and twenty-one days, a product of her mother's meticulous and detailed agenda.

That was about to change.

She watched her mother pack. Susan, her rich brown hair already coiled in her signature French twist, neatly hung another suit in the organized garment bag, then checked off the printout with each day of the week's medical conference broken into subgroups. The printout included a spreadsheet listing every event, appointment, meeting and meal, scheduled with the selected outfit, with shoes, bag and accessories.

Designer suits; Italian shoes, of course, Elizabeth thought. One must wear good cuts, good cloth. But not one rich or bright color among the blacks, grays, taupes. She wondered how her mother could be so beautiful and deliberately wear the dull.

After two accelerated semesters of college, Elizabeth thought she'd begun—maybe—to develop her own fashion sense. She had, in fact, bought jeans *and* a hoodie *and* some chunky-heeled boots in Cambridge.

With cash, so the receipt wouldn't show up on her credit card bill, in case her mother or their accountant checked and questioned the items, which were currently hidden in her room.

She'd felt like a different person while wearing them, so different she'd walked straight into a McDonald's and ordered her first Big Mac with large fries and a chocolate shake.

The pleasure had been so huge, she'd had to go into the bathroom, close herself in a stall and cry a little.

The seeds of the rebellion had been planted that day, she supposed, or maybe they'd always been there, dormant, and the fat and salt had awakened them.

But she could feel them, actually feel them, sprouting in her belly now.

"Your plans changed, Mother. It doesn't follow that mine have to change with them."

Susan took a moment to precisely place a shoe bag in the Pullman, tucking it just so with her beautiful and clever surgeon's hands, the nails perfectly manicured. A French manicure, as always—no color there, either.

"Elizabeth." Her voice was as polished and calm as her wardrobe. "It took considerable effort to reschedule and have you admitted to the summer program this term. You'll complete the requirements for your admission into Harvard Medical School a full semester ahead of schedule."

Even the thought made Elizabeth's stomach hurt. "I was promised a three-week break, including this next week in New York."

"And sometimes promises must be broken. If I hadn't had this coming week off, I couldn't fill in for Dr. Dusecki at the conference."

"You could have said no."

"That would have been selfish and shortsighted." Susan brushed at the jacket she'd hung, stepped back to check her list. "You're certainly mature enough to understand the demands of work overtake pleasure and leisure."

"If I'm mature enough to understand that, why aren't I mature enough to make my own decisions? I want this break. I need it."

Susan barely spared her daughter a glance. "A girl of your age, physical condition and mental acumen hardly *needs* a break from her studies and activities. In addition, Mrs. Laine has already left for her two-week cruise, and I could hardly ask her to postpone her vacation. There's no one to fix your meals or tend to the house."

"I can fix my own meals and tend to the house."

"Elizabeth." The tone managed to merge clipped with long-suffering. "It's settled."

"And I have no say in it? What about developing my independence, being responsible?"

"Independence comes in degrees, as does responsibility and freedom of choice. You still require guidance and direction. Now, I've e-mailed you an updated schedule for the coming week, and your packet with all the information on the program is on your desk. Be sure to thank Dr. Frisco personally for making room for you in the summer term."

As she spoke, Susan closed the garment bag, then her small Pullman. She stepped to her bureau to check her hair, her lipstick.

"You don't listen to anything I say."

In the mirror, Susan's gaze shifted to her daughter. The first time, Elizabeth thought, her mother had bothered to actually look at her since she'd come into the bedroom. "Of course I do. I heard everything you said, very clearly."

"Listening's different than hearing."

"That may be true, Elizabeth, but we've already had this discussion."

"It's not a discussion, it's a decree."

Susan's mouth tightened briefly, the only sign of annoyance. When she turned, her eyes were coolly, calmly blue. "I'm sorry you feel that way. As your mother, I must do what I believe best for you."

"What's best for me, in your opinion, is for me to do, be, say, think, act, want, become exactly what you decided for me before you inseminated yourself with precisely selected sperm."

She heard the rise of her own voice but couldn't control it, felt the hot sting of tears in her eyes but couldn't stop them. "I'm tired of being your experiment. I'm tired of having every minute of every day organized, orchestrated and choreographed to meet your expectations. I want to make my own choices, buy my own clothes, read books *I* want to read. I want to live my own life instead of yours."

Susan's eyebrows lifted in an expression of mild interest. "Well. Your attitude isn't surprising, given your age, but you've picked a very inconvenient time to be defiant and argumentative."

"Sorry. It wasn't on the schedule."

"Sarcasm's also typical, but it's unbecoming." Susan opened her briefcase, checked the contents. "We'll talk about all this when I get back. I'll make an appointment with Dr. Bristoe."

"I don't need therapy! I need a mother who *listens,* who gives a shit about how I feel."

"That kind of language only shows a lack of maturity and intellect."

Enraged, Elizabeth threw up her hands, spun in circles. If she couldn't be calm and rational like her mother, she'd be *wild.* "Shit! Shit! Shit!"

"And repetition hardly enhances. You have the rest of the weekend to consider your behavior. Your meals are in the refrigerator or freezer, and labeled. Your pack list is on your desk. Report to Ms. Vee at the university at eight on Monday morning. Your participation in this program will ensure your place in HMS next fall. Now, take my garment bag downstairs, please. My car will be here any minute."

Oh, those seeds were sprouting, cracking that fallow ground and pushing painfully through. For the first time in her life, Elizabeth looked straight into her mother's eyes and said, "No."

She spun around, stomped away and slammed the door of her bedroom. She threw herself down on the bed, stared at the ceiling with tear-blurred eyes. And waited.

Any second, any second, she told herself. Her mother would come in, demand an apology, demand obedience. And Elizabeth wouldn't give one, either.

They'd have a fight, an actual fight, with threats of punishment and consequences. Maybe they'd yell at each other. Maybe if they yelled, her mother would finally hear her.

And maybe, if they yelled, she could say all the things that had crept up inside her this past year. Things she thought now had been inside her forever.

She didn't want to be a doctor. She didn't want to spend every waking hour on a schedule or hide a stupid pair of jeans because they didn't fit her mother's dress code.

She wanted to have friends, not approved socialization appointments. She wanted to listen to the music girls her age listened to. She wanted to know what they whispered about and laughed about and talked about while she was shut out.

She didn't want to be a genius or a prodigy.

She wanted to be normal. She just wanted to be like everyone else.

She swiped at the tears, curled up, stared at the door.

Any second, she thought again. Any second now. Her mother had to be angry. She had to come in and assert authority. Had to.

"Please," Elizabeth murmured as seconds ticked into minutes. "Don't make me give in again. Please, please, don't make me give up."

Love me enough. Just this once.

But as the minutes dragged on, Elizabeth pushed herself off the bed. Patience, she knew, was her mother's greatest weapon. That, and the unyielding sense of being right, crushed all foes. And certainly her daughter was no match for it.

Defeated, she walked out of her room, toward her mother's.

The garment bag, the briefcase, the small, wheeled Pullman were gone. Even as she walked downstairs, she knew her mother had gone, too.

"She left me. She just left."

Alone, she looked around the pretty, tidy living room. Everything perfect—the fabrics, the colors, the art, the arrangement. The antiques passed down through generations of Fitches—all quiet elegance.

Empty.

Nothing had changed, she realized. And nothing would.

"So I will."

She didn't allow herself to think, to question or second-guess. Instead, she marched back up, snagged scissors from her study area.

In her bathroom, she studied her face in the mirror—coloring she'd gotten through paternity—auburn hair, thick like her mother's but without the soft, pretty wave. Her mother's high, sharp cheekbones, her biological father's—whoever he was—deep-set green eyes, pale skin, wide mouth.

Physically attractive, she thought, because that was DNA and her mother would tolerate no less. But not beautiful, not striking like Susan, no. And that, she supposed, had been a disappointment even her mother couldn't fix.

"Freak." Elizabeth pressed a hand to the mirror, hating what she saw in the glass. "You're a freak. But as of now, you're not a coward."

Taking a big breath, she yanked up a hunk of her shoulder-length hair and whacked it off.

With every snap of the scissors she felt empowered. *Her* hair, *her* choice. She let the shorn hanks fall on the floor. As she snipped and hacked, an image formed in her mind. Eyes narrowed, head angled, she slowed the clipping. It was just geometry, really, she decided—and physics. Action and reaction.

The weight—physical and metaphorical, she thought—just fell away. And the girl in the glass looked lighter. Her eyes seemed bigger, her face not so thin, not so drawn.

She looked . . . new, Elizabeth decided.

Carefully, she set the scissors down, and, realizing her breath was heaving in and out, made a conscious effort to slow it.

So short. Testing, she lifted a hand to her exposed neck, ears, then brushed them over the bangs she'd cut. Too even, she decided. She hunted up manicure scissors, tried her hand at styling.

Not bad. Not really good, she admitted, but different. That was the whole point. She looked, and felt, different.

But not finished.

Leaving the hair where it lay on the floor, she went into her bedroom, changed into her secret cache of clothes. She needed product—that's what the girls called it. Hair product. And makeup. And more clothes.

She needed the mall.

Riding on the thrill, she went into her mother's home office, took the spare car keys. And her heart hammered with excitement as she hurried to the garage. She got behind the wheel, shut her eyes a moment.

"Here we go," she said quietly, then hit the garage-door opener and backed out.

ABOUT THE AUTHOR

Nora Roberts is the #1 *New York Times* bestselling author of more than two hundred novels. She is also the author of the bestselling In Death series written under the pen name J. D. Robb. There are more than five hundred million copies of her books in print.

CONNECT ONLINE

NoraRoberts.com

NoraRoberts

Shadow Spell

Nora Roberts

BERKLEY
New York

BERKLEY
An imprint of Penguin Random House LLC
penguinrandomhouse.com

Library of Congress Cataloging-in-Publication Data

Roberts, Nora.
Shadow spell / Nora Roberts. — Berkley trade paperback edition.
pages cm. — (The Cousins O'Dwyer trilogy ; book 2) ISBN 978-0-425-25986-3 (pbk.)
1. Falconers—Ireland—Fiction. 2. Witches—Fiction. 3. Magic—Fiction.
4. Ireland—Fiction. 5. Domestic fiction. I. Title.
PS3568.O243S53 2014
813'.54—dc23
2013039243

Berkley trade paperback edition / April 2014

Printed in the United States of America
5th Printing

Book design by Kristin del Rosario

The legends and lore of Ireland come alive in the second novel in #1 *New York Times* bestselling author Nora Roberts's Cousins O'Dwyer trilogy.

Falconer Connor O'Dwyer is proud to call County Mayo home. It's where his sister, Branna, lives and works; where his cousin, Iona, has found true love; and where his childhood friends form a circle that can't be broken. But that lifelong bond is about to be changed forever by a long-awaited kiss. . . .

Meara Quinn is Branna's best friend, a sister in all but blood. Her and Connor's paths cross almost daily. She has eyes like a storm and the body of a goddess . . . things Connor has always taken for granted—until his brush with death propels them into a quick, hot tangle.

Plenty of women have found their way to Connor's bed, but none to his heart until now. Frustratingly, Meara is okay with just the heat, afraid to lose herself—and their friendship. But soon, Connor will see the full force and fury of what runs in his blood as his past rolls in like the fog, threatening an end to all he loves. . . .

"Roberts has a real flair for seamlessly melding day-to-day domestic details and the supernatural." —*Booklist*

Nora Roberts

HOT ICE
SACRED SINS
BRAZEN VIRTUE
SWEET REVENGE
PUBLIC SECRETS
GENUINE LIES
CARNAL INNOCENCE
DIVINE EVIL
HONEST ILLUSIONS
PRIVATE SCANDALS
HIDDEN RICHES
TRUE BETRAYALS
MONTANA SKY
SANCTUARY
HOMEPORT
THE REEF
RIVER'S END
CAROLINA MOON
THE VILLA
MIDNIGHT BAYOU
THREE FATES
BIRTHRIGHT
NORTHERN LIGHTS
BLUE SMOKE
ANGELS FALL
HIGH NOON
TRIBUTE
BLACK HILLS
THE SEARCH
CHASING FIRE
THE WITNESS
WHISKEY BEACH

Series

Irish Born Trilogy

BORN IN FIRE
BORN IN ICE
BORN IN SHAME

Dream Trilogy

DARING TO DREAM
HOLDING THE DREAM
FINDING THE DREAM

Chesapeake Bay Saga

SEA SWEPT
RISING TIDES
INNER HARBOR
CHESAPEAKE BLUE

Gallaghers of Ardmore Trilogy

JEWELS OF THE SUN
TEARS OF THE MOON
HEART OF THE SEA

Three Sisters Island Trilogy

DANCE UPON THE AIR
HEAVEN AND EARTH
FACE THE FIRE

Key Trilogy

KEY OF LIGHT
KEY OF KNOWLEDGE
KEY OF VALOR

In the Garden Trilogy

BLUE DAHLIA
BLACK ROSE
RED LILY

Circle Trilogy

MORRIGAN'S CROSS
DANCE OF THE GODS
VALLEY OF SILENCE

Sign of Seven Trilogy

BLOOD BROTHERS
THE HOLLOW
THE PAGAN STONE

Bride Quartet

VISION IN WHITE
BED OF ROSES
SAVOR THE MOMENT
HAPPY EVER AFTER

The Inn BoonsBoro Trilogy

THE NEXT ALWAYS
THE LAST BOYFRIEND
THE PERFECT HOPE

The Cousins O'Dwyer Trilogy

DARK WITCH
SHADOW SPELL

eBooks by Nora Roberts

Cordina's Royal Family

AFFAIRE ROYALE
COMMAND PERFORMANCE
THE PLAYBOY PRINCE
CORDINA'S CROWN JEWEL

The Donovan Legacy

CAPTIVATED
ENTRANCED
CHARMED
ENCHANTED

The O'Hurleys

THE LAST HONEST WOMAN
DANCE TO THE PIPER
SKIN DEEP
WITHOUT A TRACE

Night Tales

NIGHT SHIFT
NIGHT SHADOW
NIGHTSHADE
NIGHT SMOKE
NIGHT SHIELD

The MacGregors

THE WINNING HAND
THE PERFECT NEIGHBOR
ALL THE POSSIBILITIES
ONE MAN'S ART
TEMPTING FATE
PLAYING THE ODDS
THE MACGREGOR BRIDES
THE MACGREGOR GROOMS
REBELLION/IN FROM THE COLD
FOR NOW, FOREVER

The Calhouns

SUZANNA'S SURRENDER
MEGAN'S MATE
COURTING CATHERINE
A MAN FOR AMANDA
FOR THE LOVE OF LILAH

Irish Legacy

IRISH ROSE
IRISH REBEL
IRISH THOROUGHBRED

BEST LAID PLANS
LOVING JACK
LAWLESS

SUMMER LOVE
BOUNDARY LINES
DUAL IMAGE
FIRST IMPRESSIONS
THE LAW IS A LADY
LOCAL HERO
THIS MAGIC MOMENT
THE NAME OF THE GAME
PARTNERS
TEMPTATION
THE WELCOMING
OPPOSITES ATTRACT
TIME WAS
TIMES CHANGE
GABRIEL'S ANGEL
HOLIDAY WISHES
THE HEART'S VICTORY
THE RIGHT PATH

RULES OF THE GAME
SEARCH FOR LOVE
BLITHE IMAGES
FROM THIS DAY
SONG OF THE WEST
ISLAND OF FLOWERS
HER MOTHER'S KEEPER
UNTAMED
SULLIVAN'S WOMAN
LESS OF A STRANGER
REFLECTIONS
DANCE OF DREAMS
STORM WARNING
ONCE MORE WITH FEELING
ENDINGS AND BEGINNINGS
TONIGHT AND ALWAYS
A MATTER OF CHOICE

Nora Roberts & J. D. Robb

REMEMBER WHEN

J. D. Robb

NAKED IN DEATH
GLORY IN DEATH
IMMORTAL IN DEATH
RAPTURE IN DEATH
CEREMONY IN DEATH
VENGEANCE IN DEATH
HOLIDAY IN DEATH
CONSPIRACY IN DEATH
LOYALTY IN DEATH
WITNESS IN DEATH
JUDGMENT IN DEATH
BETRAYAL IN DEATH
SEDUCTION IN DEATH
REUNION IN DEATH
PURITY IN DEATH
PORTRAIT IN DEATH
IMITATION IN DEATH
DIVIDED IN DEATH
VISIONS IN DEATH
SURVIVOR IN DEATH
ORIGIN IN DEATH
MEMORY IN DEATH
BORN IN DEATH
INNOCENT IN DEATH
CREATION IN DEATH
STRANGERS IN DEATH
SALVATION IN DEATH
PROMISES IN DEATH
KINDRED IN DEATH
FANTASY IN DEATH
INDULGENCE IN DEATH
TREACHERY IN DEATH
NEW YORK TO DALLAS
CELEBRITY IN DEATH
DELUSION IN DEATH
CALCULATED IN DEATH
THANKLESS IN DEATH
CONCEALED IN DEATH

Anthologies

FROM THE HEART
A LITTLE MAGIC
A LITTLE FATE

MOON SHADOWS
(with Jill Gregory, Ruth Ryan Langan, and Marianne Willman)

The Once Upon Series
(with Jill Gregory, Ruth Ryan Langan, and Marianne Willman)

ONCE UPON A CASTLE
ONCE UPON A STAR
ONCE UPON A DREAM
ONCE UPON A ROSE
ONCE UPON A KISS
ONCE UPON A MIDNIGHT

SILENT NIGHT
(with Susan Plunkett, Dee Holmes, and Claire Cross)

OUT OF THIS WORLD
(with Laurell K. Hamilton, Susan Krinard, and Maggie Shayne)

BUMP IN THE NIGHT
(with Mary Blayney, Ruth Ryan Langan, and Mary Kay McComas)

DEAD OF NIGHT
(with Mary Blayney, Ruth Ryan Langan, and Mary Kay McComas)

THREE IN DEATH

SUITE 606
(with Mary Blayney, Ruth Ryan Langan, and Mary Kay McComas)

IN DEATH

THE LOST
(with Patricia Gaffney, Mary Blayney, and Ruth Ryan Langan)

THE OTHER SIDE
(with Mary Blayney, Patricia Gaffney, Ruth Ryan Langan, and Mary Kay McComas)

TIME OF DEATH

THE UNQUIET
(with Mary Blayney, Patricia Gaffney, Ruth Ryan Langan, and Mary Kay McComas)

MIRROR, MIRROR
(with Mary Blayney, Elaine Fox, Mary Kay McComas, and R. C. Ryan)

Also available . . .

THE OFFICIAL NORA ROBERTS COMPANION
(edited by Denise Little and Laura Hayden)

For my own circle,
family and friends

Coming events cast their
shadows before.

—THOMAS CAMPBELL

The ornament of a house is
the friends who frequent it.

—RALPH WALDO EMERSON

1

Autumn 1268

MISTS SPIRALED UP FROM THE WATER LIKE BREATH AS Eamon rowed the little boat. The sun shed pale, cool light as it woke from the night's rest and set morning birds to their chorus. He heard the cock crow, so arrogant and important, and the bleating of sheep as they cropped their way across the green fields.

Familiar sounds all, sounds that had greeted him every morning for the last five years.

But this wasn't home. No matter how welcoming, how familiar, it would never be home.

And home he wished for. Home brought him wishes aching down to his bones like an old man's in damp weather, longings bleeding through his heart like a lover scorned.

And under the wishing, aching, longing, bleeding, lived a simmering rage that could bubble up and scorch his throat like thirst.

Some nights he dreamed of home, of their cabin in the great woods where he knew every tree, every turn of the track. And some nights the dreams were real as life, so he could smell the peat fire, the sweet rushes of his bed with the lavender his mother wove through for good rest and good dreams.

He could hear her voice, her singing soft from below the loft where she mixed her potions and brews.

The Dark Witch, they'd called her—with respect—for she'd been powerful and strong. And kind and good. So some nights when he dreamed of home, when he heard his mother singing from below the loft, he woke with tears on his cheeks.

Hastily brushed away. He was a man now, fully ten years, head of his family as his father had been before him.

Tears were for the women.

And he had his sisters to look after, didn't he? he reminded himself as he set the oars, let the boat lightly drift while he dropped his line. Brannaugh might be the eldest, but he was the man of the family. He'd sworn an oath to protect her and Teagan, and so he would. Their grandfather's sword had come to him. He would use it when the time came.

That time would come.

For there were other dreams, dreams that brought fear rather than grieving. Dreams of Cabhan, the black sorcerer. Those dreams formed icy balls of fear in his belly that froze even the simmering rage. A fear that made the boy inside him want to cry out for his mother.

But he couldn't allow himself to be afraid. His mother was gone, sacrificing herself to save him and his sisters only hours after Cabhan had slaughtered their father.

He could barely see his father in his mind's eye, too often needed the help of the fire to find that image—the tall and proud Daithi, the *cennfine* with his bright hair and ready laugh. But he had only to close his eyes to see his mother, pale as the death to come, standing in front of the cabin in the woods on that misted morning while he rode away with his sisters, grief in his heart, fresh, hot power in his blood.

He was a boy no longer, from that morning, but one of the three, a dark witch, bound by blood and oath to destroy what even his mother could not.

Part of him wanted only to begin, to end this time in Galway on their cousin's farm where the cock crowed of a morning, and the sheep bleated in the fields. The man and witch inside him yearned for the time to pass, for the strength to wield his grandfather's sword without his arm trembling from the weight. For the time he could fully embrace his powers, practice the magicks that were his by birth and right. The time he would spill Cabhan's blood black and burning on the earth.

Still, in the dreams he was only a boy, untried and weak, pursued by the wolf Cabhan became, the wolf with the red stone of his black power gleaming at his throat. And it was his own blood, and the blood of his sisters, that spilled warm and red onto the ground.

On mornings after the worst dreams he went to the river, rowed out to fish, to be alone, though most days he craved the company of the cottage, the voices, the scents of cooking.

But after the blood dreams he needed to be away—and no one scolded him for not helping with the milking or the mucking or the feeding, not on those mornings.

So he sat in the boat, a slim boy of ten with a mop of brown hair still tousled from sleep, and the wild blue eyes of his father, the bright and stirring power of his mother.

He could listen to the day wake around him, wait patiently for the fish to take his bait and eat the oatcake he'd taken from his cousin's kitchen.

And he could find himself again.

The river, the quiet, the gentle rock of the boat reminded him of the last truly happy day he'd had with his mother and sisters.

She'd looked well, he remembered, after how pale and strained she had looked over the long, icy winter. They were, all of them, counting the days until Bealtaine, and his father's return. They'd sit around the fire then, so Eamon had thought, eating cakes and tea sweetened with honey while they listened to his father's tales of the raids and the hunting.

They would feast, so he had thought, and his mother would be well again.

So he'd believed, that day on the river when they'd fished and laughed, and all thought of how soon their father would be home.

But he'd never come, for Cabhan had used his dark magicks to slay Daithi the brave. And Sorcha, the Dark Witch—even though she'd burned him to ash, he'd killed her. Killed her and somehow still existed.

Eamon knew it from the dreams, from the prickle down his spine. Saw the truth of it in the eyes of his sisters.

But he had that day, that bright spring day on the river to remember. Even as a fish tugged on his line, his mind traveled back, and he saw himself at five years bringing a shining fish from the dark river.

Felt that same sense of pride now.

"Ailish will be pleased."

His mother smiled at him as he slid the fish into the pail of water to hold it fresh.

His great need brought her to him, gave him comfort. He baited his hook again as the sun warmed and began to thin the fingers of mists.

"We'll need more than one."

She'd said that, he remembered, that long ago day.

"Then you'll catch more than one."

"I'd sooner catch more than one in my own river."

"One day you will. One day, *mo chroi*, you'll return home. One day those who come from you will fish in our river, walk our wood. I promise this to you."

Tears wanted to come, blurred his vision of her, so she wavered in front of his eyes. He willed them away, for he would see her clear. The dark hair she let fall free to her waist, the dark eyes where love lived. And the power that shone from her. Even now, a vision only, he sensed her power.

"Why could you not destroy him, Ma? Why could you not live?"

"It was not meant. My love, my boy, my heart, if I could have spared you and your sisters, I would have given more than my life."

"You did give more. You gave us your power, almost all of it. If you'd kept it—"

"It was my time, and your birthright. I am content with that, I promise you as well." In those thinning mists she glowed, silver-edged. "I am ever in you, Eamon the Loyal. I am in your blood, your heart, your mind. You are not alone."

"I miss you."

He felt her lips on his cheek, the warmth of her, the scent of her enfolding him. And for that moment, just that moment, he could be a child again.

"I want to be brave and strong. I will be, I swear it. I will protect Brannaugh and Teagan."

"You will protect each other. You are the three. Together more powerful than I ever was."

"Will I kill him?" For that was his deepest, darkest wish. "Will I finish him?"

"I cannot say, only that he can never take what you are. What you are, what you hold, can only be given, as I gave to you. He carries my curse, and the mark of it. All who come from him will bear it as all who come from you will carry the light. My blood, Eamon." She turned her palm up, showed a thin line of blood. "And yours."

He felt the quick pain, saw the wound across his palm. And joined it with his mother's.

"The blood of the three, out of Sorcha, will lay him low, if it takes a thousand years. Trust what you are. It is enough."

She kissed him again, smiled again. “You have more than one.”

The tug on his line brought him out of the vision.

So he had more than one.

He would be brave, he thought as he pulled the fish, flapping, out of the river. He would be strong. And one day, strong enough.

He studied his hand—no mark on it now, but he understood. He carried her blood, and her gift. These, one day, he would pass to his sons, his daughters. If it wasn’t for him to destroy Cabhan, it would be done by his blood.

But he hoped, by all the gods, it was for him.

For now, he’d fish. It was good to be a man, he thought, to hunt and fish, to provide. To pay back his cousins for the shelter and the care.

He’d learned patience since being a man—and caught four fish before he rowed the boat back to shore. He secured the boat, strung the fish on a line.

He stood a moment, looking out at the water, the shine of it now under the fullness of the sun. He thought of his mother, the sound of her voice, the scent of her hair. Her words would stay with him.

He would walk back through the little woods. Not great like home, but a fine wood all the same, he told himself.

And he would bring Ailish the fish, take some tea by the fire. Then he would help with the last of the harvest.

He heard the high, sharp cry as he started back to the cottage and the little farm. Smiling to himself, he reached into his satchel, drew out his leather glove. He only had to pull it on, lift his arm, and Roibeard swooped out of the clouds, wings spread to land.

“Good morning to you.” Eamon looked into those golden eyes, felt the tug of connection with his hawk, his guide, his friend. He touched the charmed amulet around his neck, one his mother had conjured with blood magicks for protection. It carried the image of the hawk.

“It’s a fine day, isn’t it? Bright and cool. The harvest is nearly done, and we'll have our celebration soon," he continued as he walked with the hawk on his arm. "The equinox, as you know, when night conquers day as Gronw Pebr conquered Lleu Llaw Gyffes. We'll celebrate the birth of Mabon, son of Mordon the guardian of the earth. Sure there'll be honey cakes for certain. I'll see you have a bit."

The hawk rubbed its head against Eamon's cheek, affectionate as a kitten.

"I had the dream again, of Cabhan. Of home, of Ma after she gave us almost all there was of her power and sent us away to be safe. I see it, Roibeard. How she poisoned him with a kiss, how she flamed, using all she had to destroy him. He took her life, and still . . . I saw the stirring in the ashes she made of him. The stirring of them, something evil, and the glow of red from his power."

Eamon paused a moment, drew up his power, opened to it. He felt the beating heart of a rabbit rushing into the brush, the hunger of a fledgling waiting for its mother and its breakfast.

He felt his sisters, the sheep, the horses.

And no threat.

"He hasn't found us. I would feel it. You would see it, and would tell me. But he looks, and he hunts, and he waits, as I feel that as well."

Those bold blue eyes darkened; the boy's tender mouth firmed into a man's. "I won't hide forever. One day, on the blood of Daithi and Sorcha, I'll do the hunting."

Eamon lifted a hand, took a fistful of air, swirled it, tossed it—gently—toward a tree. Branches shook, and roosting birds took flight.

"I'll only get stronger, won't I?" he murmured, and walked to the cottage to please Ailish with four fish.

BRANNAUGH WENT ABOUT HER DUTIES AS SHE DID EVERY day. As every day for five years she'd done all that was asked of her. She cooked, she cleaned, tended the young ones as Ailish always seemed to have a baby at the breast or in the belly. She helped plant the fields and tend the crops. She helped in harvest.

Good honest work, of course, and satisfying in its way. No one could be more kind than her cousin Ailish and her husband. Good, solid people both, people of the earth, who'd offered more than shelter to three orphaned children.

They'd offered family, and there was no more precious gift.

Hadn't her mother known it? She would never have sent her three children to Ailish otherwise. Even in the darkest hour, Sorcha would never have given her beloved children to anyone but the kind, and the loving.

But at twelve, Brannaugh was no longer a child. And what rose in her, spread in her, woke in her—more since she'd started her courses the year before—demanded.

Holding so much in, turning her eyes from that ever-brightening light proved harder and more sorrowful every day. But she owed Ailish respect, and her cousin held a fear of magicks and power—even her own.

Brannaugh had done what her mother asked of her on that terrible morning. She'd taken her brother and sister south, away from their home in Mayo. She'd kept off the road; she'd shuttered her grief in her heart where only she could hear it keening.

And in that heart lived the need to avenge as well, the need to embrace the power inside her, and learn more, learn and hone enough to defeat Cabhan, once and done.

But Ailish wanted only her man, her children, her farm. And why not? She was entitled to her home and her life and her land, the quiet of it all. Hadn't she risked it by taking in Sorcha's blood? Taking in what Cabhan lusted for—hunted for?

She deserved gratitude, loyalty, and respect.

But what lived in Brannaugh clawed for freedom. Choices needed to be made.

She'd seen her brother walk back from the river with his fish, his hawk. She felt him test his power out of the sight of the cottage—as he often did. As Teagan, their sister, often did. Ailish, chattering about the jams they'd make that day, felt nothing. Her cousin blocked most of what she had—a puzzlement to Brannaugh—and used only the bit she allowed herself to sweeten jams or coax bigger eggs from the hens.

Brannaugh told herself it was worth the sacrifice, the wait to find more, learn more, be more. Her brother and sister were safe here—as their mother wished. Teagan, whose grief had been beyond reaching for days, weeks, laughed and played. She did her chores cheerfully, tended the animals, rode like a warrior on her big gray Alastar.

Perhaps some nights she wept in her sleep, but Brannaugh had only to gather her in to soothe her.

Except when came the dreams of Cabhan. They came to Teagan, to Eamon, to herself. More often now, clearer now, so clear Brannaugh had begun to hear his voice echo after she woke.

Choices must be made. This waiting, this sanctuary, might need to come to an end, one way or another.

In the evening she scrubbed potatoes, tender from the harvest. She stirred the stew bubbling low on the fire, and tapped her foot as her cousin's man made music on his little harp.

The cottage, warm and snug, a happy place filled with good scents, cheerful voices, Ailish's laugh as she lifted her youngest onto her hip for a dance.

Family, she thought again. Well fed, well tended in a cottage warm and snug, with herbs drying in the kitchen, babes with rosy cheeks.

It should have contented her—how she wished it would.

She caught Eamon's eye, the same bold blue as their father's, felt his power prod against her. He saw too much, did Eamon, she thought. Far too much if she didn't remember to shutter him out.

She gave him a bit of a poke back—a little warning to mind his own. In the way of sisters, she smiled at his wince.

After the evening meal there were pots to be cleaned, children to tuck into bed. Mabh, the eldest at seven, complained, as always, she wasn't sleepy. Seamus snuggled right in, ready with his dreaming smile. The twins she'd helped bring into the world herself chattered to each other like magpies, young Brighid slipped her comforting thumb in her mouth, and the baby slept before his mother laid him down.

Brannaugh wondered if Ailish knew both she and the babe with his sweet angel face would not be without magick. The birth, so painful, so *wrong*, would have ended them both in blood without Brannaugh's power, the healing, the seeing, the doing.

Though they never spoke of it, she thought Ailish knew.

Ailish straightened, a hand on her back, another on the next babe in her womb. "And a good night and happy dreams to all. Brannaugh, would you have some tea with me? I could do with some of your soothing tea, as this one's kicking up a storm tonight."

"Sure and I'll fix you some." And add the charm as she always did for health and an easy birthing. "He's well and healthy that one, and will be, I suspect, as big a handful on his own as the twins."

"It's a boy for certain," Ailish said as they climbed down from the sleeping loft. "I can feel it. I've not been wrong yet."

"Nor are you this time. You could do with more rest, cousin."

"A woman with six children and one in the pot doesn't see much rest. I'm well enough." Her gaze fixed on Brannaugh's for confirmation.

"You are to be sure, but could do with more rest all the same."

"You're a great help and comfort to me, Brannaugh."

"I hope I am."

Something here, Brannaugh thought as she busied herself with the tea. She sensed her cousin's nerves, and they stirred her own.

"Now that the harvest is in, you might settle in with your sewing. It's needed work, and restful for you. I can see to the cooking. Teagan and Mabh will help there, and I'll tell you true, Mabh's already a fine cook."

"Aye, sure and she is that. I'm so proud of her."

"With the girls seeing to the cooking, Eamon and I can help our cousin hunt. I know you'd rather I didn't take up the bow, but isn't it wise for each to do what we do well?"

Ailish's gaze veered away a moment.

Aye, Brannaugh thought, she knows and, more, feels the weight of asking us not to be what we are.

"I loved your mother."

"Oh, and she you."

"We saw little of each other the last years. Still she sent messages to me, in her way. The night Mabh was born, the little blanket my girl still holds as she sleeps was there, just there on the cradle Bardan made for her."

"When she spoke of you, it was with love."

"She sent you to me. You, Eamon, Teagan. She came to me, in a dream, asked me to give you a home."

"You never told me," Brannaugh murmured, and carried the tea to her cousin, sat with her by the peat fire.

"Two days before you came, she asked it of me."

With her hands clasped in her lap over skirts as gray as her eyes, Brannaugh stared into the fire. "It took eight for us to travel here. Her spirit came to you. I wish I could see her again, but I only see her in dreams."

"She's with you. I see her in you. In Eamon, in Teagan, but most in you. Her strength and beauty. Her fierce love of family. You're of age now, Brannaugh. Of age where you must begin to think of making a family."

"I have a family."

"Of your own, as your own mother did. A home, darling, a man to work the land for you, babes of your own."

She sipped her tea as Brannaugh remained silent. "Fial is a fine man, a good man. He was good to his wife while she lived, I can promise you. He needs a wife, a mother for his children. He has a fine house, far bigger than ours. He would offer for you, and he would open his house to Eamon and Teagan."

"How could I wed Fial? He is . . ." *Old* was her first thought, but she realized he would be no older than her Bardan.

"He would give you a good life, give a good life to your brother, your sister." Ailish picked up her sewing, busying her hands. "I would never speak of it to you if I believed he would not treat you with kindness, always. He is handsome, Brannaugh, and has a fine way about him. Will you walk out with him?"

"I . . . Cousin, I don't think of Fial in that way."

"Perhaps if you walk out with him you will." Ailish smiled as she said it, as if she knew a secret. "A woman needs a man to provide, to protect, to give her children. A kind man with a good house, a pleasing face—"

"Did you wed with Bardan because he was kind?"

"I would not have wedded him hadn't he been. Only consider it. We'll tell him we wait until after the equinox to speak to you of it. Consider. Will you do that?"

"I will."

Brannaugh got to her feet. "Does he know what I am?"

Ailish's tired eyes lowered. "You are the oldest daughter of my cousin."

"Does he know what I am, Ailish?"

It stirred in her now, what she held in, held back. Pride stirred it. And the light that played over her face came not only from the flickers of the fire.

"I am the oldest daughter of the Dark Witch of Mayo. And before she sacrificed her life, she sacrificed her power, passing it to me, to Eamon, Teagan. We are the three. Dark witches we."

"You are a child—"

"A child when you speak of magicks, of power. But a woman when you speak of wedding Fial."

The truth of that had a flush warming Ailish's cheeks. "Brannaugh, my love, have you not been content here these last years?"

"Aye, content. And so grateful."

"Blood gives to blood with no need for grateful."

"Aye. Blood gives to blood."

Setting her sewing aside again, Ailish reached for Brannaugh's hands. "You would be safe, the daughter of my cousin. And you would be content. You would, I believe it, be loved. Could you want more?"

"I am more," she said quietly, and went up to the sleeping loft.

BUT SLEEP ELUDED. SHE LAY QUIET BESIDE TEAGAN, WAITING for the murmurs between Ailish and Bardan to fade away. They would speak of this match, this good, sensible match. They would convince themselves her reluctance was only a young girl's nerves.

Just as they had convinced themselves she, Eamon, and Teagan were children, like any others.

She rose quietly, slipped on her soft boots, her shawl. It was air she needed. Air, the night, the moon.

She climbed silently down from the loft, eased the door open.

Kathel, her hound, who slept by the fire, uncurled and, without question or hesitation, went out before her.

Now she could breathe, with the cool night air on her cheeks, with the quiet like a soothing hand on the chaos inside her. Here, for as long as she could hold it, was freedom.

She and the faithful dog slipped like shadows into the trees. She heard the bubbling of the river, the sigh of wind through the trees, smelled the earth, and the tinge from the peat smoke rising from the cottage chimney.

She could cast the circle, try to conjure her mother's spirit. She needed her mother tonight. In five years, she'd not wept, not allowed herself a single tear. Now, she wanted to sit on the ground, her head on her mother's breast, and weep.

She laid a hand on the amulet she wore—the image of the hound her mother had conjured with love, with magick, with blood.

Did she stay true to her blood, to what lived in her? Did she embrace her own needs, wants, passions? Or did she set that aside like a toy outgrown, and do what would ensure the safety and future of her brother and sister?

"Mother," she murmured, "what should I do? What would you have me do? You gave your life for us. Can I do less?"

She felt the reaching out, the joining of power like a twining of fingers. Whirling around, she stared at the shadows. Heart racing, she thought: *Ma*.

But it was Eamon who stepped into the moonlight, with Teagan's hand in his.

The keen edge of her disappointment sliced like a blade through her voice. "You are to be abed. What are you thinking wandering the woods at night?"

"You do the same," Eamon snapped back.

"I am the oldest."

"I am head of the family."

"The puny staff between your legs doesn't make you head of the family."

Teagan giggled, then rushed forward, threw her arms around her sister. "Don't be angry. You needed us to come. You were in my dream. You wept."

"I am not weeping."

"In here." Teagan touched a hand to Brannaugh's heart. Her deep, dark eyes—so like their mother's—searched her sister's face. "Why are you sad?"

"I am not sad. I only came out to think. To be alone and think."

"You think too loud," Eamon muttered, still smarting over the "puny" comment.

"And you should have more manners than to listen to others' thoughts."

"How can I help it when you *shout* them?"

"Stop. We will not quarrel." Teagan might have been the smallest of them, but she didn't lack in will. "We will not quarrel," she repeated. "Brannaugh is sad, Eamon is like a man standing on hot coals, and I . . . I feel like I do when I've had too much pudding."

"Are you ill?" Brannaugh's anger whisked away. She peered into Teagan's eyes.

"Not that way. Something is . . . not balanced. I feel it. I think you do, and you do. So we will not quarrel. We are family." Still holding Brannaugh's hand, Teagan reached for Eamon's. "Tell us, sister, why you're sad."

"I . . . I want to cast a circle. I want to feel the light in me. I want to cast a circle and sit in its light with you. Both of you."

"We rarely ever do," Teagan said. "Because Ailish would we didn't."

"And she has taken us in. We owe her respect in her home. But we are not in her home now, and she need not know. I need the light. I need to speak with you within our circle, where no one can hear."

"I will cast it. I practice," Teagan told her. "When Alastar and I ride away, I practice."

On a sigh, Brannaugh ran a hand down her sister's bright hair. "It's good you do. Cast the circle, *deirfiúr bheag*."

2

BRANNAUGH WATCHED TEAGAN WORK, HOW HER SISTER pulled light, pulled fire out of herself, gave the goddess her thanks as she forged the ring. A ring wide enough, Brannaugh thought, with amusement and with gratitude, to include Kathel.

"You did well. I should have taught you more, but I . . ."

"Respected Ailish."

"And worry as well," Eamon put in, "that if we use our power too much, too strong, he'll know. He'll come."

"Aye." Brannaugh sat on the ground, looped an arm around Kathel. "She wanted us safe. She gave up everything for us. Her power, her life. She believed she would destroy him, and we would be safe. She couldn't know whatever black power he bargained with could bring him out of the ashes."

"Weaker."

She looked at Eamon, nodded. "Yes, weaker. Then. He . . . eats power, I think. He'll find others, take from them, grow stronger. She wanted us safe." Brannaugh drew a breath. "Fial wishes to wed me."

Eamon's mouth fell open. "Fial? But he's old."

"No older than Bardan."

"Old!"

Brannaugh laughed, felt some of the tightness in her chest ease. "Men want young wives, it seems. So they can bear them many children, and still want to bed with them and cook for them."

"You will not wed Fial," Teagan said decisively.

"He is kind, and not uncomely. He has a house and farm larger than Ailish and Bardan. He would welcome you both."

"You will not wed Fial," Teagan repeated. "You do not love him."

"I don't look for love nor do I need it."

"You should, but even if you close your eyes, it will find you. Do you forget the love between our mother and father?"

"I don't. I don't think to find such a thing for myself. Perhaps one day you will. So pretty you are, and bright."

"Oh, I will." Teagan nodded wisely. "As you will, as Eamon will. And we will pass what we are, what we have, to those who come from us. Our mother wanted this. She wanted us to live."

"We would live, and well, if I wed Fial. I am the oldest," Brannaugh reminded them. "It is for me to decide."

"She charged me to protect you." Eamon folded his arms across his chest. "I forbid it."

"We will not quarrel." Teagan snatched their hands, gripped hard. Flame shimmered through their joined fingers. "And I will not be tended to. I am not a babe, Brannaugh, but the same age as you when we left our home. You will not marry to give me a home. You will not deny what you are, ignore your power. You are not Ailish, but Brannaugh, daughter of Sorcha and Daithi. You are a dark witch, and ever will be."

"One day we will destroy him," Eamon vowed. "One day we will avenge our father, our mother, and we will destroy even the ash we burn him into. Our mother has told me we will, or those who come from us will, if it takes a thousand years."

"She told you?"

"This morning. She came to me while I was on the river, in the mists and the quiet. I find her there when I need her."

"She comes to me only in dreams." Tears Brannaugh wouldn't shed clogged her throat.

"You hold what you are so tight." To soothe, Teagan stroked her sister's hair. "So not to upset Ailish, so to protect us. Perhaps you only allow her to come in dreams."

"She comes to you?" Brannaugh murmured. "Not only in dreams?"

"Sometimes when I ride Alastar, when we go deep into the woods, and I hold myself quiet, so quiet, she comes. She sings to me as she used to when I was little. And it was our mother who told me we will have love, we will have children. And we will, by our blood, defeat Cabhan."

"Am I to marry Fial then, bear him the child, the blood, who will finish it?"

"No!" Tiny flames flickered at Teagan's fingertips before she remembered control. "There is no love. The love comes, then the child. This is the way."

"It is not the only way."

"It is our way." Eamon took Brannaugh's hand again. "It will be our way. We will be what we are meant, do what we must do. If we don't try, what they sacrificed for us is for nothing. They would have died for nothing. Do you want it so?"

"No. No. I want to kill him. I want his blood, his death." Struggling, Brannaugh pressed her face to Kathel's neck, soothed herself with his warmth. "I think part of me would die if I turned away from what I am. But I know all of me would if a choice I make brings harm to either of you."

"We choose, all of us," Eamon said. "One by three. We needed this time. Our mother sent us here so we could have this time. We are not children now. I think we were no longer children when we rode from home that morning, knowing we would never see her again."

"We had power." Brannaugh breathed deep, straightened. Though he was younger, and a boy for all that, her brother spoke true. "She gave us more. I asked you both to let it lie still."

"You were right to ask it—even if we woke it now and then," Eamon added with a smile. "We needed the time here, but this time is coming to a close. I feel it."

"As I do," Brannaugh murmured. "So I wondered if it meant Fial. But no, you're right, both of you. I am not for the farm. Not for kitchen magicks and parlor games. We will look, here within the circle. We will look, and see. And know."

"Together?" Teagan's face glowed with joy as she asked, and Brannaugh knew she'd held back herself, her sister and brother too long.

"Together." Brannaugh cupped her hands, brought the power up, out. And dropping her hands down like water falling, she made the fire.

And the making of it, that first skill learned, the purity of the magick coursed through her. It felt as if she'd taken her first full breath in five years.

"You have more now," Teagan stated.

"Aye. It's waited. I've waited. We've waited. We wait no more. Through the flame and the smoke, we'll seek him out, see where he lurks. You see deeper," she told Eamon, "but have a care. If he knows we look at him, he will look at us."

"I know what I'm about. We can go through the fire, fly through the air, over water and earth, to where he is." He laid a hand on the small sword at his side. "We can kill him."

"It will take more than your sword. For all her power, our mother couldn't destroy him. It will take more, and we will find more. In time. For now, we look only."

"We can fly. Alastar and I. We . . ." Teagan trailed off at Brannaugh's sharp look. "It just . . . happened one day."

"We are what we are." Brannaugh shook her head. "I should never have forgotten it. Now we look. Through fire, through smoke, with shielded sight as we invoke. To seek, to find, his eyes we blind, he who shed our blood. Now our power rises in a flood. We are the three. As we will, so mote it be."

They gripped hands, joined their light.

Flames shifted; smoke cleared.

There, drinking wine from a silver cup, was Cabhan. His dark hair fell to his shoulders, gleamed in the light of the tallows.

Brannaugh saw stone walls, rich tapestries covering them, a bed with curtains of deep blue velvet.

At his ease, she thought. He had found comfort, riches—it didn't surprise her. He would use his powers for gain, for pleasure, for death. For whatever suited his purpose.

A woman came into the chamber. She wore rich robes, had hair dark as midnight. Spellbound, Brannaugh thought, by the blind look in her eyes.

And yet . . . some power there, some, Brannaugh realized. Struggling to break the bonds that locked it tight.

Cabhan didn't speak, merely flicked a hand toward the bed. The woman walked to it, disrobed, stood for a moment, her skin white as moonshine glowing in the light.

Behind those blind eyes, Brannaugh saw the war waged, the bitter, bitter fight to break free. To strike out.

For a moment, Eamon's focus wavered. He'd never seen a grown woman fully naked, nor one with such large breasts. Like his sisters he sensed that trapped power—like a white bird in a black box. But all that bare skin, those soft, generous breasts, the fascinating triangle of hair between her legs.

Would it feel like the hair on her head? He desperately wanted to touch, just there, and know.

Cabhan's head came up, a wolf scenting the air. He rose so quickly, the silver cup upended, spilling wine red as blood.

Brannaugh twisted Eamon's fingers painfully. Though he yelped, flushed as red as the fire, he brought his focus back.

Still, for a moment, a terrible moment, Cabhan's eyes seemed to look straight into his.

Then he walked to the woman. He gripped her breasts, squeezed, twisted. Pain ran over her face, but she didn't cry out.

Couldn't cry out.

He pinched her nipples, twisted them until tears ran down her cheeks, until bruises marred the white skin. He struck her, knocking her back on the bed. Blood trickled from the corner of her mouth, but she only stared.

With a flick of his wrist, he was naked, and his cock fully erect. It seemed to glow, but not with light. With dark. Eamon sensed it was like ice—cold and sharp and horrible. And this he rammed into the woman like a pike while the tears ran down her cheeks and the blood trickled from her mouth.

Something inside Eamon burst up with outrage—a vicious, innate fury at seeing a woman treated thus. He nearly pushed through that fire, that smoke, but Brannaugh gripped his hand, twisting bone against bone.

And while he raped her—for it was nothing else—Eamon felt Cabhan's thoughts. Thoughts of Sorcha, and the terrible lust for her that he'd never quenched. Thoughts of . . . Brannaugh. Of Brannaugh, and how he would do this to her, and more. And worse. How he would give her pain before he took her power. How he would take her power before he took her life.

Brannaugh quenched the fire quickly, ended the vision on a snap. And as quickly grabbed Eamon by both arms. "I said we were not ready. Do you not think I felt you gather to go?"

"He hurt her. He took her power, her body, against her will."

"He nearly found you—he sensed something pushing in."

"I would kill him for his thoughts alone. He will never touch you as he did her."

"He wanted to hurt her." Teagan's voice was a child's now. "But he thought of our mother, not of her. Then he thought of you."

"His thoughts can't hurt me." But they'd shaken her, deep inside herself. "He will never do to me, or to you, what he did to that poor woman."

"Could we have helped her?"

"Ah, Teagan, I don't know."

"We did not try." Eamon's words lashed out. "You held me here."

"For your life, for ours, for our purpose. Do you think I don't feel what you feel?" Even the secret fear drowned in an icy wave of rage. "That it stabbed a thousand times to do nothing? He has power. Not what he had, but different. Not more, but less, and still different. I don't know how to fight him. Yet. We don't know, Eamon, and we must know."

"He's coming. Not tonight, not tomorrow, but he'll come. He knows you . . ." Eamon flushed again, looked away.

"He knows I can bear children," Brannaugh finished. "He thinks to get a son from me. He never will. But he's coming. I felt it as well."

"Then we must go." Teagan tipped her head to Kathel's flank. "We must never bring him here."

"We must go," Brannaugh agreed. "We must be what we are."

"Where will we go?"

"South." Brannaugh looked at Eamon for confirmation.

"Aye, south, as he is still north. He remains in Mayo."

"We will find a place, and there we will learn more, find more. And one day we will go home."

She rose, took both their hands again, let the power spark from one to one. "I swear by our blood we will go home again."

"I swear by our blood," Eamon said, "we or what comes from us will destroy even the thought of him."

"I swear by our blood," Teagan said, "we are the three, and will ever be."

"Now we close the circle, but never again close off what we are, what we have, what we were given." Brannaugh released their hands. "We leave on the morrow."

EYES WEEPY, AILISH WATCHED BRANNAUGH PACK HER SHAWL. "I beg you to stay. Think of Teagan. She's but a child."

"The age I was when we came to you."

"As you were a child," she said.

"I was more. We are more, and must be what we are."

"I frightened you by speaking of Fial. You cannot think we would force a marriage upon you."

"No. Oh no." Brannaugh turned then, took her cousin's hands. "You never would. It is not for Fial we leave you, cousin."

Turning, Brannaugh packed the last of her things.

"Your mother would not want this for you."

"My mother would want us to be home, happy and safe with her and our father. But that was not to be. My mother gave her life for us, gave her power to us. And now her purpose to us. We must live our lives, embrace our power, complete our purpose."

"Where will you go?"

"To Clare, I think. For now. We will come back. And we will go home. I feel it as true as life. He will not come here."

Turning back, she looked into her cousin's eyes, her own like smoke. "He will not come here or harm you or any of yours. This I swear to you on my mother's blood."

"How can you know?"

"I am one of three. I am a dark witch of Mayo, first daughter of Sorcha. He shall not come here nor harm you or yours. You are protected for all of your life. This I have done. I would not leave you unprotected."

"Brannaugh . . ."

"You worry." Brannaugh laid her hands over her cousin's hands, which rested on the mound of her belly. "Have I not told you your son is well and healthy? The birthing will go easy, and quickly as well. This I can promise as well, and I do. But . . ."

"What is it? You must tell me."

"As you love me so still you fear what I have. But you must bide me now, in this. Your son, this one to come, must be the last. He will be healthy, and the birthing will go well. But the next will not. If there is a next, you will not survive."

"I . . . You cannot know. I cannot deny my husband the marriage bed. Or myself."

"You cannot deny your children their mother. It is a terrible grieving, Ailish."

"God will decide."

"God will have given you seven children, but the price for another will be your life, and the babe's as well. As I love you, heed me."

She took a bottle from her pocket. "I have made this for you. Only you. You will put it away. Once every month on the first day of your courses, you will drink—one sip only. You will not conceive, even after you take the last sip, for it will be done. You will live. Your children will have their mother. You will live to rock their children."

Ailish laid her hands over the mound of her belly. "I will be barren."

"You will sing to your children, and their children. You will share your bed with your man in pleasure. You will rejoice in the precious lives you brought into the world. The choice is yours, Ailish."

She closed her eyes a moment. When she opened them, they turned dark, dark. "You will call him Lughaidh. He will be fair of face and hair, blue of eye. A strong boy with a ready smile, and the voice of an angel. One day he will travel and ramble and use his voice to make his living. He will fall in love with a farmer's daughter, and will come back to you with her to work the land. And you will hear his voice across the fields, for he will ever be joyful."

She let the vision go. "I have seen what can be. You must choose."

"This is the name I chose for him," Ailish murmured. "I never told you, nor anyone." Now she took the bottle. "I will heed you."

Pressing her lips together, Ailish reached into her pocket, took out a small pouch. This she pushed into Brannaugh's hand. "Take this."

"I won't take your coin."

"You *will*." The tears fell now, spilling down her cheeks like rain. "Do you think I don't know you saved me and Conall in the birthing? And even now you think of me and mine? You have given me joy. You have brought Sorcha to me when I missed her, for I saw her in you day by day. You will take the coin, and swear to me you will be safe, you will come back. All of you, for you are mine as I am yours."

Understanding, Brannaugh slipped the purse into the pocket of her skirts, then kissed Ailish on each cheek. "I swear it."

Outside Eamon did his best to make his cousins laugh. They asked him not to go, of course, asked why he must, tried to bargain with him. So he wound stories of the grand adventures he would have, smiting dragons and catching magick frogs. He saw Teagan walking with a weeping Mabh, saw her give Mabh a rag doll she'd made herself.

He wished Brannaugh would hurry, for the leave-taking was a misery. Alastar stood ready. Eamon—he was head of the family, after all, had decided his sisters would ride, and he would walk.

He would brook no argument.

Bardan came out of the little stable leading Slaine—Old Slaine now, as the broodmare was past her prime, but a sweet-natured thing for all that.

"Her breeding days are done," Bardan said in his careful way. "But she's a good girl, and she'll serve you well."

"Oh, but I can't be taking her from you. You need—"

"A man needs a horse." Bardan set his calloused hand on Eamon's shoulder. "You've done a man's work for the farm, so you'll take her. I'd give you Moon for Brannaugh if I could spare him, but you'll take Old Slaine here."

"It's more than grateful I am to you, for Slaine and all the rest. I promise you I'll treat her like a queen."

For a moment, Eamon let himself be just a boy, and threw his arms around his cousin, the man who'd been a father to him for half his life. "We'll come back one day."

"Be sure you do."

When it was done, all the farewells, the safe journeys, the tears, he swung up on the mare, his grandfather's sword and sheath secured against his saddle. Brannaugh mounted behind Teagan, leaned down once to kiss Ailish a last time.

They rode away from the farm, their home for five years, from their family—and south toward the unknown.

He looked back, waved as they waved, found himself more torn in the leaving than he'd expected. Then overhead Roibeard called, circled before spearing the way south.

This was meant, Eamon decided. This was the time.

He slowed his pace a bit, cocked his head at Teagan. "So, how does our Slaine feel about all this then?"

Teagan looked down at the mare, cocked her head in turn. "Oh, it's a grand adventure to her, to be sure, and she never thought to have another. She's proud and she's grateful. She'll be loyal to the end of her days, and do her very best for you."

"And I'll do my best for her. We'll ride through midday before we stop to rest the horses, and eat the first of the oatcakes Ailish packed for us."

"Is that what we'll be doing?" Brannaugh said.

He tossed up his chin. "You're the eldest, but I have the staff, however puny you might think it is—which it isn't at all. Roibeard shows the way, and we follow."

Brannaugh looked up, watched the flight of the hawk. Then down at Kathel who pranced along beside Alastar as if he could walk all day and through the night.

"Your guide, mine, and Teagan's. Aye, we follow. Ailish gave me some coin, but we won't be spending it unless we must. We'll be making our own."

"And just how are we doing that?"

"By being what we are." She lifted her hand, palm up, brought a small ball of flame into it. Then vanished it. "Our mother served her gift, tended us, her cabin. We can surely serve our gift, tend ourselves, and find a place to do both."

"Clare's a wild place I hear," Teagan offered.

"And what better place than the wild for such as us?" The pure joy of freedom ripened with every step. "We have our mother's book, and we'll study, we'll learn. We'll make potions and do healings. A healer is always welcome, she told me."

"When he comes, it will take more than healing and potions."

"So it will," Brannaugh said to her brother. "So we learn. We were safe five years at the farm. If our guides lead us to Clare, as it seems they will, we may have the next five there. Time enough to learn, to plan. When we go home again, we'll be stronger than he can know."

They rode through midday and into the rain. Soft and steady it fell from a sky of bruises and broodings. They rested the horses, watered them, shared oatcakes, with some for Kathel.

Through the rain came the wind as they continued their journey, past a little farm and cabin with smoke puffing out of the chimney, sending out the scent of burning peat. Inside they might be welcome, be given tea and a place by the fire. Inside the warm and dry.

But Kathel continued to prance, Roibeard to circle, and Alastar never slowed.

And even the gloomy light began to die as the day tipped toward night.

"Slaine grows weary," Teagan murmured. "She won't ask to stop, but she tires. Her bones ache. Can't we rest her a bit, find a dry place and—"

"There!" Eamon pointed ahead. Near the muddy track stood what might have been an old place of worship. Sacked now, burned down to the scorched stone by men who couldn't stop destroying what those they vanquished had built.

Roibeard circled over it, calling, calling, and Kathel bounded ahead.

"We'll stop there for the night. Make a fire, rest the animals and ourselves."

Brannaugh nodded at her brother. "The walls stand—or most of them. It should keep the wind out, and we can do the rest. It's nearly end of day. We owe Mordan and Mabon who came from her our thanks."

One wall had fallen in, they discovered, but the others stood. Even some steps, which Eamon immediately tested, circled up to what had been a second level. Whatever timber had been used had burned to ashes and blown to the winds. But it was shelter of a sort and, Brannaugh felt, the right place.

This would be the place of their first night, the equinox, when the light and the dark balanced.

"I'll tend the horses." Teagan took the reins of both. "The horses are mine, after all. I'll see to them, if you make us a place, a dry spot I'm hoping, and a good fire."

"That I'll do. We'll give our thanks, then have some tea and some of the dried venison before we—"

She broke off as Roibeard swooped down, perched on a narrow stone ledge.

And dropped a fat hare on the ground at Eamon's feet.

"Well now, that's a feast in the making. I'll clean it, Teagan tends the horses, and Brannaugh the fire."

A dry spot, she thought, and shoving back the hood of her cloak imagined one. Drew up and out what she was, thought of warm and dry—and flashed out heat so bright and hot it nearly burned them all before she drew it down again.

"I'm sorry for that. I haven't done any of this before."

"It's a cork out of a bottle," Eamon decided. "And it poured out too fast."

"Aye." She slowed it, carefully, carefully. She didn't mind the wet for herself, but Teagan was right. The old mare's bones ached, even she could feel it.

She eased back the wet, slowly, just a bit, just a bit more. It trembled through her, the joy of it. Loosed now, free. Then the fire. Magickal tonight. Other nights, as their mother had taught them, a body gathered wood, put the work into it. But tonight, it would be her fire.

She brought it, banked it.

"A bit of the oatcake, and some wine," she told her brother, her sister. "An offering of thanks to the gods for the balance of the day and night, for the cycle of rebirth. And for this place of rest.

"Into the fire," she told them. "The cake, then the wine. These small things we share with thee, we give our thanks we servants three."

"At this time where day meets night, we embrace both dark and light," Eamon continued, not sure where the words had come from.

"We will learn to stand and fight, to use our gifts for the right and the white," Teagan added.

"In this place and hour, we open to our given power. From now till ever it will be free. As we will, so mote it be."

The fire shot up, a tower, red, orange, gold, with a heart of burning blue. A thousand voices whispered in it, and the ground shook. Then the world seemed to sigh.

The fire was a fire, banked in a tidy circle on the stony ground.

"This is what we are," Brannaugh said, still glowing from the shock of energy. "This is what we have. The nights grow longer now. The dark conquers light. But he will not conquer us."

She smiled, her heart full as it hadn't been since the morning they'd left home. "We need to make a spit for the hare. We'll have that feast tonight, our first. And we'll rest in the warm and dry until we journey on."

EAMON CURLED BY THE FIRE, HIS BELLY FULL, HIS BODY warm and dry. And journeyed on.

He felt himself lift up, lift out, and fly. North. Home.

Like Roibeard, he soared over the hills, the rivers, the fields where cattle lowed, where sheep cropped.

Green and green toward home with the sun sliding quiet through the clouds.

His heart, so light. Going home.

But not home. Not really home, he realized when he found himself on the ground again. The woods, so familiar—but not. Something different. Even the air different, and yet the same.

It all made him dizzy and weak.

He began to walk, whistling for his hawk. His guide. The light changed, dimmed. Was night coming so fast?

But not the night, he saw. It was the fog.

And with it, the wolf that was Cabhan.

He heard the growl of it, reached for his grandfather's sword. But it wasn't at his side. He was a boy, ankle deep in mists, unarmed, as the wolf with the red gem glowing around his neck walked out of the fog. And became a man.

"Welcome back, young Eamon. I've waited for you."

"You killed my father, my mother. I've come to avenge them."

Cabhan laughed, a rolling, merry sound that sent ice running up Eamon's spine.

"It's spirit you have, so that's fine and well. Come avenge then, the dead father, the dead witch who whelped you. I will have what you are, and then I'll make your sisters mine."

"You will never touch what's mine." Eamon circled, tried to think. The fog rose and rose, clouding all, the woods, the path, his mind. He gripped air, fisted it, hurled it. It carved a shaky and narrow path. Cabhan laughed again.

"Closer. Come closer. Feel what I am."

He did feel it, the pain of it, the power of it. And the fear. He tried fire, but it fell smoldering, turned to dirty ash. When Cabhan's hands reached out for him, he lifted his fists to fight.

Roibeard swooped like an arrow, claws and beak tearing at those outstretched hands. The blood ran black as the man howled, as the man began to re-form into the wolf.

And another man came through the fog. Tall, his brown hair damp from the mists, his eyes deep and green and full of power and fury.

"Run," he told Eamon.

"I will not run from such as he. I cannot."

The wolf pawed the ground, showed its teeth in a terrible smile.

"Take my hand."

The man grabbed Eamon's hand. Light exploded like suns, power flew like a thousand beating wings. Blind and deaf, Eamon cried out. There was only power, covering him, filling him, bursting from him. Then with one shattering roar, the fog was gone, the wolf gone, and only the man gripping his hand remained.

The man dropped to his knees, breath harsh, face white, eyes full of magicks. "Who are you?" he demanded.

"I am Eamon son of Daithi, son of Sorcha. I am of the three. I am the Dark Witch of Mayo."

"As am I. Eamon." On a shaky laugh, the man touched Eamon's hair, his face. "I am from you. You're out of your time, lad, and in mine. I'm Connor, of the clan O'Dwyer. I am out of Sorcha, out of you. One of three."

"How do I know this to be true?"

"I am your blood, you are mine. You know." Connor pulled the amulet from under his shirt, touched the one, the same one, Eamon wore.

And the man lifted an arm. Roibeard landed on the leather glove he wore.

Not Roibeard, Eamon realized, and yet . . .

"My hawk. Not yours, but named for him. Ask him what you will. He is yours as much as mine."

"This is . . . not my place."

"It is, yes, not your time but your place. It ever will be."

Tears stung Eamon's eyes, and his belly quivered with longing worse than hunger. "Did we come home?"

"You did."

"Will we defeat him, avenge our parents?"

"We will. We will never stop until it's done. My word to you."

"I wish to . . . I'm going back. I feel it. Brannaugh, she's calling me back. You saved me from Cabhan."

"Saving you saved me, I'm thinking."

"Connor of the O'Dwyers. I will not forget."

And he flew, over the hills again, until it was soft, soft morning and he sat by Brannaugh's fire with both his sisters shaking him.

"Leave off, now! My head is circling over the rest of me."

"He's so pale," Teagan said. "Here, here, I'll fix you tea."

"Tea would be welcome. I went on a journey. I don't know how, but I went home, but 'twasn't home. I need to sort through it. But I know something I didn't. Something we didn't."

He guzzled some water Brannaugh pushed on him, then shoved the skin away again. "He can't leave there. Cabhan. He can't leave, or not far. The farther from home, from where he traded for his new powers, the less they are. He risks death to leave there. He can't follow us."

"How do you know this?" Brannaugh demanded.

"I . . . saw it in his mind. I don't know how. I saw it there, that weakness. I met a man, he's ours. I . . ." Eamon drew a long breath, closed his eyes a moment.

"Let me have some tea, will you then? A little tea, then I have a tale to tell you. We'll bide here awhile yet, and I'll tell you all. Then, aye, aye, south for us, to learn, to grow, to plan. For he can't touch us. He won't ever touch you."

Whatever boy he'd been, he was a man now. And power still simmered inside him.

3

Autumn 2013

WHEN CONNOR WOKE EARLIER THAN HE LIKED, HE hadn't expected to meet an ancestor, or the greatest enemy of his blood. He certainly hadn't anticipated starting his day with an explosion of magicks that had all but knocked him off his feet.

But, in the main, he liked the unexpected.

With the dawn barely broken, there'd been no hope his sister might be busy in the kitchen. And his skin meant too much to him to risk waking her and suggesting she might like to cook up breakfast.

More, there hadn't been a hunger, and he always woke ready to break the night's fast. Instead there'd been an odd energy, and a deep need to get out, get about.

So he'd whistled up his hawk and, with Roibeard for his companion, had taken himself into the mists and trees.

And quiet.

He wasn't a man who required a great deal of quiet. He preferred, most of the time, the noise and conversations and heat of company.

But this soft morning, the call of his hawk, the scrabble of rabbit in the brush, and the sigh of the morning breeze had been enough for him.

He thought he might walk over to Ashford Castle, let Roibeard soar in the open, over the greens there—and that would give any early-rising guests at the hotel a thrill.

Thrills often drummed up business, and he had one to run with the falconry school.

He'd aimed for that exactly, until he'd felt it—the stir of power, within and without. His own rising without his asking it, the dark stain of what was Cabhan, smudging the sweetness of the dewy pines.

And something more, something more.

He should have called his circle—his sister, his cousin, his friends, but something pushed him on, down the path, through the trees, near the wall of vines and uprooted tree where beyond lay the ruins of the cabin that had been Sorcha's. Beyond where he and his circle had battled Cabhan on the night of the summer solstice.

There the fog spread, the power thrummed, dark against white. He saw the boy, thought first and only to protect. He would not, could not, allow harm to an innocent.

But the boy, while innocent enough, had more. The something more.

Now, the fog gone and Cabhan with it, the boy gone back to his own time, his own place, Connor stayed as he was—on his knees on the damp ground, fighting to get his breath fully back into his lungs.

His ears still rang from what had sounded like worlds exploding. His eyes still burned from a light brighter than a dozen suns.

And the power merged with joined hands sang through him.

He got slowly to his feet, a tall, lean man with a thick mop of curling brown hair, his face pale yet, and his eyes deep and green as the moss with what still stirred inside him.

Best to get home, he thought. To get back. For what had come through the solstice, and hidden away till the equinox lurked still.

A bit wobbly in the legs yet, he realized, unsure if he should be amused or embarrassed. His hawk swooped by, landed with a flutter of wings on a branch. Sat, watched, waited.

"We'll go," he said. "I think we've done what we were meant to do this morning. And now, Jesus, I'm starving."

The power, he thought as he began to walk. The sheer force of it had hulled him out. Turning toward home, he sensed his sister's hound seconds before Kathel ran toward him.

"You felt it as well, did you now?" He gave Kathel's great black head a stroke, continued on. "I'd be surprised if all of Mayo didn't feel a jolt from it. My skin's still buzzing like my bones are covered with bees."

Steadier yet with hound and hawk, he walked out of the shadows of the woods into the pearly morning. Roibeard circled overhead as he walked the road with Kathel to the cottage. A second hawk cried, and Connor spotted his friend Fin's Merlin.

Then the thunder of hoofbeats broke through the quiet, so he paused, waited—felt a fresh stirring as he saw his cousin Iona, his friend Boyle astride the big gray Alastar. And Fin as well, racing with them on his gleaming black Baru.

"We'll need more eggs," he called out, smiling now. "And another rasher or two of bacon."

"What happened?" Iona, her short cap of hair tousled from sleep, leaned down to touch his cheek. "I knew you were safe, or we'd have come even faster."

"You all but flew as it is—and not a saddle between the three of you. I'll tell you inside. I could eat three pigs and top it off with a cow."

"Cabhan." Fin, his hair dark as his mount's, his eyes the dark green of Connor's when the power had taken him, turned to stare into the trees.

"Him and more. But Iona has the right of it. I'm fine and well, just starving half to death while we stand here on the road. You felt it," he added when he began to walk again.

"Felt it?" Boyle stared down at Connor. "It woke me from a sound sleep, and I don't have what the three of you do. I've no magick in me, and still whatever it was shot through me like an arrow." He nodded toward the cottage. "And it seems the same for Meara."

Connor looked over, saw Meara Quinn, lifelong friend, his sister's best mate, striding along toward them—tall and lush as a goddess in her flannel sleep pants and old jacket, he thought, and her long brown hair a tangle.

She made a picture, he mused, but then she ever did.

"She stayed the night," he told the others. "Took Iona's room as you stayed over at Boyle's, cousin. Good morning to you, Meara."

"Good morning be damned. What the bloody hell happened?"

"I'm after telling you all." He slipped an arm around her waist. "But I need food."

"Branna said you would, and she's already seeing to it. She's shaken, and pretending not to be. It was like a bleeding earthquake—but inside me. That's the devil of a way to wake."

"I'll see to the horses." Boyle slid off Alastar. "Go on in, stuff something in your belly."

"Thanks for that." Smiling again, Connor lifted his arms so Iona could drop into them from Alastar's back. Then she wrapped around him.

"Scared me," she murmured.

"You're not alone in that." He kissed the top of her head, his pretty cousin from America, the last of the three, and keeping her hand in his, went into the cottage.

The scent of bacon, of coffee, of warm bread hit his belly like a fist. In that moment he wanted to eat more than he wanted to live—and needed to eat if he wanted to live.

Kathel led the way back to the kitchen, and there Branna worked at the stove. She'd tied her dark hair back, still wore the flowered flannel pants and baggy shirt she'd slept in. That alone showed her love, he mused, as she'd have taken the time to change, to fuss with herself a little knowing there'd be company—and Finbar Burke most especially.

Saying nothing, she turned from the stove, handed him a plate holding a fried egg on toast.

"Bless you, darling."

"It'll fill the worst of the hole. There's more coming. You're cold," she said quietly.

"I hadn't noticed, but I am, yes. A bit cold."

Before she could flick a hand toward the kitchen hearth, Fin did so, and the little fire flashed.

"You're quivering some. Sit, for God's sake, and eat like a human." Voice brisk, Meara all but shoved him into a chair at the table.

"I'm not a one to brush away some fussing, and truth be told, I'd kill for coffee."

"I'll get it." Iona hurried over to the pot.

"Ah, what man can complain with three beautiful women pampering him. Thanks, *mo chroi*," he added when Iona gave him the coffee.

"You'll not be pampered long, I can promise. Sit down, the lot of you," Branna ordered. "I've nearly got this fried up. When his belly's full enough to settle him, he'll damn well explain why he didn't call for me."

"It was fast and done. I would've called for you, for all of you. It wasn't me in harm's way, I'm thinking. He didn't come for me this morning."

"And who then, when the rest of us were asleep in our beds?" When Branna would have lifted an enormous platter of food to bring to the table, Fin simply took it from her.

"Sit then, and listen. Sit," he repeated before she could snap at him. "You're as shaken as he is."

The minute the tray hit the table, Connor began to scoop eggs, sausage, bacon, toasted bread, potatoes onto his plate and into a small mountain.

"I woke early, and with an edge on," he began, and took them all through it between enthusiastic bites.

"Eamon?" Branna demanded. "The son of Sorcha? Here and now? You're sure of it?"

"As sure as I know my sister. I only thought him a boy at first, and in Cabhan's path, but when I took his hand . . . I've never felt the like, never. Not even with you, Branna, or you and Iona together. Even on the solstice when the power was a scream, it wasn't so big, so bright, so full. I couldn't hold it, couldn't control it. It just blew through me like a comet. Through the boy as well, but he held on to me, on to it. He's a rare one."

"What about Cabhan?" Iona demanded.

"It ripped through him," Fin said. "I felt it." Absently, he lifted a hand to his shoulder, where the mark of his blood, of Cabhan's blood scarred his flesh. His heart. "It stunned him, left him, I promise you, as shaken as you were."

"So he slithered away?" Boyle dug into eggs. "Like the snake he is."

"That he did," Connor confirmed. "He was gone, and with him the fog, and there was only myself and the boy. Then only myself. But . . . He was me, and I was he—parts of one. That I knew when we joined hands. More than blood. Not the same, but . . . more than blood. For a moment, I could see into him—like a mirror."

"What did you see?" Meara asked.

"Love and grief and courage. The fear, but the heart to face it, for his sisters, for his parents. For us, come to that. Just a lad, no more than ten, I'd venture. But in that moment, shining with a power he hasn't yet learned to ride smooth."

"Is it like me going to visit Nan?" Iona wondered, thinking of her grandmother in America. "A kind of astral projection? But it's not exactly, is it? It's like that, but with the time shift, much more than that. The time shift that can happen by Sorcha's cabin. You weren't by Sorcha's cabin, were you, Connor?"

"No, still outside the clearing. Near though." Connor considered. "Maybe near enough. All this is new. But I know for certain it wasn't what Cabhan expected."

"It may be he brought the boy, brought Eamon," Meara suggested. "Pulled him from his own time into ours, trying to separate him from his sisters, to take on a boy rather than a man like the sodding coward he is. The way you said it happened, Connor, if you hadn't come along, he might have killed the boy, or certainly harmed him."

"True enough. Eamon was game, by God, he was game—wouldn't run when I told him to run, but still confused, afraid, not yet able to draw up enough to fight on his own."

"So you woke and went out," Branna said, "you who never step a foot out of a morning without something in your belly, and called up your hawk. Barely dawn?" She shook her head. "Something called you there. The connection between you and Eamon, or Sorcha herself. A mother still protecting her child."

"I dreamed of Teagan," Iona reminded them. "Of her riding Alastar to the cabin, to her mother's grave, and facing Cabhan there—drawing his blood. She's mine, the way Eamon is Connor's."

Branna nodded as Iona looked at her. "Brannaugh to Branna, yes. I dream of her often. But nothing like this. It's useful, it must be useful. We'll find a way to use what happened here, what we know. He hid away since the solstice."

"We hurt him," Boyle said, scanning the others with tawny eyes. "That night he bled and burned as we did. More, I'm thinking."

"He took the rest of the summer to heal, to gather. And this morning tried for the boy, to take that power, and—"

"To end you," Fin interrupted Branna. "Kill the boy, Connor never exists? Or it's very possible that's the case. Change what was, change what is."

"Well now, he failed brilliantly." Connor polished off his bacon, sighed. "And I feel not only human again, but fit and fine. It's a pity we can't take the bastard on again now."

"You need more than a full fry in your belly to take him on." Rising, Meara gathered dishes. "All of us do. We hurt him on the solstice, and that's a satisfying thing, but we didn't finish him. What did we miss? Isn't that the thing we need? What did we not do that we need to do?"

"Ah, the practical mind."

"Someone needs to think practical," Meara tossed back at him.

"She's right. I've poured over Sorcha's book." Branna shook her head. "What we did, what we had, how we planned it, it should've worked."

"He changed the ground," Boyle reminded her. "Took the fighting ground back in time."

"And still, I can't find what we might add to it." Branna tossed a glance toward Fin, just a beat. He only gave her the most subtle shake of head. "So we'll keep looking."

"No, you sit." Iona took more dishes before Connor could do so. "Considering your dawn adventure, you get a pass at kitchen duty. Maybe I wasn't strong or skilled enough last summer."

"Do you need reminding of a whirlwind called?" Boyle asked her.

"That was more instinct than skill, but I'm learning." She glanced back at Branna.

"You are, yes, and very well indeed. You're no weak link if that's what you're thinking, nor have you ever been. He knows more than us, and that's a problem. He's lived, in his way, hundreds of years."

"That makes him older," Meara put in, "not smarter."

"We have books and legends and what was passed down generation to generation. But he lived it all, so—smarter or not—he knows more. And what he has is deep and dark. His power has no rules as ours does. He harms who he wants, no matter to it. That we can never do and be what we are."

"His power source—the stone he wears around his neck, wolf or man. Destroy it, destroy him. I know it," Fin stated, clenched a fist on the table. "I know it as truth, but don't know how it can be done. Yet."

"We'll find the way. We must," Connor said, "so we will."

Fin rose when Connor reached over the table to lay his hand on Branna's, and joined the others across the room with the clatter of dishes, the whoosh of water in the sink.

"Worrying for me won't help, and isn't needed. I don't have to look," he added, "to see."

"And if he'd harmed you and the boy, where would we be?"

"Well, he didn't, did he? And between us we gave him a solid boot in the balls. I'm here, Branna, as ever. We're meant for this, so I'm here."

"You're a thorn in my side half the time." Her hand turned under his until their fingers curled together and gripped. "But I'm used to you. You'll have a care, Connor."

"I will, of course. And the same for you."

"The same for us all."

IT AMUSED HIM, AND TOUCHED HIM WHEN MEARA FELL INTO step beside him as he left the house for the falconry school.

"Are you leaving your lorry then?"

"I am. I want to walk off that breakfast."

"You're guarding my body." He slung an arm around her shoulders, pulled her in so their hips bumped.

She'd dressed for work at the stables, rough pants and jacket, sturdy boots, and with all that hair braided back to hang through the loop of her battered cap.

And still she made a picture, he thought, the dark-eyed Meara with the gypsy in her blood.

"Your body can guard itself." She glanced up, watched the hawks circle in the heavy sky. "And you've got them keeping an eye out."

"I'm glad for your company all the same. And this gives you time to tell me what's troubling you."

"I think a mad sorcerer bent on our destruction's enough to go around."

"Something else brought you to Branna last night and had you staying through it. Is it a man giving you grief? Do you want me to lay him low for you?"

He flexed one arm, made a fist, shook it fiercely to make her laugh.

Then she sniffed. "As if I couldn't lay any I wanted low—or otherwise—myself."

He laughed in turn, sheer delight, and gave her hip another bump. "I've no doubt on that one. What is it then, darling? I can hear the buzzing in your head like a hive of angry wasps."

"You could stop listening." But she relented enough to lean against him a moment, so he caught the scent of his own soap on her skin. An oddly pleasant sort of thing.

"It's just my mother driving me half mad, which is a normal enough day in the life. Donal's got himself a girl."

"So I've heard," he said, thinking of her younger brother. "Sharon, isn't it, moved to Cong this past spring? A nice girl, from what I've seen. A pretty face, an easy smile. Don't you like her then?"

"I like her fine and well, and more to the point Donal's mad for her. It's lovely, really, to see him so taken, and happy with it, and her very much the same."

"Well then?"

"He's after moving out of the house, and in with his Sharon."

Connor considered that as they walked through the pretty morning toward work they both loved. "He's, what, twenty and four?"

"And five. And, yes, past time he moved out of his mother's house. But now my mother and my sister Maureen have their heads together and have come to the horrible conclusion I should move back in with Ma."

"Well now, that won't do, not for a minute."

"It won't." Now her sigh held relief, as he understood the simple and bare truth. "But they're laying it on like courses of brick. The guilt, the pressure, the bloody *logic* as they see it. Oh, Maureen's after saying our mother can't be left on her own, and me being the only one unhampered, so to speak, it stands I should be the one to right the ship. And Ma's right behind her with she'll have the room for me, and it would save me the rent, and how lonely she'll be without a chick or child around."

She shoved both hands in her pockets. "Bugger it."

"Do you want my opinion or only my condolences?"

She slanted a look at him, bold brown eyes both suspicious and speculative. "I'll take the opinion, though I may hurl it back in your face."

"Then here it is for you. Stay where you are, darling. You were never happy, not really, until you moved out to begin with."

"That's what I want, and what I know I should do for myself and my sanity, but—"

"If your mother's fretting about being lonely, and Maureen's fretting about your mother—who's her mother as well I'll add—being on her own, why wouldn't it be a fine idea for your mother to move in with Maureen and her family? Wouldn't it be a great help to Maureen to have her mother with her, with the children and all that?"

"Why didn't I think of that?" Meara pulled away long enough to punch Connor's shoulder, do a little dance. "Why didn't I think of that my own self?"

"You hadn't got through the courses of guilt." In an old habit, he gave her long, thick braid a tug. "Maureen's no right to push you to give up your flat, change your life just because your brother's changing his."

"I know it, but I know as well, Ma's next to helpless. She has been since my father left us. She did her best with a terrible situation, but she'll dither her way through the days, worry herself through the nights living all on her own."

"You've two brothers, two sisters," he reminded her. "There's five of you to help tend your mother."

"The smart ones got well away, didn't they? It's only me and Donal right here. But I can plant the seed in Ma's mind of moving in with Maureen. If nothing else, it should scare Maureen silent for a bit."

"There you have it." He turned, as she did, toward the stables.

Meara stopped. "Where are you going?"

"I'll walk you to work."

"I don't need my body guarded, thanks. Go on." She planted a finger in his chest, gave it a little push. "You've work of your own."

There was no harm in the day—he felt none at all. And after the early-morning clash, Connor felt Cabhan would be curled up in some dark cave, gathering.

"We've five hawk walks already booked today, and may have others before it's done. Maybe I'll see you on the paths."

"Maybe."

"If you text me when you're done for the day, I'll meet you here, walk back with you to the cottage."

"We'll see how it all goes. Mind yourself, Connor."

"I will. I do."

Because her eyebrows had drawn together, he kissed the space between them, then strolled off. Looking, to Meara's mind, like a man without a single care in the world rather than one with the weight of it on his shoulders.

An optimist to the bone, she thought, envying him a little.

But she pulled her phone out of her pocket as she took the path to the stables and her workday.

“Morning, Ma.” And smiling to herself, prepared to give her annoying sister a shot right up the arse.

4

Connor slipped through the employees' gate for the falconry school. As always, he felt a little flutter—a bit like beating wings—in his heart, along his skin. It had always been the hawk for him. That connection, like his power, came down through the blood.

He'd have preferred having some time to walk around the enclosures and aviary, greet the hawks, the big owl they called Brutus, just to see—and hear—how they all fared.

But the way he'd started his day meant he was a few minutes behind already. He saw one of his staff, Brian—skinny as a flagpole and barely eighteen—checking the feed and water.

So he only glanced around to be sure all was well as he crossed over to the offices, past the fenced-in area where his assistant, Kyra, kept her pretty spaniel most days.

"And how's it going for you today, Romeo?"

In answer, the dog wagged his whole body, clamped a gnawed blue ball in his mouth, and brought it hopefully to the fence.

"It'll have to be later for that."

He stepped into the office, found Kyra, her hair a short wedge of sapphire blue, busy at the keyboard.

"You're late."

Though she just hit five foot two, Kyra had a voice like a foghorn.

"Happy I'm the boss then, isn't it?"

"Fin's the boss."

"Happy I had breakfast with him so he knows what's what." He knocked his fist lightly on the top of her head as he moved by to a desk covered with forms, clipboards, papers, brochures, a spare glove, a tether, a bowl of tumbled stones, and other debris.

"We've had another booking come in already this morning. A double. Father and son—and the boy's just sixteen. I've put you on that, as you do better with the teenagers than Brian or Pauline. They're for ten this morning. Yanks."

She paused, sent Connor a disapproving look from her round, wildly freckled face. "Sixteen, and why isn't he in school, I want to know."

"You're such a taskmaster, Kyra. It's an education, isn't it, to travel to another country, to learn of hawks?"

"That won't teach you to add two and two. Sean's not coming in till noon, if you're forgetting. He's taking his wife in for her check with the doctor."

He looked up at that because he had forgotten. "All's well there, right, with her and the baby?"

"Well and fine, she just wants him there as they may find if it's a girl or boy today. That puts Brian on the nine with the lady from Donegal, you at the ten, and Pauline's at half-ten with a pair of honeymooners from Dublin."

She clicked and clacked at the keyboard as she laid out the

morning's schedule. Though she tended toward the bossy and brisk, Kyra was a wizard at doing a dozen things at once.

And—the fly in Connor's ointment—expected everyone else to do the same.

"I've set you on at two for another," she added. "Yanks again, a couple over from Boston. They've just come in from a stay at Dromoland in Clare, and they're having three days at Ashford before moving on. Three weeks holiday for their twenty-fifth anniversary."

"Ten and two then."

"They've been married long as I've been alive. That's something to think on."

Listening with half an ear, he sat to poke through the paperwork he couldn't palm off on her. "Your parents have been married longer yet, considering you're the youngest."

"Parents are different," she said—decisively—though he couldn't see how.

"Oh, and Brian's claiming there was an earthquake this morning, near to shook him out of bed."

Connor glanced up, face calm. "An earthquake, is it?"

She smirked, still clattering on the keyboard with nails painted with pink glitter. "Swears the whole house shook around him." She rolled her eyes, hit Print, swiveled around for a clipboard. "And he's decided it's some conspiracy, as there's not a word of it on the telly. A few mentions, so he claims, on the Internet. He's gone from earthquake to nuclear testing by some foreign power in a fingersnap. He'll be all over you about it, as he's been me."

"And your bed didn't shake?"

She flashed a grin. "Not from an earthquake."

He laughed, went back to the paperwork. "And how is Liam?"

"Very well indeed. I'm thinking I might marry him."

"Is that the way of it?"

"It might be, as you have to start on racking up those anniversaries sometime. I'll let him know when I've made up my mind."

When the phone jangled, he left her to answer, went back to clearing off a section of his desk.

So some felt it, some didn't, he thought. Some were more open than others. And some closed tight as any drum.

He'd known Kyra most of his life, he mused, and she knew what he was—had to know. But she never spoke of it. She was, despite her blue hair and the little hoop in her left eyebrow, a drum.

He worked steady enough until Brian came in and, as predicted, was full of earthquakes that were likely nuclear testing by some secret government agency, or perhaps a sign of the apocalypse.

He left Brian and Kyra batting it all around, went out to choose the hawk for the first walk.

As no one was watching, he did it the quick and simple way. He simply opened the aviary, looked into the eyes of his choice, held up his gloved arm.

The hawk swooped through, landed, coming in as obedient as a well-trained hound.

"There you are, Thor. Ready to work, are you? You do well for Brian this morning, and I'll take you out later, if I can, for a real hunt. How's that for you?"

After tethering the hawk, he walked back to the offices, transferred him to the waiting perch, tethered him there.

Patient, Thor closed his wings, sat watchful.

"We may get some wet," he told Brian, "but not a drench, I'm thinking."

"Global warming's causing strange weather around the world. It may have been an earthquake."

"An earthquake 'tisn't weather," Kyra stated.

"It's all connected," Brian said darkly.

"I think you won't see more than a shower this morning. If there's an earthquake or volcanic eruption, be sure you get Thor back home again." Connor gave Brian a slap on the shoulder. "There's your clients now, at the gate. Go on, let them in, give them the show around. I'll take Roibeard and William for the ten," he told Kyra when Brian hurried to answer the gate. "That leaves Moose for Pauline's."

"I'll set it up."

"We'll have Rex for Sean. He respects Sean, and doesn't yet have the same respect for Brian. Best not send him out with Bri yet, on their own. I'll take Merlin for the two, as he hasn't been on a walk in a few days."

"Fin's hawk isn't here."

"He's around," Connor said simply. "And Pauline can take Thor out again this afternoon. Brian or Sean, whoever you have for the last so far, can take Rex."

"What of Nester?"

"He's not feeling it today. He's got the day off."

She only lifted her beringed eyebrow at Connor's assessment of the hawk. "If you say."

"And I do."

Her round face lost its smirk in concern. "Does he need to be looked at?"

"No, he's not sick, just out of sorts. I'll take him out later, let him fly off the mood."

He was right about the shower, but it came and went as they often did. A short patter of rain, a thin beam of sun through a pocket of clouds.

By the time his double arrived, the shower had moved on, leaving the air damp and just misty enough. Truth be told, he thought as he took the father and son around, it added to the atmosphere for the Yanks.

"How do you know which one is which?" The boy—name of Taylor—gangling with big ears and knobby knuckles, put on an air of mild boredom.

"They look alike, the Harris's hawk, but they each have their own personality, their own way. You see, there's Moose, he's a big one, so he has the name. And Rex, beside him? Has a kind of regal air."

"Why don't they just fly away when you take them out?"

"Why would they be doing that? They've a good life here, a posh life come to that. And good, respectable work as well. Some were born here, and this is home for them."

"You train them here?" the father asked.

"We do, yes, from the time they're hatchlings. They're born to fly and hunt, aren't they? With proper training—reward, kindness, affection, they can be trained to do what they're born to do and return to the glove."

"Why the Harris's hawk for the walks?"

"They're social, they are. And more, their maneuverability makes them a fine choice for a walk in these parts. The Peregrines—you see here?" He walked them over to a large gray bird with black and yellow markings. "They're magnificent to be sure, and there's no faster animal on the planet when they're in the stoop. That would be flying up to a great height, then diving for its prey."

"I thought a cheetah was the fastest," Taylor said.

"Apollo here?" At the name, at Connor's subtle link, the falcon spread its great wings—had the boy impressed enough to gasp a little before he shrugged. "He can beat the cat, reaching speeds to three hundred twenty kilometers an hour. That's two hundred miles an hour in American," Connor added with a grin.

"But for all its speed and beauty, the Peregrine needs open space, and the Harris's can dance through the trees. You see these here?"

He walked them along. "I watched these hatch myself only last spring, and we've trained them here at the school until they were ready for free flights. One of their brothers is William, and he'll be with you today, Mr. Leary."

"So young? That's what, only five or six months old."

"Born to fly," Connor repeated. He sensed he'd lose the boy unless he moved things along. "If you'll come inside now, we've your hawks waiting."

"It's an experience, Taylor." The father, an easy six-four, laid a hand on his son's shoulder.

"Whatever. It'll probably rain again."

"Oh, I think it'll hold off till near to sunset. So, Mr. Leary, have you family around Mayo then?"

"Tom. Ancestors, I'm told, but no family I know of."

"Just you and your boy then?"

"No, my wife and daughter went into Cong to shop." He gave a grinning roll of his eyes. "Could be trouble."

"My sister has a shop in Cong. The Dark Witch. Maybe they'll stop in."

"If it's there and it sells something, they'll stop in. We were thinking of trying a horseback ride tomorrow."

"Oh, you couldn't do better. It's a fine ride around. You just tell them Connor said to give you a good time with it."

Stepping inside, he turned to the holding perches. "And here we have Roibeard and William. Roibeard's my own, and he's for you today, Taylor. I've had him since he was a hatchling. Tom, would you sign the forms that Kyra has ready for you, and I'll make Taylor acquainted with Roibeard."

"What kind of name is that?" Taylor demanded.

Thinks he doesn't want to be here, Connor mused. Thinks he'd rather be at home with his mates and his video games.

"Why it's his name, and an old one. He comes from hawks that hunted these very wood for hundreds of years. Here's your glove. Without it, as smart and skilled as he is, his talons would pierce your skin. You're to hold your arm up like this, see?" Connor demonstrated, holding his left arm up at a right angle. "And keep it still as we walk. You've only to lift it to signal him to fly. I'll tether him at first, until we get out and about."

He felt the boy quiver—nerves, excitement he tried to hide—as Connor signaled Roibeard to step onto the gloved arm. "The Harris's is agile and quick, as I said, and a fierce hunter, though since we'll be taking these chicken parts along"—he patted his baiting pouch—"they'll both leave off any thought of going for birds or rabbit.

"And here for you, Tom, is young William. He's a handsome one, and well behaved. He loves little more than a chance to wing through the woods, and have some chicken as a reward for the work."

"He's beautiful. They're beautiful." Tom laughed a little. "I'm nervous."

"Let's have ourselves an adventure. How's your stay at the castle?" Connor began as he led them out.

"Amazing. Annie and I thought this was our once in a lifetime, but we're already talking about coming back."

"Sure you can't come once to Ireland."

He walked them easy, making some small talk, but keeping his mind, his heart with the hawks. Content enough, ready enough.

He took them away from the school, down a path, to the hard paved road where there was an opening, with tall trees fringing it.

There he released the jesses.

"If you lift your arms. Just gentle now, sliding them up, they'll fly."

And the beauty of it, that lift in the air, that spread of wings, nearly silent. Nearly. A soft gasp from the boy, still trying to cling to his boredom as both hawks perched on a branch, folded their wings, and stared down like golden gods.

"Will you trust me with your camera, Tom?"

"Oh, sure. I wanted to get some pictures of Taylor with the hawk. With . . . Roibeard?"

"And I will. You turn, back to them, look over your left shoulder there, Taylor." Though Roibeard would answer without, Connor laid a bit of chicken on the glove.

"Gross."

"Not to the bird."

Connor angled himself. "Just lift your arm, as you did the first time. Hold it steady."

"Whatever," Taylor mumbled, but obeyed.

And the hawk, fierce grace in flight, swooped down, wings spread, eyes brilliant, and landed on the boy's arm.

Gobbled the chicken. Stood, stared into Taylor's eyes.

Knowing the moment well, Connor captured the stunned wonder, the sheer joy on the boy's face.

"Wow! Wow! Dad, Dad, did you see that?"

"Yeah. He won't . . ." Tom looked at Connor. "That beak."

"Not to worry, I promise you. Just hold there a minute, Taylor."

He took another shot, one he imagined would sit on some mantel or desk back in America, of the boy and the hawk staring into each other's eyes. "Now you, Tom."

He repeated the process, snapped the picture, listened to his clients talk to each other in amazed tones.

"You've seen nothing yet," Connor promised. "Let's move into the woods a bit. You'll all have a dance."

It never got old for him, never became ordinary. The flight of the hawk, the soar and swoop through the trees always, always enchanted him. Today, the absolute thrill of the boy and his father added more.

The damp air, fat as a soaked sponge, the flickers of light filtering through the trees, the swirl of the oncoming autumn made it all a fine day, in Connor's opinion, to tromp around the wood following the hawks.

"Can I come back?" Taylor walked back to the gates of the school with Roibeard on his arm. "I mean, just to see them. They're really cool, especially Roibeard."

"You can, sure. They'd be pleased with a bit of company."

"We'll do it again before we leave," his father promised.

"I'd rather do this than the horseback riding."

"Oh, you'll enjoy that as well, I wager." Connor led them inside at an unhurried pace. "It's pleasant to walk the woods on the back of a good horse—a different perspective of things. And they've fine guides at the stables."

"Do you ride?" Tom asked him.

"I do, yes. Though not as often as I might like. The best, of course, is hawking on horseback."

"Oh man! Can I do that?"

"That's not in the brochure, Taylor."

"It's true," Connor said as he gently transferred Roibeard to a perch. "It's not on the regular menu, so to speak. I'm just going to settle things up with your da if you want to go out, have another look at the hawks."

"Yeah, okay." He studied Roibeard another moment with eyes filled with love. "Thanks. Thanks, Connor. That was awesome."

"You're more than welcome." He transferred William as Taylor ran out. "I didn't want to say in front of the boy, but I might be able to arrange for him to have what we'd call a hawk ride. I'd need to check if Meara can lead your family—she's a hawker as well as one of the guides at the stables. And if you'd be interested."

"I haven't seen Taylor this excited about anything but computer games and music for months. If you can make it happen, that would be great."

"I'll see what I can do, if you give me a minute or two."

He leaned a hip on the desk when Tom stepped out, took out his phone. "Ah, Meara, my darling, I've a special request."

A FINE THING IT WAS TO GIVE SOMEONE THE LINGERING glow of memories. Connor did his best to do the same with his final client of the day—but nothing would quite reach the heights of Taylor and his da from America.

Between his bookings, he took the Peregrines—Apollo included—out beyond the woods, into the open for exercise and hunting. There he could watch the stoop with a kind of wonder that never left him. There he could feel the thrill of that diving speed inside himself.

As he was a social creature like the Harris's, he enjoyed doing the hawk walks, but those solo times—only himself and the birds and the air—made up his favorite part of any day.

Apollo took a crow in midstoop—a perfect strike. They could be fed, Connor thought as he sat on a low stone wall with a bag of crisps and an apple. They could be trained and tended. But they were of the wild, and the wild they needed for their spirit.

So he sat, content to wait, to watch, while the birds soared, dived, hunted, and prized the peace of a damp afternoon.

No fog or shadows here, he thought. Not yet. Not ever as he and his circle would find the way to preserve the light.

And where are you now, Cabhan. Not here, not now, he thought as he scanned the hills, rolling back and away lush and green. Nothing here now but the promise of rain that would come and go and come again.

He watched Apollo soar again, for the joy of it now, felt his own heart lift. And knew for that moment alone he would face the dark and beat it back.

Rising, he called the birds back to him, one by one.

Once all the work was done, he made a final round with the birds and checked on all that needed checking on, then shoved his own glove in his back pocket and locked the gate.

Then he wandered, at an easy stroll, toward the stables.

He sensed Roibeard first, pulled out the glove and put it on. Even as he lifted his arm, he sensed Meara.

The hawk circled once, for the pleasure of it, then swooped down to land on Connor's gloved arm.

"Did you have an adventure then? Sure you gave the boy a day he'll not be forgetting." He waited where he was until Meara rounded the bend.

Long, sure strides—a man had to admire a woman with long legs that moved with such steady confidence. He sent her a grin.

"And there she is. How'd the boy do?"

"He's mad in love with Roibeard, and expressed great affection for Spud, who gave him a good, steady ride. I had to stop once and give the sister a go at it or there'd have been a brutal sibling battle. She enjoyed it quite a lot, but not like the boy. And we won't be charging them for the few minutes of her go."

"We won't, no." He took her hand, swung it as they walked, kissed her knuckles lightly before letting it go. "Thanks."

"You'll thank me for more, as the mister gave me a hundred extra."

"A hundred? Extra?"

"That he did, as he judged me the honest sort and asked if I'd give half to you. Naturally, I told him it wasn't necessary, but he insisted. And naturally, I didn't want to be rude and refuse again."

"Naturally," Connor said with a grin, then wiggled his fingers at her.

She pulled euros from her pocket, counted them out.

"Well now, what should we do with this unexpected windfall? What do you say to a pint?"

"I say on occasion you have a fine idea. Should we round up the rest of us?" she wondered.

"We could. You text Branna, and I'll text Boyle. We'll see if we have any takers. It'd do Branna good to get out for an evening."

"I know it. Why don't you text her?"

"It's easier to say no to a brother than a friend." He met Roibeard's eyes, walked in silence a moment. And the hawk lifted off, rose up, winged away.

As Connor did, she watched the hawk for the pleasure of it. "Where's he going then?"

"Home. I want him close, so he'll fly home and stay tonight."

"I envy that," Meara said as she took out her phone. "The way you talk to the hawks, Iona to the horses, Branna to the hounds—and Fin to all three when he wants to. If I had any magic, I think that would be what I'd want."

"You have it. I've seen you with the horses, the hawks, the hounds."

"That's training, and an affinity. But it's not what you have." She sent the text, tucked the phone away. "But I'd just want it with the animals. I'd go mad if I could read people, hear their thoughts and feelings as you can. I'd forever be fighting to listen, then likely be pissed at what I'd heard."

"It's best to resist the eavesdropping."

She gave him an elbow poke and a knowing look out of dark chocolate eyes. "I know good and well you've had a listen when you're wondering if a girl might be willing if you bought her a pint and walked her home."

"That may have been the case before I reached my maturity."

She laughed her wonderful laugh. "You've not hooked fingers around your maturity as yet."

"I'm within centimeters now. Ah, and here's Boyle answering already. Iona's at the cottage practicing with Branna. He'll drag Fin with him shortly—and see if Iona will do the same with Branna."

"I like when it's all of us together. It's family."

He heard the wistfulness, swung an arm over her shoulders. "It's family," he agreed, "right and true."

"Do you miss your parents since they've settled down in Kerry?"

"I do sometimes, yes, but they're so bleeding happy there on the lake, running their B and B, and with Ma's sisters all chirping about. And they're mad about the FaceTime. Who'd've thought it? So we see them, and know what's what."

He gave her shoulder a rub as they walked the winding road to Cong. "And truth be told, I'm glad enough they're tucked away south for now."

"And here I'd be more than glad to have my mother tucked away most anywhere, and not for unselfish reasons such as your own."

"You'll get through it. It's but another phase."

"Another phase that's lasted near fifteen years. But you're right." She wiggled her shoulders as if shaking off a small weight. "You're right. I put a bug in her ear today about how she might enjoy a long visit with my sister and the grandchildren. And that's shoving the same bug straight up Maureen's arse, which she well deserves. If that doesn't stick, I'm planning to bounce her from brother to sister to brother in hopes she lands somewhere that contents her.

"I'm not giving up my flat."

"You'd go stark raving if you moved back in with your ma, and what good would that do either of you? Donal's done well by her, no question of it, but so have you. You give her your time, your ear, help with her marketing. You pay her rent."

He only lifted his eyebrows when she jerked away, narrowed her eyes.

"Be sane, Meara. Fin's her landlord, how would I not know? I'm saying you're a good daughter, and have nothing to feel selfish over."

"Wishing her elsewhere seems selfish, but I can't stop wishing it. And Fin doesn't charge half what that little cottage is worth."

"It's family," he said, and she sighed.

"How many times can you be right on one walk to the pub?" She shoved her hands in the pockets of her work jacket. "And that's enough bitching and carping from me for the same amount of time. I'm spoiling my own good day at work, and the extra fifty in my pocket."

They passed the old abbey where tourists still wandered, snapping photos. "People always tell you things. Why is that?"

"Maybe I like hearing things."

She shook her head. "No, it's because you listen, whether you want to hear it or not. I too often just tune it all out."

He stuck his hand in her pocket to give hers a squeeze. "Together we probably come average on the graph of human nature."

No, she thought. No, indeed. Connor O'Dwyer would never be average on any graph.

Then she let the worries and wondering go, walked with him into the warmth and clatter of the pub.

It was Connor who was greeted first by those who knew them—which was most. A cheery call, a flirtatious smile, a quick salute. He was the sort always welcome, and always at home where his feet were planted.

Good, easy qualities, she supposed, and something else she envied.

"You get us a table," he told her, "and I'll stand the first round."

She skirted through, found one big enough for six. Settling in, she took out her phone—Connor would be a bit of time due to conversing, she knew.

She texted Branna first.

Stop fussing with your hair. We're already here.

Then she checked her schedule for the next day. A lesson in the ring in the morning, three guideds—not to mention the daily mucking, feeding, grooming, and nagging of Boyle to make certain he'd seen to the paperwork. Then there was the marketing she'd neglected—for herself and her mother. Laundry she'd put off.

She could do a bit of the wash tonight if she didn't loiter overlong in the pub.

She checked her calendar, saw her reminder for her older brother's birthday, and added finding a gift to her schedule.

And Iona was due for another lesson in swordplay. She was coming along well, Meara thought, but now that Cabhan had put in an appearance, they'd be wise to get back to regular practice.

"Put that away now and stop working." Connor set their pints on the table. "Workday's done."

"I was checking on tomorrow's workday."

"That's your burden, Meara darling, always looking forward to the next task."

"And you, always looking to the next recreation."

He lifted his glass, smiled. "Life's a recreation if you live it right." He nodded as he spotted Boyle and Iona. "Family's coming."

Meara glanced around. And put away her phone.

5

A GOOD DAY'S WORK, A PINT, AND FRIENDS TO DRINK IT with. In Connor's estimation, there was little more to wish for. Unless it was a hot meal and a willing woman.

Though he knew the pretty blonde—name of Alice—tossing him the occasional glance would be willing enough, he contented himself with the pint and the friends.

"I'm thinking," he said, "now that Fin's joined us, you might consider combining the hawk and horse as Meara and I did today for the Yanks as a regular option."

Boyle frowned over it. "We'd need an experienced falconer as the guide, and that limits us to Meara."

"I could do it," Iona protested.

"You've only hawked a few times," Boyle pointed out. "And never on your own."

"I loved it. And you said I was a natural," she reminded Connor.

"You have a fine way with it, but you'd want to have a few goes on horseback. Even on a bike, as we do when we're giving the hawks some exercise in the winter."

"I'll practice."

"You need to be practicing more with a blade in your hand," Meara told her.

"You always kick my ass."

"I do." Meara smiled into her pint. "I do indeed."

"Our girl here's a quick study," Fin commented. "And it's an interesting idea."

"If we toyed with it . . ." Boyle sipped at his pint and considered. "The customers who booked the package would need some riding experience. The last thing we'd want is a rank novice going into a panic when a hawk lands on their arm and spooking the horse."

"Agreed there."

"The horses won't spook if I tell them not to." Iona angled her head, smiled. "Here's Branna."

She'd fussed with her hair, of course, and wore a red scarf over a jacket of strong, deep blue. The flat boots meant she'd walked from her cottage.

She ran a hand over Meara's shoulder, then dropped into the chair beside her. "What's the occasion?"

"Meara and I split a fine tip from an American today."

"Good. So you'll buy your sister a pint, won't you? I could do with a Harp."

"It's my round." Meara rose.

"She's been brooding about her mother," Connor said when she was out of earshot. "She could use a festive sort of evening. We'll have a meal, all right, and keep her mood up. I could do with some fish and chips."

"Whose stomach are you thinking of?" Branna asked.

"My stomach, her mood." He raised his glass. "And good company."

IT WAS GOOD COMPANY. SHE'D INTENDED TO HAVE ONE PINT, linger a bit, then go home, start the wash, throw together whatever was left in the larder for a quick dinner. Now she'd started on a second pint, and a chicken pie.

She'd leave her truck where it was at Branna's, walk home from the pub. Toss some wash in, make a market list—for herself and for her mother. Early to bed, and if she made the rise early enough, she could toss more wash in and be done with it.

Marketing on her lunch break. Go by her mother's after work—God help her—do her duty. Plant a few more seeds about going off to Maureen's.

Connor poked her in the ribs. "You're thinking too much. Try being in the moment. It'll amaze you."

"A chicken pie in the pub is amazing?"

"It's good, isn't it?"

She took another bite. "It's good. And what are you going to do about Alice?"

"Hmm?"

"Alice Keenan, who's signaling her churning lust across the pub like one of those flag people." She waved her arms to demonstrate.

"A pretty face, for certain. But not for me."

Meara put on a look of amazement, sent it around the table. "Are you hearing that? Connor O'Dwyer saying a pretty face isn't for him."

"Wants a ring on her finger, does she then?" Fin asked, amused.

"That she does, and as that's more than I can give, she's not for me to play with. But it is a pretty face."

He leaned toward Meara. "Now, if you were to snuggle up here, give me a kiss, she'd think, ah, well, he's taken, and stop pining for me."

"She'll have to pine, as other foolish women do." She scooped up more chicken. "My mouth's occupied at the moment."

"You put it on mine once."

"Really?" Iona pushed her plate aside, leaned in. "Tell all."

"I was but twelve."

"Just shy of thirteen."

"Just shy of thirteen is twelve." She feigned stabbing him with her fork. "And I was curious."

"It was nice."

"How could I tell?" Meara countered. "It was my first kiss."

"Aw." Iona drew in a sighing breath. "You never forget your first."

"It wasn't his."

Connor laughed, gave Meara's braid a tug. "It wasn't, no, but I haven't forgotten it, have I?"

"I was eleven. Precocious," Iona claimed. "His name was Jessie Lattimer. It was sweet. I decided we'd get married one day, live on a farm, and I'd ride horses all day."

"And what happened to this Jessie Lattimer?" Boyle wanted to know.

"He kissed someone else, broke my heart. Then his family moved to Tucson, or Toledo. Something with a *T*. Now I'm going to marry an Irishman." She angled over, kissed Boyle. "And ride horses all day."

Her eyes sparkled when Boyle linked his fingers with hers.

"Who was your first, Branna?"

The minute the words were out, the sparkle changed to regret. She knew. Of course she knew even before Branna flicked a glance at Fin.

"I was twelve as well. I couldn't let my best friend get ahead of me, could I? And like Connor for Meara, Fin was handy."

"That he was," Connor agreed cheerfully, "for he made sure he was where you were every possible waking minute."

"Not every, because it wasn't his first kiss."

"I practiced a bit." Fin tipped back in his chair with his pint. "As I wanted your first to be memorable. In the shadows of the woods," he murmured, "on a soft summer day. With the air smelling of the rain and the river. And of you."

She didn't look at him now, nor he at her. "Then the lightning struck, a bolt from the sky straight into the ground." She remembered. Oh, she remembered. "The air shook with it, and the thunder that followed. We should have known."

"We were children."

"Not for long."

"I've made you sad," Iona said quietly. "I'm sorry."

"Not sad." Branna shook her head. "A bit nostalgic, for innocence that melts faster than a snowflake in a sunbeam. We can't be innocent now, can we, with what's come. And what will come again. So . . . let's have some whiskey in our tea and take the moment—as my brother's fond of saying. We'll have some music, what do you say to that, Meara? A song or two tonight, for only the gods know what tomorrow brings."

"I'll fetch the pub fiddle." Connor rose, brushed a hand over his sister's hair as he left the table. And, saying nothing, gave her the comfort she needed.

Meara stayed longer than she'd intended, well past a reasonable time to think of doing wash or making market lists. Though she tried to brush him off, Connor insisted on walking her home.

"It's silly, you know. It's not a five-minute walk."

"Then it's not taking much of my time. It was good of you to stay because Branna needed it."

"She'd do the same for me. And it lifted my mood as well, though it didn't get the wash done."

They walked the quiet street, climbing the slope. The pubs would still be lively, but the shops were long snugged closed, and not a single car drove past.

The wind had come up, stirring the air. She caught the scent of heliotrope from a window box, and saw needle pricks of stars through the wisps of clouds.

"Did you ever think of going somewhere else?" she wondered. "Living somewhere else? If you didn't have to do what needs doing here?"

"I haven't, no. It's here for me. It's what I want and where. Have you?"

"No. I have friends who went off to Dublin, or Galway City, Cork City, even America. I'd think I could do that as well. Send money to my mother and go off somewhere, an adventure. But I never wanted it as much as I wanted to stay."

"Fighting a centuries-old sorcerer powered by evil would be an adventure for most."

"But it's no Grafton Street, is it now?" She laughed with him, turned the corner toward her flat. "Some part of me never thought it would happen. The sort of thing that happened in that clearing on the solstice. Then it did, all so fierce and fast and terrible, and there was no thinking at all."

"You were magnificent."

She laughed again, shook her head. "I can't quite remember what I did. Light and fire and wind. Your hair flying. All the light. Around you, in you. I'd never seen you like that. With your magick like the sun, all but blinding."

"It was all of us. We wouldn't have beaten him back without all of us."

"I know that. I felt that." For a moment, she just looked out at the night, at the village that had been hers all of her life. "And still he lives."

"He won't win." He walked her up the open stairs to her door.

"You can't know, Connor."

"I have to believe it. If we let the dark win, what are we? What's the purpose of it all if we let the dark win? So we won't."

She stood for a moment beside a basket from which purple and red petunias spilled. "I wish you'd let Fin drive you home."

"I have to walk off the fish and chips—and the pints."

"You have a care, Connor. We can't win without you. And besides all that, I'm used to you."

"Then I'll have a care." He reached up, seemed to hesitate, then gave her braid a familiar tug. "You have one as well. Good night to you, Meara."

"Good night."

He waited until she went in, until the door closed and locked.

He'd nearly kissed her, he realized, and wasn't entirely sure the kiss would've been . . . brotherly. Should've skipped the whiskey in his tea, he decided, if it so clouded his judgment.

She was his friend, as good a friend as he had. He'd do nothing to risk tipping the balance of that.

But now he felt edgy and unsatisfied. Perhaps he should've given Alice a whirl after all.

With so much happening, so much at stake, he couldn't be easy leaving Branna alone at night—even if Iona stayed at the cottage. And he couldn't quite feel easy bringing a woman home with him, especially given the circumstances.

All in all, he thought as he left the village behind and took that winding road on foot, it was inconvenient. And just one more reason to send Cabhan screaming into hell.

He liked women. Liked conversing with them, flirting with them. He liked a dance, a walk, a laugh. And, Jesus, he liked bedding them.

The soft and the heat, the scents and the sighs.

But such pleasures were on an inconvenient pause.

For how much longer, he wondered, as Cabhan had struck out again.

Even as he thought it Connor stopped. Stood still and quiet—body and mind—on the dark road he knew as well as the lines on his own hand. And he listened, with all of himself.

He's there, he's there. Not far, not far enough—not close enough to find, but not far enough for true safety.

He touched the amulet under his sweater, felt its shape, felt its warmth. Then he spread his arms wide, opened more.

The air whispered around him, a quiet song that danced through his hair, kissed along his skin as power rose. As his vision spread.

He could see trees, brush, hear the whisper of air through them, the beating hearts of the night creatures stirring, the faster pulses of the prey hunted. He caught the scent, the sound of water.

And a kind of smear over it—a shadow clinging to shadows. Buried in them so he couldn't separate the shapes or substance.

The river. Beyond the river, aye. Though crossing it causes pain. Water, crossing water unsettles you. I can feel you, just feel you like cold mud oozing. One day I'll find your lair. One day.

The jolt burned, just a little. Hardly more than a quick zap of static electricity. Connor drew himself in again, pulled the magick back. And smiled.

"You're weak yet. Oh, we hurt you, the boy and me. We'll do worse, you bastard, I swear on my blood, we'll do worse before we're done."

Not quite as edgy now, not quite as dissatisfied, he whistled his way home.

THE RAIN CAME AND LINGERED FOR A LONG, SOAKING VISIT. Guests of Ashford Castle—the bulk of their clientele—still wanted their hawk walks.

Connor didn't mind the rain, and marveled, as he always did, at the gear travelers piled on. It amused him to see them tromp along in colorful wellies, various slick raincoats, bundling scarves and hats and gloves, all for a bit of cool September rain.

But amused or not, he watched the mists that swirled or crawled—and found nothing in them but moisture. For now.

On a damp evening when work was done, he sat on the cottage stoop with some good strong tea and watched Meara train Iona. Their swords clashed, sharp rings though Branna had charmed them to go limp as noodles should they meet flesh.

His cousin was coming along well, he judged, though he doubted she'd ever match the style and ferocity of Meara Quinn.

The woman might have been born with a sword in her hand the way she handled one. The way she looked with one—tall and curved like a goddess, all that thick brown hair braided down her back.

Her boots, as broken-in as his own, planted on the soggy ground, then danced over it as she drove Iona back, giving her student no quarter. And those dark eyes—a prize like the gold-dust skin of her gypsy heritage—sparkled fierce as she blocked an attack.

Sure he could watch her swing a sword all day. Though he did wince in sympathy as she drove his little cousin back, back, in an unrelenting attack.

Branna came out holding a thick mug of tea of her own, sat beside him.

"She's improving."

"Hmm? Oh, Iona, yes. I was thinking the same."

Placidly, Branna sipped her tea. "Were you now?"

"I was. Stronger than she was when she came to us, and she wasn't a weakling then. Stronger though, and surer of herself. Surer, too, of her gift. Some of it's us, some of it's Boyle and what love does for body and soul, but most of it was always inside her, just waiting to blossom."

He patted Branna's knee. "We're lucky, we two."

"I've thought so a time or two."

"Lucky in who we came from. We always knew we were loved and valued. And what we have, what we are, was indeed a gift and not something to be buried or hidden away. The two of them striking swords in the rain? Not so lucky as we. Iona had and has her granny, and that's a treasure. But beyond that, for them their family's . . . well, fucked, as Meara's fond of saying."

"We're their family."

"I know it, as they do. But it's a wound that can't fully heal, isn't it, not to have the full love of those who made you. The indifference of Iona's parents, the full mess of Meara's."

"Which is worse, do you think? That indifference, which is beyond my understanding, or the full mess? The way Meara's da ran off, taking what money was left after he bollocksed all they had? Leaving a wife and five children alone, or just never giving a damn all along?"

"I think either would leave you flattened. And just look at them. So strong and full of courage."

Iona stumbled back, slipped. Her ass hit the soggy grass. Meara leaned down, offered a hand, but Iona shook her head, set her teeth. And rolled over, sprang up. Moved in, sword swinging.

Now Connor grinned, slapped his sister's leg.

"Though she be but little, she is fierce!"

"Because it's true, I'll forgive you for quoting the English bard when I've a pot of Guinness stew on the simmer."

His mind went directly to food. "Guinness stew, is it?"

"It is, and a fine round of sourdough bread with the poppy seeds you're fond of."

His eyes lit, then narrowed. "And what will I be doing to deserve it?"

"On your next free day I need you to work with me."

"I will of course."

"The magicks we made for the solstice . . . I was so certain it would work. But I missed something, just as Sorcha missed something when she sacrificed herself and poisoned Cabhan all that time ago. Every one of us since has missed something. We need to find what's missed."

"And we will. But you can't leave us out of it, Branna. You didn't miss, the whole of us did. Fin—"

"I know I have to work with him. I have, and I will."

"Does it help to know he suffers as you do?"

"A little." She leaned her head on his shoulder a moment. "Small of me."

"Human of you. A witch is as human as any, as Da always told us."

"So he did."

For a few moment they sat quiet, side by side, as swords rang.

"Cabhan's healing, isn't he?" She said it quietly, just to him. "Gathering himself for the next. I feel . . . something in the air."

"I feel it, too." Connor watched, as she did, the deep green shadows of the woods. "As his blood, Fin would feel more. Is there stew enough for the whole of us?"

She sighed in a way that told him she'd already thought of it herself. "I suppose there is. Ask them," she said as she rose, "and I'll make sure of it."

He took her hand, kissed it. "As human as any, and braver than most. That's my sister."

"The thought of Guinness stew's made you sentimental." But she gave his hand a squeeze before she went inside.

It wasn't the stew, though Christ knew it didn't hurt a thing. But he worried about her more than she knew.

Then Iona feinted left, spun, struck from the right, and it was Meara who stumbled, slipped, and landed on the wet grass.

Iona immediately let out a whoop, began to jump in circles, sword raised high.

"Well done, cousin!" he called out over Meara's strong, throaty laugh.

Iona made a flourishing bow, then on a squeak, straightened fast as the flat of Meara's sword slapped her ass.

"Well done indeed," Meara told her. "But I could've sliced open your belly while you were dancing about in victory. Finish me off next time."

"Got it, but just one more." She whooped again, jumped again. "That should do it. I'll put the swords away, and go brag to Branna."

"That's fair enough."

Iona took the swords, waved them both high, did another bow for Connor, then dashed inside.

"You trained her well," Connor commented as he rose to walk over and offer Meara what was left of his tea.

"Cheers to me."

"Did you let her knock you down?"

"I didn't, no, though I'd considered doing just that to give her a boost. Didn't prove necessary. She's always been quick, but she's learning to be sneaky as well."

She rubbed her ass. "And now I'm wet where I wasn't."

"I can fix that." He moved in a little closer, reached around her. His hands trailed lightly over the butt of her wet trousers.

Warmth seeped over, through, and his hands lingered. Something in her eyes, he thought, something in those dark, exotic eyes. He caught himself on the point of drawing her in when she stepped back.

"Thanks." She polished off his tea. "And for that as well, though I could use a glass of that wine Branna's so fond of."

"Then come in and have one. I'm calling on the others to come. There's Guinness stew and a fresh round of bread."

"I should go on." She shifted back, glanced toward her lorry. "I'm all but living here these days."

"She needs her circle, Meara. It would be a favor to me if you'd stay."

Now she looked over her shoulder, as if sensing something sneaking up behind her. "Is he coming already?"

"I can't say, not absolutely. I'll be hoping Fin can say more. So come inside and have some wine and stew, and we'll be together."

They came, as Connor knew they always would. So the kitchen filled with voices, the warmth of friends with Kathel stretched in front of the little hearth, and good, rich stew simmering on the stove.

As he'd get his Guinness in the stew, Connor opted for wine himself. Drinking it, he watched his besotted friend grin as Iona, once again, replayed her moment of victory.

Who would have thought Boyle McGraff would fall so hard, so fully? A man who said little, and in general paid more mind to his horses than the ladies. As loyal and true a friend as they came, and a brawler under the self-taught control.

And here was Boyle of the scarred knuckles and fast temper starry-eyed over the little witch who talked to horses.

"You're looking sly and satisfied," Meara commented.

"I'm enjoying seeing Boyle resemble an overgrown puppy when he looks at Iona."

"They fit well, and they'll make a good life together. Most don't."

"Ah now, not most." It pinched his heart to hear her say it, know she felt it. "The world needs lovers who fit, or how would we go on? To be only one of one for a life? That's a lonely life."

"Being one of one means being able to go as you please, and not facing being one of two, then ending up the one of one when it all goes to hell."

"You're a cynical one, Meara."

"And fine with it." She shot him a look under arched brows. "You're a romantic one, Connor."

"And fine with it."

She laughed, quick and easy, as she set the napkins she held on the table. “Branna says it’s serve yourself from the pot on the stove, so you’d best get in line.”

“That I will.”

He fetched wine for the table first to give himself a moment to open a bit, to test the air for any sense or sign before they sat and ate, and talked of magicks. Light and dark.

The stew was a bit of magick itself, but then Branna had a way.

“God, this is good!” Iona spooned up more. “I have to learn how to cook like this.”

“You’re doing well with the side dishes,” Branna told her. “And Boyle’s a steady cook. He can handle that, and you’ll do the sword fighting.”

“Maybe so. After all, I did knock Meara on her ass.”

“Will she never tire of saying it?” Meara wondered. “I see now I’ll have to knock her on her own a dozen times to dim her victory light.”

“Even that won’t.” Iona smiled, then sat back. “You didn’t do it on purpose, did you?”

“I didn’t, no, and I’m wishing I had so we could all pity you.”

“We’ll have a toast then.” Fin lifted his glass. “To you, *deifiúr bheag*, a warrior to be reckoned with. And to you, *dubheasa*,” he said to Meara, “who made her one.”

“That was smoothly done,” Branna murmured, and drank.

“Sometimes the truth is smooth. Sometimes it’s not.”

“Smooth or not, the truth’s what’s needed.”

“Then I’ll give you what I have, though it’s but little. You hurt him,” he said to Connor. “You and the boy, Eamon. But he heals. And you, the three, you feel that, as I do.”

“He gathers,” Connor said.

“He does. Gathers the dark and the black around him, and into him. I can’t say how, or we might find a way to stop it, and him.”

“The red stone. The source.”

Fin nodded at Iona. "Yes, but how did it come to him? How was it imbued, how can it be taken and destroyed? What price did he pay for it? Only he knows the answers, and I can't get through to find them, or him."

"Across the river. How far I can't say," Connor added, "but he's not on our side of it, for now."

"He'll stay there until he's full again. If we could take him on before he gains back what you and the boy took, we would finish him. I know it. But I've looked, and can't find his lair."

"Alone?" Fury fired Branna's voice. "You went off looking for him on your own?"

"That slaps at the rest of us, Fin." Boyle's voice might have been quiet, but the anger simmered under it. "It's not right."

"I followed my blood, as none of you can."

"We're a circle." It wasn't anger in Iona's voice, in her face, but a disappointment that carried a sharper sting. "We're a family."

For a moment Fin's gratitude, regret, longing rose so strong Connor couldn't block it all. He caught only the edge, and that was enough to make him speak.

"We're both, and nothing changes it. Alone isn't the way, and yet I thought of it myself. As have you," he said to Boyle. "As have all of us at one time or another. Fin bears the mark, and did nothing to put it there. Which of us can say, with truth, if we were in his place, we wouldn't have done the same?"

"I'd have done the same. Connor has the right of it," Meara added. "We'd all have done the same."

"Okay." But Iona reached over to Fin. "Now don't do it again."

"I'd take you and your sword with me as protection, but there's no purpose to it. He's found a way to cover himself from me, and I've yet to find the way under it."

"We'll work longer and harder." Branna picked up her wine again.

"All of us needed time as well after the solstice, but we've not been hiding in the dark licking our wounds. We'll work more, together and alone, and find whatever we've missed."

"We should meet like this more than we have been." With a glance around the table, Boyle spooned up more stew. "It doesn't have to be here, though Branna's far better at cooking than me. But we could meet at Fin's as well."

"I don't mind the cooking," Branna said quickly. "I enjoy it. And I'm here or over in the workshop most days, so it's easy enough."

"Easier if it was planned, and we could all give you a hand," Iona decided, then glanced around as Boyle had. "So. When shall we six meet again?"

"Now it's paraphrasing the English bard." Branna rolled her eyes. "Every week. At least every week for now. More often if we feel we should. Connor'll be working with me on his free days, as you should, Iona."

"I will. Free days, evenings, whatever we need."

There was a pause that went on just a beat too long for comfort.

"And you, Fin." Branna broke the bread she'd barely touched in half, took a bite. "When you can."

"I'll keep my schedule loose as I can."

"And all of that, all of us, will be enough," Connor determined, and went back to his stew.

6

He dreamed of the boy, and sat with him in the flickering light of a campfire ringed with rough gray stones. The moon hung full, a white ball swimming in a sea of stars. He smelled the smoke and the earth—and the horse. Not the Alastar that had been or was now, but a sturdy mare that stood slack-hipped as she dozed.

On a branch above the horse, the hawk guarded.

And he heard the night, all the whisperings of it in the wind.

The boy sat with his knees drawn in, and his chin upon them.

"I was sleeping," he said.

"And I. Is this your time or mine?"

"I don't know. But this is my home. Is it yours?"

Connor looked toward the ruins of the cabin, over to the stone marking Sorcha's grave. "It's ours, as it was hers. What do you see there?"

Eamon looked toward the ruins. "Our cabin, as we left it the morning my mother sent us away."

"As you left it?"

"Aye. I want to go in, but the door won't open for me. I know my mother's not there, and we took all she told us to take. And still I want to go in as if she'd be there, by the fire waiting for me."

Eamon picked up a long stick, poked at the fire as boys often do. "What do you see?"

It would hurt the boy's heart to tell him he saw a ruin overgrown. And a gravestone. "I see you're in your time, and I in mine. And yet . . ." He reached out, touched Eamon's shoulder. "You feel my hand."

"I do. So we're dreaming, but not."

"Power rules this place. Your mother's and, I fear, Cabhan's as well. We hurt him, you and I, so he brings no power here tonight. How long ago for you since we met?"

"Three weeks and five days more. For you?"

"Less. So the time doesn't follow. Are you well, Eamon? You and your sisters?"

"We went to Clare, and we made a little cabin in the woods." His eyes gleamed as he looked toward his home again. "We used magick. Our hands and backs as well, but we thought if we used magick we'd be safer. And dryer also," he added with a ghost of a smile. "Branaugh's done some healing as we traveled, and now that we're there. We have a hen for eggs, and that's a fine thing, and we can hunt—all but Teagan, who can't use the arrow on the living. It hurts her heart to try, but she tends the horses and the hen. We've traded a little—labor and healing and potions for potatoes and turnips, grain and such. We'll plant our own when we can. I know how to plant and tend and harvest."

"Come to me if you can, when you have need. It might be I can get you food, or blankets, whatever you need."

Some comfort, Connor thought, for a sad young boy so far from home.

"Thank you for that, but we're well enough, and have coin Ailish and Bardan gave us. But . . ."

"What? You've only to ask."

"Could I have something of yours? Some small thing to take with me? I'll trade you." Eamon offered a stone, a cobble of pure white cupped like an egg in his palm. "It's just a stone I found, but it's a pretty one."

"It is. I don't know what I have." Then he did, and reached up to take the thin leather strap with its spear of crystal from around his neck.

"It's blue tiger eye—but also called hawk's eye or falcon's eye. My father gave it to me."

"I can't take it."

"You can. He's yours as I am. He'll be pleased you have it." To settle it, he put it around Eamon's neck. "It's a fine trade."

Eamon fingered the stone, studied it in the firelight. "I'll show my sisters. They were full of wonder and questions when I told of meeting you, and how we drove Cabhan away. And a bit jealous they were as well. They want to meet you."

"And I them. The day may come. Do you feel him?"

"Not since that day. He can't reach us now, Brannaugh said. He can't go beyond his own borders, so he can't reach us in Clare. We'll go back when we're grown, when we're stronger. We'll go home again."

"I know you will, but you'll be safe where you are until the time comes."

"Do you feel him?"

"I do, but not tonight. Not here. You should rest," he said when Eamon's eyes drooped.

"Will you stay?"

"I will, as long as I can."

Eamon curled up, wrapped his short cloak around him. "It's music. Do you hear it? Do you hear the music?"

"I do, yes." Branna's music. A song full of heart tears.

"It's beautiful," Eamon murmured as he began to drift. "Sad and beautiful. Who plays it?"

"Love plays it."

He let the boy sleep and watched the fire until he woke in his own bed with the sun slipping into the window.

When he opened his fisted hand, a smooth white stone lay in his palm.

He showed it to Branna when she came down to the kitchen for her morning coffee. The sleep daze vanished from her eyes.

"It came back with you."

"We were both there, solid as we are standing here, but both in our own time. I gave him the hawk's-eye stone Da gave me—do you remember it?"

"Of course. You used to wear it when you were a boy. It hangs on the frame of your bedroom mirror."

"No longer. I wasn't wearing it, or anything else, when I got into bed last night. But in the dream, I was dressed and it was around my neck. Now it's around Eamon's."

"Each in your own time." She went to the door to open it for Kathel, returned from his morning run. "Yet you sat together, spoke together. What he gave you came through the dream with you. We have to learn how to use this."

She opened the fridge, and he saw as she pulled out butter, eggs, bacon, that the story, the puzzle of it, and her need to pick over the pieces would net him breakfast.

"We heard you playing."

"What?"

"In the clearing. We heard you. Him so sleepy he could barely hold his eyes open. And the music came, your music, came to us. He fell asleep listening to you. Did you play last night?"

"I did, yes. I woke restless, and played for a bit."

"We heard you. It carried all the way there from your room."

He caught the flicker over her face as she set bacon to sizzle in the pan. "You weren't in your room then. Where?"

"I needed some air. I just needed the night for a bit. I only went to the field behind the cottage. I felt I couldn't breathe without the air and the music."

"I wish you'd find a way to mend things with Fin."

"Connor, don't. Please."

"I love you both. That's all I'll say for now." He wandered the kitchen rubbing the little stone. "The field's too far from the clearing for the music to carry, by ordinary means."

He circled the kitchen as she sliced soda bread, as she broke eggs into the pan.

"We're tied together. We three, those three. He heard your music. Twice now I've spoken to him. Iona saw Teagan."

"And I've seen or heard none of them."

Connor paused to pick up his coffee. "Eamon mentioned his sisters were jealous as well."

"I'm not jealous. Well, a little, I admit. But it's more frustrated, and maybe a bit insulted as well."

"He took your music into dreams, and smiled as he slept when he'd been sad."

"I'll take that as something then." She plated the bacon, the eggs she'd fried. Passed it to him.

"Aren't you having some?"

"Just some coffee and toasted bread."

"Well, thanks for the trouble."

"You can pay it back with another favor." She plucked toast out of the toaster, dropped one piece on his plate, and another on a smaller one. "Carry the stone he gave you."

"This?" He'd already put it in his pocket, and now drew it out.

"Carry it with you, Connor, as you wear the amulet. There's power in it."

She took her toast and coffee to the table, waiting for him to sit with her. "I don't know, can't be sure if it's suspicion, intuition, or a true knowing, but there's power in it. Good magicks because of where it came from, when it came from, who it came from."

"All right. I'll hope the hawk's eye does the same for Eamon, and his sisters."

IT WASN'T ALL HAWK WALKS WITH EAGER TOURISTS OR giving tours to school groups. An essential part of the school involved care and training. Clean mews, clean water for baths, weight checks and a varied diet, sturdy lean-tos for weathering the birds so they might feel the air, smell it. Connor prided himself on the health, behavior, and reliability of his birds—those he helped raise from hatchlings, those who came to him as rescues.

He didn't mind cleaning the poo, or the time it took to carefully dry a wet bird's wings, the hours of training.

The hardest part of his job was, and always would be, selling a bird he'd trained to another falconer.

As arranged, he met the customer in a field about ten kilometers from the school. The farmer he knew well allowed him to bring the young hawks he trained to hunt to that open space.

He called the pretty female Sally, and tethered her to his glove to walk her about and talk to her.

"Now Fin's met this lady who wants you to be hers, and he's even seen your new home should the two of you get along. She's coming all the way from Clare. And there, I'm told, she has a fine house and a fine mews. She's done her training as well as you have yours. You'll be her first."

Sally watched him with her gold eyes, and preened on his fist.

He watched the spiffy BMW navigate the road, pull to a stop behind his truck.

"Here she is now. I expect you to be polite, make a good impression."

He put on his own game face, though his eyebrows rose a bit when the willowy blonde with a film star's face stepped out of the car.

"Is it Ms. Stanley then?"

"Megan Stanley. Connor O'Dwyer?"

The second surprise was the Yank in her voice. Fin hadn't mentioned that either.

"We're pleased to meet you."

Sally, as advised, behaved well, merely standing quiet and watching.

"I didn't realize you were an American."

"Guilty." She smiled as she walked toward Connor, and earned a point or two by studying the hawk first. "Though I've lived in Ireland for nearly five years now—and intend to stay. She's beautiful."

"She is that."

"Fin told me you raised and trained her yourself."

"She was born in the school in the spring. She's a bright one, I'll tell you that. She manned in no time at all. Hopped right on the glove and gave me a look that said, 'Well then, what now?' I have her file with me—health, weight, feeding, training. Did you hawk in America?"

"No. My husband and I moved to Clare—just outside of Ennis—and a neighbor has two Harris's Hawks. I'm a photographer, and started taking photos of them, became more and more interested. So he trained me, then helped me design the mews, the weathering area, get supplies. By his rules I wasn't to so much as think about getting a bird until I'd spent at least a year preparing."

"That's best for all."

"It's taken more than two, as there was a gap when my husband moved back to the States and we divorced."

"That's . . . difficult for certain."

"Not as much as it might've been. I found my place in Clare, and another passion in falconry. I did considerable research before I contacted Finbar Burke. You and your partner have a terrific reputation with your school."

"He's my boss, but—"

"That's not how he put it. When it comes to hawks or birds of prey, you want the eye, ear, hand, and heart of Connor O'Dwyer." She smiled again, and the film-star face illuminated. "I'm pretty sure that's a direct quote. I'd love to see her fly."

"We're here for that. I call her Sally, but if the match between you seems right, you'll call her what suits you."

"No bells, no transmitter?"

"She doesn't need them here, as she knows these fields," Connor said as he released the jesses. "But you'll want them back in Clare."

He barely shifted his arm, and Sally lifted, spread her wings. Soared.

He saw the reaction he wanted, had hoped for in Megan's eyes. The awe that was a kind of love.

"You have a glove with you, I see. You should put it on, call her back yourself."

"I didn't bring a baiting pouch."

"She doesn't need baiting. If she's decided to give you a go, she'll come."

"Now I'm nervous." Her laugh showed it as she took her glove from her jacket pocket, drew it on. "How long have you been doing this?"

"Always." He watched the flight of the bird, sent his thoughts. *If you want this, go to her.*

Sally circled, dove. And landed pretty as a charm on Megan's glove.

"Oh, you beauty. Fin was right. I won't go home without her."

And, Connor thought, she would never come to him again. "Do you want to see her hunt?"

"Yes, of course."

"Just let her know she can. Do you not talk to the birds, Ms. Stanley?"

"Megan, and yes, I do." Now her smile turned speculative as she studied Connor. "It's not something I admit to most. All right, Sally—she'll stay Sally—hunt."

The hawk rose, circled high. Connor began to walk the field with Megan, following the flight.

"So what brought you to Ireland, and to Clare?" he asked her.

"An attempt to save a marriage, which it didn't. But I think it saved me, and I'm happy with that. So it's just me and Bruno—and now Sally."

"Bruno?"

"My dog. Sweet little mutt who showed up at my door a couple years ago. Mangy, limping, half starved. We adopted each other. He's used to hawks. He doesn't bother my neighbor's.

"A dog's an asset on a hunt. Not that she needs one." As he spoke, Sally dove—a bullet from a gun. As talons flashed, Megan let out a little hiss.

"Gets me every time. It's what they do, need to do. God or the world or whatever you believe in made them to hunt and feed. But I always feel a little sorry about it. It took some time for me to stop being squeamish about feeding them during molting, but I got over that. Have you always lived in Mayo?"

"Always, yes."

They exchanged some small talk—weather, hawking, a pub in Ennis he knew well—while Sally feasted on the small rabbit she'd taken down.

"I'm half in love with her already." Megan lifted her arm, and the hawk responded, flying over to land. "Some of that's just excitement and anticipation, but I think we'll make that match you spoke of. Will you let me have her?"

"You made arrangements with Fin," Connor began.

"Yeah, I did, but he said it would be up to you."

"She's yours already, Megan." He looked from the hawk to the woman. "Else she wouldn't have come to you after her feed. You'll want to take her home."

"Yes, yes. I brought everything, with my fingers crossed for luck. I nearly brought Bruno but thought they should get acquainted before a car trip."

She looked at Sally, laughed. "I have a hawk."

"And she has you."

"And she has me. And I think she'll always have you, so would you mind if I took a picture of you with her?"

"Ah, sure if you're wanting."

"My camera's in my car." She transferred Sally to Connor, dashed back to her car. And returned with a very substantial Nikon.

"That's quite the camera."

"And I'm good with it. Go to my website and see for yourself. I'm going to take a couple, okay?" she continued as she checked setting and light. "Just relax—I don't want a studied pose. We'll have the young Irish god with Sally, queen of the falcons."

And when Connor laughed, she took three shots, fast.

"Perfect. Just one more with you looking at her."

Obliging, he looked at Sally. *You'll be happy with her,* he told the hawk. *She's been waiting for you.*

"Great. Thanks." She slung the camera around her neck. "I'll email you the best of them if you want."

"Sure I'd like that very much." He dug out one of the business cards he'd remembered to stick in his back pocket.

"And here's one of mine. My website's on it. And I wrote my

personal email on the back when I got my camera. In case you have any questions or follow-ups about . . . Sally."

"That's grand." He slipped it into his pocket.

Shortly, after helping Megan settle Sally in her container for the trip, Connor climbed back in his lorry.

"That's grand? That's all you have to say about it?" He cast his eyes to heaven as he drove. "What's come over you, O'Dwyer? The woman was gorgeous, single, clever, and a keen hawker. And she gave you an open door a kilometer wide. But did you walk through it? You didn't, no. 'That's grand' is all you said, and let that open door sit there."

Was it simply distraction, the burden of what he knew would have to be done, and the not knowing when it could or would be done? But it had always been there, hadn't it, in the back of all? And had never interfered with his romantic maneuverings.

Had it all changed so much after the solstice? He knew he'd never known fear as sharp as when he'd seen Boyle's hands burning, seen Iona on the ground bruised and bloody. When he'd known the lives of all of them depended on all of them.

Ah well, he thought, perhaps it was best to stay unentangled from those romantic maneuvers for a bit longer. No reason at all he couldn't walk through that open door at a later date.

But for now, he needed to swing by the big stables, let Fin know the deal was done. Then his sister expected him, as this was, at least in theory, his free day.

He stopped at the stables where Fin made his home in the fancy stone house with a hot tub big as a pond on the back terrace and a room on the second floor where he kept magickal weapons, books, and everything else a witch might need—especially one determined to destroy a dark sorcerer of his own blood.

Beside it stood the garage with the apartment over it where Boyle lived—and where Iona would. And the barn for the horses—some for breeding, some for use at the working stables not far off.

Some of the horses cropped in the paddock beyond the one set for jumping practice and lessons.

He spotted Meara, which surprised him, leading one out.

He hopped down from the lorry to greet Bugs, the cheerful mutt who made the barn his home, then hailed her.

"I'd hoped to see Fin, but didn't expect to see you."

"I'm fetching Rufus. Caesar was on the slate for guides today, but Iona says he's got a bit of a strain—left foreleg."

"Nothing serious, I hope."

"She says not." She looped Rufus's reins around the fence. "But we agreed to give him a bit of rest and keep an eye. Fin's round and about somewhere. I thought this was your free day."

"It is, but I had to meet a customer over at Mulligan's farm. She bought Sally—one from the brood we had last spring."

"And you're a bit sulky over it."

"I'm not sulky."

"A bit," Meara said, and bent to give Bugs a scratch. "It's hard to raise a living thing, connect and bond with it, then give it to another. But you can't keep them all."

"I know it"—though he wished otherwise—"and it's a good match. Sally took to her right off, I could see it."

"She?"

"A Yank, moved here a few years ago, and intends to stay—even after her husband, now her former husband, moved back."

Meara's lips curved; her eyebrows lifted. "A looker, is she?"

"She is. Why?"

"No why, just I could hear it in your voice. Living hereabouts?"

"No, down in Clare. Still squeamish over the hunt, but a good hand and heart with the hawk. I thought I'd let Fin know we made the deal, then I'm off to home to work with Branna, as I promised."

"I'm off as well." She unlooped the reins. "Since you'll talk to

Branna before I do, tell her Iona's after a trip to Galway City to look for a wedding dress, and soon."

"That's months off yet."

"Only six, and a bride wants to find her dress before she digs into the rest of it."

"Will they live there, do you think?"

Meara paused in the act of mounting, glanced toward Boyle's rooms over the garage. "Where else? I don't see them trying to squeeze the pair of them into Iona's room at the cottage for the long term."

He realized he'd miss her—or more them as it was now. Talk over breakfast, conversation before bed whenever the two of them stayed at the cottage.

"Boyle's place is bigger than a single room, but sure it's not big when you add children."

"You're jumping some steps ahead," Meara observed.

"Not for the likes of Boyle and Iona." Idly, he stroked the horse as he studied what Fin had built for himself—and for others as well. "They'll want a house of their own, won't they, not a couple of rooms over a garage."

"I hadn't thought of it. They'll figure it." She swung onto Rufus. "For now she's thinking bridal dresses and bouquets, as she should be. There's Fin now, with Aine."

She studied the beautiful white filly Fin led out of the barn. "Soon to be a bride herself when we breed her with Alastar."

"No white dress and bouquet for her."

"But she'll get the stud, and for some of us that's fine and enough."

She rode off on Connor's laugh. And he watched her nudge Rufus into a lope as smooth as butter before walking over to meet Fin.

His friend crouched down to give Bugs a rub, smiling as the dog wagged everywhere and made growls in his throat.

Talking to the dog, Connor knew, as he himself did with hawks,

Iona with horses, Branna with hounds. Whatever ran in Fin's blood meant he could talk to all.

"Has he complaints then?" Connor wondered.

"He's only hoping I didn't forget this." Fin reached in the pocket of his leather coat for a little dog biscuit. Bugs sat, stared up with soulful eyes.

"You're a fine boy and there's your reward."

Bugs took it delicately before trotting off in triumph.

"Takes little to please him," Connor commented.

"Well, he loves his life and would choose no other. A man would be lucky to feel the same."

"Are you lucky, Fin?"

"Some days. But it takes more than a hard biscuit and a bed in a barn to content me. But then, I have more," he added and stroked Aine's throat.

"Sure she's the most beautiful filly I've seen in my life."

"And knows it well. But then modesty in a beautiful female's usually of the false sort. I'm after riding her over, letting her and Alastar gander at each other. So how did you find Megan?"

"Another beauty for certain. They took to each other, her and Sally. She gave me the payment on the spot."

"I thought they would." He nodded, didn't glance at the check Connor handed him, just shoved it in his pocket. "She'll be back for another in a month or two."

Now Connor smiled. "I thought the same."

"And you? Will you be traveling to Clare to visit them?"

"It crossed my mind. I think no, and can only think I think no because there's too much else crossing my mind." Connor shoved fingers through his breeze-tossed hair. "I wake each morning thinking of it, and him. I never used to."

"We hurt him, but he hurt us as well. We nearly didn't get through to Iona in time. None of us will be forgetting that. For all we had together, it wasn't enough. He won't forget that."

"We'll have more next round. I'm going to work with Branna." Lightly, he laid a hand on Fin's arm. "You should come with me."

"Not today. She won't want me round today when she's thinking it'll just be the two of you together."

"Branna won't let her feelings get in the way of what must be done."

"That's God's truth," Fin agreed, and swung himself into the saddle. He let Aine dance a bit. "We have to live, Connor. Despite it, because of it, around it, through it. We have to live as best we can."

"You think he'll beat us?"

"I don't. No, he won't beat you."

Deliberately, Connor slid a hand onto Aine's bridle, looked into Fin's stormy green eyes. "Us. It's us, Fin, and will always be us."

Fin nodded. "He won't win. But before the battle, and bitter and bloody it's bound to be, we have to live. I might choose another life if I could, but I'll make the most of the one I have. I'll come to the cottage soon."

He let Aine have her head, thundered away.

With his mood mixed and unsteady, Connor drove straight to the cottage. The light filtered through the windows of Branna's workshop, bounced over the colored bottles she displayed that held her creams and lotions, serums and potions. Her collection of mortars and pestles, her tools, the candles and plants she set about were all arranged just so.

And Kathel sprawled in front of her work counter like a guard while she sat at it, her nose in the thick book he knew to have been Sorcha's.

The fire in the hearth simmered, as did something in a pot on her work stove.

Another beauty, he thought—it seemed he was surrounded by them—with her dark hair pulled back from her face, her sweater rolled up at the sleeves. Her eyes, gray as the smoke puffing from the chimney, lifted to his.

"There you are. I thought you'd be here long before this. Half the day's gone."

"I had things to see to, as I told you clear enough."

Her brows lifted. "What's bitten your arse?"

"At the moment, you are."

No, his mood wasn't mixed, he realized. It had tipped over to foul. He stalked to the jar on the counter beside the stove. There were always biscuits, and he was slightly mollified to find the soft, chewy ones she rolled in cinnamon and sugar.

"I'm here when I could get here. I had the hawk sale to deal with."

"Was it a favorite of yours— Never mind, they all are. You have to be realistic, Connor."

"I'm bloody realistic. I sold the hawk, and the buyer was beautiful, available, and interested. I'm bloody realistic enough to know I had to come back here for you and this, else I'd be having myself a good shag."

"If a shag's so bleeding important, go get it done." Eyes narrowed, she fired right back at him. "I'd rather work alone than with you pacing about horny and bitter."

"It's that it *wasn't* so bleeding important, hasn't been so bleeding important since before the solstice that worries me." He stuffed one cookie in his mouth, wagged the other in the air.

"I'm making you some tea."

"I don't want any fucking tea. Yes, I do." He dropped down onto one of the stools at her work counter, rubbed Kathel when the dog laid his great head against Connor's leg. "It's not the shag or the woman or the hawk. It's all of it. All of this. All of it, and I let it bite me in the arse."

"Some days I want to climb up on the roof and scream. Scream at everyone and everything."

Calmer, Connor bit into the second biscuit. "But you don't."

"Not so far, but it could come to it. We'll have some tea, then we'll work."

He nodded. "Thanks."

She trailed her fingers over his back as she walked around him to the stove. "We'll have good days and bad until it's done, but until it's done we have to live as best we can."

He stared at the back of her head as she put on the kettle, and decided not to tell her Fin had said the very same.

7

HE THOUGHT TO GO TO THE PUB. HE WAS TIRED OF magicks, of spells, of mixing potions. He wanted some light, some music, some conversation that didn't center on the white or the black, or the end of all he knew.

The end of all he loved.

And maybe, just maybe, if Alice happened to be about, he'd see if she was still willing.

A man needed a distraction, didn't he, when his world hung in the balance of things? And some fun, some warmth. The lovely, lovely sound of a woman moaning under him.

Most of all, a man needed an escape when the three most important women in his life decided to have a wedding-planning hen party—not a term he'd use in their hearing if he valued his skin—in his home.

But he'd no more than walked outside when he realized he didn't want the pub or the crowd or Alice. So he pulled out his phone, texted Fin on his way to his lorry.

House full of women and wedding talk. If you're there, I'm coming over.

He'd no more than started the engine when Fin texted back.

Come ahead, you poor bastard.

On a half laugh he pulled away from the cottage.

It would do him good, Connor decided, after most of a day huddled with his sister over spell books and blood magicks to be in a man's house, in male company. Sure they could drag Boyle down as well, have a few beers, maybe play a bit of snooker in what he thought of as Fin's fun room.

Just the antidote to a long and not quite satisfying day.

He took the back road, winding through the thick green woods on an evening gone soft and dusky. He saw a fox slink into the green, a red blur with its kill still twitching in its jaws.

Nature was as full of cruelty as of beauty, he knew all too well.

But for the fox to survive, the field mouse didn't. And that was the way of things. For them to survive, Cabhan couldn't. So he who'd never walked into a fight if he could talk his way out of one, had never deliberately harmed anyone, would kill without hesitation or guilt. Would kill, he admitted, with a terrible kind of pleasure.

But tonight he wouldn't think of Cabhan or killing or surviving. Tonight all he wanted was his mates, a beer, and maybe a bit of snooker.

Less than a half kilometer from Fin's, the lorry sputtered, bucked, then died altogether.

"Well, fuck me."

He had petrol, as he'd filled the tank only the day before. And he'd given the lorry a good going-over—engine to exhaust—barely a month before.

She should be running smooth as silk.

Muttering, he pulled a torch from the glove box and climbed out to lift the bonnet.

He knew a thing or two about engines—as he knew a thing or two about plumbing, about carpentry and building, and electrical work. If the hawks hadn't taken him heart and mind, he might have started his own business as a man of all work.

Still, the skills came in handy in times such as these.

He played the light over the engine, checked the battery connection, the carburetor, flicked a hand to have the key turn in the ignition, studied the engine as it attempted to turn over with an annoying and puzzling grind.

He couldn't see a single thing amiss.

Of course, he could have solved it all with another flick of his hand and been on his way to mates, beer, and possibly snooker.

But it was a matter of pride.

So he checked the connections on the fuel pump, rechecked the connection on the battery, and didn't notice the fog swimming in along the ground.

"Well it's a bloody mystery."

He started to spread his hands over the engine, do a kind of scan—a compromise before giving up completely.

And felt the dirty smudge on the air.

He turned slowly, saw that he waded ankle deep in the fog that went icy with his movement. Shadows drew in, dark curtains that blocked the trees, the road, the world. Even the sky vanished behind them.

He came as a man, the red stone around his neck glowing against the thick and sudden dark.

"Alone, young Connor."

"As you are."

Spreading his hands, Cabhan only smiled. "I've a curiosity. You have no need for a machine such as that to travel from one place to another. You have only to . . ."

Cabhan swung his arms out, lifted them. And moved two feet closer without visibly moving at all.

"Such as we respect our gift, our craft, too much to use it for petty reasons. I've legs for walking or, if needs be, a lorry or a horse."

"Yet here you are, alone on the road."

"I've friends and family close by." Though when he tested, he found he couldn't quite reach them—couldn't push through the thick wall of fog. "What have you, Cabhan?"

"Power." He spoke the word with a kind of greedy reverence. "Power beyond your ken."

"And a hovel beyond the river to hide in, alone, in the dark. I'll take a warm fire, the light of it, and a pint with those friends and family."

"You're the least of them." Pity dripped like sullen rain. "You know it, as they do. Good for a laugh and the labor. But the least of the three. Your father knew enough to pass his amulet to your sister—to a girl over his only son."

"Do you think that makes me less?"

"I know it. What do you wear? Given you by an aunt, as consolation. Even your cousin from away has more than you. You have less, are less, a kind of jester, even a servant to the others you call family, you call friends. Your great *friend* Finbar chooses one with no power over you as partner, while you labor for wages at his whim. You're nothing, and have less."

He eased closer as he spoke, and the red stone throbbed like a pulse.

"I'm more than you know," Connor replied.

"What are you, boy?"

"I'm Connor, of the O'Dwyers. I'm of the three. I'm a dark witch of Mayo." Connor looked deep into the black eyes, saw the intent.

"I have fire." He threw his right hand out, held a swirling ball of fire. "And I have air." Stabbed a finger up, twirled it, and created a small, whirling cyclone. "Earth," he said as the ground trembled. "Water."

Rain spilled down, hot enough to sizzle on the ground.

"And hawk."

Roibeard dived with a piercing call, and landed soft as a feather on Connor's shoulder.

"Parlor tricks and pets." Cabhan raised his arms high, fingers spread wide. The red gem went bright as blood.

Lightning slapped the ground inches from Connor's boots, and with it came the acrid stink of sulfur.

"I could kill you with a thought." Cabhan's voice boomed over the roar of thunder.

I don't think so, Connor decided, and only cocked his head, smiled.

"Parlor tricks and pets? I bring fire, water, earth, and air. Test my powers if you dare. The hawk is mine for all time. He and me as part of the three will fulfill our destiny. Light is my sword, right is my shield, as long ago my path was revealed. I accept it willingly."

He struck out then, with the sword formed from the ball of fire, cleaved the air between them. He felt the burn—a bolt, a blade sear across the biceps of his left arm.

Ignoring it, he advanced, swung again, hair flying in the cyclone of air, sword blazing against the dark.

And when he sliced it down, Cabhan was gone.

The shadows lifted, the fog crawled away.

"As I will," Connor murmured, "so mote it be."

He let out a breath, drew in another, tasted the night—sweet and damp and green. He heard an owl hoot on a long, inquisitive note and the rustle of something hurrying through the brush.

"Well now." For a moment, Roibeard leaned in, and their cheeks met, held. "That was interesting. What do you wager my lorry starts up easy as you please? I'm off to Fin's, so you can go ahead with me there and have a visit with his Merlin, or go back home. It's your choice, *mo dearthair.*"

With you. Connor heard the answer in his heart as much as his head. *Always with you.*

Roibeard rose into the air and winged ahead.

Still throbbing with the echoes of power—dark and light—Connor got back in the lorry. It started easy, purred, and drove smoothly the rest of the way to Fin's.

He walked straight in. A fire crackled in the hearth, and that was welcome, but no one sprawled on the sofa with a beer at the ready.

As at home there as he was in his own cottage, he started toward the back, and heard voices.

"If you want hot meals"—Boyle—"marry someone who'll make them."

"Why would I do that when I have you so handy?"

"And I was happy enough in my own place making do with a sandwich and crisps."

"And I've a fine hunk of pork in the fridge."

"Why are you buying a fine hunk of pork when you don't know what in bloody hell to do with it?"

"Why wouldn't I, again, when I have you so handy?"

Though his head ached a bit, like a tooth going bad, the exchange made Connor chuckle as he continued back.

Strange, he felt he'd already had that beer. Quite a lot of beer, as he seemed to be floating right along, but on a floor tilted just a bit sideways.

He stepped into the kitchen where the lights burned so bright they made him blink, made his head pound instead of ache. "I could do with a hunk of pork."

"There, you see?" Grinning, Fin turned—and the grin fell away again. "What happened?"

"I had a little confrontation. Jesus, it's hot as Africa in here."

He struggled out of his jacket, weaving a little, then stared at his left arm. "Look at that, will you. My arm's smoking."

When he pitched forward, his friends leaped to catch him.

"What the fuck is this?" Boyle demanded. "He's burning up."

"It's hot in here," Connor insisted.

"It's not. It's Cabhan," Fin bit off the word. "I can smell him."

"Let me get his shirt off."

"The girls are always saying that to me."

Impatient, Fin merely jerked a hand over Connor, and had him bare-chested.

Connor stared at his arm, at the huge black burn, the peeling and bubbling skin. He felt oddly detached from it all, as if he looked at some little wonder behind glass.

"Would you look at that?" he said, and passed out.

Fin pressed his hands to the burn. Despite the pain that scorched through him, he held them there. Held the burning back.

"Tell me what to do," Boyle demanded.

"Get him water. I can stop it from spreading, but . . . We need Branna."

"I'll go get her."

"It'll take too long. Get him water."

Closing his eyes, Fin opened, reached out.

Connor's hurt. Come. Come quickly.

"Water's not going to help." Still Boyle knelt down. "Either of you. It's burning your hands. I know what that's like."

"And you know it can be fixed." Sweat popped out on Fin's face, ran in a thin river down his back. "I can't know how far this might take him if I don't hold it."

"Ice? He's on fire, Fin. We can put him in a tub of ice."

"Natural means won't help. In my workshop. Get— No need," he said with relief as Branna and Iona, with a wild-eyed Meara between them, popped into the kitchen.

Branna dropped down to Connor.

"What happened?"

"I don't know. Cabhan for certain, but that's all I know. He's feverish, a bit delirious. The burn under my hands is black, deep, it's trying to spread. I'm holding it."

"Let me see it. Let me do it."

"I'm holding it, Branna. I could do more, but not, I think, all. You can." He set his teeth against the pain. "I won't let him go, not even for you."

"All right. All right. But I need to see it, feel it, know it." She closed her eyes, drew up all she had, laid her hands over Fin's.

Her eyes opened again, filled with tears, for the pain under her hands was unspeakable.

"Look at me," she murmured to Fin. "He can't, so you look for him. Be for him. Feel for him. Heal for him. Look at me." Her eyes turned the gray of lake water, calm, so calm.

"Iona, put your hands over mine, give me what you can."

"Everything I have."

"It's cool, do you feel the cool?" Branna said to Fin.

"I do."

"Cool and clear, this healing power. It washes away the fire, floods out the black."

When Connor began to shiver, and to moan, Meara dropped down, pillowed his head in her lap. "Shh now." Gently, gently, she stroked his hair, his face. "Shh now. We're here with you."

Sweat poured down Connor's face—and ran down Fin's.

Branna's breathing grew shallow as she took in some of the heat, some of the pain.

"I'm holding it," Fin said between his teeth.

"Not alone now. Healing hurts—it's the price of it. Look at me, and let it go with me. Out of him we both love, slowly, coolly, out of him, into you, onto me. Out of him, into you, onto me. Out of him, into you, onto me."

She all but hypnotized him. That face, those eyes, that voice. And the gradual lifting of the pain, the cooling of the burn.

"Out of him," she continued, rocking, rocking. "Into you, onto me. And away. Away."

"Look at me." Now he told her as he felt her hands begin to tremble over his. "We're nearly there. Boyle, in my workroom, a brown apothecary bottle with a green stopper, top shelf behind my workbench."

Gently, he eased his hands back so they could see the wound. The burn, raw and red now, was no larger than a woman's fist.

"He's cooler," Meara said, stroking, stroking. "Clammy now, but cooler, and breathing steady."

"There's no black under it, no poison under it." Iona looked from Branna to Fin and back for confirmation.

"No, it's but a nasty burn now. I'll finish it." Branna put her hands over it, sighed. "Just a burn now, healing well."

"This?" Boyle rushed in with the bottle.

"That's it." Fin took it, opening it for Branna to sniff.

"Yes, yes, that's good. That's perfect." She turned up her hands for Fin to pour the balm into them.

"Here now, *mo chroi*." She turned her hands over, gently, gently rubbed the balm on the burn—now pink, now shrinking.

As she rubbed, as she crooned, Connor's eyes fluttered open. He found himself staring up into Meara's pale face and teary eyes.

"What? Why am I on the floor? I hadn't gotten drunk yet." He reached up, brushed a tear from Meara's cheek. "Don't cry, darling." He struggled to sit up, teetered a bit. "Well, here we all are, sitting on Fin's kitchen floor. If we're going to spin the bottle, I'd like to be the one to empty it first."

"Water." Boyle pushed it on him.

He drank like a camel, pushed it back. "I could do with stronger. My arm," he remembered. "It was my arm. Looks fine now."

And seeing Branna's face, he opened his arms to her. "You tended me."

"After you scared five lives out of me." She held on tight, tight until she could trust herself. "What happened?"

"I'll tell you, but— Thanks." He took the glass Boyle offered, drank. Winced. "Jesus, it's brandy. Can't a man get a whiskey?"

"It's brandy for fainting," Boyle insisted.

"I didn't faint." Both mortified and insulted, Connor pushed the glass back at Boyle. "I fell unconscious from my wounds, and that's entirely different. I'd rather a whiskey."

"I'll get it." Meara scrambled up as Iona leaned over, pressed a kiss to Connor's cheek.

"Your color's coming back. You were so pale, and so hot. Please don't ever do that again."

"I can promise to do my best never to repeat the experience."

"What was the experience?" Branna demanded.

"I'll tell you, all of it, but I swear on my life I'm starving. I don't want to be accused of fainting again if I pass out from hunger. I'm light-headed with it, God's truth."

"I've a hunk of pork. Raw," Fin began.

"You haven't put any dinner on?" Branna pushed to her feet.

"I was thinking Boyle would cook it up, then Connor came in. We've been a bit busy with this and that since."

"You can't cook up pork in a fingersnap."

Fin tried a smile. "You could."

"Oh, save your shagging pork, and get me a platter."

"That sort of thing's in the—" Fin gestured toward the large dining area off the kitchen with its massive buffets and china cabinets and servers.

She marched in, yanked open a couple of drawers. And found a large Belleek platter. After moving a nice arrangement of hothouse lilies, she set the platter in the center of the table.

"It's a frivolous use of power, but I can't have my brother starving to death. And since I had already roasted a chicken with potatoes and carrots tonight. So."

She shot the fingers of both hands at the platter. And the air went redolent with the scents of roasted chicken and sage.

"Thank all the gods and goddesses." With that, Connor dived straight in, ripped off a drumstick.

"Connor O'Dwyer!"

"Starving," he said with his mouth full as Branna fisted her hands on her hips. "I'm serious about it. What's everyone else eating?"

"Someone set the table, for God's sake. I need to wash up." She turned to Fin. "Have you a powder room?"

"I'll show you."

She'd never been in his home, he thought. Not once would she agree to cross the threshold. It had taken her brother's need to have her step foot in it.

He showed her the powder room tucked tidily under the stairs.

"Let me see your hands." She held herself very straight while the voices and good, easy laughter flowed from the kitchen.

He held them out, their backs up. With a sigh of impatience, she gripped them and turned them over.

Blistered palms, welts along his fingers.

"The balm will take care of it."

"Stop."

She laid her hands—her palms to his palms, her fingers to his fingers.

"I'm going to thank you. I know you don't want or need thanks. I know he's your brother as much as mine. The brother of your heart, your spirit. But he's my blood, so I need to thank you."

Tears trembled in her eyes again, a glimmer over the smoke. Then she willed them back and gone. "It was very bad, very bad indeed. I can't be sure how much worse it might have been if you hadn't done for him what you did."

"I love him."

"I know it." She studied his hands, healed now, then gave them both a moment. She lifted his hands, pressed them to her lips. "I know it," she said again, and slipped inside the powder room.

As deep and true as his love ran for Connor, it was a shadow beside what he felt for her. Accepting it, Fin walked back to the kitchen, watched his circle prepare for their first meal together in his home.

"WHY DIDN'T YOU CALL US?" BRANNA ASKED WHEN THEY'D settled in with the food and Connor's tale.

"I did—or tried. There was something different in the shadows, in the fog. It was . . . like being closed into a box, tight, so there was nothing else, not even sky. I don't know how Roibeard heard me or got through unless he was already inside the box, so to speak. The stone Cabhan wore beat like a heart, and the beats of it came faster when I called the elements."

"In tune with him?" Fin wondered. "Showing excitement, temper, fear?"

"I don't think fear, as he thinks so little of me."

"Bollocks." Meara stabbed a carrot. "He was mind-fucking you so you'd think little of yourself."

"She's right on that," Boyle agreed. "Trying to get under your skin, he was. Weaken your defenses. It's a common enough tactic in a brawl."

"I saw you brawl once." Iona thought back, smiled. "You didn't say much."

"Because I was punching the stupid. But if you're thinking your opponent's got skills, maybe even better than yours, mind-fucking, as our Meara put it, it's a good tactic."

"What the bastard thinks of me either way isn't something I worry myself about." Content enough now, Connor shoveled in potatoes. "The lightning strike gave me a jolt, I confess."

"He didn't strike you because you have the amulet, and that's protection," Branna considered. "And because he wants what you have more than your death. He tried to undermine your confidence, and put bad feelings between you and me, between you and Fin."

"He failed on all counts. And here's the thing. When I struck at him, the stone glowed brighter, but then—I felt something burn—nothing like it came to be, but a quick burning. And the gem, it dimmed after that. Dimmed considerable just as I struck out again, just before he vanished, and the shadows with him."

"What he did to you took considerable from him." Branna ran her hand down Connor's arm. "To close you in, then cause you harm, to, well, show off for you as well. It cost him."

"If I'd been able to call you, if we'd all been there."

"I don't know," Branna mused.

"We do know he wasn't willing to risk it. He's not ready to take us all on again, or hasn't the balls for it." Fin looked around the table. "And there's a victory."

"He wasn't weak, I'll tell you that. I could feel it pumping out of him. The dark, and the hunger of it. I didn't see him strike, and would swear he never touched me. Yet, I felt that burn."

"Neither your jacket or shirt were scorched. But your shirt?" Boyle gestured with his fork. "Smoke came through it from the burn on your arm. Yet you're wearing it now, and there's no mark on it."

"That's grand, as I'm fond of this shirt."

"He stayed as a man," Meara added. "Because he didn't choose to use his power for the change? He needed all he had to hurt Connor. If Fin hadn't kept it from spreading until Branna got here, it would've been far worse—is that right?"

"Much worse," Branna confirmed.

"And worse, much worse, would have taken more from you—from the three. He's studied you all your lives, one way or another, so surely he knew Branna would come, and she'd put all she had into healing Connor—that Iona would add what she could. But that much worse might've put Connor down for a day or two, depleted the three of you. He wanted that, risked that. But he didn't count on Fin," Meara explained.

"I was nearly here," Connor pointed out. "He had to suss it out here's where I'd come."

Impatient, Branna shook her head. "He's watched you, studied you, but he doesn't understand Fin at all. Not at all. He can't see beyond the blood shared between them. That I would be called and come, yes, but that Fin would take the pain, the risk, the burning to stop the spread? He doesn't know you at all," she said to Fin. "He never will. In the end, that might be his undoing."

"He doesn't understand family, and because he doesn't understand, he doesn't respect. He won't win this," Connor said, and helped himself to more potatoes.

AFTER THE MEAL AND THE CLEARING UP, CONNOR DROVE Branna home, Meara with them.

"Will you be staying?" he asked Meara.

"No—unless you want me," she said to Branna. "I know we'd planned a night of it."

"Go sleep in your own bed. We'll have our night of it, and wedding plans another time. Connor will drive you home."

"I walked from the stables." Meara leaned forward to look at Connor around Branna. "You could just drop me there."

"I'll drive you home. It's late, and it's an uneasy night at best."

"I won't argue with that."

So he dropped Branna off, and waited for her to go inside, though he doubted Cabhan could manage so much as a poke with a sharp stick that night.

"She'll want just you," Meara said quietly.

"You're never out of place with us."

"No, but she'll want just you tonight. I've never seen her so frightened. We're all standing in the kitchen, with her just pulling the chicken from the oven, and laughing over something I can't even recall. Then she went white as death. It was Fin calling her, though I don't know what he said."

Gathering herself, Meara paused a moment. "But she said only, 'Connor's hurt. At Fin's.' And she grabbed my arm. Iona grabbed the other. And I was flying. A blink, an hour, I couldn't say. All these years I've known you and Branna, and I never knew the like of that. Next I know we're in Fin's kitchen, and you're on the ground, paler even than Branna.

"I thought you were dead."

"It takes more than a bit of black magick to do me."

"Stop the lorry."

"What? Ah, are you sick. I'm sorry." He swung to the side of the road, stopped. "I shouldn't be joking when—"

His words, his thoughts, the whole of his mind dropped into a void when she launched herself at him, chained her arms around him, and took his mouth like a madwoman.

Like a hot, mad, desperate woman.

Before he could act, react, think, she pulled back again.

"What— What was all that? And where's it been?"

"I thought you were dead," she repeated, and latched that hot, mad, desperate mouth to his again.

This time he acted, grabbing on to her, trying to shift her around so he could find a better hold, gain a better angle. All the while her taste pumped into him like a drug, one never sampled, one he wanted more of. All of.

"Meara. Let me—"

She jerked back again. "No. No. We're not doing this. We can't do this."

"We already did."

"Just that—" She waved her hands in the air. "That's all of it."

"Actually, there's considerable more, if you'd just—"

"No." She threw her arm out, slapped a hand to his chest to stop him. "Drive. Drive, drive, drive."

"I'm driving." He pulled back onto the road, realized he was as unsteady as he'd been after Cabhan's attack. "We should have a talk about it."

"We won't be talking about it, as there's nothing to talk about. I thought you were dead, and it's got me shaken up more than I understood because I don't want you dead."

Because he could feel the chaos inside her roiling around, he tried for ease and calm to counter it. "Sure I'm glad you don't, and glad I'm not. But—"

"There's not a 'but' about it. And nothing more to it."

She leaped out of the lorry almost before he pulled in front of her flat.

"Go home to Branna," she ordered. "She needs you."

If she hadn't said the last, he'd have marched right up to her flat, pushed his way in if necessary. Then they'd have seen what they'd have seen.

But because she was right, he waited until she'd shut herself inside. Then he drove home, more puzzled than he'd ever been about a woman.

And more stirred by one than he could remember.

8

MEARA TOLD HERSELF TO FORGET ABOUT IT. TO PUT IT aside as a moment of insanity caused by extreme stress. It wasn't every day, was it, your two good friends grabbed hold of you and took you flying so you winked out of one place, winked into another?

Where you looked at a man you'd cared for the whole of your life, and thought him dead?

Some women would have run screaming, she thought as she put her back into mucking stalls. Some would have fallen into hysterics.

All she'd done was kiss the man who wasn't dead at all.

"I've kissed him before, haven't I?" she muttered and pitched soiled hay into the barrow. "You can't know someone almost from birth, run in the same pack all along, be best mates with his sister, and not. It's nothing. It's not a thing at all."

Oh God.

She squeezed her eyes shut, leaned on her pitchfork.

Sure she'd kissed him before, and he her.

But not like that. Not like that, no. Not all hot and heavy with tongues and teeth and her heart racing.

What must he think? What did she think?

More, what the bloody, bleeding hell was she to do when next she saw him?

"Okay." Iona stepped into the stall behind her, leaned on her own pitchfork. "I've given you thirty-two minutes, by my mark. That's my limit. What's going on?"

"Going on?" Flustered, Meara tugged the brim of her cap down lower, and tossed another scoop into the barrow. "I'm pitching horse shit, as you are."

"Meara, you barely looked at me, much less spoke when we got here this morning. And you're in here muttering under your breath. If I did something to piss you off—"

"No! Of course you didn't."

"I didn't think so, but something's got you muttering and hunching off with your eyes averted."

"Maybe I've got my monthlies."

"Maybe?"

"I couldn't think fast enough if I'd been bitchy recently when I did have them. My mother—"

Iona jabbed a finger to stop her. "You didn't think fast enough there either. When it's your mother, you spew. You're not spewing, you're hiding."

"I am not." Insulted, Meara angled away. "I'm merely taking some time with my thoughts."

"Is it about last night?"

Meara straightened up like a flag pole. "What about last night?"

"Connor. Black magickal burn."

"Oh. Well, yes, of course. Of course, it's that."

Eyes narrowed in speculation, Iona circled her finger in the air. "And?"

"And? That should be enough for anyone. It would send most people into hospital with collapsed nerves."

"You're not most people." Now Iona moved in closer, crowding the space. "What happened after you left Fin's?"

"Why would anything happen?"

"There!" Iona pointed. "You looked at the ground. Something happened, and you're evading."

Why, oh why, was she such a miserable liar when it mattered? "I'm looking at the horse shit I'm not shoveling."

"I thought we were friends."

"Oh, oh, that's below the belt." It was Meara's turn to point an accusatory finger. "That sorrowful look, the little catch in your voice."

"It is," Iona admitted with a quick smile. "But it's still true."

Losing the battle, Meara leaned on her pitchfork again. "I don't know what to say about it, or do about it."

"That's why you tell a friend. You're close to Branna—and I don't mean that below the belt. If you can talk to her, I'll cover for you while you go over."

"You would," Meara said with a sigh. "I'll need to talk to her, that's clear enough. I'm not sure how. It might be better to talk to a cousin rather than a sister right off. Sort of like stepping-stones. It's just that . . ."

She stepped to the opening of the stall, looked up, looked down to be sure Boyle, Mick, or any of the stable hands weren't loitering nearby.

"It was scary, last night. And I was turned upside down right off at being whisked magickally from one kitchen to the next in a couple blinks of the eye."

"You'd never flown before? Oh God, Meara, you had to be upside down. I guess I assumed Branna would have taken you now and then. For, well, fun."

"It's not that she won't use power for a bit of fun now and then. But she's pretty bloody responsible with it."

"You don't have to tell me."

"Then we're there, where we weren't, and Connor . . . In that first moment, I thought he was dead."

"Oh, Meara." Instinctively, Iona reached out to hug her. "I knew he wasn't—that connection among the three—and I nearly lost it."

"I thought I'd—we'd—lost *him*, and my head was already spinning, my guts twisted sideways. Then Branna and Fin working on him, and you as well. And I could do nothing."

"That's not true." Iona pulled back, gave Meara a little shake. "It took us all. It took our circle, our family."

"I felt useless all the same, but that's not important. It was such a relief when he came back, and so much himself. And I thought I'd calmed and settled. But when he drove me home, it started rolling around inside me again, and before I knew it, before I could think straight, I told him to pull over."

"Were you sick? I'm so sorry."

"No, no, and he thought the same. But I went a bit mad, really. I just jumped him, right there in his lorry."

Shock had Iona's mouth falling open as she took a jerky step back. "You— You hit him?"

"No! Don't be an idjit! I kissed him. And not at all like a brother or a friend, or someone you're welcoming back from death."

"Oh." Iona drew the syllable out.

"Oh," Meara echoed, doing a restless circle around the stall. "Then, as if that wasn't enough, I pulled back. You'd think I'd've got my head back in place, but no, I did it all over again. And being a man, after all, he had no objections, and would've moved on from there if I hadn't found my sanity again."

"I shouldn't be surprised. I'm not really surprised. I thought there was something . . . but when I first got here this winter, I thought there was something between you and Boyle."

"Oh Jesus." Completely done, Meara covered her face with her hands.

"I know there wasn't, ever, anything but family, friends. So I decided the something I thought I felt between you and Connor was the same."

"It is! Of course it is. This was a result of trauma."

"A coma's a result of trauma. Making out in a truck—lorry—is a result of something else entirely."

"It wasn't making out, just a couple kisses."

"Tongues?"

"Oh bloody hell." She yanked off her cap, tossed it down, stomped on it.

"Does that help?" Iona wondered.

"No." Disgusted, Meara grabbed the cap, beat it against her thigh. "How can I tell Branna I've been snogging her brother in his lorry on the side of the road like a horny teenager?"

"The same way you told me. What about—"

"Do the two of you intend to stand around all morning, or will you be hauling that manure out?" Boyle stepped to the opening, scowled at them.

"We're nearly done," Iona told him. "And we have something we have to discuss."

"Discuss later, haul manure now."

"Go away."

"I'm the boss here."

She merely stared at him until he shoved his hands in his pockets and stalked away.

"Don't worry, I won't say anything to him."

"Oh, it doesn't matter." Mortified all over again, Meara shoveled more manure. "Connor will for certain. Men are worse than women about such matters."

"What did you say to Connor? After."

"I told him that was the end of it, and I wasn't going to talk about it."

"Right." Iona managed to hold back the laugh, but not the toothy smile. "That'll work."

"We can't have a mad, momentary impulse twisting things up. We've more important things to concern us, as a whole."

Iona said nothing for a moment, then stepped over, gave Meara another hug. "I understand. I'll go with you when you talk to Branna if you want."

"Thanks for that, but it's best I do it on my own."

"Go this morning, get it off your mind. I'll cover for you."

"It would be good to get it out and gone, wouldn't it?" And maybe her stomach would stop rolling around, she considered as she pressed a hand to it. "I'll finish up here, then run over. Once it's said, I can put it aside and concentrate on what needs doing without it nagging at me."

"I'll smooth it with Boyle."

"Tell him I've my monthlies or some other female thing. It always shuts him up."

"I'm aware," Iona said with a laugh, and went back to her own stall.

DO IT QUICK, MEARA ORDERED HERSELF AS SHE STRODE through the woods. Get it over. Branna would hardly be mad about it—more likely she'd laugh, and think it a fine joke.

That would be grand, and then she could think of it as a fine joke herself.

Imagine Meara Quinn lusting for Connor O'Dwyer. And she could admit there were little pockets of lust burning in uncomfortable places.

But a talk with Branna would quash all that, and things would be back as things should be.

Maybe she'd had a little twinge over him now and then through the years. What woman wouldn't feel a twinge or two for the likes of Connor O'Dwyer?

The man made a picture, didn't he? All long and lean and that curling mop of hair, that pretty face, that knowing grin. Add in his caring ways, for he had that as much as the pretty.

A temper to be sure, but less than hers by far. By a few thousand kilometers, truth be told. And a far happier, steadier outlook on life than most, including herself.

For all he'd faced the whole of his life, he kept that happy outlook, those caring ways. You mixed the power in, for it was an awesome thing to behold even for one who'd known and seen it all her life, and the full package of him packed a solid punch.

And he knew it well, used it well—on more than a fair share of females to her way of thinking.

Not that she held that against him. Why not pluck the flowers along the way?

For her, for sense and logic, she'd stick with being his friend rather than part of a bouquet.

She sighed, hunched her shoulders as the air chilled. She'd have to speak to him of it—foolish to tell herself otherwise. But after she'd told Branna and they'd had a good laugh over it.

She'd be able to talk to Connor, make it all a fine joke, after she told Branna.

She dug into her pocket for her gloves as the wind kicked up. And to think they'd called for a bright morning, she thought as clouds smothered the sun.

And she heard her name on the wind.

Pausing, she looked over in that direction, saw she stood at the big downed tree by the thick vines. By the place where beyond lay the ruins of Sorcha's cabin, and the land that could slip in and out of time on Cabhan's whim.

He'd never before called to her, bothered with her. Why would he? She had no power, was no threat. But he called now, and the voice that oozed seduction pulled at something inside her.

She knew the dangers, knew all the warnings and risks, yet found herself standing at the curtain of vines without realizing she'd walked to them. Found herself reaching.

She'd just have a look, just a quick look is all.

Her hand touched the vines, and a dreamy warmth came with the touch. Smiling, she started to part them while fog oozed through their tangles.

The hawk cried as it dove. It sliced a path along those vines so she stumbled back. Shuddered and shuddered with the fog swimming nearly to her knees.

Roibeard perched on the downed tree, looked at her with eyes bright and fierce.

"I was going in, have a look. Can you hear him as well? It's my name he's calling. I only want to see."

When she reached out again, Roibeard spread his wings in warning. Behind her Branna's hound let out a soft woof.

"Come with me if you like. Why don't you come with me?"

Kathel caught the hem of her jacket in his teeth, pulled her back.

"Stop that now! What's wrong with you? What's . . . What's wrong with *me*?" she murmured, swaying now, knees watery, head light.

"Bugger it." She laid an unsteady hand on Kathel's great head. "Good dog, smart and good. Let's get away from here." She looked back at Roibeard, and at the shadows dimming again as the sun struggled through the mists. "Let's all get away from here."

She kept her hand on the dog, walking fast while the hawk swooped and glided overhead. Never in her life was she so glad to see the woods behind her, and the home of the Dark Witch so close at hand.

She wasn't ashamed to run, or to fling herself, just ahead of the hound, breathless into Branna's workshop.

In the act of pouring something that smelled of sugar biscuits from vat to bottle, Branna looked up. Immediately set the pot aside.

"What is it? You're shaking. Here, here, come by the fire."

"He called me," Meara managed as Branna rushed around the work counter. "He called my name."

"Cabhan." Wrapping an arm around Meara, Branna pulled her to the fire, eased her down into a chair. "At the stables?"

"No, no, the woods. I was coming here. At the place—outside Sorcha's place. Branna, he called me, and I was going. I wanted to go in, go to him. I wanted it."

"It's all right. You're here." She brushed her hands over Meara's cold cheeks, warmed them.

"I wanted it."

"He's sly. He makes you want. But you're here."

"I might not be but for Roibeard who came out of nowhere to stop me, then Kathel who came as well, and clamped right onto my jacket to pull me back."

"They love you, as I do." Branna bent down to lay her cheek to Kathel's head, to wrap around him for a moment. "I'm going to get you some tea. Don't argue. You need it, as do I."

She got Kathel a biscuit first, then stepped outside briefly.

To thank the hawk, Meara thought. To let him know all was well, and he had her gratitude. Branna always acknowledged loyalty.

To give her own thanks, and for comfort, Meara slid off the chair to hug Kathel. "Strong and brave and true," she whispered. "There's no better dog in the world than our Kathel."

"Not a one. Sit down, catch your breath." Branna busied herself with tea when she came back inside.

"Why would he call me? What would he want with me?"

"You're one of us."

"I've no magick."

"Not being a witch doesn't mean you don't have magick. You have a heart and a spirit. You're as strong and brave and true as Kathel."

"I've never felt anything like it. It was as if everything else went away, and there was only his voice, and my own terrible need to answer it."

"I'll be making you a charm, and you'll carry it with you always."

Warm now, Meara shrugged out of her jacket. "You've made me charms."

"I'll make you another, stronger, more specific, we'll say." She brought over the tea. "Now tell me all, as carefully as you can."

When she had, Meara sat back. "It was only a minute or two I realize now. It all seemed so slow, so dreamlike. Why didn't he just strike me down?"

"A waste of a comely maid."

"I haven't been a maid in some time." She shuddered again. "And oh, what a terrible thought it is. Worse, I might have been willing."

"Spellbound isn't willing. I can only believe he'd have used you if you'd gone through—taken you to another time, used you, and done what he could to turn you."

"He couldn't do that with any spell. Not with any."

"He couldn't, no, not that. But as you said about Fin, he doesn't understand family and love." Branna gripped Meara's hand, brought it to her cheek. "He'd have hurt you, Meara, and that would have hurt us all. You'll carry the charm I make you."

"Of course I will."

"We'll need to tell the others. Boyle will need to have more of a care as well. But he has Iona and Fin. You should stay here, with Connor and me."

"I can't."

"I know you value your own space—who'd understand more—but until we've settled on what we do next, it's best if—"

"I kissed him."

"What? What?" Stunned, Branna jerked back. "You kissed Cabhan? But you said you didn't go through. What—"

"Connor. I kissed Connor. Last night. I all but molested him on the side of the road. I lost my mind for a minute, that's all it was. The flying along, the seeing him lying on Fin's kitchen floor, all the pain in his face when the healing started. I thought, he's dead, then he wasn't, then he's shaking and burning up, and then he's ripping off a drumstick and chomping into it before he's so much as put his shirt on again. It all just boiled my brain until I was all but crawling over him and kissing him."

"Well," Branna said after Meara sucked in a breath.

"But I stopped—you have to know—well, after the second time I stopped."

Though Branna's mouth quirked at the corner, her tone stayed utterly even. "The second time?"

"I— It— He— It was a mad reaction to the evening."

"And did he have a mad reaction as well—to the evening?"

"I'd have to say, thinking on it, the first one took him by surprise, and who could wonder. And the second . . . he's a man, after all."

"He is that, indeed."

"But it went no further. I'll make that clear to you. I had him drop me home and drive on. It went no further."

"Why?"

"Why?" Blank, Meara just stared. "He dropped me home as I said."

"Why didn't he go with you?"

"With me? He needed to go home, to you."

"Ah, bollocks to that, Meara." Annoyance flicked out. "I won't be used as an excuse."

"I don't mean that, not at all. I . . . I thought you'd be irritated or amused, or puzzled at least. But you're not."

"I'm none of those, no, or surprised in the least. I've wondered why it's taken the pair of you so bloody long to get to it."

"Get to what?"

"Get together."

"Together?" Pure shock had Meara surging to her feet. "Me, Connor. No, that can't be."

"And why can't it?"

"Because we're friends."

Meara sipped her tea, looked into the fire. "When I think of a lover who would touch more than my body, I think of a friend. To have only the heat without the warmth? It would do, and does, but only just."

"And what happens to the friend when the lover ends?"

"I don't know. I see our parents, Connor's and mine, happy still. Not blissful every second of every day, for who could stand that? But happy, and in tune most of the time."

"And I see mine."

"I know." Branna reached up, took Meara's hand to draw her down to sit again. "Those who made us give us each a different place to stand on it, don't they? I want, when I let myself want, that happy, that in tune. And you won't let yourself want at all because you see the ruin, the misery, and the selfishness under it all."

"He means too much to me to risk the ruin. And we've too much to fight for—as yesterday and today have proved—to tangle up our circle with sex."

"I believe Iona and Boyle have sex at every opportunity."

Now Meara laughed. "They're mad in love, and suited for it, so it's different."

"It's up to you, of course, and to Connor." And Connor, Branna thought, would very likely have a different thing or two to say about the matter. "But know I've no objection at all, if that was a worry to you. Why would I? I love you both. I'll say as well that sex is a powerful magick of its own."

"So I should sleep with Connor to aid the cause?"

"You should do what makes you happy."

"It's all a bit confusing right now to be sure what does, what doesn't. But what I have to do is get back to work before Boyle gives me the boot."

"I'll make the charm first, and Kathel and Roibeard will go back with you. Walk clear of Sorcha's place, Meara."

"Believe me, I'll do that."

"Tell Iona and Boyle what happened. Boyle will see Fin's told, and I'll speak with Connor. Cabhan's growing bold again, so we best all be on our toes."

BRANNA DIDN'T HAVE TO TELL CONNOR, AS FIN WENT BY the school that afternoon, took Connor aside.

"Is she all right? Are you sure of it?"

"I saw her myself not an hour ago. She's fine and fit as ever."

"I've been busy," Connor said. "I barely noticed Roibeard wasn't about, then when I did, I knew he was at the stables. He likes it there, with the horses. With Meara. So I thought nothing of it, and he never sent me any alarm."

"As he and Kathel were all she needed. Branna made her a charm. It's a strong one—I had Meara show me. And the woman's strong as well. Still, it's time we were all a bit more careful."

Connor paced, boots crunching on gravel. "He'd have raped her. Strong or not, she couldn't have stopped him. I've seen what he's done to women over his time."

"He didn't touch her, Connor, and won't. We'll all see to that."

"I've worried for Branna on this. He wants power, and she is full of power. Named for Sorcha's firstborn, and the first of the three in the now to be passed the amulet. And . . ."

"The woman I love, who loves me even if she won't have me. You're not alone in your worry."

"And Meara is a sister to Branna. That might be making her more appealing to him," Connor considered.

"To strike at Branna through Meara." Fin nodded. "It would be his way."

"It would. And after last night . . ."

"After what he did to you? What has that to do with Meara?"

"Nothing at all. Well, indirectly." A man shouldn't lie or evade with his mates. In any case there was more on the line than discretion. "We had a moment, Meara and I, after leaving Branna at the cottage. A moment or two in the lorry, on the side of the road."

Fin's eyebrow winged up. "You moved in on Meara?"

"The other way." Distracted, Connor twirled a finger. "She moved in on me. And moved in with great enthusiasm. Then stopped cold, said that's the end of that, and take me home. I love women, Fin. I love them top to toe, minds, hearts, bodies. Breasts. What is there about a woman's breasts?"

"How long do we have to discuss it?"

Connor laughed. "True enough. We could take hours on breasts alone. I love women, Fin, but for the life of me there's so much of them impossible to understand."

"And that discussion would take days and never be resolved." Obviously intrigued, Fin studied Connor's face. "Tell me this, did you want that to be the end of it?"

"After I got over wondering where all this had been hiding, from both of us, all our lives, no, I didn't. Don't."

"Then, *mo dearthair.*" Fin slapped Connor's shoulder. "It's up to you to follow through."

"I'm thinking on it. And now wondering if that moment or two on the side of the road might be why Cabhan took an interest in her today. Because I did, in that way? It's not far thinking."

"It's not, no. He hurt you last night. It may be he tried to hurt you again, through Meara, today. So have a care, both of you."

"I will, and I'll see she does. Ah, there's the three o'clocks. A mister and missus from Wales. Want to go along? I'll fetch you a pack and glove."

Fin started to decline, then realized it had been too long since he'd done a hawk walk with Connor. "I wouldn't mind that, but I'll get my own gear."

Connor glanced up, spotted Merlin in the sky. "Will you take him? Trust one of them with him?"

"He'd enjoy it as well."

"It'll be a bit like old times then."

When Fin went off for the gear, Connor took a quick glance at the time. As soon as he was able, he'd search out Meara. They had considerable to talk about, like it or not.

9

AS IF HER DAY HADN'T BEEN FRAUGHT ENOUGH, MEARA added on a frantic and weepy call from her mother that sent her searching out Boyle.

He sat in his office scowling as he was prone to scowl over paperwork.

"Boyle."

"Why is it the numbers never tally the first time you do them? Why is that?"

"I couldn't say. Boyle, I'm sorry to ask but I need to go. My mother's had a fire at the house."

"A fire?" He shoved up from his desk as if he'd rush off to put it out himself.

"A kitchen fire, I think. It was hard getting anything out of her, as she was near hysterical. But I did get she's not hurt, and didn't burn the place down around her. Still, I don't know how bad it all is, so—"

"Go. Go on." He rounded the desk, taking her arm, drawing her out of the office. "Let me know what's what as soon as you can."

"I will. Thanks. I'll do extra tomorrow to make up for it."

"Just go, for Christ's sake."

"I'm going."

She jumped in her lorry.

It would be nothing, she told herself. Unless it was something. With Colleen Quinn, you never knew which.

And her mother had been all but incoherent, wailing one minute, babbling the next. All about the kitchen, smoke, burning.

Maybe she was hurt.

The image of Connor, the black bubbling burn on his arm flashed through her mind.

Burning.

Cabhan. Fear spurted through her at the thought he might have played some part. Had he gone after her mother because in the end she'd resisted his call?

Meara punched the accelerator, rocketed around curves, raced her way with her heart at a gallop to the little dollhouse nestled with a handful of others just along the hem of Cong's skirts.

The house stood—no damage she could see to the white walls, the gray roof, the tidy dooryard garden. Tidy, true enough, as the small bit of garden in front and back was her mother's only real interest.

She shoved through the short gate—one she'd painted herself the previous spring, and ran up the walk, digging for her keys, since her mother insisted on locking the doors day and night in fear of burglars, rapists, or alien probes.

But Colleen rushed out, hands clasped together at her breast as if in prayer.

"Oh, Meara, thank God you've come! What will I do? What will I do?"

She threw herself into Meara's arms, a weeping, trembling bundle of despair.

"You're not hurt? For certain? Let me see you're not hurt."

"I burned my fingers." Like a child she held up her hand to show the hurt.

And nothing, Meara saw with relief, a bit of salve wouldn't deal with.

"All right then, all right." To soothe, Meara brushed a light kiss over the little burn. "That's the most important thing."

"It's terrible!" Colleen insisted. "The kitchen's a ruin. What will I do? Oh, Meara, what will I do?"

"Let's have a look, then we'll see, won't we?"

It was easy to turn Colleen around and pull her inside. Meara had gotten her height from her long-absent father. Colleen made a pretty little package—a petite, slim, and always perfectly groomed one, a fact of life that often made Meara feel like a hulking bear leading a poodle with a perfect pedigree.

No damage in the front room, another relief, though Meara could smell smoke, and see the thin haze of it.

Smoke, she thought—more relief—not fog.

Three strides took her into the compact, eat-in kitchen where the smoke hung in a thin haze.

Not a ruin, but sure a mess. And not one, she determined immediately, caused by an evil sorcerer, but a careless and inept woman.

Keeping an arm around her weeping mother, she took stock.

The roasting pan with the burned joint, now spilled onto the floor beside a scorched and soaking dish cloth told the tale.

"You burned the joint," Meara said carefully.

"I thought to roast some lamb, as Donal and his girl were to come to dinner later. I can't approve him moving in with Sharon before marriage, but I'm his mother all the same."

"Roasting a joint," Meara murmured.

"Donal's fond of a good joint as you know. I'd just gone out the back for a bit. I've had slugs in the garden there, and went to change the beer."

Fluttering in distress, Colleen waved her hands at the kitchen door as if Meara might have forgotten where the garden lay. "They've been after the impatiens, so I had to see about it."

"All right." Meara stepped over, began to open the windows, as Colleen had failed to do.

"I wasn't out that long, but I thought since I was, I'd cut some flowers for a nice arrangement on the table. You need fresh flowers for company at dinner."

"Mmm," Meara said, and picked up the flowers scattered over the wet floor.

"I came in, and the kitchen was full of smoke." Still fluttering, Colleen looked tearfully around the room. "I ran to the oven, and the lamb was burning, so I took the cloth there to pull it out."

"I see." Meara turned off the oven, found a fresh cloth, picked up the roasting pan, the charcoaled joint.

"And somehow the cloth lit, and was burning. I had to drop everything and take the pan there, where I had water for the potatoes."

Meara picked up the potatoes while her mother wrung her hands, dumped the lot in the sink to deal with later.

"It's a ruin, Meara, a ruin! What will I do? What will I do?"

The familiar mix of annoyance, resignation, frustration wound through her. Accepting that as her lot, Meara dried her hands by swiping them on her work pants.

"The first thing is to open the windows in the front room while I mop this up."

"The smoke will soil the paint, won't it, Meara, and you see the floor there, it's scorched from the burning cloth. I don't dare tell the landlord or he'll set me out."

"He'll do nothing of the kind, Ma. If the paint's soiled, we'll fix it. If the floor's damaged, we'll fix that as well. Open the windows, then put some of Branna's salve on your fingers."

But Colleen only stood, hands clasped, pretty blue eyes damp. "Donal and his girl are coming at seven."

"One thing at a time, Ma," Meara said as she mopped.

"I couldn't ring him up to tell him of the disaster here. Not while he's at work."

But you could ring me, Meara thought, as you've never understood a woman can work, does work, wants or needs to work, the same as a man.

"The windows," was all she said.

Not a mean bone in her body, Meara reminded herself as she cleaned the floor—not scorched at all, but only smudged with ash from the cloth. Not even selfish in the usual way, but simply helpless and dependent.

And was that her fault, really, when she'd been tended and sheltered the whole of her life? By her parents, then by her husband, and now by her children.

She'd never been taught to cope, had she? Or, Meara thought with a hard stare at the roasting pan, how to cook a fecking joint.

After wringing out the mop, she took a moment to text Boyle. No point in keeping him worried.

Not a fire but a burnt joint of lamb and a right mess. No harm.

Meara carted out the ruined meat to dump in the bin, scrubbed off the potatoes and set them to dry—as they were still raw because her mother had forgotten, all to the good, to turn the heat on under them.

She set the roasting pan in the sink to soak, put the kettle on for tea, all while Colleen despaired of being evicted.

"Sit down, Ma."

"I can't sit, I'm that upset."

"Sit. You'll have some tea."

"But Donal. What will I do? I've ruined the kitchen, and they're coming for dinner. And the landlord, this will put him in a state for certain."

Meara did multiplication tables in her head—the sevens, which buggered her every time. It kept her from shouting when she turned to her mother. "First, look around now. The kitchen's not ruined, is it?"

"But I . . ." As if seeing it for the first time, Colleen fluttered around. "Oh, it cleaned up well, didn't it?"

"It did, yes."

"I can still smell the smoke."

"You'll keep the windows open a bit longer, and you won't. At the worst, we'll scrub down the walls." Meara made the tea, added a couple of chocolate biscuits to one of her mother's fancy plates—and because it was her mother, added a white linen napkin.

"Sit down, have your tea. Let's have a look at your fingers."

"They're much better." Smiling now, Colleen held them up. "Branna's such a way with things, hasn't she, making up her lotions and creams and candles and so on. I love shopping in the Dark Witch. I always find some pretty little thing or other. It's a lovely little shop she has."

"It is."

"And she comes by now and then, brings me samples to try out for her."

"I know." So Colleen could have her pretty little things, Meara knew as well, without spending too much.

"She's a lovely girl, is Branna, and always looks so smart."

"She does," Meara agreed, and knew Colleen wished her daughter would dress smart instead of cladding herself for the stables.

We'll have to keep on being disappointed in each other, won't we, Ma? she thought, but said nothing more.

"The kitchen did clean up well, Meara, and thanks for that. But I haven't a thing now, or the time really, to make a nice dinner for Donal and his girl. What will Sharon think of me?"

"She'll think you had a bit of a to-do in the kitchen, so you called round to Ryan's Hotel and made a booking for the three of you."

"Oh, but—"

"I'll arrange it, and they'll run a tab for me. You'll have a nice dinner, and you'll come back here for tea and a bit of dessert—which I'll go pick up at Monk's Cafe in a few minutes. You'll serve it on your good china, and feel fine about it. You'll all have a nice evening."

Colleen's cheeks pinked with pleasure. "That sounds lovely, just lovely."

"Now, Ma, do you remember the proper way to deal with a kitchen fire?"

"You throw water on a fire. I did."

"It's best to smother it. There's the extinguisher in the closet with the mop. Remember? Fin provided it, and Donal put the brackets in so it's always right there, on the wall of the little closet."

"Oh, but I never thought of it, being that upset. And how would I remember how to use it?"

There was that, Meara thought. "Failing that, you can dump baking soda on it, or better all around, set a pot lid on it, cut off the air. Best of all, you don't leave the kitchen when you've got cooking going. You can set a timer on the oven so you're not wed to the room when you're baking or roasting."

"I meant to."

"I'm sure you did."

"I'm sorry for the trouble, Meara, truly."

"I know, and it's all fixed now, isn't it?" She laid a hand lightly over

Colleen's. "Ma, wouldn't you be happier living closer to your grandchildren?"

Meara spent some time nourishing the seed she'd planted, then went to the cafe, bought a pretty cream cake, some scones and pastries. She dropped by the restaurant, made arrangements with the manager—a friend since her school days, circled back to her mother's.

Since she had a headache in any case, she went straight home from there and rang up her sister.

"Maureen, it's time you had a turn with Ma."

After a full hour of arguing, negotiating, shouting, laughing, commiserating, she dug out headache pills, chugged them down with water at the bathroom sink.

And gave herself a long stare in the mirror. Little sleep left its mark in shadowed eyes. Fatigue on every possible level added strain around them, and a crease between her eyebrows she rubbed in annoyance.

Another day like this, she decided, she'd need all of Branna's creams and lotions—and a glamour as well—or she'd look a hag.

She needed to set it all aside for one bloody night, she told herself. Connor, Cabhan, her mother, the whole of her family. One quiet night, she decided, in her pajamas—with a thick layer of one of Branna's creams on her face. Add a beer, some crisps or whatever junky food she had about, and the telly.

She'd wish for no more than that.

Opting for the beer to begin—it wouldn't be the first time she'd taken a cold beer into a hot shower to wash away the day—she started toward the kitchen, and someone pounded on the door.

"Go away," she muttered, "whoever you are, and never come back."

Whoever it was knocked again, and she'd have ignored it again, but he followed up with:

"Open up, Meara. I know very well you're in there."

Connor. She cast her eyes to the ceiling, but went to the door.

She opened it. "I'm settling in for some quiet, so go somewhere else."

"What's this about a fire at your mother's?"

"It was nothing. Go on now."

He squinted at her. "You look terrible."

"And that's all I needed to finish off my fecking day. Thanks for that."

She started to shut the door in his face, but he put a shoulder to it. For a foolish minute, each pushed against the other. She tended to forget the man was stronger than he looked.

"Fine, fine, come in then. The day's been nothing but a loss in any case."

"Your head hurts, and you're tired and bitchy with it."

Before she could evade, he laid his hands on her temples, ran them over her head, down to the base of her skull.

And the throbbing ache vanished.

"I'd taken something for it already."

"That works faster." He added a light rub on her shoulders that dissolved all the knots. "Sit down, take your boots off. I'll get you a beer."

"I didn't invite you for a beer and a chat." The bad temper in her tone after he'd vanished all those aches and throbs shamed her. And the shame only added more bad temper.

He cocked his head, face full of patience and sympathy. She wanted to punch him for it.

She wanted to lay her head on his shoulder and just breathe.

"Haven't eaten, have you?"

"I've only just gotten home."

"Sit down."

He walked over to the kitchen—such as it was. The two-burner stove, the squat fridge, miserly sink, and counter tucked tidily enough in the corner of her living space, and suited her needs.

She grumbled rude words under her breath, but she sat and took off her boots while she watched him—eyes narrowed—poke around.

"What are you after in there?"

"The frozen pizza you never fail to stock will be quickest, and I could do with some myself for I haven't eaten either."

He peeled it out of the wrap, stuck it in the oven. And unlike her mother, remembered to set the timer. He took out a couple bottles of Harp, popped them open, then strolled back.

He handed her a beer, sat down beside her, propped his feet on her coffee table, a man at home.

"We'll start at the end of it. Your mother. A kitchen fire, was it?"

"Not even that. She burned a joint of lamb, and from her reaction, you'd think she'd started an inferno that leveled the village."

"Well then, your ma's never been much of a cook."

Meara snorted out a laugh, drank some beer. "She's a terrible cook. Why she got it into her head to have a little dinner party for Donal and his girl is beyond me. Because it's proper," she said immediately. "In her world, it's the proper thing, and she must be proper. She's bits of Belleek and Royal Tara and Waterford all around, fine Irish lace curtains at the windows. And I swear she dresses for gardening or marketing as if she's having lunch at a five-star. Never a hair out of place, her lipstick never smudged. And she can't boil a potato without disaster falling."

When she paused, drank, he patted her leg and said nothing.

"She's living in a rental barely bigger than the garden shed where she lived with my father, keeps it locked like a vault in defense against the bands of thieves and villains she imagines lie in wait—and can't think to open a bleeding window when she has a house full of smoke."

"She called for you then."

"For me, of course. She couldn't very well call for Donal, as he was at his work, and I'm just playing with the horses. At my leisure."

Then she sighed. "She doesn't mean it that way, I know it, but it *feels* that way. She never worked at a job. She married my father when she was but a girl, and he swept her up, gave her a fine house with staff to tend it, showered her with luxuries. All she had to do was be his pretty ornament and raise the children—entertain, of course, but that was being a pretty ornament as well, and there was Mrs. Hannigan to cook and maids to see to the rest."

Tired all over again, she looked down at her beer. "Then her world crashed down around her. It's not a wonder she's helpless about the most practical things."

"Your world crashed down as well."

"It's different. I was young enough to adjust to things, and didn't feel the shame she did. I had Branna and you and Boyle and Fin. She loved him. She loved Joseph Quinn."

"Didn't you, Meara?"

"Love can die." She drank again. "Hers hasn't. She keeps his picture in a silver frame in her room. It makes me want to scream bloody hell every time I see it. He's never coming back to her, and why would she have him if he did? But she would."

"It's not your heart, but hers."

"Hers holds on to an illusion, not to reality. But you're right. It's hers, not mine."

She leaned her head back, closed her eyes.

"You got her settled again?"

"Cleaned up the mess—she'd swamped the kitchen floor with water and potatoes—and I can be grateful she'd forgotten to turn the flame on under the potatoes so I didn't have that secondary disaster to deal with. She'll be having dinner at Ryan's Hotel with Donal and his girl now."

He rubbed a hand on her thigh, soothing. "On your tab."

"The money's the least of it. I rang Maureen, and had it out with her. It's her turn, fuck it all. Mary Clare lives too far. But from Maureen's, Ma could see Mary Clare and her children as well as come back here for visits. And my brother . . . His wife's grand, but it would be easier for Ma to live with her own daughter than her son's wife, I'm thinking. And Maureen has the room, and a sweet, easy-goer of a husband."

"What does your mother want?"

"She wants my father back, the life she knew back, but as that's not happening, she'd be happy with the children. She's good with children, loves them, has endless patience with them. In the end Maureen came around, for at least a trial of it. I believe—I swear this is the truth—I believe it'll be good for all. She'll be a great help to Maureen with the kids, and they love her. She'll be happy living there, in a bigger, finer house, and away from here where there are too many memories of what was."

"I think you're right on it, if it matters."

She sighed again, drank. "It does. She's not one who can live content and easy alone. Donal needs to start his life. I need to have mine. Maureen's the answer to this, and she'll only benefit from having her own mother mind the children when she wants to go out and about."

"It's a good plan, for all." He patted her hand, then rose at the buzz of the timer. "Now it's pizza for all, and you can tell me what's all this about Cabhan."

It wasn't the evening she'd imagined, but she found herself relaxing, despite all. Pizza, eaten on the living room sofa, filled the hole in her belly she hadn't realized was there until the first bite. And the second beer went down easy.

"As I told Branna, it was all soft and dreamy. I understand now what Iona meant when it happened to her last winter. It's a bit like floating, and not being fully inside yourself. The cold," she murmured. "I'd forgotten that."

"The cold?"

"Before, right before. It got cold, all of a sudden. I even took my gloves out of my pocket. And the wind came up strong. The light changed. It had been a bright morning, as they said it would, but it went gray and gloomy. Clouds rolling over the sun, I thought, but . . ."

She dug back now, mind clear, to try to see it as it had been.

"Shadows. There were shadows. How could there be shadows without the sun? I'd forgotten, didn't tell Branna. I was too wound up, I suppose."

"It's all right. You're telling me now."

"The shadows moved with me, and in them I felt warm—but I wasn't, Connor. I was freezing, but I *thought* I was warm. Is that sensible at all?"

"If you mean do I understand, I do. His magick's as cold as it is dark. The warmth was a trick for your mind, as the desire was."

"The rest is as I told you. Him calling my name, and me standing there, with my hand about to part the vines, wanting to go in, so much, wanting to answer the call of my name. And Roibeard and Kathel to my rescue."

"If you've a mind to walk from work to the cottage, or when you guide your customers, stay clear of that area, much as you can."

"I will, of course. It's habit takes me by there, and habits can be broken. Branna made me a charm in any case. As did Iona, and then Fin pushed yet another on me."

Connor dug into his pocket, pulled out a small pouch. "As I am."

"My pockets will be full of magick pouches at this rate."

"Do this. Keep one near your door here, and one in your lorry, one near your bed—sleep's vulnerable. Then one in your pocket." He put the pouch into her hand, closed her fingers over it. "Always, Meara."

"All right. That's a fine plan."

"And wear this." Out of his pocket he drew a long thin band of leather that held polished beads.

"It's pretty. Why am I wearing it?"

"I made it when I was no more than sixteen. It's blue chalcedony here, and some jasper, some jade. The chalcedony is good protection from magick of the dark sort, and the jade's helpful for protection from psychic attack—which you've just experienced. The jasper's good all around as a protective stone. So wear it, will you?"

"All right." She slipped it over her head. "You can have it back when we're done with this. It's cleverly done," she added, studying it. "But you've always been clever with your hands."

The instant the words were out, she winced inwardly at the phrase. "So, that's filled you in on the highs and lows of my day, and I'm grateful for the pizza—even if it came from my own freezer."

She started to get up, clear the dishes, but he just put a hand on her arm, nudged her back again.

"We haven't finished the circle yet, as we've been working backward. And that takes us to last night."

"I already told you nothing was meant by it."

"What you told me was bollocks."

The easy, almost cheerful tone of his voice made her want to rail at him, so she deliberately kept her tone level. "I've had enough upheaval for one day, Connor."

"Sure we might as well get it all over and done at once. We're friends, are we not, Meara?"

"We are, and that's exactly the point I'm making."

"It wasn't the kiss of a friend, even one upset and shaken, you gave me. Nor was it the kiss of a friend I gave you when I got beyond the first surprise of it."

She shrugged, to show how little it all meant—and wished her stomach would stop all the fluttering. You'd think she'd swallowed a swarm of butterflies instead of half a frozen pizza.

"If I'd known you'd be so wound up about a kiss, it wouldn't have happened."

"A man who wasn't wound up after a kiss like that would've been dead for six months. And I'm betting he'd still feel a stir."

"That only means I'm good at it."

He smiled. "I wouldn't argue with your skill. I'm saying it wasn't friend to friend, and distress. Not that alone."

"So there's a bit of lusty curiosity as well. That's not a surprise, is it? We're adults, we're human, and in the strangest of situations. We had a quick, hot tangle, and that's the end of it."

He nodded as if considering her point. "I wouldn't argue with that either, but for one thing."

"What one thing?"

He shifted so quickly from his easy slouch she didn't have an instant to prepare. He had her scooped up, shifted as well, and his mouth on hers.

Another hot tangle, fast and deep and deadly to the senses. Some part of her mind said to give him a punch and set things right, but the rest of her was too busy devouring what he gave her.

Then he tugged on her braid—an old, affectionate gesture, so their lips parted, their faces stayed close. So close the eyes she knew as well as her own took on deeper, darker hues of green with little shimmers of gold scattered through.

"That one thing."

"It's just . . ." She moved in this time, couldn't resist, and felt his heart race against hers. "Physicality."

"Is it?"

"It is." She made herself pull back, then stand—a bit safer, she thought, with some distance. "And more, Connor, we need to think, the both of us need to think. It's friends we are, and always have been. And now part of a circle that can't be risked."

"What's the risk?"

"We have sex—"

"A grand idea. I'm for it."

Though she shook her head, she had to laugh with it. "You'd be for it on an hourly basis. But it's you and me now, and with you and me what if there are complications, and the kind of tensions that can happen, that *do* happen, when sex comes through the door?"

"Done well, sex relieves the tensions."

"For a bit." Though just now the thought of it, with him, brought on plenty. "But we might cause more—for each other, for the others when we can least afford it. We need to keep ourselves focused on what's to be done, and keep the personal complications away from it as much as we can."

Easy as ever, he picked up his beer to finish it off. "That's your busy brain, always thinking what's next and not letting the rest of you have the moment."

"A moment passes into the next."

"Exactly. So if you don't enjoy it before it does, what's the point of it all?"

"The point is seeing clear, and being ready for the next—and the next after it. And we need to think about all of this, and carefully. We can't just jump into bed because we both have an itch. I care about you, and all the others too much for that."

"There's nothing you can do, not anything, that could shake my friendship. Not even saying no on this when I want you to say yes more than . . . well, more than I might want."

He stood as well. "So we'll both think on it, give it all a little time and see how we feel."

"That's the best, isn't it? It's just a matter of taking time to cool it down, think clear so we're not leaping into an impulse we could regret. We're both smart and steady enough to do that."

"Then that's what we'll do."

He offered a hand to seal the deal. Meara took it, shook.

Then they both simply stood, neither backing away, moving forward, or letting go.

"Ah hell. We're not going to think at all, are we?"

He only grinned. "Not tonight."

They leaped at each other.

10

GRAPPLING WASN'T HIS USUAL WAY, BUT THIS WAS something so . . . explosive he lost his rhythm and style. He grabbed whatever he could grab, took whatever he could take. And there was so much of her—his tall, curvy friend.

He all but ripped off her shirt to get to more.

No stopping now for either of them, for here ran needs and urges far beyond careful and rational thinking. Here was the moment, and the next and the next would have to wait.

This bright new hunger for her, just her, must be fed.

But not, he realized, standing in her living room or rolling about on the floor.

He scooped her up.

"Oh Jesus, don't try to carry me. You'll break your back."

"My back's strong enough." He turned his head to meet her mouth as he walked to her bedroom.

Crazy, she thought. They'd both gone completely mad. And she didn't give a single bleeding damn. He carried her, and though his purpose—and hers—was hurry, it was foolishly romantic.

If he stumbled, well, they'd finish things out where they landed.

But he didn't stumble. He dropped to the bed with her so the old springs squeaked in surprise, gave with a groan to nestle them both in a hollow of mattress and bedding.

And those hands, those magick hands were busy and beautiful.

She used her own to pull and yank off layers of clothes until, at last—God be praised—she found skin. Warm, smooth—with the good firm muscles of a man who used them.

She rolled with him, struggling as he did to strip off every barrier.

"Bloody layers," he muttered, and made her laugh as she fought with the buckle of his belt.

"We would, both of us, work outdoors."

"Good thing it's worth the unwrapping. Ah, there you are," he murmured and filled his hands with her bare breasts.

Firm and soft and generous. Beautiful, bountiful. He could write an ode to the glory of Meara Quinn's breasts. But at the moment, he wanted only to touch them, taste them. And feel the way her heartbeat kicked up from canter to gallop at the brush of his fingers, lips, tongue.

All that was missing was . . .

He brought light into the dark, a soft, pale gold like her skin. When her eyes met his, he smiled.

"I want to see you. Beautiful Meara. Eyes of a gypsy, body of a goddess."

He touched her as he spoke. No grappling now; he'd found his rhythm after all. Why rush through something so pleasurable when he could linger over it? He could feast on her breasts half a lifetime. Then there were her lips, soft and full—and as eager as his. And her shoulders, strong, capable. The surprisingly sweet stem of her neck. Sensitive there, just there under her jaw so she shivered when he kissed it.

He loved how she responded—a tremble, a catch of breath, a throaty moan—as he learned her body, inch by lovely inch.

Outside someone shouted out a half-drunken greeting, and followed it by a wild laugh.

But here, in the nest of the bed, there were only sighs, murmurs, and the quiet creak of the springs beneath them.

He'd taken the reins, she realized. She didn't know how it happened, as she'd never given them over to anyone else. But somewhere between the hurry and the patience, she'd surrendered them to him.

His hands glided over her as if he had centuries to pet and stroke and linger. They kindled fires along the way until her body seemed to shimmer in the heat, to glow under her skin like the light he'd conjured.

She loved the feel of him, the long back, the narrow hips, the hard, workingman's palms. He smelled of the woods, earthy and free, and the taste of him—lips, skin—was the same.

He tasted of home.

He touched where she ached to be touched, tasted where she longed for his lips. And found other secret places she hadn't known longed for attention. The inside of her elbow, the back of her knee, the inside of her wrist. He murmured to her, sweet words that reached into her heart. Another light to glow.

He seemed to know when the glow became a pulse, and the pulse a throb of need. So he answered that need, drawing the pleasure up and up before spilling her over into release.

Weak from it, dazed by the flood and the flow, she clung to him, tried to right herself.

"A moment. Give me a moment."

"It's now," he said. "It should be now."

And slid inside her. Took her mouth as he took her, deep and slow.

It should be now, he thought again. For she was open for him to fill. Warm and wet for him.

Her moan, a sound of welcome; her arms strong ropes to bind him close.

She rose to him, wrapped those long legs around him. Moved with him as if they'd come together like this, just like this, over a hundred lifetimes. In the glow he'd made, in the glow that gleamed now from what they made together, he watched her.

Dubheasa. Dark beauty.

Watched her until what they made overwhelmed him, and the pleasure deepened dark as her eyes. In the dark and the light, he surrendered to her as she had to him. And let her take him with her.

SHE LAY, BASKING. SHE'D EXPECTED—ONCE SHE'D ACCEPTED she was having sex with Connor—a rollicking rough and tumble. Instead she'd been . . . tended, pleasured, even seduced, and with a delicate touch.

And had no complaints whatsoever.

Now her body felt all loose and soft and weak in the loveliest of ways.

She'd known he'd be good at it—God knew he'd had the practice—but she hadn't known he'd be absolutely bloody brilliant.

So she could sigh now in utter satisfaction—with her hand resting on his very fine ass.

Just as she sighed, it occurred to her she couldn't possibly have measured up. She'd been taken by surprise, she thought, and surely hadn't done her best work—so to speak.

Was that why he was currently lying on her like a dead man?

She moved her hand, not quite sure now what to do or say.

He stirred.

"I suppose you're wanting me to get off you."

"Ah . . . Well."

He rolled, sprawled on his back. When he said nothing at all, she cleared her throat.

"And what now?"

"I'm thinking," he said. "That once we take a bit of a breather, we do it all over again."

"I can do better."

"Better than what?"

"Than I did. I was taken off-balance."

He trailed a finger lazily down her side. "If you'd done better, I might need weeks of a breather."

Unsure what that might mean, exactly, she pushed up enough to see his face. Since she knew what a satisfied male looked like, she relaxed again.

"So it went well for you then."

He opened his eyes, looked into hers. "I'm considering how to answer that, for if I tell the truth you might say: Since it went so well, that's all for you tonight. And I want you again before I've even caught my breath."

He slid an arm under her, drew her over, cuddled her in so they were nose to nose. "And did it go well for you?"

"I'm considering how to answer that," she said and made him grin.

"I've missed seeing you naked."

"You haven't seen me naked before tonight."

"Sure have you forgotten the night you and me and Branna and Boyle and Fin snuck out and away to swim in the river?"

"We never— Oh, that." Content, she tangled up her legs with his. "I was no more than nine, you git!"

"But naked all the same. I'll say you grew up and around very well indeed." He ran a hand down her back, over her ass, left it there. "Very well indeed."

"And you yourself, if memory serves me, were built like a puny stick. You've done well yourself. We had fun that night," she remembered. "Froze our arses, the lot of us, but it was grand. Innocent, all of us, and not a worry in the world. But he'd have been watching us, even then."

"No." Connor touched a finger to her lips. "Don't bring him here, not tonight."

"You're right." She brushed a hand through his hair. "How many, do you think, are where we are tonight who have all those years and memories between them?"

"Not many, I expect."

"We can't lose that, Connor. We can't lose what we are to each other, to Branna, to all. We have to swear an oath on it. We won't lose even a breath of the friends we've ever been, whatever happens."

"Then I'll swear it to you, and you to me." He took her hand, interlaced his fingers with hers. "A sacred oath, never to be broken. Friends we've ever been, and ever will be."

She saw the light glowing through their joined fingers, felt the warmth of it. "I swear it to you."

"And I to you." He kissed her fingers, then her cheek, then her lips. "I should tell you something else."

"What is it?"

"I've my breath back now."

And when she laughed, he rolled back on top of her.

SHE'D SHARED BREAKFAST WITH HIM BEFORE, COUNTLESS times. But never at the little table in her flat—and never after sharing the shower with him.

He could count himself lucky, she decided, that she'd picked up some nice croissants from the cafe when she'd gotten dessert for her mother.

Along with them she made her usual standby—oatmeal—while he dealt with the tea as she hadn't any coffee in the pantry.

"We're to meet tonight," he reminded her, and bit into a croissant. "These are brilliant."

"They are. I don't step foot into the cafe often as I'd buy a dozen of everything. I'll go by the cottage straight from the stables," she added. "And help Branna with the cooking if I can. It's good we're meeting regular now, though I don't know as any of us suddenly had a genius idea on what to do, exactly, and when to do it."

"Well, we're thinking, and together, so something will come."

He believed it, and the croissants only helped boost his optimism.

"Why don't I take you to the stables on my way, and just fetch you when we're both done? It'd save you the petrol, and seems foolish for us to each take our lorries."

"Then you'd have to bring me home after."

"That was the canny part of my plan." He hefted his tea as if toasting himself. "I'll bring you back, stay with you again if that's all right. Or you could just stay at the cottage."

She downed tea he'd made strong enough to break stone. "What will Branna think of this?"

"We'll be finding out soon enough. We wouldn't hide it from her, either of us, even if we could. Which we couldn't," he added with an easy shrug, "as she'll know."

"They'll all need to know." No point, Meara decided, being delicate about it all. "It's only right. Not just because we're friends and family, but because we're a circle. What we are to each other . . . that's the circle, isn't it?"

He scanned her face as she pushed oatmeal around in her bowl. "It shouldn't worry you, Meara. We've a right to be with each other this way as long as we both want it. None who care for us would think or feel otherwise."

"That's right. But then as far as my other family—my blood kin—I'd as soon not bring them into it."

"That's for you to say."

"It's not that I'm ashamed of it, Connor, you mustn't think that."

"I don't think that." His eyebrows lifted as he took a spoonful of her oatmeal, brought it up to her mouth himself. "I know you, don't I? Why would I think that, knowing you?"

"That's an advantage between us. It's that my mother would start fussing, and inviting you to dinner. I couldn't take another kitchen disaster on the heels of the last—and my finances can't take a bigger tab at Ryan's Hotel. In any case, she'll be off for her visit with Maureen soon—and unless that's a fresh disaster, it'll be a permanent move."

"You'll miss her."

"I'd like the chance to." She huffed out a breath, but ate some oatmeal before he took it into his head to feed her again. "And that sounds mean, but it's pure truth. I think I'd have a better time with her if there was some distance. And . . ."

"And?"

"I had a moment yesterday, while I was rushing over there, not sure what I'd find. I suddenly thought, what if Cabhan's been at her, as he'd been at me? It was foolish, as he's no reason to, and never has. But I thought as well of what you said about feeling better knowing your parents were away from this. I'll rest easier knowing that about my mother. This is for us to do."

"And so we will."

HE DROPPED HER OFF AT THE STABLES, THEN CIRCLED around to go home and change out of yesterday's work clothes.

He found Branna already up—not dressed for the day as yet, but having her coffee with Sorcha's spell book once again open in front of her.

"Well, good morning to you, Connor."

"And to you, Branna."

She studied him over the rim of her mug. "And how is our Meara this fine morning?"

"She's well. I've just dropped her at the stables, but wanted to change before I went to work. And wanted to see how you fared as well."

"I'm fit and fine, though I can say you look fitter and finer. You've had breakfast I take it?"

"I have, yes." But he liked the looks of the glossy green apples she'd put in a bowl, and took one. "Does this bother you, Branna? Meara and myself?"

"Why would it when I love you both, and have seen the pair of you careful to skirt round the edges of what my brilliant brain deduces occurred last night—for years."

"I never thought of her in that way before . . . Before."

"You did, but told yourself not to, which is different entirely. You'd never hurt her."

"Of course I wouldn't."

"And she'd never mean to hurt you." Which, Branna thought, was another thing different entirely. "Sex is powerful, and I think will only add to the strength and power of the circle."

"Obviously, we should've jumped into bed before this."

She only laughed. "The pair of you had to be willing and wanting. Sex only to take power? That's a selfish act, and damaging in the end."

"I can promise we were both willing and wanting." He bit into the apple, which tasted as tart and crisp as it looked. "And it's occurring to me I left you on your own last night."

"Don't insult me." Branna brushed that aside. "I can more than take care of myself and our home, as you well know."

"I do know it." He picked up the pot to top off her coffee. "And still I don't like leaving you on your own."

"I've learned to tolerate a houseful of people, even enjoy it. But as you know me you know I prize being on my own in a quiet house."

"As I'd switch the *prize* and *tolerate* around, it's a wonder we came from the same parents at times."

"It may be you were left on the doorstep and taken in out of pity. But you're handy enough to have around when a faucet's dripping or a door squeaks."

He pulled her hair, crunched his apple. "Still, you can't ask us to give you that quiet and alone too often till this is done."

"Sure I won't. I'm after making beef bourguignon for the horde of us tonight."

He raised his eyebrows. "Fancy."

"I'm in the mood for fancy, and you'll see someone brings some good red wine, and plenty of it."

"That I'll do." He tossed the apple core in the compost pail, walked over, kissed the top of her head. "I love you, Branna."

"I know it. Go on and change your clothes before you're late for work."

When he left, she sat looking away and out the window. She wanted him happy, more even than she wanted happiness for herself. And yet, knowing he was on his way to finding what he didn't yet know he wanted made her feel so painfully alone.

Sensing it, Kathel rose from beneath the table, laid his head in her lap. So she sat, stroking the dog, and returned to poring over the spell book.

IONA STEPPED INTO THE TACK ROOM WHERE MEARA organized the equipment needed for her first guided ride of the morning.

"It's coming time for another good going-over of everything in here," Meara said cheerfully. "I'm taking out a party of four, two brothers and their wives who've come to Ashford for a big family wedding on the weekend. Their niece it is, having the wedding at Ballintubber Abbey, where you and Boyle will marry next spring, then back to Ashford they'll all come for the reception."

"You and Connor had sex."

Meara looked up, and blinking dramatically began to pat herself front and back. "Am I wearing a sign then?"

"You've been smiling all morning, and singing."

"I've been known to smile and sing without having sex beforehand."

"You don't sing the whole time you're mucking stalls. And you look really, *really* relaxed, which you wouldn't, without sex, after a day like you had yesterday. Since you kissed Connor, you had sex with him."

"Some people are known to kiss without having sex. And don't you have a lesson in the ring on the schedule?"

"I have five minutes, and this is the first time I could catch you alone. Unless you want Boyle to know. It was wonderful, it was good or you wouldn't look so happy."

"It was wonderful and good, and it's not a secret. Connor and I both agree—as we're a circle, and something like this can change matters, though it won't—all should know we're together that way. Right now."

She gathered reins, bit, saddle, blanket. "So we are."

"You're good together— You're happy," Iona added, hauling up more tack herself and following Meara out. "So you're good together. Why do you say right now?"

"Because right now is right now, and who knows what tomorrow might be? You and Boyle can look forward—you're both built that way." She stepped into Maggie's stall, the mare she'd chosen for one of the women. "I'm a day-at-a-time sort on matters like this."

"And Connor?"

"I've never known him to be otherwise on any matter. That's for Caesar. Just leave it there and I'll tend to it. You have a lesson."

"At least tell me, was it romantic?"

"You've such a soft heart, Iona, but I can tell you it was. And that was unexpected, and really lovely." For a moment, just a moment, she leaned her cheek against Maggie's soft neck. "I thought, well, once it was clear we were going forward, we'd just tear in. But . . . he made the room glow. And me with it."

"That's beautiful." Iona stepped in, hugged Meara hard. "Just beautiful. Now I'm happy, too."

Iona led Alastar, her big, beautiful gray, already saddled and waiting, out of his stall, toward the ring. Smiled as she heard Meara singing again.

"She's in love," Iona murmured to her horse, and rubbed his strong neck. "She just doesn't know it yet." When Alastar nuzzled her, she laughed. "I know, she's still glowing some. I saw it, too."

Meara switched to humming as she led horses to the paddock, looped reins around the fence. She turned to go back for the last, spotted Boyle bringing Rufus along.

"Thanks for that. Since Iona's got a lesson going in the ring, I'll take the group around the paddock a bit, be sure they're as experienced as they say before we start off."

She looked up. "It's a fine day, isn't it? It's nice they've booked a full hour."

"And we've just had someone else ring up to book another four-group for noon. This wedding's bringing them along."

"I can take that as well." She had energy enough to ride and muck and groom all day and half the night. "I owe you for taking so much time away yesterday."

"We won't start owing around here," he said, "but it would help if you could as Iona's got two at half ten, Mick's doing a lesson at eleven, and with Patty at the dentist this morning, and Deborah booked for one o'clock, we're a bit squeezed. Still, I could do it myself."

"You hate doing the guideds, and I don't mind at all." She gave him a pat on the cheek, had him giving her a hard stare.

"You're a cheerful sort this morning."

"And why wouldn't I be?" she asked as four people strolled toward the stables. "It's a bright day at last, my mother's going for a long visit with a strong potential of a permanent move to Maureen's, and I had hot and brilliant sex with Connor last night."

"It's good your mother's having a visit with— What?"

Meara had to smother a snort at the way Boyle's mouth hung open. "I had sex with Connor last night, and this morning as well."

"You . . ." He trailed off, shoved his hands in his pockets, so absolutely *Boyle* she couldn't resist patting his cheek again.

"I suspect he's cheerful himself, but you can ask him yourself at the first opportunity. It's the McKinnons, is it?" Meara called out as she went, smiling all the way, to meet her morning group.

In short order, with the paperwork done, and her ignoring Boyle's questioning stares, she had her group outfitted and mounted.

"Well now, I can see you all know what you're about," she said when they'd walked and trotted around the paddock. She opened the gate for them, mounted Queen Bee.

"You've picked a fine morning, and there's no better way to see what you'll see than on the back of a horse. And how are you enjoying your stay at Ashford?" she began, sliding into easy small talk as she led them away from the stables.

She answered questions, let them chat among themselves, turned in the saddle now and again just to check—and to let them know they had her attention.

It was lovely, she thought, to ride through the woods with the sky blue overhead, with the earthy perfumes of autumn wafting on the soft and pretty breeze. The scents reminded her of Connor, had her smile brightening.

Then there he was, out and about with his own group on a hawk walk. He wore a work vest but no cap so his hair danced around his face, teased by that soft and pretty breeze. He shot her a grin as he baited his client's glove, and the wife readied her camera.

"Family of yours?" Meara asked as her group and Connor's called out to each other.

"Cousins—our husbands'." The woman—Deirdre—moved up to ride beside Meara for a moment. "We talked about trying the hawk walk ourselves."

"Sure and you should. It's a wonderful experience to take back with you."

"Do all the falconers look like that one?"

"Oh, that would be Connor who runs the school. And he's one of a kind." I had sex with him before breakfast, she thought, and shot a grin of her own back at him as she led her group on.

"Connor," she heard the woman say as she fell in behind Meara. "Jack, we should all book that hawk walk."

Under the circumstances, Meara couldn't blame her.

She led them along the river, enjoyed them, enjoyed the ride. She took them deep into the green where the shadows thickened, and out again where that blue sky shone over the trees.

When she began to circle them back, she saw the wolf.

Just a shadow in the shadows, with its paws sunk into mist. The stone around its neck gleamed like an eye even as the wolf itself seemed to waver like a vapor.

Her horse trembled under her. "Steady now," she murmured, keeping her gaze on the wolf as she stroked Queen Bee's neck. "You be steady now and the rest will follow your lead. You're the queen, remember."

The wolf paced them, coming no closer.

Birds no longer sang in the woods; squirrels no longer raced busily along the branches.

Meara took the necklace Connor had given her from under her sweater, held it out a little so the stones caught the light.

Behind her, her group chatted away, oblivious.

The wolf showed its fangs; Meara put a hand on the knife she wore on her belt. If it came, she would fight. Protect the people she guided, the horses, herself.

She would fight.

The hawk dived—from the blue, through the green.

Meara no more than blinked, and the shadow of the wolf was gone.

"Oh, there's one of the hawks!" Deidre pointed to the branch where the bird perched now, wings folded. "Did he get loose?"

"No, not at all." Meara steadied herself, put her smile back in place as she turned in the saddle. "That's Connor's own Roibeard, having a bit of fun before going back to the school."

She lifted her hand to the necklace again, and rode easily out of the woods.

11

THE MINUTE HE COULD GET AWAY, CONNOR DROVE around to the stables. Too many people about to talk, he decided immediately, but with Meara chatting with a group she'd just guided back, at least he knew just where she was and what she was doing.

He tracked Boyle down in the stalls, giving Caesar a rubdown.

"Busy days," Boyle said. "This wedding's brought in as much business as we can handle."

"And the same for us. We've our last two hawk walks of the day going now."

"We've two out ourselves, though Meara should be back anytime."

"She's just back." Absently, Connor stroked the big gelding as Boyle brushed him out. "Can you set her loose, or do you need her longer today?"

"We've the evening feedings yet, and Iona's at the big stables on a lesson."

"You'll keep her close then? I'll run back and settle my own business for the evening. Is Fin with Iona?"

"He's home if that's what you're meaning, and set to take her to your place when they're both done." Connor's tone had Boyle setting the currycomb aside. "There's a worry. What is it?"

"Cabhan. He was out today, stalking Meara on her guided. And myself a bit. Nothing came of it," Connor said when Boyle cursed. "And he wasn't quite there—not fully physically."

"Was he there or wasn't he?" Boyle demanded.

"He was, but more a shadow. It's a new thing, and something to discuss tonight when we're all together. But I'd feel easier if I knew you were with her until I'm done."

"I'll keep her with me." Boyle pulled out his phone. "And be sure Fin does the same with Iona. And Branna?"

"Roibeard's keeping a watch on all, and Merlin's with him. But I'll be happier altogether when the six of us are together at home."

IT TOOK NEAR AN HOUR TO SETTLE THE BIRDS FOR THE night, and clear up some paperwork Kyra left meaningfully on his desk. He took more time to add yet another layer of protection around the school. Cabhan had gotten into the stables once. He might try for the hawks.

By the time he'd done all that needed doing, locked up tight, the brightness had gone out of the day. Just shorter days, he thought as he stood a moment, opened himself. He felt no threat, no watchful presence. He let himself reach out to Roibeard, join with the hawk—and saw clearly the stables, the woods, the cottage, peaceful below, through his hawk's eyes.

There was Mick, squat as a spark plug, climbing into his lorry, giving a wave out the window to Patti as the girl swung onto her bike.

And there, spread below him, Fin's grand stone house, and the fields and paddocks. Iona soaring over a jump with Alastar.

A short glide, soaring on the wind and, below, Branna picking herbs in her kitchen garden. She straightened, looked up, looked, it seemed, right into his eyes.

And she smiled, lifted a hand before taking her herbs inside with her.

All's well, Connor told himself, and though there was always just a hint of regret, came fully back to earth. Satisfied, he climbed into the lorry.

He drove around to the stables—and felt a warm hum in his blood as he watched Meara come out with Boyle. She was a beauty for certain, he thought, an earthy one in a rough jacket and work pants, and boots that had likely seen hundreds of kilometers, on the ground and on horseback.

Later, he'd have the pleasure of removing those worn boots, those riding pants. And unwinding that thick braid so he could surround himself with waves of brown hair.

"Boyle, are you wanting a lift?" he called through the open window.

"Thanks, but no. I'll follow you over."

So he leaned left, shoved the door open for Meara.

She jumped in, smelling of horses and grain and saddle soap. "Christ Jesus, this was a day and a half shoved into one. The McKinnon party is leaving no stone unturned. We've got groups of them coming tomorrow up through two o'clock, with the wedding, I'm told, at five."

"The same for us."

Since she made no move, he put a hand on the back of her head, drew her over for a kiss. "Good evening to you."

"And to you." Her lips curved. "I wondered if you'd feel a little off center after thinking it over for a day."

"Not much time to think, but I'm balanced well and good."

He turned the lorry, headed away from the stables with Boyle falling in behind.

"Did you see the wolf?" he asked her.

"I did, yes. Boyle couldn't say much as we had the crew about nearly till you came, but he said you did as well. But as with me, it was more a shadow."

She shifted to face him, frowned. "Still, not only a shadow, as he bared his fangs, and I saw them clear, and the red stone. Did you send Roibeard?"

"I didn't have to; he went to you on his own. But I knew from him the wolf only kept pace with you for a minute or two."

"Enough for the horses to sense it. My biggest worry, to tell the truth, was that the horses would spook. Which they might have done, but I had a group of experienced riders. And they themselves? They saw and sensed nothing."

"I've been thinking on the whys and hows of that. I want to see what Branna and Fin and Iona have to say. And I want to ask you to stay tonight at the cottage."

"I don't have my things," she began.

"You have things at the cottage, enough to get you through. You can think of it as us taking turns. Stay tonight, Meara. Share my bed."

"Are you asking because you want me to share your bed, or because you're worried about me being on my own?"

"It would be both, but if you won't stay, I'll be sharing your bed."

"That's a fine answer," she decided. "It works well for me. I'll stay tonight."

He took her hand, leaned toward her when he stopped the lorry in front of the cottage. And could already feel the kiss moving through him before their mouths met.

The lorry shook as if from a quake, jolted as the wolf pounced.

It snarled, eyes and stone gleaming red, then with a howl echoing with triumph, leaped off. And was gone.

"Holy Jesus!" Meara managed an instant before Connor shoved out of the lorry. "Wait, wait. It might still be out there." She yanked at her own door, shoved, but it held firm against her.

"Goddamn it, Connor. Goddamn it, let me out."

He only flicked her a glance as Roibeard landed light as down on his shoulder.

In that moment, in that glance, it was like looking at a stranger, one sparking with power and rage. Light swirled around him, like a current that would surely shock to the touch.

She'd known him the whole of her life, she thought as her breath backed up in her lungs, but she'd never seen him truly, fully until that moment when the full force and fury of what ran in his blood revealed itself.

Then Branna rushed from the house, with Kathel thundering out with her. Her hair, raven black, flew behind her. She had a short sword in one hand, a ball of hot blue fire forming in the other.

Meara saw their eyes meet, hold. In that exchange she saw a bond she could never share, never really know. Not just of power and magick, but of blood and purpose and knowledge.

There she saw a kinship that ran deeper, wider even than love.

Before she'd caught her breath again, Fin's fancy car spun up. He and Iona bolted from either side. So the four of them stood, united, forming a circle, one where the light undulated and spread until it stung her eyes.

It died away, and it was only her friends, her lover, standing in front of the pretty cottage with its blaze of flowers.

Now when she pushed at the door, it sprang open—and she sprang out.

She marched straight to Connor, shoved him hard enough to knock him back a step. "Don't you ever lock me in or out again. I won't be closed off or tucked away like someone helpless."

"I'm sorry. I wasn't thinking clear. It was wrong of me, and I'm sorry for it."

"You've no right, no right to close me out of it."

"Or me," Boyle said, his face ripe with fury, when he strode up beside her. "Be grateful I don't break your head for it."

"It's grateful I am, and sorry as well."

Meara saw for the first time Alastar had come—he must have all but flown from the stables. So there was horse, hawk, and hound; the dark witches three; and the blood of Cabhan, with his own hawk standing now with Roibeard on the branch of a nearby tree.

And there was herself and Boyle.

"We're a circle or we're not."

"We are." Connor took her hands, gripped them only tighter when she started to yank them free. "We are. It was wrong of me. I jumped straight into the fury of it, and that was wrong as well. And foolish. I shut you out of it, both of you, and that showed you no respect. I'll say again, I'm sorry for it."

"All right then." Boyle shoved at his hair. "Bloody hell I could do with a beer."

"Go on in," Branna told him, glanced around at the others. "Help yourself to what you want. I need a moment with Meara. A moment with Meara," she repeated when Connor continued to grip Meara's hands. "Go, have a beer and open the wine Fin should've brought with him."

"And so I did."

Fin went to his car, fetched out three bottles. "Come on then, Connor. We could all do with a drink after this day."

"Yeah." With some reluctance Connor released Meara's hands, went inside with his friends.

"I've every right to be pissed," Meara began, and found her hands taken again.

"You do, yes, you do, but not only with Connor. I need to tell you that when I ran outside, I knew at once what he'd done, and I was relieved. I'm sorry for it, but I can't let him take full blame."

Stunned, and wounded to the core, Meara stared at Branna. "Do you think because Boyle and I don't have what you have, aren't what you are, we can't fight with you?"

"I think nothing of the kind, nor does Connor. Or Iona, and I imagine she'll be making this same confession to Boyle." When Branna let out a breath, the sound of it was regret.

"It was a moment, Meara, and the weakness was on our part, not yours. You fought with us on the solstice, and I don't want to think what might have happened without you, without Boyle. But for a moment, in the rush of it, I only thought, ah, they'll be safe. That was my weakness. It won't happen again."

"I'm still mad about it."

"I don't blame you a bit for that. But come inside, we'll have some wine and talk about all of it."

"There was nothing weak about the four of you," Meara said, but she started inside with Branna. "The power of you together was blinding. And Connor alone, before you came . . . I saw him on the solstice, but that was a blur of fear and action and violence all at once. I've never seen him as he was for that moment you speak of. Alone, with the hawk on his shoulder, and so full of what he is . . . *radiant* I suppose is the word, though it seems too soft and benign for it. I thought if I touched him now it would burn."

"He's slow to anger, our Connor, as you know. When he reaches it, it's fierce—but never brutal."

Before Branna shut the door she took a long last look at the woods, at the road, at the blaze of flowers along her cottage skirts. She went with Meara back to the kitchen where the wine was open, and the air smelled of the rich, silky sauce she'd spent a good chunk of her day preparing.

"It's near to ready," she announced and took the wine Fin poured her. "So the lot of you can make yourself useful getting the table set."

"It smells amazing," Iona commented.

"Because it is. We can talk about all of this while we feast. Connor, there's bread wrapped in the cloth there."

He got it, set it out, turned to Meara. "Am I to be forgiven?"

"I haven't gotten there yet. But I'm moving in that general direction."

"Then I'll be grateful for that."

Branna served the beef bourguignon on a long platter showcasing the herbed beef and vegetables in the dark sauce, surrounded by roasted new potatoes and garnished with sprigs of rosemary.

"It really is a feast," Iona marveled. "It must have taken hours."

"It did, so no one's allowed to bolt it down." Branna ladled it herself into her pretty shallow bowls before she sat. "And so, all of us have had a day or two." She spread her napkin across her lap before spooning up the first sample. "Meara, you should begin."

"Well, I suppose we all know where we were before this morning, but we've not been together to talk over today. I was guiding a group of four, and in fact, we rode by Connor, who had a group of his own. I took them around the longest route we use, even let them have a bit of a trot here and there, as they were all solid horsemen. It was when we'd circled back, and were coming through the woods, the narrow trail now. I saw the wolf in the trees, watching, keeping pace. But . . ."

She searched for the words. "He was like the shadows that play there, when the sun dapples through the leaves. More formed than that, but not formed. I felt I could almost see through him, though I couldn't. The horses saw or sensed, I couldn't say which, but the riders behind me, they didn't. They kept on talking together, even laughing. It was no more than a minute, and Roibeard flew in. The wolf, it didn't run away so much as fade away."

"A projection," Fin suggested.

"Not in the usual way." As he ate, Connor shook his head. "As I saw it as well. A shadow's close. My sense was of something not quite here, not quite there. Not as he was outside here, not a thing with weight and full form, but with power nonetheless."

"Something new then," Fin considered. "Balancing between two planes, or shifting between them, as he can shift time at Sorcha's cabin."

"It pulls from him though. If you watch the stone, his power source, it ebbs and flows." Meara glanced at Connor for confirmation.

"That's true enough, but as with any skill, the power of it grows as you hone it."

"The McKinnons, the people I guided," Meara continued, "they saw nothing."

"To them he was a shadow," Fin said. "Nothing more."

"A shadow spell." Branna considered it. "I've seen a thing or two in Sorcha's book that might be useful."

"And did you get the way of this from her book?" Fin asked as he ate. "For it's magick. I've had this dish at a tony restaurant in Paris, and it didn't match yours."

"It turned out well."

"It's brilliant," Boyle said.

"It is," Branna said with a laugh. "It takes forever as the sauce is fussy, and not something I'll do often. But today it gave me time to think in the back of my brain. He's pushing at Meara now as he did with Iona before. Testing the edge of things, we could say. And it's Meara, I think, because, in truth, it's Connor he wants to take a run at."

"He went for the boy first." Fin sipped wine as he considered. "A boy, an easy target he might think. But together, Connor and the boy hurt him, drove him away again. And that would be . . . disappointing."

"So he's after a bit of revenge," Boyle continued. "And got a good lick in when he took Connor on. But only a lick come to that. And next he takes aim at Meara."

"After she and Connor had their hot time in the lorry," Iona pointed out. "The power of a kiss."

"Oh, for pity's sake," Meara muttered.

"Sure it's true enough." Under the table, Connor danced his fingers up Meara's thigh and down again. "And when things progress as things do, he comes again. With a shadow spell."

"Could he do harm in that form that's not a form?" Meara wondered.

"I think yes. A delicate balance from what I know," Branna added. "And the conjurer of the spell would have to be able to shift—away, or into full form quickly—without losing that delicate balance."

"If he can do that, why didn't he come at me today? I had a knife, and I'm not helpless, but it would've been his advantage I'd think."

"He wants to unnerve you more than cause you harm," Fin told her. "Hurting you gives him some satisfaction, of course, as causing harm feeds him. But you'd be worth more to him in another area."

"He wants you," Connor said flatly, and with the bubble of that pure rage she'd seen rippling, "because I do. He thinks to seduce you—spellbind you or shake you enough so you don't fight, but run or plead—"

Her eyes fired, black suns. "Neither of those will ever happen."

"We won't underestimate him," Connor snapped back. "It's what he seeks so he can take you. And taking you the way he seeks would harm us all. He understands we're bound, but sees it as a binding for power—only that. Taking you breaks our circle. Be grateful he doesn't understand it's not just a binding for power, but one of love and loyalty. If he understood that, the power of that, he'd hunt you without ceasing."

"You've caught his eye," Fin added, "as he understands sex very well—though with none of its true pleasures or depth. It's another kind of power to him, and he has desire enough for the act of it."

"So the last day or two has been a kind of . . . mating dance?"

"That's not far from the mark," Branna said to Meara. "Sorcha writes of the weeks and weeks he tried to seduce her, bribe her, threaten her, wear down her mind and spirit. He wanted her power without question, but he wanted her body as well—and he wanted to make a child with her, I think."

"I'd slit my own throat before I'd let him rape me."

"Don't say that." The bubble of fury burst as Connor rounded on her. "Don't ever say such a thing again."

"Don't." Iona spoke quietly before Meara could fling words back. "Connor's right. Don't say that. We'll protect you. We're a circle, and we protect each other. You'll protect yourself, but you need to trust us to protect you."

"I'll say something here." Before he did, Boyle helped himself to another ladle of stew. "The four of you can't and don't fully understand what it is for Meara and me. We have our fists, our wits, a blade, instincts, strategies. But these are ordinary things. I'm not after poking at a spot still sore, but when a thought from you can lock us away, out of the mix, it comes home we've only those ordinary things."

"Boyle, you have to know—"

Fin stopped Iona, a light brush on her arm. "And I'll say something back to that—as an outsider. One step back," he insisted as Iona sent him a sorrowful look. "We're not the three, but with the three. Another delicate balance we could say. What we bring to the circle is as vital as the other end of that balance. The three might think it different from time to time, and some with the three might think different, but it is what it is, and that's for us all to remember and respect."

"You're eating at my table," Branna said quietly. "Food I made. I've given you respect."

"You have, and I'm grateful. But it's come time for you to open the door again, Branna, and let me work with you without me having to pry that door open. It's Meara we're speaking of, and the whole of it that hangs in that balance."

Branna's fingers tightened on the stem of her wineglass, then relaxed again. "You're right, and I'm sorry for it. And I see he's shaken us. That's a victory for him, and it ends now."

"We can't understand what it is not to be what we are. Iona would, I think," Connor continued, "as what she is, and has, was held back from her for so long. But I think you—and you as well, Fin—don't understand that for Branna and for me, knowing you're with us, when for Fin, going back to Paris and his fine restaurant would be an easier choice, for you, Meara, and for you, Boyle, not having power but being with us, is braver by far than going on with this, as Branna and I, and now Iona must do. We must, but you, all three of you choose. We don't forget that. Don't think, don't ever think, we do."

"We're not looking for gratitude," Boyle began.

"Well, you have it, want it or not. And admiration as well, even if there's been times, and will be again, we don't show it."

Rising, Branna got another bottle of wine, poured it all around. "For feck's sake, do you think I spend hours cooking a meal like this for myself? I do fine with a bacon sandwich. So we'll all of us stop feeling sorry for ourselves, or sorry to each other, and just be."

Very deliberately Meara scooped up more stew. "It's a gorgeous meal, Branna."

"Bloody right it is, and unless all of you want nothing but that bacon sandwich next time you come, we'll set all that business aside.

Now, why do we think Cabhan jumped on the bonnet of Connor's lorry?"

"I might be risking that bacon sandwich, though they're tasty enough," Fin said, "but answering that, for what I think myself, digs back into the other a bit."

"Answer." Branna waved a hand in the air. "I'll decide whether you eat at all next time."

"He wanted to see what would happen. He was fully formed."

"He was," Meara agreed. "Muscle, bone, and blood."

"But he was quick about it. A leap without warning—where Connor had no sense of it, nor did I, and we weren't far off. Then a leap back, wherever he's biding his time. But in that time, what did he learn?"

"I'm not following you," Boyle said.

"What did he see Connor do? Get out to face him alone—deliberately alone as he closed you and Meara inside. Protected you. And he saw Branna run out—armed, but again alone—to go to her brother."

"Then Iona and you," Meara added.

"He was gone by the time I joined, by the time we made the circle. Watching?" Fin shrugged. "I can't say for certain, but I had no sense of him."

"Nor did I," Connor said when Fin glanced at him.

"So it showed him Connor's first instinct is to protect. His woman— Oh, don't be so fragile about it," Fin said when Meara sputtered a protest. "His woman, his friend. Move the risk away and protect. Branna's is to go to Connor's side, as his would be to go to hers. But she protects as well, as she didn't move to release Meara or Boyle to increase the numbers."

"It was wrong of me as well, and I've apologized to Meara already. Now I apologize to you, Boyle."

"We've covered it all, and it's forgotten."

"He won't forget." Iona glanced around, understanding. "And he'll use what he knows, try to use it, work it in somehow."

"So we find a way to use what he knows, or thinks he knows, against him." Pleased with the idea, Meara grinned around the table. "How do we use me to trap him?"

"We won't be doing that." Connor put a firm cork in that idea bottle. "We tried it, didn't we, with Iona, and it didn't work—nearly lost her to him."

"If at first you don't succeed."

"Fuck it and try something else," Connor finished.

"I choose. Remember your own fine words. I'll ask you," she said to Fin. "Is there a way to use me to lure him?"

"I can't say—and not because I don't want to tangle with Connor, or Branna come to that. But because we'd all need time to think it through, and carefully. I'm no more willing than Connor to risk as close a call as we had with Iona on the solstice."

"I've no argument with that."

"We'll think on it, and all must agree in the end." He looked at Connor, got a nod. "And we'll work on it, use what we know, refine what we had, as it was close to the mark." He looked at Branna.

"It was, as Sorcha's poison was. But neither finished him. I can't find what we missed—and yes, we should work together. You've a good hand with potions and spells. We have until Samhain."

"Why Samhain?" Connor asked her.

"The beginning of winter, the eve of the beginning of the year itself for us—the Celts. I thought on this while making this meal. We thought the longest day—light over dark—but I think that was wrong. Maybe this is something we missed. Samhain, for we need some time, but as he's coming after one of us so blatantly, we can't take too much of it."

"On the night the Veil is thin," Connor considered. "And where it's said no password is needed to move from realm to realm. That could be it, one of the things we missed. He can pass easy as walking across the room. On that night, it may be we can do the same without struggling first to find where, or when."

"The night when the dead come to seek the warmth of the Samhain fire," Fin added, "and the comfort of their blood kin."

"The dead—ghosts now?" Meara demanded. "Witches aren't enough for us now."

"Sorcha," Branna said simply.

"Ah. You think she could come, add to the power. Sorcha, and the first three as well?"

"It's what we'll think on, work on. If we're all agreed to it."

"I like it." Boyle lifted his glass to Branna. "All Hallow's Eve it is."

"If we can hold him off that long, and learn enough," Branna qualified.

"We can. We will," Connor said decisively. "I've always been partial to Samhain—and not just for the treats. I had a fine conversation once with my great-granny on Samhain."

"Who was dead at the time, I suppose."

He winked at Meara. "Oh, gone years before I was born. When the Veil thins I'm able to see through it easier than other times. And since we're all thinking he's testing me, in particular, it might be I'm the lure we're after. And you thought of that," he said to Fin.

"It crossed my mind. We'll think a great deal more, talk it through, and work carefully. I can give you all the time you need, Branna. At any time."

"No ramblings coming up?" she asked carelessly.

"Nothing that can't be postponed or put off. I'm here till this is done."

"And then?"

He looked at her, said nothing for a long beat. "Then, we'll see what we see."

"He's only made us stronger." Iona took Boyle's hand. "Families fight, and they make mistakes. But they can come back stronger for it. We have."

"To squabbles and fuckups then."

Connor raised his glass, the rest lifted theirs, and with a musical clink, sealed the toast.

12

HE KNEW IT FOR A DREAM. IN HIS MIND'S EYE HE COULD see himself, tucked warm and naked in bed with Meara, and could—if he drifted back, feel her heart beat slow and steady against his.

Safe and warm in bed, he thought.

But as he walked the woods, the chill hung in the night air, and the clouds that flirted with the three-quarter moon deepened dark shadows.

"What are we looking for?" Meara asked him.

"I don't know till I find it. You shouldn't be here." He stopped to cup her face in his hands. "Stay in bed, sleep safe."

"You won't lock me in or away." Firmly, she gripped his wrists. "You promised it. And it's my dream as much as yours."

He could send her back, into dreams where she wouldn't remember. But it would be the same as a lie.

"Keep close then. I don't know the way here."

"We're not home."

"We're not."

Meara lifted the sword she carried so the blade caught the filtered light of the moon. "Did you give me the sword or did I bring it in myself?"

"I don't know that either." Something shimmered over his skin, teased the edges of his senses. "There's something in the air."

"Smoke."

"Aye, and more." He lifted his hand, held a ball of light. He used it as a kind of torch, dispelling shadows to better see the way.

A deer stepped onto the rough path, its rack a crown of silver, its hide a glimmer of gold. It stood a moment, statue still, as if allowing them to bask in its beauty, then turned and walked regally through the swirl of mist.

"Do we follow the hart?" Meara wondered. "As in song and story?"

"We do." But he kept the light glowing. The trees thickened, and there was the scent of green and earth and smoke as the hart moved with unhurried grace.

"Does this happen often for you? This sort of dream?"

"Not often, but it's not the first—though the first I've had company from my side of things. There, do you see? Another light up ahead."

"Barely, but yes. It could be a trap. Can you feel him, Connor? Is he here with us?"

"The air's full of magicks." So full he wondered she couldn't feel it. "The black and the white, the dark and the light. They beat like pulses."

"And crawl on the skin."

So she could feel them. "You won't go back?"

"I won't, no." But she stayed close as they followed the hart toward the light.

Connor cast himself forward, let himself see. And made out the shape, then the face in the shadowed light.

"It's Eamon."

"The boy? Sorcha's son? We're back centuries."

"So it seems. He's older, still a boy yet, but older." So Connor cast out again, this time speaking mind to mind. *It's Connor of the O'Dwyers who comes. Your blood, your friend.*

He felt the boy relax—a bit. *Come then, and welcome. But you are not alone.*

I bring my friend, and she is yours as well.

The hart drifted off into the dark as the lights merged. Connor saw the little cottage, a small lean-to for horses, a garden of herbs and medicinal plants, well tended.

They'd made a life here, he thought, Sorcha's three. And a good one.

"You are welcome," Eamon repeated, and set his light aside to clasp Connor's hand. "And you," he said to Meara. "I thought not to see you again."

"Again?"

Now the boy looked closer, looked deep with eyes as blue as the hawk's-eye stone he wore around his neck. "You are not Aine?"

"A goddess?" Meara laughed. "No indeed."

"Not the goddess but the gypsy named for her. You are very like her, but not, I see, not her at all."

"This is Meara, my friend, and yours. She is one of our circle. Tell me, cousin, how long has it been for you since you saw me?"

"Three years. But I knew I would see you again. The gypsy told me, and I saw she had the gift. She came to trade one spring morning, and told me she'd followed the magicks and the omens to our door. So she said I had kin from another time, and we would meet again, in and out of dreams."

"In and out," Connor considered.

"She said we would go home again, and meet our destiny. You have her face, my lady, and her bearing. You come from her, she who called herself Aine. So I'll thank you as I did her for giving me hope when I needed it."

He looked at Connor. "It was after our first winter here, and the dark seemed never to lift. I pined for home, despaired of seeing it again."

He'd grown tall, Connor observed, and confident. "You've made a home here."

"We live, and we learn. It's good land here, and the wild of it calls. But we, the three, must see home again before we can make our own, and keep it."

"But it's not time yet, is it? I'll trust you'll know when it is. Your sisters are well?"

"They are, and thank you. I hope your sister is the same."

"She is. We're six. The three and three more, and we learn as well. He has something new. A shadow spell, a way to balance between worlds and forms. Your mother wrote something of shadows, and my Branna studies her book."

"As does my sister. I'll tell her of this. Or will you come in. I'll wake her and Teagan as they'd be happy to meet you both."

Eamon started to turn to the cottage door.

For Meara it all happened at once.

Connor whirled and Eamon with him as if they were one form. The big gray—and it gave her a jolt to see Alastar, the same as the stallion she knew—charged from the lean-to. Almost as one, Roibeard dived, Kathel leaped.

Before she could fully turn, Connor yanked her back and behind him just as the wolf sprang.

It came from nowhere, silent as a ghost, quick as a snake.

In a blur, it dodged Alastar's flashing hooves and charged. Straight at the boy, she realized, and without thought, shoved Eamon to the side, swung her sword.

She struck air, but even that sang up her arms to her shoulders.

Then the full force of the wolf struck her, sent her flying. Pain, the shock of it, the bitter, bitter cold of it ripped through her side. Instinct—survival—had her clamping her hands around its throat to hold back the snap of its jaws.

And again, it happened at once.

The hound attacked, and light burst so bright it burned the air to red. Shouts and snarls tore through that searing curtain while her muscles quivered at the strain of holding back those snapping jaws. She heard herself scream, felt no shame in it as the wolf screamed as well.

She saw rage in its eyes, murderous and crazed, before it wavered, faded, vanished as it had come. Out of nowhere.

Her name, Connor saying it over and over and over. She couldn't get her breath, simply couldn't draw in the air—air that stank like brimstone.

Warm hands on her side, warm lips on her lips. "Let me see now, let me see. Ah, God, God. Not to worry, *aghra*, I'll fix it. Lie quiet."

"I can help you."

She heard the voice, saw the face. Branna's face, but younger. She remembered that face, Meara thought through the pain, the liquid daze of it all. Remembered it from her own youth.

"You'll look like her in a few years. Our Branna's a rare beauty."

"Lie quiet, lady. Teagan, fetch—ah well, she already is. My sister's getting the rest I need. I'm skilled, cousin," she said to Connor. "You'll trust me to this?"

"I will." But he took Meara's hand. "Here now, darling, here, *mo chroi*, look at me. At me, into me."

So she went dreaming, dreaming into those green eyes, outside of pain, outside of all but him. And him murmuring sweet things to her as he did when they loved.

Then Iona—no Teagan, the youngest—Teagan, held a cup to her lips, and the taste on her tongue, down her throat, was lovely.

Now when she drew in breath, true and deep, it tasted the same—of the green and the earth, the peat fire, and the herbs thriving nearby.

"I'm all right."

"Another moment, just another moment. How could he come here?" Brannaugh asked Connor. "We're beyond him here."

"But I'm not. Somehow I brought him, gave him passage. A trap it was after all. Using me to get to you, Eamon, and your sisters. I led him here, led him to this."

"No, he used us both, our dreams."

"And drew us in as well," Brannaugh said. "There's none of his dark left in you, my lady. Can you sit now, easy and slow?"

"I'm fine. Better than I was before the wound. You have her skill, or she has yours."

"You stood for my brother. If you hadn't risked yourself, he would be hurt, or worse, for Cabhan wanted his blood, his death."

"Your sword." Teagan laid it over Meara's legs.

"There's blood on it. I thought the strike missed."

"You struck true."

"'Tis shadow magick," Brannaugh stated.

"It is," Connor agreed. "As long as I'm here, he can come again. I do you more harm than good by staying."

"Would you take this, if you please?" Teagan held out a flower topping its bulb. "And when you can, if you'd plant this near our mother's grave. She favored bluebells."

"I will, yes, soon as I'm able. I must go, must take Meara back."

"I'm fine," she said.

"I'm not. Have a care, all of you." He wrapped his arms tight around Meara, pressed his face into her hair.

She woke in bed, sitting up with Connor's arms around her, with him rocking her as he might a baby.

"I had a dream."

"Not a dream, or not only a dream. Shh now, give me a moment."

His lips pressed onto her hair, her temples, her cheeks, all slow and deliberate.

"Let me see your side."

"It's fine. I'm fine," she insisted as he shifted her, ran his hands over her. "In fact I feel someone dosed me with a magick elixir. And I suppose that's just what happened. How did it happen? Any of it, all of it?"

"Eamon dreamed of me and I of him. He drew me to him, and I drew you with me. And likely Cabhan set the stage for it all."

His hands fisted in her hair until he carefully relaxed them again.

"To use me, my dreaming, to attack Eamon."

"You pushed me behind you."

"And you did the same with Eamon. We do what we do." On a sigh, he laid his forehead on hers. "Your sword struck his flank, and his claws yours, but he was still part in shadow so the blade drew his blood, but didn't stop him. That's my theory on it."

"He came out of the air, Connor. How do we fight what comes out of the air?"

"As we did. The light drove him back—Eamon's and mine joined, then the girls."

"He screamed," Meara remembered. "It didn't sound like an animal, but a man."

"Balancing between worlds, and forms. It's catching him when he steps off on one or the other, I think. It's near dawn. It'll be an ugly business, but I'm waking Branna. I'll leave it to you to ring up the others. This is something to share with all and straightaway."

But first he cupped her face in his hands as he had in the dreaming time. "Don't be so fucking brave next time, for the next time might kill me where I stand."

"He was just a boy, Connor, and straight in its path. And he looks like you, or you look like him. The shape of the face," she added, "his mouth, his nose, even the way he stands."

"Is that so?"

"Harder to see it yourself, I'd think, but it's very so. I'll ring Iona, then she'll be in charge of waking Boyle, who can wake Fin."

"All right." He ran his hands through her hair, long and waving as he'd released it from its braid the night before. "Whoever gets downstairs first puts on the bleeding coffee."

"Agreed." Because she could see the worry in his eyes still, she leaned in to kiss him. "Go on, you've got the worst job between us in waking Branna when the sun's barely up."

"Have the first-aid kit ready." He rolled out of bed, yanked on his pants.

As he left, Meara reached over for her phone, and saw the bluebell. Thinking of Teagan, so like the girl Iona must have been, she rose, fetched a glass of water from the bathroom, set the bulb in it.

For Sorcha, she thought, then called Iona.

She made it down first, did her duty with the coffee. She considered making oatmeal, the only breakfast meal she had a decent enough hand with. And Connor nearly always scorched the eggs if he had charge of breakfast.

She was spared when Branna came in. Her friend wore blue and green striped flannel pants with a thin green top. She'd tied a little blue sweater over it, and that somehow matched the thick socks on her feet.

Her hair spilling free to her waist, Branna marched straight for the coffee. "Don't talk to me, not a word, until I've had my coffee. Put some potatoes on the boil, and when they're soft enough, chip them up for frying."

She drank the coffee black rather than adding the good dose of cream that was her usual.

"I swear an oath, there's a time coming soon when I'll not step near a stove for a month."

"You'll have earned it. I'm not talking to anyone in particular,"

Meara said quickly as she scrubbed potatoes in the sink. "Just making some general observations."

"Bloody Cabhan," Branna muttered, as she pulled things from the fridge. "I'll kill him with my own hands, I swear *another* oath, for forcing me to see so many sunrises. The eggs are going scrambled, and whoever doesn't like it doesn't have to eat them."

Wisely, Meara said nothing, but put the potatoes on the boil.

Muttering all the while, Branna put on sausage, started on the bacon, sliced bread from the loaf for toast.

Then downed more coffee.

"I want to see your side."

Meara stopped herself from saying she was fine, simply lifted up her shirt.

Branna laid her fingers on it—how did she know the exact spot—probed for a moment. Meara felt heat slide in, and out again.

Then Branna met her eyes, just moved in and wrapped around her tight.

"It's healed perfectly. Damn it, Meara. Damn it."

"Don't start now. I've had it from Connor already. You'd think I'd been gutted instead of getting a bit of a swipe."

"What do you think he was aiming for if not your guts?" But Branna stepped back, pressed the heels of her hands to her eyes. Breathed deep before she dropped them again.

"All right then. Let's get this bloody breakfast on. Connor Sean Michael O'Dwyer! Get your arse down here and do something with this breakfast besides eat it."

As he appeared seconds later, he'd obviously been waiting for her to settle. "Whatever you like. I can do the eggs."

"You'll not touch them. Set the table as it seems I'll be cooking for six the rest of my life. And when you're done with that, you can start on the toast."

The potatoes were frying when the others arrived.

"You're all right?" Iona went straight to Meara. "You're sure?"

"I am. More than all right as I'm bristling with energy from whatever potion they gave me."

"Let me see it." Fin nudged Iona aside.

"Am I going to have to lift my shirt for everyone?" But she did so, frowning a bit as Fin laid his hand on her. "Branna's already had a poke at me."

"He's my blood. If there's even a trace of him, I'll know. And there's none." Gently, Fin drew her shirt into place again. "I wouldn't have you hurt, *mo deirfiúr.*"

"I know it. Sure there was a moment, and I wouldn't care to repeat it, but the rest? It was a fascination. You went with Iona once," she said to Boyle.

"I did, so I know the sensation. Like dreaming but more like walking, talking, doing while you dream. It makes you a bit light-headed."

"You should sit," Iona decided. "Just sit down. I'll help Branna finish breakfast."

"You'll not," Branna said definitely. "Boyle, you're the only one of the lot who doesn't have ham hands in the kitchen. Scramble up the eggs, will you, as I've nearly finished the rest."

He went over to the stove beside her, poured the beaten eggs from the bowl into a skillet where she'd melted butter.

"All right then?" he asked.

Branna leaned against him a moment. "I will be."

She turned the heat off under the potatoes, began to scoop them out with a slotted tool onto paper towels to drain. "Why didn't I feel any of it?" she wondered. "I slept straight through it all, never knowing a thing."

"Why didn't I, or Iona?" Fin countered from behind her. "It wasn't our dream; we didn't have a part in it."

"I was right in the same house, only just down the hall. I should've sensed something."

"I can see as you're the center of this world how you're deserving a piece of all of it."

When she rounded on him, eyes flashing, narrowed, Iona stepped up. "Stop it, just stop it, both of you. You're each blaming yourselves, and that's stupid. Neither of you is responsible. The only one who is, is Cabhan, so knock it off. My blood, my brother," she added before the pair of them could speak. "Blah, blah, blah. So what? We're all in this. Why don't we find out exactly what happened before we start dividing up the blame?"

"You're marrying a bossy woman, *mo dearthair*," Fin said to Boyle. "And a sensible one. Sit, Iona, and Meara as well. I'll get your coffee."

Iona sat, folded her hands neatly on the table. "That would be very nice."

"Don't bleed it out," Meara warned, and joined her.

At Branna's direction, Boyle piled eggs on the platter with the sausage, bacon, potatoes, fried tomatoes, and black pudding.

He carted it to the table while Fin served the coffee and Connor poured out juice.

"Take us through it," Fin told Connor.

"It started as they do—as if you're fully awake and aware and somewhere else all at once. In Clare we were, though I didn't know it at first. In Clare, and in Eamon's time."

He wound through the story as they all served themselves from the huge platter.

"A hart?" Branna interrupted. "Was it real, or did you bring it into it?"

"I wouldn't have thought of it. If I'd wanted a guide, I'd have pulled in Roibeard. It was a massive buck, and magnificent. Regal, and with a hide more gold than brown."

"Blue eyes," Meara added.

"You're right. They were. Bold and blue, like Eamon's, come to think of it."

"Or his father's," Branna pointed out. "In Sorcha's book she writes her son has his father's eyes, his coloring."

"You think it was Daithi," Connor considered, "or representing him. He might be given that form to be near his children, protect them as best he can."

"I hope it's true," Iona said quietly. "He was killed riding home to protect them."

"The hart that might have been Daithi's spirit guided us toward the light, and the light was Eamon. Three years in his time since we last met. He was taller, and his face fined down as it does when you're passing out of childhood. He's a handsome lad."

Now he grinned at Meara.

"He'd say that, as I told him they favor each other. Different coloring to be sure, but you'd know they're kin."

"He thought Meara was Aine—a gypsy," Connor explained. "One who'd passed through some time before, and told him they'd see home again."

"That's interesting. You have gypsy in your heritage," Iona pointed out.

"I do."

"And Fin named the filly he chose for Alastar Aine."

"I thought of that, and take it doesn't mean I resemble a horse."

"Of great beauty and spirit," Fin pointed out. "The name was hers—I never considered another. It was who she was the moment I saw her. Sure it's interesting, the connections, the overlaps."

"It's that I felt nothing while we talked, there outside the cottage. Nor did he," Connor considered. "We asked after family. I told him of the shadow spell. And it was when he asked if we'd come inside that it happened. One minute I felt nothing, then I felt him there. Just there an instant before the wolf leaped out of the air. And he felt it as well."

"You spun around together, like one person," Meara added. "It was all so fast. Connor pushed me back behind him, but it wasn't me, it was the boy, he wanted."

"And so she pushed Eamon aside, exposed herself, and swung the sword. Not even a second, no time to throw out a block of any kind. He rammed her full, clawed her. Her blood and his in the air. The hound charged. Eamon and I joined, and the girls rushed out. It was they who threw a block, stopping me from rushing forward, throwing what they had at him, so it was me who joined with them as there was nothing else to do in those few seconds. What we had was enough to give him pain, with Kathel, Roibeard, and Alastar going at him along with us. He screamed like a girl."

"Hey!"

He managed a grin at Iona. "No offense meant. Between us and Kathel, Alastar's hooves and Roibeard's talons, he went as he'd come. Gone, vanished, leaving only the stench of hell behind him. And Meara bleeding on the ground. And not two minutes, when I look back calm, not two minutes between."

"They've all been short, haven't they? Something to consider," Branna said. "It may be he only has enough power for those short bursts with this spell."

"For now," Fin added.

"For now is what we have. He hitched onto Connor's dream, slithered into it to try to get the boy—or one of the sisters if they'd greeted you, Connor. He can't get into the house, but into a dream, once you've moved out of its protection . . . I can see this. He can't get to them in that time, in that place, but could link to the dream to go there."

"Where the boy would've been vulnerable," Fin added, "in the half world of active dreaming. Then Cabhan waits on the edges of it, waits to attack—until you turn your back."

"Bloody coward," Boyle muttered.

"You said Meara spilled his blood. Where's your sword?" Branna demanded.

"At home. I never brought it here. 'Twas just in my hand in the dream."

"I'll go get it," Fin said. "Where do you have it?"

"It's on the shelf in the closet in my bedroom. I'll get you the key to the flat." When he only smiled, she sat back again. "Which you don't need at all, do you? Which is a thought that never occurred to me. Any of the four of you could walk right in as you please."

"I'll bring it. It won't take but a few moments."

"I appreciate the respect, as you know I don't approve of taking the easy way when a bit of effort and time does the job. But." Branna sighed. "We're beyond that, and it's foolish for you to drive into the village and back."

Fin merely nodded. He lifted his hand, and in a flash held Meara's sword.

Meara jolted, then laughed a little. "Well, that's brilliant, and it's so rare to see any of you do that sort of thing, I sometimes forget you can."

"Fin's a bit freer with it than Branna," Boyle pointed out.

"We all don't have the same boundaries." Fin turned the sword. "There's blood on it, and fresh enough."

"I won't have blood or swords at my table." Branna rose, took it from him. "It's enough to work with. I still have some from the solstice. But as you said, this is fresh—and it's from him when he was wounded during a shadow spell."

"I'll come back, work with you as soon as I can get away," Connor told her.

"So will I," Iona added. "We're really busy this morning, but I think my bosses might give me some flex time this afternoon."

Boyle ran a hand over Iona's cap of hair. "They might be persuaded.

I'll bring Meara back as well if you can use us. We can bring food if nothing else."

"It's quite a bit else." Branna continued to study the sword. "As there isn't enough of the fancy French stew to go full around a second time."

"We'll see to that then, Meara and myself, and come back around as soon as we can close things up at the stables. I'll send Iona off soon as I can."

"I'll come get her," Connor said. "I think we're back to no one wandering around on their own, at least for a bit. I can juggle the scheduling and be off by three if that suits."

"Well enough."

"I'll stay now." There was a beat of silence as Fin spoke. "If *that* suits."

"It does." Branna lowered the sword. "The lot of you can put my kitchen back to rights. I'll be in the workshop when you're done," she said to Fin, and walked out.

13

MEARA SPENT MOST OF HER NEXT FREE DAY AT HER mother's helping with the last of the packing up for what they were all calling The Long Visit. And as packing required making decisions—what should be taken, what should be left behind, what might be given away or simply tossed in the bin—Meara spent most of her free day with a throbbing headache.

Decisions, and Meara knew it well, put Colleen Quinn in a state of dithering anxiety. The simple choice of whether to take her trio of pampered African Violets nearly brought her to tears.

"Well, of course you'll take them." Meara struggled to find balance on a thin midway line between good cheer and firmness.

"If I leave them, you and Donal will have the bother of watering and feeding them, and if you forget . . ."

"I can promise not to forget." Because she'd take them straight to Branna, who'd know how to tend them. "But you should have them with you."

"Maureen might not want them in her house."

"Now why wouldn't Maureen want them?" Teetering on that thin line, Meara pasted a determined smile on her face as she lifted one of the fuzzy-leafed plants, pregnant with purple blooms. "They're lovely."

"Well, it's *her* house, isn't it?"

"And you're her mother, and they're your plants."

Decision made—by God—Meara set them carefully in boxes she'd begged off the market.

"Oh, but—"

"They'll ride safe in here." *Seven times seven is—bugger it—forty-nine.* "And haven't you said plants are living things, and how they respond to music and conversation and affection? They'd miss you and likely wilt, however careful I was with them."

Inspired, Meara sang "On the Road Again" as she tucked balled paper around the pots. At least that got a glimmer of a smile from Colleen.

"You've such a beautiful singing voice."

"I got it from my mother, didn't I?"

"Your father has a fine, strong voice as well."

"Hmm" was Meara's response to that as she multiplied in her head. "Well now, you'll want some of your photos, won't you, to put around your room."

"Oh." Colleen immediately linked her fingers together as she did when she didn't know whether to turn left or right. "I'm not sure, and how would I choose which. And—"

"I'll choose, then it'll be a nice surprise for you when you unpack. You know, I could do with some tea."

"Oh. I'll make some."

"That would be grand." And provide five minutes of peace.

With Colleen in the kitchen, Meara quickly snatched framed photos—captured moments of the past, of her childhood, of her siblings, and, though it didn't sit particularly well, of her parents together.

She studied one of her parents, smiling out with the lush gardens of the big house they'd once had surrounding them. A handsome face, she thought, studying her father. A fine, strapping man with all the charm in the world.

And no spine whatsoever.

She wrapped the photo to protect the glass of the frame, tucked it in the box. She might be of the opinion her mother would be better off without the constant reminder of what had been, but it wasn't her life to live.

And that life, right at the moment, fit into two suitcases, a shoulder tote, and three market boxes.

There would be more if the move became permanent—a word Colleen wasn't ready to hear. More packing to do, but much more than that, Meara was sure, more life to be lived.

Considering the job done—or nearly enough—she went back to the kitchen. And found her mother sitting at the tiny table, weeping quietly into her hands.

"Ah, Ma."

"I'm sorry, I'm sorry. I haven't made the tea. I feel at sea, Meara. I've lived in Cong and hereabouts all my life. And now . . ."

"It's not far. You'll not be far." Sitting, Meara took her hands. "Not even a full hour away."

Colleen looked up, tearfully. "But I won't see you or Donal as I do."

"It's just a visit, Ma."

"I may never come back here. It's what you're all thinking for me."

With little choice, Meara shouldered the guilt. "It's what we're all thinking you'll want once you're there a little while. If you stay in Galway with Maureen and Sean and the kids, we'll visit. Of course we will. And if you're not happy there, you'll come back here. Haven't I said I'll see the cottage is right here for you?"

"I hate this place. I hate everything about this place."

Stunned, Meara opened her mouth, then shut it again without an idea what to say.

"No, no, that's not right, that's not true." Rocking herself, Colleen pressed her hands to her face. "I love the gardens. I do. I love seeing them, front and back, and working in them. And I'm grateful for the cottage, for it's a sweet little place."

Taking a tissue from her pocket, Colleen dabbed away the tears. "I'm grateful to Finbar Burke for renting it to me for far less than a fair price—and to you for paying it. And to Donal for staying with me so long. To all of you for seeing someone rang me every day to see how I was doing. For taking me on little holidays. I know you've all conspired so I'll move off to Galway with Maureen for my own good. I'm not altogether stupid."

"You're not stupid at all."

"I'm fifty-five years old, and I can't roast a joint of lamb."

Because that brought on another spate of weeping, Meara tried another tact. "It's true enough you're a bloody terrible cook. When I'd come home from school and smell your pot roast cooking, I'd ask God what I'd done to deserve such punishment."

Colleen goggled for a long minute, tears shimmering on her cheeks. Then she laughed. The sound was a bit wild, but it was a laugh all the same.

"My mother's worse."

"Is that even possible?"

"Why do you think your grandda hired a cook? We'd have starved to death. And bless her, Maureen's not much better."

"That's why they invented take-away." Hoping to stem more weeping, Meara rose to put the kettle on. "I never knew you hated living here."

"I don't. That was wrong and ungrateful. I've a roof over my head, and a garden I'm proud of. I've good neighbors, and you and Donal close. I've hated it's all I have—another's property my daughter pays to keep around me."

"It's not all you have." How blind had she been, Meara wondered, not to see how it would score her mother's pride to live in a rental her child paid for?

"It's only a place, Ma. Just a place. You have your children, your grandchildren, who love you enough to conspire for your happiness. You have yourself, a terrible cook, but a brilliant gardener. You'll be a boon to those grandchildren."

"Will I?"

"Oh, you will. You'll be patient with them, and sincerely interested in their doings and their thoughts. It's different with a parent, isn't it? They have to consider constantly whether to say yes or no, now or later. They have to discipline and enforce as well as love and tend. You'll only have to love, and they'll soak all that up like sponges."

"I do miss having them closer, having the time to spoil them."

"So here's your chance."

"What if Maureen objects to the spoiling?"

"Then I'm off to Galway to kick her arse."

Colleen smiled again as Meara made the tea. "You've always been my warrior. So fierce and brave. I'm hoping I'll have grandchildren from you to spoil one day."

"Ah well."

"I've heard you and Connor O'Dwyer are seeing each other."

"I've been seeing Connor O'Dwyer all my life."

"Meara."

No avoiding it, Meara thought, and brought the tea to the little table. "We're seeing each other."

"I'm as fond of him as I can be. He's a fine man, and so handsome as well. A good heart and a kind nature. He comes to see me now and then, just to see how I'm faring, and to ask if there's any little thing he can do around the place."

"I didn't know, but it's like him."

"He has a way about him, and though I know the way of the world, I can't approve of . . . that is, the sex before marriage."

Holy Mary, Meara prayed, have mercy and spare me from the sex talk.

"Understood."

"I feel the same with Donal and Sharon, but . . . A man's a man, after all, and they'll want such things with or without Holy Matrimony."

"As do women, Ma, and I hate to break the news to you, but I'm a woman grown."

"Be that as it may," Colleen said primly, "you're still my daughter. And despite what the Church says on such matters, I'll hope you'll have a care."

"You can rest easy there."

"I'll rest easy when you're happy and married and starting a family in a home of your own. I'm as fond of Connor as I can be, as I said, but it's a fact he's an eye for the ladies. So have a care, Meara."

When she heard the front door open, Meara offered desperate thanks. "And here's Donal set to take you to Galway," she said brightly. "I'll get another cup for his tea."

SHE THOUGHT TO GO HOME, STARE AT THE WALLS UNTIL SHE felt less frazzled and guilty and generally out of sorts. And ended up driving straight to Branna's.

The minute she'd dashed into the workshop, she saw she'd made a mistake.

Branna and Fin stood together at the big work counter, their hands poised over a silver bowl. Whatever brew it contained glowed, a hard orange light that swirled up a thin column of smoke.

Branna held up a finger of her free hand, a signal to wait.

"Yours and yours and me and mine, life and death together twine. Blood and tears cast and shed mixed together thick and red. Fire and smoke will bubble true and seal your fate with this brew."

It bubbled up, frothed over, a virulent orange.

"Damn it!" Branna stepped back, fisted her hands on her hips. "It's still not right. It should go red, bloodred. Murderous red, and thick. We're still missing something."

"It's damn well not my blood," Fin said. "I've given you a liter already."

"A few drops is all, don't be such a baby." Obviously frustrated, Branna shoved at the hair she'd bundled on top of her head. "I've taken mine and Connor's and Iona's as well, haven't I?"

"And there's three of you to my one."

"Plus what we've used from the vial we have of his from the solstice, and what we're using from the sword."

"You can have mine if you need it," Meara offered. "Otherwise it seems I'm just in the way."

"You're not. It might be we can use another eye, another brain on this. But we're having a break so I can think on this," Branna decided. "We'll have some tea."

"You're upset," Fin said to Meara as Branna mopped up the counter. "You saw your mother off to Galway today."

"Just a bit ago, yes, and with much of the weeping and gnashing of teeth."

"I'm sorry." Immediately Branna came around the counter, rubbed Meara's arm. "I was blocked off in my own frustrations and didn't give a thought to yours. It was hard."

"In some ways more and in others less than I expected. But altogether exhausting."

"I've things I could do and leave the two of you to talk."

"No, don't go on my account. And this gives me the chance to talk to you about the rental."

"It's nothing you need worry over. As I told you, I can hold it until she's decided what she wants to do. It's been hers near to ten years now."

"It's good of you, Fin. I mean it."

Saying nothing, Branna walked over to make the tea.

"I think she won't be back—not to live," Meara said. "I think the change will boost her. The grandchildren, particularly the grandchildren, as she'll be living with some and closer to the rest. Added to it, Maureen's Sean will make a fuss over her, as he's always had a soft spot there. And the fact is, she's not happy on her own. She needs someone not just for conversation but direction, and Maureen will give her both."

"Then stop feeling guilty about it," Fin advised.

"I'm wading in it for a bit." Doing just that, Meara pressed her fingers to her eyes. "She cried so, and said things I didn't know were in her mind or her heart. She's grateful to you, Fin, for the cottage, for the ridiculously low rent you've charged all these years—and I never thought she had any idea about the money at all. But she did, she's grateful, and so am I."

"It's nothing, Meara."

"It is, to her, to me. I couldn't have managed my own rent and hers if hers hadn't been cheaper than dirt even with Donal kicking in, and then there'd have been murder for certain. So you kept her alive and me out of prison, so you'll take the gratitude that's given."

"You're welcome." Then he went to her, drew her in, as she'd started to cry. "Enough now, darling."

"It's just she started crying again when Donal and I loaded her things into the lorry, and she clung to me as if I were going off to war. Which I am, I suppose, but she doesn't know. I swear she's turned a blind eye to what three of my closest friends are about all these years, and now is only somewhat concerned that Connor and I are having sex outside Holy Matrimony."

Though he couldn't help the smile, Fin rubbed her back. "It sounds like a very full day for you."

"Ending with me booting my own mother out of her home."

"You did no such thing. You helped her break a chain that's kept her locked here when she'll be happier in a house filled with family. I'll wager she'll thank you for it before the year's out. Here now, *dubheasa*, dry your eyes."

He stepped back, patted his pockets, then pulled out a handkerchief swirling with color, and made her laugh.

"What's all this?"

"Always a rainbow after the storm." Then plucked an enormous and bright pink daisy from her hair. "And flowers from the rain."

"You'd make a fecking fortune at birthday parties."

"I'll keep that for backup."

"And I'm a complete git."

"Not at all." He gave her another hug. "Only a half a git at best."

He caught Branna's eye over Meara's head. And the smile she sent him stabbed straight into his heart.

SHE DRANK HER TEA, ATE THREE OF BRANNA'S LEMON biscuits, and though she knew next to nothing of writing spells and making potions, did her best to help.

She ground herbs using mortar and pestle—sage, fleabane, rosemary for banishing. She measured out the dust of a crushed black fluorite crystal, snipped lengths of copper twine, marking all amounts precisely in Branna's journal.

By the time Connor arrived, with Iona and Boyle with him, all the ingredients Branna and Fin had chosen were ready.

"We've failed twice with this today," Branna told them, "so we'll hope it's true third time's the charm. Plus we've had Meara's hand in it this time, and that's for luck."

"An apprentice witch are you?" Connor nipped her in for a kiss.

"Hardly, but I can grind and measure."

"Did you see your mother on her way?"

"I did, and mopped her up after she cried her buckets. Then came here where Fin mopped me up in turn."

"Be happy." This time Connor kissed her forehead. "For she will be."

"I'm closer to believing it as Donal texted me not an hour ago to say Maureen's family gave her a queen's welcome, with streamers and flowers, cake and even champagne. I can be a little shamed for not thinking Maureen had it in her to make the fuss, but I'll get past that the first time she pisses me off. Donal says she's giddy as a girl—Ma, not Maureen, so that's a cloud gone from over my head."

"We'll go up and take her out to dinner once we can get away easy."

A good heart, her mother had said. And a kind nature.

"You'd be taking a chance as you're having sex with her daughter outside Holy Matrimony."

"What?"

"I'll explain later. I think Branna wants your blood."

"From all," Branna countered. "As we took from all for the spell before the solstice."

"It didn't finish it." Boyle frowned at the bowl as Branna carefully added ingredients. "Why should this?"

"We have his blood—from the ground, from the blade," Fin said.

"That adds his power to it, it adds the dark, and the dark we'll use against him."

"Cloak the workshop, Connor." Branna measured salt into the bowl. "Iona, the candles if you will. This time we'll do it all together as we're all here, and within a circle.

"Within and without," she began, "without and within, and here the devil's end we'll spin." Taking up a length of copper, she twisted it into the shape of a man. "In shadows he hides, in shadows we'll bide and trap his true form inside. There to flame and burn to ash in the spell we cast."

She set the copper figure on the silver tray with vials, a long crystal sphere, and her oldest athame.

"We cast the circle."

Meara had seen the ritual dozens of times, but it always brought a tingle to her skin. The way a wave of the hand would set the wide ring of white candles to flame, and how the air seemed to hush and still within their ring.

Then stir.

The three and Fin stood at the four points of the compass, and each called on the elements, the god and goddesses, their guides.

And the fire Iona conjured burned white, a foot off the floor with the silver bowl suspended over it.

Herbs and crystals, blessed water poured from Branna's hand—stirred by the air Connor called. Black earth squeezed from Fin's fist dampened by tears shed by a witch.

And blood.

"From a heart brave and true." With her ritual knife Iona scored Boyle's palm. "To mix with mine as one from two."

And scored her own, pressed her hand to his.

"Life and light, burning bright," she said as she let the mixed blood slide into the bowl.

Connor took Meara's hand, kissed her palm. "From a heart loyal and strong." He scored her palm, his. "Join with mine to right the wrong. Life and light, burning bright."

Branna turned to Fin, started to take his hand, but he drew it back, and pulled down the shoulder of his shirt.

"Take it from the mark."

When she shook her head, he gripped her knife hand by the wrist. "From the mark."

"As you say."

She laid the blade on the pentagram, his curse and heritage.

"Blood that runs from this mark, mix with mine. White and dark." When she laid her cut hand on his shoulder, flesh to flesh, blood to blood, the candle flames shot high, and the air trembled.

"Dark and white, power and might, light and life burning bright."

The blood ran in a thin river down her hand, into the bowl. The potion boiled, churned, spewing smoke.

"In the name of Sorcha, all who came before, all who came after, we join our power to make this fight. We cast thee out of shadow and into light."

She tossed the copper figure into the bubbling potion, where it flashed—orange and gold and red flame, a roar like a whirlwind, a thousand voices calling through it.

Then a silence so profound it trembled.

Branna looked into the bowl, breathed out. "It's right. This is right. This can end him."

"Should I release the fire?" Iona asked her.

"We'll leave it to simmer, one hour, then off the flame overnight to cure. And on Samhain, we choke him with it."

"We're done for now then?" Meara asked.

"Done enough so I want to clear my head and drink a good glass of wine."

"Well then, we'll be back in a minute. I just need to . . ." She was already pulling Connor from the room. "Just need Connor for a moment."

"What is it?" He worried, as she had a death grip on his hand while she pulled him out the back of the workshop, through the kitchen. "Are you upset? I know the ritual was intense, but—"

"It was. It was. It was." She all but chanted it, dragging him on through the living area, up the stairs.

"Was it the blood? I know it can seem harsh, but I promise you it's needed to make the potion, to bespell it."

"No. Yes. Jesus. It was all of it!" Breathless, she shoved him into his bedroom, then back against the door to slam it.

Then she covered his mouth with hers, all but fusing their lips with the heat pouring from her.

"Oh," he managed, finally clueing in as she ripped his sweater up and away.

"Just give me." She peeled off the insulated shirt under the sweater, latched her teeth on his bare shoulder. "Just give me."

He'd have slowed things down—a bit—but she was already unhooking his belt, and what was a man to do?

He started tugging up her sweater—undressing a woman was one of the great pleasures of life—got tangled up with her very busy hands. He considered just ripping it away, then—

"Ah, to hell with all that."

The next thing Meara knew she was naked, and so was he.

"Yes, yes, yes." She gripped his hair, assaulted his mouth, moaned with pleasure when he took her breasts.

She'd never been so wild with lust, never known such quaking, roiling need. Perhaps something in the swirling air, the pulse of the fire, the stunning rise and merging of powers and magicks had punched into her.

All she knew was she'd had to have him or go mad.

He still tasted of it, that exotic flavor of magick—potent, seductive, edging toward the dark. She felt the ripples of it still working in him, not yet tamped down.

And wanted that, wanted him, wanted all.

His hands weren't patient now, but greedy and rough and quick. She wanted that as well, craved being touched and taken as if his life depended on it.

It felt as if hers did.

He whipped her around, forced her back to the door. She had an instant to look into his eyes—fierce and feral—before he drove into her.

She'd thought she'd go mad if he didn't take her, and now, being taken, went mad.

Her hips jackhammered, challenging him to match her ferocious pace. Her nails bit into him—back, shoulders—her teeth gnawed and scraped. Little pains, quick and hot, that fired into a crazed pleasure that enslaved him. His blood beat hammer strikes under the skin, so he thrust into her harder, faster, deeper in a brutal, breathless rhythm.

She cried out, a sound that joined shock and greed. And again, this time his name with a kind of wonder. When he gripped her hips, lifted her, she locked her legs around his waist.

He ravaged her throat, filled himself with the taste of her as he filled her with his lust until the last frayed tether snapped.

He broke, swore he felt the very air shatter like glass as she tightened around him, as her final cry died off into a shuddering sigh.

Limp, they slid down to the floor in a sweaty tangle of limbs.

"God. My sweet God." She drew in air like a drowning woman surfacing.

Struggling for breath, he managed a grunt, then flopped off her to lie on his back with his eyes closed and his chest heaving.

"Is the floor shaking?"

"I don't think so." He opened his eyes, stared at the ceiling. "Maybe. No," he decided. "I think we are—or more what you could call vibrating. There are bound to be aftershocks after an earthquake, I'm told."

He reached out blindly to pat her, and his hand landed on her breast. A fine place. "Are you all right then?"

"I'm not all right. I'm amazing and amazed. I feel like I've gone flying again. It was the way you looked—like you'd been lit up from the inside, and your hair flying around in the wind you'd made, and the power of it all beating like tribal drums. I couldn't help it. I'm sorry, but I couldn't control myself."

"You're forgiven. I'm a forgiving sort of man."

She sighed out a laugh, laid a hand over his. "And now here we are, naked and spent on your floor—and your room's a disaster of a mess as always."

He turned his head, glanced around. Not a disaster, exactly, he calculated. True enough there were shoes and boots and clothes and books scattered around. And he'd never seen the point—a severe and sharp bone of contention between him and his sister—on making a bed when you were only going to get back in it again.

To please her, he waved a hand, had the shoes and boots and clothes and books—and whatever else lay on the floor—pile up in a corner. He'd deal with it all—at some point.

But for now he waved his hand again, had rose petals raining down. She laughed, grabbed a handful from the air, then scattered them over his hair.

"You're a foolish romantic, Connor."

"There's not a thing foolish about romance." He drew her over, pillowed her head on his shoulder. "There, that's altogether better."

She couldn't argue, and yet. "We should go down. They'll be wondering what we're up to."

"Oh, I'll wager they know perfectly well what we're up to. So we'll take a little time."

A little, she decided. "I'll need my clothes again—from wherever you sent them."

"I'll get them back to you. But not quite yet."

She let herself be content with her head pillowed on his shoulder, and the air full of rose petals.

14

AS SEPTEMBER TICKED ON TO OCTOBER, BRANNA DRAgooned Connor and Iona into helping harvest the vegetables from her back garden. She set Iona on picking the fat pea pods, Connor to digging potatoes, while she pulled carrots and turnips.

"It smells so good." Iona straightened to sniff at the air. "In the spring when we planted, it all smelled fresh and new, and that was wonderful. And now it smells ripe and ready, and that's a different wonderful."

Connor sent Iona a baleful stare as he shoveled. "Say that when she has you scrubbing all this, and boiling or blanching or whatever the bloody hell it is."

"You don't complain when you eat the meals I make all winter with the vegetables I jar or freeze. In fact . . ."

She moved over, plucked a plump plum tomato from the vine, sniffed it. "I've a mind to make my blue cheese and tomato soup tonight."

Knowing his fondness for it, Branna smiled when Connor gave her the eye. "That's a canny way to keep me working."

"I'm a canny sort."

Harvesting put her in a fine mood. She might pluck and pick through the summer, but the basics of bounty she'd jar up for the coming winter gave her a lovely sense of accomplishment.

And the work, as far as Branna was concerned, only added to it.

"Iona, you could pick a good pair of cucumbers. I'll be making some beauty creams later, and I'll need them."

"I don't know how you manage to do so much. Keep the house, a garden, cook, make all the stock for your shop—run a business. Plot to destroy evil."

"Maybe it's magick." Enjoying the scent of them, the feel of them in her hand, Branna added more tomatoes to her bucket. "But it's the truth I love what it is I do, so most times it's not much like working."

"Tell that to the man with the shovel," Connor complained, and was ignored.

"You've plenty dished on your own plate," Branna said to Iona. "You don't seem to mind spending each day shoveling away horse dung, hauling bales of hay and straw, riding about the woods nattering to tourists who likely ask most of the same questions daily. Add all the studying and practice you've done on the craft since last winter when you could barely spark a candlewick."

"I love it all, too. I have a home and a place, a purpose. I have family and a man who loves me." Lifting her face to the sky, Iona breathed deep. "And I have magick. I only had hints of that, only had Nan as real family before I came here."

She shifted to the cucumbers, selected two. "And I'd love to be able to plant a little garden. If I learned how to can things, then I'd feel I'd done my part when Boyle ends up doing most of the cooking."

"There's room enough for one at Boyle's. Do you plan on staying there once you're married?"

"Oh, it's fine for now. More than fine for the two of us, and close to everything and everyone we want to be close to. But . . . we want to start a family, and sooner rather than later."

Branna adjusted the straw hat she wore more for the tradition of it than as a block from the sun that peeked in and out of puffy white clouds on a day that spoke more of summer than fall.

"Then you'll want a house, and not just rooms over Fin's garage."

"We're thinking about it, but neither of us wants to give up being close to all of you, or the stables, so we're just thinking about it." Bending back to her work, Iona picked a bright yellow squash. "There's the wedding to plan first, and I haven't even decided on my dress or the flowers."

"But you have what you want in mind for both."

"I have a sort of vision of the dress I want. I think— Connor, fair warning, as this will bore you brainless."

"The potatoes have already done that." He plucked them out of shoveled dirt for the bucket.

"Anyway, I want the long white dress, but I think more a vintage style than anything sleek and modern. No train or veil, more simple but still beautiful. Like something your grandmother might have worn—but a bit updated. Nan would give me hers, but it's ivory and I want white, and she's taller—and, well, it's not really it, as much as I'd love to wear a family dress."

She picked a cherry tomato, popped it warm into her mouth. "God, that's good. Anyway, I've been looking online, to get the idea, and after Samhain, I'm hoping you and I and Meara can go on a real hunt."

"I'd love it. And the flowers?"

"I've gone around and around on that, too, then I realized . . . I want your flowers."

"Mine?"

"I mean the look of your flowers, your gardens."

Straightening again, Iona waved a hand toward the happy mix of zinnias, foxglove, begonias, nasturtiums. "Not specific types or colors. All of them. All that color and joy, just the way you manage to plant them so they look unstudied and happy, and stunning all at once."

"Then you want Lola."

"Lola?"

"She's a florist, has a place just this side of Galway City. She's a customer of mine. I send her vats of hand cream as doing up flowers is murder on the hands. And she'll often order candles by the gross to go with her arrangements for a wedding. She's an artist with blooms, I promise you. I'll give you her number if you want it."

"I do. She sounds perfect."

Iona glanced toward Connor. He crouched on the ground studying a potato as if it had the answer to all the questions printed on its skin.

"I warned you I'd bore you brainless."

"No, it's not that. It got me thinking about family, about gardens and flowers. And the bluebell Teagan asked me to plant at her mother's grave. I haven't done it."

"It's too much of a risk to go to Sorcha's cabin now," Branna reminded him.

"I know it. And still, it's all she asked. She helped heal Meara, and all she asked was that I plant the flowers."

Setting down her bucket, Branna crossed over to him, crouched down so they were face-to-face. "And we will. We'll plant the bluebell—a hectare of them if that's what you want. We'll honor her mother, who's ours as well. But none of us are to go near Sorcha's grave until after Samhain. You'll promise me that."

"I wouldn't risk myself, and by doing that risk all. But it weighs on me, Branna. She was just a girl. And with the look of you, Iona. And I'm looking at you," he said to Branna, "just like I looked at Sorcha's Brannaugh, and I could see how she'd be in another ten years, and see how you were at her age. There was too much sorrow and duty in her eyes, as too often there's too much in yours."

"When we've done what we've sworn to do, the sorrow and duty will be done." She gave his grubby hand a squeeze. "They'll know it just as we do. I'm sure of that."

"Why can't we see, you and me together? And with Iona the three? Why can't we see how it ends?"

"You know the answer to that. As long as there's choice, the end is never set. What he has, and all that's gone before, it blurs the vision, Connor."

"We're the light." Iona stood with her bucket of pods, garden soil staining the knees of her jeans. And the ring Boyle had given her sparkling on her finger. "Whatever he comes with, however he comes, we'll fight. And we'll win. I believe that. And I believe it because you do," she told Connor. "Because with your whole life leading to this, knowing it did, you believe. He's a bully and a bastard hiding behind power he bartered for with some devil. What we are?" She laid a hand on her heart. "What we have is from the blood and from the light. We'll cut him down with that light, and send him to hell. I know it."

"Well said. And there." Branna gave Connor a poke. "That's our own Iona's St. Crispin's Day speech."

"It was well said. It's just a mood hanging over me. A promise not yet kept."

"One that will be," Branna said. "And it's not just that and digging potatoes that's put you in a mood—a sour one that's rare for you. Have you and Meara had a fight?"

"Not at all. It's all grand. I might worry here and there at the way Cabhan's taken too fine an interest in her. When it's one of us, we have weapon for weapon, magicks to magicks. She's only wit and spine, and a blade if she's carrying one."

"Which serves her well, and she wears your protective stones, carries the charms we made. It's all we can do."

"I had her blood on my hands." He looked down at them now, saw the wet red of Meara's blood rather than the good, dark soil. "I find I can't get around it, get past it, so I'm after texting her a half dozen times a day, making up some foolish reason, just to be sure she's safe."

"She'd knock you flat for that."

"I know it well."

"I worry about Boyle, too. And Cabhan hasn't paid any real attention there. It's natural," Iona added, "for us to have concerns about the two people we care about who don't have the same arsenal we do." She looked at Branna. "You worry, too."

"I do, yes. Even knowing there's nothing we can do we haven't done, I worry."

"If it helps, I promise I'm with her a lot during the workday. And when she takes out a group—ever since the wolf shadowed her—I braid a charm into her horse's mane."

Connor smiled. "Do you?"

"She indulges me, and so does Boyle. I've been adding them to all the horses as often as I can manage. It makes me feel better when we have to leave them at night."

"I gave her some lotion the other day, asked her to use it every day, to test it for me." Now Branna smiled. "I charmed it."

"The one that smells of apricots and honey? It's lovely." He kissed Branna's cheeks. "So that's thanks on a magickal and a romantic sort of level. I should've known the pair of you would add precautions. For me, she's never out of Roibeard's sight unless she's in mine."

"Well, give her over to Merlin for an hour or so—Fin would be willing. And go hawking." With a hand on his shoulder for a boost, Branna rose. "Put the potatoes in the little cellar and take your hawk out for a bit. I expect you could both use the time."

"What about the boiling and blanching and all the rest?"

"You're dismissed."

"And the soup?"

She laughed, gave him a light knock on the head with her fist. "Here's my thought. Tell Boyle I'll need Meara around here in . . ." Branna looked up at the beaming sun, calculated the time. "Three hours will work. Then the rest of you should be here by half-six. We'll have your soup, and a rocket salad as I'll have Iona cut it fresh, some brown bread, and cream cake."

"Cake? What occasion is this?"

"We'll have a *céili*. It's long past time we had a party here."

Brushing his hands on his pants, Connor pushed to his feet. "I can see I need to develop a sour mood more often."

"It won't work a second time. Go store those potatoes, go find your hawk, and be back here at half-six."

"I'll do all that. Thanks."

She went back, picked more tomatoes as now she'd be making the soup for six, and glanced over at Iona after Connor had gone.

"He doesn't know yet," Iona said. "He'd tell you if he did. You if no one else. So he doesn't know he's in love with her."

"He doesn't know yet, but he's coming around to it. Sure he's loved her all his life, so realizing it's another sort of love than he let himself believe takes some time."

Branna looked toward the cottage, thought of him, thought of Meara. "She's the only one he'll ever want a life with, or a lifetime. Others have and could touch his heart, but none but Meara could break it."

"She never would."

"She loves him, and always has. And he's the only one she'll ever want a life with, or a lifetime. But she hasn't his faith in love or its power. If she can trust herself and him, they'll make each other. If she can't, she'll break his heart and her own."

"I believe in love and its power. And I believe that when given the choice, Meara will reach for it, hold on to it, and treasure it."

"I hope more than I hope for almost anything else you're right." Branna let out a breath. "Meanwhile, the two of them haven't yet figured why no one else in the world has ever made them feel as they do now. The heart, it's a fierce and mysterious thing. Let's get all this inside, scrubbed off. I'll show you how to start the soup, then we'll see how much we can jar before Meara comes."

SHE ARRIVED, TIMELY AND OUT OF SORTS.

Once she'd stalked through to the kitchen, she fisted her hands on her hips, frowned at the shining jars of colorful vegetables cooling on the counter, the soup simmering low on the stove.

"What's all this? If you've called me here to do kitchen work, you're to be sorely disappointed. I've had enough work altogether today."

"We're nearly done," Branna said pleasantly.

"I'm having a beer." Meara completed her stalk to the fridge, yanked out a bottle of Smithwick's.

"Is everything all right at the stables?"

Meara snarled at Iona. "All right? Oh, sure it's been more than all right with us having a summer day in October and every blessed soul within fifty kilometers deciding nothing would do but they ride a horse today. If I wasn't taking out a group, I was doing rubdowns or hauling saddles in, hauling them out."

She waved the beer in the air before opening it. "And didn't Caesar take it in his head to bite Rufus on the arse, and this after I told the Spanish lady riding him to give the horses some space. So then I had a near hysterical Spanish lady on my hands, and I can barely understand her as she's hysterical *in* Spanish, and doing half the talking with her hands so the reins are flying about giving Caesar the notion she wants a fine gallop."

"Oh God." Iona spoiled the attempt to sound concerned by choking off a laugh.

"Oh sure it's an amusement to you."

"Only a little, because I know it's all right, and you wouldn't have put her on Caesar if she couldn't ride."

"For all her hysterics, she rode like a bloody conquistador, and I have a suspicion she angled for the gallop all along. Fortunately, I was on your Alastar, and caught up with her easy. Grinning wide she was, though she tried to turn that around when I got hold of Caesar's bridle and pulled him up. And I swear to you—"

Now she pointed, face livid. "I swear to you the two horses had a hearty laugh over it all." She chugged down beer. "And after that one I had five teens. Five girl teens. And that I can't talk about at all or I might have Spanish hysterics myself. And you." She pointed again, an accusing jab at Iona. "You've a free day to play about in the gardens as you're sleeping with the boss."

"I'm such a slut."

"Well, there you are." Meara drank again. "And that's why I won't be doing any kitchen work or garden work, and if there's spells or enchantments to be done, I'll require another beer at the very least."

Branna glanced over toward the jars at a trio of tiny pops—a sign the lids had sealed. "That's a good sound. There's no work at all. We're having the day off."

This time Meara drank slowly. "Has she fallen under a spell herself?" she asked Iona. "Or has she been into the whiskey?"

"Neither, but there should be whiskey later. We're having a *céili*."

"A *céili*?"

"I've the first of my harvesting done, and the jarring as well. We've had a summer day in October." Branna dried off her hands, laid the cloth out. "So have your singing voice ready, Meara, and put on your dancing shoes. I'm in the mood for a party."

"Are you sure this isn't a spell?"

"We've worked and worried, planned and plotted. It's time we took a night. We'll hope he hears our music, and it burns his ears."

"I won't argue with that." More contemplatively now, Meara took another sip of beer. "I hate to risk spoiling this rare mood of yours, but I should tell you I saw him twice today—the shadow. First of the man, and next the wolf. Just watching, no more than that. But sure it's enough to play on the nerves."

"He does it for that, so we'll show him he can't stop us from living. And speaking of just that, I'll need you both upstairs."

"You're full of surprises and mystery," Meara decided. "Do the others know you're after having a party?" she asked as they started upstairs.

"Connor will let them know."

Branna led them into her bedroom, where, unlike Connor's, everything was perfectly in place.

She had the largest space—built to her specifications when she and Connor expanded the cottage. She'd painted the walls a deep forest green, and with the dark, tree-bark trim, she often thought it was like sleeping in the deep woods. She'd chosen the art carefully, following fancy with paintings of mermaids and faeries, dragons and elves.

She'd indulged herself with the bed, with a Celtic trinity knot carved into its high head- and footboard. A garden of pillows mounded on its thick white duvet. A chest, built and painted by her great-grandfather sat at its foot and held the most precious of the tools of her craft.

She fetched a long hook from her closet and, fitting it into the little slot in the ceiling, drew down the attic door and steps.

"I need to get something. I'll only be a minute."

"It always feels so peaceful in here." Iona walked to the windows that looked out over fields and woods to the roll of green hills beyond.

"They do good work between them, Branna and Connor. I envy her en suite bath with that big tub and the hectare of counter. Of course if I had that much counter in my bath, I'd clutter it up. And hers has . . ."

Meara went to the door, peeked in. "A pretty vase of calla lilies, fancy soaps in a dish, three fat white candles on gorgeous silver holders. I'd say it was witchcraft, but she's just brutal about tidiness."

"I wish some of it would rub off on me," Iona said as Branna came down the steps with a big white box. "Oh, let me help you."

"I've got it, 'tisn't heavy." She laid the white box on the white duvet. "So when we talked about weddings, and dresses and flowers and all of that, I had this thought."

After opening the box, she folded back layers and layers of tissue paper, then lifted out a long white dress.

Iona's gasp was exactly the reaction she'd hoped for.

"Oh, it's beautiful. Just gorgeous."

"It is, yes. My great-grandmother wore it on her wedding day, and I thought it might suit for yours."

Eyes wide, Iona took a quick step back. "I couldn't. I couldn't, Branna, it should be for you, for yours. It was your great-grandmother's."

"And she's your blood as well as mine. It wouldn't suit me, though it's lovely. The style's not for me. And she was petite, as you are."

Head cocked, Branna held the dress in front of Iona. "I'll ask you to try it on—indulge me in that. If it doesn't suit, if it isn't what pleases you, no harm done."

"Try it on then, Iona. You're frothing to."

"Okay, okay! Oh, this is fun." She began to strip, all but dancing as she did. "I never thought I'd be trying on a wedding dress today."

"You've the unders for a honeymoon." Meara raised her brows at Iona's lacy pale blue bra and matching panties.

"I've bought an entire new supply. It's proven to be an excellent investment." She laughed as Branna helped her step into the dress.

"Button up the back, will you, Meara?" Branna said as Iona carefully slid her arms in the thin lace sleeves.

"There are a million of them, and so tiny, and pretty like pearls."

"She was Siobhan O'Ryan, who married Colm O'Dwyer, and was

an aunt to your own grandmother, Iona, if I've got it all straight. The length's good as you'll be wearing heels, I imagine." Branna fluffed the tiers of lace-edged tulle.

"It might've been made for you the way it fits." Meara continued to fasten buttons.

"Oh, it's so beautiful." Smiling at herself in Branna's long mirror, Iona brushed fingertips over the lace bodice, down the tiered column of skirt.

"There! That's the lot,' Meara said as she did up the last buttons at the base of Iona's neck. "You look a picture, Iona."

"I do. I really do."

"The skirt's perfect, I think." Nodding, Branna walked around Iona as her cousin swayed this way and that to make the skirt sweep. "Soft, romantic, just enough fuss but not too much. But I'm thinking the bodice could use some altering. It's far too old-fashioned and far too modest. Vintage is one thing, covering you to the chin's another."

"Oh, but we can't change it. You've kept it all these years."

"What can be changed can be changed back again. Turn around here once." She turned Iona herself, putting her back to the mirror. "These should go." Branna swept her hands down the sleeves, vanishing them, glanced at Meara.

"Altogether better already. And the back here? Don't you think . . ."

Branna pursed her lips as Meara traced a low vee, then with a nod, traced it herself to open the back to just above the waist. "Yes, she's a lovely strong back and should show it off. Now the bodice."

Head angling this way, that way, Branna walked a circle around Iona. "Perhaps this . . ." She changed the bodice to a straight line just above the breasts with thin straps.

Meara folded her arms. "I like it!"

"Mmm, but it's not quite right." Thinking, imagining, Branna tried an off-the-shoulder style, with a hint of cap sleeves. Stepped back to study with Meara.

They both shook their heads.

"Can I just—"

"No!" And both of them snapped out the denial as Iona started to peek over her shoulder.

"The first you did was better by far."

"It was, but . . ." Branna closed her eyes a moment until the image formed. Then opening them, she waved her hands slowly over the bodice.

"That!" Meara laid a hand on Branna's shoulder. "Don't touch it. Let her look now."

"All right. If you don't like it, you've only to say. Turn around, have a look."

And the look said it all. Not just a contented smile now, but a stunned gasp followed by a luminous glow.

Bride-white lace formed a strapless bodice with the curve of a sweetheart neckline. From the nipped waist, the lace-edged tulle fell in soft, romantic tiers.

"She likes it," Meara said with a laugh.

"No, no, no. I love it more than I can say. Oh, Branna." Tears glimmered now as she met her cousin's eyes in the glass.

"The back was my notion," Meara reminded her, and had Iona angling to look. "Oh! Oh, Meara. It's fabulous. It's wonderful. It's the most beautiful dress in the world."

She spun around in it, laughed through the tears. "I'm a bride."

"Almost. Let's play a bit more."

"Oh please." As if to protect, Iona crossed her arms over the bodice. "Branna, I love it exactly as it is."

"Not with the dress, for it couldn't be more perfect for you. No veil you said, and I agree. What about something like this?"

She ran a finger over Iona's cap of sunny hair so Iona wore a rainbow of tiny rosebuds on a sparkling band. "That suits the dress, and you, I think—and something for your ears. Your Nan might have just the thing, but for now . . ." She added tiny diamond stars.

"That works well."

A dress, Branna thought, suited to the shower of sunlight and the glimmer of the moon. Suited for a day of love and promises, and a night of rejoicing.

"I don't have the words to thank you for this. It's not just the dress—how it looks, which is beyond anything I hoped for. But that it's from family."

"You're mine," Branna told her, "as is Boyle." She slid an arm around Meara's waist. "Ours."

"We're a circle as well, we three." Meara took Iona's hand. "It's important to know that, and value that. Beyond all the rest, we're a circle as well."

"And that's beyond anything I once hoped for. On the day I marry Boyle, my happiest day, you'll both stand with me. We'll stand, we three, the three and all six. Nothing can ever break that."

"Nothing can or will," Branna agreed.

"And now I see why you decided to celebrate. Spanish hysterics be damned," Meara announced. "I'm in the mood to sing and put my dancing shoes on."

15

THE KITCHEN SMELLED OF COOKING, AND THE PEAT FIRE in the hearth. It glowed with light, shoving the bright, celebrational glow against the dark that pressed against the windows. The dog stretched by the fire, big head on big paws, watching his family with an amused eye.

There was music, full of pipes and strings, rollicking out of the little kitchen iPod while they put the finishing touches on the meal. Voices mixed and mingled, song and conversation as Connor swung Iona around in a quick dance.

"I'm still so clumsy!"

"You're not at all," he told her. "You're only needing more practice." He twirled her once, and twice on her laugh, then passed her smoothly to Boyle. "Give her a spin, man. I've primed her for you."

"And I'll break her toes when I trod on her feet."

"You're light enough on them when you've a mind to it."

Boyle only smiled and lifted his beer. "I haven't had enough pints for that."

"We'll tend to that as well." Connor grabbed Meara's hand, sent her a wink, then executed a quick complicated step, boots clacking, clicking on the glossy wood floor.

And Meara angled her head—a silent acceptance of the challenge. Mirrored it. Two beats later they clicked, stomped, kicked in perfect unison to the music, and, Iona thought, to some energetic choreography in their minds.

She watched them face each other, torsos straight and still while their legs and feet seemed to fly.

"It's like they were born dancing."

"I can't say about the Quinns," Fin commented, "but the O'Dwyers have always been musical. Hands, feet, voices. The best *céilies* hereabouts have forever been hosted by the O'Dwyers."

"Magickal," she said with a smile.

His gaze slid toward Branna, lingered a moment. "In all ways."

"And what about the Burkes? Do they dance?"

"We've been known to. Myself, I do better at it with my hands on a woman. And since Boyle's not making the move, I'm obliged to."

He surprised Iona by pulling her to him, circling her fast, then dropping into steps that took the dance into a half time. After a moment's fumbling, she caught on, matched him well enough, with his arms guiding her.

"I'd say the Burkes hold their own."

When he twirled her around, she levitated herself a few inches off the floor and made him laugh.

"As does the American cousin. I'm looking forward to dancing with you at your wedding. It may be I'll have to be standing in for the groom on that, while he stands on the sidelines."

"Now I see I've no choice in the matter, or find myself shown up by Finbar Burke."

Boyle snatched Iona away, solved the issue of his less talented feet by lifting her off hers and turning circles.

And Branna found herself facing Fin.

Connor saw the moment, squeezed Meara's hand in his.

"Will you?" Fin asked.

"I'm about to put dinner on the table."

He said, "Once," and took her hand.

They had a way, Connor thought, a smooth way of flowing along with the music, in time, in step, as if they'd been made to move together.

His soft heart ached for them, both of them, for it was love ashimmer in their steps. Around the kitchen, they turned, flowed, turned, eyes for each other only, easy and happy as they'd once been.

Beside him, Meara stopped as he had, and leaned her head against his shoulder.

For one lovely moment, all was right in the world. All was as it had been once, how it might be yet again.

Then Branna stopped, and though she smiled, the lovely moment shattered.

"Well now, I hope you've all worked up an appetite."

Fin murmured something to her, in Irish, but too soft and low for Connor to understand. Her smile fell toward sorrow as she turned away.

"We'll have more music after our meal, and there's wine aplenty." Movements brisk, Branna turned the music down. "Tonight's not for work or worries. We've food fresh from the garden tonight, and our own Iona made the soup."

That pronouncement brought on a long, hushed silence that hung until Iona rolled out a laugh. "Come on! I'm not that bad a cook."

"Of course you're not," Boyle said with the air of a man facing a hard, unhappy task. He went to the stove, spooned up a taste straight from the pot. Sampled, lifted his eyebrows, sampled again. "It's good. It's very good indeed."

"I don't know if a man in love's to be trusted," Connor considered. "But we'll eat."

They ate a bounty from the garden, kept the conversation light and away from all things dark. Wine flowed freely.

"And how's your mother faring in Galway?" Fin asked Meara.

"I'm not ready to say she's there to stay, but closer to it. I had a talk with my sister, who's that surprised it's a happy arrangement—for now in any case. My mother's working in the garden, and keeping it in trim. And she's struck up a bit of a friendship with a neighbor who's a keen gardener herself. If you could hold the cottage a bit longer—"

"As long as you need," Fin interrupted. "I've a mind to do a few updates there. When you've time enough, Connor, we could talk about a bit of work on the place."

"I've always time enough for that. I've missed the challenge and fun of building and fixing since we finished off the cottage. Did you truly do the soup, Iona, for it's more than good." So saying, he took another ladle from the tureen.

"Branna watched me like Roibeard, and took me through it step by step."

"I'm hoping you'll be remembering the steps, as I'll be asking you to make it at home."

Pleased, Iona grinned at Boyle. "We'll have to plant tomatoes. I'm pretty good with a garden. We could try some next year—in patio pots."

"Sure maybe we'll find something with a bit of land by then, and you can have a proper garden."

"It may be you'll be too busy with weddings and honeymoons next spring to plant tomatoes," Meara pointed out.

"And we've more than enough here to share," Branna added. "You haven't found a place that suits you more than where you are?"

"Not yet, and no hurry on it," Boyle said, glancing at Iona.

"None," she confirmed. "We like being close to all of you, and to the stables. In fact, we're both set on staying close, so until we find something that hits all the notes, we like just where we are."

"Building your own tends to hit those notes, as I've reason to know." Fin poured more wine, all around.

"You wrote a bloody opera when you built your house," Boyle commented.

"Sure what fun it was to have a hand in that," Connor remembered. "Though Fin was as fussy as your aunt Mary about everything from a run of tile to cabinet pulls.

"That's what makes it a satisfying endeavor, if you're in no particular hurry. There's land behind my own place," Fin continued, "where a house could be tucked nicely in the trees if someone liked the notion of that. And I'd be willing to sell a parcel to good neighbors."

"Are you serious?" Iona's spoon clattered against her bowl.

"About good neighbors, yes. I've no wish to be saddled with poor ones, even with plenty of space between."

"A cottage in the woods." Eyes shining, Iona turned to Boyle. "We could be excellent neighbors. We could be *amazing* neighbors."

"When you bought all that, you said it was to keep people from planting houses around you."

"People are one thing," Fin said to Boyle. "Friends and family—and partners—there's another thing entirely. We can take a look around some time or another if you've any interest."

"I guess now's too soon," Iona said with a laugh. "But then I don't have a single idea how to design or build a house."

"Sure you're lucky you have a couple of cousins who do," Connor pointed out. "And I know some good workmen here and about if you decide to go that way. Which would suit me down to the ground," he added, "if I've a vote in it. I can go hawking back there as I do, and have the benefit of stopping in for a bowl of soup."

"He thinks with his stomach," Meara commented. "But he's right enough. It would be a lovely spot for a cottage, and just where you want it to be. It's a fine notion, Fin."

"A fine notion, but he's yet to talk price."

Fin smiled at Boyle, lifted his glass. "We'll get to that—after your bride's had a look."

"A canny businessman he's always been," Branna said. "She'll fall in love and pay any price." But she said it with humor, not sting. "And it is a fine notion. More, it's saved me a quandary, for the field behind here is for Connor. But with Iona being family, I've been torn about it—even though . . . I've walked it countless times, and it never said Iona. I could never see you and Boyle making your home there, though you'd have been in sight of our own, and it's a pretty spot with a lovely view of things. I never could understand the way of that. Now I do. You'll have your cottage in the woods."

She lifted her glass in turn. "Blessed be."

BRANNA BROUGHT OUT HER VIOLIN AFTER THE MEAL, AND joined her voice with Meara's. Only happy tunes, and lively ones. Connor fetched the boden drum from his room, added a tribal beat. To Iona's surprise and delight, Boyle disappeared for a few moments and came back with a melodeon.

"You play?" Iona gaped at Boyle, at the little button accordion he held. "I didn't know you could play!"

"I can't, not a note. But Fin can."

"I haven't played, not a note, in years," Fin protested.

"And who's fault is that?" Boyle shoved the instrument at him.

"Play it, Fin," Meara encouraged. "Let's have a proper *seisiún*."

"Then no complaints when I make a muck of it." He glanced at Branna. After a moment she shrugged, tapped her foot, and began something light and jumpy. With a laugh, Connor danced fingers and stick over the colorful drum.

Fin caught the time and the tune, joined in.

Music rang out, paused only for more wine or a discussion of what should be next. Iona scrambled up for a notepad.

"I need the names of some of these! We'll want some of them at the wedding reception. They're so full of fun and happy." Imagining herself in her perfect wedding dress, dancing to all that lively joy with Boyle, surrounded by friends and family, she beamed at him. "The way our life together's going to be."

At Meara's long, exaggerated *awwww*, Boyle kissed Iona soundly.

So in the warm, bright kitchen there was laughter and song, a deliberate and defiant celebration of life, of futures, of the light.

Outside, the dark deepened, the shadows spread, and the fog slunk along the ground.

In its anger, and its envy, it did what it could to smother the house. But protections carefully laid repelled it so it could only skulk and plot and rage against the brilliance—searching, searching for any chink in the circle.

Meara switched to water to wet her throat, brought a glass over to Branna. She felt suddenly tired, and a little drunk. It was air she needed more than water, she thought. Air cool and damp and dark.

"After Samhain," Connor said, "we'll have a real *céilie*, invite the neighbors and those all around as Ma and Da did. Near Christmas, do you think, Branna?"

"With a tree in the window, and lights everywhere. With enough food to set the tables groaning. I've a fondness for Yule, so that would suit me."

It was rare for Connor to slide into her mind, but he did now.

He's close, circling close, pressing hard. Do you feel him?

Branna nodded, but kept smiling. *The music draws him like a wasp to the light. But we're not ready, not altogether ready to take him on.*

Here's a chance to try, and we shouldn't miss taking it.

Then tell the others, this way. We'll try the chance, and hope surprise is enough.

Connor saw, as Branna did, that Fin already felt that pressure, those dark fingers scrabbling against the bright. He saw Iona jolt, just a little, as he slid his thoughts into her head.

Her hand squeezed Boyle's.

He glanced toward Meara.

The instant he realized she wasn't there he felt her, *saw* her reach out to open the front door of the cottage.

The fear gripped his throat like claws, all but drawing blood. He shouted for her, in his mind, with his voice, and rushed out of the room.

Nearly half asleep, floating on the shadows soft and dim, she stepped outside. Here's what she needed, here's what she had to have. The dark, the thick and quiet dark.

Even as she started to draw in a deep breath, Connor caught her around the waist, all but threw her back into the cottage.

Everything shook—the floor, the ground, the air. To her stunned eyes, the dark mists outside the door bowed inward as if something large and terrible pushed its weight against them. Boyle slammed the door on it, and the dull roar—like an angry surf—that rolled with it.

"What happened? What is it?" Meara shoved against Connor, who'd thrown his body over hers.

"Cabhan. Stay back," Branna snapped, and flung the door open again.

A storm raged outside, the shadows twisting, knotting. Under them came a kind of high shriek and a rumble that was thousands of wings beating.

"Bats, is it?" Branna said in disgust. "Try as you might," she shouted, fists clenched at her sides. "Try your worst, then try again. But this is *my* home, and never will you cross the threshold."

"Jesus," Meara whispered as the mists thinned enough for her to see the bats. Like a living, undulating wall, red eyes gleaming, spiked wings beating.

"Stay here." Connor shouted against the din, then leaped up to join his sister. And with him, Iona and Fin moved to form a line.

"In our light you'll twist and turn," Connor began.

"In our flame you'll scorch and burn," Iona continued.

"Here merge the power of one and three," Fin added.

"As we will, so mote it be," Branna finished.

Meara, dragged back by Boyle, watched as the bats lit like torches. Hated herself for cringing as they screamed, as they burst, as smoking bodies twisted.

Ash fell like black rain, whipped in the terrible wind.

Then all went quiet.

"You're not welcome here," Branna murmured, then firmly shut the door.

"Are you hurt?" With the danger passed, Connor dropped to his knees beside Meara.

"No, no. God, did I let it in? Did I open us up to that?"

"Nothing got in." But Connor gathered her up, pressed his lips to her hair. "You opened nothing but the door."

"I had to. Felt I couldn't breathe, and wanted—craved—the dark and quiet." Shaken, she balled her hands, pressed them to her temple. "He used me again, tried to use me against all of us."

"And failed," Iona said crisply.

"He sees you as weak. Look at me now." Fin crouched down to her. "He sees you as weak as you're a woman, and no witch. But he's wrong, as there's nothing weak about or in you."

"And still he used me."

"He wanted you to go out, beyond the protections and charms." Connor brushed her hair away from her face. "He tried to lure you out, away from us. Not to use you, darling, but to harm you. For he's enraged by what we're doing here. The music, the light, the simple joy of it all. He'd have hurt you, if he could, for only that."

"You're sure of it? The music, the lights?" Meara looked from

Connor to Branna, and back. "Well then. We'll play louder, and if you'd do me a favor considering, use what you will to make the lights brighter."

Connor kissed her, helped her to her feet. "No, not a bit of weak in or about you."

LATE INTO THE NIGHT WHEN THEY'D PLAYED THEMSELVES out, Connor held her close against him in his bed. He couldn't seem to let her go. The image played in his mind—the dazed look on her face as she'd stepped from light to dark.

"It's mind tricks he's using, and he's enough of them, enough in him to slither through the shields." As he spoke, he traced a finger over the beads she wore. "We'll work on something stronger."

"He doesn't go after Boyle the same way. Is Fin right? It's because I'm not a man?"

"He preys on women more, doesn't he? He killed Sorcha's man to be sure, but he killed Daithi to torment her, to break her heart and spirit. And he tormented her again and again over that last winter. The history of it says he took girls from the castle and around."

"Yet it's the boy, Eamon, he's tried to get to."

"Take out the boy, and he'd see the girls as more vulnerable to him. He wants Brannaugh—both the one who was and our own. I feel it whenever I let him in."

She shifted. "Let him in?"

"Into my head—a bit. Or when I'm able to slip through, as he does, and get into his. It's cold, and it's dark, and so full of hunger and rage it's hard to understand any of it."

"But letting him in, even for a moment, is dangerous. He could see your thoughts as well, couldn't he—use them against us? Against you."

"I've ways around that. He doesn't have what I have, or only a whisper of it. What Eamon has as well, and he'd love to drain the boy of his power, take it for his own."

Idly, he stroked her hair, loose from its braid. Despite all, he found himself oddly content to just be with her, bodies warm and close, voices hushed in the dark.

"He bothered us so little before Iona came. With Fin he's been relentless since the day the mark burned into Fin's shoulder."

"He never speaks of it, our Fin, or rarely."

"To me he does," Connor told her, "and sometimes to Boyle. But no, even then it's rare. Things changed all around when Cabhan's mark came on him. And changed all around again when Iona came. He pushed at her those weeks, as she was not only a woman but so new and inexperienced, just learning all she had in her and how to use it. He thought her weak as well."

"She proved him wrong."

"As you have more than once already." He kissed her forehead, her temple. "But he won't stop trying. Harming you harms us all. That he can see well enough, even if he can't understand it, as he's never loved in the whole of his existence. How is it, do you think, to exist for so long, so many lifetimes, and never know love, giving it, being given it?"

"People live without it—or do for one lifetime—and don't torment and kill."

"I'm not meaning it as an excuse." Now he propped up on his elbow to look down at her. "He can bespell a woman and take her body, and her power if she has it. Lusting without love—without any love for anything or anyone—that's the dark. Those who go through their time with only that? I think they must be sad creatures, or evil ones. It's the heart that gets us through the hard times, and gives us joy."

"Branna says your power comes through your heart." Lightly, Meara traced a cross on it.

"That's her thinking, and it's true enough. I couldn't be if I couldn't feel. He feels. Lust and rage and greed, with nothing to lighten it. Taking what we are won't be enough. It will never be enough. He wants us to know the dark he knows, to suffer in it."

It made her want to shudder, so she stiffened herself against it. "You found that in his mind?"

"Some of it. Some I can just see. And for a moment tonight, I knew what he felt—and it was a kind of terrible joy that he would take you from me, from us. From yourself."

"You were inside me—in my head. He never called my name, not this time, but you did. I heard you call my name, and I stopped for just an instant. I felt like I stood on the edge of something, pulled in both directions. Then I was under you on the floor, so I don't know which way I'd have gone."

"I know, and not only because there's no weakness in you. Because of this." He lowered his head, met her lips lightly, lightly with his. "Because it's more than lust."

Nerves rose, a shiver of wings in her belly. "Connor—"

"It's more," he whispered, and took her mouth.

Soft, so soft and tender, his lips coaxing hers to give, seducing degree by aching degree. If his power came from the heart, he used it now, saturating her in pure feeling.

She would have said no—no, it wasn't the way for her, couldn't be the way. But he was already gliding her along on the sweet, onto the shimmer, into the shine.

His hands, light as air, skimmed over her, and even with such a delicate touch kindled heat.

Quiet, so quiet and stirring, his words asking her to believe what she never had. To trust what she both feared and denied.

In love, its simplicity, its potency. Its permanence.

Not for her. No, not for her—she thought it, but drifted on its silky clouds. What he gave, what he brought, what he promised, was irresistible.

For a moment, for a night, she gave herself to it. Gave herself to him.

So he took, but gently, and gave more in return.

He'd known, in the instant she'd stood between Cabhan's dark and his light, he'd known the full truth of love. He'd understood it came weighted with fear, and with risks. He'd known he might be lost in the maze of it, accepted he would work through its shadows, draw on its light and live his life riding its ups, its downs, its stretches of smooth, its sudden bumps.

With her.

A lifetime of friendship hadn't prepared him for this change, this tidal shift from easy love to what he felt for her.

The one. The only. And this he would cherish.

He didn't ask for the words back—they would come. But for now her yielding was enough. Those breathy sighs, the tremors, the thick, unsteady beat of her heart.

She rose up, swimming up and over a wave of pleasure so absolute it seemed to fill her body with pure white light.

Then it was him filling her, giving her more, and more and more until tears blurred her vision. As she peaked, as she clung for glorious moments to that bright and brilliant edge, she heard his voice, once again, in her mind.

This is more, he said to her. *This is love.*

"WHY DOES IT MAKE YOU SO UNEASY?"

"What?" Meara stared at him, then looked around. "Where are we? Is— Is that Sorcha's cabin? Are we dreaming?"

"More than a dream. And love is more than the lie you try to believe it is."

"It's Sorcha's cabin, but it stands under the vines that grow around it. And this isn't the time to talk about love and lies. Did he bring us here?"

She drew her sword, grateful the dream that wasn't a dream provided it.

"Love's the source of the light."

"The moon's the source of the light, and we can be glad it's full wherever and whenever we are." She turned a slow circle, searching shadows. "Is he near? Can you feel him?"

"If you can't yet believe you love me, you should believe I love you. I've never told you a lie, or not one that mattered, in your life."

"Connor." She sheathed her sword, but left her hand on the hilt. "Have you lost your senses?"

"I've gained them." He grinned at her. "It's your senses lost because you haven't the nerve to pick them up and hold them."

"I'm the one with the sword so mind what you say about my nerve."

He only kissed her before she shoved him away. "Not a weak thing in or about you. Your heart's stronger than you think, and it's going to be mine."

"I'm not going to stand here, of all places, and talk nonsense with you. I'm going back."

"That's not the way." Connor took her arm as she turned.

"I know the way well enough."

"That's not the way," he repeated. "And it's not yet time, as here he comes now."

Her fingers tightened on the hilt of her sword. "Cabhan."

Connor stilled her sword hand before she could draw, and took the white cobble out of his pocket. It glowed like a small moon in his palm.

"No. It's Eamon who comes."

She watched him ride into the little clearing, not a boy now, but a man. Very young, but tall and straight and so like Connor her heart jerked.

He wore his hair longer and braided back. He came quietly astride a tough-looking chestnut who, to her eye, could have galloped halfway across the county without losing its wind.

"Good evening to you, cousin," Connor called out.

"And to you and your lady." Eamon dismounted smoothly. Rather than tether the horse, he simply laid the reins over its back. The way the chestnut stood, like a carved statue in the moonlight, it was clear it wouldn't stray or bolt away from its master.

"It's been some time for you," Connor observed.

"Five years. My sisters and their men bide at Ashford. Brannaugh has two children, a son and a daughter, and another son comes any day. Teagan is with child. Her first."

He looked to the cabin, then over to his mother's gravestone. "And so we've come home."

"To fight him."

"'Tis my fondest wish. But he is in your time, and that is a truth that cannot be denied."

Tall and straight, with the hawk's eye around his neck, Eamon looked over at his mother's grave again.

"Teagan came here before me. She saw the one who will come from her. Saw her watching while Teagan faced Cabhan. We are the three, the first, but what we are, what we have, we will pass to you. This is all I can see."

"We are six," Connor said. "The three and three more. My lady, my cousin's man, and a friend, a powerful friend." And since the boy was now a man, Connor thought, the time had come to speak of it. "Our friend Finbar Burke. He is of Cabhan's blood."

"He is marked?" Like Meara, Eamon laid a hand on the hilt of his sword.

"Through no act of his own, no wish of his own."

"The blood of Cabhan—"

"I would trust him with my life, and have. I would trust him with the life of my lady, and I love her beyond reason—though she doesn't believe it. We are six," Connor repeated, "and he is one of us. We will fight Cabhan. We will end him. I swear it."

Connor drew Meara's sword and, taking it, stepped over to the gravestone. He scored his palm, let the red drip onto the ground. "I swear by my blood we will end him."

He reached in his pocket, unsurprised to find the bluebell. He used the sword to dig a small hole, and planted it. "A promise given and kept."

He stirred the air with a finger, pulled the moisture out of it, and let blood and water pour on the ground.

Stepping back, he watched with the others as the flower grew, and the blooms doubled.

"I rode away from her." Eamon stared at the grave. "There was no choice, and it was her will and her wish. Now I come home a man. Whatever I can do, whatever power is given me, I will do, I will use. A promise kept." He held out a hand to Connor. "I cannot trust this spawn of Cabhan's, but I trust you and yours."

"He is mine."

Eamon looked at the grave, at the flowers, at the cabin. "Then you are six." He touched his amulet, the twin of Connor's, then the stone on the leather binding Connor had given him. "All we are is with you. I hope we'll see each other again, when this is done."

"When it's done," Connor agreed.

Eamon mounted his horse, then smiled at Meara. "You should believe my cousin, my lady, as what he speaks, he speaks from his heart. Farewell."

He turned his horse, rode off as quietly as he'd come.

Meara started to speak—and woke with a jolt in Connor's bed.

He sat beside her, a half smile on his face as he studied his bloodied palm.

"Jesus Christ. You never know where you'll end up when you lie down beside the likes of you. Mind yourself! You'll get blood on the sheets."

"I'll fix it." He rubbed palm to palm, stanched the blood, closed the shallow wound.

"What was that about?" she demanded.

"A bit of a visit with family. Some questions, some answers."

"What answers?"

"I'm after figuring that out. But the flower's planted, as Teagan asked of me, so that's enough for now. He looked fine and fit, didn't he, our Eamon?"

"You'd say so as you've a resemblance. Cabhan would know they'd come back."

"They don't end him, but neither does he end them. Like the flowers, that's enough to know for now. It's for us to end, I know that as well."

"And how do you know?"

"I feel it." He touched a finger to his heart. "I trust what I feel. Unlike you for instance."

After an impatient glance she shoved out of bed. "I have to go to work."

"You've time for a bite to eat. You needn't worry as there's not enough time for me to poke at you properly about my feelings and yours. But there'll be time for that soon enough. I love you to distraction, Meara, and while it comes as a surprise to me, I'm happy being surprised."

She grabbed up her clothes. "You're romanticizing the whole business, and cobbling it all together with magicks and risks and blood and sex. I expect you'll come to your senses before long, and for now, I'm using the loo, and getting myself ready for work."

She marched off.

He grinned after her, amused he had such a fine view of her backside as she stalked through the door of the bath he shared with Iona.

He'd come to his senses, he thought—though it had taken most of his life to get there. He could wait for her to come to hers.

Meanwhile . . . He studied his healed palm. He had some thinking to do.

16

WOMEN WERE A CONSTANT PUZZLE TO CONNOR'S mind, but their mysteries and secret ways accounted for some of their unending appeal to him.

He considered the woman he loved. Courageous and straightforward as they came on all matters—except those of the heart. And there she turned as fearful as a trapped bird, and just as likely to fly off and away given the smallest opening.

And yet that heart held strong and loyal and true.

A puzzle.

He'd spooked her, no question of that, with his declaration of feelings. He loved her, and for him true love came once and lasted forever.

Still, as he'd rather see her fly free—for now—than batter herself against the cage, he roused Boyle.

Having Boyle go into the stables with Meara—earlier than either needed to be—accomplished two things. She'd have his friend with her, and the three would have some time to talk alone.

Rain blew across the trees and hills, shivered against the windows. He let the dog out, walked out himself, circling the cottage—as they'd done the night before—checking to be certain no remnants of Cabhan's spell remained.

His sister's flowers bloomed, bold, defiant colors against the gloom with the grass beyond them a thick green blanket. And all he felt in the air was the rain, was the wind, was the strong, clear magicks he'd helped light himself in a ring around what was theirs.

When he paused at Roibeard's lean-to, the hawk greeted him with a light rub of his head to Connor's cheek. That was love, simple and easy.

"You'll keep an eye out, won't you?" Connor skimmed the back of his knuckle down the hawk's breast. "Sure you will. Take some time for yourself now, and have a hunt with Merlin, for we're all safe for the moment."

In answer, the hawk spread his wings, lifted. He circled once, then soared to the woods, and into them.

Connor walked around again, went in through the kitchen door—holding it open as Kathel came up behind him.

"Done your patrol, have you then? And so have I." He gave the dog a long stroke, a rub along the ears. "I don't suppose you'd go up and give our Branna a nudge to get me out of making breakfast?"

Kathel simply gave him a look as dry as any hound could manage.

"I didn't think so, but I had to try it."

Accepting his fate, Connor fed the dog, freshened the water in the bowl. He lit the fires, in the kitchen, in the living room, even in the workshop, then had to calculate he could stall no more, and got down to it.

He set bacon sizzling, sliced up some bread, beat up eggs.

He was just pouring the eggs into the pan when Iona and Branna came in together—Iona dressed for work, Branna still in her sleep clothes with that before-my-coffee scowl in her eyes.

"Everyone's up so early." Knowing the rules, Iona let Branna get to the coffee first. "And Boyle and Meara already gone."

"She wanted to change, and promised Boyle she'd fix him some breakfast for taking her around."

"Mind those eggs, Connor, you'll scorch them," Branna said, as she did whenever he made breakfast.

"I won't."

"Why is it you have to turn up the flame to hellfire to cook every bloody thing?"

"It's faster is why."

And damn it, he nearly did scorch them because she'd distracted him.

He dumped them on a plate with the bacon, tossed on some toast, then plopped it all in the middle of the table. "If you'd stirred yourself sooner, you could've made them to your liking. Now you'll eat them from mine, and you're welcome."

"It looks great," Iona said brightly, and finger combing her cap of bright hair, sat.

"Ah, don't pander to him just because he's made a meal, and for the first time in weeks." Branna sat with her, gave Kathel's ears a scratch.

"It's not pandering if you're hungry." Iona filled her plate. "We're going to get cancellations today." She nodded toward the steady, soaking rain. "Not only rain, but a cold one, too. Normally I'd be sorry about that, but today I think we could all use the extra time."

She sampled some eggs. They were very . . . firm, she decided.

"If it's as slow as I think it may be," she continued, "I can probably get off early. I can come work with you, Branna, if you want."

"I've some stock to finish up as I didn't work on it yesterday. I'll need to get it done and run it into the shop. But I'll be here by noon,

I'd think. Fin and I've finished the changes to the potion we used on the solstice. It's stronger than it was, but the spell needs work, as does the timing, and the whole bloody plan."

"We've got time."

"The days click by. And he's growing bolder and bolder. What he tried last night—"

"Didn't work, did it now?" Connor countered. "What are his devil bats now but ash blown by the wind, washed by the rain? And it gave me a notion or two, the whole business of it."

"You've a notion, have you?" Branna lifted her coffee.

"I have, and a story to tell as well. I looked for Eamon in dreams, and he for me. So we found each other."

"You saw him again."

He nodded at Iona. "I did, and pulled Meara into it with me. He was a man, about eighteen, as he said it had been five years since he'd last seen me. His Brannaugh has two children with a third to come, and Teagan is carrying her first."

"She was pregnant—Teagan," Iona added, "when I saw her, in my own dream."

"I remember, so this would have been for me the same time in their world as it was for you. It was, for me as for you, at Sorcha's cabin."

"You know better than to go there," Branna snapped, "in dreams or no."

"I can't tell you in truth if it was my doing or his, for I promise you I don't know even now. But I knew we were safe there, for that time, or I would have pulled it back. I wouldn't have risked Meara again."

"All right. All right then."

"They'd come home," he continued, and lathered toast with jam, "and that was bittersweet. They know they'll fight Cabhan, and they know they won't win, won't end him, as he's here in our time, our place. I told him we were six, and that one of our six had Cabhan's blood."

"And did that float well?" Branna wondered.

"He knows me." Connor tapped a hand on his heart. "And he trusts me. So in turn, he trusts mine, and Fin is mine. He had the pendant I gave him as well as the amulet we share. I had the little stone he gave me, and when I took it out, it glowed in my palm. You had the right of that, Branna. It has power."

"Well, I wouldn't put it in a sling and play David to Cabhan's Goliath, but it's good to keep it with you."

"So I do. And more, I had the bluebell."

"Teagan's flower," Iona added.

"I planted it, fed it with my blood, with water I drew from the air. And the flowers bloomed there on Sorcha's grave."

"You kept your word." Iona brushed a hand over his arm. "And you gave them something that mattered."

"I told him we'd end it, as I believe we will. And I think I know something that we missed on the solstice. Music," he said, "and the joy of it."

"Music," Iona repeated even as Branna sat back, speculation in her eyes.

"What drew him here last night, so enraged, so bold? Our light, yes, and we'll have that. Ourselves, of course. But we made music, and that's a light of its own."

"A joyful noise," Iona said.

"It is that. It blinds him—with that rage against the joy. Why couldn't it bind him as well?"

"Music. We made music that night last spring, do you remember, Iona? Just you and I and Meara here. I brought out my fiddle, and we played and sang, and he lurked outside, all shadows and fog. Drawn to it," Branna said, "drawn to the music even as he hated it—hated that we had it in us to make it."

"I remember."

"Oh, I can work with this." Branna's eyes narrowed, her lips curved. "Aye, this will be something to stir into the pot. It's a good thought, Connor."

"It's brilliant," Iona said.

"I tend to agree with that." Grinning, Connor shoveled in the last of his eggs.

"I'm sure Meara said the same."

"She may, when I tell her. I only came around to it this morning," he added, "and she was in a fired hurry to get on her way."

"Why was that? I've still got nearly a half an hour before I have to get to work." And because she did, Iona rose for a second cup of coffee. "If she'd waited, Boyle and I could've . . . Oh." Her eyes rounded. "Did you have a fight?"

"A fight, no. She went into a fast retreat, as I expected she would, when I told her I loved her. Being Meara, it'll take her a bit of time to settle into it all."

"You figured it out." Dancing back, Iona wrapped her arms around him from behind his chair. "That's wonderful."

"It wasn't a matter of figuring . . . Maybe it was that," he reconsidered. "And she's some slower on coming to the conclusion. She'll be happier when she does, and so will I. But for now, there's a certain enjoyment in watching her try to squirm around it."

"Have a care, Connor," Branna said quietly. "It's not a stubborn nature or a hard head that holds her back. It's scars."

"She can't live her life denying her own heart because her shite of a father had none."

"Have a care," Branna repeated. "Whatever she says, whatever she thinks she believes, she loved him. She loves him still, and that's why the hurt's never gone all the way quiet."

Irritation walked up his spine. "I'm not her father, and she should know me better."

"Oh no, darling, it's that she's afraid she is—she's like her father."

"Bollocks to that."

"Of course." Branna rose, began to clear. "But that's the weight she carries. As much as I love her, and she loves me, I've never been able to lift it away, not altogether. That's for you to do."

"And you will." Iona pushed away from the table again to help. "Because love, if you just don't let go, beats anything."

"I won't be letting go."

Iona paused to kiss the top of his head. "I know it. The eggs were good."

"I wouldn't go as far as that," Branna said, "but we'll do the washing up since you cooked . . . after a fashion."

"That's fine then, as I need to call Roibeard in and get on to work."

He got his jacket from the peg, and a cap while dishes clattered. "I do love her," he said as the words felt so fine, "I love her absolutely."

"Ah, Connor, you great git, so you always have."

He went out into the rain thinking his sister was right. So he always had.

A FOUL MOOD, AN EDGY MANNER, AND A TENDENCY TO snipe equaled an assignment to the manure compost pile.

A filthy day for a filthy job, Meara thought as she changed into her oldest muck boots, switched her jacket for one of the thicker barn coats. But then again she was feeling fairly filthy. And since she couldn't deny she'd picked a fight with Boyle—after snapping at Mick, snarling at Iona, and brooding her way through the rest of the morning—she couldn't blame Boyle for banishing her to shit duty.

But she did in any case.

He'd given her guided to Iona—hardy souls from the midlands who weren't put off by the sodding rain. Mick had a ring lesson, so the sodding rain didn't matter for that, not a bit. Nor did it matter to

Patty, who was cleaning tack, or to Boyle, who'd closed himself off in his office.

So it was left to her to tromp around in the sodding rain, and to the majestic turning of the shit pile.

She wrapped a scarf around her neck, pulled a cap low on her head, and clomped her way out—carting a shovel and a long metal stick—well behind the stables to what was not-so-lovingly referred to as Shite Mountain.

A stable of horses produced plenty for the mountain, and this by-product—if she wanted to use a fancy term—had to be dealt with. And wiser, eco-minded souls did more than deal. They used.

It was a process she approved of, on normal days. On days she wasn't pissed off at the world in general. On days when it wasn't raining fecking buckets.

Manure, properly treated, became compost. And compost enriched soil. So Fin and Boyle had built an area—far enough the odors didn't carry back—to do just that.

When she reached Shite Mountain, she cursed, realizing she left her iPod and earbuds back at the stable. She wouldn't even have music to distract her.

All she could do was mutter as she pulled the old, empty feed bags off the big pile, and began to use the shovel to turn the manure.

Proper compost required heat to kill the seeds, the parasites, to turn manure into a rich additive. It was a job she'd done countless times, so she continued automatically, adding fertilizer to help break down the manure, turning the outer layers into the heart and the heat, making a second pile, adding ventilation by shoving the stick down deep.

At least she didn't have to drag out the hose as the sodding rain added all the water required to the mucky mix.

Mucky mix, she thought, putting her back into it. That's just what Connor had tossed them into.

Why did he have to bring love into it? Love and promises and notions of futures and family and forever? Hadn't it all been going well? Hadn't they been doing fine and well with sex and fun and friendship?

Now he'd said all those words—and said many of them in Irish. A deliberate ploy, she thought as she shoveled and turned and spread. A ploy to twist up her heart. A ploy to make her sigh and surrender.

He'd made her weak—he had, he had—and she didn't know what to do with weakness. Weakness was an enemy, and he'd set that enemy on her. And more, he'd made her afraid.

And she'd started it all, hadn't she? Oh, she only had herself to blame for the situation, for the trouble it was bound to cause all around.

She'd kissed him first, she couldn't deny it. She'd taken him into her bed, changing what they were to each other.

Connor was a romantic—she'd known that as well. But the way the man flitted from woman to woman, she couldn't be blamed entirely for never expecting proclamations of love.

They had enough to deal with, didn't they? The time to All Hallow's Eve grew shorter every day, and if they had a true and solid plan for that, she'd yet to hear it.

Connor's optimism, Branna's determination, Fin's inner rage, Iona's faith. They had all that, and Boyle's loyalty as well as her own.

But those didn't amount to strategy and tactics against dark magicks.

And instead of keeping his brain focused on finding those strategies and tactics, Connor O'Dwyer was busy telling her things like she was the beat of his heart, the love of all his lifetimes.

In Irish. In Irish while he did impossible things to her body.

And hadn't he looked her straight in the eye in the morning, after they woke from that strange dreamworld, and said straight out he loved her?

Grinned at her, she thought now, steaming up. As if turning her world upside down was a fine and funny joke.

She should've knocked him out of bed onto his arse. That's what she should've done.

She'd set things right with him, by God she would. Because she wouldn't be weak, not for him or anyone. She wouldn't be weak and afraid. Wouldn't have her heart twisted up so she made promises she'd only break.

She wouldn't let herself become soft and foolish like her mother. Helpless to care for herself. Shamed and mourning the betrayal dealt like an axe blow by a man.

More—worse—she wouldn't let herself become careless and selfish like her father. A man who would make promises, even keep them as long as his life stayed smooth. Who would heartlessly break them, and the hearts of those who loved him, when the road roughened.

No, she'd be no man's wife, no man's burden, no man's heartbeat. Especially not Connor O'Dwyer's.

Because, God help her, she loved him far too much.

She felt a sob rising up, brutally choked it back.

A temporary thing, she promised herself as she spread the bags over the compost piles again. This kind of burning in the heart couldn't last.

No one could survive it.

She'd be herself again soon, and so would Connor. And all this would be like one of those strange dreams that weren't dreams.

She told herself she was steadier now, that the physical labor had done her good. She'd go back, smooth things over with Mick, especially, and the others as well.

"You've done your penance," she said out loud, stepped back, turned.

And her father smiled at her.

"So here you are, my princess."

"What?"

A bird sang in the mulberry tree, and the roses bloomed like a fairyland. She loved the gardens here, the colors, the scents, the sounds of the birds, the song of the fountain as the water poured into the circling pool from a jug held by a graceful woman.

And loved all the odd corners and shaded bowers where she could hide away from her siblings if she wanted to be alone.

"Lost in dreams again, and didn't hear me calling." He laughed, the big roll of it making her lips curve even as tears stung her eyes.

"You can't be here."

"A man's entitled to take a pretty day off to be with his princess." Smiling still, he tapped the side of his nose with his index finger. "It won't be long before all the lads in the county will start coming around, then you won't have time for your old da."

"I always would."

"That's my darling girl." He took her hand, drew her arm through the crook of his. "My pretty gypsy princess."

"Your hand's so cold."

"You'll warm it up." He began to walk with her, around the stone paths, through the roses and the creamy cups of calla lilies, the aching blue of lobelia with the sun showering down like the inside of a broken pearl.

"I came just to see you," he began, using that confidential voice, adding the sly wink as he did when he had secrets to tell her. "Everyone's in the house."

She glanced toward it, the three fine stories of brick, painted white as her mother had wished. More gardens surrounded the large terrace, then led to a smooth green lawn where her mother liked to have tea parties in good summer weather.

All tiny sandwiches and frosted cakes.

And her room there, Meara thought, looking up. Yes, her room right there, with its French doors and little balcony. A Juliet balcony, he called it.

So she was his princess.

"Why is everyone in the house? It's such a bright day. We should have a picnic! Mrs. Hannigan could make up some bridies, and we can have cheese and bread, and jam tarts."

She started to turn, wanted to run to the house, call everyone out, but he steered her away. "It's not the day for a picnic."

For a moment she thought she heard rain drumming on the ground, and when she looked up, it seemed a shadow passed over the sun.

"What is that? What is it, Da?"

"It's nothing at all. Here you are." He broke a rose from the bush, handed it to her. She sniffed at it, smiled as the soft white petals brushed her cheek.

"If not a picnic, can't we have some tea and cake, like a party, since you're home?"

He shook his head slowly, sadly. "I'm afraid there can be no party."

"Why?"

"None of the others want to see you, Meara. They all know it's your fault."

"My fault? What is? What have I done?"

"You consort and conspire with witches."

He turned, gripping her shoulders hard. Now the shadow moved over his face, had her heart leaping in fear.

"Conspire? Consort?"

"You plot and plan, having truck with devil's spawn. You've lain with one, like a whore."

"But . . ." Her head felt light, dizzy and confused. "No, no, you don't understand."

"More than you. They are damned, Meara, and you with them."

"No." Pleading, she laid her hands on his chest. Cold, cold like his hands. "You can't say that. You can't mean that."

"I can say it. I do mean it. Why do you think I left? It was you, Meara. I left you. A selfish, evil trollop who lusts for power she can never have."

"I'm not!" Shock, like a blow to the belly, staggered her back a step. "I don't!"

"You shamed me so I couldn't look upon your face."

The sobs came now, then a gasp as the white rose in her hand began to bleed.

"That's your own evil," he said when she threw it to the ground. "Destroying all who love you. All who love you will bleed and wither. Or escape, as I did. I left you, shamed and sickened.

"Do you hear your mother weep?" he demanded. "She weeps and weeps to be saddled with a daughter who would choose the devil's children over her own blood. You're to blame."

Tears ran down her cheeks—of shame, of guilt and grief. When she lowered her head, she saw the rose, sinking in a puddle of its own blood.

And rain, she realized, falling fast and hard.

Rain.

She swayed a little, heard the bird singing in the mulberry, and the fountain cheerfully splashing.

"Da . . ."

And the cry of a hawk tore through the air.

Connor, she thought. Connor.

"No. I'm not to blame."

Drenched by the rain, freed by the cry of the hawk, she swung out with the shovel. Though she took him by surprise, he leaped back so it whooshed by his face.

A face no longer her father's.

"Go to hell." She swung again but the ground seemed to heave under her feet. As it did she swore something pierced her heart.

On her sharp cry of pain, Cabhan bared his teeth in a vicious smile. And he spilled into fog.

She managed a shaky step forward, then another. The ground continued to heave, the sky turned and turned over her head.

From a distance, through the rain and the fog, she heard someone calling her name.

One step, she told herself, then another.

She heard the hawk, saw the horse, a gray blur speeding through the mists, and the hound streaking behind him.

She saw Boyle running toward her as if devil dogs snapped at his heels.

And as the world spun and spun, she saw with some amazement Connor leap off Alastar's bare back.

He shouted something, but the roaring in her head muffled the sound.

Shadows, she thought. A world of shadows.

They closed in and swallowed her.

She swam through them, choked on them, drowned in them. She heard her father laugh, but cruelly, so cruelly.

You're to blame, selfish, heartless girl. You have nothing. You are nothing. You feel nothing.

I'll give you power, Cabhan promised, his voice a caress. *It's what you truly want, what you covet and crave. Bring me his blood, and I'll give you power. Take his life, and I'll give you immortality.*

She struggled, tried to claw her way through the shadows, back to the light, but couldn't move. She felt bound, weighed down while the shadows grew thicker, thicker so she drew them in with every breath.

Every breath was colder. Every breath was darker.

Do what he asks, her father urged her. *The witch is nothing to you; you're nothing to him. Just bodies groping in the dark. Kill the witch. Save yourself. I'll come back to you, princess.*

Then Connor reached for her hand. He glowed through the shadows, his eyes green as emeralds.

Come with me now. Come back with me. I need you, aghra. *Come back to me. Take my hand. You've only to take my hand.*

But she couldn't—didn't he see—she couldn't. Something snarled and snapped behind her, but Connor only smiled at her.

Sure you can. My hand, darling. Don't look back now. Just take my hand. Come back with me now.

It hurt, it hurt, to lift that heavy arm, to strain against binding she couldn't see. But there was light in him, and warmth, and she needed both so desperately.

Weeping, she lifted her arm, reached out for his hand. It was like being pulled by her fingertips out of thick mud. Being dragged a centimeter at a time, and painfully, while some opposing force pulled her back.

I've got you, Connor said, his eyes never leaving hers. *I won't let you go.*

Then she felt as if she exploded, a cork out of a bottle, into the clear.

Her chest burned, burned as if her heart had turned into a hot coal. When she tried to draw in air, it seared up into her throat.

"Easy now, easy. Slow breaths. Slow. You're back now. You're safe. You're here. Shh now, shh."

Someone sobbed, wrenching, heartrending. It took her minutes to realize the sounds came from her.

"I've got you. We've got you."

She turned her face into Connor's shoulder—God, God, the scent of him was like cool water after a fire. He lifted her.

"I'm taking her home now."

"My house is closer," she heard Fin say.

"She'll be staying at the cottage until this is finished, but thanks. I'm taking her home now. But will you come? When you can, will you come?"

"You know I will. We all will."

"I'm with you now, Meara." She heard Branna's voice, felt Branna's hand stroke her hair, her cheek. "I'm right here with you."

She wanted to speak, but nothing came out but those terrible, tearing sobs.

"Go with them," Boyle said. "Go with them, Iona. It should be the three with her. I'll see to Alastar. Take the lorry and go with them."

"Come soon."

Meara turned her head enough to see Iona running for Boyle's lorry, climbing behind the wheel. Running through the rain, through the mists while the world rocked back and forth, back and forth like the deck of a ship in a storm.

And the pain in her chest, in her throat, in every part of her burned like the fires of hell.

She wondered if she'd died. If she'd died damned as the father who wasn't her father had said.

"Shh now," Connor said again. "You're alive and you're safe, and you're with us. Rest now, darling. Just rest now."

On his words, she slipped into warm sleep.

17

SHE HEARD VOICES, MURMURING—SOFT, SOOTHING. SHE felt hands, stroking—light, gentle. It seemed she floated on a warm pallet of air with the scents of lavender and candle wax all around. Bathed in light, she knew peace.

Murmuring became words, garbled and indistinct, as if spoken through water.

"It's rest she needs now. Rest and quiet. Let the healing do its work." Branna's voice, so weary.

"She's some color back, doesn't she?" And Connor's, anxious, shaky.

"She does, and her pulse is steady again."

"She's strong, Connor." Now Iona, a bit hoarse as if from sleep or tears. "And so are we."

Then she drifted again, floating, floating into comforting silence.

Waking was like a dream.

She saw Connor sitting beside her, eyes closed, his face illuminated by the glow of the candles all around the room. It was as if he'd been painted in pale, luminous gold.

Her first conscious thought was it was ridiculous for a man to be that handsome.

She started to say his name, but before she could speak it, his eyes opened, looked directly into hers. And she knew by the color, the intensity of the green, more than the candlelight illuminated him.

"There you are." When he smiled the intensity faded, and it was only Connor and candlelight. "Lie still and quiet, just for a moment."

He held his hands over her face, closed his eyes again, as he skimmed them down, over her heart, back again. "That's good. That's fine now."

He removed something from her forehead, her collarbone, leaving the faintest tingle behind.

"What is that?" Was that her voice? That frog croak?

"Healing stones."

"Was I sick?"

"You were, but you're doing well now."

He lifted her a little, removed stones from under her back, under her hands, put them in a pouch and closed it tightly.

"How long was I asleep?"

"Oh, near to six hours now—not long in the grand scheme."

"Six hours? But I was . . . I was . . ."

"Don't look for it yet." His tone, brisk, cheerful, had her frowning. "You'll be a bit foggy yet, and feel weak and shaky. But it'll pass, I promise you. And here, you'll drink this now. Branna left it for you to drink—and all of it—as soon as you woke."

"What is it?"

"What's good for you."

He propped her up on pillows before taking the stopper from a slim bottle filled with red liquid.

"All of that?"

"All." He put the bottle in her hands, cupped his own around them to guide it to her lips. "Slow now, but every drop of it."

She prepared for medicine, and instead sipped the cool and lovely. "It's like liquid apples, blossoms and all."

"That's some of it. All now, darling. You need every drop."

Yes, more color in her cheeks now, Connor thought. And her eyes were heavy, but clear. Not blind and staring as they'd been when she'd succumbed to Cabhan's spell, when she'd lain lifeless on the wet grass.

The image flashed back into his mind, made his hands shake. So he pushed it aside, looked at her now.

"You'll have some food next." It took every ounce of will to keep his voice steady and carve a little cheer into it. "Branna's made up some broth, and we'll see how you do with that and some tea first."

"I think I'm starving, but I can't really tell. I feel I'm only half here. But better. The drink was good."

She handed him back the bottle; he set it aside as carefully as a man placing a bomb.

"Food next." He managed a smile before he laid his lips on her forehead. Then simply couldn't move.

She felt him tremble, reached for his hand. He gripped hers so hard she had to bite back a gasp. "It was bad?"

"It's fine now. All's well now. Oh God."

He pulled her to him, so tight. He'd have pulled her inside him if he could. "It's all right now, it's all fine now," he said over and over, to comfort himself as much as her.

"I don't know how he got past the protection. It wasn't strong enough. I didn't make it strong enough. He took the necklace from you, and I never believed he could. He took it away, and stole your breath. I should've done more. I will do more."

"Cabhan." She couldn't quite remember. "I was . . . turning the manure. The compost. And then . . . I wasn't. I can't see it clear."

"Don't fret." He brushed at her hair, at her cheeks. "It'll come back when you're stronger. I'll make you another necklace, a stronger one. I'll have the others help me, as what I did with the other wasn't enough."

"The necklace." She reached up where it should have hung around her neck. Remembered. "It's in my jacket. I took it off, didn't I?"

As she struggled to remember, Connor slowly eased away.

"You took it off?"

"I was that mad. I took it off, stuffed it in my jacket pocket. I snapped at poor Mick—and everyone else as well, so Boyle . . . Yes, Boyle sent me out to the compost pile. I put on one of the barn coats, left my own jacket behind."

"You weren't wearing it at all? And the pocket charms I made you?"

"In my pocket—in the jacket I left in the stables. I didn't give it a thought because . . . Connor."

He stood abruptly, and in his face she saw only cold rage.

"You took it off, left it behind because I gave it to you."

"No. Yes." It was all such a muddle. "I wasn't thinking properly, don't you see? I was so angry."

"Because I love you, you were angry enough to go out, without protection."

"I wasn't thinking of it that way. I wasn't thinking at all. I was stupid. I was beyond stupid. Connor—"

"Well then, it's done, and you're safe enough now. I'll send Branna up with the broth."

"Connor, don't go. Please, let me—"

"You need the quiet now to finish the healing. I'm not able to be quiet now, so I can't be with you."

He went out, closed the door between them.

She tried to get up, but her legs simply wouldn't hold her. Now she, a woman who'd prided herself on her strength, her health, had to crawl back into bed like an invalid.

She lay back, breath unsteady, skin clammy, and her heart and mind spinning with the consequences of one careless act done in temper.

When Branna came in with a tray she could have wept with frustration.

"Where's he gone?"

"Connor? He needed some air. He's been sitting with you for hours."

Branna arranged the tray—an invalid's tray with feet so it would sit over the lap of the sick and the weak. Meara stared at it with absolute loathing.

"You'll feel stronger after the tea and broth. It's natural to be shaky and weak just now."

"I feel I've been sick half my life." Then she looked up, cleared her own frustrations enough to see the fatigue and worry in Branna's eyes. "I'm poor at it, aren't I? Never been sick more than a few hours. You've seen to that. You always have. I'm so sorry, Branna. I'm so sorry for this."

"Don't be foolish." Eyes weary, hair bundled up messily, Branna sat on the side of the bed. "Here now, have some of the broth. It's the next step."

"In what?"

"Getting back to yourself."

Since she wanted that—she couldn't mend things with Connor when she could barely lift a spoon—she began to eat. The first taste was like ambrosia.

"I thought I was starved, but I couldn't really feel much of anything. It's wonderful to feel hungry, and this is brilliant. I can't piece it all together. I remember it, most of it, clear enough until I started back to the stables, then it goes dim."

"Once you feel yourself again, you'll remember. It's a kind of protection."

"Oh God." Meara squeezed her eyes shut.

"Is there pain? Darling—"

"No, no—not that kind. Branna, I did something so stupid. I was upset, in a black temper so I just couldn't think sensible. Connor—well, he said he loved me. The kind of love that leads to marriage and babies and cottages on the hill, and it just threw me into upheaval altogether. I'm not fit for that sort of thing—everyone knows it."

"No one knows anything of the sort, but I won't argue you think it. You should stay calm, Meara." Branna stroked a hand along Meara's leg. "Rest easy now to help yourself be well again."

"I can't be calm and rest easy when Connor's gone off as mad at me as he's ever been. And worse, even worse."

"Why would he be mad at you?"

"I took it off, Branna." Her fingers rubbed at her throat, where the necklace should be. "I wasn't thinking, I swear. I was just caught up in the temper. So I took off the necklace he gave me and pushed it into my pocket."

The hand stroking to soothe stilled. "The blue chalcedony with the jade and jasper beads?" Branna said carefully.

"Yes, yes. I just shoved it into my pocket, along with the charms. And I was picking fights with everyone within arm's reach until Boyle had enough of me. He sent me out to the compost, and as it's filthy work, and it was raining buckets, I switched my jacket for a barn coat. I didn't think—didn't even remember I'd taken the necklace off, you see. I wouldn't have gone out without it. I swear, even in a mad, I wouldn't have done that purposely."

"You took off what he gave you out of love, what he gave you to protect you, what he loves, from harm. You cut through his heart, Meara."

"Oh, Branna, please." She sobbed in air as Branna rose, walked to the window to stare out at the dark. "Please don't turn me away."

Branna spun back, her own temper bright in her eyes. "That's a cold and cruel thing to say."

All the color dropped out of Meara's cheeks again. "No. No. I—"

"Cold and cruel and selfish. You've been my friend, my sister in all but blood since my first memory. But you could think I'd turn you away?"

"No. I don't know. I'm so confused, so twisted up inside."

"The tears are good for you." Voice brisk now, Branna nodded. "You don't shed them often, and they're good for you now. A kind of purging. There are five people in this house—no, that's not true as Iona and Boyle have gone off now that you're awake to pack up your things for you."

"Pack up my—"

"Quiet. I've not finished. Those five people love you, and not one of us deserves you're thinking we would stop because you've done something hurtful."

"I'm sorry. I'm sorry."

"I know you are. But I'm here, Meara, standing between you and Connor, loving you both. He blamed himself, you see, for not giving you stronger protection."

"I know." Her voice hitched and shook on every word. "He said. I remembered. I told him. He left me."

"He left the *room*, Meara, you idjit. He's Connor O'Dwyer, as good and loyal and true a man as there ever was. He's not your bleeding father or a man anything like him."

"I don't mean . . ." It flooded back, the force and clarity of it leaving her gasping for air.

"Calm. Be calm." Branna rushed to her, gripped her hands, pushed her will against the panic. "You will be calm, and breathe easy. In my eyes, look in my eyes. There's calm, and there's air."

"I remember."

"Calm first. No harm comes here, and no dark. We scried the candles, laid the herbs and stones. Here is sanctuary. Here is calm."

"I remember," she said again, and calmly. "He was there."

"You'll let yourself settle a bit, and as much as I want to know it all, we'll wait until we're all together. You'll only have to tell it once."

And Connor, Branna thought, deserved to hear it all.

"What did he do to me? Can you tell me that? How bad was it?"

"Drink the broth first."

Impatient, and stronger already, Meara just lifted the bowl, drank it down straight. And made Branna laugh a little.

"Now you've done it."

"Tell me— Oh!"

It was like a jolt of electricity, or a good, quick orgasm, or a direct hit by a lightning bolt. Energy shot straight into her, rocking her back.

"What *is* that?"

"Something you're meant to drink slowly, but leave it to you."

"I feel I could sprint all the way to Dublin. Thank you."

"You're welcome. We'll just leave this for later." Cautious now, Branna moved the tea out of reach.

"I could eat a cow and still have room for pudding." But she reached for Branna's hand. "I'm sorry. Truly."

"I know it. Truly."

"Tell me, will you, what he did to me? Was it poison, like Connor?"

"It wasn't, no. You were open and defenseless, and he would know it. He used his shadows, and I think it blocked it all for a time. But they cleared enough, for he can't keep that box, as Connor called it, shut tight for long. The lot of us were coming. He'd have known that as well, so he acted quickly and with cruelty. The spell he cast, you could call it a kind of Sleeping Beauty, but it's not so pretty as a fairy tale. It's a kind of death."

"I . . . He killed me."

"No, it's not so clean. He took your breath; he stopped your heart. It's a kind of paralysis that anyone who didn't know would take for death. Without intervention, it could last for days or weeks. Even years. Then you would wake."

"Like, what, a zombie?"

"You would wake, Meara, and you would be mad. You would claw or dig your way out if you could, or die raving. Or . . . he would come for you, at a time of his own choosing, and make you his creature."

"Then I would be dead," Meara declared. "All that I am would be gone. He couldn't have done this to me if I'd worn the protection Connor gave me."

"No. He could hurt you, he could try to draw you to him, but he couldn't cast such a spell on you when you're protected." She paused a moment. "It was Connor who breathed life back into you. He reached you first. He brought you back—your breath, your heart. Then the rest of us came together as he pulled you out of the sleep. Even in those few minutes, Meara, you'd been drawn deep. You could only sob and sob, and shake. He had to slide you into sleep again, healing sleep, so you could be calm while we worked."

"The candles, the stones, the herbs. The words. I heard you—you and Connor and Iona."

"Fin as well for a bit."

Five people who loved her, Meara thought, all sick and afraid because she'd been foolish.

"He could've broken us, because I was childish."

"That's true enough."

"I'm shamed and sorry, Branna, and so I'll say to all. But if I could speak with Connor first."

"Of course you should."

"Could you help me clean up a bit?" She managed a wobbly smile. "I've been a bit dead, and probably look it."

BECAUSE IT CONTINUED TO RAIN, CONNOR SAT IN BRANNA'S workshop, drinking his second beer and brooding at the fire.

When Fin walked in, he scowled. "You'd be wise to feck off. I'm not fit company."

"That's a pity." Fin dropped into a chair with a beer of his own. "You said she'd waked and was better—but little else. Branna's yet to come back down, and as Iona and Boyle just came in with cases of her things, I'd like to know just what the bloody hell better might be."

"Awake, aware. She drank the potion, and her color was good when I left her."

"All right then." Fin took a sip of beer, waiting for the rest. When it didn't come, he prepared to pry the lid off, then Boyle came in.

And better yet.

"I hauled clothes and boots and Christ knows, enough for a month or more that Iona swears is all essential. Then I was dismissed, which is just fine with me."

He dropped down, as Fin had, with a beer.

"Branna said she'd rallied well, and was having a shower. A hell of a thing, a scare like that. A hell of a thing." He drank deep from the beer. "I sent her out there. She was snappish and snarly, and I'd had enough of it, and sent her off to Shite Mountain. I should've kept her inside, working on tack. I shouldn't have—"

"It's not your fault." Connor shoved up, paced around. "Don't take any kind of blame on this, for it's not yours. She took it off. I told her I loved her. And to think I was entertained at the way she stormed about after, claiming she had to get to the stables straightaway."

"So, that's why I lost a full hour's sleep this morning. And," Boyle added, "that's what crawled up her arse like a scorpion."

"She took what off?" Fin asked, circling back.

"The necklace, the blue chalcedony with jasper and jade I gave her for protection. She took it off, went out without it, because I told her I loved her."

"Ah, God." Fin rolled his eyes heavenward. "Women. Women drive men to madness, and is there any doubt as to why? Why, the question should be, do we want them about when they devil us at every turn?"

"Speak for your own women," Boyle suggested. "I'm more than fine with my own."

"Give it time," Fin said darkly.

"Ah, feck off. She was in a temper," Boyle added, watching Connor. "It was foolish and reckless, but, well, as someone who's a temper of his own, it's the easiest thing in the world to do the foolish and reckless when caught up in one."

"We could have lost her."

"That will never happen," Fin vowed.

"She was gone, for moments—that might as well have been years for me." It shook Connor, belly deep, to think it. To know it. "You saw it yourself, Boyle, as you reached her seconds after I did."

"And in those seconds it felt as if the blood drained out of my body. I wanted to start CPR, and you tossed me back with a flick of your hand."

"I'm sorry for that."

"No need. You knew what needed to be done, and I was in the way. You breathed light into her. I've never seen the like."

Seeing it again, Boyle took a breath of his own.

"You're straddling our girl on the ground, calling out for gods and goddesses, and your eyes, I swear to you, went near to black. And the wind's whirling, the others come running, and you lifted your arms up, like a man grabbing on to a lifeline. And you pulled light out of the rain, pulled it out of the rain, into yourself so you burned like a torch. Then you breathed it into her. Three times you did that, burning hotter every time so I near expected you to go to flame."

"Three times is needed," Fin said. "With fire and light."

"And I saw her draw in air. Her hand moved, just a bit in mine." Boyle took another long drink. "Christ."

"I owe you all," Meara said from the doorway. She stood with her hands clasped, her hair loose, and her eyes filled with emotion. "I have to ask if I could have a moment alone to speak to Connor. Just a few moments, if you wouldn't mind."

"Of course not." Boyle got up quickly, moved to her, hugged her hard. "You look fine." Drawing back, he gave her back a hearty pat, then walked straight out.

Fin got up more slowly, studying the tears swirling in her eyes. He said nothing at all, but kissed her lightly on the cheek before going out.

Connor stood where he was. "Did Branna give you leave to be up and about?"

"She did. Connor—"

"It's best if you tell what happened to all, at one time."

"I will. Connor, please, forgive me. You have to forgive me. I couldn't bear it if you didn't, couldn't bear knowing I ruined it all. I was wrong, in every way wrong, and I'll do anything, anything you need or want or ask to mend this with you."

Her shame, her sorrow poured out, all but pooled at his feet. And still he couldn't bring himself to move toward her.

"Then answer me one question with truth."

"I won't lie to you, whatever the truth costs. I never have lied to you."

"Did you take off what I gave you because you thought I might have used it to hold you, to keep you with me, to make you feel for me?"

Shock ripped through the sorrow, pushed her one stumbling step back. "Oh no, God no. You would never do such a thing. I would never think any such thing, never of you. Never, Connor, on my life."

"All right." That, at least that, stanched the worst of a bleeding heart. "Be calm again."

"It was temper," she said, "temper and . . . fear. Honest, be honest," she ordered herself. "Fear more than anything, and that sparked the temper, and together the roar of it made me blind and deaf to any sort of sense. I swear to you, I *swear* I never meant to go out without it. I forgot. I was so turned around and wound up, that when Boyle booted me out, I changed jackets without a thought I'd left all the protection in the other."

She had to stop, press her fingers to her eyes. "Read me. Go in here—" She moved her fingers to her temple. "Read my thoughts, for you'd find the truth."

"I believe you. I know when I hear the truth."

"But will you forgive me?"

Was it as hard for her to ask, he wondered, as for him to accept? He thought perhaps it was. And still they needed to clear it all before the answers.

"I gave you something that mattered to me because you mattered."

"And I was careless with it, and with you. Careless enough to cost us all." She took a step toward him. "Forgive me."

"I give you love, Meara, of the kind I've never given to another. But you don't want it."

"I don't know what to do with it, and that's a different thing. And I'm afraid." She pressed both hands to her heart. "I'm afraid because I can't stop what's happening in me. If you don't forgive me, if you can't forgive me, I think something inside me would die of grief."

"I forgive you, of course."

"You're more than I deserve."

"Ah, Meara." He sighed it. "Love isn't a prize given on merit, or something to be taken back when there's a mistake. It's a gift, as much for the giver as the one who's given it. The day you'll take it, hold it, you won't be afraid."

He shook his head before she could speak. "It's enough. You're more weary than you know, and you've still a tale to tell. You should sit, and we'll see what Branna's cooked up as, Jesus, it's been a long time since breakfast."

When he crossed to her, she reached for his hand. "Thank you.

For the light, for the breath, for my life. And thank you, Connor, for the gift."

"Well now, that's a start," he told her, and led her back to the kitchen.

SHE TOLD THE STORY HALTINGLY WHILE SHE DUG INTO THE spaghetti and meatballs—a particular favorite. It seemed she couldn't get enough to eat or drink—though she found even a few sips of wine made her unsteady.

"You'll do better with water tonight," Branna told her.

"I think part of me knew it wasn't real, but it looked and felt and smelled and sounded so real. The gardens, the fountain, the paths, just as I remember them. The house, the suit my father wore, the way he tapped his finger to the side of his nose."

"Because he built the spell on your thoughts and images." Fin poured her more water.

"The way he called me princess." Meara nodded. "And how it could make me feel like one when he paid special attention to me. He was . . ."

It pained her to speak of it. "He was the fun in our home, you see. His big laugh, and how he'd slip us extra pocket money or a bit of chocolate like it was a secret shared. I worshiped him, and that all came back, those feelings, as we walked around the garden with a bird singing in the mulberry tree."

She had to stop a moment, gather herself. "I worshiped him," she repeated, "and he left us—left me—with never a backward glance. Sneaking off like a thief, and indeed it turned out he was just that, as he took everything of value he could with him. But there, in the gardens, it was all as it had been before. The sun shining, and the flowers, and feeling so happy.

"Then he turned on me, so quickly. He'd left because of me, he said, because I was friends with you. I'd shamed him by consorting, conspiring—he used those words—with witches. I was damned for it."

"A trick, using some of your thoughts again," Branna explained, "then twisting them."

"My thoughts? But I never thought he left because we were friends."

"But you've thought, more than once, his leaving was your fault. I don't have to slip into your mind to know it," Connor added.

"I know it's not true. I'm meaning I know he didn't leave because of me."

"And still it can make you doubt yourself." Iona sent her a look of understanding. "Make you wonder, when you're feeling low, what it is about yourself they can't love. I know how it is, and how hard it is to accept someone who should love you absolutely, doesn't. Or not enough. But it wasn't me, and it wasn't you. It was them, the lack in them."

"I know it, but you're right. Sometimes . . . The rose he gave me began to bleed, and he said I was a whore for lying with a witch. But I certainly never had before my father left us. And God, come to it, the man was too much of a coward ever to say such things to anyone's face."

She paused, stared down at her plate. "He was so weak, my father. It's hard admitting you loved something—someone so weak."

"We can't choose our parents," Boyle said, "any more than they can choose us. We all just have to muddle through best we can."

"And loving . . ." Connor paused until she lifted her eyes to his. "It's never something to be ashamed of."

"What I loved was an illusion, as much as what I saw today. But I believed in both, for a while. And with this, today, I felt things change when he said those things to me, those hard things he, for all his flaws, would never have said. I heard the rain again, and I heard Roibeard, and I knew him for a lie. I had the shovel. I hadn't when I walked with him, but now I did again. I swung it at him, swung it at his head, but he was quick. I swung it again, but the world started to turn and rock. And you, Connor, riding up like a demon on Alastar, and Boyle running from the stables, and Kathel and . . . He smiled at me—Cabhan now and nothing like my father."

She saw it clearly now, that cruelly handsome face smiling. "And it felt like something stabbed my heart—so sharp and cold—as he smiled and swirled away in the fog."

"Black lightning," Boyle stated. "That's what it looked like to me, just a flash of it from the stone he wears."

"I didn't see it." Meara lifted her water glass, drained it again. "I tried to walk, but it was like swimming through the mud. I felt sick and dizzy, and I couldn't feel the rain now as the shadows closed so thick.

"I couldn't get out of them, couldn't seem to move, couldn't call out. And there were voices in the shadows. My father's, Cabhan's. Threats, promises. I . . . He said, he would give me power. If I took Connor's life, he'd give me immortality."

She groped for Connor's hand, comforted when he took it. "I couldn't get out, and it all got darker and darker. I couldn't speak or move, as if bound up, and it was so bitter cold. Then you were there, Connor, talking to me, and there was light. You were the light. You told me to take your hand. I didn't know how, but you said to take your hand."

"And you did."

"I didn't think I could, it hurt so. But you kept saying I could. Kept telling me to take your hand and go with you."

She linked fingers with him now, a strong grip.

"When I did, it was like being pulled out of a pit while something fought to drag me back, pulled out and out, and the light, it was blinding. Then I felt the rain again. It hurt, everything, all at once. My body, my heart, my head. The shadows were horrible, but I wanted to go back where I didn't feel the pain."

"Part of it was shock," Branna said. "And what he'd used to take you. Then the abrupt yank back. It's why Connor put you to sleep."

"I owe you all."

"We're a circle," Boyle began. "Nothing's owed."

"No, I do. Owe you for coming for me—and yes, any of us would for the other. And I owe you my apology for being so foolish as to give him the chance to take me. And doing that put us all at risk."

"It's done." Boyle reached over, poked her shoulder.

"It is," Branna agreed. "Now you'll have some tea and quiet up in bed."

"I've slept enough."

"Not nearly enough, but you can take your tea out by the fire until you're ready to go up."

"I'll tuck you up."

Meara frowned at Fin. "I can move my arse from here to there."

"Now then, you're not after an argument after such a fine apology, are you?" He settled it by going around the table, plucking her right out of her chair. "You're a sturdy girl, Meara Quinn."

"Oh, am I now?"

He shot Connor a grin over his shoulder, carted her into the sofa. He gave the fire a little boost with a finger flick, then set her down, pulled the pretty throw over her while she eyed him balefully.

"I hate being tended."

"So do I, like poison. That's why I'm doing it. You deserve a bit of a pinch."

"Go on then, make me feel guiltier than I already do."

"No need for that." He sat down, just above her hip, gave her a brief study. And pulled the blue chalcedony out of his pocket. "I thought you might want this."

"Oh. How did you—"

"It was a quick trip to the stables to fetch your jacket, and this out of the pocket." He dangled it by the band. "Do you want it or no?"

"I do, very much."

He laid it around her neck himself. "Have more of a care with it, and with him."

"I will." She looked up, into his eyes. "I swear it. Thank you. Thank you, Fin."

"You're welcome, and maybe we'll see if there's any cakes to go with that tea."

He started out, glanced back. She held the stones in her palm, stroked them gently with a finger.

Love, he thought. It could make you a fool or a hero. Or both at once.

18

MEARA WOKE IN CONNOR'S BED. ALONE. THREE WHITE candles glowed in clear glass domes on his dresser. Some magickal health thing, she supposed—as the scent of lavender—sprigs of it under the pillow along with more crystals—was likely meant for health and restful sleep.

The last she remembered, as she scanned back, she'd stretched out on the sofa downstairs, tucked in by Fin, waiting for the others to come in for their tea.

She wondered if they had.

It annoyed her she'd dropped off again like a sick child. And annoyed her more to find herself alone in bed.

When she eased out of bed, she found her legs a little wobbly, which added a third annoyance. She'd felt so strong after drinking the broth, found it lowering to realize she wasn't fully recovered.

Someone had changed her into her nightwear, and that was lowering as well.

She walked, a bit drunkenly, into the bath, peered at herself in the mirror over the sink. Well, it was God's holy truth she'd looked better, but she'd looked worse.

She frowned as she saw her toothbrush, the creams she used, other toiletries tucked neatly into a basket on the narrow counter.

They'd moved her in, hadn't they, while she slept. Just packed her up, settled her in without so much as a by-your-leave.

Then she remembered why, and sighed.

She deserved it, and had no ground to stand on. She'd put herself and everyone else at risk, given them hours of worry. No, she wouldn't question the decision; she wouldn't complain.

But she would damn well find Connor.

She cracked open the door leading to Iona's room. If Boyle and Iona had gone to Boyle's, as they did most nights now, Connor would be using this room. Though he should be using his own, with her.

Rain pattered, and without even a hint of moonlight she waited for her eyes to adjust to the dark before she tiptoed into the room. She heard breathing, moved closer. She had a mind to just crawl right in with Connor, and they'd see what he had to say about it.

Then as she leaned over the bed for a closer look, she clearly saw Iona, tucked up with Boyle, her head on his shoulder.

A sweet picture, she thought—and a private one. But before she could back away, Iona whispered, "Are you feeling sick?"

"Oh, no, no, I'm sorry." Meara hissed it out. "So sorry. I woke, and I came in looking for Connor. I didn't mean to wake you."

"It's all right. He's on the sofa downstairs. Do you need anything? I can make you some tea to help you sleep again."

"I feel like I've slept a week."

"And some of us haven't slept through one bloody night," Boyle muttered. "Go away, Meara."

"I'm going. I'm sorry."

She went out through the hall door, heard the rumble of Boyle's voice, the murmur of Iona's laugh before she shut it behind her.

Fine for them, she thought, all curled up warm together, and here she was sneaking around in the middle of the night trying to find her man.

She was halfway down the steps before it struck her.

Her man? When had she started thinking of Connor as "her man"? She was fuddled up, that was all, just fuddled up from magicks dark and light. She wasn't thinking any way at all, not clearly, and should probably go straight back up to bed.

Sleep it all off.

But she wanted him, that was the hell of it. She wanted her head resting on his shoulder as Iona's was on Boyle's.

She made her way down.

He'd wrapped himself up in the throw on the sofa that was too short for him so his feet ended up propped on the arm of it, and his face half smashed into the pillow angled on the other arm.

The only way a man could be near to comfortable under the circumstances would be by drinking himself unconscious first. She shook her head, set her hands on her hips, and wondered how he managed to look so fecking adorable, considering.

They'd banked the fire so it burned low with simmering coals red as a beating heart. The light flickered over him, adding a bit of the devil to the adorable.

Regardless, she had some words to say to him, and he was about to hear them.

She started forward, eyes on his face, and tripped over the boots he'd tossed aside.

She landed on him, hard and full, getting an elbow in the belly for her trouble. So the first word she said to him was *oof*.

And his response was a muttered, "What the fuck!" as he levered up, grabbed her shoulders as if prepared to give her a good toss. Then he said, "Meara?" and pushed the hair out of her face.

"I tripped over your gigantic boots and into your bony elbow."

"You may have collapsed one of my lungs. Here." He shifted her, managed to sit with her half sprawled over his lap.

It was far from the way she'd intended things to go.

"Are you feeling sick then?"

Even as he lifted a hand to her brow as if to check for fever, she batted it aside. "Why is everyone thinking I'm sick? I'm not sick. I woke, that's all there is to it. I woke as I've slept most of a day and half a night away."

"You needed to," he said, altogether reasonable. "Do you want some tea?"

"I can see to my own tea if I'm in the mood for bloody tea."

"Sure you're in some mood or the other."

Tears wanted to fight their way through the annoyance, and she wouldn't have it. "You said you'd forgiven me."

"I did. I have. Here now, you're cold."

She batted again as he started to wrap the throw around her. "Leave off, will you leave off fussing over me." Those insistent tears kept pushing up, shocking, shaming, stupefying her. "Just leave off."

She tried to push away, roll up and off, but he wrapped his arms around her, held her in, held her tight. "Just calm yourself down, Meara Quinn. Be still a moment. Be quiet a moment."

The effort of trying to pull away exhausted her, left her out of breath and ever closer to tears. "All right, I'm calm."

"Not yet, but in a moment. Take a breath or two." He rocked her gently, looked toward the fire, boosted the flames.

"Don't tend to me, Connor. It makes me want to blubber."

"Blubber away then. It's all reaction, Meara, all natural from what was done to you, and what needed to be done to counter it."

"When will it stop?"

"It's less than it was, isn't it now? And will be even less in the morning with more calm, more rest. Have a bit of patience."

"I hate patience."

He laughed, brushed his lips over her hair. "That I know, but you have it. I've seen it myself."

But she had to dig and dig deep for it, Meara thought. Connor simply owned it, like the color of his eyes, the timbre of his voice.

"I don't hate your patience," she murmured.

"That's good to know as it would be a hard thing to rid myself of it to please you. Tell me now, did something wake you, or did you wake natural?"

"I just waked, and you weren't there." She heard it, the petulance in her voice. She could only hope that was part of the reaction as well, or else she'd learn to hate herself before much longer.

"If you forgive me, why are you sleeping down here with your feet hanging over the end of the sofa?"

"You needed quiet and rest, that's all." Because he trusted her calm now, he managed to shift them both so they wedged together in the corner of the sofa, looking toward the fire. "You were asleep before we brought out the tea, and never stirred when I carried you up, and Branna got you in your nightclothes. It's healing, darling, the sleep's a healing thing, and your mind and body, even your spirit took what it needed."

"I thought you didn't want to be with me, and I hunted you down to fight about it."

"Then I'm glad you tripped over my boots as this is nicer than a fight."

"I'm sorry."

"There's no need to keep being sorry." He traced a finger over the stones around her neck.

"Fin went to the stables and got it for me."

"I know."

"I won't take it off again."

"I know."

Trust, patience, forgiveness. No, she didn't deserve him, she thought, and pressed her face to his throat. "I hurt you."

"You did, yes."

"How do you love so easy, Connor? So free and easy. I don't mean how it always was with us, or how it is for you with Branna."

"Well, I'm new with it myself, so I don't know for certain. I can say it was like holding something you've had so long and is just another part of you. Then tilting that something a little. You know how you hold a piece of glass, then change the angle just a bit, and it catches the sun, makes that beam? You can kindle a fire that way, just tilting the glass. Something like that, and what was already there tipped and caught all the light."

"It could tip another way, and lose it again."

"Why would it when the light's so lovely? Do you see the fire there?"

"I do, of course."

"All it takes is a bit of tending, a stir, more fuel, and it'll burn day and night and night and day, give you light and warmth."

"You could forget to stir it, or run out of fuel."

Laughing, he nuzzled at her neck. "Then you'd be careless, and shame on you for it. Love needs tending, is what I'm saying. It's some work to keep the light and the warmth, but why would you want to be cold in the dark?"

"No one would want to, but it's easy to forget to tend things."

"I expect sometimes both tend, and other times one may tend more as the other forgets for a bit, then it might shift over again."

It was all a matter of balance, he thought, with some care and effort tossed in.

"What's easy isn't always what's right, and it may take a reminder here and there. Over it all, Meara, I've never known you to just settle on the easy. You've never been afraid of the work."

"What I can lift or carry or clean or put my back into, no. But emotional work is another matter."

"I haven't seen you shirk on that area either. You don't credit yourself near enough. Friendships take tending as well, don't they? How have you managed to remain such good, strong friends, not only with me, but Branna, Boyle, Fin, now Iona? Then there's family," he said before she could comment. "And families take considerable tending. You've done more than many would for yours."

"Yes, but—"

"And grumbling about it doesn't matter," he said, anticipating her. "It's the doing that counts at the end of the day."

He kissed her between the eyes. "Trust yourself."

"That's the hard part."

"Well then, practice. You didn't learn how to ride a horse by standing back and wondering if you might fall off."

"I've never in my life fallen off a horse."

"There, you see my point in it all."

It was her turn to smile. "Aren't you the clever one?"

"That makes you the lucky one, to have such a clever man in love with you. With patience enough to let you practice until you catch up."

"It makes my heart shake when you say it," she admitted. "It makes me so afraid when you say it to me my heart shakes."

"Then you'll tell me when it stops shaking and grows warm instead. Now try to sleep again."

"Here?"

"Here's where we are, and we're cozy, aren't we? And the fire's nice. Do you see the stories in the fire?"

"I see the fire."

"There're stories in the embers, in the flames. I'll tell you one."

He spoke of a castle on a hill, and a brave knight on a white stallion. Of a warrior queen skilled with bow and sword who rode the sky on a golden dragon.

All so fanciful, she thought, and so pretty she nearly saw what he drew with his words.

And she drifted off to sleep again with a smile on her face, and her head pillowed on his shoulder.

IT TOOK THREE DAYS BEFORE SHE WAS ABLE TO BE UP AND awake more than down and asleep. She spent the whole of the first day in bed, on the sofa, or doing what small chores Branna would assign her. But by the second, she felt able to return to the stables for part of the day, help with grooming, feeding.

And made her apologies to her coworkers.

By the third, she'd found Meara again.

It felt so good she sang as she shoveled shit.

"Look at you, giving Adele a run for her money."

"The woman's got a brilliant throat." Meara paused, smiled back at Iona who leaned on the open stall door. "Sure I never really understood that saying about how at least you have your health. Never really sick a day in my life. A strong constitution and a best friend who's a witch with exceptional healing powers saw to that. Now that I've been down, I'm learning to give thanks for being up again."

"You look great."

"And feel even better."

Meara wheeled the barrow out of the stall, and Iona stepped in to sweep it out. With their changed positions, Meara glanced right, left, to be certain they were alone.

"Since I'm better, will you tell me how bad it all was?"

"You don't remember? You had all the details before, once you came out of it."

"No, I remember. What I'm meaning is how bad was it, Iona? How close did he come to destroying me? I didn't feel right asking Branna or Connor before," she added when Iona hesitated. "But I'm on my feet now, and I'm asking you. Knowing the whole of it's the last of the healing I think I'll need."

"It was very bad. I've never dealt with anything like that before. Well, I don't think the others had either, but they knew more about it. The first moments, from what Branna told me, were critical. The deeper you went under, the harder it would be to bring you back, and the more likely . . . there could have been a kind of brain damage."

"A madness."

"Of a kind, I think. And memory loss, a psychosis. Branna said Connor reaching you so quickly made all the difference."

"So he saved my life, and my sanity as well."

"Yes. After that, the next hour or two were critical points. Branna knew just what to do, or she bluffed really well while barking out orders to Connor and me. I didn't realize how scared I was until we were finished; it was all just do, and do now. Then Fin came and having him added to it. And Boyle. He sat, held your hand right through the ritual. It took over an hour, and you were so white and pale and still. Then your color started to come back, not much, but a little."

"I'm making you cry. I don't mean to make you cry."

"No, it's okay." Iona dashed the tears away, and together they cut the binding on the fresh bale. "Your color came back, and Boyle said he felt your fingers move in his. And that's when I realized how scared I'd been—when the worst, according to Branna, was over."

"He put me down hard," Meara said as she loosened the straw with a pitchfork. "That's a tick in his column."

"Maybe, but we brought you back, and here you are spreading fresh straw for Spud's stall. That's a bigger tick in ours."

The silver lining, Meara mused. Iona could always find one. And maybe it was time she started searching them out herself.

"I'm after keeping it that way. I'll be putting in some time with my sword. I need the practice."

Needed practice, she thought as they moved to the next stall, on many things.

CONNOR DID SOME CLEANING OF HIS OWN, BUT WHAT HE considered end-of-the-day work. Birds must be fed, and as with horses, their area cleaned regularly of droppings. According to his personal calendar it was time for the hawks' bath to be cleaned and sanitized.

He wanted the labor. He'd needed the sheer physicality and mindless rote of it the last day or so while Meara recovered. It took effort to maintain his own calm, for her sake, to add some cheer to keep her spirits up when she'd been weakened and tired, and so unlike herself.

With some women you brought flowers or chocolate. With Meara—not that some blossoms and candy were out of place—she did better with bits and pieces of village gossip, or tales of work, of the people who'd come by the schools or stables.

He'd done his best to supply her, to prop his boots up, lift a pint and regale her with stories—some of which he embellished, others he made up of whole cloth.

And what he'd wanted to do was hunt Cabhan down, to dare the bastard to show himself. He wanted to whip a wind so fierce it would rend his bones and freeze his blood.

The thirst for vengeance ran so strong he was constantly parched.

And knew better, Jesus, knew better, he thought as he scrubbed the tub while the birds perched and watched him. But knowing and feeling weren't the same thing at all. He could hope that the labor burned the thirst out of him.

Then he saw her, walking across the wide gravel yard. He left everything, went out and through to meet her.

"What are you doing walking about alone?" he demanded.

"I could ask the same of you, but as I know what you'll say to that I won't and avoid it all. Iona and Boyle dropped me off before they went to Cong for a pint and a meal, so I haven't been alone at all, as I'm not now."

She glanced around. "You're late at this, aren't you, Connor? Where's everyone else?"

"We finished up the last hawk walk, and I sent the lot of them on. Brian had some studying for this online class he's taking, and Kyra had herself a hot date. And for the rest, I thought they could use an extra hour free."

"And you wanted some time alone with your friends," she added with a nod toward the hawks.

"There was that as well. I have to finish up here, since I've started it all."

"I'll come back with you, if that's all right. Then you'll give me a lift back to the cottage."

He walked her back. The birds ruffled a bit at the visitor, gave her a long stare.

"I haven't had time to visit much in the last months," she commented. "The young ones don't know me, or not well."

"They'll come to." He got back down to finish the cleaning. "How'd the day all go for you then?"

"Just as it should. I took out two guideds." She angled her head at his sharp look, pulled out the stones she wore from under her scarf. "And Iona insisted I take Alastar—*and* she braided fresh charms in his mane. I saw nothing but the woods and the trail. I won't be reckless, Connor. For my own sake, yes, but also because I never want to put you or the others through what I put you through once already."

She paused a moment. “I need the work and the horses as you need the work and the hawks.”

“You’re right. I hope he felt you. I hope he felt how strong and able you are, despite him.”

He began to fill the tub, listened to the water pour.

“You think I don’t know you’re angry,” she said quietly. “But I do know it. I’m angry as well. I’ve wanted to end him, always, because it’s needed, because of you and Branna and Fin. But now I don’t only want to end him—I want to give him pain and misery first, to *know* he suffers. I don’t tell Branna as she’d never approve. For her it’s only about right and wrong, light and dark—birthright and blood. And I know that’s how it should be, but I want his pain.”

From his crouch, he looked up at her. “I would give it to you, and more. I would give you his agony.”

“But we can’t.” Hunkering down beside him, she touched his arm lightly. “Because Branna’s got the right of it, and because it would change you. To seek revenge only? To seek to cause pain and suffering to pay him back for what he did to me? It would change you, Connor. I think it wouldn’t change me, but that’s the lack in me.”

“It’s not a lack at all.”

“It’s how I’m built, so we’ll all have to live with it. But you’re the light, and there’s reason for that. End him, it must be done. But it must be done as it should be done. And if there’s pain, it’s because it had to be, not because you willed it.”

“You’ve done some thinking on this.”

He measured out the additives, then as he always did, stirred the water with his hands over the surface, adding that light she spoke of, for the health and well-being of his birds.

“God, yes, and far too much on it. And in thinking far too much on it, I came to understand you needed to know I felt as you do, but it isn’t what I want from you, or for myself. I want what we are, the six of us. I want us to be right. And when we end him, and it’s done, for us to know we were right. I want no shadows over us, no shadows over you. That's revenge enough for me."

"I love you, Meara. I love that you'd understand this, come clear to it, and tell me. I've been torn, in a way I've never been."

"Don't be. Know I'm telling you what's in my heart. I want us to be right."

"Then we will be."

Satisfied, relieved, she nodded. "And it's time to talk of it all again. I know you've all let it go the last few days."

"You weren't up to it."

"I'm more than up to it now." She pushed up, flexed her biceps to make him smile. "So we'll talk again, the six of us."

"Tonight?"

"Tonight, tomorrow night if need be. We'll see what the others say."

"I'll finish up then." He looked at her, smiled.

For some women it was flowers, he thought, or chocolate.

For Meara?

"Hold your arms out."

"What? Why would I?"

"Because I ask you. Hold your arms out."

She rolled her eyes, but did as he asked. He stretched his hands toward the birds, the young ones, sent his thoughts to them.

With the flow of his hands, they lifted, a soft whoosh of wings—the young hawks—and rose up to circle her, to make her laugh.

"Hold still, and don't worry about your jacket or your skin, I've taken that in the measure."

"What— Oh!"

They landed light and graceful along her outstretched arms.

"We've trained them well, though this isn't in their lessons. Still they don't seem to mind it. And they'll know you, Meara, now they will."

"They're beautiful. They're so beautiful. When you look in their eyes you think they know more than we do. So much more."

She laughed, and at the sound of it, the terrible thirst that had dogged him for days finally eased.

19

THEY HAD TEA, WITH WHISKEY FOR THOSE WHO WANTED it, in the living room of the cottage. Branna set out a plate of gingerbread biscuits and considered her domestic duties done.

"Where do we begin?" she wondered. "Do we still agree on Samhain?"

"It gives us a fortnight," Boyle pointed out. "And from what I can see we could use the time. But . . ."

"But." Fin opted for whiskey and poured himself two fingers, neat. "He's come at us hard. We weren't ready for him, and that's clear enough."

"It was my fault."

"Fault isn't the point of it, Meara," Fin interrupted. "He lurks and slithers about at his will, and could come at any one of us in a moment of vulnerability. He's been at Iona, and now at you. From the pattern of it, if we don't end this, he'll go at Branna next."

"Let him come." Branna calmly took a sip of tea.

"You're far too cocksure of yourself," Fin snapped back. "Arrogance isn't power or a weapon."

"You've never had trouble wrapping yourself in it good and tight."

"Stop." Connor stretched his legs out, shook his head. "The pair of you. Save the pokes and barbs for when we've time for them. He may well go at Meara again, but she won't be foolish a second time."

"My oath on that."

"And it's just as likely he could take a pass at Boyle, or Fin or myself if he saw an opportunity."

Risking having an accusation of arrogance tossed at him, Connor shrugged. "And though I think Fin's right, if he tires of going for Meara, he'll turn his attentions on Branna, knowing that doesn't speak to what we do, when we do it, and how we send him on to hell for all and done."

"He's right. Protecting ourselves, that's defense—and it's essential," Iona added. "But it's our offense that needs to be perfected."

"She's been watching matches with me." Boyle gave her a quick grin. "We were close the last we went for him, sent him off bleeding and howling. But it wasn't enough. What will be?"

"The potion's stronger than it was, and that makes it a risk. One we'll have to take." Fin flicked a glance at Branna, got her nod.

"We thought to take him by surprise on the solstice," Connor pointed out, "and he took us. Even then, as Boyle said, we got close to it. If we make our stand at Sorcha's cabin, he'll have the advantage of shifting the time, and we couldn't know when he'd take us, or if he could, as he did, manage to separate us so we'd end up scattered, using power to reform again."

"If not there," Meara asked, "where?"

"It's a place of power, for us as well as him. I think it must be there. But you're right, Connor," Branna added. "We can't be separated. I'm thinking the three as a unit, and Fin, Boyle, and Meara as another—and those joined in a way that can't be broken. This we can do—and this we *will* do this time."

"Can we block him from the time shift?" Iona wondered.

"We could, I think, if we knew how he does it. But to counter such a spell, we'd need the elements of it. It's working blind there," Branna said in frustration.

"We shift first." Connor leaned forward, took a biscuit. "You're not the only one who can study and ponder and plot." He gestured toward Branna with the biscuit, then bit in. "But you're the only one who can make such brilliant gingerbread. We take the offensive, and shift from the start."

"And how, scholar, should we find the way to do that—which will take considerable doing—would we lure him to when we are?"

"We know the way to do it already," he reminded his sister. "Iona did it herself when she'd no more than gotten her toe dipped in her own magickal waters."

"I did?" After a blink, Iona pumped her fist in the air. "Go, me."

"I've done it myself," he added, "alone and with Meara, and met our long-ago cousins."

"Dream travel?" Branna put down her teacup. "Oh, Connor, that's a reckless thing."

"It's reckless times, and we'd have to be smart about it."

"It's bloody brilliant," Fin said, and earned Connor's grin, Branna's scowl.

"He's talking of casting a dream net over the six of us at once."

"I know it. That's what's bloody brilliant. He'd have to be on the same level, wouldn't he, to come at us? And it would be in the time and place of our choosing."

"He couldn't turn it on us," Connor pointed out, "as he wouldn't know the elements of the spell we cast, any more than we know the elements of his. It's him who'd have to come to us, and he'd lose the power to shift our ground."

"Give me a moment." Boyle lifted a hand, then used it to scratch his head. "Are you saying we'd go against Cabhan in our sleep?"

"A dream spell's different from natural sleep. It's not like you're lying there snoring them off. You've done a bit of it yourself," Connor recalled. "Pulled in with Iona into her dream—and didn't you give the bastard a good punch in the face while you were at it?"

"I did, and woke with his blood on my knuckles. But a dream battle? I've accepted all the lot of you can do as I've lived with it most of my life, but this strains the tether."

"He'd never expect it," Meara speculated. "Can it really be done?"

"All six at once, and with no one left behind at the wheel you could say." Struggling to look at the pros, the cons, the balance of them, Branna shoved both hands through her hair. "Sure it's nothing I've ever done. I'd be easy trying it with the three, facing him off that way, and the three of you back here—Fin at that wheel for certain to steer us back should we lose balance or direction."

"It's the six of us," Meara said decisively, "or not at all."

"Meara, I'm not talking this through in the way of insulting you. Any of you. But dream casting six together, and two of them without powers."

"Not so cocksure now?" Fin asked, with just a little bite.

"Oh, feck off," Branna snapped.

"And back at you, darling, for suggesting that I or Boyle or Meara would stay back like obedient pups while you waged the war."

"That's not my meaning."

"It's how it feels." Meara turned to Connor. "And you?"

"The six of us," he said without hesitation, "or none at all."

"All or none," Boyle agreed.

"Yes." Nodding, Iona took his hand. "If anyone can work out how it can be done, Branna, it's you."

"Ah, Jesus, bloody hell, let me think." She shoved the teacup aside, poured whiskey—more generously than Fin had.

She tossed it back like water.

"I've always admired your head for whiskey," Fin said as she shoved to her feet to pace.

"Be quiet. Just be quiet. Six at once," she repeated as she paced, "in the name of Morrigan, it's madness. And two of them armed with nothing but wit and fist and sword for all that. And one of them bearing Cabhan's mark. Just shut up about it," she snapped at Fin, who'd said nothing at all, "it's fact."

"They're armed with more than wit and fist and sword, and have more than a mark unearned." Connor spoke quietly. "They have heart."

"Do you think I don't know it? Do you think I don't value it, above all?" She stopped, closed her eyes a moment. Sighed. "You've turned this upside down on me, Connor. I need to work my way through it. It's not like one of us going into a magickal dream and taking along the one lying with us, the one we've been intimate with. And that has its own risks, as both Boyle and Iona know well."

"It's not, no. This would be a deliberate and conscious thing, a planned thing, a casting of our own." Connor lifted his hands, spread them, palms up. "With as many protections as we can build into the spell. But there'll be risks, yes, but risks however we go about it. And on Samhain, when the Veil thins, is the perfect time for this."

He rose, went to her, took her hands. "You'd leave them behind if you could—and I would as well. That's for love and friendship—and because this is a burden and duty that came to us. To you, to me, to Iona. Not to them."

He kissed her hands lightly. "But that would be wrong for so many reasons. We're a circle, three by three. It was always meant to be the six of us, Branna. I believe that."

"I know it. It's clear to me as well."

"You fear you'll fail them. You won't. You won't, and the burden of it isn't yours alone."

"We've never done it before."

"I'd never floated so much as a feather before I came here," Iona reminded her. "And now?"

She lifted her hands, palms up. The sofa where she sat beside Boyle rose smoothly, soundlessly, did a slow circle, then lowered back to the ground.

"Fair play to you," Fin said, amused.

"You taught me, you and Connor. You opened me to what I have and what I am. We'll figure out how to do it, and do it."

"All right. All right. I can't stand one against five. And it is a bloody brilliant idea. Reckless and frightening and brilliant. I know a potion I could tinker with that should work, and we'll write the spell—and I'll need every hour of that fortnight."

"And you have us to help you tinker," Connor pointed out.

"I'll need you all as well. Still, I'd be easier if we have what would be a kind of control outside the dream net."

"Would they have to be right here—with us, I mean?" Meara asked.

"Physically you're meaning?" Connor glanced over at her, considered. "I don't see why."

"Then you have your father, the two of you. And there's Iona's grandmother. That's blood and purpose shared, isn't it? And love as well."

"And more bloody brilliance!" On a laugh, Connor turned to Meara, plucked her straight out of her chair to spin her around. "That would do, and do very well. Branna?"

"It could—no, it would. And if I'd cleared the buzzing out of my head, I'd have seen it. Iona's Nan, our da, and . . ."

She turned to Fin. "Your cousin Selena. Would she be willing? Three's a better number than two, and gives it all power and blood from each of us. Three would balance, I'd think, should we need to be righted again."

"She would be more than willing. She's in Spain, but I'll contact her. I'll speak with her about it."

"Then that part's settled. I'll study on it."

"I have been," Connor told her. "The potion, to open the vision, shared by all inside the ritual circle. Best done outside, in the air. We take our guides as well, the horse, the hound, the hawk."

Branna started to speak, reconsidered. "You have studied on it."

"I have. Fin, your horse, your hawk—and I don't suppose you can come up with a hound in the next fortnight? Three for three."

"I have one. I have Bugs."

"Little Bugs?" Iona began, thinking of the barn dog at the big stables.

"Little as you are, game as you are. Three for three," Fin repeated with a nod. "Horse for Boyle, hawk for Meara, hound, such as he is, for me. It's well thought, Connor."

"It's you who must link them to the others, as they come from you."

"So I will."

"And so inside the circle, our circle and our guides," Connor said. "Our circle, the six, hands joined as the spell is spoken, as the spell is cast. And minds linked as well, which I will do. Minds, hearts, hands linked, and we go together, on the dream, to the night of All Hallow's Eve, to Samhain, in the year Sorcha's Brannaugh, Eamon, and Teagan returned to Mayo."

"Their presence adds power." Branna sat again, reached for a cookie herself. "The night the Veil thins. We may draw their power, and Sorcha's with ours. No, he could never expect this. There's time enough to perfect the potion and the spell. And then, to draw him there. That's for Meara."

"It's for me?"

Branna huffed at her brother. "You haven't spoken to her of it."

"Between one thing and the other, no. It's you he wants to use this go," Connor told her, "so it's you who'll use him. You'll sing him there."

"Sing?"

"Music, light, joy—emotions. Flames to his moth," Connor explained. "When he comes, it must be as quick as we can make it, giving him no time to slip away again."

"We go much as we did on the solstice," Branna began.

"No." Now Fin pushed to his feet. "We failed there, didn't we?"

"We have a new strategy, a stronger weapon."

"And if he once again manages to draw the three apart again, even if only for a moment? If the spell, the ritual, the end, must come from you, then he must be held off while you cast him out. We engage him. Boyle, Meara, and I. We cost him blood and pain before. We'll do worse this round. We'll do worse while you do what's best."

"Do you want his end, Fin, or do you want his blood?"

"I want both, and so do you, Branna. You can't shed it for gain or for joy."

"Nor should you."

"And I won't. We won't. But we'll shed it and worse in defense of the three. In defense of the light. If there's joy in it as well? A witch is still human for all that."

"I'm with Fin on it," Boyle said. "Iona's mine. And all of you my family. I'll stand for her, for you. I won't stand back."

"They've said what I'd say." Meara shrugged. "So that's done." She set her hands on her knees. "So, as I have it, in a fortnight's time, we'll all—including horses, hounds, hawks, go dreaming ourselves back a few centuries. I'll sing, and like the Pied Piper's tune to rats, that will lure Cabhan. Three of us fight, three of us cast the spell to destroy him. When the job's done we take our bows, then wake up back here where we should take another bow for certain, as we've vanquished evil. Then I suppose we should all go to the pub for a pint."

"That puts it all in a nutshell," Connor decided.

"All right then. I think there should be whiskey all around as we're all raving lunatics." She let out a breath, picked up a biscuit and bit in. "But at least one of us does indeed make brilliant gingerbread."

Amused, Connor poured whiskey all around, lifted his glass, tapped it to Meara's. "Whether we're victorious or buggered, there's no five others I'd rather stand with. So fuck it all. *Sláinte.*"

And they drank.

THEY HAD WORK TO DO AND PLENTY OF IT. BRANNA BARELY left her workshop. If her nose wasn't in a spell book—Sorcha's, her great-grandmother's, her own—she was at her work countertesting potions or writing spells.

When the life around them allowed, Connor joined her, or Iona or Fin. Meara found herself in the position of fetching, carrying, cooking—or splitting that chore with Boyle.

As often as she could she pulled one of them out for sword practice.

And all watched the woods, the fields, the roads for any sign.

"It's been too quiet." Meara easily parried Connor's advance on one of the rare occasions she managed to drag him away from work or witchcraft.

"He's watching, and waiting."

"That's just it, isn't it? He's waiting. I've barely seen a shadow of him for days now. He's keeping his distance. He's waiting for us to make the move as he knows we've one to make."

She thrust, feinted, then swung up, nearly disarming him.

"You're not paying attention in the least," she complained. "If these blades weren't charmed I could've sliced your ear off."

"Then I'd only half hear your voice, and that would be a pity."

"We should go at him, Connor."

"We've a plan, Meara. Patience."

"It's not about patience, but strategy."

"Strategy, is it?" He twirled his free hand, stirred a little cyclone of air. When she glanced toward it, he moved in, and had his sword to her throat. "How's that?"

"Well, if you're after cheating—"

"And Cabhan will play nicely, of course."

"Point taken." She stepped back. "What I'm saying is we should feint." She jabbed, shifted, jabbed again. "Make him think we've gone at him, let him score a point or two. He'll think we've made our move, so he won't expect it when we do."

"Hmm. That's . . . interesting. Have you anything in mind?"

"You're the witch, aren't you, so you and your like would have to come up with the ritual of it."

Lowering her sword, she worked through what she'd only half baked in her head.

"But what if we did it near here—near the cottage where we could retreat, as retreat would be part of it. Let him think he's routed us."

"That's a hard swallow, but I see where you're going. Come on then." He grabbed her hand, pulled her into the workshop where Branna funneled a pale blue liquid into a slim bottle. Iona crushed herbs with mortar and pestle.

"Meara's an idea."

Eyebrows drawn together, Branna focused on the liquid sliding gracefully into the bottle. "I'm still working on the last idea that's come around."

"It's perfect, Branna." Iona stopped as Branna slid a crystal stopper into the bottle.

"And how many dream spells for six, and their guides, have you cast?"

"This will be my first." But Iona smiled. "And it's perfect. You should have seen the stars," she told Connor and Meara. "Tiny blue stars rising up, circling around the cauldron as she finished it."

"I think it's right." Branna rubbed the small of her back. "I added the amethyst as you suggested, Connor, and I think it's right. It needs to cure out of the light for at least three days."

She lifted it, carried it over to a cupboard.

"Let me make you some tea," Iona began, but Branna shook her head.

"Thanks, but no. I've had enough tea these last days to do me for six months. I'm after some wine."

"Then we'll have some wine while you hear Meara's idea. Better, don't you feel like cooking something?" Connor tried out a winning smile. "Aren't you feeling a longing for your own kitchen, darling? This is the sort of idea that goes well with a good bowl of soup, and the full circle of us."

Meara gave him a shove. "I think it's a good idea, and it should be heard by everyone. But I can make the soup while you sit and have your wine."

"I'll make it, because despite the fact that my brother's thinking with his belly, I do miss my kitchen. We've vegetables in the garden still." She pointed at Connor. "Go fetch some."

"What's your pleasure?"

"Any and all. I'll make it up as I go. And since you've had some fine idea, Meara, you can tell me of it while I have the wine. I don't see why I should wait for the others. Leave that, Iona. We'll get back to it. Let's have a little kitchen time."

Meara thought she was doing some making it up as she went as well. And by the time everyone arrived, she'd refined things a bit.

"So," she finished, "by doing something now without any real stake in winning, we'd have him thinking we'd made our attack, bungled it, or at least failed at it. We're forced to retreat to the cottage—where we're protected. Confused-like, you know? And bitter. If we've had our arse handed to us, he wouldn't think we'd launch another attack in a matter of days."

"If we go halfway, he could do real damage," Boyle pointed out. "Why not go full-out?"

"We still need the time left for the plan we settled on. I've been working the spell around the night we chose," Branna explained. "I wouldn't want to try it on another. It must be Samhain."

"Her point is by losing we have a better chance of winning." Connor gave Boyle a bump on the shoulder. "And I know losing, even by design, goes down hard."

"We'd have to make it flashy. He won't be fooled by something that looks weak and tossed together." But Fin smiled. "And we could give plenty of flash. Fire and storm, quake and flood. We throw the elements at him. It wouldn't be right—not on its own in any case, but it would be loud and strong and it would feel bloody fierce."

"A call to the elements." Now Branna began to smile. "Oh, we could make it fierce indeed. Even rock him on his heels a bit. We'd need to shield, for we've neighbors here. The field—the rise behind the gardens."

"That's farther than I'd thought," Meara began. "If we're going to be routed, that's a long road to retreat and safety."

"We don't retreat," Connor said. "At least not at a run. We fly."

"Fly?" Meara let out a long breath. "I think I'll have some more wine on that notion."

"That makes a statement, too." Iona did the honors with the wine. "We're defeated, and have to fly to safety. When would we try it?"

"We're on a waning moon." Connor glanced toward the window. "That could be useful. I'd like a go at it tonight, but I think closer to the real attack. Two nights more? If we get any singes from it, we'd have time to mend them."

"Two nights more." Branna walked over to stir her soup.

EVEN A FEINT REQUIRED PLANNING.

The three added more protection around the house. If Cabhan

believed them weakened, he might try to come in for the coup de grace. They couldn't afford a single chink.

Meara thought of it as a kind of play. Though some would be scripted, and she'd gone over her part of it a dozen times and more, some would have to be written and delivered on the spot.

"I'm nervous," she confessed to Connor. "More nervous than I was on the solstice."

"You'll be fine. We all will. Remember defense is the first goal here. Offense is just a happy bonus."

"It's nearly time." As if to warm them, she rubbed her hands together. "He may not even come."

"I think he will. He'll believe you're weak, and that we're fractured. He'll see a chance, want to take it. It's family he doesn't understand, and the bonds of friendship. But he'll understand what we lure him with."

He took her hand, walked with her into the workshop where the others had already gathered.

Even for this, Meara thought, the ritual must be kept.

So they lighted the ritual candles, watched while the smoke from the cauldron rose in a pale blue.

Branna took the ritual cup she placed in the circle, and spoke words familiar now.

"This we drink, one cup for six, from hand to hand and mouth to mouth to fix with wine our unity. Six hearts, six minds as one tonight as we prepare to wage this fight. Sip one, sip all, and show each one here answers the call."

Three times they passed the cup, hand to hand, mouth to mouth.

"A circle are we, two rings forming one three by three. Tonight we ask for strength and power to see us through the dark hour. Four elements we will call to bring about Cabhan's fall. Fire, earth, water, air we'll stir into a raging sea. As we will, so mote it be."

The three closed the circle.

"We're ready. The circle's been cast, the spell begun. If we have time to cast a circle on the rise, so much the better." Branna looked at Meara. "You'll know when to start."

She hoped so.

They walked to the rise, carrying candles, cauldron, weapons, and wands, shielded from sight—but for Cabhan's. Connor told her they'd left a window for him.

As they topped the rise, he reached for her hand. She pulled sharply away.

And the play began.

20

I TOLD YOU TO STAY CLEAR OF ME."

"Ah now, Meara, it was just a pint in the pub."

"Talk runs like a river, Connor, so I know just how you spent your time in the pub." She sent him a look of absolute disgust. "And while I was barely able to stand after what was done to me. On your account done to me."

"Jesus, Meara, it was just a bit of a flirt. Some conversation, a bit of fun."

"Have all the fun and *conversation* you want, but don't think you'll come cozying up to me after." Deliberately she quickened her pace. "I know your ways. Who better?"

"What do you want?" He hunched his shoulders as they climbed the gentle rise. "I needed a bit of a breather, is all, after being cooped up day after day in the cottage or slammed with work at the school. You could do little but sleep for hours at a go."

"And why was that?" She stopped, rounded on him. "It's you and your magicks put me flat, isn't it?"

He planted his feet, glared back at her. "It's me and my magicks saved your bleeding life!"

"And while I was clinging to that life, you're off *conversing* with Alice Keenan at the pub."

"Enough, enough, enough!" Branna blasted at both of them. "There's no time for this. Didn't I tell you my star chart has tonight as our best chance to finish this? We can't do what needs doing with the two of you sniping at each other."

"I'm here, aren't I?" Meara jerked up her chin. "I'm here putting my life on the line yet again because I said I would. I keep my word. Unlike some."

"A man buys a girl a pint, and suddenly he's a liar?"

"Lay the candles, Connor." Branna shoved them at him. "And focus on what's at hand. By the gods, couldn't you have waited till we'd done this before sniffing around Alice Keenan?"

On an outraged hiss, Meara dumped her pack on the ground. "Oh, so it's fine and well for him to run around behind me after I've been useful?"

"That's not what I meant," Branna said, her tone sharp, dismissive. "Stop acting the gom."

"Now I'm the gom? You would take his part, even knowing he was off with that sleveen."

"Stop, will you all stop?" Iona put her hands over her ears.

"Best stay out of it," Boyle advised.

"I can't stay out of it. They're my family, and I can't take any more of this sniping and bickering. Give me those." She snatched the candles from Connor, began to secure them in a circle on the rise. "How can we work together, do what we've all sworn to do, if we're fighting?"

"Easy for you to say." Meara slammed a hand on the hilt of her sword. "When you've Boyle acting the lap dog for you at every turn."

"I'm no one's dog, Meara, and mind yourself."

"Didn't I tell you tonight wasn't the time?" Fin drew his athame out of its sheath, examined it in the light of the waning moon.

"If I said up, you'd say down," Branna shot back. "For the spite of it."

"And wasn't it you who said it must be the solstice? And here we are, months later, at your bidding again."

"And I wonder still how much you held back that night. If my bidding was done, you would never be here, you would never be with us."

"Branna, that's too much." Connor laid a hand on her shoulder. *He's coming,* he told her, told the others. *Fast.*

"Too much or not enough hardly matters now. We're here."

Branna swept her hand out, lighted the candles. She set the bowl at the northmost point.

Behind her, Connor touched his fingers lightly to Meara's.

She drew in a breath, and braced for it.

Fog dropped, a thick curtain, and with it came a bitter, bone-deep cold. A roaring ripped through it, shivered over the high grass.

Even as she drew her sword, Connor whipped her aside.

She felt something streak by her, grazing her arm, leaving a frigid burn of pain behind. She didn't have to feign the fear and confusion. Both rose up in her like a flood.

Then Connor's voice sounded in her head. *I'm with you. I love you.*

She spun, moving back-to-back with Boyle, readied to attack or defend.

The ground trembled under her feet as Fin called to earth.

"Danu, goddess and mother, by your power will this earth quake and shudder."

Even protected by the ritual, Meara nearly pitched forward when the ground heaved.

"On Acionna, on Manannan mac Lir I call," Branna shouted. "On Cabhan's head your wrath will fall."

Rain poured out of the sky, as if some deity had turned the course of a raging river.

Through the fog, the deluge, she saw glowing streaks of black winging like arrows. And to her shock, the fog hissed. It curled around her leg like a snake. Instinctively she sliced out at it, rent it. Black blood splattered from the mists.

Balls of fire catapulted out, burning the black arrows to cinder on Iona's call. "Power of fire in Brighid's name to scorch the dark with light and flame."

She felt Boyle lurch, whirled to defend, and saw him hack at a thorny tendril of fog striking toward Fin.

She dove under, sliced and struck, then had to cling to the ground as it heaved up under her.

"Sidhe, heed your servant, your son, and with your breath bring his damnation."

She watched Connor, a flame within the flames lift his arms high. As she struggled to her feet she saw the boiling sky above open. And whirl.

Came the lightning, spearing out of the dark to strike the quaking earth. Even the rain sparked with fire. She saw Iona fall, saw Boyle spring over to lift her. Flames shot from her hands at the wolf, at the man, at the twisting, snaking branches of fog.

She fought her way through, back toward the circle where the candles still glowed like beacons. Back toward Connor, who'd gripped Branna's hand, then Iona's, so the three of them lit, candles themselves.

It howled, the wolf.

It laughed, the man.

The candles, wax and witch, sputtered and began to dim.

"Pull it back!" Branna shouted. "We've lost it. We've lost the night. It's drained from us. Flee, while we can."

Connor gripped Meara around the waist—strong hands, face

fierce, sheened with sweat, with blood. "I'll steer clear of you after I save your life a second time."

Spinning through the air, showers of stars, sparks of fire. Light so brilliant she had to squeeze her eyes tight, turn her head.

Falling, too fast, too fast, so the speed sucked the air from her lungs.

The next she knew she was sprawled over Connor on the kitchen floor with his heart galloping under her like a runaway horse.

A terrible roar swept over, around, rattling the windows. Great fists pounded at the doors, the walls, so the cottage shook. For a moment Meara braced for it to collapse on their heads.

Then there was silence.

The others lay, like survivors of some terrible smashup. Kathel leaped over her to Branna, licked at her face, whined.

"I'm all right, there now. We're all right."

"That should convince him we'd gone to war tonight, as it bloody well convinced me." Connor stroked Meara's hair as he shifted her. "Are you hurt?"

"I don't know. I don't think so. You're bleeding."

He swiped his fingers over a gash on his temple. "Didn't dodge fast enough."

"Here, let me see to it." Branna scooted over. "Iona—"

"I know what you need." As she ran toward the workshop, Meara tugged up her trouser leg, saw the livid bruise circling just above her ankle.

"Here, let me see to that." Even as Branna tended him, Connor reached out, laid his hands on the bruising.

"The fog—it turned to snakes. And thorns. It grew thorns."

"Not thorns, teeth." Fin, his face shiny with sweat, sat on the kitchen floor with his back braced against a cupboard.

"You're hurt. A bit of that for Connor's head," Branna snapped to Iona as she pushed up to go to Fin. "See that it's clear and clean. Were you bitten?" she demanded of Fin.

"I'm just winded."

She pressed her hand to his chest. "It's more. Let me see."

"I'll tend to myself when I've my breath back."

"Oh, bollocks." With a flash of her hand, she stripped him to the waist.

"If you're after getting my clothes off, we could do with some privacy."

"Shut it." She looked over her shoulder, spoke urgently. "Iona, the balm!"

"I'll see to myself," Fin began.

"I'll put you under if you don't be still, be quiet. You know I can and will. Connor, I need you."

"How bad is it?"

He saw for himself when he pushed across the kitchen floor.

Raw and black puncture wounds ran down both sides of Fin's torso, as if a monstrous jaw had closed over him.

"They're not deep." Branna's voice stayed low and steady. "Thank the gods for that. And the poison . . ." She looked up sharply. "What did you do to stop the spread of it?"

"I'm his blood." Breathing labored, Fin spoke slowly, almost too precisely. "What he makes from his weakens in mine."

"There's pain," Connor said.

"There's always pain." But he hissed out a breath as Branna worked deeper. "Christ Jesus, woman, your healing's worse than the wound."

"I have to draw it out, weakened or not."

"Look at me, Fin," Connor ordered.

"I'll take my own pain, thanks."

Connor merely gripped Fin's jaw in his hand, turned his head.

He's taking the pain, Meara realized. Taking Fin's pain so the healing goes quickly. And so, she knew, Branna couldn't take it herself.

Boyle got out the whiskey, so she stood to fetch glasses. Then sitting on the floor again, passed them out when Branna sat back, nodded.

"That will do."

"A bit more of a dust-up than we reckoned on." Mirroring Fin, Connor leaned back against the cupboards. His own face shone now, from the sweat of the effort, of the pain. "But we singed his ass more than a bit, and we're safe and whole."

"He'll think we're cowed," Branna said. "He'll think we're bickering among ourselves, licking our wounds, questioning if we should ever try such a thing again."

"And when we go at him in two days' time, we'll burn him to ashes before he knows we've duped him. A fine show, one and all." He lifted his glass. "A notion of brilliance, Meara my darling, and one that may have turned the tide good and hard. It's hardly a wonder I love you."

He drank, as did the others, but Meara held her glass and studied him.

"No taste for your whiskey?" he asked her.

"I'm waiting for my heart to shake. It may be I'm in a bit of shock. Why don't you tell me again? We'll see if it gets through."

He set his glass aside, walked over on his knees to where she sat on the floor. "I love you, Meara, and ever will."

She downed the whiskey, set the glass down, rose up on her knees to face him. "No, it's not shaking. But really, what sort of weak and foolish heart shakes in fear of love. Will yours?" She laid her hand on his chest. "Let's see if it does. I love you, Connor, and ever will."

"It may have stopped for a second." He closed his hand over hers, held it to him. "But there's no fear, there's no doubt. Do you feel that? It's dancing, with joy."

She laughed. "Connor O'Dwyer of the dancing heart. I'll take you." She threw her arms around him, met his mouth with hers.

"Would you like us to move along then?" Boyle replied. "Give the two of you your privacy there on the kitchen floor?"

"I'll let you know," Connor murmured, then went back to kissing his love.

He stood, plucked her up, swept her up, gave her a toss to make her laugh again. "On second thought, we'll get out of your way."

He carried her from the room on more laughter.

"It's what you've always wanted," Fin said to Branna.

"What I knew could be, felt should be, and yes, what I wanted." She let out a sigh. "I'll put on the kettle."

LATER, WRAPPED UP WITH MEARA IN BED, THE HOUSE QUIET around them, and moonlight coming through the window, Connor asked her.

"Was it the battle that did it? The knowing of life and death that steadied your heart?"

"You took his pain."

"What? Who?"

"Down in the kitchen. Though he didn't want it of you, you wouldn't let him hurt, so you took Fin's pain. I thought, That's who he is, down into it. A man who'd take on the pain of a friend—or anyone else for that matter. A man of power, of kindness. Of fun and music and loyalty. And he loves me."

She laid a hand on his cheek. "I've loved you as long as I can remember, but I wouldn't let myself have it, have that gift you spoke of, or give it. That was fear.

"And I thought, when I watched you tonight, in the horrible heat of battle, in the bright lights of the kitchen, how can I let myself be too afraid to have what I love? Why do I keep convincing myself I might be like my father, or let what he did define the whole of my life? I owe Cabhan a debt."

"Cabhan?"

"He thought to hurt and shame and shake me by bringing the image of my father to me. And he did, right enough, but that was from me. And seeing plain what I held in me, I could start seeing the truth. He didn't leave me, or my mother, or the rest of us. He left his own shame and his mistakes and failures because he couldn't stand and look at them in the mirror."

"You always stand, you always look."

"I try, but I didn't look from the right angle. I didn't let myself tip the glass. It's my mother who stayed, with the shame he left her with, who lived—in her own dithering way—with mistakes and failures that were his. And she stood, and stayed, for me and my family, even after we were grown. She's happy now, free of that whether she knows it fully or not. I'm free of it as well. So I owe Cabhan a debt. But it won't stop me from doing all I can to send him to hell."

"Then I owe him a debt alongside you. And we'll send him to hell together."

IT WAS HARD OVER THE NEXT TWO DAYS OUTSIDE OF THE cocoon of the cottage to stop himself from radiating joy. He had to go about his work, and avoid contact with Meara until they were inside that sanctuary.

He felt Cabhan probing once or twice, but lightly, cautiously. And there were bruises there, oh yes, they'd given the bastard a few bruises for his trouble.

He'd come into it weaker than he'd been—and thinking their circle damaged when it was stronger and more vital than it had ever been.

And yet.

"You have doubts," he said to Branna. Only hours remained, so he'd come home to help however he could.

"It's a good scheme."

"And still?"

She took out the dream potion, padded it carefully in a silver box that had come down through their family, placing it alongside the bloodred brew she hoped would end Cabhan.

"A feeling, and I don't know if it's a true one. I wonder if I was so confident on the solstice that now I doubt when it's time to try again. Or if there's truly something I'm not seeing, not doing that needs seeing, needs doing."

"It's not only on your shoulders, Branna."

"I know it. Whatever Fin thinks, I know that very well." She gathered the tools she'd cleansed and charmed to wrap in a roll of white velvet.

She opened a drawer, took out a smaller silver box. "I have something for you, whatever tonight brings."

Curious, he opened it, saw the ring, the deep glow of the ruby in hammered gold. "This came to you, down from our great-grandmother."

"Now it's yours if you want it for Meara. She's my sister, and that bind only tightens when you give her the ring. Another circle, and it should be hers. But only if it's what you want."

He came around the work counter, drew her in. "After the night's done. Thank you."

"I want it ended, now more than ever. I want to see you and Meara make your lives together."

"We'll end it. We're meant to."

"Your heart's talking."

"It is, and if your head wasn't talking so bloody loud, you'd hear your own." He drew her back. "If you won't trust your heart, trust your blood. And mine."

"I am."

He gathered his own tools and readied himself for the night to come.

They met at the big stables, and at Fin's request, Connor saddled Aine, the white filly Fin bought to breed with Alastar.

"I thought Fin was taking Baru, his stallion."

Connor glanced back at Meara. She wore sturdy boots, rough pants, a thick belt with her sword and sheath carried on it. He knew Iona had braided charms in her hair.

And she wore his necklace over a flannel shirt.

"So he is. We're to take Aine, and Iona and Boyle take Alastar. The third horse makes the getting there easier."

"So we're riding to Sorcha's cabin."

"In a way. You're prepared for what's to come?"

"As well as I can be."

He reached across the saddle for her hand. "We'll come through it."

"I believe that."

Together, they led the horse out to join the others in the pale light of a crescent moon. "Once we're there it must go quickly, without a missed step. My father, Iona's grandmother, Fin's cousin, they'll have ahold of things, and they'll bring us back should things go wrong."

"You'll bring me back," she said.

Once he'd mounted, she swung up behind him. He glanced at Boyle and Iona already on a restless Alastar.

Wants to be going, he does, to be doing.

He saw Fin gather up the little mutt, mount the black stallion, then hold his hand down to Branna.

"It's hard for her," Connor murmured. "To go with him this way."

"Hard for him as well."

But Branna mounted, then signaled to Kathel. The hound raced off. Overhead Roibeard called, and Fin's Merlin answered.

"Hold on to me," Connor advised, and the three horses leaped forward in a gallop.

Then they flew.

"Sweet Jesus!" Meara's big laugh followed the exclamation. "This is brilliant! Why haven't we done this before?"

The wind streamed by, cool and damp, while clouds winked over the moon and away again. The air filled with the scent of spice and earth, of things going bold before they settled down to rest.

They flew, riding the air above that earth, into the deep, and straight through the vines to Sorcha's cabin.

"Quickly now," Connor told her.

He had to leave her to move to Branna and Iona, to cast the circle, a hundred candles, the bowls, the cauldron.

Branna opened the silver box, removed the dream potion.

"Spirits ride upon this night. We come to join them with our light. In this place and in this hour, we call upon bright things of power. We are the three, and are three more. Together we walk through the door and into the dreaming there to find the meaning of our destiny. So we drink one by three and one by three."

She poured the potion into a silver cup, lifted it up. Lowered it, sipped.

"Body, blood, mind, and heart, into the dreaming we depart."

She passed the cup to Fin. He sipped, repeated the words, and then to Iona, and around the circle.

It tasted of stars, Connor thought as he took his turn, one by three.

He joined hands, his sister's, Meara's, and with her circle said the words.

"With right, with might, with light we seek the night. A dream-walk back in time, Cabhan's evil to unwind. To the time of the return of Sorcha's three. As we will, so mote it be."

There wasn't a floating as he'd experienced before, but a kind of swimming through mists and colors with voices murmuring behind, before, and images just on the edges of his vision.

When the mists cleared, he stood as he had been, with his circle, and his hand clasped with Meara's, his other with Branna's.

"Did we go back?"

"Look there," Connor said to Meara.

Vines covered the cabin, but it stood. And bluebells bloomed on the ground beneath the gravestone.

The horses stood with the hawks on branches above them. Kathel sat calm as a king beside Branna, while Bugs quivered a little between Fin's boots.

"We're all here, as we should be. You'll call him now, Meara."

"Now?"

"Start," Branna confirmed, and took out the vial filled with red. "Draw him in."

Inside the vial brilliance pulsed and swirled. Liquid light, magick fire.

"In the center of the circle." Connor took her by the shoulders, kissed her. "And sing, whatever happens."

She had to steady herself, calm her heart, then open it.

She'd chosen a ballad, sang in Irish though he doubted she knew the meaning of all the words. Heartbreaking they were, and as beautiful as the voice that lifted over the clearing, into the night, and across all the dreaming time.

He'd ask her to sing it for him, he decided, when they were done with dark things, when they were alone. She would sing it again, for him.

"He hears," Fin whispered.

"It's a night that calls to black and white, to dark and light. He'll come."

Branna stepped out of the circle, then Connor, then Iona.

"Whatever happens," Connor said again. "Sing. He's coming."

"Aye." Fin stepped out of the circle, leaving Boyle to guard Meara.

He drew a sword, and set it to burning.

It came on the fog, a shadow that became a wolf. It stalked toward the line of four witches, then whirled and leaped at the circle.

Boyle blocked Meara's body with his, but the wolf leaped back from the fireball Iona threw.

It paced the clearing, eyed the horses until Alastar pawed the ground, then it rose up to a man.

"Do you think to try for me again? Do you think to destroy me with song and your weak white magick?" He waved a hand and the flame on Fin's sword died.

Fin simply lifted it, caught the fire again.

"Try me," Fin suggested, and stepped forward in front of the three.

"My son, blood of my blood, you are not my enemy."

"I am your death." Fin leaped forward, swinging out, but cleaved only fog.

The rats came, a boiling flood of them, red eyes feral. Those that streamed to the circle screamed as they flashed into flame. But Meara saw one of the candles gutter out.

Now she drew her sword and sang.

Aine reared, hooves flashing. Her eyes rolled in fear. Fin grabbed her reins, used the sword to set a ring of fire around her. While the two stallions crushed the rats, the hawks dived for them.

The bats spilled out of the sky.

Connor saw another candle wink out.

"He's attacking the circle to get to her. It must be now, Branna."

"We have to pull him closer."

Connor threw his head back, called the wind. The torrent of it tore through those thin wings until the air filled with smoke and screaming.

Meara's voice wavered as a single twisted body fell at the circle's edge, and a third candle went out.

"Steady, girl," Boyle murmured.

"I'm steady." Drawing in air, she lifted her voice over the screams.

"I'll slice open your throat and rip your heart out through it."

Cabhan, his eyes nearly as red as his stone, threw black lightning at the circle.

Boyle took an opening, jabbed through with his knife, drew first blood. The explosion of air knocked him back. The blood on the tip of his knife hit the ground and sizzled black as pitch.

"It has to be now," Connor shouted, and began the chant.

The power rose up, clear heat. Again he heard voices, not only Meara's and Iona's, but others. Distant, murmuring, murmuring through the thinning Veil. Over them Meara's song rang, filled his heart with more.

Fin swept his sword so the candles reignited, so the flames ran straight.

The rats turned away, flowing toward the three. Cabhan dropped to all fours. The wolf charged Kathel.

Connor felt Branna's fear, turned with her as did Iona to shoot power toward the wolf. But the ground heaved under it—Fin's work. Kathel's jaws snapped over the wolf's shoulder, and Roibeard dived.

It screamed, fought its way clear to run toward the trees beyond the clearing.

"Cut it off," Connor shouted. "Drive it back." But his heart stopped when both Boyle and Meara ran clear of the circle to join Fin.

It darted right, turned and, desperate, began to charge. Meara's sword flamed. The tip of it scorched fur before the wolf checked, turned again.

Out of the corner of his eye, Connor caught movement. He glanced over, saw three figures by the cabin. A wavering vision, as their voices struggled to reach through the Veil.

Then he knew only his sister, Iona, only the three and the hot rush of power.

She suspended the vial in front of them, and with hands linked, minds linked, powers linked, they hurtled it toward the wolf.

The light exploded, a thousand suns. It charged into him, through him.

"By the power of three you are ended. With our light your dark is rended. With our light this web is spun, with our blood you are undone. No life, no spirit, no magicks left for thee. As we will so mote it be."

The light flashed again, brighter still. It bloomed in his eyes, simmered in his blood. And through it, again, he saw three figures. One held out a hand to him, reaching. Reaching.

Then they were gone, and so was the light. The dark fell, lifted only by moonglow and the circle of candles. Breaking his link with the three, Connor rushed to Meara.

"Are you hurt? Anywhere?"

"No, not a bit."

"You weren't to stop singing, you weren't to step out of the circle."

"My throat got dry." She smiled, her face smeared with soot, and threw her arms around him. "Did we end it? Did we end him?"

"Give me a moment." Ash and blood littered the ground, tiny splotches of black still burned. "By the gods what's left of him should be here. Give me a moment."

"He's not. I can feel him." Fin swiped blood from his face. "I can feel him, I can smell him. I can find him. I can finish him."

"You can't leave the clearing." Branna grabbed his arm. "You can't or you may not get back."

Face fierce, Fin wrenched his arm free. "What difference does it make if I end him, end this?"

"This isn't your place."

"And it isn't your choice."

"Nor can it be yours," she said, and flung him back into the circle. "Connor."

"Bloody hell."

With considerable regret, he rushed Fin, pinned him, and got a fist in his face for the trouble before Boyle joined in.

"Quickly." Branna laid a hand on Connor's shoulder, took Meara's hand, nodded to Iona as the men grappled on the ground.

She closed her eyes, broke the spell.

Through the dark and light again, through the colors and mists to the clearing with the ruins of a cabin and the call of an owl.

"It wasn't for you to stop me."

"Not only her," Connor said, rubbing his jaw as he eyed Fin. "It was for all of us. We can't do without you."

"Can you be sure?" Meara demanded. "Can you be sure we didn't finish him?"

Saying nothing, Fin stripped off his coat, yanked the sweater under it over his head. The mark on his shoulder showed raw and red, beating like a heart.

"What is this?" Branna demanded. "You feel his pain?"

"Your blood saw to that. He's wounded, but who can say if it's mortal. I could have finished him."

"If you'd left the clearing, you'd have been lost," Connor said. "You're with us, Fin. Your place, your time is here. We didn't finish him. I felt him as well before Branna broke the spell. But not here, not now. And this time, we've some bumps and bruises and nothing more—if we're not counting your fist in my face—and he's battered and bleeding and torn, half blind as well—I got that much. He may not survive the night."

"I can ease the pain."

Fin only stared at Branna. "I'll keep it all the same."

"Fin." Iona stepped forward, rose to her toes to cup his face in her hands. "*Mo dearthair.* We need you with us."

After a moment's struggle, Fin lowered his forehead to hers, sighed. "Ah well."

"We should go back." Meara handed Bugs to Fin, where the dog wiggled in his arms and lapped at his face. "We may not have finished it, but we did good work tonight. And for myself, I sang my throat dry as the moon."

"It's not finished." Branna crossed over to Sorcha's gravestone, traced a finger over the words carved there. "Not yet finished, but it will be. I swear it will be."

They mounted, filthy, weary. Connor hung back, just a bit, looking over his shoulder at the clearing before they went through the vines. "I saw them—I need to tell the others."

"Saw who?"

"The three. Sorcha's three—the shadows of them. Eamon with a sword, Brannaugh with a bow, Teagan with a wand. Some part of them was there, came through and into the dreaming. They tried to get through to us."

"We could have used them—more than their shadows."

"That's the truth all around." He turned Aine toward home. "I thought, for a moment and more, I thought we'd done it."

"So did I. You wanted to go with Fin. Wanted to go with him and finish it, whatever the cost."

"I did, but I couldn't."

"Because it wasn't meant."

"More than that. I couldn't leave you." He stopped Aine so he could turn to her, touch her face. "I couldn't and wouldn't leave you, Meara, not even for that.

"I've something for you."

He dug in his pocket, pulled out the silver box, opened it so the ruby pulled at the moonlight.

"Oh, but, Connor—"

"It's a fine ring, and I'll see that it fits—as you fit me, and I fit you. It's come down through the family. Branna passed it to me so I could give it to you."

"You're proposing to me on horseback when we both smell of brimstone?"

"It strikes me as romantic and memorable. Look here." He slid it onto her finger, gave it a little tap. "See, it fits, as I said. You'll have to marry me now."

She looked at the ring, back at him. "I suppose I will then."

He caught her in a kiss as sweet as it was awkward.

"Hold on now," he told her.

And they flew.

SEEKING ITS LAIR, IT CRAWLED OVER THE GROUND, MORE shadow than wolf, more wolf than man. Its black blood scorched the earth behind it.

It knew only pain and hate and a terrible thirst.

And the terrible thirst was vengeance.

Keep reading for an excerpt from

THE COLLECTOR

SHE THOUGHT THEY'D NEVER LEAVE. CLIENTS, ESPECIALLY new ones, tended to fuss and delay, revolving on the same loop of instructions, contacts, comments before finally heading out the door. She sympathized because when they walked out the door they left their home, their belongings, and in this case their cat, in someone else's hands.

As their house sitter, Lila Emerson did everything she could to send them off relaxed, and confident those hands were competent ones.

For the next three weeks, while Jason and Macey Kilderbrand enjoyed the south of France with friends and family, Lila would live in their most excellent apartment in Chelsea, water their plants, feed, water and play with their cat, collect their mail—and forward anything of import.

She'd tend Macey's pretty terrace garden, pamper the cat, take messages and act as a burglary deterrent simply by her presence.

While she did, she'd enjoy living in New York's tony London

Terrace just as she'd enjoyed living in the charming flat in Rome—where for an additional fee she'd painted the kitchen—and the sprawling house in Brooklyn—with its frisky golden retriever, sweet and aging Boston terrier and aquarium of colorful tropical fish.

She'd seen a lot of New York in her six years as a professional house sitter, and in the last four had expanded to see quite a bit of the world as well.

Nice work if you can get it, she thought—and she could get it.

"Come on, Thomas." She gave the cat's long, sleek body one head-to-tail stroke. "Let's go unpack."

She liked the settling in, and since the spacious apartment boasted a second bedroom, unpacked the first of her two suitcases, tucking her clothes in the mirrored bureau or hanging them in the tidy walk-in closet. She'd been warned Thomas would likely insist on sharing the bed with her, and she'd deal with that. And she appreciated that the clients—likely Macey—had arranged a pretty bouquet of freesia on the nightstand.

Lila was big on little personal touches, the giving and the getting.

She'd already decided to make use of the master bath with its roomy steam shower and deep jet tub.

"Never waste or abuse the amenities," she told Thomas as she put her toiletries away.

As the two suitcases held nearly everything she owned, she took some care in distributing them where it suited her best.

After some consideration she set up her office in the dining area, arranging her laptop so she could look up and out at the view of New York. In a smaller space she'd have happily worked where she slept, but since she had room, she'd make use of it.

She'd been given instructions on all the kitchen appliances, the remotes, the security system—the place boasted an array of gadgets that appealed to her nerdy soul.

In the kitchen she found a bottle of wine, a pretty bowl of fresh fruit, an array of fancy cheeses with a note handwritten on Macey's monogrammed stationery.

Enjoy our home!

—Jason, Macey and Thomas

Sweet, Lila thought, and she absolutely would enjoy it.

She opened the wine, poured a glass, sipped and approved. Grabbing her binoculars, she carried the glass out on the terrace to admire the view.

The clients made good use of the space, she thought, with a couple of cushy chairs, a rough stone bench, a glass table—and the pots of thriving flowers, the pretty drops of cherry tomatoes, the fragrant herbs, all of which she'd been encouraged to harvest and use.

She sat, with Thomas in her lap, sipping wine, stroking his silky fur.

"I bet they sit out here a lot, having a drink, or coffee. They look happy together. And their place has a good feel to it. You can tell." She tickled Thomas under the chin and had his bright green eyes going dreamy. "She's going to call and e-mail a lot in the first couple days, so we're going to take some pictures of you, baby, and send them to her so she can see you're just fine."

Setting the wine aside, she lifted the binoculars, scanned the buildings. The apartment complex hugged an entire city block, and that offered little glimpses into other lives.

Other lives just fascinated her.

A woman about her age wore a little black dress that fit her tall, model-thin body like a second skin. She paced as she talked on her cell phone. She didn't look happy, Lila thought. Broken date. He has to work late—he says, Lila added, winding the plot in her head. She's fed up with that.

A couple floors above, two couples sat in a living room—art-covered walls, sleek, contemporary furnishings—and laughed over what looked like martinis.

Obviously they didn't like the summer heat as much as she and Thomas or they'd have sat outside on their little terrace.

Old friends, she decided, who get together often, sometimes take vacations together.

Another window opened the world to a little boy rolling around on the floor with a white puppy. The absolute joy of both zinged right through the air and had Lila laughing.

"He's wanted a puppy forever—forever being probably a few months at that age—and today his parents surprised him. He'll remember today his whole life, and one day he'll surprise his little boy or girl the same way."

Pleased to end on that note, Lila lowered the glasses. "Okay, Thomas, we're going to get a couple hours of work in. I know, I know," she continued, setting him down, picking up the half glass of wine. "Most people are done with work for the day. They're going out to dinner, meeting friends—or in the case of the killer blonde in the black dress, bitching about not going out. But the thing is . . ." She waited until he strolled into the apartment ahead of her. "I set my own hours. It's one of the perks."

She chose a ball—motion-activated—from the basket of cat toys in the kitchen closet, gave it a roll across the floor.

Thomas immediately pounced, wrestled, batted, chased.

"If I were a cat," she speculated, "I'd go crazy for that, too."

With Thomas happily occupied, she picked up the remote, ordered music. She made a note of which station played so she could be sure she returned it to their house music before the Kilderbrands came home. She moved away from the jazz to contemporary pop.

House-sitting provided lodging, interest, even adventure. But writing paid the freight. Freelance writing—and waiting tables—had kept her head just above water her first two years in New York. After she'd fallen into house-sitting, initially doing favors for friends, and friends of friends, she'd had the real time and opportunity to work on her novel.

Then the luck or serendipity of house-sitting for an editor who'd taken an interest. Her first, *Moon Rise*, had sold decently. No bust-out bestseller, but steady, and with a nice little following in the fourteen-to-eighteen set she'd aimed for. The second would hit the stores in October, so her fingers were crossed.

But more to the moment, she needed to focus on book three of the series.

She bundled up her long brown hair with a quick twist, scoop and the clamp of a chunky tortoiseshell hinge clip. While Thomas gleefully chased the ball, she settled in with her half glass of wine, a tall glass of iced water and the music she imagined her central character, Kaylee, listened to.

As a junior in high school, Kaylee dealt with all the ups and downs—the romance, the homework, the mean girls, the bullies, the politics, the heartbreaks and triumphs that crowded into the short, intense high school years.

A sticky road, especially for the new girl—as she'd been in the first book. And more, of course, as Kaylee's family were lycans.

It wasn't easy to finish a school assignment or go to the prom with a full moon rising when a girl was a werewolf.

Now, in book three, Kaylee and her family were at war with a rival pack, a pack that preyed on humans. Maybe a little bloodthirsty for some of the younger readers, she thought, but this was where the path of the story led. Where it had to go.

She picked it up where Kaylee dealt with the betrayal of the boy she thought she loved, an overdue assignment on the Napoleonic Wars and the fact that her beautiful blond nemesis had locked her in the science lab.

The moon would rise in twenty minutes—just about the same time the Science Club would arrive for their meeting.

She had to find a way out before the change.

Lila dived in, happily sliding into Kaylee, into the fear of exposure, the pain of a broken heart, the fury with the cheerleading, homecoming queening, man-eating (literally) Sasha.

By the time she'd gotten Kaylee out, and in the nick, courtesy of a smoke bomb that brought the vice principal—another thorn in Kaylee's side—dealt with the lecture, the detention, the streaking home as the change came on her heroine, Lila had put in three solid hours.

Pleased with herself, she surfaced from the story, glanced around.

Thomas, exhausted from play, lay curled on the chair beside her, and the lights of the city glittered and gleamed out the window.

She fixed Thomas's dinner precisely as instructed. While he ate she got her Leatherman, used the screwdriver of the multi-tool to tighten some screws in the pantry.

Loose screws, to her thinking, were a gateway to disaster. In people and in things.

She noticed a couple of wire baskets on runners, still in their boxes. Probably for potatoes or onions. Crouching, she read the description, the assurance of easy install. She made a mental note to e-mail Macey, ask if she wanted them put in.

It would be a quick, satisfying little project.

She poured a second glass of wine and made a late dinner out of the fruit, cheese and crackers. Sitting cross-legged in the dining room, Thomas in her lap, she ate while she checked e-mail, sent e-mail, scanned her blog—made a note for a new entry.

"Getting on to bedtime, Thomas."

He just yawned when she picked up the remote to shut off the music, then lifted him up and away so she could deal with her dishes and bask in the quiet of her first night in a new space.

After changing into cotton pants and a tank, she checked the security, then revisited her neighbors through the binoculars.

It looked like Blondie had gone out after all, leaving the living room light on low. The pair of couples had gone out as well. Maybe to dinner, or a show, Lila thought.

The little boy would be fast asleep, hopefully with the puppy curled up with him. She could see the shimmer of a television, imagined Mom and Dad relaxing together.

Another window showed a party going on. A crowd of people—well-dressed, cocktail attire—mixed and mingled, drinks or small plates in hand.

She watched for a while, imagined conversations, including a whispered one between the brunette in the short red dress and the bronzed god in the pearl gray suit who, in Lila's imagination, were having a hot affair under the noses of his long-suffering wife and her clueless husband.

She scanned over, stopped, lowered the glasses a moment, then looked again.

No, the really built guy on the . . . twelfth floor wasn't completely naked. He wore a thong as he did an impressive bump and grind, a spin, drop.

He was working up a nice sweat, she noted, as he repeated moves or added to them.

Obviously an actor/dancer moonlighting as a stripper until he caught his big Broadway break.

She enjoyed him. A lot.

The window show kept her entertained for a half hour before she made herself a nest in the bed—and was indeed joined by Thomas. She switched on the TV for company, settled on an *NCIS* rerun where she could literally recite the dialogue before the characters.

Comforted by that, she picked up her iPad, found the thriller she'd started on the plane from Rome, and snuggled in.

OVER THE NEXT WEEK, SHE DEVELOPED A ROUTINE. THOMAS would wake her more accurately than any alarm clock at seven precisely when he begged, vocally, for his breakfast.

She'd feed the cat, make coffee, water the plants indoors and out, have a little breakfast while she visited the neighbors.

Blondie and her live-in lover—they didn't have the married vibe—argued a lot. Blondie tended to throw breakables. Mr. Slick, and he was great to look at, had good reflexes, and a whole basket of charm. Fights, pretty much daily, ended in seduction or wild bursts of passion.

They suited each other, in her estimation. For the moment. Neither of them struck Lila as long-haul people with her throwing dishes or articles of clothing, him ducking, smiling and seducing.

Game players, she thought. Hot, sexy game players, and if he didn't have something going on, on the side, she'd be very surprised.

The little boy and the puppy continued their love affair, with Mom, Dad or nanny patiently cleaning up little accidents. Mom and Dad left together most mornings, garbed in a way that said high-powered careers to Lila.

The Martinis, as she thought of them, rarely used their little terrace. She was definitely one of the ladies-who-lunch, leaving the apartment every day, late morning, returning late afternoon usually with a shopping bag.

The Partiers rarely spent an evening at home, seemed to revel in a frantic sort of lifestyle.

And the Body practiced his bump and grind regularly—to her unabashed pleasure.

She treated herself to the show, and the stories she created every morning. She'd work into the afternoon, break to amuse the cat before she dressed and went out to buy what she thought she might like for dinner, to see the neighborhood.

She sent pictures of a happy Thomas to her clients, picked tomatoes, sorted mail, composed a vicious lycan battle, updated her blog. And installed the two baskets in the pantry.

On the first day of week two, she bought a good bottle of Barolo, filled in the fancy cheese selections, added some mini cupcakes from an amazing neighborhood bakery.

Just after seven in the evening, she opened the door to the party pack that was her closest friend.

"There you are." Julie, wine bottle in one hand, a fragrant bouquet of star lilies in the other, still managed to enfold her.

Six feet of curves and tumbled red hair, Julie Bryant struck the opposite end of Lila's average height, slim build, straight brown hair.

"You brought a tan back from Rome. God, I'd be wearing 500 SPF and still end up going lobster in the Italian sun. You look just great."

"Who wouldn't after two weeks in Rome? The pasta alone. I told you I'd get the wine," Lila added when Julie shoved the bottle into her hand.

"Now we have two. And welcome home."

"Thanks." Lila took the flowers.

"Wow, some place. It's huge, and the view's a killer. What do these people do?"

"Start with family money."

"Oh, don't I wish I had."

"Let's detour to the kitchen so I can fix the flowers, then I'll give you a tour. He works in finance, and I don't understand any of it. He loves his work and prefers tennis to golf. She does some interior design, and you can see she's good at it from the way the apartment looks. She's thinking about going pro, but they're talking about starting a family, so she's not sure it's the right time to start her own business."

"They're new clients, right? And they still tell you that kind of personal detail?"

"What can I say? I have a face that says tell me all about it. Say hello to Thomas."

Julie crouched to greet the cat. "What a handsome face he has."

"He's a sweetheart." Lila's deep brown eyes went soft as Julie and Thomas made friends. "Pets aren't always a plus on the jobs, but Thomas is."

She selected a motorized mouse out of Thomas's toy basket, enjoyed Julie's easy laugh as the cat pounced.

"Oh, he's a killer." Straightening, Julie leaned back on the stone-gray counter while Lila fussed the lilies into a clear glass vase.

"Rome was fabulous?"

"It really was."

"And did you find a gorgeous Italian to have mad sex with?"

"Sadly no, but I think the proprietor of the local market fell for me. He was about eighty, give or take. He called me *una bella donna* and gave me the most beautiful peaches."

"Not as good as sex, but something. I can't believe I missed you when you got back."

"I appreciate the overnight at your place between jobs."

"Anytime, you know that. I only wish I'd been there."

"How was the wedding?"

"I definitely need wine before I get started on Cousin Melly's Hamptons Wedding Week From Hell, and why I've officially retired as a bridesmaid."

"Your texts were fun for me. I especially liked the one . . . 'Crazy Bride Bitch says rose petals wrong shade of pink. Hysteria ensues. Must destroy CBB for the good of womankind.'"

"It almost came to that. Oh no! Sobs, tremors, despair. 'The petals are pink-pink! They have to be rose-pink. Julie! Fix it, Julie!' I came close to fixing her."

"Did she really have a half-ton truckload of petals?"

"Just about."

"You should have buried her in them. Bride smothered by rose petals. Everyone would think it was an ironic, if tragic, mishap."

"If only I'd thought of it. I really missed you. I like it better when you're working in New York, and I can come see your digs and hang out with you."

Lila studied her friend as she opened the wine. "You should come with me sometime—when it's someplace fabulous."

"I know, you keep saying." Julie wandered as she spoke. "I'm just not sure I wouldn't feel weird, actually staying in— Oh my God, look at this china. It has to be antique, and just amazing."

"Her great-grandmother's. And you don't feel weird coming over and spending an evening with me wherever, you wouldn't feel weird staying. You stay in hotels."

"People don't live there."

"Some people do. Eloise and Nanny did."

Julie gave Lila's long tail of hair a tug. "Eloise and Nanny are fictional."

"Fictional people are people, too, otherwise why would we care what happens to them? Here, let's have this on the little terrace. Wait until you see Macey's container garden. Her family started in France—vineyards."

Lila scooped up the tray with the ease of the waitress she'd once been. "They met five years ago when she was over there visiting her grandparents—like they are now—and he was on vacation and came to their winery. Love at first sight, they both claim."

"It's the best. First sight."

"I'd say fictional, but I just made a case for fictional." She led the way to the terrace. "Turned out they both lived in New York. He called her, they went out. And were exchanging 'I dos' about eighteen months later."

"Like a fairy tale."

"Which I'd also say fictional, except I love fairy tales. And they look really happy together. And as you'll see, she's got a seriously green thumb."

Julie tapped the binoculars as they started out. "Still spying?"

Lila's wide, top-heavy mouth moved into a pout. "It's not spying. It's observing. If people don't want you looking in, they should close the curtains, pull down the shades."

"Uh-huh. Wow." Julie set her hands on her hips as she scanned the terrace. "You're right about the green thumb."

Everything lush and colorful and thriving in simple terra-cotta pots made the urban space a creative oasis. "She's growing tomatoes?"

"They're wonderful, and the herbs? She started them from seeds."

"Can you do that?"

"Macey can. I—as they told me I could and should—harvested some. I had a big, beautiful salad for dinner last night. Ate it out here, with a glass of wine, and watched the window show."

"You have the oddest life. Tell me about the window people."

Lila poured wine, then reached inside for the binoculars—just in case.

"We have the family on the tenth floor—they just got the little boy a puppy. The kid and the pup are both incredibly pretty and adorable. It's true love, and fun to watch. There's a sexy blonde on fourteen who lives with a very hot guy—both could be models. He comes and goes, and they have very intense conversations, bitter arguments with flying crockery, followed by major sex."

"You watch them have sex? Lila, give me those binoculars."

"No!" Laughing, Lila shook her head. "I don't watch them have sex. But I can tell that's what's going on. They talk, fight, pace around with lots of arm waving from her, then grab each other and start pulling off clothes. In the bedroom, in the living room. They don't have a terrace like this, but that little balcony deal off the bedroom. They barely made it back in once before they were both naked.

"And speaking of naked, there's a guy on twelve. Wait, maybe he's around."

Now she did get the glasses, checked. "Oh yeah, baby. Check this out. Twelfth floor, three windows from the left."

Curious enough, Julie took the binoculars, finally found the window. "Oh my. Mmmm, mmmm. He does have some moves. We should call him, invite him over."

"I don't think we're his type."

"Between us we're every man's type."

"Gay, Julie."

"You can't tell from here." Julie lowered the glasses, frowned, then lifted them again for another look. "Your gaydar can't leap over buildings in a single bound like Superman."

"He's wearing a thong. Enough said."

"It's for ease of movement."

"Thong," Lila repeated.

"Does he dance nightly?"

"Pretty much. I figure he's a struggling actor, working part-time in a strip club until he gets his break."

"He's got a great body. David had a great body."

"Had?"

Julie set down the glasses, mimed breaking a twig in half.

"When?"

"Right after the Hamptons Wedding Week From Hell. It had to be done, but I didn't want to do it at the wedding, which was bad enough."

"Sorry, honey."

"Thanks, but you didn't like David anyway."

"I didn't not like him."

"Amounts to the same. And though he was so nice to look at, he'd just gotten too clingy. Where are you going, how long will you be, blah blah. Always texting me, or leaving messages on my machine. If I had work stuff, or made plans with you and other friends, he'd get upset or sulky. God, it was like having a wife—in the worst way. No dis meant to wives, as I used to be one. I'd only been seeing him for a couple months, and he was pushing to move in. I don't want a live-in."

"You don't want the wrong live-in," Lila corrected.

"I'm not ready for the right live-in yet. It's too soon after Maxim."

"It's been five years."

Julie shook her head, patted Lila's hand. "Too soon. Cheating bastard still pisses me off. I have to get that down to mild amusement, I think. I hate breakups," she added. "They either make you feel sad—you've been dumped; or mean—you've done the dumping."

"I don't think I've ever dumped anyone, but I'll take your word."

"That's because you make them think it's their idea—plus you really don't let it get serious enough to earn the term 'dump.'"

Lila just smiled. "It's too soon after Maxim," she said, and made Julie laugh. "We can order in. There's a Greek place the clients recommended. I haven't tried it yet."

"As long as there's baklava for after."

"I have cupcakes."

"Even better. I now have it all. Swank apartment, good wine, Greek food coming, my best pal. And a sexy . . . oh, and sweaty," she added as she lifted the glasses again. "Sexy, sweating dancing man—sexual orientation not confirmed."

"Gay," Lila repeated, and rose to get the takeout menu.

THEY POLISHED OFF MOST OF THE WINE WITH LAMB KABOBS—then dug into the cupcakes around midnight. Maybe not the best combination, Lila decided, considering her mildly queasy stomach, but just the right thing for a friend who was more upset about a breakup than she admitted.

Not the guy, Lila thought as she did the rounds to check security, but the act itself, and all the questions that dogged the mind and heart after it was done.

Is it me? Why couldn't I make it work? Who will I have dinner with?

When you lived in a culture of couples, it could make you feel less when you were flying solo.

"I don't," Lila assured the cat, who'd curled up in his own little bed sometime between the last kabob and the first cupcake. "I'm okay being single. It means I can go where I want, when I want, take any job that works for me. I'm seeing the world, Thomas, and okay, talking to cats, but I'm okay with that, too."

Still, she wished she'd been able to talk Julie into staying over. Not just for the company, but to help deal with the hangover her friend was bound to have come morning.

Mini cupcakes were Satan, she decided as she readied for bed. So cute and tiny, oh, they're like eating nothing, that's what you tell yourself, until you've eaten half a dozen.

Now she was wired up on alcohol and sugar, and she'd never get to sleep.

She picked up the binoculars. Still some lights on, she noted. She wasn't the only one still up at . . . Jesus, one forty in the morning.

Sweaty Naked Guy was still up, and in the company of an equally hot-looking guy. Smug, Lila made a mental note to tell Julie her gaydar was like Superman.

Party couple hadn't made it to bed yet; in fact it looked as though they'd just gotten in. Another swank deal from their attire. Lila admired the woman's shimmery orange dress, and wished she could see the shoes. Then was rewarded when the woman reached down, balancing a hand on the man's shoulder, and removed one strappy, sky-high gold sandal with a red sole.

Mmm, Louboutins.

Lila scanned down.

Blondie hadn't turned in yet either. She wore black again—snug and short—with her hair tumbling out of an updo. Been out on the town, Lila speculated, and it didn't go very well.

She's crying, Lila realized, catching the way the woman swiped at her face as she spoke. Talking fast. Urgently. Big fight with the boyfriend.

And where is he?

But even changing angles she couldn't bring him into view.

Dump him, Lila advised. Nobody should be allowed to make you so unhappy. You're gorgeous, and I bet you're smart, and certainly worth more than—

Lila jerked as the woman's head snapped back from a blow.

"Oh my God. He hit her. You bastard. Don't—"

She cried out herself as the woman tried to cover her face, cringed back as she was struck again.

And the woman wept, begged.

Lila made one leap to the bedside table and her phone, grabbed it, leaped back.

She couldn't see him, just couldn't see him in the dim light, but now the woman was plastered back against the window.

"That's enough, that's enough," Lila murmured, preparing to call 911.

Then everything froze.

The glass shattered. The woman exploded out. Arms spread wide, legs kicking, hair flying like golden wings, she dropped fourteen stories to the brutal sidewalk.

"Oh God, God, God." Shaking, Lila fumbled with the phone.

"Nine-one-one, what is your emergency?"

"He pushed her. He pushed her, and she fell out the window."

"Ma'am—"

"Wait. Wait." She closed her eyes a moment, forced herself to breathe in and out three times. Be clear, she ordered herself, give the details.

"This is Lila Emerson. I just witnessed a murder. A woman was pushed out a fourteenth-story window. I'm staying at . . ." It took her a moment to remember before she came to the Kilderbrands' address.

"It's the building across from me. Ah, to the, to the west of me. I think. I'm sorry, I can't think. She's dead. She has to be dead."

"I'm dispatching a unit now. Will you hold the line?"

"Yes. Yes. I'll stay here."

Shuddering, she looked out again, but now the room beyond the broken window was dark.

ABOUT THE AUTHOR

Nora Roberts is the #1 *New York Times* bestselling author of more than two hundred novels. She is also the author of the bestselling In Death series written under the pen name J. D. Robb. There are more than five hundred million copies of her books in print.

CONNECT ONLINE

NoraRoberts.com

NoraRoberts

Blood Magick

Nora Roberts

BERKLEY
NEW YORK

BERKLEY
An imprint of Penguin Random House LLC
penguinrandomhouse.com

Library of Congress Cataloging-in-Publication Data

Roberts, Nora.
Blood magick / Nora Roberts. — Berkley trade paperback edition
p. cm. —(Cousins O'Dwyer trilogy; book three)
ISBN 978-0-425-25987-0 (paperback)
1. Buisnesswomen—Fiction. 2. Witches—Fiction. 3. Magic—Fiction.
4. Ireland—Fiction. 5. Domestic fiction I. Title.
PS3568.O243B5465 2014
813'.54—dc23
2014012909

Berkley trade paperback edition / November 2014

PRINTED IN THE UNITED STATES OF AMERICA
9th Printing

Book design by Kristin del Rosario

From #1 *New York Times* bestselling author Nora Roberts comes a trilogy about the land we're drawn to, the family we learn to cherish, and the people we long to love. . . .

County Mayo is rich in the traditions of Ireland, legends that Branna O'Dwyer fully embraces in her life and in her work as the proprietor of The Dark Witch shop, which carries soaps, lotions, and candles for tourists, made with Branna's special touch.

Branna's strength and selflessness hold together a close circle of friends and family—along with their horses and hawks and her beloved hound. But there's a single missing link in the chain of her life: love. . . .

She had it once—for a moment—with Finbar Burke, but a shared future is forbidden by history and blood. Which is why Fin has spent his life traveling the world to fill the abyss left in him by Branna, focusing on work rather than passion.

Branna and Fin's relationship offers them both comfort and torment. And though they succumb to the heat between them, there can be no promises for tomorrow. A storm of shadows threatens everything that their circle holds dear. It is Fin's power, loyalty, and heart that will make all the difference in an age-old battle between the bonds that hold their friends together and the evil that has haunted their families for centuries.

"There is a kind of poetry to the writing in this Nora Roberts story . . . [that] captures your imagination and finds a home in your heart."

—Fresh Fiction, on *Dark Witch*

Nora Roberts

HOT ICE
SACRED SINS
BRAZEN VIRTUE
SWEET REVENGE
PUBLIC SECRETS
GENUINE LIES
CARNAL INNOCENCE
HONEST ILLUSIONS
DIVINE EVIL
PRIVATE SCANDALS
HIDDEN RICHES
TRUE BETRAYALS
MONTANA SKY
SANCTUARY
HOMEPORT
THE REEF
RIVER'S END
CAROLINA MOON
THE VILLA
MIDNIGHT BAYOU
THREE FATES
BIRTHRIGHT
NORTHERN LIGHTS
BLUE SMOKE
ANGELS FALL
HIGH NOON
TRIBUTE
BLACK HILLS
THE SEARCH
CHASING FIRE
THE WITNESS
WHISKEY BEACH
THE COLLECTOR
TONIGHT AND ALWAYS
THE LIAR
THE OBSESSION

Series

Irish Born Trilogy

BORN IN FIRE
BORN IN ICE
BORN IN SHAME

Dream Trilogy

DARING TO DREAM
HOLDING THE DREAM
FINDING THE DREAM

Chesapeake Bay Saga

SEA SWEPT
RISING TIDES
INNER HARBOR
CHESAPEAKE BLUE

Gallaghers of Ardmore Trilogy

JEWELS OF THE SUN
TEARS OF THE MOON
HEART OF THE SEA

Three Sisters Island Trilogy

DANCE UPON THE AIR
HEAVEN AND EARTH
FACE THE FIRE

Key Trilogy

KEY OF LIGHT
KEY OF KNOWLEDGE
KEY OF VALOR

In the Garden Trilogy

BLUE DAHLIA
BLACK ROSE
RED LILY

Circle Trilogy

MORRIGAN'S CROSS
DANCE OF THE GODS
VALLEY OF SILENCE

Sign of Seven Trilogy

BLOOD BROTHERS
THE HOLLOW
THE PAGAN STONE

Bride Quartet

VISION IN WHITE
BED OF ROSES
SAVOR THE MOMENT
HAPPY EVER AFTER

The Inn BoonsBoro Trilogy

THE NEXT ALWAYS
THE LAST BOYFRIEND
THE PERFECT HOPE

The Cousins O'Dwyer Trilogy

DARK WITCH
SHADOW SPELL
BLOOD MAGICK

The Guardians Trilogy

STARS OF FORTUNE
BAY OF SIGHS
ISLAND OF GLASS

eBooks by Nora Roberts

Cordina's Royal Family

AFFAIRE ROYALE
COMMAND PERFORMANCE
THE PLAYBOY PRINCE
CORDINA'S CROWN JEWEL

The Donovan Legacy

CAPTIVATED
ENTRANCED
CHARMED
ENCHANTED

The O'Hurleys

THE LAST HONEST WOMAN
DANCE TO THE PIPER
SKIN DEEP
WITHOUT A TRACE

Night Tales

NIGHT SHIFT
NIGHT SHADOW
NIGHTSHADE
NIGHT SMOKE
NIGHT SHIELD

The MacGregors

PLAYING THE ODDS
TEMPTING FATE
ALL THE POSSIBILITIES
ONE MAN'S ART
FOR NOW, FOREVER
REBELLION/IN FROM THE COLD
THE MACGREGOR BRIDES
THE WINNING HAND
THE MACGREGOR GROOMS
THE PERFECT NEIGHBOR

The Calhouns

COURTING CATHERINE
A MAN FOR AMANDA
FOR THE LOVE OF LILAH
SUZANNA'S SURRENDER
MEGAN'S MATE

Irish Legacy

IRISH THOROUGHBRED
IRISH ROSE
IRISH REBEL

LOVING JACK
BEST LAID PLANS
LAWLESS

BLITHE IMAGES
SONG OF THE WEST
SEARCH FOR LOVE
ISLAND OF FLOWERS
THE HEART'S VICTORY
FROM THIS DAY
HER MOTHER'S KEEPER
ONCE MORE WITH FEELING
REFLECTIONS
DANCE OF DREAMS
UNTAMED
THIS MAGIC MOMENT
ENDINGS AND BEGINNINGS
STORM WARNING
SULLIVAN'S WOMAN
FIRST IMPRESSIONS
A MATTER OF CHOICE

LESS OF A STRANGER
THE LAW IS A LADY
RULES OF THE GAME
OPPOSITES ATTRACT
THE RIGHT PATH
PARTNERS
BOUNDARY LINES
DUAL IMAGE
TEMPTATION
LOCAL HERO
THE NAME OF THE GAME
GABRIEL'S ANGEL
THE WELCOMING
TIME WAS
TIMES CHANGE
SUMMER LOVE
HOLIDAY WISHES

Nora Roberts & J. D. Robb

REMEMBER WHEN

J. D. Robb

NAKED IN DEATH
GLORY IN DEATH
IMMORTAL IN DEATH
RAPTURE IN DEATH
CEREMONY IN DEATH
VENGEANCE IN DEATH
HOLIDAY IN DEATH
CONSPIRACY IN DEATH
LOYALTY IN DEATH
WITNESS IN DEATH
JUDGMENT IN DEATH
BETRAYAL IN DEATH
SEDUCTION IN DEATH
REUNION IN DEATH
PURITY IN DEATH
PORTRAIT IN DEATH
IMITATION IN DEATH
DIVIDED IN DEATH
VISIONS IN DEATH
SURVIVOR IN DEATH
ORIGIN IN DEATH
MEMORY IN DEATH
BORN IN DEATH
INNOCENT IN DEATH
CREATION IN DEATH
STRANGERS IN DEATH
SALVATION IN DEATH
PROMISES IN DEATH
KINDRED IN DEATH
FANTASY IN DEATH
INDULGENCE IN DEATH
TREACHERY IN DEATH
NEW YORK TO DALLAS
CELEBRITY IN DEATH
DELUSION IN DEATH
CALCULATED IN DEATH
THANKLESS IN DEATH
CONCEALED IN DEATH
FESTIVE IN DEATH
OBSESSION IN DEATH
DEVOTED IN DEATH
BROTHERHOOD IN DEATH
APPRENTICE IN DEATH

Anthologies

FROM THE HEART

A LITTLE MAGIC

A LITTLE FATE

MOON SHADOWS

(with Jill Gregory, Ruth Ryan Langan, and Marianne Willman)

The Once Upon Series

(with Jill Gregory, Ruth Ryan Langan, and Marianne Willman)

ONCE UPON A CASTLE

ONCE UPON A STAR

ONCE UPON A DREAM

ONCE UPON A ROSE

ONCE UPON A KISS

ONCE UPON A MIDNIGHT

SILENT NIGHT

(with Susan Plunkett, Dee Holmes, and Claire Cross)

OUT OF THIS WORLD

(with Laurell K. Hamilton, Susan Krinard, and Maggie Shayne)

BUMP IN THE NIGHT

(with Mary Blayney, Ruth Ryan Langan, and Mary Kay McComas)

DEAD OF NIGHT

(with Mary Blayney, Ruth Ryan Langan, and Mary Kay McComas)

THREE IN DEATH

SUITE 606

(with Mary Blayney, Ruth Ryan Langan, and Mary Kay McComas)

IN DEATH

THE LOST

(with Patricia Gaffney, Mary Blayney, and Ruth Ryan Langan)

THE OTHER SIDE

(with Mary Blayney, Patricia Gaffney, Ruth Ryan Langan, and Mary Kay McComas)

TIME OF DEATH

THE UNQUIET

(with Mary Blayney, Patricia Gaffney, Ruth Ryan Langan, and Mary Kay McComas)

MIRROR, MIRROR

(with Mary Blayney, Elaine Fox, Mary Kay McComas, and R. C. Ryan)

DOWN THE RABBIT HOLE

(with Mary Blayney, Elaine Fox, Mary Kay McComas, and R. C. Ryan)

Also available . . .

THE OFFICIAL NORA ROBERTS COMPANION

(edited by Denise Little and Laura Hayden)

For Kat,

one of the brightest lights in my life

How far away the stars seem,
and how far is our first kiss,
and, ah, how old is my heart.

—WILLIAM BUTLER YEATS

It will have blood; they say,
blood will have blood.

—WILLIAM SHAKESPEARE

1

Summer 1276

ON A BRIGHT DAY AS SUMMER FADED, BRANNAUGH gathered herbs, flowers, foliage, all for salves and potions and teas. They came to her, neighbors, travelers, for their hopes and healings. They came to her, the Dark Witch, as once they'd come to her mother, with aches in body, in heart, in spirit, and paid with coin or service or trade.

So she and her brother, her sister, had built their lives in Clare, so far from their home in Mayo. Far from the cabin in the woods where they had lived, where their mother had died.

So she had built her life, more contented, more joyful than she'd believed possible since that terrible day their mother had given them all but the dregs of her own power, had sent them away to be safe as she sacrificed herself.

All grief, Brannaugh thought now, all duty and fear as she'd done what was asked of her, as she'd led her younger brother and little sister away from home.

They'd left love, childhood, and all innocence behind.

Long years. The first few spent, as their mother had bid, with their cousin and her man—safe, tended, welcomed. But the time had come, as time does, to leave that nest, to embrace who and what they were, and would ever be.

The Dark Witches three.

Their duty, their purpose above all else? To destroy Cabhan, the dark sorcerer, the murderer of their father, Daithi the brave, of their mother, Sorcha. Cabhan, who had somehow survived the spell the dying Sorcha had cast.

But on such a bright day in summer's end, it all seemed so far away—the terrors of that last winter, the blood and death of that last spring.

Here, in the home she'd made, the air smelled of the rosemary in her basket, of the roses planted by her husband on the birth of their first child. The clouds puffed white as lambs across the blue meadow of the sky, and the woods, the little fields they'd cleared, as green as emeralds.

Her son, not yet three years, sat in a patch of sun and banged on the little drum his father had made him. He sang and hooted and beat with such joyous innocence her eyes burned from the love.

Her daughter, barely a year, slept clutching her favored rag doll while guarded by Kathel, their faithful hound.

And another son stirred and kicked in her womb.

From where she stood she could see the clearing, and the little cabin she, Eamon, and Teagan had built near to eight years before. Children, she thought now. They'd been but children who could not embrace childhood.

They lived there still, close. Eamon the loyal, so strong and true. Teagan, so kind and fair. So happy now, Brannaugh thought, and Teagan so in love with the man she'd married in the spring.

All so peaceful, she thought, despite Brin's banging and hooting.

The cabin, the trees, the green hills with their dots of sheep, the gardens, the bright blue sky.

And it would have to end. It would have to end soon.

The time was coming—she felt it as sure as she felt the babe's kicks in her womb. The bright days would give way to the dark. The peace would end in blood and battle.

She touched the amulet with its symbol of a hound. The protection her mother had conjured with blood magicks. Soon, she thought, all too soon now, she would need that protection again.

She pressed a hand to the small of her back as it ached a bit, and saw her man riding toward home.

Eoghan, so handsome, so hers. Eyes as green as the hills, hair a raven's wing that curled to his shoulders. He rode tall and straight and easy on the sturdy chestnut mare, his voice lifted—as often it was—in song.

By the gods, he made her smile, he made her heart lift like a bird on the wing. She, who had been so sure there could be no love for her, no family but her blood, no life but her purpose, had fallen deeper than oceans for Eoghan of Clare.

Brin leaped up, began to run as fast as his little legs could manage, all the while calling.

"Da, Da, Da!"

Eoghan leaned down, scooped the boy up in the saddle. The laugh, the man's, the boy's mixed, flew toward her. Her eyes stung yet again. In that moment, she would have given all of her power, every drop given her, to spare them what was to come.

The baby she'd named for her mother whimpered, and Kathel stirred his old bones to let out a soft woof.

"I hear her." Brannaugh set down her basket, moved over to lift her waking daughter, snuggled her in with kisses as Eoghan rode up beside her.

"Look here, would you, what I found on the road. Some little lost gypsy."

"Ah well, I suppose we should keep him. It may be he'll clean up fine, then we can sell him at the market."

"He might fetch us a good price." Eoghan kissed the top of his giggling son's head. "Off you go, lad."

"Ride, Da!" Brin turned his head, beseeched with big dark eyes. "Please! Ride!"

"A quick one, then I want me tea." He winked at Brannaugh before setting off in a gallop that had the boy shouting with delight.

Brannaugh picked up her basket, shifted young Sorcha on her hip. "Come, old friend," she said to Kathel. "It's time for your tonic."

She moved to the pretty cottage Eoghan with his clever hands and strong back had built. Inside, she stirred the fire, settled her daughter, started the tea.

Stroking Kathel, she doused him with the tonic she'd conjured to keep him healthy and clear-eyed. Her guide, her heart, she thought, she could stretch his life a few years more. And would know when the time came to let him go.

But not yet, no, not yet.

She set out honey cakes, some jam, and had the tea ready when Eoghan and Brin came in, hand in hand.

"Well now, this is fine."

He scrubbed Brin's head, leaned down to kiss Brannaugh, lingered over it as he always did.

"You're home early," she began, then her mother's eye caught her son reaching for a cake. "Wash those hands first, my boy, then you'll sit like a gentleman for your tea."

"They're not dirty, Ma." He held them out.

Brannaugh just lifted her eyebrows at the grubby little hands. "Wash. The both of you."

"There's no arguing with women," Eoghan told Brin. "It's a lesson you'll learn. I finished the shed for the widow O'Brian. It's God's truth her boy is useless as teats on a billy goat, and wandered off to his own devices. The job went quicker without him."

He spoke of his work as he helped his son dry his hands, spoke of work to come as he swung his daughter up, set her to squealing with delight.

"You're the joy in this house," she murmured. "You're the light of it."

He gave her a quiet look, set the baby down again. "You're the heart of it. Sit down, off your feet awhile. Have your tea."

He waited. Oh, she knew him for the most patient of men. Or the most stubborn, for one was often the same as the other, at least wrapped inside the like of her Eoghan.

So when the chores were finished, and supper done, when the children tucked up for the night, he took her hand.

"Will you walk out with me, lovely Brannaugh? For it's a fine night."

How often, she wondered, had he said those words to her when he wooed her—when she tried flicking him away like a gnat in the air?

Now, she simply got her shawl—a favorite Teagan had made her—wrapped it around her shoulders. She glanced at Kathel lying by the fire.

Watch the babes for me, she told him, and let Eoghan draw her out into the cool, damp night.

"Rain's coming," she said. "Before morning."

"Then we're lucky, aren't we, to have the night." He laid a hand over her belly. "All's well?"

"It is. He's a busy little man, always on the move. Much like his father."

"We're well set, Brannaugh. We could pay for a bit of help."

She slanted him a look. "Do you have complaints about the state of the house, the children, the food on the table?"

"I don't have a one, not for a single thing. I watched my mother work herself to bones." As he spoke he rubbed the small of her back, as if he knew of the small, nagging ache there. "I wouldn't have it of you, *aghra*."

"I'm well, I promise you."

"Why are you sad?"

"I'm not." A lie, she realized, and she never lied to him. "A little. Carrying babies makes a woman a bit daft from time to time, as you should know. Didn't I weep buckets when carrying Brin when you brought in the cradle you'd made? Wept as if the world was ending."

"From joy. This isn't joy."

"There is joy. Only today I stood here, looking at our children, feeling the next move in me, thinking of you, and of the life we have. Such joy, Eoghan. How many times did I say no to you when you asked me to be yours?"

"Once was too many."

She laughed, though the tears rose up in her throat. "But you would ask again, and again. You wooed me with song and story, with wildflowers. Still, I told you I would be no man's wife."

"None but mine."

"None but yours."

She breathed in the night, the scent of the gardens, the forest, the hills. She breathed in what had become home, knowing she would leave it for the home of childhood, and for destiny.

"You knew what I was, what I am. And still, you wanted me—not the power, but me."

Knowing that meant all the world to her, and knowing it had opened the heart she'd determined to keep locked.

"And when I could no longer stop myself from loving you, I told you all there is, all of it, refusing you again. But you asked again. Do you remember what you said to me?"

"I'll say it to you again." He turned to her, took her hands as he had on the day years before. "You're mine, and I am yours. All that you are,

I'll take. All that I am, I'll give. I'll be with you, Brannaugh, Dark Witch of Mayo, through fire and flood, through joy and grief, through battle and through peace. Look in my heart, for you have that power. Look in me, and know love."

"And I did. And I do. Eoghan." She pressed against him, burrowed into him. "There is such joy."

But she wept.

He stroked, soothed, then eased her away to see her face in the pale moonlight. "We must go back. Go back to Mayo."

"Soon. Soon. I'm sorry—"

"No." He touched his lips to hers, stilled her words. "You will not say so to me. Did you not hear my words?"

"How could I know? Even when you spoke them, when I felt them capture my heart, how could I know I would feel like this? I would wish with all I am to stay, just stay. To be here with you, to leave all the rest behind and away. And I can't. I can't give us that. Eoghan, our children."

"Nothing will touch them." Again he laid a hand on her belly. "Nothing and no one. I swear it."

"You must swear it, for when the time comes I must leave them and face Cabhan with my brother and sister."

"And with me." He gripped her shoulders as fire and fierceness lit his eyes. "Whatever you face, I face."

"You must swear." Gently she drew his hands back down to her belly where their son kicked. "Our children, Eoghan, you must swear to protect them above all. You and Teagan's man must protect them against Cabhan. I could never do what I must do unless I know their father and their uncle guard and protect them. As you love me, Eoghan, swear it."

"I would give my life for you." He rested his brow on hers, and she felt his struggle—man, husband, father. "I swear to you, I would give my life for our children. I will swear to protect them."

"I am blessed in you." She lifted his hands from her belly to her lips. "Blessed in you. You would not ask me to stay?"

"All that you are," he reminded her. "You took an oath, and that oath is mine as well. I am with you, *mo chroi*."

"You are the light in me." On a sigh, she rested her head on his shoulder. "The light that shines in our children."

She would use all she was to protect that light, all that came from it, and at last, at last, vanquish the dark.

SHE BIDED, TAKING EACH DAY, HOLDING IT CLOSE. WHEN HER children rested, when the one inside her insisted she rest as well, she sat by the fire with her mother's spell book. Studied, added her own spells, her own words and thoughts. This, she knew, she would pass down as she passed the amulet. To her children, and to the child who came from her who would carry the purpose of the Dark Witch should she and Eamon, Teagan fail.

Their mother had sworn they—or their blood—would destroy Cabhan. She had seen, with her own eyes, one of their blood from another time, had spoken to him. And she dreamed of another, a woman with her name, who wore the amulet she wore now, who was, as she was, one of three.

Sorcha's three would have children, and they would have children in turn. So the legacy would continue, and the purpose with it, until it was done. She would not, could not, turn away from it.

She would not, could not, turn away from the stirrings in her own blood as summer drew down.

But she had children to tend, a home to tend in turn, animals to feed and care for, a garden to harvest, the little goat to milk. Neighbors and travelers to heal and help.

And magicks, bright, bright magicks, to preserve.

So with her children napping—and oh, Brin had put up a battle heroic against closing his eyes—she stepped outside for a breath.

And saw her sister, her bright hair braided down her back, walking up the path with a basket.

"You must have heard me wishing for your company, for I'm after some conversation with someone more than two years of age."

"I've brown bread, for I baked more than enough. And I was yearning for you as well."

"We'll have some now, as I'm hungry every minute of every day." Laughing, Brannaugh opened her arms to her sister.

Teagan, so pretty with her hair like sunlight, her eyes like the bluebells their mother had prized.

Brannaugh gathered her close—then immediately drew her back again.

"You're with child!"

"And you couldn't give me the chance to say so to you myself?" Glowing, beaming, Teagan grabbed hold for another strong embrace. "I was only just sure of it this morning. I waked, and I knew there was life in me. I haven't told Gealbhan, for I needed first to tell you. And to be sure of it, absolutely sure. Now I am. I'm babbling like a brook. I can't stop."

"Teagan." Brannaugh's eyes welled as she kissed her sister's cheeks, as she remembered the little girl who'd wept on that dark morning so long ago. "Blessed be, *deirfiúr bheag*. Come inside. I'll make you some tea, something good for you and the life in you."

"I want to tell Gealbhan," she said as she went in with Brannaugh, took off her shawl. "By the little stream where he first kissed me. And then tell Eamon he'll again be an uncle. I want music and happy voices. Will you and Eoghan bring the children this evening?"

"We will, of course, we will. We'll have music and happy voices."

"I miss Ma. Oh, it's foolish, I know, but I want to tell her. I want to tell Da. I'm holding a life inside me, one that came from them. Was it so with you?"

"Aye, each time. When Brin came, and then my own Sorcha, I saw her for a moment, just for a moment. I felt her, and Da as well. I felt them there when my babes loosed their first cry. There was joy in that, Teagan, and sorrow. And then . . ."

"Tell me."

Her gray eyes full of that joy, that sorrow, Brannaugh folded her hands over the child within her. "The love is so fierce, so full. That life that you hold, not in your womb, but in your arms? The love that comes over you? You think you know, then you do, and what you thought you knew is pale and weak against what is. I know what she felt for us now. What she and Da felt for us. You'll know it."

"Can it be more than this?" Teagan pressed a hand to her middle. "It feels so huge already."

"It can. It will." Brannaugh looked out at the trees, at the rioting gardens. And her eyes went to smoke.

"This son in you, he will not be the one, though he'll be strong and quick to power. Nor will the son that comes from you after him. The daughter, the third, she is the next. She will be your one of the three. Fair like you, kind in her heart, quick in her mind. You will call her Ciara. One day she will wear the sign our mother made for you."

Suddenly light-headed, Brannaugh sat. Teagan rushed over to her.

"I'm well; I'm fine. It came over me so quick I wasn't ready. I'm a bit slower these days." She patted Teagan's hand.

"I never looked. I didn't think to."

"Why should you think to? You've a right simply to be happy. I wouldn't have spoiled that for all the worlds."

"You haven't. How could you spoil anything by telling me I'll have a son, and another, and a daughter? No, sit as you are. I'll finish the tea."

They both glanced toward the door as it opened.

"Sure he has the nose for fresh bread, has Eamon," Teagan said as their brother walked in with his brown hair tousled, as always, around a heartbreakingly handsome face.

With a grin he sniffed the air like a hound. "I've a nose, for certain, but didn't need it to make my way here. You've enough light swirling around the place to turn up the moon. If you're after doing a spell so bright, you might've told me."

"We weren't conjuring. Only talking. We're having a bit of a *céili* at the cabin this evening. And you can keep Brannaugh company when I leave, so I can have time to tell Gealbhan he's to be a father."

"As there's bread fresh, I can— A father is it?" Eamon's bold blue eyes filled with delight. "There's some happy news." He plucked Teagan off her feet, gave her a swing, then another when she laughed. He set her down in a chair, kissed her, then grinned at Brannaugh. "I'd do the same with you, but it's like to break my back, as you're big as a mountain."

"Don't think you'll be adding my jam to that bread."

"A beautiful mountain. One who's already given me a handsome nephew and a charming niece."

"That might get you a dollop."

"Gealbhan will be overjoyed." Gently, as he was always gentle with Teagan, he brushed his fingers down her cheek. "You're well then, are you, Teagan?"

"I feel more than wonderful. I'm likely to cook a feast, which will suit you, won't it?"

"It will, aye, it will."

"And you need to be finding the woman to suit you," Teagan added, "for you'd make a fine father."

"I'm more than fine with the two of you providing the children so I can be the happy uncle."

"She's hair like fire, eyes like the sea in storms, and a shimmer of power of her own." Brannaugh sat back, rubbing a hand over the mound of her belly. "It comes in waves these days. Some from him, I'm thinking—he's impatient." Then she smiled. "It's good seeing the woman who'd take you, Eamon. Not just for a tumble, but for the fall."

"I'm not after a woman. Or not one in particular."

Teagan reached out, laid a hand on his. "You think, and always have, you're not to have a woman, a wife, as you've sisters to protect. You're wrong, and always have been. We are three, Eamon, and both of us as able as you. When you love, you'll have no say in it."

"Don't be arguing with a woman who carries a child, especially a witch who does," Brannaugh said lightly. "I never looked for love, but it found me. Teagan waited for it, and it found her. You can run from it, *mo dearthair*. But find you it will.

"When we go home." Her eyes filled again. "Ah, curse it, I'm watering up every time I take a breath it seems. This you have to look to, Teagan. The moods come and go as they will."

"You felt it as well." Now Eamon laid a hand on Brannaugh's so the three were joined. "We're going home, and soon."

"At the next moon. We must leave on the next full moon."

"I hoped it would wait," Teagan murmured. "I hoped it would wait until you're finished birthing, though I knew in my head and my heart it would not wait."

"I will birth this son in Mayo. This child will be born at home. And yet . . . This is home as well. Not for you," she said to Eamon. "You've waited, you've bided, you've stayed, but your heart, your mind, your spirit is ever there."

"We were told we would go home again. So I waited. The three, the three that came from us. They wait as well." Eamon ran his fingers over the blue stone he wore around his neck. "We'll see them again."

"I dream of them," Brannaugh said. "Of the one who shares my name, and the others as well. They fought and they failed."

"They will fight again," Teagan said.

"They gave him pain." A fierce light came into Eamon's eyes. "He bled, as he bled when the woman named Meara, the one who came with Connor of the three, struck him with her sword."

"He bled," Brannaugh agreed. "And he healed. He gathers again. He pulls in power from the dark. I can't see where, how, but feel only. I can't see if we will change what's to come, if we can and will end him. But I see them, and know if we cannot, they will fight again."

"So we go home, and find the way. So they who come from us won't fight alone."

Brannaugh thought of her children, sleeping upstairs. Safe, innocent still. And the children of her children's children, in another time, in Mayo. Neither safe, she thought, nor innocent.

"We will find the way. We will go home. But tonight, for tonight, we'll feast. We'll have music. And we three will give thanks to all who came before us for the light. For the lives," she said, with a hand light on his sister's belly, and one on her own.

"And tomorrow." Eamon stood. "We begin to end what took the lives of our father, of our mother."

"Will you bide with Brannaugh? I would speak with Gealbhan now."

"Give him only the joy today." Brannaugh rose with her sister. "Tomorrow is soon enough for the rest. Take today for joy alone, for time is so short."

"I will." She kissed her sister, her brother. "Eoghan must bring his harp."

"Be sure he will. We'll fill the wood with music and send it flying over the hills."

She sat again when Teagan left, and Eamon nudged her tea toward her. "Drink it. You're pale."

"A bit tired. Eoghan knows. I've talked with him, and he's ready to leave—leave all he built here. I never thought it would be hard to go back. Never knew I would be torn in two ways."

"Gealbhan's brothers will tend the land here, for you and for Teagan."

"Aye, and it's a comfort. Not for you, the land here it's never been for you." Here again was sorrow and joy mixed into one. "You will stay in Mayo, whatever comes. I can't see what we will do, Eoghan and I, the children. But Teagan will come back here, that I see clear. This is her place now."

"It is," he agreed. "She will ever be a dark witch of Mayo, but her home and heart are for Clare."

"How will it be for us, Eamon, not to be together as we have been all our lives?"

His eyes, the wild blue of their father's, looked deep into hers. "A distance in space means nothing. We are always together."

"I'm weepy and foolish, and I dislike it very much. I hope this mood is a brief one or I might curse myself."

"Well, you were given to tempers and sharp words toward the end of carrying young Sorcha. It may be I prefer the weeping."

"I don't, that's for certain." She drank the tea, knowing it would settle her. "I'll add a bit more to the tonic I give Kathel and Alastar, for the journey. Roibeard does well without it yet. He's strong."

"He's hunting now," Eamon said of his hawk. "He goes farther each time. He goes north now, every day north. He knows, as we do, we'll travel soon."

"We will send word ahead. We will be welcome at Ashford Castle. The children of Sorcha and Daithi. The Dark Witches will be made welcome."

"I'll see to that." He sat back with his own tea, smiled at her. "Hair like fire, is it?"

As he'd wanted, she laughed. "Oh, and you'll be struck dumb and half blind, I promise you, when you meet."

"Not I, my darling. Not I."

2

FOR THE CHILDREN IT WAS AN ADVENTURE. THE IDEA OF a long journey, of the traveling to a new place—with the prize of a castle at the end of it, had Brin especially eager to go, to begin.

While Brannaugh packed what they'd need, she thought again of that long-ago morning, rushing to do her mother's bidding, packing all she was told to pack. So urgent, she thought now, so final. And that last look at her mother, burning with the power left in her, outside the cabin in the woods.

Now she packed to go back, a duty, a destiny she'd always accepted. Eagerly wished for—until the birth of her first child, until that swamping flood of love for the boy who even now raced about all but feverish in his excitement.

But she had a task yet to face here.

She gathered what she needed—bowl, candle, book, the herbs and stones. And with a glance at her little boy, felt both pride and regret.

"It is time for him, for this," she told Eoghan.

Understanding, he kissed her forehead. "I'll take Sorcha up. It's time she was abed."

Nodding, she turned to Brin, called him.

"I'm not tired. Why can't we leave now and sleep under the stars?"

"We leave on the morrow, but first there are things we must do, you and I."

She sat, opened her arms. "First, come sit with me. My boy," she murmured, when he crawled onto her lap. "My heart. You know what I am."

"Ma," he said and cuddled into her.

"I am, but you know, as I've never hidden it from you, what I am besides. Dark witch, keeper of magicks, daughter of Sorcha and Daithi. This is my blood. This is your blood as well. See the candle?"

"You made the candle. Ma's make the candles and bake the cakes, and Da's ride the horses."

"Is that the way of it?" She laughed, and decided she'd let him have that illusion for a little while more. "Well, it's true enough I made the candle. See the wick, Brin? The wick is cold and without light. See the candle, Brin, see the wick. See the light and flame, the tiny flame, and the heat, the light to be. You have the light in you, the flame in you. See the wick, Brin."

She crooned it to him, over and over, felt his energy begin to settle, his thoughts begin to join with her.

"The light is power. The power is light. In you, of you, through you. Your blood, my blood, our blood, your light, my light, our light. Feel what lives in you, what waits in you. See the wick, it waits for your light. For your power. Bring it. Let it rise, slow, slow, gentle and clean. Reach for it, for it belongs to you. Reach, touch, rise. Bring the light."

The wick sparked, died away, sparked again, then burned true.

Brannaugh pressed a kiss to the top of his head. There, she thought, there, the first learned. And her boy would never be just a child again.

Joy and sorrow, forever entwined.

"That is well done."

He turned his face up, smiled at her. "Can I do another?"

"Aye," she said, kissed him again. "But heed me now, and well, for there is more to learn, more to know. And the first you must know, must heed, must vow is you harm none with what you are, what you have. Your gift, Brin? An' it harm none. Swear this to me, to yourself, to all who've come before, all who will come after."

She lifted her athame, used it on her palm. "A blood oath we make. Mother to son, son to mother, witch to witch."

Solemn-eyed, he held out his hand to her, blinked at the quick pain when she nicked it.

"An' it harm none," he said when she took his hand, mixed her blood with his.

"An' it harm none," she repeated, then gathered him close, kissed the little hurt, healed it. "Now, you may do another candle. And after, together, we will make charms, for protection. For you, for your sister, for your father."

"What of you, Ma?"

She touched her pendant. "I have what I need."

IN THE MORNING MISTS, SHE CLIMBED ONTO THE WAGON, her little girl bundled at her side. She looked at her boy, so flushed with delight in the saddle in front of his father. She looked at her sister, fair and quiet astride Alastar; her brother, their grandfather's sword at his side, tall and straight on the horse he called Mithra. And Gealbhan steady and waiting on the pretty mare Alastar had sired three summers before.

She clucked to Gealbhan's old plow horse, and with Brin letting out a whoop, began. She looked back once, just once at the house she'd come to love, asked herself if she would ever see it again.

Then, she looked ahead.

A healer found welcome wherever she went—as did a harpist. Though the baby heavy in her belly was often restless, she and her family found shelter and hospitality along the wild way.

Eoghan made music, she or Teagan or Eamon offered salves or potions to the ailing or the injured. Gealbhan offered his strong back and calloused hands.

One fine night they slept under the stars as Brin so wished, and there was comfort in knowing the hound, the hawk, the horse guarded what was hers.

They met no trouble along the way, but then she knew the word had gone about. The Dark Witches, all three, journeyed through Clare and on to Galway.

"The word would reach Cabhan as well," Eamon said as they paused in their travels to rest the horses, to let the children run free for a time.

She sat between him and Teagan while Gealbhan and Eoghan watered the horses and Eamon dropped a line into the water.

"We're stronger than we were," Teagan reminded him. "We journeyed south as children. We go north children no more."

"He worries." Brannaugh stroked her belly. "As you and I carry more than we did."

"I don't doubt your power or your will."

"And still you worry."

"I wonder if it must be now," Eamon admitted, "even knowing it must be now. I feel it as both of you, and yet would be easier if there was time for both of you to have proper lyings-in before we face what we must face."

"What's meant is meant, but in truth I'm glad we'll break our journey for a day or so with our cousins. And by all the gods I'll be happy to have a day off that bloody wagon."

"I'm dreaming of Ailish's honey cakes, for no one has a finer hand with them."

"Dreaming with his belly," Teagan said.

"A man needs to eat. Hah!" He pulled up the line, and the wriggling fish who'd taken the hook. "And so we will."

"You'll need more than one," Brannaugh said, and reminded them all of those same words their mother spoke on a fine and happy day on the river at home.

They left the rugged wilds of Clare, pushed by fierce winds, sudden driving rains. They rode through the green hills of Galway, by fields of bleating sheep, by cottages where smoke puffed from chimneys. Roibeard winged ahead, under and through layers of clouds that turned the sky into a soft gray sea.

The children napped in the wagon, tucked in among the bundles, so Kathel sat beside Brannaugh, ever alert.

"There are more cottages than I remember." Teagan rode beside her on the tireless Alastar.

"The years pass."

"It's good land here—I can all but hear Gealbhan thinking it."

"Would you plant yourself here then? Does it speak to you?"

"It does. But so does our cabin in the woods in Clare. And still, the closer we come to home, the more I ache for it. We had to put that aside for so long, all of us, but now . . . Do you feel it, Brannaugh? That call to home?"

"Aye."

"Are you afraid?"

"Aye. Of what's to come, but more of failing."

"We won't." At Brannaugh's sharp look, Teagan shook her head. "No, I've had no vision, but only a certainty. One that grows stronger as we come closer to home. We won't fail, for light will always beat the dark, though it take a thousand years."

"You sound like her," Brannaugh murmured. "Like our mother."

"She's in all of us, so we won't fail. Oh, look, Brannaugh! That tree there with the twisted branches. It's the very one Eamon told our cousin Mabh came to life each full moon, to scare her. We're nearly to Ailish's farm. We're all but there."

"Go on, ride ahead."

Her face lit so she might've been a child again, Teagan tossed back her head and laughed. "So I will."

She rode to her husband, let out a fresh laugh, then set off in a gallop. Beside Brannaugh, Kathel whined, quivered.

"Go on then." Brannaugh gave him a stroke.

He leaped out of the wagon, raced behind the horse with the hawk flying above them.

It was a homecoming, for they'd lived on the farm for five years. Brannaugh found it as tidy as ever, with new outbuildings, a new paddock where young horses danced.

She saw a young boy with bright hair all but wrapped around Kathel. And knew when the boy smiled at her, he was Lughaidh, the youngest and last of her cousin's brood.

Ailish herself rushed over to the wagon. She'd grown a bit rounder, and streaks of gray touched her own fair hair. But her eyes were as lively and young as ever.

"Brannaugh! Oh look at our Brannaugh! Seamus, come over and help your cousin down from the wagon."

"I'm fine." Brannaugh clambered down herself, embraced her cousin. "Oh, oh, it does my heart good to see you again."

"And mine, seeing you. Oh, you're a beauty, as ever. So like your mother. And here's our Eamon, so handsome. My cousins, three, come back as you said you would. I've sent the twins off to get Bardan from the field, and Seamus, you run over and tell Mabh her cousins are here."

Teary-eyed, she embraced Brannaugh again. "Mabh and her man have their own cottage, just across the way. She's near ready to birth her first. I'm to be a granny! Oh, I can't stop my tongue from wagging. It's Eoghan, aye? And Teagan's Gealbhan. Welcome, welcome all of you. But where are your children?"

"Asleep in the wagon."

Nothing would do but for Ailish to gather them up, to ply them with the honey cakes Eamon remembered so fondly. Then Conall, who'd been but a babe in arms when last she'd seen him, took her children off to see a new litter of puppies.

"They'll be fine, my word on it," Ailish said as she poured out tea. "He's a good lad, is Conall—one you helped bring into the world. We'll let the men see to the horses and that, and you'll both take your ease awhile."

"Praise be." Brannaugh sipped the tea, let it and the fire warm her, soothe her. "I'm sitting in a chair that's not moving."

"Eat. You've another in you who needs the food as well."

"I'm starving all the day and half the night. Teagan's not as hungry—yet. But she will be."

"Oh, are you carrying?" Delight glowed on her face as Ailish stopped her fussing with tea, laid her hands over her own heart. "My sweet little Teagan, to be a mother. The years, where do they go? You were but a babe yourself. Will you stay? Will you stay until your time comes?" she asked Brannaugh. "It's still a distance to Mayo, and you're close. I can see you're close."

"A day or two only, and so grateful for it. The babe will be born in Mayo. It's meant. It's what must be."

"Must it?" Ailish gripped Brannaugh's hand, then Teagan's in turn. "Must it? You've made your lives in Clare. You're women, mothers. Must you go back to the dark that waits?"

"We're women, and mothers, and more. We can turn our back on none of it. But don't fret, cousin. Don't think of it. We have today, with tea and cakes and family."

"We will come back again." When they looked at her, Teagan pressed a hand to her heart. "I feel it so strong. We will come back again. Believe that. Believe in us. I think faith only makes us stronger."

"If that's so, you'll have all of mine."

They had music and feasting and family. And for a night and a day peace. Still Brannaugh found herself restless. Though her man slept in the bed Ailish had provided them, she sat by the fire.

Ailish came in, wearing her night-robes and a thick shawl.

"You need some of the tea you always made for me when I was so close to the end, and the babe so heavy in me I couldn't sleep."

"I look for her in the fire and smoke," Brannaugh murmured. "I can't help the looking, I miss her so. More as we near home. I miss my father; it's an ache. But my mother is a kind of grieving that won't end."

"I know it." Ailish sat beside her. "Does she come to you?"

"In dreams. There are moments, but only moments. I long to hear her voice, to have her tell me I'm doing right. That I'm doing what she'd want of me."

"Oh, my love, you are. You are. Do you remember the day you left us?"

"I do. I hurt you by leaving."

"Leaving always hurts, but it was what was right—I've come to know it. Before you left you told me of Lughaidh, the babe I carried. You said he must be the last, for neither I nor a babe would live through another birthing. And you gave me a potion to drink, every moon until the bottle was empty. So there would be no more children for me. It grieved me."

"I know." And knew it more poignantly now that she had her own children. "You are the best of mothers, and were one to me."

"I would not have lived to see my children grown, to see my oldest girl ripe with her own child. To see, as you told me, Lughaidh, so bright and sweet, with a voice—as you said—like an angel."

Nodding, Ailish studied the fire in turn, as if seeing that day again in the smoke and flame. "You laid protection over me and mine, gave me the years I might not have had. You are what she would want. Even as it grieves me that you will go, you will face Cabhan, I know you must. Never doubt she is proud of you. Never doubt, Brannaugh."

"You comfort me, Ailish."

"I will have faith, as Teagan asked. Every night I will light a candle. I will light it with the little magick I have so that it shines for you, for Teagan, for Eamon."

"I know you fear the power."

"It's my blood as well. You are mine as you were hers. This I will do, every sunset, and in the small light I'll put my faith. Know it burns for you and yours. Know that, and be safe."

"We will come back. In that I will have faith. We will come back, and you will hold the child now inside me."

THEY JOURNEYED ON, WITH A LITTLE SPOTTED PUP GIVEN the children with much ceremony, and with promises for a longer visit when they returned.

The air grew colder, the wind brisk.

More than once she heard Cabhan's voice, sly and seductive, trailing on that wind.

I wait.

She would see Teagan look out over the hills, or Eamon rubbing his fingers over his pendant—and know they heard as well.

When the hawk veered off, and Alastar strained to follow, Kathel leaped out of the wagon, trotted off on a fork in the road.

"It's not the way." Eoghan pulled his horse up by the wagon. "We would make Ashford by tomorrow, but that is not the way."

"No, not the way to Ashford, but the way we must go. Trust the guides, Eoghan. There's something we must do first. I feel it."

Eamon drew up on the other side. "Near home," he said. "All but near enough to taste. But we're called."

"Aye, we're called. So we answer." She reached out, touched her husband's arm. "We must."

"Then we will."

She didn't know the way, yet she did. With her mind linked with the hound's she knew the road, the turns, the hills. And oh, she felt him reaching out, that darkness, hungry and eager to take what she was, and more.

The hazy sun slid down toward the western hills, but still they rode. Her back ached from the hours in the wagon, and a thirst rose up in her. But they rode.

She saw the shadow of it in the oncoming dark—the rise of it with fields around. A place of worship, she thought, she could feel that.

And a place of power.

She stopped the wagon, breathed the air.

"He can't get through. It's too strong for him to push through."

"Something here," Eamon murmured.

"Something bright," Teagan said. "Strong and bright. And old."

"Before us." Grateful for the help, Brannaugh let her husband lift her from the wagon. "Before our mother. Before any time we know."

"A church." Gealbhan reached up to lift Teagan from the saddle. "But no one's here."

"They're here." Weary, Teagan leaned against him. "Those who came before us, those who sanctified this ground. They will not let him pass. This is a holy place."

"Tonight, this is ours." Brannaugh stepped forward, lifted her hands. "Gods of light, goddesses bright, we call to you across the night. By the power you have given, by the purpose we are driven, we seek your blessing. A night within your walls before whatever fates befall, this respite, this resting. We are Sorcha's three. Dark witches come to thee. By thy will, so mote it be."

Light bloomed like sun, shining through the windows, the doors that opened with a wind like breath. And warmth poured out.

"We are welcome here." Smiling, she lifted her daughter, and all the fatigue from the long journey fell away. "We are welcome."

Brannaugh settled the children to sleep on pallets she made on the floor of the church. And was grateful to find both of them too weary to whine or argue, for her momentary energy already flagged.

"Do you hear them?" Eamon whispered.

"Even I hear them." Eoghan scanned the church, the stone walls, the wooden seats. "They sing."

"Aye." Gealbhan picked up the pup to soothe it. "Soft, lovely. As angels or gods might sing. This is a holy place."

"It offers more than sanctuary for the night." A hand pressed to her back, Brannaugh rose. "It offers the blessing, and the light. We were called by those who've come before us, to this place, on this night."

Teagan touched her fingers lightly, reverently, to the altar. "Built by a king for a kindness given. A promise kept. Built here near a pilgrim's walk. This abbey called Ballintubber."

She lifted her hands, smiled. "This much I see." She turned to her husband. "Aye, this is a holy place, and we'll seek the blessing of those who called us."

"Like the king," Brannaugh said, "we have a promise to keep. Eoghan, my love, would you fetch me my mother's book?"

"I will, aye—if you will sit. Just sit, Brannaugh. You're too pale."

"I'm weary, in truth, but I promise you this must be done, and we will all be better for it. Teagan—"

"I know what we need. I'll—"

"Sit," her brother insisted. "I'll get what we need, and the both of you will take your ease for a moment. Gealbhan, I swear by the gods, sit on the pair of them if they don't rest for a bit."

Gealbhan had only to touch his wife's cheek, to take Brannaugh's hand to have them heed. "What must be done?" he asked Teagan.

"An offering. An asking. A gathering. He cannot come here. Cabhan cannot come here, or see here. Here he has no power. And here, we can gather ours together."

"What do you need?"

"You are the best of us." She kissed his cheek. "If you would help Eamon, I promise you Brannaugh and I will bide here, will rest."

When he'd gone, she turned quickly to Brannaugh. "You have pain."

"It's not the birthing pains. You'll learn the babe often gives you a bit of a taste of what's coming. This will pass. But the rest is welcome. What we will do here will take strength."

They took an hour, to rest, to prepare.

"We must cast the circle," she told Eoghan, "and make the offering. Do not fear for me."

"Would you ask me not to breathe?"

"It is your love, your faith, and Gealbhan's with yours we need."

"Then you have it."

They cast the circle, and the cauldron floated over the fire they made. Water flowed from Teagan's hands into the cauldron. Brannaugh added herbs, Eamon crushed stones.

"These come from the home we made."

"And these." Teagan opened a pouch, poured in the precious. "From the home we seek. Small things, a dried flower, a pebble, a bit of bark."

"More than gold or silver treasured. We offer to you. Here, a lock of hair from my firstborn."

"A feather from my guide." Eamon added it to the now bubbling cauldron.

"This charm my mother made me."

"Ah, Teagan," Brannaugh murmured.

"She would wish it." Teagan added it to the offering.

"To you we give what we hold dear, and add to them this witch's tear. And seal with blood this brew to show our hearts are true."

And each with a sacred knife offered their blood, and with it the bubbling cauldron boiled and smoked.

"Father, mother, blood of our blood and bone of our bone, we orphans have faith forever shown. Grant us here in this holy place, in this holy hour the might and right of your power. With your gift we cannot fail and over Cabhan will prevail. Imbue us now, we witches three. As we will, so mote it be."

The wind had stirred inside the walls. The candlelight gone brilliant. But at the final words the three spoke together, the wind whirled, the light flashed.

The voices that had murmured, rang out.

With her siblings Brannaugh clasped hands, with them she dropped to her knees.

It ripped through her, the light, the voices, the wind. And the power.

Then came silence.

She rose again, and with Teagan and Eamon turned.

"You were alight," Eoghan said in wonder. "Like candles yourselves."

"We are the three." Teagan's voice rose and echoed in the humming silence. "But there are many. Many before us, many who come after."

"Their light is ours; ours is theirs." Eamon lifted his arms, his sisters' high. "We are the three, and we are one."

Filled with light, fatigue vanished, suffused, Brannaugh smiled. "We are the three. We cast our light over the dark, we seek it out of its shadows. And we will prevail."

"By our blood," they said together, "we will prevail."

IN THE MORNING, IN THE SOFT LIGHT OF DAY, THEY SET OUT again. They traveled the road with green hills rising, with water shining blue under a welcoming sun. Toward the grand gray stones of Ashford they rode, where the gates were open for them, the bridge drawn down, and the sun shined bright over the water, over the land of their birth.

And so Sorcha's children came home.

3

Winter 2013

BRANNA O'DWYER WOKE TO A GRAY, SOGGY, RELENTLESS rain. And wished for nothing more than to burrow in and sleep again. Mornings, she had always felt, came forever too soon. But like it or not, sleep was done, and with its leaving came a slow and steady craving for coffee.

Annoyed, as she was often annoyed by morning, she rose, pulled thick socks over her feet, drew a sweater over the thin T-shirt she'd slept in.

Through habit and an ingrained tidiness, she stirred up the bedroom fire so the licks of flame would cheer the room, and with her hound, Kathel, having his morning stretch on the hearthrug, she made her bed, added the mounds of pretty pillows that pleased her.

In her bath, she brushed out her long fall of black hair, then bundled it up. She had work, and plenty of it—after coffee. She frowned at herself in the mirror, considered doing a bit of a glamour, as the restless night surely showed. But didn't see the point.

Instead, she walked back into the bedroom, gave Kathel a good rub to get his tail wagging.

"You were restless as well, weren't you now? I heard you talking in your sleep. Did you hear the voices, my boy?"

They walked down together, quiet, as her house was full as it was too often these days. Her brother and Meara shared his bed, and her cousin Iona shared hers with Boyle.

Friends and family all. She loved them, and needed them. But God be sweet, she could've done with some alone.

"They stay for me," she told Kathel as they walked down the steps of the pretty cottage. "As if I can't look after myself. Have I not put enough protection around what's mine, and theirs, to hold off a dozen Cabhans?"

It had to stop, really, she decided, heading straight toward her lovely, lovely coffee machine. A man of Boyle McGrath's size could hardly be comfortable in her cousin Iona's little bed. She needed to nudge them along. In any case, there had been no sign nor shadow of Cabhan since Samhain.

"We almost had him. Bugger it, we nearly finished it."

The spell, the potion, both so strong, she thought as she started the coffee. Hadn't they worked on both hard and long? And the power, by the gods, the power had risen like a flood that night by Sorcha's old cabin.

They'd hurt him, spilled his blood, sent him howling—wolf and man. And still . . .

Not done. He'd slipped through, and would be healing, would be gathering himself.

Not done, and at times she wondered if ever it would be.

She opened the door, and Kathel rushed out. Rain or no, the dog wanted his morning run. She stood in the open doorway, in the cold, frosty December air, looking toward the woods.

He waited, she knew, beyond them. In this time or in another, she couldn't tell. But he would come again, and they must be ready.

But he wouldn't come this morning.

She closed the door on the cold, stirred up the kitchen fire, added fuel so the scent of peat soothed. Pouring her coffee, she savored the first taste, and the short time of quiet and alone. And, a magick of its own, the coffee cleared her head, smoothed her mood.

We will prevail.

The voices, she remembered now. So many voices rising up, echoing out. Light and power and purpose. In sleep she'd felt it all. And that single voice, so clear, so sure.

We will prevail.

"We'll pray you're right about it."

She turned.

The woman stood, a hand protectively over the mound of her belly, a thick shawl tied around a long dress of dark blue.

Almost a mirror, Branna thought, almost like peering into a glass. The hair, the eyes, the shape of the face.

"You're Brannaugh of Sorcha. I know you from dreams."

"Aye, and you, Branna of the clan O'Dwyer. I know you from dreams. You're my blood."

"I am. I am of the three." Branna touched the amulet with its icon of the hound she was never without—just as her counterpart did the same.

"Your brother came to us, with his woman, one night in Clare."

"Connor, and Meara. She is a sister to me." Now Branna touched her heart. "Here. You understand."

"She saved my own brother from harm, shed blood for him. She is a sister to me as well." With some wonder on her face, Sorcha's Brannaugh looked around the kitchen. "What is this place?"

"My home. And yours for you are very welcome here. Will you sit? I would make you tea. This coffee I have would not be good for the baby."

"It has a lovely scent. But only sit with me, cousin. Just sit for a moment. This is a wondrous place."

Branna looked around her kitchen—tidy, lovely, as she'd designed it herself. And, she supposed, wondrous indeed to a woman from the thirteenth century.

"Progress," she said as she sat at the kitchen table with her cousin. "It eases hours of work. Are you well?"

"I am, very well. My son comes soon. My third child. She reached out; Branna took her hand.

Heat and light, a merging of power very strong, very true.

"You will name him Ruarc, for he will be a champion."

It brought a smile to her cousin's face. "So I will."

"On Samhain, we—the three and three more who are with us—battled Cabhan. Though we caused him harm, burned and bled him, we didn't finish him. I saw you there. Your brother with a sword, your sister with a wand, you with a bow. You were not with child."

"Samhain is yet a fortnight to come in my time. We came to you?"

"You did, at Sorcha's cabin where we lured him, and in your time, as we shifted into it to try to trap him. We were close, but it wasn't enough. My book—Sorcha's book—I could show you the spell, the poison we conjured. You may—"

Brannaugh held up a hand, pressed the other to her side. "My son comes. And he pulls me back. But listen, there is a place, a holy place. An abbey. It sits in a field, a day's travel south."

"Ballintubber. Iona weds her Boyle there come spring. It is a holy place, a strong place."

"He cannot go there, see there. It is sacred, and those who made us watch over it. They gave us, Sorcha's three, their light, their hope and strength. When next you face down Cabhan, we will be with you. We will find a way. We will prevail. If it is not to be you, there will come another three. Believe, Branna of the O'Dwyers. Find the way."

"I can do nothing else."

"Love." She gripped Branna's hand hard. "Love, I have learned, is another guide. Trust your guides. Oh, he's impatient. My child comes today. Be joyful, for he is another bright candle against the dark. Believe," she said again, and vanished.

Branna rose, and with a thought lit a candle for the new light, the new life.

And with a sigh, accepted her alone was at an end.

So she started breakfast. She had a story to tell, and no one would want to hear it on an empty stomach. Believe, she thought—Well, she believed it was part of her lot in life to cook for an army on nearly a daily basis.

She swore an oath that when they'd sent Cabhan to hell she'd take a holiday, somewhere warm, sunny—where she wouldn't touch a pot, pan, or skillet for days on end.

She began to mix the batter for pancakes—a recipe new to her she'd wanted to try—and Meara came in.

Her friend was dressed for the day, a working day at the stables, in thick trousers, a warm sweater, sturdy boots. She'd braided back her bark brown hair, sent Branna a cautious look with her dark gypsy eyes.

"I promised I'd see to breakfast this morning."

"I woke early, after a restless night. And have already had company this morning."

"Someone's here?"

"Was here. Drag the others down, would you, so I'll tell my tale all at once." She hesitated only a moment. "Best if Connor or Boyle rings up Fin, and asks if he'd come over as well."

"It's Cabhan. Is he back?"

"He's coming, right enough, but no."

"I'll get the others. Everyone's up, so it won't take long."

With a nod, Branna set bacon sizzling in a pan.

Connor came first, and her brother sniffed the air like Kathel might do.

"Be useful," she told him. "Set the table."

"Straightaway. Meara said something happened, but it wasn't Cabhan."

"Do you think I'd be trying my hand with these pancake things if I'd gone a round with Cabhan?"

"I don't." He fetched plates from the cupboard. "He stays in the shadows. He's stronger than he was, but not full healed. I barely feel him yet, but Fin said he's not full healed."

And Finbar Burke would know, Branna thought, as he was Cabhan's blood, as he bore the mark of Sorcha's curse.

"He's on his way," Connor added.

When she only nodded, he went to the door, opened it for Kathel. "And look at you, wet as a seal."

"Dry him off," Branna began, then sighed when Connor simply saw to the task by gliding his hands over the wet fur. "We've towels in the laundry for that."

Connor only grinned, a quick flash from a handsome face, a quick twinkle in moss green eyes. "Now he's dry all the faster, and you don't have a wet towel to wash."

Iona and Boyle came in, hand in hand. A pair of lovebirds, Branna thought. If anyone had suggested to her a year before that the taciturn, often brusque, former brawler could resemble a lovebird, she'd have laughed till her ribs cracked. But there he was, big, broad-shouldered, his hair tousled, his tawny eyes just a little dreamy beside her bright sprite of an American cousin.

"Meara will be right down," Iona announced. "She had a call from her sister."

"All's well?" Connor asked. "Her ma?"

"No problems—just some Christmas details." Without being asked she got out flatware to finish what Connor started, and Boyle put the kettle on for tea.

So Branna's kitchen filled with voices, with movement—and she could admit now that she'd had coffee—with the warmth of family. And then excitement as Meara dashed in, grabbed Connor and pulled him into a dance.

"I'm to pack up the rest of my mother's things." She did a quick stomp, click, stomp, then grabbed Connor again for a hard kiss. "She's staying with my sister Maureen for the duration. Praise be, and thanks to the little Baby Jesus in his manger!"

Even as Connor laughed, she stopped, pressed her hands to her face. "Oh God, I'm a terrible daughter, a horrible person altogether. Dancing about because my own mother's gone to live with my sister in Galway and I'll not have to deal with her on a daily basis myself."

"You're neither," Connor corrected. "Are you happy your mother's happy?"

"Of course, I am, but—"

"And why shouldn't you be? She's found a place where she's content, where she has grandchildren to spoil. And why shouldn't you kick up your heels a bit, as she won't be ringing you up twice a day when she can't work out how to switch out a lightbulb?"

"Or burns another joint of lamb," Boyle added.

"That's the bloody truth, isn't it?" So Meara did another quick dance. "I'm happy for her, I am. And I'm wild with joy for my own self."

When Fin came in Meara launched herself at him—and gave Branna a moment to adjust herself, as she had to do whenever he walked in her door.

"You've lost a tenant, Finbar. My ma's settled once and done with my sister." She kissed him hard as well, made him laugh. "That's thanks to you—and don't say you don't need it—for the years of low rent, and for holding the little cottage in case she wanted to come back to Cong."

"She was a fine tenant. Kept the place tidy as a church."

"The place looks fine now, it does, with the updates we've done." As Iona took over the table setting, Connor grabbed his first coffee. "I expect Fin will have someone in there, quick as you please."

"I'll be looking into it." But it was Branna he looked at, and into. Then saying nothing, took Connor's coffee for himself.

She kept her hands busy, and wished to bloody hell she'd done that little glamour. No restless night showed on his face, on that beautiful carving of it, in the bold green eyes.

He looked perfect—man and witch—with his raven black hair damp from the rain, his body tall and lean as he shed his black leather jacket, hung it on a peg.

She'd loved him all her life, understood, accepted, she always would. But the first and only time they'd given themselves to each other—so young, still so innocent—the mark had come on him.

Cabhan's mark.

A Dark Witch of Mayo could never be with Cabhan's blood.

She could, would, and had worked with him, for he'd proven time and again he wanted Cabhan's end as much as she. But there could never be more.

Did knowing it pained him as it did her help her through it? Maybe a bit, she admitted. Just a bit.

She took the platter heaped with pancakes she'd already flipped from the skillet out of the warmer, added the last of them.

"We'll sit then, and eat. It's your Nan's recipe, Iona. We'll see if I did her proud."

Even as she lifted the platter, Fin took it from her. And as he took it, his eyes met and held hers. "You've a story to go with them, I'm told."

"I do, yes." She took a plate full of bacon and sausage, carried it to the table. And sat. "Not an hour ago I sat here and had a conversation with Sorcha's Brannaugh."

"She came here?" Connor paused in the act of sliding a stack of pancakes onto his plate. "Our kitchen?"

"She did. I'd had a restless night, full of dreams and voices. Hers among them. I couldn't be sure of the place as it was vague and scattered as dreams can be." She took a single pancake for herself. "I was here, getting my first cup of coffee, and I turned around. There she was.

"She looks like me—or I like her. That was a jolt of surprise, just how close we are there—though she was heavily pregnant. Her son comes today—or not today, as in her time it was still a fortnight to Samhain."

"Time shifts," Iona murmured.

"As you say. They'd gone to Ballintubber Abbey on the way here. That's where the dream took me."

"Ballintubber." Iona shifted to Boyle. "I felt them there, remember? When you took me to see it, I felt them, knew they'd gone there. It's such a strong place."

"It is, yes," Branna agreed. "But I've been there more than once, as has Connor. I never felt them."

"You haven't been since Iona's come," Fin pointed out. "You haven't been there since the three are all in Mayo."

"True enough." And a good point, she was forced to admit. "But I will, we will. On your wedding day, Iona, if not before. She said the others, those before us, guard the place, so Cabhan's barred from it. He can't go in, see in. It's a true sanctuary if we find we need one. They, who came before, gave light and strength to the three. And hope—I think she needed that most."

"And you," Iona said, "all of us. Hope wouldn't hurt us either."

"I'm more for doing than hoping, but it gave her what she needed. I could see it. She said—in the dream, and here—we will prevail. To believe that, and they'll be with us when we face Cabhan again. To find the way. To know, if it isn't for us to finish, another three will come. We will prevail."

"Though it takes a thousand years," Connor added. "Well then, I'm fine with hope, fine with doing. But I'll be buggered if I wait a thousand years to see the end of Cabhan."

"Then we find the way, in the here and the now. I had pancakes once when I went to Montana in the American West," Fin commented. "They called them something else . . ."

"Flapjacks, I bet," Iona suggested.

"That's the very thing. They were brilliant. These are better yet."

"You've rambled far and wide," Branna said.

"I have. But I'm done with rambling until this is done. So, like Connor, a thousand years won't suit me. We find the way."

Just like that? Branna thought and struggled against annoyance. "She said they'd be with us, next time we faced him down. But they were there on Samhain, and still he got away from us."

"Only just there, or barely," Connor remembered. "Shadows like? Part of the dream spell we cast, that could be. How would we bring them full—could it be done? If we could find *that* way, how could we not end him? The first three, and we three. And the three more with us."

"Time's the problem." Fin sat back with his coffee. "The shifts. We were there on Samhain, but from what you say, Branna, they were not. So they were but shadows, and unable to take part. We have to make the times meet. Our time or theirs, but the same. It's interesting, an interesting puzzle to solve."

"But what time and when?" Branna demanded. "I've found two, and each should have worked. The solstice, then Samhain. The time should have been on the side of light. The spells we worked, the poison we created, all done to mesh with that specific time and place."

"And both times we wounded him," Boyle reminded her. "Both times he bled and fled. And the last? It should've been mortal."

"His power's as dark as ours is light," Iona pointed out. "And the source of it heals him. Longer this time. It's taking longer."

"If we could find his lair." Connor's face turned grim. "If we could go at him when he's weakened."

"I can't find him. Even the two of us together failed," Fin reminded him. "He has enough, or what feeds him has enough to hide. Until he slithers out again, and I—or one of us—can feel him, we wait."

"I'd hoped by Yule, but that's nearly on us." Branna shook her head. "I'd hoped we could take him on by Yule, though that was more from a wanting it done than a knowing it was the time. I haven't found it in the stars. Not yet anyway."

"It seems to me we have an outline of the work needed." Boyle lifted a shoulder. "Finding the day, the time. Finding the way to bring the first three into it, if that's a true possibility."

"I believe it is." Fin looked at Branna.

"We'll study on it, work on it."

"I've time this morning."

"I have to go into the shop, take stock in. I'm barely keeping up with the holidays."

"I can help tomorrow, my off day," Iona offered.

"I'll take it."

"I want to finish a little shopping myself," Iona added. "My first Christmas in Ireland. And Nan's coming. I can't wait to see her, and to show her the house—well, what there is of it." She leaned into Boyle. "We're building a house in the woods."

"She changed her mind on the tiles in the big bath again," Boyle told the room at large.

"It's hard to decide. I've never built a house before." She looked at Branna. "Help me."

"I told you there's little I'd love more. Give me tomorrow, and we'll spend an hour or so over wine at day's end for looking at tile and paint samples and so on."

"Connor and I start talking about what we might want our place to look like, sitting in the field above the cottage here. And my brain goes to mush instantly." Meara swirled a bite of pancake in syrup. "I can't really get my mind around the building of a place, and the knowing down to the color of paint on the walls."

"Well, come for the wine and we'll play with yours as well. And speaking of houses," Branna added as she saw the door opening to her early-morning thoughts. "The lot of you have places—Boyle's, Meara's. There's no need for all of you to pack yourself in here every night."

"We're better together," Connor insisted.

"And there wouldn't be the idea that sleeping at Meara's flat would mean oatmeal for breakfast most mornings?"

He grinned. "It would be a factor."

"I've a fine way with oatmeal." Meara poked him.

"That you do, darling, but did you taste these pancakes?"

"I confess even my famous oatmeal can't rise up to them. You're after a bit of space," Meara said to Branna.

"I wouldn't mind some, now and again."

"We'll work on that as well."

"It seems we've plenty to be working on." Boyle rose. "I'd say we have to start with clearing up Branna's kitchen, and getting to the work that makes our living."

"When will you be back from your shop business?" Fin asked Branna.

She'd hoped the divergence of talk had distracted him off that, and should have known better. More, she admitted, avoiding working with him couldn't be done. Not for the greater good.

"I'll be back by two."

"Then I'll be here at two." He rose, picked up his plate to take it to the sink.

MAKING A LIVING HAD TO BE DONE, AND IN TRUTH, BRANNA enjoyed the making of hers. Once her house was empty and quiet, she went up to dress for the day, banked her bedroom fire to a simmer.

Down in her workshop she spent the next hour wrapping the fancy soaps she'd made the day before. Adding the ribbons and dried flowers to the bottles of lotions she'd already poured.

Candles she'd scented with cranberry she tucked into the fancy gift boxes she'd bought for the holiday traffic.

After a check of the list her manager had given her, she added salve, bath oil, various creams, noted down what needed replenishing, then began to carry boxes out to her car.

She'd intended to leave the dog home, but Kathel had other plans and jumped right in the car.

"After a ride, are you? Well, all right then." After one last check, she slid behind the wheel, and took the short drive to the village of Cong.

The rain and the cold discouraged any tourists pulled to the area in December. She found the steep streets empty, the abbey ruins deserted. Like a place out of time, she thought, with a smile.

She loved it, empty in the rain, or full of people and voices on a fine day. While she sold straight out of her workshop from time to time—especially to those who might come in hoping for a charm or spell—she'd chosen to place her shop in the village where the tourists and locals could easily breeze in. And as she was ever practical, where they might exchange some euros for what she made herself.

She parked in front of the whitewashed building, the corner shop on the pretty side street where the Dark Witch was housed.

Kathel jumped out behind her, waited patiently despite the rain while she unloaded the first box of stock. She elbowed open the door to a cheery ring of bells, walked into the lovely scents, the pretty lights of what she'd made herself, for herself.

All the lovely bottles, bowls, boxes on shelves, candles flickering to add atmosphere—and that lovely scent. Soft colors to soothe and relax, bold ones to energize, hunks of crystal placed just so for power.

And of course, the fuss for the holiday with the little tree, the greenery and berries, some ornaments she bought from a woman in Dublin, the jeweled wands and stone pendants she bought from a Wiccan catalog because people expected such things in a shop called the Dark Witch.

And there was Eileen, her pixie-sized body up on a step stool, cleaning a high shelf. Eileen turned, her bold green glasses slipping down her pug of a nose.

"Well now, it's the lady herself, and glad I am to see you, Branna.

I hope you've come with more of those cranberry candles, for I sold the very last of them not fifteen minutes ago."

"I have two dozen more, as you asked. I would've thought too many, but if we're fully out, you were right again."

"It's why you made me manager." Eileen stepped down. She wore her dark blond hair in a scoop, dressed always smart—today in tall boots under a pine green dress. She was barely five feet altogether, and had borne and raised five strapping sons.

"More in the car then? I'll go fetch them in."

"You won't, no, as there's no need for both of us to be drenched." Branna set the first box down on the spotless counter. "You can unpack and keep Kathel company, for he insisted on coming along."

"He knows where I keep special treats for lovely, good dogs."

His tail wagged as she spoke, and he sat politely, all but grinned at her.

Branna went out into the rain again, Eileen's laugh trailing behind her.

It took three trips, and a truly thorough drenching.

She waved her hands, down from her hair to her feet, drying herself as Connor had dried the dog that morning. Something she would have done for few outside her own circle.

Eileen didn't so much as blink, but continued to unpack the stock. Branna had chosen Eileen to run her shop, and manage the part-time clerks, for many practical reasons. But not the least of them was the wisps of power she sensed in the woman, and Eileen's acceptance of all Branna was.

"I had four hearty tourists—in from the Midlands—come to see *The Quiet Man* museum, have lunch at the pub. They stopped in, and dropped three hundred and sixty euros among them before they headed out again."

And not the least of those practical reasons, Branna thought now, was Eileen's knack of guiding the right customer to the right products.

"That's fine news on a rainy morning."

"Will you have some tea then, Branna?"

"No, but thanks." Instead, Branna pushed up her sleeves and helped Eileen unpack and place the stock. "And how's it all going?"

As she'd hoped, Eileen kept her mind off her troubles by catching her up with village gossip, with news of her sons, her husband, daughters-in-law (two, and another in June), grandchildren, and all else under the sun.

A scatter of customers came in during the hour she worked, and didn't leave empty-handed. And that was good for the spirit as well as the pocketbook.

She'd built a fine place here, Branna reminded herself. Full of color and light and scent, and all tidily arranged as her organized soul demanded—and as artfully displayed as her sense of style could wish.

And she thanked the gods again for Eileen and the others who worked for her, that they dealt with the customers, and she could have her time in her workshop to create.

"You're a treasure to me, Eileen."

Eileen's face flushed with pleasure. "Ah now, that's a lovely thing to say."

"A true one." She kissed Eileen's dimpled cheek. "How fortunate are we as we both get to do what we love and are bloody good at, every day? If I had to work the counter and such as I did in the first months I opened, I'd be mad as a hatter. So you're my treasure."

"Well, you're mine in turn, as having an employer who leaves me to my own ways is a gift."

"Then I'm leaving you to it now, and we'll both go on with what we love and do bloody well."

When she and Kathel left, Branna felt refreshed. A trip to her shop tended to lift her mood, and today's had lifted it higher than most. She drove through the rain on roads as familiar as her own kitchen, then sat a moment outside her cottage.

A good morning, she thought, despite the dreariness of the day. She'd spoken to her cousin, one of the first three, and at her own kitchen table. She would think and think long and hard on the hope and faith needed.

She'd taken good stock into her shop, spent an hour and more with a friend, watched people take away things she'd made with her own hands. Into their homes those things would go, she mused. Or to others as gifts and mementos. Good, useful things, and pretty besides, for she valued the pretty as much as the useful.

And thinking just that, she lifted a hand and had the tree in her front window, the lights around the windows of her shop twinkling on.

"And why not add some pretty and some light to a dreary day?" she asked Kathel. "And now, my boy, we've work to do."

She went straight to her workshop, boosted the fire while Kathel made himself comfortable on the floor in front of it.

She'd told Fin she'd be back by two, knowing she'd planned to return by noon. A bit later than her plan, she noted, but she still had near to two hours of quiet and alone before she had him to deal with.

After donning a white apron, she made ginger biscuits first because it pleased her. While they cooled and their scent filled the air, she gathered what she needed to make the candle sets on the new list Eileen had given her.

It soothed her, this work. She wouldn't deny she added a touch of magick, but all for the good. All in all it was care, it was art, and science.

On the stove she melted her acid and wax, added the fragrance oils, the coloring she made herself. Now the scents of apple and cinnamon joined the ginger. With a dollop she fixed the wicks in the little glass jars with the fluted edges, held them straight and true with a slim bamboo stick. The pour required patience, stopping to use another stick to poke into the apple-red wax to prevent pockets of air from forming. So she poured, poked until the little jars were filled and set aside for cooling.

A second batch, white and pure and scented with vanilla, and a third to make the scent—for three was a good number—green as the forest and perfumed with pine. Seasonal, she thought, and the season on them, so a half dozen sets should do.

The next she made perhaps she'd bring in spring.

Satisfied with the work, she glanced at the clock, saw it was nearly half-two. So the man was late, but that was fine as she'd had time to finish as she'd wanted.

But she'd be damned if she'd wait for him on the next job of work.

She took off her apron, hung it up, made herself some tea, and took two biscuits from the jar. With them, she sat, opened Sorcha's book, her own, her notebook, her laptop.

In the quiet alone, she began to study all they'd done before, and how they might do it better.

He came in—fully thirty-five minutes late—and drenched. She barely spared him a glance, and said, firmly, "Don't track up my floor."

He muttered something she ignored, dried himself quickly. "There's no point in being annoyed I'm later than I said. One of the horses took sick and needed tending."

She often forgot he had work of his own. "How bad?"

"It was bad enough, but she'll be all right. It's Maggie, and a sudden stable cough. The medicine might have righted her, but . . . well, I wouldn't risk it."

"You wouldn't, no." And there, she knew him. His softest spot was for animals, for anything and anyone who needed tending. "And couldn't." And it had been bad enough, she could see that now as well in the fatigue in his eyes.

"Sit. You need some tea."

"I wouldn't mind it, or a couple of those biscuits I smell. The ginger ones?"

"Sit," she said again, and went to turn up the heat on the kettle.

But he wandered around, restless.

"You've been working, I see. New candles not yet set."

"I've a shop to fill. I can't spend every moment of my day on bloody Cabhan."

"You can spend it taking offense from me where none was meant. And as it happens I want some candles for myself."

"Those just made are for gift sets."

"I'll have two of those then, as I've gifts to buy, and for more . . ." He wandered over to some shelves. "I like these you have here in the mirror jars. They'd shine in the light." He lifted one, sniffed at it. "Cranberries. It smells of Yule, so that suits, doesn't it? I'd have a dozen."

"I don't have a dozen of those, exactly, on hand. Just the three you see there."

"You could make the rest."

She made the tea, slanted him a look. "I could. You'll have to wait for them until tomorrow."

"That'll do. And these tapers as well, the long white ones, the smaller red."

"Did you come to work or to shop?"

"It's a fine thing to do both in one place, at one time." He took what he wanted, set it all on her counter for later.

After he sat, lifted his tea, he looked directly into her eyes. Her heart might have skipped, just once, but she ignored it.

"On the other side of the river, as we knew before. He gathers in the dark, in the deep. A cave, I think, but when and where I don't know, not for certain."

"You looked for him. Bloody, buggering hell, Fin—"

"Through the smoke," he said, coolly. "No point thrashing about on a filthy day like this. I looked through the smoke, and like smoke, it hazed and blurred. But I can tell you he's not as weak as he was, even days ago. And something's with him, Branna. Something . . . else."

"What?"

"Whatever, I think, he bargained with to be what he is, to have what he has. It's darker yet, deeper yet, and I think . . . I don't know," he murmured, rubbing his shoulder where the mark dug into him. "I think it plays him, I think it uses him as much as he uses it, and in his weakness I could see that much. More than I have before. It's a sense only, this other. But I know, and for certain, he heals, and he will come again before much longer."

"Then we'll be ready. What did we miss, Fin? That's the question. So, let's find the answer."

He bit into a biscuit, smiled for the first time since he'd come in. "I might need more than two of these to sustain me while going over these bloody books again."

"There's more in the jar if you need them. Now." She tapped her book. "The potion first."

4

IT PAINED HIM TO LOOK AT HER—SO CLOSE, BUT DISTANT as Saturn. It sustained him, far more than ginger biscuits, to see her face, hear her voice, catch her scent, just hers, among the others wafting through her workshop.

He'd tried everything he knew to kill his love for her. He reminded himself she'd turned from him, cast him aside. He'd taken other women, tried to fill the abyss she'd left in him with their bodies, their voices, their beauty.

He'd left his own home, often for months at a go, just to put himself away from her. Traveling, rambling, to places near and far, foreign and familiar.

He'd made his fortune, and a good, solid one, with work, with time, with wit and grit. He'd built a fine home for himself, and had seen to it his parents had all they needed, though they'd moved to New York City to be near his mother's sister. Or, he often thought, to be away of any talk or thought of magicks and curses. For that he couldn't blame them.

No one could say he'd wasted his life or his skills—magickal or otherwise. But nothing he'd done had eroded even a fraction of that love.

He'd considered a potion, a spell, but he knew love magick, to bring it or remove it—held consequences far beyond the single person who wished for it, or wished it gone.

He would not, could not, use his gift to ease his heart.

Was it worse or better, he often wondered, knowing she loved him as well, she suffered as well? Some days, he admitted, he found some solace in that. Other days it buggered the living hell out of him.

But for now neither of them had a choice. They must be together, work together, join together for the single purpose of destroying Cabhan, for defeating him, for ending him.

So he worked with her, through argument and agreement, in her lovely workshop over endless cups of tea—and finally a bit of whiskey in it—poring over the books, writing out a new spell neither of them was satisfied with, and again, going over every step of the two previous battles.

And neither of them devised anything new, found another answer.

She was the canniest witch he knew—and all too often the strictest in her ethics. And beautiful with it. Not just the face and form, all that glorious hair, those warm gray eyes. What she was, the power and presence of it, added more, and her unstinting devotion to her craft, to her gift—to family—more still.

He was doomed to love her.

So he worked with her, then paid for the candles—full price, he thought with amusement, for the gods knew Branna O'Dwyer was a practical witch, and left her to drive home through the steady rain.

He checked on Maggie first, pleased with her progress. He gave the sweet-natured mare half an apple and some of his time and attention. He visited the rest of the horses, giving them time as well. He had pride in what he'd built here, in what he and Boyle had built here and at the rental stables. Pride, too, in the falconry school nearby.

Connor ran it like a dream, Fin thought.

If not for Cabhan, he could leave tomorrow for India or Africa, for America or Istanbul, and know Boyle and Connor would take care of all they'd built.

Once Cabhan was done, he'd do just that. Pick a spot on the map, and go. Get away, see something new. Anything but here for a bit, for here was all he loved far too deeply.

He gave the little stable dog Bugs a treat, then on impulse picked him up, took him along to the house. Fin imagined they'd both enjoy the company.

He liked his quiet and alone as much as Branna did hers—or nearly. But the nights were so bleeding long in December, and the chill and dark so unrelenting. He couldn't pop up to Boyle's above the garage as he'd often done in the past, and he expected Boyle and his Iona would end up at Branna's even though she tried to discourage it.

They would guard her, as he could not.

That alone stirred rage and frustration he had to shove back down.

He set the dog down inside the house, flicked a hand to the fire to have the flames snapping, another toward the tree he'd put in the big front window.

The dog pranced around, his joy at being inside so palpable, Fin smiled and settled a little. Yes, they'd both do well with the company.

He wandered back toward the kitchen, its light bright on all the gleaming surfaces, got himself a beer.

She'd only been in his home once, and only as Connor was there, and hurt. But he could see her there. He'd always seen her there. It ground his pride to admit he'd built the place with her in mind, with the dreams they'd once woven together in mind.

He carried a few of her candles into the dining room, put the tapers in silver holders, set out some of the mirrored ones. Yes, they caught the light well, he decided. Though she'd be unlikely to see her work in his space.

He thought of making some food, but put it off as he purely hated to cook. He'd slap something together later, he decided, as a trip to the pub for a meal didn't appeal with the rain thrashing.

He could go downstairs, wile away some of the evening with sports on the big TV, or kill time with a game or two. He could stretch out with another beer in front of the fire with a book that wasn't all magicks and spells.

"I can do whatever I bloody well please," he told Bugs. "And it's my own fault, isn't it, that nothing pleases me. Maybe it's just the rain and the dark. What would please me is a hot beach, some blasting sun, and a willing woman. And that's not altogether true, is it?"

He crouched, sent Bugs into paralytic joy by giving him a belly rub. "Would we were all so easily happy as a little stable dog. Well, enough of this. I'm tired of myself. We'll go up and work, for the sooner this is done, the sooner I'll find if that hot beach is the answer after all."

The dog followed him, slavishly devout, as he walked back, then up the wide stairs to the second floor. He thought of a hot shower, maybe a steam as well, but turned directly into his workroom. There he lit the fire as well, flames shimmering in a frame of deep green tourmaline while the dog explored.

He'd designed every inch of the room—with some help from Connor—the black granite work counters, the deep mahogany cabinetry, the wide plank cypress floors that ran throughout the house. Tall, arched windows, with the center one of stained glass that created the image of a woman in white robes bound by a jeweled belt. She held a wand in one hand, a ball of flame in the other while her black hair swirled in an unseen wind.

It was Branna, of course, with the moon full behind her and the deep forest surrounding her. The Dark Witch watched him with eyes, even in glass, full of power and light.

He had a heavy antique desk—topped by a state-of-the-art computer. Witches didn't fear technology. A cabinet with thick and carved doors held weapons he'd collected the world over. Swords, a broadaxe, maces, foils, throwing stars. Others held cauldrons, bowls, candles, wands, books, bells, athames, and still others various potions and ingredients.

She would have liked the room, he thought, for when it came to work as well as living, he was nearly as ruthlessly tidy as she.

Bugs looked up at him, tail wagging hopefully. Reading him, Fin smiled.

"Go ahead then. Make yourself at home."

The dog wagged more fiercely, then ran over and leaped onto a curved divan, circled about, and settled down with a sigh of utter contentment.

Fin worked into the night, dealing with practical matters such as charms—protection needed refreshing with regularity—on tonics and potions. Something specifically for Maggie. He cleansed some crystals—what he thought of as housework—as that needed doing as well.

He'd have forgotten supper altogether, but he felt the dog's hunger. He went down, Bugs on his heels, put together a sandwich, some crisps, sliced up an apple. As he'd neglected to bring in any food for the dog, he simply shared the meal, amusing them both by tossing bits of sandwich for Bugs to snatch out of the air as handily as he did the bugs from which he'd earned his name.

Considering the practical again, he let the dog out, kept his mind linked with Bugs so he'd know if the little hound headed back to the stables after the practical was seen to.

But Bugs pranced right back to the kitchen door, sat, and waited until Fin opened it for him.

"All right then, it seems you're spending the night. And that being the case, it's God's truth you could use a shower even more than I. You carry the stables with you, little friend. Let's take care of that."

In the bath, the shower nearly had Bugs scrambling off, but Fin was quick. And laughing, carted the dog in with him. "It's just water. Though we're going to add soap all around."

Bugs trembled, lapped at the spray coming out of the many jets, wiggled against Fin's bare chest when Fin rubbed in some of the liquid soap.

"There you see, not so bad now is it?" He stroked gently to soothe as well as clean. "Not so bad at all."

He gestured toward the ceiling. Lights streamed, soft colors, music flowed in, soft and lilting. He set the dog down, gave himself the pleasure of the hot jets while the dog lapped at the wet tiles.

Fin was quick, but not quite quick enough to dry the dog before Bugs shook himself, shooting drops all over the bath. His own laugh echoed in the room as the little dog shot him a look of satisfaction.

With that mess sorted out, he moved into the bedroom, tossed down one of the big pillows that grouped on the sofa in his sitting area. But the dog, fully at home now, jumped onto the big, high bed, stretched out like a potentate at his ease.

"Well, at least you're clean."

He climbed in himself, decided on a book rather than TV to ease him toward sleep.

By the time Fin turned off the light, Bugs was quietly snoring. Fin found the sound of it a small comfort, and wondered how pathetic it was when a snoring dog eased the lonely.

In the dark, with the fire down to glowing embers, he thought of Branna.

She turned to him, her hair a black curtain, all silk spilling over her bare shoulders. The fire flickered now, gold flames that turned her eyes to silver with that gold dancing in them.

And she smiled.

"You yearn for me."

"Day and night."

"And here you want me, in your big bed, in your fancy house."

"I want you anywhere. Everywhere. You torture me, Branna."

"Do I?" She laughed, but the sound wasn't cruel. It was warm as a kiss. "Not I, Finbar, not I alone. We torture each other." She trailed a finger down his chest. "You're stronger than you were. As am I. Do you wonder, would we be stronger together?"

"How can I think, how can I wonder, when I'm so full of you?"

He took her hair in his hands, pulled her to him. And God, oh God, the taste of her after so long, after a lifetime, was like life after death.

He rolled over, pressing her under him, going deeper into the wonder of it. Her breasts, fuller, softer, sweeter than he remembered, and her heart drumming under his hands as she arched up to him.

A blur and storm of the senses—the feel of her skin, silk like her hair and warm, so warm, chasing away all the cold. The shape of her, the lovely curves, the sound of her breathing his name, moving, moving under him, chasing away all the lonely.

His blood beat for her; his own heart pounded as she tangled her hands in his hair as she used to, as she ran them down his back. Gripped his hips, arched up. Opened.

He plunged in. The light exploded, white, gold, sparking like fire—all the world afire. Wind whipped in a torrent to send that fire into a roar. For an instant, one breath, the pleasure struck.

Then came the lightning. Then came the dark.

He stood with her in the storm, her hand gripped in his.

"I don't know this place," she said.

"Nor do I. But . . ." Something, something he knew, somewhere deep. Too deep to reach. Thick woods, whirling winds, and somewhere close the rush of a river.

"Why are we here?"

"Something's close," was all he said.

She turned up her hand, held a small ball of flame. "We need light. Can you find the way?"

"Something's close. You should go back. It's the dark that's close."

"I won't go back." She touched her amulet, closed her eyes. "I feel it."

When she started forward, he tightened his hold on her hand. He would find a way to shield her, if needed. But the urgency to move on pulled him.

Thick trees, deep shadows that seemed to glow with the dark. No moon, no stars, only that wind that sent the night screaming.

In it, something howled, and the howl was hungry.

Fin wished for a weapon, dug deep for power, drew a blade, and set the blade on fire.

"Dark magicks," Branna murmured. She, too, seemed to glow, alight with her own power. "All around. This is not home."

"Not home, but near enough. Not now, but long ago."

"Yes, ago. His lair? Could it be? Can you tell?"

"It's not the same. It's . . . other than that."

She nodded as though she'd felt the same. "We should call the others. We should have our circle in full. If this is his place."

"There." He saw it, dark against dark, the mouth of a cave hunched in a hillside.

He would not take her in, Fin thought. Would not take her there, for within was death. And worse.

Even as he thought it, the old man stepped out. He wore rough robes, worn hide boots. Both his hair and beard were a long tangle of gray. Both madness and magick lived in his eyes.

"You are too soon. You are too late." As he spoke he held up a hand. Blood dripped from it, blood spread over his rough robes.

"It's done. Done, as I am done. You are too soon to see it, too late to stop it."

"What is done?" Fin demanded. "Who are you?"

"I am the sacrifice. I am the sire of the dark. I am betrayed."

"I can help you." But as Branna started forward, power roared out of the cave. It swept her back, Fin with her, sent the old man falling to the ground where his blood pooled black on the earth.

"Dark Witch to be," he said. "Cabhan's whelp to come. There is no help here. He has eaten the dark. We are all damned."

Fin pushed to his feet, tried to shove Branna back. "He's in there. He's in there. I can feel him."

But as he made to leap toward the cave, she grabbed at him. "Not alone. It isn't for you alone."

He whirled toward her, all but mad himself. "He is mine; I am his. Your blood made it so. It's your curse I carry, and I *will* take my vengeance."

"Not for vengeance." She wrapped herself around him. "For that would damn you. Not for vengeance. And not alone."

But he woke alone, covered with sweat, the mark on his arm burning like a fresh brand.

And could still smell her on the sheets, on his skin. In the air.

The dog quivered against him, whining.

"It's all right now." Absently, he stroked. "It's done for now."

He showered off the sweat, grabbed pants, an old sweater, pulling the sweater on as he went downstairs. He let the dog out, barely noticed the rain had stopped and weak winter sunlight trickled down.

He needed to think, and clearly, so started for coffee. Cursed at the banging on his front door.

Then thought of Maggie, hurried to answer even as he thought her out, settled himself the mare was doing well.

He opened the door to Branna.

She walked through it, shoving him back with both hands.

"You had no right! Bloody bastard, you had no right pulling me into your dream."

He grabbed her hands by the wrists before she could shove him again. And he thought again she all but glowed, but this was pure fury.

"I didn't—or not by intent. For all I know you pulled me into yours."

"I? What bollocks. You had me in your bed."

"And willing enough while you were." As he had her hands she couldn't slap him, but she had power free enough, and shot him back two full steps with it. It burned a bit as well. "Stop it. You'd best cool yourself off, Branna. You're in my home now. I don't know if I pulled you, you pulled me, or if something else pulled us together. And I can't shagging think as I haven't had so much as a cup of fucking coffee."

With that, he turned, strode off toward the kitchen.

"Well, neither have I." She strode after him. "I want you to look at me."

"And I want my fucking coffee."

"Look at me, Finbar, damn it. Look at me and answer this. Did you pull me into your dream, into your bed?"

"No." He shoved a hand through his hair. "I don't know, I just don't know, but if I did, I did it in my fecking sleep and not meaning to. Bugger it, Branna, I wouldn't bespell you. Whatever you think of me you shouldn't think that. I'd never use you that way."

She took a breath, then a second. "I do know it. I apologize, for of course I know it when I calm myself. I'm sorry, I am. I was . . . upset."

"Small wonder. I'm not doing so well myself."

"I could do with coffee myself, if you don't mind."

"Right."

He walked over to the coffeemaker—the type she'd been toying with indulging in, as it did all the fancy coffees and teas and chocolates besides.

"Will you sit?" He lifted his chin toward the little glassed-in bump where she imagined he took his coffee in the morning.

She slid onto one of the benches thickly padded in burnt orange, studied the turned wooden bowl—as glossy as glass—full of sharp red apples.

They were adults, she reminded herself, and couldn't shy away from discussing what had happened in that big bed.

"I won't, and can't, blame you or any man for where his mind goes in sleep," she began.

"I won't, and can't, blame you or any woman for where hers goes." He set her coffee, served in an oversized white mug, on the table in front of her. "For it could've been you as easily as me."

She hadn't thought of it, and found herself baffled into silence for a moment. To give herself time to think, she tried the coffee, found it doctored exactly as she liked.

"That's fair enough. Fair enough. Or, as I didn't give myself the chance to think of it before this, it could've been other powers entirely."

"Others?"

"Who can say?" More frustrated than angry now, she threw up her hands. "What we know is I came or was brought to your bed, and in this dreaming state we began what healthy people might begin."

"Your skin's as soft as rose petals."

"Hardly a wonder," she said lightly, "as I use what I make, and I make fine products."

"For those moments, Branna, it was as it once was with us, and more besides."

"For those moments, both bespelled. And what happened, Fin, when we joined? In that moment? The lightning, the storm, the light then the dark, and we were thrown into another place and time. Can it be clearer, the price paid for those moments?"

"Not to me, not clear at all. What did we learn, Branna? Go back to it."

She folded her hands on the table, deliberately, firmly, set emotion aside. "All right. Into the dark, thick woods, no moon or stars, great wind moaning through the trees."

"A river. The rush of it somewhere behind us."

"Yes." She closed her eyes, took herself back. "That's right, yes. The river behind, power ahead. The dark of it, and still we went toward it."

"The cave. Cabhan's lair, I know it."

"We saw nothing of him."

"I felt him, but . . . it wasn't as it is now. Something else." He shook his head. "It isn't clear at all, but though I don't know where we were, I sensed something familiar all the same. As if I should have known. Then the old man was there."

"I didn't know him."

"Nor did I, but again it felt as if I should. We were too soon to see, he said, and too late to stop it. Riddles. Just fecking riddles."

"A time shift, I'm thinking. We weren't in the now, but not when we could know more. He called himself the sacrifice."

"And the sire of the dark. He bled and bled. Mad and dying, but there was power in him. Fading, but there."

"Cabhan's sacrifice?" Branna wondered, then sat rod straight. "Cabhan's sire?" she said even as she saw the same thought in Fin's eyes. "Could it be?"

"Well, he was whelped from someone. Ah, Cabhan's whelp, he called me, and you Dark Witch to be. He knew us, Branna, though we'd yet to be born in his time. He knew us."

"He didn't make Cabhan what he is." She shook her head, let herself feel again what she'd felt. "There wasn't enough in him for that. But . . ."

"In the cave, there was more." Calmer now, Fin relaxed the hand he'd fisted on the table. "Did the old man conjure more than he could deal with, bring the dark in, give it a source?"

"Cabhan's blood—his sire. And the sire's blood spilling out. His life spilling onto the ground. In sacrifice? God, Fin, did Cabhan kill his own father, sacrifice his own sire to gain the dark?"

"It must be blood," Fin murmured. "It must always be blood. The dark demands it; even the light requires it. Too soon to see. If we had stayed, would we have found him, just coming into the power he has? Just coming in, and not fully formed?"

"It happened then, as the old man lay dying. It erupted, didn't it, heaving us back, breaking whatever spell had taken us. And it was cold, do you remember, did you feel? It was brutally cold for an instant before it was done, and I woke in my own bed."

Fin pushed up, restless, pacing. "He couldn't have wanted us there—Cabhan. Couldn't have wanted us anywhere near his lair, or to have us gain any knowledge of his origin."

"If we've the right of it."

"He didn't bring us there, Branna. Why would he? The more we know, the more we can use to end him. Other powers you said. And I say other powers sent us there, whether those powers are without or within us."

"Why only we two? Why not the six of us?"

"Dark Witch to be, Cabhan's whelp?" He shrugged. "You know very well you can't always logic out magicks. We need to go back, learn more."

"I'm not after having sex with you so we can travel back in time to Cabhan's cave."

"But you'd give your life for it." He waved her off before she could speak. "I don't want sex as a magickal tool, even with you. And I want to be full in control on the next journey, not taken by other forces or means. I have to think on it."

"I'll have your oath."

"What?" Distracted, he glanced back, watched her rise from the table, her hair long, loose, a bit wild. Her eyes somehow calm and fierce at once.

"Your oath, Finbar. You won't go back alone. You won't move on this without me, without our circle. You aren't alone and won't act alone. Your word on it, here and now."

"Do you see me so reckless, so hell-bent on my own destruction?"

"I see you as I did on Samhain when you would have left our circle and safety to go after Cabhan alone, even at the risk of never coming back to your own place and time. Do you think so little of us, Fin? So little you'd step away and leave us behind?"

"I think everything of you, and the others, but he's my blood, not yours." The words held a bitter taste, but were all truth. "And still I won't act alone. I won't because if I go wrong I'd risk you, and the others. Everything."

"Your hand on it." She held out her own. "Your hand on it, to seal the oath."

He took her hand in his. Light streamed out between their fingers, sizzled and snapped like a wick just fed the flame.

"Well. Well, now," he said quietly. "That hasn't happened in some time."

She felt the heat, the spread of it through her—both comfort and torment. Would it grow, she wondered, if she moved to him, if she reached for him?

She drew her hand from his, stepped back.

"I need to tell the others before they scatter for the day. You're welcome to come."

"You'll deal with it." And he needed some distance from her. "I've things to do."

"All right then." She started back, him with her, to his front door. "I'll be working with Iona today, and we'll see what we can do. It might be best for us to meet, all of us, but not tonight. A little time more to sort through it all. Tomorrow night if it suits you."

"You'll be cooking."

"My lot in life."

He wanted to run his hand over her hair, just feel it as he'd felt it in the dream. But he didn't touch her. "I'll bring wine."

"Your lot in life." She stepped through the door when he opened it for her, then turned, stood for a moment with the morning mists around her. "You've built a good house, Fin. Handsome for certain, but it has a fine, strong feel to it."

"You've seen hardly more than the kitchen."

"Well now, that's the heart of a home. If you could come tomorrow at around three, we could work before the others come for supper."

"I'll work it out, and be there."

He waited while she walked to her car, surprised when she stopped, looked back again with a quick, saucy smile.

"I should've mentioned, your skin's not far off from rose petals, but in a manly way, of course."

When he laughed, the tension in his belly eased even as she drove away from him.

5

AFTER BRANNA TOLD HER TALE, ASKED HER CIRCLE TO think on its meanings, she put in another request.

"I'd like the house cleared of men tonight, if you don't mind, and to spend it with my women here, with wine and paint samples and such. If you could do me a favor, Connor, Boyle, would you invade Fin's house, and stay there? Do whatever men do with an evening free of females. I don't want to know what that might be."

When Connor hesitated, she drilled her finger in his belly. "And don't be after thinking the three of us need the protection of men. Two of us are witches same as you, and the other could kick your arse into next week if you riled her."

"I take pains not to rile her. All right then. What do you say, Boyle, we'll drag Fin off to the pub, then stagger back to his place?"

"I'm for it. He'll want the company, I expect," he said with a glance at Branna.

"Want it or not, he needs it. I'll be in the workshop. Iona, when you're done here, I'll put you to work."

"I'll be here by six," Meara told her, and waited until Branna left the room. "A terrible hard thing for both of them. I don't know how they stand up to it. So let's give them some fun and ease tonight at least."

"That we can do." Boyle rubbed a hand on Meara's shoulder, turned to Iona. "It's good you'll be with her today."

She hoped she could help, would know what to say—what not to say. And when Iona went into the workshop, Branna was already at the stove, with a dozen mirrored bowls set out on the counter.

"I've an order for these, so want to get them done straight off, and I've a mind to make up some sets—the small bottles—of hand lotion and scrubs and soaps. Put them together in the red boxes they sent me too many of, tie them with the red-and-green-plaid ribbon. Eileen can put them on special, as the company didn't charge me for the overstock as it was their mistake. Some will wait till the final moment for the holiday shopping, so they should move well enough."

Iona went with instinct, crossed over, and, saying nothing, put her arms around her cousin.

"I'm all right, Iona."

"I know, but only because you're so strong. I wouldn't be. Just so you know, I'd get behind you if you just needed to cut loose."

"Cut what loose?"

On a half laugh, Iona eased back. "I mean rant, rave, curse the heavens."

"No point in it."

"The ranting, raving, cursing *is* the point. So whenever you need to, I've got your back. I'll get the bottles, the boxes. I know where they are."

"Thanks for that—for all of that. Would you mind running the little sets into the shop once we've done them? I'd like them out as soon as we can."

"Sure. But do you just want them in stock, or do you want me out of here?"

Her cousin, Branna thought, had finely honed instincts. "Both, but you, just for a little while. I'm glad to have you, but for just a little while I could do with some alone. And when you come back, we can begin the more essential work between us."

"All right." Iona got out the boxes, began to assemble them. "How many of these?"

"Half dozen, thanks."

"I think you're right if you want my opinion."

"About the boxes?"

"No, not about that. About what happened. About it being another power that pulled you and Fin together."

"I'm not sure I'm right, or I've concluded just that."

"It's what I think." She brushed at her cap of bright hair, glanced up. "Maybe—I hope I don't push too hard on a sore spot—but maybe both you and Fin want to be together, maybe that wanting stirs up from time to time, and maybe last night, for whatever reason, was one of those times."

"A lot of maybes in your certainty, cousin."

"Circling around the sore spot, I guess. There's no maybe in the wanting or the stirring. I'm sorry, Branna, it's impossible not to see it or feel it, especially the more we all bind together for this."

Branna kept her hands busy, her voice calm. "People want all manner of things they can't have."

Sore spot, Iona reminded herself, and didn't push on it. "What I mean is, it's very possible the two of you were a little vulnerable last night, that your defenses or shields were lowered some. And that opened the door, so to speak, to that other power. Not Cabhan, because that absolutely makes no sense."

"It hurt us." And left a terrible aching behind. "He lives to hurt us."

"Yes, but . . ." Iona shook her head. "He doesn't understand us. He doesn't understand love or loyalty or real sacrifice. Lust, sure. I don't doubt he understands you and Fin are hot for each other, but he'd never understand what's under it. Sorcha would."

Branna stopped working on the candles, stared at Iona. "Sorcha."

"Or her daughters. Think about it."

"When I think about it, I'm reminded Sorcha's the very one who cursed all that came from Cabhan, which would be Fin."

"That's true. She was wrong, but that's true. And sure, maybe, considering he killed her husband, tore her from her own children, she'd do the same thing again. But she knew love. She understood it, she gave her power and her life for it. Don't you think she'd use it if she could? Or that her children would?"

"So she, or they, cast the dreaming spell? Where we were together, and all defenses down, so we came together."

She began to walk about, deliberately, running it over in her mind. "And when we did, used the power of that to send us back. But both too soon and too late."

"Okay, think about that. Sooner, whatever happened in that cave might have pulled you in, beyond what you could fight. Later, you wouldn't have spoken with the old man—potentially, and I think right again—Cabhan's father."

Iona got out the ribbon, the bottles as Branna worked in silence.

"I think you saw what you were meant to see, that's what I'm saying. I think we need to find a way to see more—that's the work. They can't hand it to us, right? And I think—sore spot—it had to be only you and Fin together because the two of you need to resolve—not gloss over or bury or ignore—your feelings."

"Mine are resolved."

"Oh, Branna."

"I can love him and be resolved to living without him. But I see now too much of it was hazed in my mind. All that feeling I couldn't quite set down. You have good points here, Iona. We saw what we were meant to see, and we work from that."

She glanced over, smiled before she poured more scented wax. "You've learned a great deal since the day you came to that door, in all that rain, in that pink coat, babbling away with your nerves."

"Now if I could only learn to cook."

"Ah well, some things are beyond our reach."

She finished the candles, and together she and Iona made up the half dozen pretty gift sets. When her cousin set off to Cong, Branna took her solitude with tea by the fire, with Kathel's head in her lap.

She studied the flames, let her thoughts circle. Then with a sigh, set her tea aside.

"All right then, all right." She held her hands out to the fire. "Clear for me and let me see, through the smoke and into the fire, take me where the light desires."

Images in the flames, voices through the smoke. Branna let herself drift toward them, let them pull her, surrendered to the call she'd felt in the blood, in the bone.

When they cleared, she stood in a room where another fire simmered, where candles flickered. Her cousin Brannaugh sat in a chair singing softly to the baby at her breast. She looked up, her face illuminated, and said, "Mother?"

"No." Branna stepped out of the shadows. "No, I'm sorry."

"I wished for her. I saw her when my son came into the world, saw her watching, felt her blessing. But only that, and she was gone. I wished for her."

"I asked the light to take me where it willed. It brought me here." Branna moved closer, looked down at the baby, at his down of dark hair, and soft cheeks, his dark, intense eyes as he suckled so busily at his mother's breast.

"He's beautiful. Your son."

"Ruarc. He came so quick, and the light bloomed so bright with his birthing. I saw my mother in it even as Teagan guided him out of me and into the world. I thought not to see you again, not so soon."

"How long for you?"

"Six days. We stay at Ashford, are welcome. I have not yet gone to the cabin, but both Teagan and Eamon have done so. Both have seen Cabhan."

"You have not."

"I hear him." She looked toward the window as she rocked the baby. "He calls to me, as if I would answer. He called to my mother, now to me. And to you?"

"He has, will again, I imagine, but it will do him no good. Do you know of a cave, beyond the river?"

"There are caves in the hills, beneath the water."

"One of power. A place of the dark."

"We were not allowed beyond the river. Our mother, our father both forbade it. They never spoke of such a place, but some of the old ones, at gatherings, I heard them speak of Midor's cave, and would make the sign against evil when they did."

"Midor." A name, at least, Branna thought, to work from. "Do you know of Cabhan's origins? There is no word of it in the book, in Sorcha's book."

"She never spoke of it. We were children, cousin, and at the end, there was no time. Would it help to know?"

"I'm not sure, but knowing is always better than not. I was there, in a dream. With Fin. Finbar Burke."

"Of the Burkes of Ashford? No, no," she said quickly. "This is the one, the one of your circle who is Cabhan's blood. His blood drew him to this place, and you with him?"

"I don't know, nor does he. He is not Cabhan, he is not like Cabhan."

Now Sorcha's Brannaugh looked into her own fire. "Does your heart speak, cousin, or your head?"

"Both. He's bled with us. You saw yourself, or will on Samhain night. And you will judge for yourself. Midor," she repeated. "The light brought me here, and it may be for only this. I've never heard of

Midor's cave. I think this may be buried in time, but I know how to pick up a shovel and dig."

They both looked toward the tall window as the howling rose up outside.

"He hunts and stalks." Brannaugh held her son closer. "Already since we've come home a village girl's gone missing. He pushed the dark against the windows, swirls his fog. Beware the shadows."

"I do, and will."

"Take this." Shifting the baby, she held out her hand, and in it a spear of crystal clear as water. "A gift for you, and a light."

"Thank you. I'll keep it with me. Be well, cousin, and bright blessings to you and your son."

"And to you. Samhain," she murmured as Branna felt herself pulled away. "I will tip my arrows with poison, and do all in my power to end him."

But you won't, Branna thought as she sat in front of her own fire again, studying the crystal in her hand. Not on Samhain.

Another time, gods willing, but not on Samhain.

She rose, tucking the gift into her pocket. Choosing her laptop over the books, she began to search for Midor's cave.

"I COULDN'T FIND A BLOODY THING THAT APPLIED TO THIS." Branna sat, poking at the salad she'd made to go with a pretty penne and a round of olive bread.

"I'm not sure you can Google the cave of a sorcerer from the twelfth or thirteenth century." Meara slathered butter on the bread.

"You can Google near to every bleeding thing."

"Is it an Irish name? Midor?" Iona wondered.

"Not one I've heard. But he might've come from anywhere, from the bowels of hell for all we know, and ended up dying in front of that cave."

"What about the mother?" Iona gestured with her wine. "Midor had to sire Cabhan—if we've got that right—with someone. Where's the mother? Who's the mother?"

"There's nothing, just nothing about any of this in Sorcha's book, in my great-grandmother's. Maybe it's not important after all." Branna fisted her chin on her hand. "And bollocks to that. Some of it must be or Fin and I wouldn't have gone to that shagging cave."

"We'll figure it out. Ah, this pasta's brilliant," Meara added. "We will figure it out, Branna. Maybe it's Connor's absolute faith rubbing off, but I believe it. Things are starting up again, you see? You having visits with Sorcha's Brannaugh, you and Fin going on dreamwalks after a bit of a dream shag."

Iona hunched her shoulders, then relaxed them again when she saw from Branna's face Meara handled it just right.

"Wasn't much of a shag," Branna admitted. "It took premature ejaculation to a new level entirely. Fate's a buggering bitch, I say. It's all, Here you are, Branna, remember this? Then it's, Well, remembering's all you'll get. And it's back to the blood and the dark and the evildoings for you."

"You're tired of it." Iona reached over, rubbed her arm.

"Tonight I am, that's for certain. No one's ever touched me like Fin, and I'm tired enough of it tonight to say so out loud. No one, not my body or my heart or my spirit besides. And no one will. Knowing that, well, it can make you tired."

Iona started to speak, but Meara shook her head, silenced her.

"I didn't need to be reminded of it. It was cruel, but magick can be. Here's a gift, and oh, look what you are, what you have. But you can never be sure what you'll pay for it."

"He's paid as well," Meara said gently.

"Sure I know it. More than any other. It was easier when I could be angry or feel betrayed. But what needs doing can't be done with anger and hard feelings. Letting them go brings back so much. Too much. So I have to ask how do I do what needs doing when I feel all this? It needs to be let go as well."

"Love's power," Iona said after a moment. "I think even when it hurts, it's power."

"That may be. No, that *is*," Branna corrected. "But how to use it and not be swallowed by it, that's a fine, thin line, isn't it? And right now I feel weighed and unbalanced and . . ."

She trailed off, laid a hand lightly on Iona's, the other on Meara's. "Beware the shadows," she murmured, looking out the window where they dug deep pockets in the wall of fog.

"No, sit easy," she said when Meara started to rise. "Just sit easy. He can't come in to what's mine, try as he might. But I'm sitting here in my own kitchen acting the gom. Sitting here, sniveling away so he can slide around my walls and windows, feeding on my self-pity. Well, he's fed enough."

She shoved away from the table, ignoring Iona's quick, "Wait!" Striding straight to the window, she flung it open, and hurled out a ball of fire, then another, then two at once while the fury of her power snapped around her.

Something roared, something inhuman. And the fog lit like tinder before it vanished.

"Well now." Branna closed the window with a little snap.

"Holy shit." Iona standing, a ball of fire on her palm, let out a shaky breath. "Holy shit," she repeated.

"I don't think he liked the taste of that. And I feel better." After dusting her hands, palm to palm, she came back, sat, picked up her fork. "You should put that fire out now, Iona, and finish your pasta." She sampled her first bite. "For it's brilliant if I say so myself. And, Meara, if you wouldn't mind texting Connor. Just letting them know to have a care, though I don't think Cabhan's up to tangling with them tonight."

"Sure I'll do that."

"He thought to take a little swipe at the women," Branna said as she ate. "He'll forever underestimate women. And he thought to lap up some of my feelings. Now he'll choke on them. It's light he can't abide." With a flick of her fingers the light in the room glowed just a little brighter. "And joy, and we'll have some of that, for it's not much makes me happier than picking out colors and finishings and the like."

She scooped up more pasta. "So, Iona, have you thought of travertine for the master bath?"

"Travertine." Iona let out another breath, and managed, "Hmmm."

"And we've still details on your wedding to see to, and have barely talked of yours, Meara. There's joy here." She took her friends' hands again. "The kind women know. So let's have more wine and talk of weddings and making stone and glass into homes."

CONNOR READ THE TEXT FROM MEARA. "CABHAN'S BEEN AT the cottage. No," he said quickly as both his friends pushed back from the table. "He's gone. Meara says Branna sent him off with his tail burning between his legs."

"I'll see better outside, out of the light and noise. We'll be sure," Fin added, and rose, walked out of the warmth of the pub.

"We should go back," Boyle insisted.

"Meara says not to. Says that Branna needs her evening with just the women, and swears they're safe, tucked up inside. She wouldn't brush it off, Boyle."

He opened himself, did what he could to block out the voices, the laughter around him.

"He's not close." He looked to Fin for verification when Fin came back.

"He's that pissed, and still on the weak side," Fin said. "Away from the cottage now, away from here. I should've felt him. If we'd been there . . ."

"Only shadows and fog," Connor put in. "It's all he'd risk yet. But the pub's done for us, isn't it? Back to your house?"

"Easy enough to keep watch from there, whether Branna likes it or not."

"I'm with you. No, I've got this." Boyle dug out some bills, tossed them down. "You never got around to talking to Connor as you wanted."

"About what?" Connor asked.

Fin merely swung on his jacket, and bided his time as half the pub had something to say to Connor before he left. The man drew people like honey drew flies, Fin thought, and knew he himself would go half mad if he had that power.

Outside, they squeezed into Fin's lorry as they'd decided—after considerable discussion—one would do them.

"It's the school I wanted to discuss," Fin began.

"There are no problems I can think of. Is it adding the hawking on horseback, as I've given that considerate thought?"

"We can talk about that as well. I've had partnership papers drawn up."

"Partnership? Is Boyle going into it with you?"

"I've got enough on my plate with the stables, thanks all the same," Boyle said, and tried to find space to stretch out his legs.

"Well, who'd you partner with then? Ah, tell me it's not that idjit O'Lowrey from Sligo. He knows his hawks sure enough, but on every other point he's a git."

"Not O'Lowrey, but another idjit altogether. I'm partnering with you, you git."

"With me? But . . . Well, I run the place, don't I? There's no need for you to make me a partner."

"I'm not having the papers for need but because it's right and it's time. I'd've done it straight off, but you were half inclined to building, as much as you're for the hawks. And running the school might not have suited you, the paperwork of it, the staffing and all the rest of the business. But it does, otherwise you could've just done the hawk walks, and the training. But the whole of it's for you, so well, that's done."

Connor said nothing until Fin stopped in front of his house. "I don't need papers, Fin."

"You don't, no, nor do I with you. Nor does Boyle or me with him. But the lawyers and the tax man and all of them, they need them. So we'll read them over, sign them, and be done with it. It'd be a favor to me, Connor."

"Bollocks to that. It's no favor to—"

"Would the pair of you let me out of this bloody lorry if you're going to fight about it half the night as I'm stuck between you?"

Fin got out. "We'll pour a couple more pints in him, and he'll be signing the papers and forgetting he ever did."

"There aren't enough pints in all of Mayo for me to forget a bloody thing."

The edge in Connor's voice had Boyle shaking his head, leaving them to it. And had Fin laying his hands on Connor's shoulders.

"*Mo dearthair*, do you think I do this out of some sense of obligation?"

"I don't know why you're doing it."

"Ah, for feck's sake, Connor. The school's more yours than mine, and ever was. It wouldn't *be* but for you, as much as I wanted it. I'm a man of business, am I not?"

"I've heard tell."

"And this is business. It's also the hawks, which are as near and dear to me as you." He lifted his arm, gloveless. In moments Merlin, his hawk, landed like a feather on his wrist.

"You care for him when I'm away."

"Of course."

Fin angled his head so the hawk rubbed against him. "He's part of me, as Roibeard is part of you. I trust you to see to him, and Meara to see to him. When this is done, with Cabhan, I can't stay here, not for a while in any case."

"Fin—"

"I'll have to go, for my own sanity. I'll need to go, and I can't say, not now, if I'll come back. I need you to do this favor, Connor."

Annoyed, Connor gave Fin a hard poke in the chest. "When this is over, you'll stay. And Branna will be with you, as she once was."

"Ending Cabhan won't take away the mark." Fin lifted his arm again, sent Merlin lifting off, spreading his wings in flight. "She can't be mine, not truly, while I bear it. Until I can rid myself of it I can't ask her to be mine. And I can't live, Connor, I swear to you, knowing she's hardly more than a stone's throw away every night and never to be mine. Once I thought I could. Now I know I can't."

"I'll sign your papers if it's what you want. But I'm telling you now, looking eye to eye, when this is done—and it will be done—you'll stay. Mark it, Finbar. Mark what I say. I'll wager you a hundred on it, here and now."

"Done. Now." He slung an arm around Connor's shoulders. "Let's go have a pint and see if we can talk Boyle into making us something to eat as we didn't get that far at the pub."

"I'm for all of that."

SHE COULDN'T SLEEP. LONG AFTER THE HOUSE WAS QUIET, Branna wandered through it, checking doors and windows and charms. He was out there, lurking. She felt him like a shadow over a sunbeam. As she walked back upstairs, she trailed a hand over Kathel's head.

"We should sleep," she told him. "Both of us. There's more work to be done tomorrow."

In the bedroom she built up the fire, for warmth, for the comfort of its light. She could walk through those flames in her mind, she considered, but knew whatever visions came might not bring warmth and comfort.

She'd had enough of the chill for now.

Instead, once Kathel settled, she took out her violin. He watched her as she rosined her bow, thumping his tail as if in time. That alone made her smile as she walked to the windows.

There she could see out, toward the hills, toward the woods, into the sky where the moon floated in and out of clouds, and stars flickered like distant candles.

And he could see in, she thought, see her standing behind the glass, behind the charms. Out of his reach.

And that turned her smile potent.

Look all you want, she thought, for you'll never have what I am.

She set the violin on her shoulder, closed her eyes a moment while the music rose up in her.

And she played, the notes lifting out of her heart, her spirit, her blood, her passions. Slow, lilting, lovely, power sang through the strings, shimmered its defiance against the glass, against the dark.

Framed in the window, the firelight dancing behind her, she played what both lured and repelled him while her hound watched, while her friends slept, while the moon floated.

In his bed, alone in the dark, Fin heard her song, felt what lifted out of her heart pierce his own.

And ached for her.

6

SHE TOOK THE MORNING FOR DOMESTIC TASKS, TIDYING and polishing her house to what Connor often called her fearful standards. She considered herself a creature of order and sense, and one happiest when her surroundings echoed not only that order, but her own tastes.

She liked knowing things remained where she wanted them, a practical matter to her mind that saved time. To be at her best, she required color and texture and the pretty things that brightened the heart and appealed to the eye.

Pretty things and order required time and effort, and she enjoyed the housewifely duties, the simple and ordinary routine of them. She appreciated the faint scent of orange peel once the furniture was polished with the solution she made for herself and the tang of grapefruit left behind once she'd scrubbed her bath.

Fluffed pillows offered welcome as a soft, pretty throw arranged just so offered comfort and eye appeal.

Once done she refreshed candles, watered plants, filled her old copper bucket with more peat for the fire.

Meara and Iona had set the kitchen to rights before they'd gone off to the stables, but . . . not quite right enough to suit her.

So while laundry chugged away in the machines, she fussed, making a mental list of what she wanted at the market, a secondary list of potential new products for her shop. Humming while she planned, she finished the last of the housework with mopping the kitchen floor.

And felt him.

Though her heart jumped she made herself turn slowly to where Fin stood in the doorway that led to her shop.

"A cheerful tune for scrubbing up."

"I like scrubbing up."

"A fact that's always been a mystery to me. As is how you manage to look so fetching doing it. Am I wrong? Did we agree to work this morning?"

"You're not wrong, just early." Deliberately she went back to her mopping. "Go put the kettle on in the workshop. I'm nearly done."

She'd had her morning, Branna reminded herself, her time alone to do as she pleased. Now it was time for duty. She'd work with Fin as it needed to be done. She accepted that, and had come to accept him as part of her circle.

Duty, she thought, couldn't always be easy. Reaching a goal as vital as the one sought required sacrifice.

She put away her mop and bucket, put the rag she'd tucked in the waistband of her pants in the laundry. After taking just one more minute to gird herself for the next hours, went into her workshop.

He'd boosted the fire, and the warmth was welcome. It wasn't as odd as it once had been to see him at her workshop stove, making tea.

He'd shed his coat, stood there in black pants and a sweater the color of forest shadows with the dog standing beside him.

"If you're wanting a biscuit we'd best clear it with herself first," he told the dog. "I'm not saying you didn't earn one or a bit of a lie-down by the fire." He stopped what he was doing, grinned down at the dog. "Afraid of her, am I? Well now, insulting me's hardly the way to get yourself a biscuit, is it?"

It disconcerted her, as always, that he could read Kathel as easy as she.

And as she had with him in the kitchen, he sensed her, turned.

"He's hoping for a biscuit."

"So I gather. It's early for that as well," she said with a speaking look to her dog. "But he can have one, of course."

"I know where they are." Fin opened a cupboard as she crossed the room. Taking out the tin, he opened it. Before he could offer it, Kathel rose up, set his paws on Fin's shoulders. He stared into Fin's eyes for a moment, then gently licked Fin's cheek.

"Sure you're welcome," Fin murmured when the dog lowered again, accepted the biscuit.

"He has a brave heart, and a kind one," Branna said. "A fondness and a great tolerance for children. But he loves, truly loves a select few. You're one of them."

"He'd die for you, and knows I would as well."

The truth of it shook her. "That being the case we'd best get to work so none of us dies."

She got out her book.

Fin finished the tea, brought two mugs to the counter where she sat. "If you're thinking of changing the potion we made to undo him, you're wrong."

"He's not undone, is he?"

"It wasn't the potion."

"Then what?"

"If I knew for certain it would be done already. But I know it brought him terror, gave him pain, great pain. He burned, he bled."

"And he got away from us. Don't," she continued before he could speak. "Don't say to me you could have finished him if we'd let you go. It wasn't an option then, and will never be."

"Has it occurred to you that's just how it needs to be done? For me, of his blood, for me, who bears his mark, to finish what your blood, what cursed me, to end him?"

"No, because it isn't."

"So sure, Branna."

"On this I am. It's written, it's passed down, generation by generation. It's Sorcha's children who must end him. Who will. For all those who failed before us, we have something they lacked. And that's you."

She used all her will to keep her mind quiet as she spoke, to keep her words all reason.

"I believe you're essential to this. Having one who came down from him working to end him, working with the three, this is new. Never written of before in any of the books. Our circle's the stronger with you, that's without question."

"So sure of that as well?"

"Without question," she repeated. "I didn't want you in it, but that was my weakness, and a selfishness I'm sorry for. We've made our circle, and if broken . . . I think we'll lose. You gave me your word."

"That may have been a mistake for all, but still I'll keep it."

"We can end him. I know it." As she spoke, she took the crystal from her pocket, turned it in the light. "Connor, Iona, and I, we've all seen the first three. Not in simple dreams, but waking ones. We've connected with them, body and spirit, and that's not been written of before."

He heard the words, the logic in them, but couldn't polish away the edges of frustration and doubt. "You put great store in books, Branna."

"So I do, for words written down have great power. You know it as I do." She laid her hand on the book. "The answers are here, the ones already written, the ones we'll write."

She opened the book, paged through. "Here I wrote you and I dream-traveled to Midor's cave, and saw his death."

"It's not an answer."

"It will lead to one, when we go back."

"Back?" Now his interest kindled. "To the cave?"

"We were taken there. We'd have more, learn more, see more, if we took ourselves. I can find nothing about this man. The name meant nothing to Sorcha's Brannaugh. We need to seek him out."

He wanted to go back, thought of it every day, and yet . . . "We have neither the place nor the time. We'd have no direction, Branna."

"It can be done, it can be worked. With the rest of our circle here to bring us back if needed. Cabhan's sire, Fin, how many answers might he have?"

"The answers of a madman. You saw the madness as well as I."

"You'd go back without me if you could. But it must be both of us."

He couldn't deny it. "There was death in that cave."

"There's death here, without the answers. The potion must be changed—no, not the essence of it, in that you're right. But what we made, we made specific to Samhain. Would you wait until Samhain next to try again?"

"I would not, no."

"I can't see the time, Fin, can you? I can't see when we should try for him again, and without that single answer, we're blind." She pushed up, wandered the room. "I thought the solstice—it made good logic. The light beats back the dark. Then Samhain, when the veil thins."

"We saw them, the first three. The veil thinned, and we saw them with us. But not fully," he added before she could.

"I thought, is it the solstice, but the winter? Or the spring equinox? Is it Lammas or Bealtaine? Or none of those at all."

Temper, the anger for herself in failing, bubbled up as she whirled back to him. "I see us at Sorcha's cabin, fighting. The fog and the dark, Boyle's hands burning, you bleeding. And failing, Fin, because I made the wrong choice."

On a half laugh—just a touch of derision in it, he arched his eyebrows. "So now it's all yours, is it?"

"The time, that choice, *was* mine, both of them. And both of them wrong. All my careful calculations, wrong. So more's needed to be certain this time. This third time."

"Third time's the charm."

Huffing out a breath, she smiled a little. "So it's said. What we need may be there, for the taking, if we go back. So, will you go dreaming with me, Fin?"

To hell and back again, he thought.

"I will, but we'll be sure of the dream spell first. Sure of it, and of the way back. I won't have you lost beyond."

"I won't have either of us lost. We'll be sure first, of the way there, and the way back. It's Cabhan's time, his origins—we agree on that?"

"We do." So Fin sighed. "Which means you'll be after bleeding me again."

"Just a bit." Now she lifted her eyebrows. "All this fuss over a bit of blood from a man who so recently claimed he'd die for me?"

"I'd rather not do it by the drop."

"No," she said when he started to pull off his sweater. "Not from the mark. His origins, Fin. He didn't bear the mark at his beginning."

"The blood from the mark's more his."

She did what she did rarely, stepped to him, laid a hand over the cursed mark. "Not from this. Yours from your hand, mine from mine, so our blood and dreams entwine."

"You've written the spell already?"

"Just pieces of it—and in my head." She smiled at him, forgetting herself enough to leave her hand on his arm. "I do considerable thinking when I clean."

"Come to my house and think your fill, as your brother left the room he uses there a small disaster."

"He's the finest man I know, along with the sloppiest. He just doesn't see the mess he makes. It's a true skill, and one Meara will have to deal with for years to come."

"He says they're thinking the solstice—the summer—for the wedding, and having it in the field behind the cottage here."

"They're both ones for being out of doors as much as possible, so it suits them." She turned away to fetch a bowl and her smallest cauldron.

"They suit each other."

"Oh, sure they do, however much that surprised the pair of them. And with Boyle and Iona before them, we'll have spring and summer weddings, new beginnings, and the gods willing, the rest far behind us."

She got out the herbs she wanted, already dried and sealed, water she'd gathered from rain on the full moon, extract distilled from valerian.

Fin rose, got down a mortar and pestle. "I'll do this," he said, measuring herbs.

For a time they worked in easy silence.

"You never play music in here," he commented.

"It distracts me, but you can bring in the iPod from the kitchen if you're wanting some."

"No, it's fine. You played last night. Late in the night."

Startled, she looked up from her work. "I did. How do you know?"

"I hear you. You often play at night, late in the night. Often sad and lovely songs. Not sad last night, but strong. And lovely all the same."

"It shouldn't carry to you."

His gaze lifted, held hers. "Some bonds you can't break, no matter how you might wish it, no matter how you might try. No matter how far I traveled, there were times I'd hear you play as if you stood beside me."

It tugged and tore at her heart. "You never said."

He merely shrugged. "Your music brought me home more than once. Maybe it was meant to. Bowl or cauldron?" he asked.

"What?"

"The herbs I've crushed. For the bowl or the cauldron?"

"Bowl. What brought you home this last time?"

"I saw Alastar, and knew he was needed. I bargained and bought him, arranged for him to be sent. But it wasn't time for me. Then I saw Aine, and knew she was for Alastar, and . . . more. Her beauty, her spirit, called to me, and I thought, she must come home, but it wasn't time for me. Then Iona came to Ireland, came to Mayo, walked by Sorcha's clearing through the woods to you. In the rain, she walked in a pink coat, so full of excitement and hope and magicks yet untapped."

Stunned, Branna stopped her work. "You saw her."

"I saw she came home, and came to you, and knew so must I. He would see, and he would know. And he would come, and with the three I might finally end him."

"How did you see Iona—even to her pink coat?" Flummoxed, Branna pushed her hands at her hair, loosened pins she had to fix in again. "She's not your blood. Do you ask yourself how?"

"I ask myself many things, but don't always answer." He shrugged again. "Cabhan knew her for of the three, so it may be through him I saw, and I knew."

"It should remind you, when you doubt, the blood you share makes our circle stronger." She lit the candles, then the fire under the little cauldron. "Slow heat builds to a steady boil. We'll let that simmer while we write the spell."

When Connor came in he kept his silence, as magicks swam through the air. Branna and Fin stood, hands outstretched over the cauldron while smoke rose pale blue.

"Sleep to dream, dream to fly, fly to seek, seek to know." She spoke the words three times, and Fin followed.

"Dream as one, as one to see, see the truth, truth to know."

Stars flickered through the smoke.

"Starlight guide us through the night and safe return us to the light." Branna lifted a hand, and with the other gestured toward a slim, clear bottle.

Liquid rose from the cauldron, blue as the smoke, shining with stars, and in one graceful flow, poured into the bottle. Fin capped it.

"That's done it. We've done it." She let out a breath.

"Another dreaming spell?" Now Connor crossed the room. "When do we go for him?"

"It's not for that, not yet." Branna shoved her hands through her hair again, muttered a curse at herself, and this time just pulled the pins out. "What time is it? Well, bloody hell, where did the day go?"

"Into that." Fin pointed to the bottle. "She nearly ate my head when I was so bold as to suggest we take an hour and have lunch."

"She'll do that when she's working," Connor agreed, giving Fin a bolstering pat on the shoulder. "Still, there's always supper." He gave Branna a hopeful smile. "Isn't there?"

"Men and their bellies." She took the bottle to a cupboard so it could cure. "I'll put something together as it's best we all talk through what Fin and I worked out today. Get out of my house for a bit."

"I've only just got into the house," Connor objected.

"You're after a hot meal and wanting me to make it, so get out of the house so I can have some space to figure on it."

"I just want a beer before—"

Fin took his arm, grabbed his own coat. "I'll stand you one down the pub as I could use the air and the walk. And the beer."

"Well then, since you put it that way."

When Kathel trotted to the door with them, Branna waved at the three of them. "He could use the walk himself. Don't come back for an hour—and tell the others the same."

Without waiting for an answer, she turned and walked through to her kitchen.

Spotless, she thought, and so beautifully quiet—a lovely thing after hours of work and conjuring. She would've enjoyed a glass of wine by the fire, and that hour without a single thing to do, so she had to remind herself she enjoyed the domestic tasks.

She put her hands on her hips, cleared her head of clutter.

All right then, she could sauté up some chicken breasts in herbs and wine, roast up some red potatoes in olive oil and rosemary, and she had green beans from the garden she'd blanched and frozen—she could do an almondine there. And since she hadn't had time to bake more yeast bread, and the lot of them went through it like ants at a picnic, she'd just do a couple quick loaves of beer bread. And that was good enough for anyone.

She scrubbed potatoes first, cut them into chunks, tossed them in her herbs and oil, added some pepper, some minced garlic and stuck them in the oven. She tossed the bread dough together—taking a swig of beer for the cook, and with plenty of melted butter on top of the loaves, stuck them in with the potatoes.

As the chicken breasts were frozen, she thawed them with a wave of her hand, then covered them with a marinade she'd made and bottled herself.

Satisfied things were well under way, she poured that wine, took the first sip where she stood. Deciding she could use some air, a little walk herself, she got a jacket, wrapped a scarf around her neck, and took her wine outside.

Blustery and cold, she thought, but a change from all the heat she and Fin had generated in the workshop. As the wind blew through her hair, she walked her back garden, picturing where her flowers would bloom, where her rows of vegetables would grow come spring.

She had some roses still, she noted, and the pansies, of course, who'd show their cheerful faces right through the snow or ice if they got it. Some winter cabbage, and the bright orange and yellow blooms of Calendula she prized for its color and its peppery flavor.

She might make soup the next day, add some, and some of the carrots she'd mulched over so they'd handle the colder weather.

Even in winter the gardens pleased her.

She sipped her wine, wandered, even when the shadows deepened, and the fog teased around the edges of her home.

"You're not welcome here." She spoke calmly, and took out the little knife in her pocket, used it to cut some of the Calendula, some hearty snapdragons, a few pansies. She'd make a little arrangement, she thought, of winter bloomers for the table.

"I will be." Cabhan stood, handsome, smiling, the red stone of the pendant he wore glowing in the dim light. "You'll welcome me eagerly into your home. Into your bed."

"You're still weak from your last *welcome*, and delusional besides." She turned now, deliberately sipped her wine as she studied him. "You can't seduce me."

"You're so much more than the rest of them. We know it, you and I. With me, you'll be more yet. More than anyone ever imagined. I will give you all the pleasure you deny yourself. I can look like him."

Cabhan waved a hand in front of his face. And Fin smiled at her.

And oh, it stabbed her heart as if she'd turned the little knife on herself. "A shell only."

"I can sound like him," he said in Fin's voice. *"Aghra, a chuid den tsaol."*

The knife twisted as he said the words Fin used to say to her. *My love, my share of life.*

"Do you think that weakens me? Tempts me to open to you? You are all I despise. You are why I am no longer his."

"You chose. You cast me away." Suddenly he was Fin at eighteen, so young, so full of grief and rage. "What would you have me do? I never knew. I never deceived you. Don't turn from me. Don't cast me aside."

"You didn't tell me," Branna heard herself say. "I gave myself to you, only you, and you're his blood. You're his."

"I didn't know! How could I? It came on me, Branna, burned into me. It wasn't there before—"

"Before we loved. More than a week ago, and you said nothing, and only tell me now, as I saw for myself. I am of the three." Tears burned the back of her eyes, but she refused to let them thicken her voice. "I am a Dark Witch, daughter of Sorcha. You are of Cabhan, you are of the black and the pain. You're lies, and what you are has broken my heart."

"Weep, witch," he murmured. "Weep out the pain. Give me your tears."

She caught herself standing in front of him, on the edge of her ground, and his face was Cabhan's face. And that face was lit with the dark as the red stone glowed stronger.

Tears, she realized, swam in her eyes. With all her will she pulled them back, held her head high. "I don't weep. You'll have nothing from me but this."

She jabbed out with the garden knife, managed to stab shallowly in his chest as she grabbed for the pendant with her other hand. The ground trembled under her feet; the chain burned cold. For an instant his eyes burned red as the stone, then the fog swirled, snapped out with teeth, and she held nothing but the little knife with blood on its tip.

She looked down at her hand, at the burn scored across her palm. Closing her hand into a fist she drew up, warmed the icy burn, soothed it, healed it.

Perhaps her hands trembled—there was no shame in it—but she picked up the flowers, the wineglass she'd dropped.

"A waste of wine," she said softly as she walked toward the house.

But not, she thought, a waste of time.

She'd stirred the potatoes, taken the bread from the oven, and had poured a fresh glass of wine before the rest of her circle began wandering in.

"What can I do," Iona asked as she washed her hands, "that won't give anyone heartburn?"

"You could mince up that garlic there."

"I'm good at mincing, also chopping."

"Mincing will do."

"Are you all right?" Iona said under her breath. "You look a little pale."

"I'm right enough, I promise you. I have something to tell all of you, but I'd as soon wait until I have this all done."

"Okay."

She focused on cooking, on letting the voices flow around her while she worked. She didn't have to ask for help—others set the table, poured wine, arranged food on platters or in bowls.

"Do you have a marketing list?" Meara asked as those bowls and platters made their way around the table. "And if not, if you could make one, I'll be doing the marketing for you—unless you object."

"You're doing my marketing?"

"The lot of us will be taking turns on it, from now on. Well, as long as you're stuck doing most of the cooking. It's gone past cleaning up after being a fair trade-off. So we'll see to the marketing."

"I have a list started, and planned to go to the market tomorrow."

"It'll be my turn for that, if that's all right with you."

"Sure it's fine with me."

"If there's anything you want taken into your shop, I can haul it in for you at the same time."

She started to speak, then looked around the table, narrowed her eyes. "What's all this then, doing the marketing, taking in my stock?"

"You look tired." At Connor's eye-roll and sigh, Boyle scowled. "Why dance around it?"

"Thank you so much for pointing it out to me," Branna snapped back.

"You want the truth or want it fancied up?" Boyle's scowl only deepened. "You look tired, and that's that."

Eyes narrowed still, she ran her hands down her face, did a glamour. Now she all but glowed. "There, all better."

"It's under it where you're tired."

She started to round on Fin, and Connor threw up his hands. "Oh leave off, Branna. You're pale and heavy-eyed, and we're the ones looking at you." He jabbed a finger when she started to rise, sent a little shove across the table to put her back in her chair.

She didn't need the glamour now to bring the flush to her cheeks. "Want to take me on, do you?"

"Just stop it, both of you," Iona ordered. "Just stop. You have every reason to look tired, with all you're doing, and we have every right to take some of the load off. It's just marketing, for God's sake, and cleaning up and *chores*. We're doing it so you can have some time to breathe, damn it. So stop being so snarly about it."

Branna sat back. "Doesn't seem so long ago it was an apology coming out of your mouth every two minutes or less. Now it's orders."

"I've evolved. And I love you. We all love you."

"I don't mind the marketing," Branna said, but calmly now. "Or the chores—very much. But I'm grateful to pass some of it on for the time being as we'll all be busy with more important matters, and Yule's all but on us. We should have light and joy for Yule. We will have."

"Then it's settled," Iona stated. "If anybody wants to say anything else about it, I'm cooking tomorrow." She forked up some chicken, smiled. "I thought that would close the subject."

"Firmly." Branna reached over to squeeze her hand. "And there's another subject entirely needs discussion. Cabhan was here."

"Here?" Connor shoved to his feet. "In the house?"

"Of course not in the house. Be sane. Do you think he could get through the protection I've laid—and you as well? I saw him outside. I went out in the back garden to check on the winter plantings, and to get some air as I'd been working inside all day. He was bold enough to come to the edge of the garden, which is as far as he can step. We spoke."

"After Connor and I went down to the pub." Fin spoke coolly. "And you're just telling us of it now?"

"I wanted to get supper on as there's enough confusion in that with the kitchen full of people. And once we sat, the conversation began on my haggard self."

"I never said haggard," Boyle muttered.

"In any case, I'm telling you now, or would if Connor would stop checking out all the windows and come back to the table."

"And you wonder I don't like leaving you on your own."

She shot arrows at her brother with the look. "Mind yourself or you'll be trying to make such insulting remarks with a tongue tied in knots. I was wandering the garden, with a glass of wine. The light changed, the fog came."

"You didn't call for us."

This time she pointed a warning finger at her brother. "Leave off interrupting. I didn't call, no, because I wanted to know what he had to say, and I wasn't in trouble. He couldn't touch me, and we both knew it. I wouldn't risk my skin, Connor, but more, you—all of you—should know I'd never risk the circle, what we have to do. Not for curiosity, not for pride. For nothing would I risk it."

"Let her finish." Though Meara was tempted to give Connor's leg a kick under the table, she gave it a comforting squeeze instead. "Because we do know it. Just as we knew he'd try for Branna before it was done."

"A poor try, at least this time," Branna continued. "The usual overtures. He'd make me his, give me more power than I could dream of and more bollocks of the same sort. He was still hurting a bit, hiding it, but the red stone was weaker. But he still has power up his sleeve. He changed to Fin."

In the silence, Fin lifted his gaze from his wineglass, and the heat of it clashed with Branna's. "To me?"

"As if his illusion of you would shatter all my defenses. But he had a bit more. He's canny, and he's been watching us for a lifetime. He changed again, back to when you were eighteen. Back to the day . . ."

"We were together. The first time. The only time."

"Not that day, no, but the week after. When I learned of the mark. All you felt and said, what I felt and said, all there as it had been. He had enough to make me feel it, to draw me to the edge of my protection. He fed on that so the stone glowed deeper, as did his arrogance, as he didn't understand I had more than enough to take out my garden knife and give him a good jab with it. As I did I grabbed the chain of the stone, and I saw fear. I saw his fear. Back he went to fog, so I couldn't hold it, couldn't work fast enough to break the chain.

"It's ice. So cold it burns," she murmured, studying her palm. "And holding it, for that instant, I felt the dark of him, the hunger, and most I felt the fear."

Connor snatched her hand.

"I saw to it," she assured him as he scanned for injuries. "You could see the links of the chain scored across my palm."

"But you wouldn't risk yourself."

"I didn't. Connor, he couldn't touch me. And had he been quick enough to lay a hand on me when I grabbed the chain, the advantage would have been mine."

"Certain of that, are you?" Fin rose, came around the table, held out his hand. "Give it to me. I'll know if there's any of him left."

Without a word, Branna put her hand in his, stayed quiet as she felt the heat run under her skin, into her blood.

"And if he'd gotten the knife from you?" Boyle asked. "If he'd used it against you, sliced at your hand or arm when you held the chain?"

"Gotten the knife from me?" She picked up her table knife. And held a white rose. "He gave me an opportunity. I took it, and gave him none." She looked at Fin. "He put nothing in me."

"No." He released her hand, walked back and sat. "Nothing."

"He fears us. I learned this. What we've done, the harm we caused him, gives him fear. He gained some strength from my emotions, I won't deny it, but he bled for it, and he ran."

"He'll come back." Fin kept his eyes on hers as he spoke. "And fear will have him strike more violently at the source of the fear."

"He'll always come back until we end him. And while he may strike more violently, the more he fears, the less he is."

7

HE THOUGHT TO GO OFF HAWKING. HE'D SADDLE BARU, Fin decided over his morning coffee with dawn barely broken in the eastern sky. Saddle up his horse, whistle up his hawk, and go off. A full morning for himself.

They had the dream potion, and though there was more work, he needed—God he needed some time and distance from Branna. One bleeding morning could hardly matter.

"We'll take it, won't we?" he said to Bugs, who sprawled on the floor joyfully gnawing on a rawhide bone Fin had picked up at the market in a weak moment. "You can go along so I'll have the full complement. Horse, hound, hawk. I'm in the mood for a long, hard gallop."

And if Cabhan was drawn to him, well, it wasn't as if he'd gone out looking. Precisely.

He glanced toward the door at the knock. One of the stablemen, he expected, as they'd come to the back. But he saw Iona through the glass.

"An early start?" he said as he opened the door to her.

"Oh yeah, bright and." Her smile shone bright as Christmas. "I'm picking Nan up at the airport."

"Of course, I'd forgotten she was coming. From now till the New Year, is it?"

"For Christmas—Yule—and staying until the second of January. I wish it was longer."

"You'll be glad to see her. So will we all. And she'll be back, won't she, in the spring for your wedding?"

"That's an absolutely. I couldn't convince her to stay straight through, but that's probably for the best anyway. Considering."

"Out of harm's way."

"Still. And she won't be talked into staying at Branna's while she is here. I'm taking her to her friend Margaret Meeney. Do you know her?"

"She taught me my letters and sums, and will still tell me not to slouch if she spots me in the village. A born teacher was Mrs. Meeney. Do you want coffee?"

"Thanks, but I've had my quota. Oh, there's Bugs. Hey, Bugs."

When she crouched down to give the dog a rub, Fin struggled with mild embarrassment. "He comes wandering in now and again."

"It's nice to have the company. Mrs. Meeney didn't teach me my letters and sums." She looked up at Fin. "I didn't grow up with you like the others. I don't have the same history."

"It doesn't change what we are now."

"I know, and that's a constant miracle to me. This family. You're my family, Fin, but I don't have the history with you or Branna the others do, so maybe I can say what the others can't, or say it in a different way. He used you, what happened between you, to try to get to her. That hurt you as much as her."

She straightened. "It would be easier to walk away, leave this to the three. But you don't. You won't. Part of it's because of your own need to right a wrong—a wrong done to you. Part's for family, for your circle, your friends. And all the rest, all the parts of the rest, that's for Branna."

He leaned back against the counter, slipped his hands into his pockets. "That's a lot of parts."

"There are a lot of parts to you. I didn't grow up with you, didn't watch you and Branna fall in love, or go through the pain of what pulled you apart. But I see who you are now, both of you. And from where I'm standing, she's wrong not to let herself have love, have joy. It makes all the sense in the world, but it's still wrong. And you're wrong, Fin. You're wrong for believing—and deep down you do—she's doing it to punish you. If that were true, Cabhan couldn't have used you to hurt her.

"I should go."

"You've such kindness in you." He pushed off the counter, then cupped her chin, kissed her. "Such light. If you could cook I swear I'd turn Boyle into a mule and steal you away for my own."

"I'm keeping that in reserve. We'll have Christmas, we'll have family. I know you, and Branna, too, would rather move on this dream spell right away. But Connor was right last night. We'll take our family time, have the holiday with color and light and music. Throw that in his face first."

"We were outvoted on it, and I can see it from your side."

"Good." She reached for the door, turned back. "You need to have a party. This fabulous house begs for it. You should have a party for New Year's Eve."

"A party?" The quick switch unbalanced him. "Here?"

"Yes, a party; yes, here. I don't know why I didn't think of it before. Time to sweep out the old, ring in the new. Definitely a New Year's Eve party. I'll text Boyle. We'll help you throw it together."

"I—"

"Gotta go."

She shut the door, and quickly, leaving him frowning after her. "Well, Christ, Bugs, it looks like we're having a party."

He decided to think about it and all that entailed later. He still wanted that ride. He'd get out, give Baru his head, let Merlin soar and hunt. Give little Bugs the time of his young life.

And on the way home, he'd stop by the stables, and stop again by the falconry school, put some time in each. If there was enough of the day left after all of that, he'd check to see if he could be of use in Branna's workshop. Though he assumed she'd be as pleased as he to have a full day apart.

Out in the stables while he saddled his big black, he had a conversation with Sean that ranged from horses, a feed order, to women, to football, and back to horses.

He paused as he led Baru out. "It may be I'm having a party for New Year's Eve."

Sean blinked, pushed back his cap. "At the big house here?"

"Sure that would be the place."

"Hah. A party at the big house—fancy-like?"

"Not altogether fancy." He hadn't thought of it either way—and supposed he should have consulted Iona since it was her doing. "Just scrape the horse shite off your boots."

"Hah," Sean said again. "And would you be having music then?"

Fin blew out a breath. "It seems only right there'd be music. And there'd be food and drink as well before you ask. Nine o'clock seems right." He scooped Bugs off the ground, swung into the saddle.

"A party at the big house," Sean said as Fin kicked Baru straight into a gallop.

When Fin glanced back, he saw his longtime stable hand, hands on hips, studying the house as if he'd never seen it before.

Which said, Fin supposed, it was long past time for a party.

Bugs vibrated excited delight as they thundered off, the horse sent out waves of pleasure at the chance to run, and overhead the hawk called out, high and bright, as it circled.

And long past time for this, he realized.

Though part of him yearned for the woods, the smell of them, the song of the trees in the breeze, he headed for open. So he took to the fields, the gentle rise of hill, let the horse run over the green while the hawk soared the blue.

He pulled out, put on his glove. He and Merlin wouldn't need it, but it was best if someone rambled by. He lifted his arm, lifted his mind. The hawk dived, did a pretty, show-off turn that made Fin laugh, then glided like a feathered god to the glove.

The dog quivered, watched them both.

"We've taken to each other, you see. That's the way of it. So you're brothers now as well. Will you hunt?" he asked Merlin.

In answer the hawk rose up, calling as he circled the field.

"We'll walk a bit." Fin dismounted, set Bugs down.

The dog immediately rolled in the grass, barked for the fun of it.

"He's young yet." Fin patted Baru's neck when the horse gave the hound a pitying glance.

Here's what he'd needed, Fin thought as he walked with the horse. The open, the air. A cold day for certain, but clear and bright for all that.

The hawk went into the stoop, took its prey.

Fin leaned against Baru, gazing out over the green, the brown, the slim columns of smoke rising from chimneys.

And this, he thought, he missed like a limb when he was off wandering. The country of his blood, of his bone, of his heart and spirit. He missed the green, the undulating hills, the gray of the stone, the rich brown of earth turned for planting.

He would leave it again—he would have to when he'd finished what he needed to finish. But he would always come back, pulled to Ireland, pulled to Branna, pulled . . . Iona had said it. Pulled to family.

"They don't want you here."

Fin continued to lean on the horse. He'd felt Cabhan come. Maybe had wanted him to.

"You're mine. They know it. You know it. You feel it."

The mark on his shoulder throbbed.

"Since the mark came on me, you've tried to lure me, draw me. Save your promises and lies, Cabhan. They bore me, and I'm after some air and some open."

"You come here." Cabhan walked across the field on a thin sea of fog, black robes billowing, red stone glowing. “Away from them. You come to me.”

“Not to you. Now or ever.”

“My son—”

“Not that.” Anger he’d managed to tamp down boiled up. “Now or ever.”

“But you are.” Smiling, Cabhan pulled the robe down his shoulder, exposed the mark. “Blood of my blood.”

“How many women did you rape before you planted your seed, a seed that brought you a son?”

“It took only the one destined to bear my child. I gave her pleasure, and took more. I will give Branna to you, if she is what you want. She’ll lie with you again, and as often as you choose. Only come to me, join with me, and she can be yours.”

“She’s not yours to give.”

“She will be.”

“Not while I breathe.” Fin held out a hand, palm forward, brought the power up. “Come to me, Cabhan. Blood to blood, you say. Come to me.”

He felt it, that tug-of-war, felt the heat as his power burned. Saw, as Branna had, a flicker of fear. Cabhan took a lurching step forward.

“You do not summon me!”

Cabhan crossed his arms, wrenched them apart. And broke the spell. “They will betray you, shun you. When you lie cold, your blood on the ground, they will not mourn you.”

He folded into the fog, lowered, hunched, formed into the wolf. Fin saw his sword in his mind’s eye, in its sheath in his workshop. And lifting his hand, held it.

Even as he called the others, called his circle, the wolf lunged.

But not at him, not at the man holding a flaming sword and burning with power. It lunged at the little dog quivering in the high grass.

“No!”

Fin leaped, swung. Then met, sliced only fog, and even that died away with the dog bleeding in the grass, his eyes glazed with shock and pain.

"No, no, no, no." He started to drop to his knees. The hawk called; the horse trumpeted. Both struck out at the wolf that had re-formed behind Fin.

With a howl, it vanished again.

Even as he knelt, Branna was there.

"Oh God." He reached down, but she took his hands, nudged them away.

"Let me. Let me. My strength is healing, and hounds are mine."

"His throat. It tore his throat. Harmless, he's harmless, but it went for him rather than me."

"I can help. I can help. Fin, look at me, look in me. Fin."

"I don't want your comfort!"

"Leave it to her." Connor crouched down beside him, laid a hand firmly on his shoulder. "Let her try."

Already grieving, for he felt the life slipping away, he knelt in helpless rage and guilt.

"Here now, here." Branna crooned it as she laid her hands on the bloodied throat. "Fight with me now. Hear me, and fight to live."

Bugs's eyes rolled up. Fin felt the dog's heart slow.

"He suffers."

"Healing hurts. He has to fight." She whipped her gaze to Fin, all power and fury. "Tell him to fight, for he's yours. I can't heal him if he lets go. Tell him!"

Though it grieved him to ask, Fin held his hands over Branna's. *Fight.*

Such pain. Branna felt it. Her throat burned with it, and her own heart stuttered. She kept her eyes on the eyes of the little hound, poured her power in, and the warmth with it.

The deep first, she thought. Mend and mend what was torn. In the cold field, the wind blowing, sweat beaded on her forehead.

From somewhere, she heard Connor tell her to stop. It was too much, but she felt the pain, the spark of hope. And the great grief of the man she loved.

Look at me, she told the dog. *Look in me. In me. See in me.*

Bugs whimpered.

"He's coming back, Branna." Connor, still scanning the field, still guarding, laid a hand on Branna's shoulder, gave her what he had.

The open wound narrowed, began to close.

Bugs turned his head, licked weakly at her hand.

"There now," she said gently. "Yes, there you are. Just another moment. Just a bit more. Be brave, little man. Be brave for me another moment."

When Bugs wagged his tail, Fin simply laid his brow against Branna's.

"He'll be all right. He could do with some water, and he'll need to rest. He . . ."

She couldn't help it, couldn't stop herself. She wrapped her arms around Fin, held him.

"He's all right now."

"I owe you—"

"Of course you don't, and I won't have you say it, Fin." She eased back, framed his face with her hands. For a moment they knelt, the dog gamely wagging his tail between them.

"You should take him home now."

"Yes. Home."

"What happened?" Connor asked. "Can you tell us? We told Iona not to come. Christ, she's driving her grandmother from the airport in Galway."

"Not now, Connor." Branna pushed to her feet. "We'll get the details of it later. Take him home, Fin. I have some tonic that would do well. I'll get it for you. But rest is all he really needs."

"Would you come with me?" He hated to ask, to need to ask, but still feared for the little dog. "Look after him for just a bit longer, just a bit to be sure?"

"All right. Of course. Connor, you could ride Baru back, and take the hawks, take Kathel. I'll be home soon."

"Well, I—"

But Branna put her hand in Fin's. She, Fin, and the little dog winked away together.

"Well, as I was saying." Connor ran his fingers through his hair, looked up to where Fin's hawk and his own Roibeard circled. He gave Kathel's head a pat, then swung onto Baru. "I'll just see to the rest."

IN HIS KITCHEN, THE DOG SNUGGLED IN HIS ARMS, FIN TRIED to sort out what to do next.

"I should bathe this blood off him."

"Not in there," Branna said, all sensibilities shocked when he walked to the kitchen sink. "You can't be washing up a dog in the same place you wash up your dishes. You must have a laundry, a utility sink."

Though he didn't see the difference, Fin changed directions, moved through a door and into the laundry with its bright white walls and burly black machines. Opening a cupboard, he reached for laundry soap.

"Not with that, for pity's sake, Fin. You don't bathe a dog with laundry soap. You're wanting dish soap—the liquid you'd use for hand washing."

He might have pointed out the bloody dish soap was under the bloody kitchen sink where he'd intended to wash the dog in the first place. But she was bustling about, pulling off her coat, notching it on a peg, pushing up her sleeves.

"Give me the dog; get the soap."

Fine then, he thought, just fine. His brain was scattered to bits in any case. He fetched the soap, stepped back in.

"You're doing fine," she murmured to Bugs, who stared up at her with adoration. "Just tired and a little shaky here and there. You'll have a nice warm bath," she continued as she ran water in the sink. "Some tonic, and a good long nap and you'll be right as rain."

"What's right about rain, I've always wondered." He dumped soap in the running water.

"That's enough—enough, Fin. You'll have the poor thing smothered in bubbles."

He set the bottle on the counter. "I've something upstairs—a potion—that should do for him."

"I'll get him started here if you'll get it."

"I'm grateful, Branna."

"I know. Here now, in you go. Isn't that nice?"

"He's fond of the shower."

With the dog sitting in the sea of bubbles looking, to Fin's eye, ridiculous, Branna turned.

"What?"

"Never mind. I'll get the tonic."

"The shower, is it?" she murmured when Fin left, rubbing her hands over the dog. Bugs lapped at the bubbles, at her hand, and brought on a very clear image of Fin, wearing nothing but water, laughing as he held the dog in a glass-walled shower where the jets streamed everywhere and steam puffed.

"Hmmm. He's kept in tune, hasn't he? Still some of the boy in there though, showering with a dog."

It amused her, touched her, which wasn't a problem. It stirred her, which was.

Fin brought back a pretty bottle with a hexagon base filled with deep green liquid. At Branna's crooked finger, he unstopped it, held it out for her to sniff.

"Ah, yes, that's just what he needs. If you have a little biscuit, you'd add three—no, let's have four—drops to it. It'll go down easier that way, and he'll think it a treat."

Without thinking, Fin reached in his pocket, took out a thumb-sized dog biscuit.

"You carry those in your pocket—what, in case you or the dog here get hungry?"

"I didn't know how long we'd be out," he muttered, and added the drops.

"Set it down to soak in. We could use an old towel."

He set off again, came back with a fluffy towel the color of moss.

"Egyptian cotton," Branna observed, and smoothly lifted the dog out, bundled him up before he could shake.

"I don't have an old towel. And it'll wash, won't it?"

"So it will." She rubbed the dog briskly, kissed his nose. "That's better now, isn't it? All clean and smelling like a citrus grove. An Egyptian one. Give him his treat, Fin, for he's a good boy, a good, brave boy."

Bugs turned those adoring, trusting eyes on Fin, then gobbled down the offered treat.

"He could do with some water before . . ." She glanced down, and stared. Truly horrified. "Belleek? You're using Belleek bowls for the dog's food and water."

"They were handy." Flustered, he took the dog, tossed the towel on the counter, then set Bugs down by the water bowl.

The dog drank thirstily, and noisily, for nearly a full minute. Let out a small belch then sat, stared up at Fin.

"He only needs a warm place to sleep for a while," Branna told him.

Fin picked the dog up, snagged a pillow from the sofa in the great room, tossed it down in front of the fire.

Egyptian cotton, Belleek bowls, and now a damask pillow, Branna thought. The stable dog had become a little prince.

"He's tired." Fin stayed crouched down, stroking Bugs. "But he doesn't hurt. His blood's clear. There's no poison in him."

"He'll sleep now, and wake stronger than he was. I had to give him a boost to bring him back. He'd lost so much blood."

"He'll have a scar here." Gently, Fin traced a finger over the thin, jagged line on the dog's throat.

"As Alastar carries one."

Nodding, Fin rose as the dog slept. "I'm in your debt."

"You're not, and insult us both by saying it."

"Not insult, Branna, gratitude. I'll get you some wine."

"Fin, it can't be two in the afternoon."

"Right." He had to scrub his hands over his face, try to find his balance again. "Tea then."

"I wouldn't say no." And it would keep him busy, she thought as he walked back into the kitchen, until he settled a little more.

"He's for the stables. It's been two years, thereabouts, since he wandered in. I wasn't even here. It was Sean cleaned him up, fed him. And Boyle who named him."

"Could be he wandered here for a reason, more reason than a bed of straw and scraps and some kind words. He's in your home now, sleeping on a damask pillow in front of the fire. You took him on Samhain."

"He was handy, like the bowls."

"More than that, Fin."

He shrugged, measured out tea. "He has a strong heart, and I never thought Cabhan would pay him any mind. He's . . ."

"Harmless. Small and harmless and sweet-natured."

"I brought him in one night. He has a way of looking at you, so I brought him in."

Yes, still some of the boy, she thought, and all the kindness born in him. "A dog's good company. The best, to my mind."

"He chases his tail for no good reason but it's there. I haven't any biscuits," he realized after a quick search. "Of the human sort."

"Tea's fine. Just the tea."

Understanding he'd want to be close to the dog, she took a chair in view of the fire, waited until he'd brought the tea, sat with her.

"Tell me what happened."

"I wanted a ride, a good, fast ride. The hills, the open."

"As I wanted to walk in my garden. I understand the need."

"You would. I thought to ride, to do some hawking, and took Bugs along to give him an adventure. Christ Jesus."

"Your horse, your hawk, your hound." She could almost see the guilt raging around him, hoped to smooth it down again. "Why wouldn't you? You're the only one of us who can link to all three."

"I wasn't looking for Cabhan, but in truth, I was more than pleased he found me."

"As I was, walking in my garden. I understand that as well. Did he attack?"

"He started with his blather. I'm his blood, the lot of you will betray me, shun me, and so on. You'd think he'd be as bored with all that as I, but he never stops. Though this time out he promised to give you to me, should I want you, and that was fresh."

Branna angled her head, and her voice was dry as dust. "Oh, did he now?"

"He did. He understands desire well enough. Understands the hungers of lust, but nothing of the heart or spirit. He knows I want you, but he'll never understand why. I turned it on him. Began to draw him to me. It surprised him I could, for a moment, I could, and it threw him off. I called for the three—for we'd promised that—and as he became the wolf I pulled the sword from the cupboard upstairs, enflamed it."

He paused a moment, got his bearings. "I could have held him off, I'm sure of it. I could have engaged him, with Baru and Merlin with me, until you came and we went at him together. But he didn't come at me. He streaked to the side, had Bugs by the throat. All so fast. I went at him, struck at him, but he shifted away. He went for the dog who barely weighs a stone, tore his throat, then vanished away before I could strike a single blow. He never came at me."

"But he did. He struck at your heart. Baru, Merlin, yourself? There's a battle. The little dog, a strike at you with no risk to himself. A fecking coward he's always been, will always be."

"He rounded behind me when I went to the dog."

Because, Branna knew, Fin thought of the dog before his own safety. "He knew you would go to the hurt and the helpless. Go to what's yours."

"I would have faced him man to man, witch to witch." Now Fin's eyes fired, molten green, as rage overcame guilt. "I wanted that."

"As we all do, but that's not his way. You may come from him, but you're not of him. He keeps at you, as he can't conceive you'd make the choice not to be."

"You left me because I'm of him."

"I left you because I was shocked and hurt and angry. And when that cleared, because I'm sworn." She closed a hand around her pendant. "I'm sworn by Sorcha and all who came after her, down to me, and Connor and Iona, to use all we are to rid the world of him."

"And all who come from him."

"No. No." Outrage would have come first at any other time, but she still felt his guilt under everything else he felt. "You come from him, but you're one of us. I've come to know that was meant. I've come to believe none who've come before us succeeded because none who came before had you. Had his blood with them. None of them had you, Fin, with your power, your loyalty, your heart."

He heard the words, believed she meant them. And yet. "I'm one of you, but you won't be with me."

"How can I think of that, Fin? How can I think of it when even now I can feel the urgency of what we're sworn to do building again? I can't see beyond that, and when I do, when I let myself think about what might be once this is done, I can't see any of the life we once thought we'd make together. We were so young—"

"Bollocks to that, Branna. What we felt for each other was older than time. We weren't the young and foolish playing at love."

"How much easier would it have been if we had been? How much easier now? If we only played at it, Fin, we wouldn't be bound to think of tomorrows. What future could we have? What life, you and I?"

He stared into the fire, knowing again she spoke the truth.

And yet.

"None, I know it, and still that feels like more than either of us have without the other. You're the rest of me, Branna, and I'm tired enough right now to stop pretending you're not."

"You think I don't mourn what might have been?" Hurt radiated through her, into the words. "That I don't wish for it?"

"I have thought that. I've survived thinking that."

"Then you've been wrong, and it may be I'm too tired as well to pretend. If it was only my heart, it would be yours."

She took an unsteady breath as he turned his gaze from the fire to her face.

"It can't be anyone else's. It's already lost. But it isn't only that, and I can't act on *might be.* When my father gave me this?" She held up the pendant. "I had a choice. He told me I had a choice, to take it or not. But if I took it, the choice was done. I would be one of the three, and sworn to try, above all, to end what Sorcha began. I won't betray you, Fin, but neither will I betray my blood. I can't think of wants and wishes, I can't reach for *might be*s. My purpose was set before I was born."

"I know that as well." There were times the knowing it emptied him out. "Your purpose takes your head, your power, your spirit, but you can't separate your heart from the rest."

"It's the only way I can do what needs to be done."

"It's a wonder to me you believe all who've come before you would want you unhappy."

"I don't, of course, I don't. It's that I believe all who've come before need me to do what must be done, what each of us have sworn. I . . ." She hesitated, not at all sure she knew how to say what was in her. "I don't know, Fin, I don't, if I know how to do what I must and be with you. But I can swear it's not wanting to hurt or punish you. It may have been long ago when I was so young and so hurt and frightened. But it's not that, not at all."

He sat silent for a time, then looked back at her. "Tell me this. This one thing. Do you love me?"

She could lie. He would know it for a lie, but the lie would serve. And a lie was cowardly.

"I've loved no one as I loved you. But—"

"It's enough. It's enough to hear you say what you haven't said to me in more than a dozen years. Be grateful I owe you a debt." There was fire behind his eyes, burning hot. "I owe you for what lies sleeping there, else I'd find a way to get you into my bed, and put an end to this torment."

"Seduction? Persuasion?" She tossed back her hair, rose. "I go to no man's bed unless and until it's my clear choice."

"Of course, and one made only with your head. For such a clever woman you can be amazingly thick."

"Now that you're back to insulting me, I'll be on my way. I've work I'm neglecting."

"I'll drive you. I'll drive you," he said even as she prepared to blast him. "There's no point giving Cabhan another target today should he still be around. And I'll stay and work with you, as agreed. The purpose, Branna, is mine as well, however different our thoughts on the life we live around that purpose."

She might still have blasted him—she could work up a head of steam quickly and keep it pumping. But she caught the quick and concerned glance he sent the dog.

Bugger it.

"That's fine then, as there's plenty of work. Bring the dog. He'll sleep through the ride, then Kathel can look after him."

"I'd feel better about it. Oh, and there's another thing. Iona tells me I'm having a party here for New Year's Eve. So there's that."

"A party?"

"Why does everyone say it back to me as if I've used a foreign tongue?"

"That may be because I don't recall you ever having a party."

"There's a first time," he muttered, and got the dog.

8

SHE BLAMED THE DOG. HE'D SOFTENED HER UP, AND FIN, with his fancy towels and bowls and utter love for a stable dog, had marched right through her defenses.

She'd said more than she'd meant to, and more than she'd admitted to herself. Words had as much power as deeds to her mind, and now she'd given them to him when it might have been more rational, more practical to keep them to herself.

But that was done, and she knew well how to shore up her defenses. Where Finbar Burke was concerned she'd been doing so for more than a decade.

And in truth, there was too much to do, too much going on around her, to fret about it.

They'd had a lovely, quiet Yule, made only more special by Iona's grandmother joining them. As they observed the solstice and the longest night, she could begin looking toward spring.

But Christmas came first.

It was a holiday she particularly enjoyed—all the fussiness of it. She liked the shopping, the wrapping, the decorating, the baking. And this year in particular, all the work of it gave her a short respite from what she'd termed to Fin her *purpose*.

She'd hoped they'd host a big *céili* during the season, but it seemed too mixed with risks with Cabhan lurking. Next year for certain, she promised herself. Next year, she'd have her parents and other cousins, neighbors and friends and the rest.

But this year, it would be her circle, and Iona's Nan, and that was a fine thing, and a happy one.

With her breads and biscuits baked, along with mince pie she'd serve with brandy butter, she checked the goose roasting in the oven.

"Your kitchen smells of my childhood." Mary Kate, Iona's grandmother, came in. Her face, still flushed from cold, beamed as she crossed the room to kiss Branna's cheek. "Iona's slipping some gifts under the tree, and likely shaking a few as well. I thought I'd see what I could do to help."

"It's good to see you, and I'm more than grateful to have a pair of skilled hands in here."

Trim and stylish in a bright red sweater, Mary Kate walked over to sniff at pots. "I'm told you've taught Iona to cook a thing or two, which was more than I could do."

"She's willing, and getting better at the able. We'll have some wine first, before we get down to it. It's Christmas, after all. Did you get by to see the new house?"

"I did. Oh, it's going to be fine, isn't it? And finished, they tell me, by the wedding—or near enough. It's a light in my heart to see her so happy."

She took the wine Branna offered. "I wanted a moment alone with you, Branna, to tell you what it means to me you and Connor gave her a home, a family."

"She's family, and a good friend as well."

"She's such a good heart. It was hard for me to send her here. Not to Ireland, not to you." Mary Kate glanced toward the front of the house. "But to what it would all mean. To send her, knowing what it could mean, and what I know it does. I thought to write to you, to tell you she was coming, and then I thought no, for that would be in the way of asking you, an obligation, to take her in, to help her hone her gifts. And it should be a choice."

Once more Branna thought of Fin. "Do we have one?"

"I believe we do. I chose to give her the amulet, though it grieved me to do it. Once done it can't be taken back. But it was hers to wear, hers to bear. I knew the first time I held her. I held you and Connor when you were only babes. And knew, as your father knew, and your aunt. And now the three of you are grown, and the time's here, as it wasn't with me and your father, your aunt."

She walked to the window, looked out. "I feel him. He won't bother with me—Iona frets over that, but he won't bother with me. I'm nothing to him now. But I've power enough to help if help's needed."

"We may, when the day comes."

"But that isn't today." Mary Kate turned again, smiled again. "So today I'll help in the kitchen." She took a long sip of wine. *"Nollaig Shona Duit."*

"We'll see it is." Branna tapped her glass to Mary Kate's. "A very happy Christmas."

IT TOOK A LITTLE MAGICK TO EXPAND THE TABLE TO FIT seven people and all the food, but she'd wanted a feast—and no more talk of Cabhan.

"We won't be eating like this tomorrow at my sister's," Meara announced as she sampled Branna's stuffing. "Between Maureen and my mother, we may be in a runoff for the worst cook in Ireland."

"So we'll fill up tonight, eat careful there, and be back here for leftovers." Connor stabbed a bite of goose.

"It's my first major holiday with Boyle's family." Happiness rolled off Iona as she looked around the table. "I'm taking bread pudding—and I won't be in the runoff, as Nan walked me through it. We're going to pick a holiday, Boyle, for us to host. Make a tradition. How're things going on New Year's, Fin?"

"They're coming."

"I could make bread pudding."

He smiled, adoring her. "I'm having it catered."

"Catered?"

He flicked a glance at Branna's instant shock. "Catered," he said firmly. "I look at a menu, say, this, and that, and some of these, hand over the money, and it's done."

"You'll enjoy the party more without having to fuss," Mary Kate said lightly.

"It's for certain everyone will, as they'd enjoy it less if I'd tried my hand at making the food."

"God's truth," Boyle said, with feeling. "He's hired Tea and Biscuits for the music."

"You hired a band?"

This time Fin shrugged at Branna. "People want music, and they're a good band. If guests want to pick up a fiddle or pipe or break out in song, that's fine as well."

"It'll be good *craic*," Connor decreed.

"How many are coming?" Branna wondered.

"I don't know, precisely. I just set the word out."

"You could have half the county there!"

"I didn't set word that far out, but if that's the case, the caterer will be busy."

"Patrick and I used to have parties that way," Mary Kate remembered. "Oh, we couldn't afford a caterer in those days, but we'd just set the word out with friends and neighbors. It's friendly. A good *céili*."

"Branna's not happy with the idea altogether," Connor put in.

"She'd rather we didn't have any sort of party until we've done with Cabhan."

"We won't bring him to the table tonight," Branna said in a tone that brooked no argument. "Did I hear Kyra got a ring for Christmas, Connor?"

"You did, and you've ears to the ground, as she only got it last night, I'm told. She's flashing what there is of it everywhere." Thinking of their office manager, he wagged his fork at Fin. "Be sure you get into the school and make over it like it was the Hope Diamond. She gets her nose out of joint easy."

"I'll be sure to do that. My ear to the ground tells me that Riley—you remember Riley, Boyle, as his face ran into your fist some months back."

"He earned it."

"He did, and it seems he earned the same again from one Tim Waterly, who owns a horse farm in Sligo. I've had some dealings with Tim, and we've dealt together well. You'd think him a mild-mannered sort of man, but in this case, Riley's face ran into Tim's fist during a lively discussion on if trying to pass off moldy hay was good business practice."

"He's a fucker is Riley, right enough. I'm begging your pardon, Nan."

"No need, for a man who'd try to sell moldy hay, or worse, mistreat a horse as he did your sweet mare Darling, is a fucker indeed. Would you pass me those potatoes, Meara? I think I've room for another bite of them."

They ate their way through the feast, and some groaned their way through the cleanup, but somehow managed pie or trifle or some of both. There was Fin's champagne, and gifts exchanged. Delighted hugs, and a pause as carolers wandered by.

And no sign of Cabhan, Branna thought as she checked out the windows yet again.

When she slipped out to the kitchen to check from there, Fin followed her.

"If you don't want Cabhan brought up, stop looking for him."

"I'm after another bottle of champagne."

"You're after worrying yourself to distraction. He's burrowed in, Branna. I've my own way of looking."

He got out the bottle himself, set it on the counter.

"I just want tonight to be . . . unspoiled."

"And it is. I've something for you."

He turned his hand, empty, turned it again, and held out a box wrapped in gold paper and topped with an elaborate silver bow.

"We've exchanged our gifts."

"And one more yet. Open it, and I'll open this." He turned to the champagne.

Thrown off yet again, she unwrapped the box, opened it as Fin drew the cork with a muffled *pop*.

She knew the bottle was old—and beautiful. Its facets streamed with light, shimmering with it so it seemed to glow in her hand. It had held power once, she thought, long ago. Then traced a finger over the glass stopper. A dragon's head.

"It's stunning. It's old and stunning and still hums with power."

"I found it in a fussy antiques shop in New Orleans, though it didn't come from there. It had passed from hand to hand long before it came to that fussy shop where they had no idea what it was. I knew it for yours as soon as I picked it up. I've had it a few years now as I wasn't sure how to give it so you'd accept it."

She stared down at the bottle. "You think I'm hard."

"I think nothing of the sort. I think you're strong, and that makes it hard for both of us. Still, I couldn't leave it in that shop where they didn't know what they had, and not when I knew it for yours."

"And you know when I look at it, I'll think of you."

"Well, there is that advantage to it. All the same, it's for you."

"I'll keep it in my room, and despite my better sense I'll think of you when I look at it." She couldn't risk her lips on his, but brushed hers to his cheek, and for a moment rested her cheek to his as she'd once done so often, so easily. "Thank you. I— Oh, she had it made very particularly. I have a glimmer here," she murmured, staring at the bottle. "The dragon was hers, I think. And she had this made, just so, to hold . . . to hold tears. A witch's tears—so precious and powerful when shed for joy, when shed in sorrow."

"Which did this hold?"

"I can't see it, but I'll think joy, as it's Christmas, and a beautiful gift. It should hold joy." She set it carefully on the counter. "We should have champagne, and we should have music. And I won't check the windows any more tonight."

THAT NIGHT, LATE, SHE PUT THE BOTTLE ON HER DRESSER, and, sliding into bed, watched it catch all the golds of the fire.

And thought of him. And thinking of him, laid a charm under her pillow to block dreams. Her heart was too full to risk dreams.

THINGS NEEDED DOING, BRANNA THOUGHT AS SHE SPENT the day—happily alone—in her workshop. She'd enjoyed every minute of Yule, of Christmas. Gathering with her circle, preparing the food, making music together. She'd loved the trip to Kerry on Christmas Day, didn't feel the least guilty she'd magickly flown to see her parents, to spend time with them and other family. And had felt warmer yet, as Connor did the same, with Meara.

It had done her spirit good to see her parents so happy with this new phase of their lives. Boosted her confidence to recognize their complete faith in her, in Connor.

But now it was back to practical matters again. To the work that earned her living. To the work that was her destiny, that was life or death.

She replenished some of her most popular lotions and creams, worked on the pretty travel candles that all but flew off her shop's shelves.

Then she gave herself the pleasure of experimenting with new scents, new colors, new textures. She could focus her mind on her senses, how did this look, what mood did this scent evoke, how did this feel on the skin?

She glanced up when the door opened, found herself happy to see Meara come in.

"Well now, this is perfectly timed. Take off your gloves, would you, and try this new cream."

"It's an ugly day out there, all cold, blowing rain." She pulled off her cap, unwound her scarf—tossed her thick brown braid behind her back. "And in here it's warm and smells like heaven. A fine change from the damp and the horse shite."

She hung up her coat, walked over to Branna, held out bare hands. "Oh, that's lovely." She rubbed in the cream, sniffed at her hands. "Just lovely and cool, and it smells like . . . air. Just fresh air, like you'd find on the top of a mountain. I like the color of it in the bowl, too. Pale, pale blue. Like blue ice."

"A perfect name for it. Blue Ice, it is. It's made for working hands and feet. I thought to do it in a sturdy sort of jar. The sort men wouldn't fuss about having for themselves. I'm thinking of doing a line of it. A scrub as well, a gel for the shower, cake and liquid soap. Again with packaging women will like, but men won't feel insults their testicles."

"I don't know how you think of all of it."

"If I didn't, I might have spent the day in the cold rain and horse shite with you." She walked over to put on the kettle. "And I feel as we come to the end of the year, it's time to think of new. Just yesterday my mother asked if I couldn't create some products exclusive for their little B and B. Some they could use as amenities for the guests—then sell in full size. And after year's end, I'm going to see what I can do about that."

"It was lovely seeing your mother yesterday, and your father as well, and the rest. Connor sprang it on me all at once. Why don't we fly down and see my ma and da for a bit before we're off to Galway? I'm saying how I'd love to see them, and shouldn't we ring them up first, but he just takes my hand, and *pop* we're there." She laid a hand on her belly. "I don't think I'll ever get used to that mode of traveling."

"It meant a lot to them, and to me, to have you both there for a few hours."

"Christmas means family, and if we're lucky, friends as well."

"And yours? Your family?"

"Ah, Branna, my mother's thriving at Maureen's. She's happier than I've seen her in years. Roses in her cheeks, a sparkle in her eye. She showed me her bedroom, and I have to give Maureen full marks there, as it's as fussy and pretty as Ma would want."

Meara sighed, but it was a sound of contentment. "Having us all in one place meant the world to her, that I could see. And didn't Maureen take me off to a corner to tell me how good it is for Ma to be there—I even let her go on about it, as if it had been her notion all along."

"It's a weight off you."

"A heavier one than I knew. And she's so pleased I won't be having sex with Connor much longer outside Holy Matrimony." Laughing, Meara sat by the fire. "She's already talking more grandchildren."

"And you?" Branna brought over a tray with steaming tea and sugar biscuits.

"I want them, of course, but likely not as quickly as will suit her. A bridge to cross at a later time." She sipped at her tea. "I'm glad you said I'd timed it well, coming in on you. I wanted to talk to you. Just you and me."

"Is there a problem?"

"That's what I want to ask you. I don't remember a time we weren't friends as it all started when we were still in nappies."

Branna took a bite of a sugar biscuit, grinned. "And may be in nappies again before we're done."

Meara snorted out a laugh. "That's a thought. As we're forever, you and I, we can say things maybe others can't. So I want to say this to you. Could it be good for you, Branna, this dream linking you're about to do with Fin?"

"We all agreed—"

"No, no, I'm not asking as part of the circle. I'm asking only as your friend, your sister. Nappie to nappie, we'll say."

"Ah, Meara."

"I'm thinking only of you now, as it's only you and me here. It's intimate, this dreaming together. I know and understand that well. It's a lot to ask of yourself, Branna, of your heart, your feelings."

"Dealing with Cabhan comes ahead of all that."

"Not for me. Not between me and you. I know you'll do it regardless, but I want to know how you feel about it all—friend to friend, and woman to woman besides. How you feel, and what I can do to help you."

"How I feel?" Branna loosed a long breath. "I feel it must be done, that it's the best way we have. And I know there'll be hurt, for it is intimate as you say. I know Fin and I must work together for the good of all, and I've accepted that."

"But?"

She sighed, knowing she could tell Meara whatever she held in her heart. "Since he came back months ago, since he's stayed all these months, and I've seen him fight and bleed with us, it's harder to hold back what I feel for him, and always have felt. It's harder to set aside what I know he feels for me, and always has felt. What we do next will make it harder still, on both of us. And I can only be grateful knowing you're there, you understand."

"Couldn't Connor go with him, or Boyle, or any of us?"

"If it was meant to be Connor or Boyle or any of us, it wouldn't have been me pulled into the dream that took us to Midor's cave. I can deal with it, Meara, as he can, though I know it's no easier for him than for me."

"He loves you, Branna, as deep as any man can love. I know it hurts you for me to say it."

"No, you don't hurt me." Branna rubbed a hand on Meara's thigh. "I know he loves me, or some part of him does. Some part always will. Love's powerful, and it's vital, but it's not all."

"Do you blame him still for his lineage?"

"It was easier when I did, when I was so young, so shattered, I could. But not blaming him doesn't change the facts of it all. He's Cabhan's blood. He bears the mark, and that mark came on him, manifested after we'd been together. If there's any of that lingering in me that blames him, well, it blames myself as well."

"I wish you wouldn't," Meara replied. "I wish you wouldn't take on blame, either of you."

"My blood, his blood. He bears the mark as much because of Sorcha as Cabhan, doesn't he? I think now that we're older and know more than we did, we both understand we're not meant to be together."

"If we defeat Cabhan, would you still feel that way? Still believe you couldn't be with him, and happy?"

"How can I say? How can I know? It's fate that drew us together, and fate pulled us apart. Fate decides these things."

"I don't believe that for a minute," Meara said, with heat. "We decide our own fate, by our choices, our actions."

Branna smiled, sat back. "You've a point there. Of course we're not merely puppets. But fate deals the hand, to my way of thinking. How we play the cards matters, but we only have the ones we're dealt. What would I do if fate hadn't dealt me you? I wouldn't have a friend who'd know to come give me her shoulder."

"It's always here for you."

"I know it. I'm built to stand on my own, but God, it's good to lean now and then. I can wish I didn't love him. I can wish I could look back at the girl I'd been and say, well now, she had her fling and her disappointment, her bit of heartbreak. Now she's moved on. But whatever cards I hold, he's one of them. And ever will be."

"We could take more time, try to find another way."

"We've waited too long already. We deserved to take the time for family and friends, but it's time to turn back to duty. I'm prepared for it, I promise you."

"Would you want me to stay after it's done? I mean after all of it, for me to stay. Me and Iona?"

"We'll see how it all goes. But it's a comfort to me to know, should I be needing you, you and Iona would be here. Before we worry if I'll be needing comfort, we go back, Fin and I, and find what this Midor is to Cabhan and Cabhan to him. And if the fates deal the cards, we learn how and when to stop him."

She tipped her head to Meara's shoulder. "I know Fin to be a good man, and that steadies me. I once tried to believe he wasn't, because it made it simpler, but that was wrong and foolish. At the end of it all, if I can know I've loved a good man, I can be satisfied with that."

9

SHE'D PREPARED FOR IT, EMOTIONALLY, MENTALLY. Branna told herself the spell, the dreamwalk, was not only a necessary step, but could and should go forward without personal issues.

She and Fin had reached a place, hadn't they, over the past months where they could work together, talk together without anger or heartache?

They were adults now, far from the starry-eyed children they'd been. She had a duty to her bloodline. And Fin, to his credit, had unstinting loyalty to their circle.

It would be enough.

And still as they gathered together in her workshop, long after dark settled, she had to hold back trepidation.

"Are you sure about this?" Connor brushed a hand down her back, earned a quick look and a mental push.

Stay out of my head.

He left his hand warm on the small of her back. "There's still time to find another way."

"I'm completely sure, and this is the best way. Fin?"

"Agreed."

"Cousin Mary Kate, are you certain you don't want to join the circle?"

"You should go as you've been, and know I'll be here to help should you need it."

"Nan's our backup." Iona gave her grandmother's hand a squeeze, then stepped forward.

They cast the circle, for ritual and respect, for protection and unity. Together Branna and Fin stepped inside it. He wore his sword on his belt, she a ritual knife.

This time, this deliberate time, they wouldn't go unarmed.

"From this cup we drink this brew so together in dreams we ride." Branna sipped the potion, handed the cup to Fin.

"With this drink we travel through another time and place side by side." Fin drank, handed off the cup to Connor.

"Within our circle, hand in hand, we travel over sky and land." They spoke together, eyes locked, as Branna felt the power rising up.

"Into dreams, willingly, there to seek, there to see Cabhan's origin of destiny. Full faith, full trust in thee and me, as we will, so mote it be."

Fin held out his hand; Branna put hers in it.

In a flash of light, in a burst of bright power, they flew.

Through the wind and the whirling, fast, so fast it whisked the breath from her lungs. She had a moment to think they'd made the potion too strong, then she stood, swaying a little, in the starry dark. Her hand still gripped in Fin's.

"A bit too much essence of whirlwind."

"Do you think so?"

She shot him a smirking glance. His hair looked as wild as hers felt. Though his sharp-featured face seemed grim, satisfaction mixed with it.

She felt about the same herself.

"There's no point in sarcasm, as you had as much to do with the formula as I." Branna shook her hair out of her eyes. "And it got us here, for that's the cave."

In the cold, starry dark, the mouth of the cave pulsed with red light. She heard a low hum, like a distant storm at sea from within. But without, nothing moved, nothing stirred.

"He's in there," Fin told her. "I can feel it."

"He's not alone. I can feel that. Something wicked, that brings more than a pricking of thumbs."

"I should go in alone, assess things."

"Don't insult me, Finbar. Side by side or not at all."

To settle it, she started forward. Fin kept a firm grip on her hand, laid the other on the hilt of his sword. "If it turns on us, we break the spell. Without hesitation, Branna. We don't end here."

She might have swayed toward him, such were the needs the dream spell stirred. But she steadied herself, stood her ground. "I've no intention of ending here. We've work to do in our own time and place."

They stepped into the mouth of the cave, the pulsing light. The hum grew louder, deeper. Not like a storm at sea, Branna realized. But like something large, something alive, waiting at rest.

The cave widened, opened into tunnels formed with walls damp enough to drip so the steady *plop* of water on stone became a kind of backbeat to the hum. Fin bore left, and as Branna's instincts said the same, they moved quietly into the tunnel.

His hand, she thought, was the only link to the warm and the real, and knew he felt the same.

"We can't be sure when we are," Branna whispered.

"After the last time we dreamed." He shook his head at her look. "I don't know how I know, but I know. It's after that, but not long after."

Trust, she reminded herself. Faith. They continued on with the humming growing deeper yet. She could all but feel it inside her now, like a pulse, as if she'd swallowed the living dark.

"It pulls him," Fin murmured. "It wants to feed. It pulls me through him, blood to blood." He turned to her, took her firmly by the shoulders. "If it—or he—draws me in, you're to break the spell, get out, get back."

"Would you leave me, or any of us, to this?"

"You, nor any of the others come from him. You'll swear it, Branna, or I'll break it now and end it before it's begun."

"I'll end it, I swear it." But she would drag him back with her. "I'll swear it because they won't draw you in. You won't allow it. And if we stand here arguing over it, we won't have to break the spell, it'll end on its own time without us learning a bloody thing."

Now she took his hand. A spark shot between their palms before they moved forward.

The tunnel narrowed again, and turned into what she recognized as a chamber—a workshop of sorts for dark magicks.

The bodies of bats, wings stretched, were nailed to the stone walls like horrific art. On shelves skeletal bird legs, heads, the internal organs of animals, others she feared were human, bodies of rats, all floated in jars filled with viscous liquid.

A fire burned, and over it a cauldron bubbled and smoked in sickly green.

To the left of it stood a stone altar lit by black tallows, stained by the blood of the goat that lay on it, its throat slit.

Cabhan gathered the stream of blood in a bowl.

He looked younger, she realized. Though his back was to them as he worked, he struck her as younger than the Cabhan she knew.

He stepped back, knelt, lifted the bowl high.

"Here is blood, a sacrifice to your glory. Through me you feed, through you I feed. And so my power grows."

He drank from the bowl.

The hum throbbed like a beating heart.

"It's not enough," Fin murmured. "It's pale and weak."

Alarmed, Branna tightened her grip on his hand. "Stay with me."

"I'm with you, and with him. Goats and sheep and mongrels. If power is a thirst, quench it. If it's hunger, eat it. If it's lust, sate it. Take what you will."

"More," Cabhan said, raising the bowl again. "You promised more. I am your servant, I am your soldier. I am your vessel. You promised more."

"More requires more," Fin said quietly, his eyes eerily green. "Blood from your blood, as before. Take it, spill it, taste it, and you will have more. You will be me, I will be thee. And no end. Life eternal, power great. And the Dark Witch you covet, yours to take. Body and power to our will she must bend."

"When? When will I have more? When will I have Sorcha?"

"Spill it, take it, taste it. Blood from your blood. Into the cup, through your lips. Into the cauldron. Prove you are worthy!"

All warmth had drained from Fin's hand. Branna pressed it between hers, gave him what she could.

"I am worthy." Cabhan set the bowl down, rose to take up a cup. He turned.

For the first time Branna saw the woman in the shadows. An old woman, shackled and shivering in the bitter cold.

He walked to her, taking the cup.

"Have mercy. On me, on yourself. You damn yourself. He lies. He lies to you, lies to all. He has chained you with lies as you have chained me with iron. Release me, Cabhan. Save me, save yourself."

"You are only a woman, now old, your puny powers leaking. And of no value but this."

"I am your mother."

"I am already born," he said, and slit her throat.

Branna cried out in shock and horror, but the sound drowned in the rising roar. Power swam in the air now, black as pitch, heavy as death.

He filled the cup, drank, filled it again. This he carried to the cauldron, poured through the smoke. And the smoke turned red as the blood.

"Now the sire's with it," Fin said, and Cabhan went to a bottle, poured its contents into the cauldron.

"Say the words." Fin's fingers, icy in Branna's, flexed, unflexed. "Say the words, make the binding."

"Blood unto blood I take so the hunger I will slake and the power here we make. From the dam and from the ram mix and smoke and call dark forces to invoke my name, my power, my destiny. Grant to me life eternal and sanctuary through this portal. I am become both god and demon and reign hereby over woman and man. Through my blood and by my power, I will take the Dark Witch unto me. I am Cabhan, mortal no more, and by these words my humanity I abjure."

He reached through the smoke, into the cauldron, and with his bare hand, pulled out the amulet and its bloodred stone.

"In this hour by dark power I am sworn."

He lifted the amulet over his head, laid the glowing stone on his chest.

The wind whirled into a roar as Cabhan, his eyes glowing as red as the stone, lifted his arms high. "And I am born!"

From the altar leaped the wolf, black and fierce. It sprang toward Cabhan, sprang into him with a deafening scream of thunder.

Something howled in triumph, and even the stones trembled.

He turned his head. Through the dark, through the shadows, his eyes, still glowing, met Branna's.

She lifted a hand when his arms shot out toward her, prepared to block whatever magicks he hurled. But Fin spun her around, wrapped around her. Something crashed, something burned.

And he broke the spell.

Too fast, too unsteady. Branna clung to Fin as much to warm him—his body burned so cold—as to keep herself from spinning away.

She heard the voices first—Connor's steady as a rock and calm as a summer lake—guiding her. Then Iona's joining his.

Don't be letting go now, Connor said inside her head. *We've got you. We've got both of you. Nearly home now. Nearly there.*

Then she was, dizzy and weak-limbed, but home in the warmth and the light.

Even as she drew a breath, Fin slipped out of her grip, went down to his knees.

"He's hurt." Branna went down on her own. "Let me see. Let me see you." She took his face, pushed back his hair.

"Just knocked the wind out of me."

"The back of his sweater's smoking," Boyle said, moving in and quickly. "Like Connor's shirt that time."

Before Branna could do so herself, Boyle pulled the sweater up and off. "He's burned. Not so deep as Connor's, but near the whole of his back."

"Get him down, face-first," Branna began.

"I'm not after sprawling down on the floor like a—"

"Have a nap." With that snapped order, Branna laid a hand on his head, put him under. "Face-first," she repeated, and had Connor and Boyle laying him out on the workshop floor.

She passed her hands over the scorching burns covering his back. "Not deep, no, and the poison can't mix with his blood. Just the cold, the heat, the pain. I'll need—"

"This?" Mary Kate offered her a jar of salve. "Healing was my strongest art."

"That's it exactly, thanks. We'll be quick. It hasn't had time to dig into him. Iona, would you take some? I've a bit of a burn on my left arm. It's nothing, but we'll want to keep it nothing. You know what to do."

"Yes." Iona shoved up Branna's sleeve. "It's small, but it looks angry."

But it cooled the moment Iona soothed on the salve. The faint dizziness passed as well as her cousin added her own healing arts. Steadier, she could focus fully on Fin.

"That's better, isn't it? Sure that's better. We could do with a whiskey, if you don't mind. We went a little faster than I'd calculated, and coming back was like tumbling off a building."

"I've already got it," Meara told her. "He looks all clear again."

"We'll just be making sure." With her hands on him, Branna searched for any deeper injury, any pocket of dark. "He'll do." Relief stung the back of her throat, rasped through her voice. "He's fine." She laid her hand on his head again, lingered just a moment. "Wake up, Fin."

His eyes opened, looked straight into hers. "Fuck it," he said as he pushed up to sit.

"I'm sorry for it, as it's rude to give sleep without permission, but I wasn't in the mood to argue."

"She was burned, too," Iona said, knowing it would shift Fin's temper. "On her left arm."

"What? Where?" He'd already grabbed Branna's arm, shoved her sleeve up.

"Iona saw to it. It was barely there at all, as you shoved me behind you, covered over me as if I wasn't capable of blocking an attack."

"You couldn't have, not that one. Not with the new power so full and young, and him flying on it like an addict on too much of a hard drug. He had more in that moment than he has now, or I think ever since. And he hungers for that wild high again."

Connor crouched down. "I'll say this. Thank you for looking after my sister."

"Now I'm ungracious." Branna sighed. "I'm sorry for that as well. I'm still turned around. I do thank you, Fin, for sparing me."

She took the whiskeys from Meara, handed him one.

"He took you for Sorcha. In the dark, near to hallucinating, he felt you—when the power came full, he felt you, but took you for Sorcha. He meant to . . ."

"Drink some of that."

"So I will." Fin tapped his glass to hers, drank. "He meant to disfigure you if he could, so no one would see your beauty, so your husband, he thought, would turn from you. I saw his mind in that moment, and the madness in it."

"A man would have to be mad to slit his own mother's throat, then drink her blood."

"That's purely disgusting," Meara decided. "And still if we're going to hear about it, I'd rather hear all at once, and when we're all sitting down."

"That's the way. Fin, put on your sweater now so you can sit at the table like a civilized man." Mary Kate handed him the sweater. "I'll just look around the kitchen, Branna, see what you might have I can put together, as I'll bet everyone could do with a bit of food."

While Mary Kate put together a wealth of leftovers from the Christmas feast, Branna sat—relieved not to be doing the fixing—so she and Fin could tell the story.

"His own mother." Shaking his head, Boyle picked up one of the pretty sandwiches Mary Kate put together.

"Just a woman, and old, so he said. He had no feelings for her. There was nothing in him for her. There was nothing in him," Fin continued, "but the black."

"You heard what spoke to him."

Frowning, Fin turned to Branna. "You didn't?"

"Only a humming, as we heard when we got there, when we went into the cave. A kind of . . . thrumming."

"I heard it." Absently, Fin rubbed at his shoulder, at the mark. "The promises for more power, for eternal life, for all Cabhan could want. But to gain it, he had to give more. Sacrifice what was human in him. It started with the father."

"Do you know it or think it?" Connor asked him.

"I know it. I could see inside his head, and I could feel the demon trapped in the stone, and its needs, its avarice. Its . . . glee at knowing it would soon be free again."

"Demon?" Meara picked up the wine she'd opted for. "Well now, that's new—and terrifying."

"Old," Fin corrected. "Older than time, and it waited until it found a vessel."

"Cabhan?"

"It's still him," Fin told Boyle. "It's Cabhan right enough, but with the other a part of him, and hungry always for power and for blood."

"The stone's the source, as we thought," Branna continued. "It came from the blood of the father and the mother Cabhan sacrificed for power. Conjuring it, pledging to it, he took in this . . . well, if Fin says demon, it's a demon right enough."

"Why Sorcha?" Iona wondered. "Why was he so obsessed with her?"

"For her beauty, and her power, and . . . the purity, you could say, of her love for her family. He wanted, craved the first two, and wanted to destroy the last."

Fin rubbed his fingers on his temple, attempting to ease the pounding still trapped inside his head.

"She rejected him, time and again," he continued, though the pounding refused to be abated. "Scorned him and his advances. So he . . ."

Surprised when Mary Kate stepped behind him, stroked her hands along temples, along the back of his neck where he hadn't realized more pain lodged, he lost his thread.

And the headache drifted away.

"Thank you."

"You're more than welcome."

She gave him a grandmotherly kiss on the top of the head before she sat again. It flustered him, and showed him just where Iona got her kind and open heart.

"Ah. His lust for her, woman and witch, became obsession. He would turn her, take what she had, and he believes no spell, no magicks can stop him, can touch him. Her power could cause him harm, threaten his existence, and her rejection burned his pride."

"Then there were three," Branna calculated. "And with the three the power, and the threat, increases. We can end him."

"In that moment, in the cave, when he took in the demon, and the black of it, he believed nothing could or ever would. But what's in him knows better. It lies to him, as his mother warned him. It lies."

"We can hurt him, bloody him, burn him to ash, but . . ." Connor shrugged. "Unless we destroy the amulet as well, unless we can destroy the demon joined with him, he'll heal, he'll come back."

"It's good to know." Iona spread some cheese on a cracker. "So how do we destroy the stone, the demon?"

"Blood magick against blood magick," Branna decided. "White against dark. As we have been, but perhaps with a different focus. We have to find the right time, and be sure of it. I'm thinking it must be Sorcha's cabin, as before, to draw what she had into it, but we need to find a way to trap him, to keep him from escaping again so it can be finished. And if we can do that, it would be Fin who needs to destroy the stone, the source."

"I felt the pull, of the demon, of the witch. And the far stronger one when they united. I felt the . . . appeal, the lust for what they'd give me."

"And feeling that, risked yourself to shield me. It's for you to do when the time comes," Branna said briskly. "We've only to figure out the hows and the whens. Mary Kate, are you certain you have to go back to America, for it's a joy to me to have someone else fixing a meal around here."

Understanding the need to shift the conversation, Mary Kate smiled. "I do, I'm afraid, but I'll be back for Iona's wedding, and before it enough to help with some of the doings. And it might be, I'm thinking, I'll stay."

"Stay?" Iona reached around the table, grabbed her hands. "Nan, do you mean you'd stay in Ireland?"

"I'm doing some thinking about it. I stayed in America after your grandda died for your mother, then for you. And I love my house there, my gardens, the views out my window. I have good friends there. But . . . I can have a house here, and gardens, and pretty views out my windows. I have good friends here. And I have you. I have all of you, and more family besides."

"You could live with us. I showed you where we're putting on the room for you to have when you visit. You could just live there, with us." Iona looked at Boyle.

"Of course, and we'd love that."

"You've a sweet heart," Mary Kate said to Iona, "and you've a generous one, Boyle. But if I come to stay, to live, I'll take my own place. Close by, be sure of that. In the village most like, where I can walk to the shops and see my good friends, and visit with you in your fine new home as often as you please."

"I've a cottage and no tenant," Fin commented, and had Mary Kate lifting her eyebrows.

"I've heard as much, but it's some months till April."

"It's easy to rent it to tourists for short spells who want something in the village, something self-catering. You might have a look at it before you go back to America."

"I'll do just that, and should confess I've already had a peek in the windows." She grinned. "It's cozy as a kitten, and so nicely updated."

"I'll see you get a key, and you can go in, look around whenever you like."

"I'll do that. I should go. Margaret will start worrying if I'm much later."

"I'll drive you in." Boyle started to rise.

"I'll do it." Fin stood instead. "I'll give you the key, and drop you round your friend's. I need to be home myself."

"I'll get my coat. No, the lot of you stay where you are," Mary Kate insisted. "I don't mind being escorted from the house by a handsome young man."

When they'd left, Iona got to her feet. "I'm going to draw you a bath."

Branna's eyebrows shot up. "Are you?"

"A bath with some of your own relaxation salts, and Meara's going to make you a cup of tea. I'd like to send Connor and Boyle to Fin's to do the same for him—"

"I'm not drawing a bath for Fin Burke," Boyle said, definitely.

"But the two of them are going to clean up in here, just the way you like it. So you can get some rest, good rest, and put all this out of your mind for the rest of the night."

"I wouldn't argue with her once she gets the steam up," Boyle advised.

"I wouldn't mind a bath, or the tea."

"That's settled then." Iona walked out.

"And I wouldn't mind you leaving the kitchen as it is if one of you would go check on Fin," Branna said. "This was more of a strain on him than it was on me, and I'll confess, I'm worn through from it."

"I'll give him a few minutes, then go over," Connor told her. "I'll stay if that's what he needs, or stay till I'm sure he's settled. We can still see to the kitchen. Go on up now, don't worry."

"Then I will. Good night."

Meara waited until Branna was out of earshot, Kathel by her side, then walked over to put the kettle on. "You're the one who's worrying, Connor."

"She didn't eat, not a thing." He glanced toward the kitchen doorway, stuck his hands in his pockets as if he couldn't quite figure out what to do with them. "She only pretended to eat. There were shadows under her eyes that weren't there at the start of the spell. Then letting you and Iona fuss over her without putting up a fight? She's worn to the bone, that's what.

"You'll look after her, won't you, Meara? You and Iona will see to her. I won't be long at Fin's unless I'm needed. And we'll stay here tonight."

"Give Fin what he needs, and we'll see to Branna."

"Without making it like you're seeing to her."

She shot the fretting brother a glance. "I've known her near as long as you, Connor. I think I know how to handle Branna O'Dwyer as much as any can. We'll give her a bit of female time, then leave her alone. She'll do best with the quiet and alone."

"True enough. I'll run over to Fin's, and be back as soon as I can."

"If you need to stay, you've only to let us know." She turned her face for a kiss when he came over, smiled at his quick, hard hug.

She finished up Branna's tea while Connor put on his outdoor gear, and turned to Boyle when they were alone. "It looks like you're left with the dirty dishes." Meara gave him a quick pat on the shoulder as she sailed out.

He looked around the empty kitchen, sighed. "Ah, well." And rolled up his sleeves.

CONNOR WALKED STRAIGHT INTO FIN'S AS HE HAD SINCE the day the front door went up. Before, come to that, as he'd installed the door himself.

He found Fin with another whiskey in front of the living room fire, the little stable dog Bugs curled up sleeping at his feet.

"I've orders to check in on you," he announced, and thought it was good he had. Fin looked as worn and bruised as Branna.

"I'm fine, as you can see plain enough."

"You're not, as I see plain enough," Connor corrected, and helped himself to a whiskey, then a chair. "Iona's after drawing Branna a bath, and Meara's making her tea. She's letting them, which tells me she needs the fussing. What do you need?"

"And if I ask it, you'll give it?"

"You know I will, though it's a mortifying thought I may be drawing your bath and tucking you up."

Fin didn't smile, only shifted his gaze from whatever he saw in the fire, met Connor's eyes. "It was a hard pull, a bloody brutal pull. For a moment I could feel all it promises. That power beyond what any of us hold. It's black and it's cold, but it's . . . seductive. And all I have to say is, I'll take it."

"You didn't. And you won't."

"I didn't, this time. Or times before, but it's a call to the blood. And to the animal that's inside all of us. So I'll ask you for something, Connor, as you're my friend as near as much a brother to me as you are to Branna."

"I'm both."

"Then you'll swear to me, on your own blood, on your heart where your magick roots, if I turn, if the pull is too much and I fall, you'll stop me by whatever means it takes."

"You'd never—"

"I need you to swear it," Fin interrupted, eyes fierce. "Otherwise I'll need to go, I'll need to leave here, leave her—leave all of you. I won't risk it."

Connor stretched out his legs, crossed his boots at the ankles, stared at them for several moments.

Then slowly, he lifted his gaze to Fin's.

"Listen to yourself. You want his end more than the three, more than the three we come from, but you'd step away, on the chance you've put in your block of a head you could fall when you've stood all this time."

"You weren't in the cave. You didn't feel what I felt."

"I'm here now. I've known you near to all our lives, before the mark came on you and after. I know who you are. And because I do, I'll swear it to you, Fin, if that's what you need. What I have comes from my heart, as you said, and my heart knows you. So you'll have your brood, and I'll say you've earned it. And tomorrow we'll be back to it."

"All right then." Steadier now, Fin sipped his whiskey. "I have earned a brood."

"That you have, and I'll brood with you until I finish my whiskey." Connor sipped and sat awhile in silence. "We both love her," he said.

Fin leaned back, shut his eyes. "That's the fucking truth."

And love, Connor knew well, pulled stronger than any dark promises.

10

FIN CONSIDERED HIMSELF SOCIABLE ENOUGH. HE KNEW when to stand a round in the pub, was a good guest who could make conversation at dinner. If he had mates over to watch a match or play some snooker, he provided plenty of beer and food and didn't fuss about the mess made.

He hadn't been raised in a barn, after all, so he understood as well as any man the basic expectations and duties when hosting a party.

Iona reeducated him.

In midafternoon on the last day of the year, she came to his door with her sunlight crown of hair tucked into a bright blue cap he remembered her Nan had knit her for Christmas. And loaded down with shopping bags.

"Didn't we just have Christmas?"

"Party supplies." She pushed some bags in his hand, carried the rest with her as she walked back to his kitchen. After dumping them on the center island, she pulled off her coat, scarf, hat, gloves, then her boots—and took all of them into his laundry room.

"We've got candles," she began.

"I have candles. I bought some from Branna not long before Yule."

"Not enough, not nearly." Both firmness and pity lived in Iona's shake of the head. "You need them everywhere."

She dug into a bag, started taking things out. "These are for the living room mantel. You'll get a twelve-hour burn, so you want to light them about a half hour before you expect people to start coming."

"Do I?"

"You do," she said definitely. "They'll set a pretty, celebrational yet elegant atmosphere. These are for the powder room up here, and for the bathroom downstairs, and the main bath upstairs. No one should go into your master suite unless invited, but there's extra so you should put some there, just in case. And these are guest towels—pretty, simple, and disposable."

She laid out a wrapped stack of white napkins embossed with silver champagne flutes.

"So people don't have to dry their hands on the same cloth towel someone else dried their hands on."

Fin let out a quick laugh. "Seriously now?"

"Fin, look at my face." She pointed to it. "Deadly serious. I got some extra candles for your dining room in case you didn't have enough there, and others for the mantel on your lower level. Now, it's essential you make sure there's plenty of TP in the bathrooms. Women hate, loathe, and despise when they're sitting there and there's no TP."

"I can only imagine. Fortunately."

"I plan to do an hourly check on the bathrooms, so it shouldn't be a problem."

"You're a comfort to me, Iona."

She laid her hands on his cheeks. "I got you into this, and I said I'd help. I'm here to help. Now. The caterers will pretty much take over the kitchen, and they'll know what they're doing. I checked on them, and they're supposed to be stellar. Good choice."

"Thanks. I do what I can."

She only smiled. "We'll just want to be sure the servers understand they'll need to cover your lower level with food and drink because you're going to have a lot of people gathering down there to play games, dance, and hang out. You'll have fires going, of course."

"Well, of course."

"I know everyone will have plenty to eat and drink. It's not called The Night of the Big Portion or . . . wait." She closed her eyes a moment. "Or *Oiche ne Coda Moire*, for nothing."

Now he grinned at her. "You handled the Irish brilliantly."

"I've been practicing. We don't have to get into the New Year's Eve tradition of cleaning the house—I read up on Irish traditions—because yours is already spotless. You're as scary as Branna there, so I'm going to put these candles where they belong, and the guest towels, and oh—" She reached into another bag. "I picked up these pretty mints and these candied almonds. The colors are so pretty, and it's a nice thing to have here and there in little bowls. Oh, and Boyle's picking up the rolling rack I borrowed from Nan's friend's daughter."

"A rolling rack?" For reasons he didn't want to explore, he got the immediate image of a portable torture device.

"For hanging coats. You have to do something with people's coats, so we're borrowing the rack. It should work fine in the laundry room. One of us will take people's coats as they come in, hang them up, get them when people want to leave. You can't just toss them on the couch or on a bed."

"I hadn't given it a thought. I'm lucky to have you."

"You are, and it's also good practice. I'm already planning a blow-out party next summer when our house is finished and furnished, and we're settled in."

"I'm already looking forward to it."

"We'll have finished Cabhan by then. I believe it. We won't be working every day as we are now on how and when. We'll just be living. I know it's been a hard week, on you and Branna especially."

"It's not meant to be easy."

Carefully, Iona tidied the stacks of guest towels. "Have you seen her today?"

"Not today, no."

"This morning she said she was going to try some calculations on finishing this a year from the day I arrived—the day I first went to the cottage to meet her."

He considered. "There's a thought."

"And she looked as doubtful it's right as you do, but it's something to consider. So we will. But not tonight. Tonight is party time."

"Hmm. What's in this other bag here?"

"Ah, well . . . some people like silly party hats and noisemakers."

He opened the bag, stared in at colorful paper hats, sparkly tiaras. "I'm going to tell you right out of the gate. Though I adore the very ground you walk on, I won't be wearing one of these."

"Completely optional. I thought we could put them in a couple big baskets for anyone who wants them. Anyway, I'm going to set all this up, then I'm going to work with Branna for an hour or two before I deck myself out in my party clothes. I'll be here an hour early for finishing touches."

She carted out candles, and he looked deeper into the bag full of paper hats. No, he wouldn't be wearing one, but he'd put himself up as her second in command now, help her with her candles and fussing.

Then he'd take an hour himself for some calculations of his own.

LATER, WHEN THE CATERERS INVADED AND HE'D ANSWERED dozens of questions, made far too many decisions on details he hadn't considered, he closed himself off in his room for a blessed half hour to dress in the quiet. He wondered what his odds were of staying closed in, considered Iona's cheerful determination and calculated them at nil.

Where had he been this time last year? he wondered. The Italian Alps, near Lake Como. He'd spent three weeks or so there. He'd found it easier to spend holidays away from home, to celebrate them in his own way with strangers.

Now he'd see how he managed not only to be home, but to have those he knew in his home.

Maybe he dawdled a little longer than necessary, then dressed in black jeans and black sweater, started downstairs.

He heard voices, music, laughter. Glanced at his watch to see if he'd completely miscalculated the time. But no, he had forty minutes yet before guests were due.

Candles in red glass holders glowed on his mantel above a crackling fire. His tree shined. A bouncy reel played out of his speakers. The massive candlestand he'd bought in some faraway place stood in a corner, cleverly filled with votives that radiated more light.

Light and music, he thought, his circle's weapon against the dark.

Iona had been right. She'd been perfectly right.

He started back, noted she'd set more candles in his library, still more in the space he'd fashioned into a music room.

She'd come up with flowers as well—little glass jars of roses tied with silver ribbons.

He found her and Meara, along with some of the catering staff, busy in the dining area.

Another fire, more candles, more roses, silver trays and crystal dishes filled with food, chafing dishes holding more.

And all the sweets displayed on his buffet—the cakes and biscuits and pastries. Offerings of cheeses under a clear dome.

Iona, in a short sheath of dark, deep silver, had her hands on her hips as she took—he had no doubt—eagle-eyed stock. Beside her, Meara had her hair tumbling loose over the shoulders of a gown the color of carnelian that clung to her curves.

"I think I've made a mistake," he said and had both his friends turning to him. "Why have I invited people here tonight when I could have two beautiful women all to myself?"

"That's just the sort of charm that will have all your guests talking about this party for months," Iona told him.

"I was going to say bollocks, but it's charming bollocks," Meara decided. "Your home looks absolutely amazing on top of it all."

"I didn't have much to do with it."

"Everything," Iona corrected. "You just let me play with fire." Laughing, she walked over, hooked her arm in his. "And Cecile and her team are the best. Honestly, Cecile, the food looks too good to eat."

Cecile, a tall blonde in black pants and a vest over a crisp white shirt, flushed with pleasure. "Thanks for that, but eating it's just what we want everyone to do. We did some stations downstairs as Iona suggested," she told Fin. "And have a bar set up there as well. We'll have servers passing through regularly up here, down there, to be sure all your guests are well seen to."

"It all looks brilliant."

"You haven't seen downstairs." Iona led him to the stairs and down. "I went a little mad with the candles, and got nervous, so I did a protection spell. They can't burn anything or anyone."

"You think of everything."

More candles and greenery, pretty food and flowers. He walked to the bar, to the fridge behind it and took out a bottle of champagne.

"You should have the first drink."

"I'll take it."

He opened the champagne with a muffled *pop*, poured her a flute, then poured one for himself. "It was a happy day when you came into our lives, *deirfiúr bheag*."

"The happiest of my life."

"To happy days then."

She tapped her glass to his. "To happy days, for all of us."

Within the hour it seemed he had half the village in his house. They swarmed or gathered, gawked or settled right in. They filled plates and glasses, sat or stood in his living room or, as Iona had predicted, wandered downstairs where the band he'd hired began their first set.

He found himself happy enough with a beer in his hand to move from conversation to conversation. But of all the faces in his house, there was one he didn't see.

Then as if he wished it, she was there.

He came back upstairs to do his duty with his main-floor guests, and she was there, standing in his kitchen chatting with the caterers.

She'd left her hair down, a black waterfall that teased the waist of a dress of velvet the color of rich red wine. He thought Iona could have found a hundred more candles and still not achieved the light Branna O'Dwyer brought into his home.

He got a glass of champagne, brought it to her. "You'll have a drink."

"I will indeed." She turned to him, eyes smoky, lips as red as her dress. "You throw a fine party, Fin."

"I do, as I follow Iona's orders."

"She's been half mad with excitement and anxiety over tonight, having pushed you into it. And all but bought me out of candles. I see she made good use of them."

"They're everywhere, as she commanded."

"And where is our Iona?"

"She's downstairs. Meara's down there as well, and Boyle and Connor, and Iona's Nan." But he guided her toward the dining area as he spoke. "Will you eat?"

"Sure I will as it looks delicious, but not just yet."

"Do you still have a weakness for these?" He picked up a mini cream puff drenched in powdered sugar.

"A terrible one, which I usually deny. But all right, not tonight." She took it, tried a small bite. "Oh, that's a sinful wonder."

"Have two. *Oiche na Coda Moire.*"

She laughed, shook her head. "I'll come back for the second."

"Then I'll take you down to your circle, and the music."

He offered a hand, waited until she put hers in it. "Will you dance with me, Branna? Put yesterday and tomorrow aside, and dance with me tonight?"

She moved with him toward the music, the warmth, the glowing light.

"I will."

SHE NEARLY HADN'T COME. SHE TRIED TO FIND REASONS TO stay away, or failing that to simply pay a courtesy visit, then slip out again. But every reason devised rang the same way in her ears.

As cowardice. Or worse, pettiness.

She couldn't be so petty, so cowardly as to snub him because it distressed her to be in his home, to see, to feel the life he'd built himself without her.

Her choice, without him. Her duty, without him.

So she'd come.

She'd spent a great deal of time on her hair, her makeup, the whole of her appearance. If she was to celebrate the end of one year, the beginning of another in his house, in his company, she'd bloody well look amazing doing it.

She found the downstairs of his home, what she thought of as a play area, so very him. Good, rich colors mixed with neutrals, old refurbished furniture mixed with the new. Small pieces obviously bought on his rambles. And plenty of entertainment.

The absurdly big wall TV, the snooker table, the old pinball machine and jukebox along with a gorgeous fireplace of Connemara marble topped by a thick, rough plank for a mantel.

The musicians played lively tunes near a mahogany bar he told her he found in Dublin. Though the space was roomy, furniture had been pushed back to make more room yet for dancing.

When he drew her into a dance, it was yesterday with all its innocent joy, with its simplicity and possibilities. But she pushed aside the pang it brought, told herself to let this one night be a time out of time.

She looked up at him laughing. "Now you've done it."

"What's that I've done?"

"Hosted the party of the year and now will be expected to do the same next. And next."

Mildly horrified, he glanced around. "I thought to pass that torch to Iona and Boyle."

"Oh no, they'll have their own. But I'm thinking you own New Year's Eve now. I see your Sean wearing a party hat, over there kicking up the heels of clean and shiny boots, and Connor's Kyra and her boyfriend—fiancé now—with him wearing a shirt that matches the color of her frock and a cardboard king's crown on his head. And there's my Eileen dancing with her husband as if they were but sixteen, and the years, the children with them yet to come. You built a house that can hold most of the village for a party, and now you've done it."

"I never thought of that."

"Sure it's too late now. And there I see Alice giving you the seductive eye, as she's resigned to Connor being lost to her. You should give her a dance."

"I'd rather dance with you."

"And you have. Do your duty, Finbar, give her a twirl. I've people I should talk with."

She stepped back from him, turned away. If she danced with him again, and too often, the people she should talk with would begin talking about them.

"Isn't it great?" Iona grabbed her, did a quick circle. She'd donned a pink tiara that announced 2014 in sparkles. "It's such a good party. I just have to do my hourly bathroom sweep and I'll be back."

"Bathroom sweep?"

"Checking TP and guest towel supplies, and so on."

"I'm putting you in charge of every party I may have."

"You're a natural with parties and gatherings," Iona countered. "Fin's new at it. So am I, but I think I have a knack."

"God help us," Boyle said, and kissed the top of her head.

Branna enjoyed the music, the bits of conversation. After she slipped back upstairs, she enjoyed some of the food, and some time with those who sought more quiet in Fin's living room or the great room.

It gave her time to see more of his house, to feel the flow of it. And the chance to check out the windows, to open herself enough to search for any sense of Cabhan.

"He won't come."

She turned from the tall French doors of his library toward Fin, who stepped through the doorway.

"You're so sure?"

"Maybe there's too much light, too many people, the voices, the thoughts, the sounds, but he won't come here tonight. Maybe he's just burrowed in, waiting for the year to pass, but he won't come tonight. I wish you wouldn't worry."

"Being vigilant isn't the same as worrying."

"You worry. It shows."

Instinctively, she reached up to rub her fingers between her eyebrows where she knew a line could form. And made him smile.

"You're perfectly beautiful. That never changes. It's in your eyes, the worry."

"If you say he won't come tonight, I'll stop worrying. I like this room especially." She ran her hand over the back of a wide chair in chocolate leather. "It's for the quiet, and a reward."

"A reward?"

"When work's done, it's for settling down in a good chair like this with a book and the fire. With rain pattering down, or the wind blowing, or the moon rising up. A glass of whiskey, a cup of tea—what's your pleasure—and a dog at your feet."

She did a turn, holding out a hand. "All these books to choose from. A good warm color for the walls—you did well there—with all the dark wood to set it off."

She angled her head when he gave her a half smile. "What?"

"I built it with you in mind. You always used to say, when we were building our dream castle, how it had to have a library with a fire and big chairs, with windows the rain could drip down or the sun could creep through. It should have glass doors leading out to a garden so on a bright day you'd step out, and find a spot outside to read."

"I remember." And saw it now. He'd made one of her imaginings come to life.

"And there should be a room for music," Fin added. "There would be music throughout the house, but a room just for it where we'd have a piano and all the rest. The children could take their lessons there."

He glanced back. "It's just over there."

"Yes, I know. I saw it. It's lovely."

"There was part of me thought if I built it, if I kept you in mind, you'd come. But you didn't."

So clear now that she let herself see, the house was what they'd dreamed of making together.

"I'm here now."

"You're here now. What does that mean for us?"

God, her heart was too full of him, here in this room he'd conjured out of dreams.

"I tell myself what it can't be. That's so clear, so rational. I can't see what it can or might."

"Can you say what you want?"

"What I want is what can't be, and that's harder than it was, as I've come to believe that's through no fault of yours or my own. It was easier when I could blame you or myself. I could build a wall with the blame, and keep it shored up with the distance when you spent only a few days or few weeks here before you went off again."

"I want you. Everything else comes behind that."

"I know." She let out a breath. "I know. We should go back. You shouldn't be so long away from your guests."

But neither of them moved.

She heard the shouting, the rise of voices, the countdown. Behind her, the mantel clock began to strike.

"It's going onto midnight."

Only seconds, she thought, between what was and what is. And from there what would be. She took a step toward him. Then took another.

Would she have walked by him? she asked herself when he pulled her to him. No. No, not this time. At least this one time.

Instead she linked her arms around his neck, looked into his eyes. And on the stroke of midnight met his lips with hers.

Light snapped between them, an electric jolt that shocked the blood, slammed into the heart. Then shimmered into an endlessly longed-for warmth.

Oh, to feel like this, to finally feel like this again. To finally have her body, her heart, her spirit united in that longing, that warmth, that singular wild joy.

His lips on her lips, his breath with her breath, his heart on her heart. And all the sorrow blown away as if it never was.

He'd thought once what he felt for her was all, was beyond what anyone could feel. But he'd been wrong. This, after all the years without her, was more.

The scent of her filling him, the taste of her undoing him. She gave as she once had, everything in a simple kiss. Sweetness and strength, power and surrender, demand and generosity.

He wanted to hold on to her, hold on to that moment until the end of his days.

But she pulled back, stayed a moment, brushed a hand over his cheek, then stepped back from him.

"It's a new year."

"Stay with me, Branna."

Now she laid a hand on his heart. Before she could speak, Connor and Meara turned into the room.

"We were just—"

"Going," Meara finished Connor's sentence. "Going back right now."

"Right. Sure, we weren't even here."

"It's all right." Branna left her hand on Fin's heart another moment, then let it fall away. "We're coming back now. Fin's been too long away from his own party. We'll go toast the New Year. For luck. For light. For what may be."

"For what should be," Fin said, and walked out ahead of them.

"Go with him," Meara suggested, and moved into Branna. "Are you all right then?"

"I am. But it's God's truth I could do with a drink, and as much as it goes against my nature, a lot of noise and people."

"We'll get all of that."

When she put an arm around Branna's waist, Branna leaned into her a moment. "How could I love him more now than once I did? How could it be so much more in me for him when what was, was everything?"

"Love can fade and die. I've seen it. It can grow and build as well. I think when it's real and meant, it can only grow bigger and stronger."

"It's not meant to be a misery."

"No. It's what we do with it that's the misery or the joy, I think, not the love."

Branna sighed, gave Meara a long look. "When did you get so bloody wise about it?"

"Since I let myself love."

"Let's go toast to that then. To you letting yourself love, to Iona's party skills, to the New bloody Year, to the end of Cabhan. I feel I might want to get a wee bit snackered."

"What kind of friend would I be if I didn't get snackered right along with you? Let's find some champagne."

11

HE WAS MORE THAN DONE WITH PEOPLE. AT HALF-TWO in the morning, far too many of them lingered in his house, cozied up as if they'd stay till spring. He considered just going upstairs, shutting himself in, leaving them to it. He was brutally tired, and more, that moment—that incredible moment with Branna had cross-wired his emotions so he didn't know what he felt.

So it seemed easier all around to shut it all off and feel nothing at all.

She seemed perfectly content to sit, sip champagne, chat with whoever remained. But that was Branna, wasn't it? Strong as steel.

The best thing for him would be a few hours' escape in sleep. They'd be back to Cabhan in the morning—or later in the morning. And the sooner the better. Ending him would fulfill his obligations. Ending Cabhan would end his own personal torment.

So he'd slip away—no one would miss him by this point.

Then Iona stepped up, as if she'd read his mind, twined her arm with his, took his hand.

"The problem with throwing a really great party is people don't want to leave."

"I do."

She laughed, squeezed his hand. "We're down to the diehards, and we'll start nudging them along. Your circle won't leave you alone with them. Give it about twenty minutes. What you should do is go around, start gathering up the empties since the caterers left a couple hours ago. It's a sign it's time to go."

"If you say."

"I do." To demonstrate, she began picking up bottles and glasses, gave Boyle a telling look that had him doing the same.

In moments a handful of those diehards readied to go with many thanks and wishes for a happy and prosperous New Year. And in the case of a few, such as Sean, heartfelt if somewhat sloppy hugs.

Party magicks, Fin decided, and started on discarded tea and coffee cups.

He carted them up to the kitchen, said good-bye to another handful. Two birds, he decided, he'd have the party debris dealt with, and move out the stragglers.

Though it took thirty minutes rather than Iona's predicted twenty, he wouldn't complain.

"That's the last of them," Iona announced.

"Thank the gods."

"You gave a lot of people a fun and memorable evening." She tipped onto her toes to kiss his cheek. "And you had one yourself."

"I'm happy to remember it now that it's done. And thank you for all you did."

"Couldn't have had a better time of it." She glanced around the living room, nodded. "And we're not leaving you with much of a mess. Branna, I can ride with you if you want, just leave my car here. I'm not taking Nan to the airport until afternoon tomorrow, so I can come back for it easily."

"Best you ride with Boyle."

"We'll make a caravan of it," Connor said as he shrugged into his coat. "A short drive for certain, but it's still the dead of night. Branna can follow you and Boyle out, and Meara and I will come up behind."

"I'm not driving home tonight at all. I'm staying here."

Branna looked at Fin as she spoke. He wasn't sure how he kept his feet when she'd rocked him back so stunningly on his heels.

"Well then!" Brightly, Meara smiled, and jammed her cap on her head. "We'll be off. Good night, and happy New Year."

"But," Connor began as she all but dragged him to the door with Iona pushing Boyle behind him.

"Would you let me get my coat on?" Boyle complained even as Iona firmly closed the door behind the four of them.

Fin stood exactly where he was. Only one thought managed to eke through the logjam in his mind. "Why?"

"I decided for this time, this place, I wouldn't think about yesterday or about tomorrow. It may be we'll both come to regret it, but I want to be with you. I always have, likely always will, but this is only tonight. There can't be any promises or building dream castles this time around, and we both know that. But there's need, and there's finally trust again."

"You're content with that?"

"I find I am, and God knows I've turned it all over a hundred different ways, but I find I am content with that. We're both entitled to make this choice. You asked me to stay with you. I'm saying I will."

So much of the turmoil inside him settled into calm even as all the resignation he'd carried for years dropped away to make room for a tangle of joy and anticipation.

"Maybe I changed my mind on it."

She laughed, and he saw the light sparkle in her smoky eyes. "If that's the case, I wager I can change it back again quick enough."

"It seems the least I can do is give you that chance." He held out a hand. "I won't kiss you here or we'd end up on the floor. Come to bed, Branna."

She put her hand in his. "We've never been in a bed together, have we? I'm curious about yours. I resisted going upstairs and poking around during the party. It took heroic willpower."

"You've never lacked that." He brought her hand to his lips. "I've imagined you here a thousand times. A thousand and a thousand times."

"I couldn't do the same, as even my heroic will wouldn't have held up against the imagining." Amazed at her own calm, she kissed his hand in turn. "I knew when Iona walked into my workshop you'd come back. You'd be a part of this, a part of me again. I asked why, why, when I'd found my life, made myself content with it, fate should put you back into it again."

"What was the answer?"

"I've yet to get one, and still can't stop the asking. But not tonight. It's so grand, your home. All these rooms, and the all but heartbreaking detail of every centimeter of space."

And none of it, he thought, so much home as the kitchen of her cottage.

He opened the door of his bedroom, kissed her hand again, then drew her in. Rather than turn on the lights, he flicked his wrist.

The fire kindled in the hearth, and candles flickered to life.

"Again grand," she said. "A grand male sanctuary, but warm and attractive instead of practical and Spartan. Your bed's glorious." She moved to it, trailed fingers over the massive footboard. "Old, so old. Do you dream of those who've slept here?"

"I cleansed it so I wouldn't feel I shared the bed with strangers from other times. So, no, I don't dream of them. I've dreamed of you when I've slept here."

"I know it, as I had a moment in that bed with you in dreams."

"Not just then. A thousand and a thousand times."

She turned to him, looked at him in the light and shadow of dancing flames. The heart she'd lost to him so many years before swelled inside her. "We won't dream tonight," she said, and opening her arms, went to him.

The nerves that had hummed just under her skin dissolved. Body to body with him, mouth to mouth with him, her world simply righted.

This, of course, the single missing link in the chain of her life.

For tonight, if it could only be tonight, she would give herself a gift. She would only feel. She would open herself, heart, body, mind, and feel what she'd struggled against for so long.

Tomorrow, if need be, she'd tell herself it was only the physical, only a way to relieve the tension and strain between them for the greater good. But tonight, she embraced the truth.

She loved. Had always loved, would always love.

"I've missed you," she murmured. "Ah, Finbar, I've missed you."

"Ached for you." He brushed his lips over her cheeks, brought them back to hers.

She clung as they lifted inches off the floor, then a foot, circling. With a laugh, she flung her arms up, scattered stars above them.

"By firelight and starlight, by candle flame, tonight, what I am, is yours."

"And what you are, is cherished."

He lowered them to the bed, sank into the kiss.

With her, at last with her, free to drink deep and deep from her lips, free to feel her body under his, to see her hair spread out.

The gift she gave them both, too magnificent to rush. So he would savor her gift, and give all he had in return.

He took his hands slowly up her body, gently captured her breasts. No longer the budding girl etched in his memory, but the bloom.

New memories here to layer over what had been.

He pressed his lips to her throat, lingered over the scent of her caught there, just there, that had haunted his days and nights. His again, to take in like breath.

As he slid the dress down her shoulders, she arched to ease his way. Her skin, white as milk, caught the gold of his firelight, the silver of her stars. He undressed her as if uncovering the most precious of jewels.

Her heart fluttered under his touch. Only he had ever been able to bring her that sensation, one of both nerves and pleasure. Each time he kissed her, it was slow and deep, as if worlds could spin away and back again while he savored.

"You've more patience than you did," she managed as her blood began to sing under her skin.

"You're more beautiful than you were. I never thought it possible."

She caught his face in her hands a moment, fingers skimming up into his hair, then she shifted to rise above him with stars sparkling over her head.

"And you." She drew his sweater up, off. "Witch and warrior. Stronger than the boy I loved." She spread her hands over his chest. "Wounded, but ever loyal. Valiant."

When he shook his head, she brought his hands up, pressed them to her own heart. "It matters to me, Fin, more than I can tell you. It matters." She lowered to press her lips to his lips, to press her lips to his heart.

She'd broken his heart, as he'd broken hers. She didn't know what fate would grant them, even if those hearts could be truly mended. But tonight she wanted him to know she knew his heart, and valued it.

To change the mood she danced her fingers along his left ribs. Fin jumped like a rabbit.

"Bloody hell."

"Ah, still a weakness there, I see. That one small spot." She reached for it again, and he caught her wrist.

"Mind yourself, as I recall a weakness or two of yours."

"None that make me squeal like a girl, Finbar Burke." She shifted again as he reared up, wrapped her legs around his waist, her arms around his neck. "Still would rather a fist in the face than a tickle along the ribs."

"The one's less humiliating."

She shook back her hair, laughed up at the ceiling.

"Do you remember—"

She looked back at him, met his eyes. It was all there, in that instant, looking out at her. His craving for her, and the love wrapped around it. Past and present collided, rushed through her like a hot wind, sparking her own terrible, burning need.

"Oh God, Fin."

No more patience, no more careful explorations. They came together in a fury, all wild need and desperation. Rough hands rushed over her, took greedily while her own yanked and pulled to free him of the rest of his clothes.

Nothing between them, she thought now. She couldn't bear even air between them. Their mouths came together in heat and hunger as they rolled over the bed to find more of each other.

She closed her teeth over his shoulder, dug her fingers into his hips.

"Come inside me. I want you inside me."

When he drove into her, the world stopped. No breath, no sound, no movement. Then came thunder, a hoarse roar of it, charging like a beast from the hills. And lightning, a flash that lit the room like noon.

With her eyes locked on his, she gripped his hands.

"It's for us to say tonight," she said. "It's for us tonight." She arched toward him. "Love me."

"Only you. Always you."

He gave himself over to the need, to her demand, to his own heart.

When they came together, they were the thunder, they were the lightning. And over their heads her stars shone the brighter.

WHEN HE WOKE, THE SUN WAS UP AND STREAMING. A BRIGHT day for the start of a new year. And Branna lay sleeping beside him.

He wanted to wake her, to make love with her in that streaming sunlight as they had in the dark and through to the soft kiss of dawn.

But shadows haunted her eyes. She needed sleep, and quiet, and peace. So he only touched her hair, and smiled, reminding himself she could be annoyed at best, ferocious at worst, on waking.

So he got out of bed, pulled on his pants, and slipped out of the room.

He'd work. He wanted work, wanted to find the way to end all of it, to resolve it once and for all. And to find the way to break the curse a dying witch had laid on him, so long before.

If he could break the curse, remove the mark, he and Branna could be together, not for a night, but a lifetime.

He'd given up believing that could be. Until this New Year, until the hours spent with her. Now that hope, that faith was back inside him, burning bright.

He would find a way, he told himself as he went to his workshop. A way to end Cabhan and protect the three, and all that came from them. A way to erase the mark from his body, and purge his blood of any trace of Cabhan.

Today, the first day of the New Year, he'd renew that quest.

He considered the poison they'd created for the last battle. Strong and potent, and they'd come close. The injuries to Cabhan—or what inhabited him—had been great. But not mortal. Because what empowered Cabhan wasn't mortal.

A demon, Fin thought, paging through his own books. One freed by blood sacrifice to merge with a willing host. A host with power as well.

Blood from the sire.

He sat to make notes of his own.

Blood from the dam.

Shed by the son.

He wrote it all down, the steps, the words, what he'd seen, and what he'd felt.

The red stone created by blood magicks of the darkest sort, of the most evil of acts. The source of power, healing, immortality.

"And a portal," Fin murmured. "A portal for the demon to pass through, and into the host."

They could burn Cabhan to ash as Sorcha had, but wouldn't end him without destroying the stone, and the demon.

A second potion, he considered, and rose to pace. One conjured to close this portal. Trap the demon inside, then destroy it. Cabhan couldn't exist without the demon, the demon couldn't exist without Cabhan.

He pulled down another book, one of the journals he kept when he traveled. With his hands braced on the work counter, he leaned over, reading, refreshing himself. Considering what might be done.

"Fin."

Engrossed, his mind on magicks dark and bright, he glanced over. She wore one of his oldest shirts, a faded chambray he sometimes tossed on to work in the stables. Bare feet, bare legs, tumbled hair, and a look in her eyes of astonished sorrow.

His heart skipped—just the sight of her—even before he followed her gaze to the window, to the stained-glass image of her.

He straightened, hooked his thumbs in his front pockets. "It seemed right somehow, to have the Dark Witch looking over my shoulder when I worked here. Reminding me why I did."

"It's a constant grief to love like this."

"It is."

"How do we go on, as that may never change?"

"We take what we have, and do whatever we can to change it. Haven't we lived without each other long enough?"

"We are what we are, Fin, and some of that is through no choice of our own. There can't be promises between us, not for tomorrows."

"Then we take today."

"Only today. I'll see to breakfast." She turned to go, glanced back. "You've a fine workshop here. Like the rest of the house, it suits you."

She went down. Coffee first, she told herself. Of a morning, coffee always made things clearer.

She'd begun the New Year with him, something she'd sworn would never happen. But she'd made that oath in a storm of emotion, in turmoil. And had kept it, she admitted, as much for self-preservation as duty.

And now, for love, she'd broken it.

The world hadn't ended, she told herself as she worked Fin's very canny machine. Fire hadn't rained from the sky. They'd had sex, a great deal of lovely sex, and the fates appeared to accept it.

She'd woken light and bright and loose and . . . happy, she admitted. And she'd slept deeper and easier than she had since Samhain.

Sex was energy, she considered, gratefully taking those first sips of coffee. It was positive—when done willingly—a bright blessing and a meeting of basic needs. So sex was permitted, and she could thank the goddesses for that, and would.

But futures were a different matter. She wouldn't make plans again, let herself become starry-eyed and dreaming. Today only, she reminded herself.

It would be more than they'd had before, and would have to be enough.

She hunted in his massive fridge—oh, she'd love having one so big as this—and found three eggs, a stingy bit of bacon, and a single hothouse tomato.

Like today only and sex, it would have to be enough.

She heard him come in as she finished cobbling together what she thought of as a poor man's omelette.

"Your larder is a pitiful thing, Fin Burke. A sad disgrace, so you'll make do with what I could manage here, and be grateful."

"I'm very grateful indeed."

She glanced around. He'd put on a black long-sleeved tee, but his feet remained as bare as hers. And he had a smile on his face.

"You seem very happy for a miserly bit of bacon and tomato scrambled up with a trio of eggs."

"You're wearing only my old shirt and cooking at my stove. I'd be a fool not to smile."

"And a fool you've never been." She stuck a second mug on his coffee machine, pressed the proper buttons. "This one here is far better than mine. I should have one. And your jam was old as Medusa, and just as ugly. You'll make do with butter for your toast. I've started you a list for the market. You'll need to—"

He whirled her around, lifted her to the tips of her toes, and ravished her mouth. When she could think, she thought it fortunate she'd taken the eggs off the heat, or they'd have been scorched and ruined.

But since she had, she gave as good as she got in the kiss.

"Come back to bed."

"That I won't as I've taken the time and trouble to make a breakfast out of your pitiful stores." She pulled back. "Take your coffee. I'm plating this up before it goes cold. How do you manage breakfast on your own?"

"Now that Boyle's rarely available for me to talk into frying one up, I get whatever's handy. There's the oatmeal packs you make up in the microwave."

"A sad state of affairs." She put a plate in front of him, sat with her own. "And with such a lovely spot here to have your breakfast. I think, once Boyle and Iona are in their house, you'd be able to see their lights through the trees from here. It meant something to them, you selling them the land."

"He's a brother to me, and he's lucky for all that, as otherwise I might have snatched Iona up for my own. Though she can't cook for trying."

"She's better than she was. But then she had nowhere to go but up in that department. She's stronger every day. Her power's still young and fresh, but it has a fierceness to it. It may be why fire's hers."

This was good, she thought, and this was sweet. Sitting and talking easy over coffee and eggs.

"Will her grandmother take your cottage to rent?" she asked him.

"I think she will."

Branna toyed with her eggs. "There's connections everywhere between you and me, and us. I put it all out of my mind for a very long time, but I've had to ask myself in these last months, why so many of them? Beyond you and me, Fin. There's always been you and Boyle and Connor, and Meara as well."

"Our circle," he agreed, "less one till Iona came."

"That she would come as fated as the rest. And didn't you have that cottage when Meara's mother needed it, and now for Iona's Nan? You and Boyle and the stables, you and Connor with the falconry school. Land you owned where Boyle and Iona will live their life. You've spent more time away than here these past years, and still you're so tightly linked. Some may say it's just the way of things, but I don't believe that. Not anymore."

"What do you believe?"

"I can't know for certain." Poking at the eggs on her plate, she stared off out the window. "I know there are connections again, the three now, the three then. And each of us more closely linked to one of them. And didn't Eamon mistake our Meara for a gypsy he knew—name of Aine as you named the white filly you brought back to breed with Alastar? I feel Boyle has some connection there as well, some piece of it, and if we needed we'd find that connection to Teagan of the first three."

"It's no mystery." He rubbed his shoulder. "It's Cabhan for me."

"I think it's more, somewhere. You're from him, of his blood, but not connected in the way I am with Sorcha's Brannaugh, or Connor with Eamon and so on. If you were, I can't see how you'd have known to bring Alastar back for Iona, and Aine back for Alastar."

"I didn't bring Aine back for Alastar, not altogether, or not only. I brought her back for you."

The mug she'd lifted stilled in midair. "I . . . I don't understand you."

"When I saw her, I saw you. You used to love to ride, to fly astride a horse. I saw you on her, flying through the night with the moon bursting full in the sky. And you, lit like a candle with . . ."

"What?"

"As you are in the window upstairs, just as I saw you years before when I had it done. A wand in one hand, fire in the other. It came and went like a fingersnap, but was clear as day. So I brought her back for you, when you're ready for her."

She said nothing, could say nothing for a moment. Then she rose, went to the door, and let in the little dog she'd sensed waiting.

Bugs wagged around her feet, then dashed to Fin.

"Don't feed him from the table," she said absently as she sat again. "It's poor manners for both of you."

Fin, who'd been about to do just that, looked down at the hopeful dog.

You know where the food is, little man. Let's not ruffle the lady's feathers.

Happy enough, Bugs raced off to the laundry, and his bowls.

"I'll ride her when we next face Cabhan, and be the stronger for it. You brought us weapons, for both Alastar and Aine are weapons against him. You've bled with us, conjured with us, plotted with us, to end him. If your connection was with him, strongest with him, how could you do these things?"

"Hate for him, and all he is."

Branna shook her head. Hate didn't make courage or loyalty. And what Fin had done took both.

"I was wrong to try to block you out in the beginning of this, and it was selfishly done. I wanted to believe that connection, you to Cabhan, but it's not there. Not in the way he'd want, not in the way he needs. Your connection is with us. I don't understand the why of it, but it's truth."

"I love you."

Oh, her heart warmed and ached at the words. She could only touch his hand. "Love is powerful, but it doesn't explain, in a logical way, why your feelings for me link you so tight with the others."

She leaned forward now, her breakfast forgotten. "Between the first three and us, I've found no others who've been so tightly woven together. No others who've gone back dreaming to them, or had them come. Others have tried and failed, but none have come so close as we to ending him. I've read no tales in the books of one of the three riding on Alastar into battle, with Kathel and Roibeard with them. And none that speak of a fourth, of one who bears the mark, joining them. It's our destiny, Fin, but you're the change in it. I believe that now. It's you who make our best chance to finish it, you who bear his mark and come from his blood. And still, I can't see the why of it."

"There are choices, you know well, to be made with power, and with blood."

"I feel there's more, but that alone may be enough."

"It won't be enough to destroy Cabhan. Or I mean to say we won't succeed in destroying him, no more than Sorcha could, without destroying what he took into him."

She nodded, having come to the same conclusion. "The demon he bargained with."

"The demon who used him to gain freedom. Blood from his sire, from his mother, shed by him, drunk by him, used by him with the demon's demands and promises, to create the stone."

"And the power source."

"Not just a power source, I think. A portal, Branna, the entry into Cabhan."

"A portal." She sat back. "There's a thought. Through the stone conjured with the blackest of blood magicks, into the sorcerer who made the bargain. There sits the power, and the way into the world. If a portal can be opened . . ."

"It can be closed," Fin finished.

"Yes, there's a thought indeed. So it becomes steps and stages. Weaken and trap Cabhan so he can't slip away and heal again. And as he—the host—is weak and trapped, close the portal, trapping the demon, who *is* the source. Destroy it, destroy Cabhan for good and all."

She picked up her fork again, and though the eggs had gone cold, ate. "Well then, all that's left is figuring out how it's to be done, and when it can be done, and doing it."

"I've a few thoughts, and may have more when I finish reading up. I spent some time with a Shaolin priest some years ago."

"A . . . You worked with a Shaolin priest? In China?"

"I wanted to see the wall," he said with a shrug. "He had some thoughts on demons, as a kind of energy. And I've spent some time here and there with shamans, other witches, a wise man, an Aborigine. I kept journals, so I'll be reading through."

"It seems you've had quite the education in your travels."

"There are places in the world of such strong energy, such old power. They call to people like us. Only today," he said, reaching over for her hands. "But if there are ever tomorrows, I'd show you."

Since she couldn't answer, she only squeezed his hands, then rose to clear the plates. "It's today that needs us. I've never given a thought to destroying demons, and in truth never believed they existed in our world. Which is, I see now, as shortsighted as those who can't believe in magicks."

"I'll see to the clearing up here. It's the rule in your own house, and a fair one."

"All right then. I should get home, and start reading up on demons myself."

"It's the first day of the New Year," he said as he walked to her. "And a kind of holiday."

"Not for the likes of us, with what's coming. And I've work besides to earn my living. You may have staff and all that to see to most, but I'd think you've a living to earn as well."

"We've no lessons today, and the guided rides and hawk walks are a handful only between them both. And I've a couple hours yet before I'm to meet with Boyle, then Connor."

She angled her face up to his. "It's a fortunate man you are to have such leisure time."

"Today it is. I'm thinking you may have an hour yet to spare."

"Well, your thinking isn't—" She broke off, narrowed her eyes as the shirt she'd worn winked away, leaving her naked. "That was rude and inhospitable."

"I'll show you great hospitality, *aghra*." Closing his arms around her, he flew them both back into bed.

12

SHE DIDN'T LEAVE UNTIL MIDDAY, AND FOUND KATHEL outside playing run and tumble with Bugs. She ignored the fact that those who worked in the stables would have seen her car still parked when they'd arrived that morning.

The juice would begin to flow from the grapevine, but it couldn't be helped. She gave Bugs a quick rub, told him he was welcome to come with Fin anytime at all and play with Kathel.

Then she whistled her own dog into the car, and drove home.

She went straight upstairs to change out of her party dress and into warm leggings, a cozy sweater, and soft half boots. After bundling her hair up, she considered herself ready to work.

In her workshop, she put the kettle on, lit the fire. And feeling a shift in the air, whirled around.

Sorcha's Brannaugh stood, a quiver on her back, her own Kathel at her heel.

"Something changed," she said. "A storm came and blew through the night. Thunder raged, lightning flamed even through a fall of snow. Cabhan rode the storm until the stones of the castle shook."

"Are you harmed? Any of you?"

"He could not get past us, and will not. But another maid is missing, and a kinswoman, and I fear the worst for her. Something changed."

Yes, Brannaugh thought, something changed. But first there were questions. "What do you know of demons?"

Sorcha's Brannaugh glanced down as Branna's Kathel went to hers, and the hounds sniffed each other.

"They walk, they feed, they thirst for the blood of mortals. They can take many forms, but all but one is a lie."

"And they search out, do they not," Branna added, "those willing to feed them, to quench that thirst? The red stone, we've seen its creation, and we've seen the demon Cabhan bargained with pass through it and into him. They are one. Sorcha couldn't end Cabhan because the demon lived, and healed him. They healed, I think, each other."

"How did you see?"

"We went in a dream spell, myself and Finbar Burke."

"The one of Cabhan's blood. You went with him, to Cabhan's time, to his lair. How can there be such trust?"

"How can there not? Here is trust," she said, gesturing to the dogs who'd gone to wrestling on the floor. "I know Fin's heart, and would not know all we do now without him."

"You've been with him."

"I have." And though she felt her cousin's concern, even disapproval, she wouldn't regret it. "The storm came to you. I heard it when I joined with Fin, and I thought fate clashed at the choice we made. But you say it was Cabhan who rode the storm, and you felt it was his power, or rage, that shook the stones. It may be the joining angered him—this speaks true to me. What angers him only pleases me."

"I know what it is to love. Have a care, cousin, on how that love binds you to one who carries the mark."

"I've had a care since the mark came on him. I won't shirk my duty. My oath on it. I believe Fin may be the true change, the weapon always needed. With him, as no three has before, we will end this. Cabhan, and what made him what he is now. It must be both, we believe that, or it will never end. So, what do you know of demons?"

Brannaugh shook her head. "Little, but I will learn more. You will call him by his name. This I have heard. You must use his name in the spell."

"Then we'll find his name. How long since last we talked in your time?"

"Today is La nag Cearpairi."

Day of the Buttered Bread, Branna realized. New Year's Day. "As it is here. We are on the same day, another change. This will be our year, cousin, the year of the three. The year of the Dark Witch."

"I will pray for it. I must go, the baby's waking."

"Wait." Branna closed her eyes again, brought the image into her mind from the box in her attic. Then held out a small stuffed dog. "For the baby. A gift from his cousins."

"A little dog." As she petted it, Sorcha's Brannaugh smiled. "So soft it is, and clever."

"It was mine, and well loved. Bright blessings to you and yours this day."

"And to you and yours. I will see you again. We will be with you when it's needed, in that I will have faith, and trust." She laid her hand on her dog's head, and they faded away.

Branna lowered her hand to her own dog's head, stroked. "Once I thought to give the little dog to my own baby. But since that's not to be, it seemed a fine gift for my cousin's." Kathel leaned his great body against her in comfort. "Ah, well, we've work to do, don't we? But first I think you've earned a biscuit for being so welcoming to our cousin's hound."

She got one for him, smiled when he sat so politely. "How lucky am I to have so many loves in my life." She leaned down, pressed a kiss to the top of his head, then offered the biscuit.

Content in the quiet, she made her tea, and she sat with her spell books, looking for whatever she might find on demons.

She had the whole of the afternoon to herself, a precious thing, so mixed work and reading with some baking to please herself. She put a chicken on the boil, thinking chicken soup with chunky vegetables and thick egg noodles would go well. If she didn't have a houseful, she could freeze most of it for when she did.

With dusk she shifted her books to the kitchen so she could continue to work as she monitored her soup. She'd just rewarded herself with a glass of wine when Iona came in.

"Boy, I could use one of those. I took Nan back, got weepy—sad she had to go home, so happy she's coming back. And I thought I was done for the day." She poured the wine. "But Boyle texted me they'd had a group of twelve who'd celebrated New Year's at Ashford, decided they'd finished feeling hungover and wanted guided rides. So it was back to work."

She took her first sip. "And I'm babbling about all that—can babble about more if necessary—to keep from asking about you and Fin if you don't want to be asked."

"You may have gleaned we had sex."

"I think we all gleaned that was a strong probability. Are you happy, Branna?"

Branna went to stir the soup. "I can say, without question, I've had a long-nagging itch thoroughly scratched, and I'm not sad about it. I'm happy," she said when Iona just waited. "Today, I'm happy and that's enough."

"Then I'm happy." She stepped closer, gave Branna a hug. "What can I do to help? In any area."

"I've dinner under control. You could sit there, read over my notes, see what you think of it all."

"Okay. Boyle and I were going to eat out, and stay at his place—and Connor and Meara the same. We thought you'd have plans with Fin and wanted to give you room. But you've got that vat of soup going, so . . ."

"Don't change plans on my account. I'd already thought of freezing the bulk of it. I was in the mood to make soup, and give my head time to think that way." She didn't mention she'd made no plans with Fin—and wouldn't mind a night alone.

"You're planning to keep seeing him—being with him, I mean."

"A day at a time, Iona. I won't think on it further than that."

"All right, but I may as well tell you Fin was by to talk through some business with Boyle and he looked . . . happy. Relaxed."

"Sex will relax you in the aftermath. We've an understanding, Fin and I. We're both content with it."

"If you are, I am." Iona sat, started to read.

Branna tested the soup, considered, then added more rosemary.

At the table, Iona said, "A portal! It makes so much sense. It's an evil stone, created from human sacrifice—through patricide, matricide—what better way for a demon to transport into Cabhan? It *all* makes sense. Sorcha burned him to ash. We had him on the ropes—we had him bleeding under the damn ropes, but we didn't deal with the demon. How do we?"

"Read on," Branna suggested. She considered having her soup in her pajamas. Maybe even on a tray in her room while she read a book that had nothing to do with magicks, evil, or demons.

"A second poison," Iona muttered, "a kind of one-two punch. And a spell that closes the portal. How do we close a portal opened through human sacrifice? That's going to be tricky. And . . . Call the demon by his name." She looked up and over at Branna. "You know its name?"

"I don't, not yet. But it was the advice given me by Brannaugh of the first three. She came to me today. And I've written all that down as well, but the most important part to my thinking is it was the same day for her as it is for us. For her today was the first day of the year.

I think if we can somehow stay balanced that way, we'll draw more from each other."

"Do we know any demonologists?"

"Not offhand, but . . . I suspect we could find one should we need one. I think it might be more simple and basic than that."

"What's simple and basic about finding out a demon's name?"

"Asking it."

Iona flopped back in the chair, gave a half laugh. "That would be simple. We could all come here, or all meet in the pub if you want to go over this tonight."

"I think you can pass it all on well enough."

"Then I will. When's Fin coming by? I don't want to be in the way."

"Oh . . ." Branna went back to the soup. "We didn't set any specific time. It's best if we keep it more casual-like."

"Gotcha. I'm going to go up, grab a shower, and change. I'll just ask Boyle to swing by and get me. The four of us can put our heads together on it, and talk it to death with you and Fin later."

"That would suit me very well."

Evasive, Branna thought when alone again. She preferred evasive to deceptive. She hadn't absolutely said she expected Fin. And it would give her brain a rest not to have to talk it all through, to give it all a day or two to stir around in her head first.

Maybe she'd rest her brain with the telly instead of a book. Watch something fun and frivolous. She couldn't think of the last time she'd done only that.

"I'm heading out!" Iona called back. "Text me if you need me."

"Have a good time."

Branna waited until she heard the door close, then, smiling to herself, got out a container to freeze all but a bowl of the soup.

A bowl of soup, a glass of wine, followed by a bit of the apple crumble she'd baked earlier. A quiet house, old pajamas, and something happy on the telly.

Even as she thought what a lovely idea it all was, the door opened.

Fin, with Bugs on his heel, came in with a ridiculously enormous bouquet of lilacs. The scent of them filled the air with spring and promise. She wondered where he'd traveled for them, and arched her eyebrows.

"And I'm supposing you're thinking a forest of flowers buys your way into dinner and sex?"

"You always favored lilacs. And both Boyle and Connor did mention going off tonight to give us the cottage to ourselves. Who am I to disappoint my mates?"

She got out her largest vase, began to fill it while Bugs and Kathel had a cheerful bout of wrestling. "I'm after a bowl of soup in front of the telly."

"I'd be more than happy with that."

She took the lilacs, breathed them in—remembered doing the same on a long-ago spring when he'd brought her an equally huge bouquet of them.

"I baked an apple crumble to follow."

"I'm fond of apple crumble."

"So I recall." And so, she thought, this explained why she'd had a yen to bake one. "I had myself a fine plan for the evening. An all but perfect one for me." She laid the flowers aside a moment, turned to him. "All but perfect, and now it is. It's perfect now you're here."

She walked into his arms, pressed her face into his shoulder. "You're here," she murmured.

BRANNA THOUGHT OF IT AS REFOCUSING. WEEKS AND WEEKS of studying, charting, calculating had brought her no closer to a time and date for the third and, please the gods, last battle with Cabhan. She rarely slept well or long, and she had eyes to see the lack of sleep had begun to show.

Pure vanity if nothing else demanded a change of direction.

Now that she was bedding Fin and being bedded by him, very well, thank you very much, she couldn't say she'd gotten more sleep, but she'd rested considerably better in those short hours.

Still, she'd gotten no further, not on the when or precisely the how. So, she'd refocus.

Routine always steadied her. Her work, her home, her family, and the cycle that spun them together. A new year meant new stock for her shop, meant seeds to be planted in her greenhouse flats. Negative energies should be swept out, and protection charms refreshed.

Added to it she had two weddings to help plan.

She spent the morning on her stock. Pleased with her new scents, she filled the containers she'd ordered for the Blue Ice line, labeled all, stacked them for transport to the village with the stack of candles she'd replenished from the stock Iona had decimated for Fin's party.

After a check of her list, she made up more of the salve Boyle used at the stables. She could drop that by if the day went well, and thinking of it, added a second jar for the big stables.

A trip to the market as well, she decided. Despite it being Iona's turn for it, Branna thought she'd enjoy a trip to the village, a drive in the air. The dinner with the rest of her circle after their night away hadn't accomplished much more than emptying her container of soup, so the stop by the market was necessary.

With a glance at the clock she calculated she could be back in two hours, at the outside. Then she'd try her hand at creating a demon poison. Wrapped in her coat, a bold red and blue scarf, and the cashmere fingerless gloves she'd splurged on as a Yule gift to herself, she loaded up her car.

As Kathel was nowhere in sight, she sent her mind to his, found him spending some quality time with Bugs and the horses. She gave him leave to stay till it suited him, then drove herself to Cong.

She spent half her allotted time in the village, loitering with Eileen in the shop. More time in the market, buying supplies and exchanging gossip with Minnie O'Hara, who knew all there was to know—including the fact that on New Year's Eve Young Tim McGee (as opposed to his father Big Tim, and his grandfather Old Tim) had gotten himself drunk as a pirate. And so being had serenaded Lana Kerry—she who had broken off their three-year engagement for lack of movement—below her flat window with songs of deep despair, sadly off key.

It was well known Young Tim couldn't sing a note without causing the village dogs to howl in protest. He had begun this at near to half-three in the morning, and until the French girl in the flat below—one Violet Bosette who worked now in the cafe—opened her own window and heaved out an old boot. For a French girl, Minnie considered, her aim was dead-on, and she clunked Young Tim right upside the head, knocking him flat on his arse where he continued to serenade.

At which time Lana came out and hauled him inside. When they'd emerged near to dinnertime the next day, the ring was on Lana's finger once more, and a wedding date set for May Day.

It was a fine story, Branna thought as she drove out of the village again, especially as she knew all the participants but the French girl with good aim.

And it had been worth the extra time spent.

She took the long way around just for the pleasure of it, and was nearly within sight of the stables when she saw the old man on the side of the road, down on his knees and leaning heavily on a walking stick.

She pulled up sharply, got out.

"Sir, are you hurt?" She started toward him, began to search for injuries or illness with her mind.

Then stopped, angled her head. "Have you fallen, sir?"

"My heart, I think. I can bare get my breath. Will you help me, young miss?"

"Sure and I'll help you." She reached out a hand for his, and punched power into it. The old man flew back in a tumble.

"Do you think to trick me with such a ploy?" She tossed back her hair as the old man lifted his head, to look at her. "That I couldn't see through the shell to what's inside?"

"You stopped, outside your protection." As the old man rose, he became Cabhan, smiling now as the red stone pulsed light.

"Do you think I'm without protection? Come then." She gestured with an insulting wiggle of her fingers. "Have a go at me."

The fog spread, nipping like icy needles at her ankles; the sky darkened in a quick, covering dusk. Cabhan dropped to the ground, became the wolf, and the wolf gathered itself, leaped.

With a wave of hands, palms out, Branna threw up a block that sent the wolf crashing against the air, falling back.

Poor choice, she thought, watching it as it stalked her. For in this form she could read Cabhan like the pages of a book.

She probed inside, searched for a name, but sensed only rage and hunger.

So when he charged as wolf from the right, she was prepared for the man rushing in from the left. And she met fire with fire, power with power.

It surprised her the earth itself didn't crack from the force that flew out of her, the force that flashed out at her. But the air snapped and sizzled with it. She held, held, while the muscles of her body, the muscles of her power ached with the effort. While she held, the brutal cold of the fog rose higher.

Though her focus, her eyes, her magicks locked with his, she felt his fingers—its fingers—crawl up her leg.

Sheer insult had force. She swung what she had out at him so it struck like a fist. Though it bloodied his mouth, he laughed. She knew she'd misjudged, let temper haze sense, when he lunged forward and closed his hands over her breasts.

Only an instant, but even that was far too much. Now she merged temper, intellect, and skill and called the rain—a warm flashing flood that washed away the fog and burned his skin where the drops fell.

She braced for the next attack, saw it coming in his eyes, then she heard, as he did, the thunder of hoofbeats, the high, challenging cry of the hawk, the ferocious howl of the hound.

"Soft and ripe and fertile. And in you I'll plant my seed and my son."

"I'll burn your cock off at the root and feed it smoldering to the ravens should you try. Oh, but stay, Cabhan." She spread her arms, stopped the rain, held a wand of blinding light and a ball of fire. "My circle comes to greet you."

"Another time, Sorcha, for I would have you alone."

Even as Fin slid from his still-racing Baru, his sword flaming, Cabhan swirled into mists.

Fin and Kathel reached her on a run, and Fin gripped her shoulders. "Did he hurt you?"

"I'm not hurt." But as she said it she realized her breasts throbbed, a dark throb like a rotted tooth. "Or not enough to matter."

She laid one hand on Fin's heart, the other on Kathel's head. "Be easy," she said as the others came up on horseback or in lorries. The hawks—Roibeard and Merlin—landed together on the roof of Boyle's lorry. Before she could speak through the rapid-fire questions, she saw Bugs running for all he was worth down the road to her.

"Brave heart," she crooned, and crouched to gather him up when he reached her. "It's too open here," she told the others. "And I'm right enough."

"Connor, will you see to Branna's car? She'll ride with me. My house is closest."

"I can drive perfectly well," Branna began, but he simply picked her up, set her in the saddle, then swung up behind her.

"You take too much for granted," she said stiffly.

"And you're too pale."

She held Bugs safe as Baru lunged forward.

If she was pale, Branna thought, it was only because it had been an intense battle, however short. She'd get her color back, and her balance with it quickly enough.

No point in arguing, she decided, as the lot of them were worried for her—as she'd have been for any of them in the same case.

When they reached the stables, Fin swung down, plucked her off, and called out to an openmouthed Sean, "See to the horses."

Since she deemed it more mortifying to struggle, Branna allowed him to carry her into his house.

"You've made a scene for no reason, and will have tongues wagging throughout the county."

"Cabhan going at you in the middle of the road in the middle of the day is reason enough. You'll have some whiskey."

"I won't, but I'd have some tea if it's no trouble to you."

He started to speak, then just turned on his heel, leaving her on his living room sofa as he strode off to the kitchen.

In the moment alone, she tugged at the neck of her sweater, looked down at herself. She could clearly see the imprint of Cabhan's fingers on her skin over the top of her bra. She rose, deciding the matter would be best dealt with in private.

And the rest of her circle, along with her dog, crowded in.

"Don't start. I want the powder room a moment first." She sent a look at Meara, at Iona, the request clear in her eyes.

So they followed her into the pretty little half bath under the stairs.

"What is it?" Iona demanded. "What don't you want them to see?"

"I'd as soon my brother and your fiancé don't get a gander of my breasts." So saying she stripped off the sweater. And on Meara's hiss of breath, the bra.

"Oh, Branna," Iona murmured, lifted her hands. "Let me."

"If you'd lay your hands over mine." Branna covered her own breasts. "I could do it myself, but it'll be faster and easier with your help."

Branna searched inside herself, brought up the warmth of healing, sighed into it when Iona joined her, and again when Meara just put an arm around her waist.

"It's not deep. He only had me for a fraction of a second."

"It hurts deep."

Branna nodded at Iona. "It does, or did. It's easing already, and my own fault for giving him even that small opening."

"I think it'll go faster, hurt less if you look into me. If you boost what I can do with what you have. Just for this, okay? Look at me, Branna. Look into me. The hurt lifts out, let it go. The bruising eases. Feel the warm."

She let it go, opened herself, twined what she had with Iona.

"It's clear. He's left no mark on or in you. You're . . ." Iona paused, still searching for injury. And her eyes widened.

"Oh, Branna."

"Ah, well, I supposed that's next." She unhooked her pants, let them fall to reveal the streaks of bruising up her inner thighs.

"Bloody bastard," Meara muttered and took Branna's hand in a strong grip.

"It was the fog, a kind of sly attack. More a brush than a squeeze, so it's not as dark or painful. Have at it, Iona, if you wouldn't mind."

She let herself go again, let herself drift on the warmth Iona gave her until even the echo of pain faded.

"He wanted to frighten me, to attack me on the level women fear most. But he didn't frighten me." Calmly Branna hooked her pants again, slipped into her bra, then her sweater. "He enraged me, which gave him the same chance to rush my defenses and find that one small chink. It won't happen a second time."

She turned to the mirror over the sink, gave herself a hard look—and a very light glamour.

"There, that's done the job. Thank you, both of you. I'll see if Fin's made a decent cup of tea and tell you all what happened."

She stepped out. Connor stopped pacing the foyer, strode straight to her, caught her up against him.

"I'm fine, I promise. I . . . No prying into my head, Connor, you'll only annoy me."

"I've a right to be certain my sister's unharmed."

"I've said I am."

"He left the mark of his hands, black as pitch, on her breasts."

At Meara's words, Branna twisted around, astonished by the betrayal.

"There's no holding things back." Meara stiffened her spine. "It's not fair or right, and not smart, either. You'd say so yourself if it was me or Iona."

When Connor started to pull up her sweater, Branna slapped his hands away. "Mind yourself! Iona and I took care of it. Ask her yourself if you can't take my word."

"There's not a trace of him in or on her," Iona confirmed. "But he'd put his marks on her, up her thighs, on her breasts."

"He put his hands on you." Fin spoke with a quiet that roared like thunder.

Branna closed her eyes a moment. She hadn't sensed him come up behind her. "I let him rile me, so it's my own fault."

"You said you weren't hurt."

"I didn't know I was until I got back here and had a look. It was nothing near what Connor dealt with, or Boyle, or you. He bruised me, and where he did is a violation as he meant it to be."

Fin turned away, walked to the fire, stared into it.

It was Boyle who moved to Branna, put an arm around her waist. "Come on now, darling. You'll sit down and have your tea. You'd do better with some whiskey in it."

"My sensibilities aren't damaged. I'm not so delicate as that. But thank you. Thank all of you for coming so quickly."

"Not quick enough."

She gave Connor's arm a squeeze when he sat beside her. "That's likely my doing as well, and I'll confess it, as Meara—and rightfully—has shamed me into bare truth. I wanted just a moment or two, and took it before I called for you. And before you all rain down on my head, it *was* but a moment or two, and I had good reason."

"Good reason?" Fin turned back. "Not to call your circle?"

"For a moment," she repeated. "I'm well protected."

Rage, pure and vicious, burned in his eyes. "Not so well he couldn't put his hands on you, and leave marks behind."

"My own fault. I'd hoped he'd change into the wolf, and he did. The hound is mine, and a wolf is the same. I thought I might be able to pull out the name of the demon, now that we know we're looking for one. But it wasn't long enough, and all I found was the black, and the greed. I need longer. I believe, I promise you, I could dig out the name if I had longer."

She picked up her tea, sipped, and found it strong enough to battle a few sorcerers on its own. And that was fine with her.

"He came as an old man, looking ill and sick on the side of the road. He thought to trick me, and did—but only for a handful of seconds, and only because I'm a healer and it's my call and my duty to help those who need it."

"Which he knew very well," Connor said.

"Of course. But he persists in thinking of women, whatever their power, as less, as weak, and as foolish. So I turned the trick on him, pretended I thought him an old helpless man, then knocked him head over arse.

"It's true I should have called for you right at that moment, and you have my word on it, I won't take even that little time again before I do. He did what I hoped, as I said, came at me as the wolf."

She took them through it, left out no detail, then set the tea aside.

Connor drew her tight against him. "Feed his cock to the ravens, will you?"

"It's what came to me at the time."

"And the stone?"

"Brilliantly bright at the start of it. And bright again when he took hold of me. But when my rain burned him, it went muddy."

She took another breath. "And there came a kind of madness in his eyes. He called me Sorcha. He looked at me, and he saw her, as Fin said when he saw me in the cave. It's still Sorcha for him."

"Centuries." Eyes narrowed, Boyle nodded. "Being what he is, wanting what he wants and never getting it. It would breed a madness, and she's the center of it for him."

"And now you are," Fin finished. "You have the look of her. I've enough to see his thoughts to know he sees her in you."

"She is in me, but there was a confusion in that madness. And confusion is a weakness. Any weakness is an advantage for us."

"I saw him, glimpses when I took out a guided this morning," Meara said.

"I saw him, too, on one of mine. I didn't have a chance to tell anyone." Iona puffed out a breath. "He's feeling strong again, and getting bolder."

"Easier to end him when he's not hiding," Boyle pointed out. "I have to get back to the stables. I can spare either Meara or Iona if you need, Branna."

"I'm fine now, and I . . . Oh bloody hell!" She pushed to her feet. "I'd been marketing, and all I bought is still in the car."

"I'll see to it," Connor told her.

"And put everything where I won't find it? I bought a fine cut of beef, and had in mind to roast it."

"With the little potatoes and carrots and onions all roasting with it?"

Meara cast her eyes to the ceiling. "Connor, only you would think of your stomach when your sister's barely settled."

"As he knows I'm fine, and if I wasn't, cooking would settle me the rest of the way."

"We'll bring it in here." Fin spoke in a tone that brooked no argument. "If you've a mind to cook, you can cook here. If you need something I don't have, we'll get it. I've some work in the stables, and more upstairs, but someone will be close."

He walked out, she assumed to bring in her groceries.

"Give him a break." Iona spoke quietly, got up herself, rubbed a hand on Branna's arm. "Giving him a break doesn't make you weak, won't make him think you are. It'll just give him a break."

"He might have asked what I wanted to do."

Connor kissed her temple. "You might have asked the same of him. We'll be off then, and back in time for dinner. If you need anything, you've only to let me know."

When they all left, Branna sat back down and had a good brood into the fire.

13

BRANNA DECIDED, GIVEN THE CIRCUMSTANCES, SHE'D just call what she needed to her. It seemed the best place to work on her research and studies would be the breakfast nook in his kitchen, and that way all would be close to hand when the roast was in the oven.

He kept his distance from her, and his silence—and both, she knew bloody well, were deliberate acts. Let him have his temper, she thought. She had one of her own, and the cold shoulder he offered only kept it stirred on a simmer.

On top of it all, it irritated her not to be able to stamp out the pleasure of cooking a real meal in his kitchen. It had such a nice flow to it, such fine finishes, such canny little bits of businesses such as the pot filler near the cooktop should she have a big pot to fill and not want to haul it from sink to stove.

And the cooktop she coveted. Then she might've had a six-burner commercial grade herself if she'd envisioned cooking for so many so often.

It didn't seem right a man who didn't cook himself should have a kitchen superior to hers—and she'd considered her own a dream of style and efficiency.

So she brooded about that while she let the meat marinate, and set up her temporary desk in his nook.

Another cup of tea, a couple of biscuits—store-bought, of course—and her dog along with Bugs snoring under the table. She passed the time working on the formula for the second poison—ingredients, words, timing—sent a long email to her father in case he knew, or knew anyone who knew, more of demons than she could uncover.

By the time Fin came in, grubby from the stables, she'd abandoned her books and sat at his counter peeling carrots.

He got out a beer, said nothing.

"You're the one who put me in this kitchen." She didn't snap, but the edge of one colored her tone. "So if you're going to cling to your anger with me, take yourself elsewhere."

He stood in a ragged jacket and sweater more ragged yet, jeans giving way at one knee and boots that had seen far better days. His hair mussed and windblown around the cool expression on his face.

It only egged on her own temper he could look so bloody sexy.

"I'm not angry with you."

"You've an odd way of showing your cheerful feelings then, as you've been in and out of the house twice and said not a word to me."

"I'm buying a couple more hacks for the guideds and working a deal on selling one of the young hawks to a falconer. It's my business, one that keeps all this running, and I came in and up to my office so I wouldn't be talking terms in front of the hands and the young girl in for her afternoon lesson."

He tipped the beer toward her, then drank. "If it's all the same to you."

"It's all the same, and still the same I'm saying to take your temper somewhere else. It's a bloody big house."

"I like them big." He walked over, stood on the other side of the island. "I'm not angry with you, so don't be a fecking idjit."

She felt the very blood kindle under her skin. "A fecking idjit is it now?"

"It is from where I'm standing."

"Then if you insist on standing there, it's me who'll go elsewhere." She slapped down the peeler, shoved back, and got halfway to the doorway before he took her arm.

She gave him a jolt that would've knocked him back to the opposite side of the room if he hadn't been ready for it. "Cool yourself down, Branna, as I've been working on doing these past hours."

Her eyes were smoke, her voice a fire simmering. "I won't be called an idjit, fecking or otherwise."

"I didn't say you were, only advised you not to be." His tone was cool as January rain. "And for the third time, I'm not angry with you. And *rage* is too tame a word for what I hold in me for him, for the bastard who put his hands on you."

"He poisoned Connor, near to killed Meara, and Iona, he's burned Boyle's hands black and laid you out on my kitchen floor. But you're more than raged because he now knows the shape of my teats?"

He took her shoulders, and she saw now he spoke the truth. What lived in his eyes was more than rage. "Battle wounds, and fair or foul they're won in battle. This wasn't any of that. You've only just let me touch you again, and he does this? You can't see the deliberation, the timing? Doing this so you'd think of my blood, of my origins when next I want to touch you?"

"That's not—"

"And you can't see, can't think with that clever brain that he had contact with you? Physical contact, and with it might have pulled you out of the here and now to where he willed?"

She started to speak, then held up both hands until he released her. And she went back, sat again. "You can call me a fecking idjit now, as I've earned it. I didn't think of either, but I can see it clear enough now. I didn't think of the first, as you have nothing to do with what he did, what he tried to do to me. I wouldn't think of him when you touched me, Fin. That's where you have it wrong. He meant you to think it, and there it seems he succeeded."

She reached for his beer, then shook her head. "I don't want beer."

Saying nothing, he turned, took the wine stopper out of the bottle of Pinot Noir she'd used in the marinade. When he poured her a glass, she sipped slowly.

"As for the second, I'm well rooted. He may think he has enough to pull me when and where he wills. I can promise you he doesn't. I took precautions there when he tried luring Meara, and we fully understood how he can shift in time. You can trust me on this."

"All right."

She lifted her eyebrows. "Just that?"

"It isn't enough?"

"He meant to frighten and humiliate me, and did neither. Perhaps he did also mean to twist my sensibilities so I wouldn't want your touch, but he failed there as well. But he appears to have well succeeded in enraging you. This he understands, the rage. You're bedding me now, and you won't have me touched by another."

"It's not that, Branna." Calmer—marginally—he shoved his fingers through his hair. "Well, not just that. It's what touched you."

"He'd only understand the possession. He'd never understand your remorse, your guilt, for no matter how many times you show him you reject his part of you, it's all he sees there. He can't see past your blood. You must. We all must. I do or however I felt about you, I couldn't have let you touch me."

"It's his blood I want. I want it dripping from my hands."

"I know it." Understood it, she admitted, and had felt the same herself more than once. "But that's vengeance, and vengeance won't defeat him. Or not vengeance alone, for whatever we are, we're human, too, and he's more than earned that thirst from us."

"I can't be calm about it. I don't know how you can be."

"Because I looked in his eyes today, closer than you are now to me.

I felt his hands burning cold on me. And it wasn't fear running through me. It has been; there's been fear mixed in, even with the power so full and bright. But not today. We're stronger, each one of us alone, stronger than he is, even with what's in him. And together? We're his holocaust."

He skirted the counter, laid his hands on her shoulders again. Gently now. "We must stop him this time, Branna, whatever it takes."

"And I believe we will."

Whatever it takes, he thought again, and brushed his lips to her brow. "I need to keep you from harm."

"Do you think I need protection, Fin?"

"I don't, no, but that doesn't mean I won't give it. It doesn't mean I don't need to give it."

He kissed her brow again.

Whatever it takes.

HE HAD BUSINESSES TO RUN, AND THE WORK DIDN'T WAIT until it was convenient for him. Ledgers had to be balanced, calls had to be made or returned, and it seemed there was forever some legal document to read and sign.

He'd learned early that owning a successful business required more than the owning of it, and the dream. He could be grateful Boyle and Connor handled the day-to-day demands—and all the paperwork, time, and decision-making on the spot that engendered. But it didn't leave him off the hook.

Even when he traveled, he stayed keyed in—via phone or Skype or email. But when he was home, he felt obliged to get his hands dirty. That held the pleasure of grooming horses as he prized that physical contact and mental bond. More than using a currycomb or hoof pick, the grooming or feeding or exercising gave him an insight into each horse.

Nor did he mind cleaning up for the birds at the school or spending time carefully drying wet feathers. He'd gained a great deal of satisfaction in having a hand training the younger ones, and had found himself bonding particularly with a female they'd named Sassy—as she was.

Though the days grew slowly longer, there rarely seemed enough hours in them to do all he wanted or needed to do. But he knew where he wanted to be, and that was home.

Nearly a year now, he thought as he stood with Connor in the school enclosure, kicking a blue ball for Romeo, their office manager's very enthusiastic spaniel. The longest straight stretch for him since he'd been twenty.

Business and curiosity and the need for answers would call him away again, but no more, he hoped, for months at a time. For the first time since the mark had come on him, he felt home again.

"I'm thinking the winter, and the slower demand, makes the best time to experiment with the hawk rides we talked of before."

"We'd offer something more than special to those who come here for some adventure." Connor gave the ball a kick, sent the dog racing. "I've worked out the pricing on it, should we give it a go, and Boyle grumbled as he does so it seemed in line."

"As do I. It'll require a different waiver, and some adjustment on the insurance end of things, and I'll see to that."

"Happy not to pick up that torch."

Fin took his turn to boot the ball. "The other end is scheduling, which I'll leave to you and Boyle to coordinate. We've got Meara and yourself as experienced riders and hawkers, and Iona's done well with the hawking."

"And none better on a horse. So that gives us three who could take the point on a combination. You'd be four."

Fin glanced over as Connor grinned at him. "I haven't run a guided since . . . not since the first few months Boyle and I were getting it all off the ground."

"Sure you could go out anytime, I'm certain, with one of the others, as a kind of apprentice."

Connor set to kick, and for the hell of it Fin blocked, took the ball himself, added some footwork remembered from boyhood before he sent it flying.

"After a match then?" Connor asked.

"I'll take you on when I've time, and that'll be after I've done a draft of a new brochure for you and Boyle to have a look at. Meanwhile, you should have another who can hawk and ride and handle a small group—as I think we'd keep this combination, at least at the start to groups of six and under. Who strikes you?"

"I've some with more hawking experience, but I'd say our Brian. He's the most eager to learn the new, try the different."

"Then you'll speak to him, and if he's keen on it, he can start training, see how it all goes. We'll want to try it a few times, with just staff or friends. If *that* all goes well, we'll begin to offer the package in March, we'll say. By the equinox, as a goal."

"A good time to work out any kinks in the wire."

"And now, I'm after taking Sassy out for a bit. I'll go to the stables, get a mount, and we'll see how she does with a horse and rider. Merlin will come along as he'll keep her in line. And I want to see how they get on. I think to breed them."

Connor grinned. "I was going to speak to you about just that. It's the right match, to my mind. They're well suited—his dignity and her sassiness. I think they'd produce a grand clutch for us."

"We'll let them decide."

Fin got a baiting pouch as the female still looked for the reward, and pulling on a glove, fixed Sassy's jesses. She preened a bit, pleased to be chosen, and cocked her head, eyeing him with a look he could only deem flirtatious.

"Sure you're a fetching one, aren't you now?" He walked out the gates with her, and turning toward the stables, called for Merlin.

His hawk soared overhead, then went into a long, graceful swoop Fin could only deem a bit of showing off. On his arm, Sassy spread her wings.

"Want to join him, do you? Then I'll trust you to behave and go where I lead you." He loosened the jesses, lifted his arm, and watched her lift into the sky.

They circled together, added a few playful loops, and he thought, yes, he and Connor had the right of it. They matched well.

He enjoyed the walk, the familiar trees, the turn of the path, the scents in the air. Though he'd hoped he would, he felt nothing of Cabhan, and traveled from school to stables with only the hawks for company.

He thought the stables made a picture, spread as they were with the paddock, the lorries and cars, and Caesar's majestic head lifted out the open stall window. The horse sent Fin a whinny of greeting so he went directly over to stroke and rub, have a short conversation before going inside.

He found Boyle in the office, glowering at the computer.

"Why do people ask so many stupid questions?" Boyle demanded.

"You only think they're stupid as you already know the answers." Fin sat on a corner—about the only clear area—of the desk. "I've just come from Connor at the school," he began, and spoke with Boyle about the plans for the new package.

"Iona's keen on it, that's for certain. And Brian, well, he's young, but from what I've seen and heard, he works hard, and I know he rides well enough. I'm willing to give it a go."

"Then we'll smooth out the details. Unless you need me here, I'm taking Caesar. We'll try a hawk ride as I've Merlin and a young female along with me. I'll map out a potential route."

"Have a care. Iona and I went by the new house to see the progress early this morning. She saw the wolf, the shadow wolf, slinking through the trees."

"You didn't?"

"No, I was turned away, and talking with one of the carpenters. She said it came closer than it had before, though she's put protection around the house."

"I'll have a look myself."

"I'd be grateful."

Fin saddled Caesar, who was eager to be off as he understood he'd get a run out of it instead of the usual plod. After he'd led the horse out, mounted, he walked a distance away, then baited his glove, called to Sassy.

She landed prettily, gobbled the bit of chicken as if she'd been starved for a month, then settled into it. She and Caesar exchanged one long stare, then the horse turned his head away as if the hawk was nothing to do with him.

"That's a fine attitude," Fin decided, and to test both horse and hawk, kicked into a gallop.

It startled the hawk, who spread her wings—another picture—and would have risen off the glove if Fin hadn't soothed her.

"You're fine. It's just another way to fly." She fidgeted some, not entirely convinced, but stayed on the glove. Satisfied, Fin dropped into a canter, turned toward the woods before he signaled her to lift.

She soared to a branch where Merlin already waited.

"Well done, well done indeed. You'll lead, Merlin, and we'll follow."

His hawk looped through the trees; the female followed. Keeping to a dignified walk, Fin led the horse through.

For the next half hour he took her through the paces, bringing her back to the glove, letting her go again.

The chilly, damp air opened for a thin drizzle of rain, but none of them minded it. Here was freedom for all in a kind of game.

He mapped out the route in his head, thought it would make a fine loop for the package, showing off how the hawks could dance through the trees, and return time and time to the glove without breaking the horse's easy pace.

Close enough here to hear the river murmur, far enough there to feel as though you rode hawking into another time. And he could smell snow coming. By nightfall, he thought, and it would grace the greens and browns, lie still and quiet for a time.

And come spring, the blackthorn would bloom, and the wildflowers Branna gathered for pleasure and for magicks.

Come spring, he thought—he hoped—he could walk through the woods with her, in peace.

And thinking of her, he changed direction. The hawks and horse could settle down outside her cottage awhile while he worked with her.

When he moved onto a clear path, he let Caesar canter again, then laughed as he saw Bugs running, tongue lolling.

"Now with the hound I've all three. We'll just go by, stop in Branna's. She might have something for all of you. Then we'll take a look at Boyle's new house before going on home."

Apparently fine with that plan, Bugs raced along beside the horse.

Fin slowed again as they approached the big downed tree, and the thick vines that barred most from the ruins of Sorcha's cabin.

Bugs let out a low growl.

"Oh aye, he's coming around now. I feel him as well."

Fin ordered Sassy to stay in the air, called Merlin to the glove.

Fog snaked through the vines. Fin held out his free hand, levitated the dog up to sit in front of him in the saddle.

He felt the pull, the almost cheerful invitation to come through, to bask in all that could be, all the dark gifts offered.

"If that's the best you have . . ." With a shrug, Fin started to turn the horse.

The wolf burst out of the vines, gleaming black, red stone pulsing. Caesar shied, reared, but Fin managed to keep his seat, and snatched the dog before Bugs lost his.

To Fin's surprise, Sassy went into a stoop, swooped over the wolf, then up again where she perched in a tree, staring down at it.

Clever girl, he thought. Fierce and clever girl.

"I'll say again, if that's the best you have . . ."

Fin took Caesar into a charge, and shot down a hand to split the earth open under the wolf. As the horse leaped over it, the wolf vanished.

Fin heard the laughter behind him, turned the horse.

Cabhan floated above the open earth on a blanket of fog.

"Far from the best, boy. You've yet to taste my best. Spare yourself, for in the end you'll come to me. I know your blood."

Fin fought the urge to charge again, but he'd been in business long enough to know a turned back could pack a harder punch.

So he simply turned Caesar, walked away without hurry.

"Spare yourself." It came as a whisper, not a shout. "And when I've finished with you, I will bind the dark witch you lust for to you for eternity."

The urge to turn and charge grew with fury.

Without looking back, Fin healed the earth, and moved forward and out of the woods.

Fin tethered the horse outside the cottage and, dismounting, pressed his cheek to Caesar's. "You earned your name today, as you never hesitated to charge when I asked it of you." Like a magician, he held out his hand, showed it empty, then turned his wrist and produced an apple.

While Caesar crunched his treat, Fin called Sassy to glove. "And you, so brave for one so young. You'll hunt." He signaled to Merlin. "You'll hunt together in Branna's field, and you can stay awhile in Roibeard's lean-to. And you." He bent to rub Bugs. "I'll wager there's a biscuit inside for the likes of you."

With the dog, Fin walked to the workshop and in.

"There's my reward," he said as Branna took a tray of biscuits out of the little workshop oven.

"You timed that exceedingly well." She laid the tray on the top of the stove, turned. "Something happened," she said immediately.

"Not of great import, but here's a hound who's earned a biscuit if you have one."

"Of course." She got two from the jar, as Kathel had already stirred himself from his nap by the fire to greet his small friend.

"I'd rather this sort," Fin said and plucked up one of the human variety she already had cooled on a rack. "I had business to see to at home, then at the school and around to the stables. We're doing the hawk-and-horse package come spring."

"That's all well and good, but what happened?"

"I took hawk and horse out myself. Caesar and Merlin and a pretty female name of Sassy who will mate with Merlin when she's ready for it."

"And how does she feel about that?" Branna put the kettle on as Fin already grabbed a second biscuit.

"She likes the look of him, and he of her. I was after mapping out a couple of routes that might suit the package, and Bugs joined in as we passed near the big stables. With them I turned this way, thinking to work with you for an hour or two, and passed by the entrance to Sorcha's cabin."

"You could've avoided that spot."

"True enough. I didn't want to avoid it. And because I didn't, I learned the hawk I chose for Merlin will be his match."

He told her, accepted the tea, and actively considered trying for a third biscuit.

"He grows more arrogant," Branna said.

"Enough to taunt, which is all this business was. He wanted me to come at him again, and it occurred to me that denying him that was more of an insult."

"He wants us to know none of us can take a simple walk in the woods without risk. Taunting," Branna agreed, "in hopes to destroy our morale, close us in."

"He's more confident than he was, or so it strikes me."

"We've bloodied him twice, more than twice, and the last time nearly destroyed him."

"But we didn't," Fin pointed out. "And he heals, and knows he's only to reach his lair again to heal. Knows he can battle us time and time again, and come back time and time again. If you're a gambling man, the odds would be at some point we'll lose the day. It's time again, Branna, and he has that in his pocket."

"He doesn't believe he can be destroyed—or he doesn't believe what's in him can. But I'm working on that."

She walked over, tapped her finger on her notebook. "I called on my father, and he called on others, and I've put together ingredients and the mixing of them I think will take the demon. I've been working on the words of the spell along with it. We need the name. I don't believe this will work without calling the demon by name, and those who consulted with my father confirm that."

Fin palmed the third biscuit, then stepped closer to read over her shoulder.

"Dried wing of bat—best from Romania?"

"I'm told."

"Tail hairs from a pregnant yak." Fin arched a brow. "No eye of newt or tongue of dog. Apologies," he said to both Kathel and Bugs.

"You may joke about the English bard's witches three, but I've formulated this from the best sources I can find."

"Wolfsbane, Atropa belladonna berries—crushed—tincture of Amazonian angel's trumpet, conium petals from Armenia, sap from the manchineel tree. I know some of these."

"All poisons. All of them natural poisons. We have some of this in what we've devised for Cabhan, but there are a number of ingredients here that are more exotic than I've worked with before. I'll have to send for some, obviously. It requires water blessed by a priest, which is easy enough. Blood remains the binding agent. It's yours we'll need. Your blood, some of your hair, and nail clippings."

He only grunted.

"I'd started on the amounts, and the orders. My sources conflict somewhat on both, but we'll find the right mix. And the words need to be right. The potion will be black and dense when we have it right. It will hold no light, reflect no light."

He reached up, massaged her shoulders. "You're knotted up. You should be pleased, not tense. This is brilliant progress, Branna."

"None of it will have a hope of working unless we choose the right time, and there I've made no progress at all."

"I've thought on it. Ostara? The equinox. We tried the summer solstice, for light. Ostara is light as well, the balance of it tipping to the light."

"I come back to it, again and again." She pushed her hands through her hair to secure loosened pins. "But it won't hold for me as the other tries did. It should be right; maybe it is and I just can't see it through the other elements."

He turned her, still rubbing her shoulders. "We might try devising the spell, and the potion with Ostara as the time, and see if it holds then. Providing we find a pregnant yak."

She smiled as he'd hoped. "My father tells me he knows a man who can acquire anything, for a price."

"Then we'll pay the price, and we'll begin. I've still got an hour or so, and I'll help with the spell. But tonight, I think you could use a distraction, having your mind off all this."

"Is that what you think?"

"I think you should come out to dinner with me. I've a place in mind you'll like, very much."

"Out to dinner? And what sort of place would this be?"

"A very fancy place. Romantic and elegant, and where the food is a god." He twined some of her loosened hair around his finger. "You could wear the dress you wore New Year's Eve."

"I've more than one dress, and would consider going skyclad to be served food fit for gods that I don't make myself."

"If you insist, but I'd rather see to getting you skyclad myself after dessert."

"Are we having a date, Finbar?"

"We are. Dinner at eight, though I'll pick you up at seven so you'll have some time to enjoy the city before we eat."

"The city? What city?"

"Paris," he said, and kissed her.

"You want us flying off to Paris for a meal?"

"A brilliant meal—in the City of Light."

"Paris," she repeated, and tried to tell herself it was frivolous and foolish, but just couldn't. "Paris," she said again, and kissed him back.

14

WHAT WAS IT LIKE? PARIS," IONA ADDED. "WE HAVEN'T had a chance to talk about it without the guys around since you went."

"It was lovely. A bit breathtaking really. The lights, the voices, the food and wine, of course. For a few hours, another world altogether."

"Romantic?" Iona tied pretty raffia bows around softly colored soaps, and boldly colored ones.

"It was."

"I wonder why that part of it worries you."

"I'm not after romance. It's the sort of thing that weakens resolve and clouds sense." Branna measured out ground herbs. "It's not something I can risk now."

"You love each other."

"Love isn't always the answer." While Iona helped with store stock, Branna focused on more magickal supplies. Another battle would come, other attacks were likely. She wanted a full store of medicinals on hand, for any contingency.

"It is for you, and I'm glad of it." She added precisely six drops of extract of nasturtium to the small cauldron. "It adds to what you are, strengthens your purpose."

"You think it weakens yours."

"I think it can, and now more than ever that can't be allowed. Both Fin and I know we can live without each other. We have done so, and well enough. We know what we have now may only be for now. Whatever the rest, with or without, waits until Cabhan is finished."

"You're happier with him," Iona pointed out.

"And what woman isn't happier when she can count on a good shag with some regularity?" After Iona's snort, she held up a finger for silence, then holding her hands over the cauldron, brought the brew to a fast boil. Murmuring now, drawing light down with one hand, a thin shower of blue rain with the other. For an instant a rainbow formed, then it, too, slid into the pot.

Branna took the brew down to the slowest of simmers.

Satisfied, she turned, found Iona studying her.

"Watching you work," Iona explained. "It's all so pretty, so graceful, with power just flowing all around."

"We'll want this restorative on hand, as well as the balms and salves I've been stocking up." Branna tapped the door to a cupboard she thought of as her war chest.

"Hope for the best, but prepare for the worst."

"A good policy."

"It's what you're doing with Fin?"

"Being with him—and not just for the sex—lets me remember all the reasons I fell in love with him. He has such kindness—and I wanted to forget that of him. His humor, his focus, his loyalty. I want to remember all that now, for the comfort of it, and for the unity.

Remembering who he is means I can give him all my trust in this. All of it. And I'm not sure, no matter how I tried, I did before. Because I can and do, there'll always be some best to hold on to."

"Is he coming today?"

"I told him no need. We're still shy some of the ingredients so we can't begin to make the poison as yet. He has his work as I have mine. And I appreciate you giving me so much of your off day."

"I like playing with your store stock—and the more I can do, the more time you have for demon poisons. I want to take Alastar out later, and was hoping you'd want to go for a ride with us."

"A ride?"

"I've seen you ride, and Meara mentioned you don't take much time for it, the way you once did."

She hadn't, Branna thought, as it reminded her of Fin. But now . . . He'd brought Aine for her, and she hadn't given herself the pleasure of testing the bond with the horse.

"If what needs doing is done, I would. And if the pair of us rode out for pleasure, it's a nose-thumbing in Cabhan's direction."

"We're seeing him every day now." Idly, Iona stacked the pretty soaps into colorful towers. "Skulking around."

"I know it. I see him as well. He tests my borders often now."

"I dreamed of Teagan last night. We talked."

"And you're just telling me of it?"

"It was like a little visit. Sitting in front of the fire, drinking tea. She's showing, and she let me feel the baby kick. She told me about her husband, and I talked about Boyle. And it struck me—what you'd said about all of us being connected—her husband and Boyle are so alike. In temperament, his love of horses and the land."

"Boyle's connected to the three through the man Teagan married? Yes, that could be."

"We didn't talk of Cabhan, and isn't that odd? We just drank tea and talked of her husband, the baby to come, Boyle, the wedding plans. At the end of the dream, she gave me a little charm, and said it was for Alastar."

"Do you have it?"

"I put it on his bridle this morning before I came. I had a charm in my pocket, one I'd made for Alastar, so I gave it to her."

"We've exchanged tokens, each of us with each of them. I think it's more than courtesy. Something of ours in their time, and something of theirs in ours. We'll want all three gifts with us when we face Cabhan again."

"We're still not sure when."

"It's a frustration to me," Branna admitted. "But it can't be done until we have all we need to destroy the demon. I have to believe we'll know when we must."

"Demons and visits in dreams with cousins from centuries ago. Battles and whirlwinds and weddings. My life is so different from what it was a year ago. I've been here nearly a year now, and it feels as if the life I led before was barely there. Is it silly—and unrealistic—for me to plan and cook a kind of anniversary dinner for Boyle? Surprise him with it—and I mean something he can actually eat without pretending it doesn't suck."

Both amused and touched, Branna glanced over while Iona rearranged her towers. "Of course it's not."

"I can still see him just the way it was when he first rode up on Alastar. The way both of them just shot straight into me. Now they're mine. I want to mark the day."

"So you will."

Something brushed the edge of her thoughts. Branna paused, waited for it to come, and the door jangled open.

One of her neighbors, a cheerful, grandmotherly type, stepped inside.

"Good day to you, Mrs. Baker."

"And to you, Branna, and here's Iona as well. I hope I'm not a bother to you."

"Not at all. Would you have some tea?" Branna offered.

"I wouldn't mind it, if it's no trouble. It's tea I've come for—if you've the blend you make for head colds. It would save me a trip to the village if you've some on hand I can buy from you."

"I do, of course. Here, take off your coat, and sit by the fire. Have you a cold coming on?"

"Not me, but my husband has one full blown, and is driving me mad with his complaints. I swear a cup of tea by your fire here with women who know better than to think their life's finished because they've got a cold in the head would save my sanity. Oh, and aren't these soaps as pretty as candy in a jar."

"I can't decide which is my favorite, but this one's leading the charge." Iona held up a bold red cake for Mrs. Baker to sniff.

"That's lovely. I'm going to treat myself to one of these as a reward for not knocking himself unconscious with a skillet."

"You deserve it."

"A bit of the sniffles and men are more work than a brood of babies. You'll be finding that out for yourself soon enough, with the wedding coming."

"I'm hoping to get a good skillet as a wedding gift," Iona said, and made Mrs. Baker laugh until she wheezed.

Accepting the invitation, she took off her coat, her scarf, and settled herself by the fire. "And here's your Kathel—it's a fine thing, a dog, a fire, a cup of tea. I thought I saw him when I started over, prowling along the edge of the woods, even called out a greeting to him before I saw it wasn't our Kathel at all. A big black dog for certain, and for a moment I thought: Well, God in heaven, that's a wolf. Then it was gone." She snapped her fingers. "Old eyes, I imagine, playing tricks."

After a quick glance at Iona, Branna brought over tea and biscuits. "A stray perhaps. Have you seen it before?"

"I haven't, no, and hope not to again. It gave me gooseflesh, I admit, when it turned its head toward me after I called out, thinking it was Kathel. I nearly turned round and went back inside—which should prove it gave me the shivers, as inside I've Mr. Baker's whining.

"Oh, Branna, what a treat! I couldn't be more grateful."

"You're very welcome. I've a tonic you could add to Mr. Baker's tea. It's good for what troubles him, and will help him sleep."

"Name your price."

They entertained Mrs. Baker, rang up the sale of tea and tonic, and gave the pretty soap as a gift. And Branna sent Kathel out with her, to be certain she got home safe.

"Did he show himself to her," Iona said the minute they were alone, "or is his . . . presence—would that be it—just more tangible?"

"I'm wondering if he got careless, as that's another possibility. Prowling around as she said, hoping to trouble us, and he didn't shadow himself from others. As he doesn't want the attention of others, I think it was carelessness."

"He's impatient."

"It may be, but he'll just have to wait until we're ready. I'm going to finish this restorative, then we'll take ourselves off. We'll have that ride."

"You're hoping he'll take a run at us."

"I'm not hoping he won't." Branna lifted her chin in defiance. "I'd like to give him a taste of what two women of power can do."

BRANNA WASN'T DISAPPOINTED FIN HAD BUSINESS ELSEwhere. If he'd been at home or in the stables, he wouldn't have cared for the idea of her and Iona going out at all, or would have insisted on going with them.

She wore riding boots she hadn't put on in years, and had to admit it felt good. And what felt even better was saddling Aine herself.

"We don't know each other well as yet, so I hope you'll let Iona know if you've any problems with me." She took a moment to come around the filly's head, stroke her cheeks, look into her eyes.

"He'd have wanted you for your beauty and grace alone, for you have both in full measure. But he sensed you were for me, and I for you. If that's the way of it, I'll do my best for you. That's an oath. I made this for you today," she added, and braided a charm into Aine's mane with a bright red ribbon. "For protection, as mine or not, I'll protect you."

"She thinks you're nearly as pretty as she is," Iona told Branna.

With a laugh, Branna stepped over to adjust the stirrups to her liking. "Now then that's a fine compliment."

"With you on her back, you'll make a picture—which is something she's happy to make for Alastar."

"Let's make one then." With Iona she led the horses out of the stables, vaulted into the saddle as if it had been only yesterday.

"Do we have a plan?" Iona leaned over the saddle to pat Alastar's neck.

"Sometimes it's best to take things as they come."

They walked to the road, with Kathel and Bugs prancing along with them.

"I can't call the hawk," Iona said.

"They'll come if needed. Though that would've been a thought, wouldn't it, to ride out with all the guides. What do you say to a canter?"

"I say yay."

Graceful, Branna thought again when Aine responded and broke into a bright canter. And flirtatious, Branna added, as she didn't need to have Iona's gift to interpret the way Aine tossed her mane.

She glanced back, saw that the faithful Kathel slowed his own pace to stay with Bugs, felt her lips curve at the happiness beaming from both of them.

So she let herself just enjoy.

The cool air, with a sharpness in it that told her more snow would come. The scent of the trees and horses, the steady beat of hooves.

Maybe she had taken too little time for too long a time if a little canter down the road brought her such a lift in spirit.

She felt in tune with the horse. Fin would be right, she admitted, as he was never wrong on such matters. For whatever reason, Aine would be hers, and the partnership between them began now.

They turned onto the path into the trees where the air was cooler yet. Small pools of snow lay in shadows where they'd formed in a previous fall, and a bird chattered on a bough.

They slowed to an easy trot.

"She's hoping, and so's Alastar, we'll head to some open before it's done for a gallop."

"I wouldn't mind it. I haven't gone this way in more than a year. I'd nearly forgotten how lovely it can be in winter, how hushed and alone."

"I'll never get used to it," Iona told her. "Could never take any of it for granted. I don't know how many guideds I've done through here this last year, and still every one is a wonder."

"It doesn't bore you, a horsewoman of your skills, just plodding along?"

"You'd think it would, but it doesn't. The people are usually interesting, and I'm getting paid for riding a horse. Then . . ." Iona wiggled her eyebrows. "I get to sleep with the boss. It's a good deal all around."

"We could circle around on the way back, go by your house."

"I was hoping you'd say that. They were supposed to—maybe—start putting up drywall today. Connor's been a champ, making time to get over there and pitch in."

"Sure he loves the building, and he's clever with it."

In unison they turned to walk the horses along the river.

The air chilled, and Branna saw the first fingers of fog.

"We've company," she murmured to Iona.

"Yeah. Okay."

"Keep the horses calm, won't you, and I'll do the same with the hounds."

He came as a man, handsome and hard, dressed in black with silver trim. Branna noted he'd been vain enough to do a glamour as his face glowed with health and color.

He swept them a deep bow.

"Ladies. What a grand sight you make on a winter's day."

"Do you have so little to occupy yourself," Branna began, "that you spend all your time sniffing about where you're not welcome."

"But you see I've been rewarded, as here are the two blooms of the three. You think to wed a mortal," he said to Iona. "To waste your power on one who can never return it. I have so much more for you."

"You have nothing for me, and you're so much less than him."

"He builds you a house of stone and stick when I would give you a palace." He spread his arms, and over the cold, dark water of the river swam a palace shining with silver and gold. "A true home for such as you, who has never had her own. Always craved her own. This I would give you."

Iona dug deep, turned the image to black. "Keep it."

"I will take your power, then you will live in the ashes of what might have been. And you." He turned to Branna. "You lay with my son."

"He isn't your son."

"His blood is my blood, and this you can never deny. Take him, be taken, it only weakens you. You will bear my seed one way or the other. Choose me, choose now, while I still grant you a choice. Or when I come for you, I will give you pain not pleasure. Choose him, and his blood, the blood of all you profess to love, will be on your hands."

She leaned forward in the saddle. "I choose myself. I choose my gift and my birthright. I choose the light, whatever the price. Where Sorcha failed, we will not. You'll burn, Cabhan."

Now she swept an arm out, and over that cold, dark river a tower of fire rose, and through the flame and smoke the image of Cabhan screamed.

"That is my gift to you."

He rose a foot off the ground, and still Iona held the horses steady. "I will take the greatest pleasure in you. I will have you watch while I gut your brother, while I rip your cousin's man in quarters. You'll watch me slit the throat of the one you think of as sister, watch while I rape your cousin. And only then when their blood soaks the ground will I end you."

"I am the Dark Witch of Mayo," she said simply. "And I am your doom."

"Watch for me," he warned her. "But you will not see."

He vanished with the fog.

"Those kind of threats—" Iona broke off, gestured toward the flaming towers, the screams. "Would you mind?"

"Hmm. I rather like it, but . . ." Branna whisked it away. "They're not threats, not in his mind, but promises. We'll see he breaks them. I'd hoped he'd take wolf form, at least for a few moments. I want the name of what made him."

"Satan, Lucifer, Beelzebub?"

Branna smiled a little. "I think not. A lesser demon, and one who needs Cabhan as Cabhan needs it. The pair of them left a stink in the air. Let's have that gallop now, and go by and see your house."

"The sticks and stones?"

"Are solid and strong. And real."

Iona nodded. "Branna, what if . . . if while you're with Fin you got pregnant?"

"I won't. I've taken precautions." With that she urged Aine into a gallop.

SHE GAVE AINE A CARROT AND A RUBDOWN, SO WHEN FIN came into the stables he found both her and Iona.

"I'm told you went for a ride."

"We did, and it reminded me how I enjoy it." She leaned her cheek to Aine's. "You did say she and I should get acquainted."

"I didn't have in mind you going off alone."

"I wasn't alone. I was with Iona and she with me, with Aine and Alastar and the dogs altogether. Oh, don't try to slither out because he's glowering," she said to Iona. "You're tougher than that. We had a conversation with Cabhan—no more really than a volley of harsh words all around. We'll tell you and the others the whole of it."

"Bloody right you will." He started to grab Branna's arm, and Aine butted him in the shoulder with her head.

"Taking her side now?"

"She's mine, after all. And knows as well as I do we had no trouble, and took no more risks than any of us do when taking a step out of the house. I suppose you'll want a meal with the telling."

"I could eat," Iona said.

"We'll have it all here," Fin told them.

"With what?"

He took Branna's arm now, but casually. "You've given me lists every time I turn around. There's enough in the kitchen to put together a week of meals."

"As it should be. All right then. Iona, would you mind telling the others while I see what I can put together in Finbar's famous kitchen?"

"You went out looking for him," Fin accused.

"I didn't, no, but I didn't go out not expecting to find him."

"You knew he'd come at you."

"He didn't come at us, not in any way as you mean. Only words. A kind of testing ground on his part, I'm thinking. I'd hoped he'd come as the wolf, so I could try to get the name, but he was only a man."

Inside, she took off her coat, handed it to Fin. "And we did have a lovely ride around it, coming back so I could see the progress on Iona's house. It's going to be lovely, just lovely. An open kind of space, and still a few snug little places for the cozy. Coming back here that way, I had a different perspective on this house. That room with all the windows that juts toward the woods. It must be a lovely place to sit and look out, all year long. Private enough, and steps from the trees."

She rummaged in the refrigerator, freezer, cupboards as she spoke.

"I've a recipe for these chicken breasts Connor's fond of. It gives them a bite." Head angled, she sent him a challenging look. "Can you take a bite, Fin?"

"Can you?" He pulled her to him, nipped her bottom lip.

"I give good as I get. And you might get more yet if you pour me some wine."

He turned, found a bottle, studied the label. "Do you understand what it would have done to me if he'd hurt you?"

"None of us can think like that. We can't. What we feel for each other, all of us for each other, is strong and true and deep. And we can't think that way."

"It's not thinking, Branna. It's feeling."

She laid her hands on his chest. "Then we can't feel that way. He weakens us if he holds us back from taking the risks we have to take."

"He weakens us all the more if we stop feeling."

"You're both right." Iona came in. "We have to feel it. I'm afraid for Boyle all the time, but we still do what we have to do. We feel it, and we keep going."

"You've a good point. You feel, but you don't stop," she said to Fin. "Neither can I. I can promise you I'll protect myself as best I can. And I'm very good at it."

"You are that. I'm going to open this wine, Iona. Would you have some?"

"Twist my arm."

"After you've done the wine, Fin, you can scrub up the potatoes."

"Iona," Fin said smooth as butter, "you wouldn't mind scrubbing the potatoes, would you, darling?"

Before Branna could speak, Iona pulled off her coat. "I'll take KP. In fact, whatever you're making, Branna, you could walk me through it. Maybe it'll be the anniversary dinner for Boyle."

"This is a little rough and ready for that," Branna began, "but . . . Well, that's it! For the love of . . . Why didn't I think of it before?"

"Think of what?" Iona asked.

"The time. The day we end Cabhan. Right in front of my face. I need my book. I need my star charts. I need to be sure. I'll take the table here for it—it shouldn't take long."

She grabbed the wine Fin had just poured, and walking toward the dining area, flicked fingers in the air until her spell books, her laptop, her notepad sat neatly on one side. "Iona, you'll need to quarter those potatoes once scrubbed, lay them in a large baking dish. Get the oven preheated now, to three hundred and seventy-five."

"I can do that, but—"

"I need twenty minutes here. Maybe a half hour. Ah . . . then you'll pour four tablespoons, more or less, of olive oil over the potatoes, toss them in it to coat. Sprinkle on pepper and crushed rosemary. Use your eye for it, you've got one. In the oven for thirty minutes, then I'll tell you what to do with them next. I'll be finished by then. Quiet!" she snapped, dropping down to sit before Iona could ask another question.

"I hate when she says more or less or use your eye," Iona complained to Fin.

"I've an eye as well, but I promise it's worse than your own."

"Maybe between us, we'll make one good one."

She did her best—scrubbed, quartered, poured, tossed, sprinkled. And wished Boyle would get there to tell her if it looked right. On Fin's shrug, she stuck it in the oven. Set the timer.

Then she drank wine and hoped while she and Fin studied Branna.

She'd pulled one of her clips from somewhere and scooped up her hair. The sweater she'd rolled to her elbows as she worked from book to computer and back again, as she scribbled notes, made calculations.

"What if she's not done when the timer goes off?" Iona wondered.

"We're on our own, as she'd skin us if we interrupted her now."

"That's it!" Branna slapped a hand on her notebook. "By all the goddesses, that's it. It's so fecking simple, it's so bloody *obvious*. I looked right through it."

She rose, strode back, poured a second glass of wine. "Anniversary. Of course. When else could it be?"

"Anniversary?" Iona's eyes went wide. "Mine? The day I came, met you? But you said that hadn't worked. The day I met Boyle? That anniversary?"

"No, not yours. Sorcha's. The day she died. The anniversary of her death, and the day she took Cabhan to ash. That day, in our time, is when we end it. When we will. Not a sabbat or esbat. Not a holy day. Sorcha's day."

"The day the three were given her power," Fin stated. "The day they became, and so you became. You're right. It was right there, and not one of us saw it."

"Now we do." She raised her glass. "Now we can finish it."

15

SHE FELT REVIVED, REENERGIZED. BRANNA ACTIVELY enjoyed preparing the meal—and Iona did very well with her end of it—enjoyed sitting around Fin's dining room with her circle, despite the fact that the bulk of the dinner conversation centered on Cabhan.

Now, in fact, maybe because of it.

Because she could see it clear, how it could and would be done. The when and the how of it. Risks remained, and they'd face them. But she could believe now as Connor and Iona believed.

Right and light would triumph over the dark.

And was there a finer way to end an evening than sitting in the steaming, bubbling water of Fin's hot tub drinking one last glass of wine and watching a slow, fluffy snowfall?

"You've been a surprise to me, Finbar."

He reclined across from her, lazy-eyed. "Have I now?"

"You have indeed. Imagine the boy I knew building this big house with all its style and its luxuries. And the boy a well-traveled and successful man of business. One who roots those businesses at home. I wouldn't have thought a dozen years back I'd be indulging myself in this lovely spot of yours while the snow falls."

"What would you have thought?"

"Considerably smaller, I'd have to say. Your dreams grew larger than mine, and you've done well with them."

"Some remain much as they were."

She only smiled, glided her foot along his leg under the frothy water.

"It feels we could be in some chalet in Switzerland, which I like, but I wonder you didn't put this in that room with all the windows, the way it's situated so private and opening to the woods."

He drank some wine. "I had that room built with you in mind."

"Me?"

"With the hope one day you'd marry me as we planned, live here with me. And make your workshop there."

"Oh, Fin." His wish, and her own, twined together to squeeze her heart.

"You like the open when you work, the glass so you can look out, the feel of being out, is what appeals to you. Snug enough inside, but with that open to bring the out in to you. So the glass room facing the woods gives you the private and the open at once."

She couldn't speak for a moment, didn't want her voice to shake when she did. "If I had the magicks to change what is, to transform them into what I'd wish them to be, it would be that, to live and to work here with you. But we have this."

She set her wineglass in the holder, flowed over to him, to press body to body. "We have today."

He skimmed a hand down her hair, down to where it dipped and floated over the water. "No tomorrows."

"Today." She laid her cheek against his. "I'm with you, you're with me. I never believed, or let myself believe, we could have this much.

Today is the world for me, as you are. It may never be enough, and still." She drew back, just a little. "It's all."

She brushed his lips with hers, slid into the kiss with all the tenderness she owned.

She would give him all she had to give him. And all was love. More than her body, but through her body her heart. It had always been his, would always be, so the gift of it was simple as breathing.

"Believe," she murmured. "Tonight."

Sweetly, for with her practical bent she could forget the sweet, she offered the kiss, to stir, to soothe.

Her only love.

He knew what she offered, and knew what she asked. He would take, and he would give. And setting aside the wish for more, he would believe tonight was everything.

Here was magick in having her soft and yielding, her sigh warm against his cheek as they embraced. The heat rose through him, around him, with the snow a silent curtain to close out all the world but them.

He took her breasts, gently, gently, as he could still see in his mind the violent marks what shared his blood had put on her. He swore as her heart beat against his hand, he would never harm her, would give his life to keep her from harm.

Whatever came tomorrow, he'd never break the oath.

Her hands glided over him, and her fingers brushed against the mark he carried. Her touch, even so light, brought on a bone-deep ache there. A price he'd pay without question.

The water, a steady drumbeat in the hush of the night, swirled around them as their hands drifted under it to give pleasure.

Her breath caught, shaking her heart with the meeting of emotion and sensation, the rise of need and wonder.

How could tenderness cause such heat—a wire in the blood, a fire in the belly—and still have her wish to draw every moment into forever?

So when she straddled him, took him deep, and deep and deep, she knew she would never take another. Whatever the needs of the body, no other could touch her heart, her soul. Combing her fingers through his hair, she held his face as she moved over him so he could see her, see into her, and know.

On their slow climb, the swirling water glowed, a pool of light to bathe them and surround them. As they fell, holding tight, the light flowed out against the dark to illuminate the soft curtain of snow.

Later, lax and sleepy in his bed, she curled against him. As tonight became tomorrow, she held fast to what she loved.

IT TOOK MORE PRECIOUS DAYS BEFORE BRANNA COULD acquire all the ingredients, in quantities to allow for experimenting, needed for the poison.

Connor looked on as she sealed them in individual jars on her work counter.

"Those are dangerous, Branna."

"As well they need be."

"You'll take precautions." His face only went stony when she shot him a withering glance. "So you always do, I know full well. But I also know you've never worked with such as this, or concocted such a lethal brew. I've a right to worry about my sister."

"You do, but you needn't. I've spent the days waiting for all of this to arrive to study on them. Meara, take him off, would you? The pair of you should be off to work, not hovering around me."

"If we can't use the stuff until near to April," Meara argued, "can't you wait to make it?"

"As Connor's so helpfully pointed out, I've never done this before. It may take some time to get it right, and I might even have to send out for more before we're sure of it. It's a delicate business."

"Iona and I should do this with you."

Patience, Branna ordered herself, and dug some out of her depleting stores.

"And if the three are huddled in here, hours a day, maybe for days on end, Cabhan will know we're brewing up something. It's best we all continue our routines." Struggling against annoyance, as his worry for her was from love, she turned to him. "Connor, we talked all this through."

"Talking and doing's different."

"We could mix up the routines a bit," Meara suggested, caught between them. "One of us can stay for an hour or two in the morning, another can come around midday, and another come round early from work."

"All right then." Anything, Branna thought, to move them along. "But not this morning as you're both on the schedule. I'm only going to be making powders, distilling. Preparing the ingredients. And I know what I'm about. Added to it, I expect Fin by midday, so there's two of us at it already."

"That's fair enough," Meara said before Connor could argue, and grabbed his hand. "I've got to get on or Boyle will be down my throat and up my arse at the same time. Branna, you'll let us know if you need any help."

"Be sure I will."

Connor strode over, gave Branna a quick, hard kiss. "Don't poison yourself."

"I thought I would just for the experience, but since you ask so nicely . . ."

She breathed a sigh of relief when the door closed behind them, then found Kathel sitting, staring at her.

"Not you as well? When did I all at once become an idjit? If you want to help, go round on patrol." She marched to the door, opened it. "I'm after cloaking the workshop and locking up besides. It wouldn't do to have someone wander in for hand balm while I'm doing this work. Be helpful, Kathel," she said in a more cajoling tone, "and you'll tell me if you find Cabhan's anywhere near."

Another sigh of relief when she'd shut the door behind him.

She cloaked the glass so none but who she chose could see inside. She charmed the doors so none but who she chose could enter.

And turning back to the counter, began—carefully—with wolfsbane.

It was painstaking work, as one of the precautions involved psychically cleansing each ingredient.

Some said those who practiced the dark arts sometimes imbued poisonous plants with the power to infect strange illnesses by only a touch or an inhale of scent.

She didn't have the time or inclination to fall ill.

After cleansing, she rejarred the entire plant, or crushed petals or berries, or distilled.

From outside, Fin watched her as if through a thin layer of gauze. She'd been wise to cloak her workplace, he thought, as even from here he recognized belladonna, and angel's trumpet—though he could only assume the latter was Amazonian.

She worked with mortar and pestle because the effort and the stone added to the power. Every now and then he caught a quick glimmer of light or a thin rise of dark from the bowl or from a jar.

Both dogs flanked him. He wasn't certain if Bugs had come along for himself or for Kathel, but the little stable mutt sat and waited as patiently as Branna's big hound.

Fin wondered if he'd ever watch Branna through the glass without worry. If that day ever came, it wouldn't be today.

He moved to the door, opened it.

She'd put on music, which surprised him as she most often worked in silence, but now she worked to weeping violins.

Whatever she told the dogs stopped their forward motion toward her so they sat again, waited again. Taking off his coat, so did he.

Then she poured the powder she made through a funnel and into a jar, sealed it.

"I wanted to get that closed up before the dogs began milling around, wagging tails. I wouldn't want a speck of dust or a stray hair finding its way into the jars."

"I thought you'd have banished any speck of dust long before this."

She carried the funnel, mortar, pestle to a pot on the stove, carefully set them inside the water steadily boiling inside.

"I tend to chase them away with rag or broom as it's more satisfying. Is it midday?"

"Nearly one in the afternoon. I was delayed. Have you worked straight through since Connor and Meara left this morning?"

"And with considerable to show for it. No, don't touch me yet." She stepped to her little sink, scrubbed her hands, then coated them with lotion.

"I'm keeping my word," she told him, "and being overly cautious."

"There's no *overly* with this. And now you'll have a break from it, some food and some tea."

Before she could protest, he took her arm to steer her out and into her own kitchen.

"If you're hungry, you might have picked up some take-away while you were out. Here, you'll have a sandwich and be thankful for it."

He only pulled out a chair, pointed. "Sit," he said, and put the kettle on.

"I thought you wanted food."

"I said you'd have food, and I wouldn't mind some myself. I can make a bloody sandwich. I make a superior sandwich come to that, as it's what I make most."

"You're a man of some means," she pointed out. "You might hire a cook."

"Why would I do that when I can get a meal here more than half the time?"

When he opened the refrigerator, she started to tell him where he might find the various makings, then just sat back, decided to let him fend for himself.

"Did Connor put a bug in your ear?"

"He didn't have to. It would be better if you worked with someone rather than alone. And better as well if you stopped to eat."

"It seems I'm doing just that."

She watched him build a couple of sandwiches with some rocket, thinly sliced ham, and Muenster, toss some crisps on the side. He dealt with the tea, then plopped it all down on the table without ceremony.

Branna rose to get a knife as he'd neglected to cut hers in half.

"Well, if you have to be dainty about it."

"I do. And thanks." She took a bite, sighed. "I didn't realize I was hungry. This part of it's a bit tedious, but I got caught up all the same."

"What else is to be done?"

"On this first stage, nothing. I have the powders, the tinctures and extracts, some of the berries and petals should be crushed fresh. I cleansed all, and that took time, as did boiling all the tools between each ingredient to avoid any contamination. I think it should rest, and I'll start mixing tomorrow."

"We," he corrected. "I've cleared my days as best I can, and unless I'm needed at the stables or school, I'm with you until this is done."

"I can't say how long it will take to perfect it."

"Until it's done, Branna."

She shrugged, continued to eat. "You seem a bit out of sorts. Did the meeting not go well?"

"It went well enough."

She waited, then poked again. "Are you after buying more horses or hawks?"

"I looked at a yearling, and sealed a deal there as I liked the look of him. With Iona, we've drawn more students for the jumping ring. I thought to have her train this one, as he comes from a good line. If she's willing it may be we can expand that end of things, put her in charge of it."

Branna lifted her eyebrows. "She says she's content with the guideds, but I think she'd be thrilled with this idea. If you're thinking this, she must be a brilliant instructor."

"She's a natural, and her students love her. She's only three young girls regular as yet, but their parents praise her to the skies. And we've two of those students because she started with one, and the word spread around."

Branna nodded, continued to eat as Fin lapsed into silence.

"Will you tell me what's troubling you?" she asked him. "I can see it, hear it, under the rest. If it's something between us—"

"Between us we have today, as agreed." He heard the edge in his own voice, waved the words away. "It's nothing to do with that, with what's between us. Cabhan's coming into my dreams," he told her. "Three nights running now."

"Why haven't you told me?"

"What's to be done about it?" Fin countered. "He hasn't pulled me in. I think he doesn't want that battle and the energy it would cost him, so he slips and slithers into them, making his promises, distorting images. He showed me one of you last night."

"Of me."

"You were with a man with sandy hair and pale blue eyes, an American accent. Together, in a room I didn't know, but a hotel room I'd say. And you laughing as you undressed each other."

She gripped her hands together under the table. "His name was David Watson. It would've been near to five years ago now when he was in Cong. A photographer from New York City. We enjoyed each other's company and spent two nights together before he went back to America.

"He's not the only one Cabhan could show you. There aren't many but more than David Watson. Have you taken no women to bed these past years, Finbar?"

Darkly green, just a bit dangerous, his eyes met hers. "There have been women. I tried to hurt none of them, and still most knew they were solace or, worse, somehow, placeholders. I never thought or expected you'd not had . . . someone, Branna, but it was hard to have no choice than to watch you with another man."

"This is how he bleeds you. He doesn't want you dead, as he hopes to merge what you have with what he has, to hold you up as son, when you're nothing of the kind. So this is how he damages you without leaving a mark."

"I'm already marked, or neither of us would have been with others. I know his purpose, Branna, as well as you. It doesn't make it go down easier."

"We can try to find what will block him out."

Fin shook his head. "We've enough to do already. I'll deal with it. And there's something else, I can't quite see or hear, but only feel there's something else trying to find a way in as well."

"Something?"

"Or someone, and I wouldn't block without knowing. It's like something pushing against him, trying to find room. I can't explain it. It's a feeling when I wake that there's a voice just out of my hearing. So I'll listen for it, see what it says."

"You might do better with a good night's sleep than listening for voices. I can't change the last years, Fin."

He met her eyes. "Nor can I."

"Would it be easier on you if we weren't together now? If we went back to working together only? If he couldn't use me as a weapon against you, it—"

"There's nothing harder than being without you."

She rose, went around the table to curl in his lap. "Should I give you the names of those I've been with? I could add their descriptions as well, so you'll know what to expect."

After a long moment, he gave her hair a hard tug. "That's a cruel and callous suggestion."

She tipped her head back. "But it nearly made you smile. Let me help you sleep tonight, Fin." She brushed her lips over his cheek. "You'll do better work for it. Whatever's trying to get in along with him can wait."

"There was a redhead name of Tilda in London. She had eyes like bluebells, a laugh like a siren. And dimples."

Eyes narrowed, Branna slid a hand up his throat, squeezed. "Balancing the scales, are we?"

"As you've yet to witness Tilda's impressive agility, I'd say the scales are far from balanced. But I should sleep better tonight for mentioning her."

He dropped his forehead to Branna's. "I won't let him damage me, or us."

Iona rushed in the back door, said, "Oops."

"We're just having some lunch," Branna told her.

"So I see. You'd both better come take a look at this." Without waiting, she hurried through and into the workshop.

When Branna and Fin joined her, they stood looking out the window at the line of rats ranged just along the border of protection.

Branna laid a hand on Kathel's head when he growled.

"He doesn't like not being able to see in," she said quietly.

"I started to flame them up, but I thought you should see first. It's why I came around the back."

"I'll deal with it." Fin started for the door.

"Don't burn them there where they are," Branna told him. "They'll leave ugly black ash along the snow, then we'll have to deal with that—and it's lovely just now."

Fin spared her a look, a shake of his head, then stepped out coatless.

"The neighbors." On a hiss of frustration, Branna threw up a block so no one could see Fin.

And none too soon, she noted, as he pushed out power, sent the rats scrabbling while they set up that terrible high-pitched screaming. He drove them back, will against will, by millimeters.

Branna went to the door, threw it open, intending to help, but saw she wasn't needed.

He called up a wind, sent them rolling and tumbling in ugly waves. Then he opened the earth like a trench, whirled them in. Then came the fire, and the screams tore the air.

When they stopped he drew down the rain to quench the fire, soak the ash. Then simply pulled the earth back over them.

"That was excellent," Iona breathed. "Disgusting but excellent. I didn't know he could juggle the elements like that—boom, boom, boom."

"He was showing off," Branna replied. "For Cabhan."

Fin stood where he was, in the open, as if daring a response.

He lifted his arm high, called to his hawk. Like a golden flash Merlin dived down, then, following the direction of Fin's hand, bulleted into the trees.

Fin whirled his arms out, in, and vanished in a swirl of fog.

"Oh God, my God, Cabhan."

"It wasn't Cabhan's fog," Branna said with forced calm. "It was Fin's. He's gone after him."

"What should we do? We should call the others, get to Fin."

"We can't get to Fin as we can't know where he is. He has to let us, and he isn't. He wants to do this on his own."

He flew, shadowed by the fog, his eyes the eyes of the hawk. And through the hawk watched the wolf streak through the woods. It left no track and cast no shadow.

As it approached the river it gathered itself, leaped up, rose up, sprang over the cold, dark surface like a stone from a sling. As it did, the mark on Fin's arm burned brutally.

So Cabhan paid a price, he thought, for crossing water.

He followed the wolf, masked by his own fog until he felt something change in the air, something tremble. He called to Merlin, slowed his own forward motion, seconds before the wolf vanished.

FIN MIGHT HAVE WANTED TO HANDLE THINGS ON HIS OWN, but Iona called the others anyway. Placidly, silently, Branna brewed a pot of tea.

"You're so calm." Iona paced, waiting for something to happen. "How can you be so calm?"

"I'm so angry it feels my blood's on fire. If I didn't bank it with calm, I might burn the place to the ground."

Stepping over, Iona wrapped her arms around Branna from behind. "You know he's all right. You know he can take care of himself."

"I know it very well, and it changes nothing." She patted Iona's hand, moved to get a dish for biscuits while her angry heart beat fists against her ribs. "I never asked why you're home so early."

"We decided we could start the whole shift rotation today. I have a lesson at the big stables at four, but Boyle could spare me until." Iona rushed to the door. "Here they are now. And, oh! Here's Fin. He's fine."

When Branna said nothing, Iona opened the door. "Get inside," she snapped to Fin. "You don't even have a jacket."

"I was warm enough."

"You'll be warmer yet if I kick your arse," Boyle warned him. "What's all this about taking off after Cabhan on your own, in some fecking funnel of fog."

"Just a little something I've been working on, and an opportunity to test it out." Fin shook back his hair, rolled his shoulders. "Brawling with me won't change anything, but I'm open to it if it helps you."

"I'll be the one holding you down while he does the arse kicking." Connor yanked off his coat. "You've no right going off after him on your own."

"Every right in this world and any."

"We're a circle," Iona began.

"We are." Because it was Iona, Fin tempered his tone. "And each of us individual points of it."

"Those points are connected. What happens to you, affects us all." Meara glanced over at Branna, who continued to fuss with tea and biscuits. "All of us."

"He never knew I was there, couldn't see I was following, watching where he went. I was cloaked. It's what I've been working on, and the point of trying it."

"Without letting any of us know what you were about?" Connor tossed out.

"Well, I didn't know for certain it would work till I tried, did I?"

He walked to Branna. "I used some of what I have of him in me to conjure the fog. It's taken weeks—well, months, come to that—for me to perfect it as I only had bits of time here and there to give to it. Today, I saw a chance to try it. Which isn't so different, if you're honest, from taking a ride out into the woods just to see what may be."

"I wasn't alone."

"Nor was I," he countered just as coolly. "I had Merlin, and used his eyes to follow. He's taunted us, and you gave him back a bit, for you know, as we all should, if we look to be doing nothing at all, he'll know we're doing a great deal more. Why else did I make such a show of dispatching the rats?"

Irritation vibrating around him, he turned, lifted his hands. "Is there so little trust here?"

"It's not lack of trust," Iona told him. "You scared us. I thought at first Cabhan had ambushed you, but Branna said you'd made the fog yourself. But we couldn't see you, we didn't know where you were. It scared us."

"For that, *deirfiúr bheag*, I'm sorry. I'm sorry for causing you a minute of fear on my account, any of you, but you most especially who stood for me almost before you knew me."

Iona released a sigh. "Is that your way of getting out of trouble?"

"It's only the truth." He moved to her, kissed her forehead. "I admit I followed the moment, saw a chance, took it. And taking it, we know more than we did, if that's any balance to the scales."

"He's right," Branna said before anyone else could speak. "It may take time for me to cool my anger, as it may for the rest of you, but if we're practical—and we can't be otherwise—Fin's right. He used what he has and is. I wondered why you showed off so blatantly for Cabhan. It was a bit embarrassing."

At Fin's cocked brow, she gestured to Connor. "Take this tea tray by the fire, would you? The jars on the work counter are sealed, but I don't want food near them."

"He used the elements, one after the other, fast—zap, zap," Iona explained. "Wind, fire, earth, water. It was pretty awesome."

"Considerable overkill," Branna said tartly, "but I see the purpose now."

"Since it's done, it's done." Boyle shrugged, took a mug of tea. "I'd like to hear what we know that we didn't, and as no one's in a bloody battle, I've only a few minutes for it, as I've work still to do."

"He ran as the shadow wolf, leaving no tracks in the snow. Fast, very fast, but running, not flying. I think he conserves the energy." Fin took a biscuit, then paced as he spoke. "He only flew to get over the river, and as he spanned it, my mark burned. It costs him to cross the water, and now I know when I feel that, as I have before, he's crossed back to our side of it. He took the woods again, turned toward the lake. It tired him, as he ran a long way, then I felt the change, felt it coming so slowed, pulled Merlin back toward me. The wolf vanished. He'd shifted into another time. His own time, I'd say. And his lair."

"Can you find the way back? Sure and you can find the way back," Connor continued, "or you wouldn't look so fecking smug about it."

"I can find the way to where the wolf shifted, and I think we'll find Cabhan's lair isn't far from there."

"How soon can we go?" Meara demanded. "Tonight?"

"I happen to be free," Connor said.

"Not tonight." Branna shook her head. "There are things to prepare for if we find it. Things we could use. What we find, if anything, would be in our time. But . . ."

"You're after going back, once we find it, on going back to his time." Boyle frowned into his tea. "And take him on there?"

"No, not that. We don't have all we need, and the time has to be our choosing. But if we could leave something in his cave—block it from him, use it to see him there. Hear him. We could get the name. And we might learn his plans before he acts on them."

"Not all of us," Fin countered. "It's too risky for all of us to go back. If we were trapped there, it's done for us. Only one goes."

"And you think that should be you."

He nodded at Branna. "Of course. I can go back, leaving no trace in the cloak of the fog, take your crystal, as that's what's best for seeing, and be out again."

"And if he's in there?" Iona gave Fin a light punch on the shoulder. "You could be done."

"That would be why a couple of us—at least a couple," Connor calculated, "find a way to draw him out, keep him busy." He grinned at Meara. "Would you be up for that?"

"I'd be raring for it."

"So . . ." Grabbing a biscuit, and another for his pocket, Boyle considered. "The four of us go where Fin followed today, and hunt from there. Connor and Meara catch Cabhan's attention so he's after them, and the lair's clear of him. If we find it, Fin takes this crystal, shifts in time back to the fecking thirteenth century, plants the thing in the cave, comes back, and we're all off to the pub for a round."

"That's the broad strokes of it." Branna patted his arm. "We'll fix the small, and important details of it. So we don't go until we do. None of us go near the place." She looked directly at Fin. "Is that agreed?"

"It is," he said, "and I've some ideas on a few of the details."

"As have I." Satisfied, and only a little angry still, Branna took a biscuit for herself.

16

It would take nearly a week before Branna was fully satisfied, and those days took precious hours away from perfecting the poison. Still, she considered it all time well spent.

The timing would be tight, and the circle would be separated at several stages—so every step of every stage had to be carefully plotted.

They chose early evening, so routines could hold and they'd still have an hour or more of light before dusk.

In her workshop, Branna carefully placed the crystal she'd chosen and charmed in a pouch.

"You must place it high, facing the altar, where it will reflect what's below," she told Fin. "And you must move there and back quickly."

"So you've already said."

"It bears repeating. You'll be tempted to linger—as I would be in your place—to see what else you might find, what else you might learn. The longer you're there, in his place and in his time, the more chance there is of you leaving some trace, or of him sensing you."

She placed the pouch in a leather bag, then held up a vial. "Should it go wrong, should he come back before you're done, this should disable him for a few moments, long enough for you to get back to me, Iona, Boyle in our time. It's only if there's no choice."

She pouched the vial, added it to the bag. Stared down at it as she wished what he needed to do didn't need to be done. "Don't risk all for the moment."

"As all includes you, you can be sure I won't."

"Touch nothing of his. Don't—"

"Branna." He cupped her face until their eyes met. "We've been over it all."

"Of course. You're right. And it's time." She handed him the bag, went to get her jacket. "Iona and Boyle will be here any minute."

"When this is done we'll have a window to look in on him as he too often looks in on us. And we'll be able to give all the time needed to the poison that will end it."

"I'm uneasy, that's the truth." She didn't know if it helped to say it, but did know it was foolish, and maybe dangerous, to pretend. "The closer we come to the end of it, and I believe we will end it, there's a pull and tug in me. It's more than confidence and doubt. I don't understand my own feelings, and it makes me uneasy."

"Be easy about this. If for now, only this."

She could only try, as there was no room for doubts, and no time to delay as Iona and Boyle pulled up outside.

She picked up a short sword, fixed the sheath to her belt. "Best be prepared," was all she said as Iona and Boyle came in.

"Connor and Meara are on their way."

"Then we'd best be on ours." Branna reached for Fin's hand, then Boyle's. When Iona took Boyle's other hand, they flew.

Through the cool and the damp, through the wind and over the trees, across the river, then the lake with the castle of Ashford shining behind them.

They landed softly, in a stand of trees, in a place she didn't recognize.

"Here?"

"It's where I lost him. It's been hundreds of years since Midor and his cave," Fin pointed out. "Some houses not far, some roads, but as with Sorcha's cabin, I think the place where Cabhan was made will remain, in some form."

"There's a quiet here." Eyes watchful, Boyle studied the lay of the land. "A kind of hard hush."

Feeling the same, Fin nodded. "We're a superstitious breed, we Irish, and wise enough to build around a faerie hill without disturbing it, to leave a stone dance where it stands. And to keep back from a place where the dark still thrums."

He glanced over at Boyle. "We agreed to stay together, but it's fact we'd cover more ground if we split up."

"Together," Branna said firmly, as she'd expected him to suggest it. "And if the dark still thrums?" She drew out a wand with a tip of glass-clear crystal. "The light will find it."

"I don't recall that being in the plan."

"Best to be prepared," she repeated. She lifted her wand to the sky until the tip pulsed light. And watched Merlin circle above them.

"Between my wand and your hawk, we should find the lair. It pulls north."

"Then we go north." Boyle took Iona's hand in his again, and the four of them headed north.

ON THE OTHER SIDE OF THE RIVER CONNOR AND MEARA walked in the woods. He'd linked with Roibeard, who swooped through the trees, and with Merlin, who watched the rest of the circle travel another wood.

"It's a pleasure to finally have some time to go hawking with you. It's been too long since we just took an hour for it."

"I need to practice more," Meara responded, easy and casual, though her throat was dry. "So I'm full ready when we add the package."

"We could've come on horseback."

"This will do." She lifted a gloved arm for Roibeard, and though the hawking was a ploy, enjoyed having him.

"Would you want a hawk of your own?" Connor asked her.

She glanced at him in genuine surprise. "I've never thought of it."

"You should have your own. A female if you find one who speaks to you. Your hawk and mine could mate."

The idea brought a smile as it seemed a lovely thought, and a normal one. "I've never tended to a hawk on my own."

"I'd help you, but you'd do well with it. You've helped often enough with Merlin when Fin's gone rambling. We could build a place for them when we build our house. If you're still in the mind to build one."

"I've hardly thought of that either, as I'm barely making strides on the wedding." She let Roibeard fly again. "And there's Cabhan to worry about."

"We won't think of him today," Connor said, though both of them thought of little else. "Today we follow Roibeard's dance. Give us a song, Meara, something bright to lift Roibeard's wings."

"Something bright, is it?" She took his hand, swung his arm playfully as they walked. But she wanted that connection, the physical of it, as they both knew the music could bring Cabhan.

They'd planned on it.

She decided on "The Wild Rover," as it was bright enough, and had a number of verses to give Cabhan time to be drawn in, if it was to happen.

She laughed when Connor joined her on the chorus, and any other day would have prized the walk with him, with the hawk, with the song in the pretty woods where the snowmelt left the ground so soft and pools of white still clung to the shady shadows.

When he squeezed her hand, she knew the ploy had worked. And it was time for their part of the scheme.

Her voice didn't falter as she saw the first wisps of fog slithering over the ground, nor when Roibeard landed on a branch nearby—a golden-winged warrior poised to defend.

"I could still your voice with a thought."

Cabhan rose from the fog, and smiled his silky smile when Meara stopped singing to draw her sword. "And so I have. You risk your lady, witch, strolling through the woods without your sister to fight for you."

"I've enough to protect my lady, should she need it. But I think you know she does well protecting herself. Still . . ." Connor ran a finger down Meara's blade, set it alight. "A little something more for my lady."

"What manner of man has his woman stand in front of him?"

"Beside him," Connor corrected, and drew a sword of his own, enflamed it.

"And leaves her unshielded," Cabhan said and hurled black lightning at Meara.

Connor sent it crashing to the ground with a hard twist of wind. "Never unshielded."

ACROSS THE WATER, THE PULSE OF BRANNA'S WAND QUICKened. "Close now."

"There." Fin pointed to a wild tangle of thickets edged with thick black thorns, snaking vines dotted with berries like hard drops of blood. "In there is Midor's cave. I can feel the pull, just as I felt the burn when Cabhan crossed the river. The way's clear."

"It doesn't look clear," Iona said. "It looks lethal." Testing, she tapped the flat of her sword on one of the thorns, listened to the metallic clink of steel to steel. "Sounds lethal."

"I won't be going through them, but through time. Though when this is done we'll come back here, all of us, and burn those thorny vines, salt and sanctify the ground."

"Not yet." Branna took his arm. "Connor hasn't told me Cabhan's taken the bait."

"He has. He's nearly there, and the sooner I'm in and out, the less time Connor and Meara have to stand against him. It's now, Branna, and quick."

Though it filled her with dread, they cast the circle, and she released Fin's hand, accepted it would be done.

"In this place," she chanted with the others, "of death and dark, we send the one who bears the mark through space, through time. Powers of light send him through, let our wills entwine. Send him through, and send him back by the light of the three."

"Come back to me," Branna added, though it hadn't been part of the spell.

"As you will," Fin said, his eyes on hers, "so mote it be."

His fog swirled, and he was gone.

"It won't take long." To comfort, Iona put her arm around Branna's shoulders.

"It's so dark. It's so cold. And he's alone."

"He's not." Boyle took her hand, held it firmly. "We're right here. We're with him."

But he was alone in the cold and the dark. The power here hung so thick and dank he felt nothing beyond it. Black blood stained the ground where Cabhan had shackled and killed his mother.

He scanned the horror of jars, filled with the pieces of the woman who'd birthed him, which Cabhan had preserved for his dark magicks.

The world Fin knew, his world, seemed not just centuries away, but as if it didn't exist. Freeing the demon, giving it form and movement had drawn the cave into its own kind of hell where all the damned burned cold.

He smelled brimstone and blood—old blood and new. It took all his will to resist the sudden, fierce need to go to the altar, take up the cup that stood below a cross of yellowing bones, and drink.

Drink.

Sweat coated his skin though his breath turned to clouds in the frigid air that seemed to undulate like a sea with the fetid drops sliding down the walls and striking the floor in a tidal rhythm.

Something in its beat stirred his blood.

His hand trembled as he forced himself to reach into the bag, open the pouch, take out the crystal.

For a moment Branna was there—warm and strong, so full of light he could slow his pulse again, steady his hands. He rose up within the fog, up the damp wall of the cave. He saw symbols carved in the stone, recognized them from Ogham, though he couldn't read them.

He laid the crystal in a chink, along a fingertip of ledge, and wondered if Branna's charm could be strong enough to hide it from so much dark.

Such deep, fascinating dark, where voices chanted, and those to be sacrificed screamed and wept for a mercy that would never be given.

Why should mercy be given to the less? Their cries and screams of torment were true music, a call to dance, a call to feed.

The dark must be fed. Embraced. Worshipped.

The dark would reward. Eternally.

Fin turned to the altar, took a step toward it. Then another.

"IT'S TAKING TOO LONG." BRANNA RUBBED HER ARMS TO fight a cold that dug into her bones and came from fear. "It's nightfall. He's been more than half an hour now, and far too long."

"Connor?" Iona asked. "He's—"

"I know, I know. He and Meara can't hold Cabhan much longer. Go to Connor, you and Boyle go to Connor and Meara, help them.

I'll go through for Fin. Something's wrong, something's happened. I haven't been able to feel or sense him since he went through."

"You'll not go in. Branna, you'll not." Boyle took her shoulders, gave her a little shake. "We have to trust Fin to get back, and we can't risk you. Without you, it ends here, and not for Cabhan."

"His blood could betray him, however much he fights it. I can pull him out. I have to try before. Ah, God, Cabhan, he's coming back. Fin—"

"Can we pull him back, the two of us?" Iona gripped Branna's hand. "We have to try."

"With all of us, we might . . . Oh, thank the gods."

When Fin, his fog thin and faded, fell to his knees on the ground at her feet, Branna dived for him.

"He's coming," Fin managed. "It's done, but he's coming. We have to go, and quickly. I could use some help."

"We've got you." Branna wrapped her arms around him, looked at Iona, at Boyle, nodded. "We've got you," she repeated, and held on to him as they flew.

His skin was ice, and she couldn't warm it as she pulled him over treetops, over the lake, and the castle aglow with lights.

She brought him straight to the cottage, set the fire to roaring before she knelt in front of him. "Look at me. Fin, I have to see your eyes."

They glowed against the ice white of his face, but they were Fin's, and only his.

"I brought nothing back with me," he told her. "Left nothing of me. Only your crystal."

"Whiskey." But even as she snapped it out, Boyle sat beside Fin, cupped Fin's hands around the glass.

"I feel I've walked a hundred kilometers in the Arctic without a single rest." He gulped down whiskey, let his head fall back as Connor and Meara came in.

"Is he hurt?" Connor demanded.

"No, only half frozen and exhausted. Are you?"

"A few singes, and I'll see to them."

"He's already seen to mine." Meara moved straight to Fin. "Clucking like a mother hen over me. What can we do for you, Fin?"

"I'm well enough."

"You don't look it. Should I get one of your potions, Branna?"

"I don't need a potion. The whiskey's fine. And you're doing some clucking yourself, Mother."

Meara dropped into a chair. "The way you are makes a ghost look like it's had ten days in the tropics."

Warming bit by painful bit, Fin smiled at her. "You're not looking rosy yourself."

"He kept going at her," Connor said, and surprised Meara by lifting her up—strapping girl that she was—taking her place, then cuddling her on his lap. "He'd go for me, but that was for show. He wanted our Meara, to hurt her, so kept hammering against her protection, looking for the slightest chink. At first we tried to draw it all out, give the rest of you time, but it went on longer than we thought, and it was get serious about it, or fall back."

"Connor made a tornado." Meara spun a finger in the air. "A small one you could say, but impressive. Then turned it to fire. And that sent Cabhan on his way."

"We couldn't hold him longer," Connor finished.

"It was long enough. We'll all have some whiskey," Branna decided. "Let me see where you're burned, Connor, and I'll tend to it."

"I'll do it." Iona nudged Branna back down. "Stay with Fin."

"I'm well enough," Fin insisted. "It was the cold, that was the most of it. It's so sharp, so bitter it carves the life out of you. Enervates. It's more than it was," he said to Branna. "More than we saw and felt."

She sat on the floor, took one of the glasses Boyle passed around. "Tell us."

"It was darker, darker than it was when we went in the dreamwalk. Colder, and the air thick. So thick you couldn't get a full breath. There was a cauldron on the fire, and it smelled of sulphur and brimstone. And there were voices chanting. I couldn't make out the words, not enough of them, but it was in Latin, and some in old Irish. As were the screams, the pleading that rose up with them. Those being sacrificed. All of that, a kind of echo, in the distance. Still, I could smell the blood."

He took a drink, gathered himself again. "There was a pull to it, from in me. A wanting of it, stronger than before, this pull and tug in two directions. I put the crystal up, a little notch in the stones, high on the wall across from the altar."

Now he turned the glass in his hands, staring down into the amber of the whiskey as if seeing it all again.

"And when I no longer had it with me, the need was more. Bigger. The pull more alluring, you could say. There was a cup on the altar, and in it blood. I wanted it. Coveted it. Innocent blood, that I could smell. The blood of an innocent, and if I only took it, drank it, I would become what I was meant to become. Why was I resisting that? Didn't I want that—my own destiny, my own glory? So I stepped toward the altar, and went closer yet. All the chanting filled the cave, and those screams were almost like music to me. I reached for the cup. I held my hand out to take it. Finally just take it."

He paused, knocked back the rest of the whiskey. "And through all the screaming, the chanting, the pulsing of that thick air, I heard you." He looked down at Branna. "I heard you. 'Come back to me,' you'd said, and what was in me wanted that more than all the rest. Needed that more than the blood I could already taste in the back of my throat.

"So I backed away, and the air, it got colder yet, and was so thick now it was like wet rags in my lungs. I was dizzy and sick and shaky. I think I fell, but I said the words, and I was out, I was back."

He set the glass aside. "You need to know the whole of it, the full of it. How close I came. No more than a fingerbrush away from turning, and once turned, I would have turned again on all of you."

"But you didn't take it," Iona said. "You came back."

"I wanted it. Something in me was near to desperate for it."

"And still you didn't take it," Connor pointed out. "And here you sit, drinking whiskey by the fire."

"I would've broken trust with you—"

"Bollocks," Branna interrupted and surged to her feet. "Bollocks to that, Finbar. And don't sit there saying you came back for me, for you didn't come back for me alone, or for any of us alone. You came back as much for yourself. For the respect you have for who you are, for your gift, and for your abhorrence of all Cabhan is. So bollocks. I didn't let myself trust you in the beginning of this, and you proved me wrong time and time again. I won't have it, I'm telling you, I won't have you sit here after all that and not trust yourself.

"I'm going to heat up the stew. We all need to eat after this."

When she sailed out, Meara nodded, rose. "That says it all and plainly enough. Iona, let's give Branna a hand in the kitchen."

When they left, Boyle went for the whiskey, poured more in Fin's glass. "If you're going to feel sorry for yourself, you'd do better doing it a bit drunk."

"I'm not feeling sorry for myself, for fuck's sake. Did you hear what I said to you?"

"I heard it, we all heard it." Connor stretched out his legs, slouched down in the chair with his own whiskey. "We heard you fought a battle, inward and outward, and won it. So cheers to you. And I'll tell you something I know as easy as I know my own name. You'd slit your own throat before you'd do harm to Branna, or to any one of us. So drink up, brother, and stop acting the gom."

"Acting the gom," Fin muttered, and because it was there, drank the whiskey.

And because they knew him, his friends let him brood.

He waited until they were all in the kitchen, until everyone had taken a seat but himself.

"I'm grateful," he began.

"Shut the feck up and sit down to eat," Boyle suggested.

"You shut the feck up. I'm grateful and have a right to say as much."

"So noted and acknowledged." Branna ladled stew in his bowl. "Now shut the feck up and eat."

He sampled some of the hearty beef and barley stew, felt it slide down to the cold still holding in his belly, and spread warmth again.

"What's in it besides the beef and barley and potatoes?"

Branna shrugged. "There's none of us here couldn't do with a little tonic after this day."

"It's good." Connor spooned some up. "More than good, so here's another, Fin, advising you to shut the feck up."

"Fine and well." Fin reached for the bread on the dish. "Then I won't tell you the rest of it, since you're not interested."

"What rest?" Iona demanded.

It was Fin's turn to shrug. "I've shut the feck up, as advised."

"I didn't tell you to or so advise you." Meara smiled sweetly. "I'm interested enough so you can talk to me."

"All right then, to your interest, Meara, there were carvings on the walls in the cave. Old ones. Ogham script."

"Ogham?" Connor frowned. "Are you sure of it?"

As it made him feel himself again, Fin ate more stew. "I'm speaking with Meara here."

"Oh, give it over." But Boyle laughed as he helped himself to the bread. "Ogham then? What did it say?"

Fin spared him a long, dry look. "My talents are many but don't stretch far enough to read Ogham. But it tells us the cave's been used, and as the script was high on the walls, and with magickal symbols here and there as well, very likely for dark purposes long before Cabhan's time."

"Some places are inherent for the dark, or for the light," Branna speculated.

"What I felt there was all of the dark, like . . . a rooting place for it. The shadows moved like living things. And on the altar, as I was close enough to see, there were bones in a dish along with the cup of blood. Three black candles, and a book with a hide cover. Carved on it is the mark." He touched his shoulder. "This mark."

"So it goes back, the mark, before Teagan threw the stone and scarred Cabhan. Before Sorcha cursed him." Iona angled her head. "A symbol of the demon in him? Or of his own dark places? I'm sorry," she said quickly.

"No need." Fin picked up his spoon again. "Near the book was a bell, again silver, with a wolf standing on its hind legs as a handle."

"Bell, book, and candle, bones and blood. The symbol of Cabhan's mark, the symbol of the wolf." Branna considered. "So he had these things, symbols of what he became. Old things?"

"Very old, all but the candles. And they . . . made from human tallow mixed with blood."

"Can it get more disgusting?" Meara wondered.

Connor gave her a pat. "I expect it can."

"His tools," Branna speculated, "perhaps passed down from father to son, or mother to son or daughter. Passed down to him, and then used for the dark. Though we can't say if his sire didn't dabble in such, or why he would've chosen the cave for his own."

"He might've been a guardian," Meara suggested. "Someone with power who guarded the demon or whatever it is, and kept it imprisoned."

"True enough," Branna agreed. "Whether or not Cabhan came from light or dark, or something between them, he made his choice."

"There's more," Fin told her. "A wax figure of a woman, bound hand and foot with black cloth, kneeling as in supplication."

"Sorcha." Branna shook her head. "His obsession with her started long ago. But he could never bind her or bring her to her knees."

"Nearly eight hundred years is a long time to hold an obsession or a grudge," Iona pointed out. "I'd say it's been madness that started long ago."

"I'd agree."

"And more," Fin said again. "The figure had blood smeared on its belly, between its legs."

Carefully, Branna set her spoon down. "She lost a child, early that winter. She miscarried, and was never fully well again. She had some terrible illness she couldn't heal. Tearing pains in the belly."

"He killed her child?" Even with centuries of distance, Iona's eyes filled. "Inside her? Could he do that?"

"I don't know." Shaken, Branna rose, got wine for herself and brought the bottle to the table. "If she didn't guard against it, in just the right way? If he found some way to . . . She had three children to tend to, and her husband off with the men of their clan. Cabhan hounding her. She may have given him some vulnerable spot to use, had a moment when she wasn't fully vigilant."

"We will be." Fin touched a hand to hers. "We'll give him nothing, and we'll take all. This is yet more he must answer for."

"She was grieving. You can hear her tears in her book when she wrote of the loss. Yes," Branna said quietly. "He must answer for this, and for all."

17

SHE INCREASED HER EFFORTS. IT COULDN'T BE RUSHED—no, working with a lethal mix couldn't be hurried. But Branna spent every minute she could on concocting the poison.

Whoever from her circle spent time in her workshop took on a task—magickal or otherwise. She herself rarely went out, beyond a walk through her winter gardens to clear her head of formulas and spells and poisons.

Even on those brief walks, Branna obsessed whether five drops of tincture from the angel's trumpet were too much or four too little. Should the crushed berries be freshly used, or allowed to steep in their juices?

"It matters," she muttered, half to herself as she meticulously lined up the jars for the day's attempt. "One drop off, and we start again."

"You said the four drops didn't work yesterday, so do the five," Connor suggested.

"And if it should be six?" Frustrated, she stared at the jars as if she could will them to tell her the secret. "Or is the other recipe I found the true one, the one that calls for five death cap mushrooms, taken from under an oak?"

"The more poison the better, if you're asking me."

"It can't be more or less. It's not like cooking up a kitchen-sink soup." Though she heard the testiness in her own voice, she simply couldn't smooth it out. "It *must* be right, Connor, and I feel this may be our only chance. If we fail, at best we have to wait another year before trying again. At worst, the demon finds a way to shield himself when he finds we've a way to attack it."

"You're fretting far too much, Branna. It's not your way to fret and second-guess."

He was right, of course, and fretting, she admitted as she pressed her fingers to her eyes, tended to block more than open.

"I feel an urgency, more than I have. A knowing, Connor, this *must* be the time, or our time is done. And the thought we might only go on slapping at Cabhan as we have, for our lifetime, only hold him off until we pass this duty to the next three? It's not bearable. You'll have children with Meara. Would you want to weigh one or more of them with this?"

"I wouldn't, no. Of course, I wouldn't. We won't fail."

He put his hands on her shoulders, rubbed them. "Ease your mind a bit. You'll block your own instincts—and they're a strength—if you pour in all this doubt."

"This will be the third time I've tried creating the brew. The doubt's there for a reason."

"Then put it aside. This recipe, that recipe, put that aside as well. What do you think—how does it feel to you? Maybe it's not like throwing together a soup, but you've been mixing potions since you were four."

Deliberately, he closed the books, knowing full well by now she could recite it all by rote in any case. "What do you say—not just from the head this time, but from the belly?"

"I say . . ." She shoved impatiently at her hair. "Where the devil is Fin? I need his blood for this, and I want it fresh."

"He said he'd be here before noon, so he will. Why don't I work on the order with you, and the words? Then when he comes, you'll bleed him, and begin."

"All right, all right."

Time to stop fussing and fiddling and *do*, she ordered herself.

"The blessed water would be first. I've got 'First we pour the water blest to form the pool for all the rest. Belladonna berries crushed and steeped, stirring juices slow and deep. Hair from a pregnant yak mixed with manchineel tree sap to dissolve the wing of bat. Angel's trumpet, wolfsbane petals, add them in and wait to settle. Then . . ."

"What do you think, Branna?" Connor prompted.

"Well, I think I rushed it last time. I think this stage needs to work, to boil a bit."

"So . . . Stir and boil and bubble and stir . . ."

"Until the rise of smoke occurs—yes, I rushed it. It should boil and steam a bit. All right." With a firm nod, she wrote more notes. "The mushrooms, we'll try the mushrooms as—what the bloody hell, it feels right."

"There we are now." Connor gave her an elbow poke of encouragement.

"Caps of death soft and white, bring about eternal night. No, no, not for a demon." She crossed it out, started again. "Caps of death three plus two, spread your poison through this brew."

"Better," Connor agreed.

"And the conium petals. Ah, pretty petals sprinkled in, let this lethal magick begin."

"Deadly magick's better, I think."

"Yes, deadly." She made the change. "Blood to bind it, drop by drop, and the demon heart will stop. Power of me, power of three, here fulfill our destiny. As we will, so mote it be."

She dropped the pencil on the counter. "I'm not sure."

"I like it—it sounds right. It's strong enough, Branna, but not fussy. It's death we're dealing, so there's no need for frills."

"You've a point there. Bloody hell, it needs to thicken, go black. I need to add that. Blacken, thicken under my hands . . ."

"To make this poison for the damned," Connor finished.

"I quite like that," she considered. "I want to write it all up fresh."

"If you can't start until Fin's here, why don't you—" He broke off, turning to the door as Fin came in. "Well, here he is now. She's after bleeding you, mate."

Fin stopped in his tracks. "I gave more than enough yesterday, and the day before."

"I want fresh."

"She wants fresh," Fin grumbled and tossed off his coat. "What are you doing with what's left I bled for you yesterday, and the day before that?"

"It's safe—and you never know when it might be useful. But I want to start it all fresh today. I've changed some of the spell."

"Again?"

"Yes, again," she said in as irritable a tone as he. "It needed work. Connor agreed—"

"I'm not in this." Connor held up his hands. "The two of you sort this out. In fact, now that you're here, Fin, I'm off. It's Boyle, I think, who's coming in a bit later, so he can sweep up the leavings if the two of you battle."

He grabbed his coat, his cap, his scarf, and was out the door with Kathel slipping out with him—as if the dog agreed some distance wouldn't hurt a thing.

"Why are you so cross?" Branna demanded.

"Me? Why are you? You've got that I'm-annoyed-at-every-fecking-thing between your eyebrows."

Only more annoyed, Branna rubbed her fingers to smooth out any such line. "I'm not annoyed—yes, I bloody well am, but not at every fecking thing, or at you. I'm not used to failing so spectacularly the way I am with this damnable brew."

"Not getting it right isn't failing."

"Getting it right is success, so its opposite is failing."

"They called it practicing magicks for a reason, Branna, and you know it full well."

She started to snap, then just sighed. "I do know it. I do. I thought I'd come closer the first few times than I have. If I keep missing by so wide a mark, I'll need to send for the ingredients again."

"So we start fresh." He walked to her, kissed her. "Good day to you, Branna."

She let out a half laugh. "And good day to you, Finbar." Smiling, she picked up her knife. "And so . . ."

She expected him to roll up his sleeve, but he pulled off his sweater.

"Take it from the mark," he told her. "As you did for the poison for Cabhan. From the mark, Branna, as you should have done the first time with this."

"I should have, it's true. It hurts you, it burns you, when I take blood from there."

"Because the purpose is the enemy of the mark. Take it from there, Branna. Then I want a damn biscuit."

"You can have half a dozen."

She stepped to him with the ritual knife and the cup.

"Don't block it." He drew her eyes to him. "The pain may be part of it. We'll let it come, and let it go."

"All right."

She was quick—quick was best—and scored across the pentagram with the tip of her blade. She caught the blood in the cup—felt the pain though he made no sound, no movement.

"That's enough," she murmured, and set the knife aside to pick up the cloth she had ready, pressed it to the wound.

Then, putting the cup by the jars, turned back to him to gently heal the shallow wound.

Before he knew what she was about—perhaps before she did—Branna pressed a kiss to the mark.

"Don't." Stunned, appalled to the marrow, he jerked back. "I don't know how it might harm you, what it might do."

"It will do nothing to me, as you did nothing to earn it. I spent years trying to blame you for it, and should have blamed Sorcha—or more, her grief. She harmed you—she broke our most sacred oath, and harmed you, and many before you. Innocents. I'd take it from you if I could."

"You can't. Do you think I haven't tried?" He yanked on his sweater again. "Witchcraft, priests, wise women, holy men, magicks black and white. Nothing touches it. I've been to every corner of the world where there was so much of a whisper of a rumor the curse could be broken."

His rambles, she realized. This was their basis. "You never said—"

"What could I say?" he countered. "This visible symbol of what runs inside me can't be changed, it can't be removed by any means I've tried. No spell, no ritual can break the curse she cast with her dying breaths. It can't be burned off, cut off or out of me. Considered lopping my arm off, but feared it would just sear in on another part of me."

"You— Good God, Fin."

He hadn't meant to say so much, but couldn't take back the words. "Well, I was more than a bit drunk at the time, fortunately, as cursed is cursed, two-armed or one, despite what seemed desperately heroic at two and twenty, when shattered on the best part of a bottle of Jameson."

"You won't harm yourself," she said, shaken to the core. "You won't think of it."

"No point in it, as I've been told time and again when all attempts failed. The curse of a dying witch—and one who'd sacrificed herself for her children, to protect them from the darkest of purposes?—it's powerful."

"When this is done, I would help you find a way—all of us—"

"It's for me, if there is a way, and I won't ever stop looking, as because of this you can't give me tomorrows. I can't ask for them or give them to you. We could never have children." He nodded. "I see you know that, too. Neither of us would bring a child into the world knowing he would carry this burden."

"No." Despair, and brutal acceptance, twisted her heart. "And when this is done . . . you'll go again."

"When this is done, could either of us be together as we are, knowing we'd never have the life we once imagined? Knowing this"—he touched his shoulder—"stands between us even after Cabhan's end? As long as I wear it, he doesn't truly end, and Sorcha's curse goes on, in me. So I'll never stop looking for a way."

"So her curse comes back threefold. You, me, and the life we might have had."

"We have today. It's more than I believed I'd have with you again."

"I thought it would be enough." She walked into his arms, held tight.

"We'd best not waste it."

"No, we won't waste it." She lifted her face, lifted her lips to his. "If I could wish it, we'd be ordinary."

He could smile. "You could never be ordinary."

"Just a woman who makes soaps and candles, and has a pretty shop in the village. And you just a man who has the stables and the falconry. If I could wish it. But . . ."

As she did, he looked at the counter, with the spell books, the jars. "If we were ordinary, we couldn't do what has to be done. Best try the spell or you'll be bleeding me again saying the blood's not fresh enough."

Duty, she thought, and destiny. Neither could be shirked.

She got the cauldron, lit its fire low.

The long, painstaking process took precision and power—step by careful step. Branna ordered herself to put all the previous failures aside, to treat this as the first attempt. The toxic brew bubbled and smoked as both she and Fin held their hands over the cauldron to slowly, slowly stir.

She drew a breath as they approached the final step.

"Blacken, thicken under my hands," she said.

Fin followed. "To make this poison for the damned."

"Power of me," they said together as with the words the brew bubbled forcibly. "Power of three, here fulfill our destiny. As we will, so mote it be."

She felt the change, the spread of power and will, from her, from Fin. They reached for each other, linking that power and that will, letting it merge and, merging, increase.

Blocking all else, she focused only on that merging, that purpose, while her heart began a hard, quick tattoo in her breast, while the warmth and scents of her workshop faded away.

All light, bright and brilliant, rising in her, flowing from her. Blooming with what rose and flowed from him.

A meeting, physical, intimate, psychic, potent that built like a storm, ripped through her like a climax.

Her head fell back. She lifted her arms, palms up, fingers spread.

"Here, a weapon forged against the dark. Fired by faith and light. On the Dark Witch's sacrificial ground, three by three by three will stand against the evil born in the black. Blood and death follow. Bring horse, hawk, hound together, and say the name. Ring bell, open book, light candle, say the name. Into fire white, all light, blinding bright, cast the stone and close the door. Blood and death follow. Be it demon, be it mortal, be it witch, blood and death follow."

Her eyes, which had gone black, rolled back white. Fin managed to catch her before she fell, simply folded like a puppet with its strings nipped.

Even as he swept her up, she pressed a hand to his shoulder.

"I'm all right. Just dizzy for a minute."

"You'll sit right here." He laid her on the little sofa in front of the fire, then going to her stock, scanned until he found what he wanted.

He didn't bother to put the kettle on, but made tea with a snap of his fingers, poured six drops of the tonic into it, then brought it to her.

"Drink and don't argue," he ordered. "It's your own potion."

"I was there, all the light and power rising up, and the brew stirring in the cauldron, thickening, bubbling. Then I was watching myself, and you, and hearing the words I spoke without speaking them. I've had flashes of what's to come before—all of us have—but nothing so strong or overtaking as that. I'm all right now, I promise you."

Or nearly, she thought and drank the laced tea.

"It's only when it left me, it was like being emptied out entirely for just a moment."

"Your eyes went black as the dark of the moon, and your voice echoed as if from a mountaintop."

"I wasn't myself."

"You weren't, no. What came in you, Branna?"

"I don't know. But the strength and the light of it was consuming. And, Fin, it was beautiful beyond the telling. It's all that we are, but so brilliantly magnified, a thousand suns all around and inside at once. It's the only way I know to tell you."

She drank more tea, felt herself begin to settle again. "I want to write it down, everything I said. It wouldn't do to forget."

"I won't be forgetting it, not a word."

She smiled. "Best to write it down in any case. A weapon forged—it must have worked then."

"The poison's black and thick as pitch."

"We have to seal it, keep it in the dark, and charm the bottle to hold it."

"I'll take care of it."

"No, no, we conjured it together, and there's something to that,

I think. So we should do the rest together as well. I'm altogether fine, Fin, I promise you."

She set the tea aside, got to her feet to prove her words. "It should be done quickly. I wouldn't want the poison to turn and have to go through the whole business again."

He kept an eye on her until he was fully satisfied.

After they sealed the spell, she took two squat bottles, both opaque and black, from the cabinet under her work counter.

"Two?"

"We made enough, as I thought it wise to have a second. If something should happen to the first—before or during—we'll have another."

"Smart and, as always, practical." When she started to get out a funnel, he shook his head. "I don't think this is something we do that way. I understand, again, your practicality, but I think, for this, we stay with power."

"You may be right. One for you, then, one for me. It should be quickly done, then stopped tight, again sealed." She touched one of the bottles. "Yours." Then the other. "Mine." And walked back to stand with him by the cauldron. "Pot to bottle, leaving no trace on the air, no drop on the floor."

She linked one hand with his, held the other out, as he did. Two thin streams of oily black rose out of the cauldron, arched toward the bottles, slid greasily in. When the stream ended, they floated the stoppers up, in.

"Out of light, sealed tight, open only for the right."

Relieved, Branna flashed white fire into the cauldron to burn any trace left behind. "Better safe," she said as she moved to take the bottles, store them deep in a cupboard where she kept the jars of ingredients used, and the poison already prepared for Cabhan. "Though I'll destroy the cauldron. It shouldn't be used again. A pity, as it's served me well." Then she charmed the door of the cupboard. "It will only open for one of our circle."

She went to another cupboard, took out a pale green bottle basketed in silver filigree, then chose two wineglasses.

"And what's this?"

"It's a wine I made myself, and put by here for a special occasion—not knowing what that might be. It seems it's this. We've done what we must, and I'll tell you true, Fin, I wasn't sure we would or could. Each time I thought I was certain of it, we'd fail. But today?"

She poured the pale gold wine in both glasses, offered him one. "Today we haven't failed. So . . ."

Understanding, he touched his glass to hers. "We'll drink to today." He sipped, angled his head. "Well now, here's yet another talent, for this is brilliant. Both light and bold at once. It tastes of stars."

"You could say I added a few. It is good," she agreed. "We've earned good this day. And as I recall, you've earned a biscuit."

"Half a dozen was the offer," he remembered, "but now I think we've both earned something more than biscuits." He swung an arm around her waist. "You'd best hold on to your wine," he warned, and took her flying.

IT MADE HER GIDDY, THE SURPRISE AND SPEED OF IT. MADE her hunger as his mouth took hers on the flight. She let out a gasping laugh when she found herself sprawled under him on a huge bed draped with filmy white curtains.

"So this is what we've earned?"

"More than."

"I've lost my wine."

"Not at all." He gestured so she looked over, saw a table holding the glasses. And saw both bed and table floated on a deep blue sea.

"Now who's practical? But where are we? Ah, it's so warm. It's wonderful."

"The South Seas, far away from all but us, and circled so not even the fish might see."

"The South Seas, on a floating bed. There's a bit of madness in you."

"When it comes to you. An hour or two with you, Branna, in our own window into paradise. Where we're warm and safe, and you're naked." And so she was in a fingersnap. Before she could laugh again, he slid his hands up and over her breasts. "By the gods, I love having you naked and under me. We've done what we must," he reminded her. "Now we take what we want."

His mouth came down on hers, hot and possessive, to send the need sizzling through her like a lit fuse. She answered, not with surrender, but equal fire and force.

The magicks merged still pulsed through them, bright and fierce, so each opened to it, and each other.

The crazed rush of his lips over her skin, brewed a storm of lust. The urgency of her seeking hands whipped the storm into a whirlwind. They tumbled over the bed as it rocked over the wide, rolling sea while inside them waves of need rose and broke only to rise again, an endless tide.

If this was his madness, she'd take it willingly, and flood him with her own. Love, beyond reason, simply swamped her. And here, in this window of alone he'd given them, she could ride on it. Here, where there was only the truest of magicks, she could offer it back to him.

Her body quaked, her heart trembled. So much to feel, so much to want. When a cry of pleasure broke from her, it carried across the blue into forever.

To have her, completely, where no one could touch them. To give her the fantasy she so rarely took for herself, and to know she reached for, took, accepted all he felt for her, would ever feel for her. That alone filled him with more than all the powers, all the magicks, all the mysteries.

No words needed. All she felt lived in her eyes, all he felt mirrored back to him from hers.

When he filled her, it was a torrent of pleasure and love and lust. When she closed tight, so tight around him, it was unity.

They drove each other hard and fast, in a world only theirs with the deep blue sea rocking beneath them. She lay with him, lulled by the quiet lap of water against the bed, the warmth of the sun, the scent of the sea. And the feel of him against her, hot, slick skin to skin.

"Why this place," she asked him, "of all the places?"

"It seemed beyond all we have and know together. We have the green and the wet in us, and wouldn't cast it out. But this? The warm and the blue? A bit of the fanciful for someone who rarely gifts herself with it. And all gods know, Branna, the winter's been cold and hard."

"It has. But at the end of it, we'll have more than spring. We'll have duty done, and the light and breath that comes from it. When it's done . . ."

He lifted his head, looked into her eyes. "Ask."

"Bring me back here again, for both of us, when what's done is done. And before you go wherever you must. Bring me back."

"I will. You'll want to go home now."

"No. No, let's stay awhile." She shifted, sat up, and reached for the glasses. "We'll finish our wine and enjoy the sun and the water. Let's take the fancy of this a little longer. For there'll be little time or chance for it once we return."

She leaned her head on his shoulder, sipped the starry wine, and watched the sea that spread to the far horizon.

18

WHEN THE SIX OF THEM MANAGED TO COME TOGETHER, Branna opted for a quietly celebrational meal of rack of lamb, roasted butternut squash, and peas with butter and mint.

"Sure I didn't expect such a fuss," Connor said as he took charge of carving the chops from the rack. "Not that I'm complaining."

"It's the first time we've sat down, the six of us, in near to a week," Branna pointed out. "We've all talked here and there, and we all know what's been done and where we are. The brew's curing well. I checked it only this afternoon." She took a dollop of the squash for her plate, passed the bowl. "Connor and I made a second bottle of the poison needed for Cabhan, so like the demon's brew, we'll have that in case something goes amiss."

"I'm not going to think of misses." Meara handed off the peas to Boyle. "Near to a year now that evil bastard's been dogging us—longer I know for the three, but in this year he's taunted and attacked with barely a respite. Third time's the charm, isn't it? I'm believing in that—and thinking that every time I see him when I'm out on a guided."

"Today?" Branna asked.

"Today, and every day now, lurking in the woods, even keeping pace for a time. A little closer to the track, it seems. Close enough that twice now, Roibeard's flown in and taken a dive at him. It. Whatever the bloody hell."

"He does it to rattle us," Boyle pointed out. "It's best not to rattle."

"True enough." With the chops severed, Connor took two for himself. "He's getting stronger or bolder, or both. I've seen him skulking about when out on a hawk walk. But today, our Brian mentioned he'd seen a wolf cross the path."

"As Mrs. Baker saw him," Branna added.

"Indeed. Now with Brian, who tends to think an errant wind may be a sign of the apocalypse, it was easy enough to convince him he'd only caught sight of a stray dog. But it's a concern he's showing himself to others."

"Would he hurt them?" Iona demanded. "We can't let him hurt an innocent."

"He would." Fin kept his calm. "It's more likely he'll keep whatever he has for us, but he would and could hurt others. Someone else with power might tempt him, for that would be a kind of feeding."

"Or a woman." Boyle waited a beat, then nodded when no one spoke. "We all know he has needs in that area. So would he take a woman, and if we think he may, how can we stop it?"

"We can spread the protection farther than we have," Branna began. "If he decided to slake that thirst it would be with the young and attractive. The vulnerable. We can do what we can."

"It's not how I'd go about it." Fin sliced lamb from the bone very precisely. "He can shift his times, he can go when and where he likes. Why draw more attention to where he is, and what he plans here? In his place I'd go back, a hundred years or more, take what I wanted, do what I wished, and set no alarm around here."

"So, we can't do anything about it, can't help whoever he'd hurt," Iona said.

"We'll destroy him," Branna reminded her. "And that's doing all there is to do."

"But it's a month before the anniversary of Sorcha's death."

"He's had eight hundred years to do his worst." Boyle laid a hand over Iona's. "We can only deal with now."

"I know it. I know, and still we can only do so much. There's so much power here, but we're helpless to stop him from doing harm."

"I look through the crystal every morning," Branna told her. "And every night. Often more than that. I've seen him working, and seen some of the spells he conjures. There's blood, always, but I've yet to see him bring a mortal or witch into his cave. I've yet to see or hear anything that would help us."

"It's all we can do now." Connor looked around the table. "Until we do more. It's a month, and that feels long, but in fact, we've more things to gather before that time's up. We need the brew and spell for the cauldron to destroy the stone. With light, as Branna prophesied."

"I've a fine one for that," Branna assured him. "And only need you and Iona to finish it with me. It's for the three to do," she explained to all.

"And so we will," Connor responded. "But we don't yet have the name, and without it, we can't finish it off, no matter the poison, no matter the light."

"Lure out the wolf," Branna considered. "Long enough for me, or Fin come to that, to search its mind and find it."

"We can't know, in that form, if he'd have the name in his mind," Fin pointed out. "Cabhan sleeps, at some point he must sleep."

"You think to go into his dreams?" Connor shook his head. "There's too deep a risk, Fin. And more for you than any of us."

"If Branna watches the crystal, and we know when he sleeps, I might join with him with the rest of you ready to pull me out."

"I won't be a part of it. I won't," Branna said when Fin turned to her. "We can't, and I won't, risk you, and risk all, and for this last piece we've weeks yet to find on our own, another way. You barely pulled yourself away the last time."

"It's not the same as that."

"I'm with Branna on this," Boyle put in. "He'd twist you more than any of the rest of us. If it comes down to it, and we have only that way, it must be someone else. Any one of us here."

"Because you don't trust me."

"Don't play the donkey's arse," Boyle said coolly. "There's not a one at this table who doesn't trust you with their lives, and the lives of those they love."

"You're valued." Scowling, Meara leaned toward Fin. "And that's the why of it. And it's too late not to play the donkey's arse, as you just did."

"Apologies, but it's fact what you see as risk is also advantage, as I could get into his dreams, and out again, quicker than any of us."

"It's off the table." Connor deliberately continued to eat. "And shoving it on again only spoils a fine meal. In any case, I've a thought on all this, if anyone wants to hear it."

"He has thoughts." Smiling now, Meara gave him an elbow nudge. "I've been a witness to the occasion."

"And my thought is, we might try Kathel. We might have Kathel go along with me, or with Meara or Iona during the walks or guideds. It may be Kathel can find what's going on in the mind of the wolf, and then Branna could find it from Kathel."

"That's not as foolish as it sounds," Branna considered.

"Thanks for that." Connor helped himself to another chop.

"I can give him leave to go, then we can see. I've been wondering about the vision I had, the words I spoke that weren't my own when we finished the brew. Three and three and three."

"Well, the three here, the three in their own time," Connor said, "and Fin with Boyle and Meara. It seems clear."

"It felt more. It's hard to say, but it felt more. And even if it's so simple, we've got to bring Sorcha's three together with us, at the time, in that place. It's our time, that *was* clear. Not theirs, but ours, so we have to keep Cabhan closed in to that."

"Bell, book, candle." Iona pushed peas around her plate. "Basic tools. And the need for our guides to be there."

"Blood and death follow." Meara picked up the wine, topped off her glass, then Iona's. "We've known that all along. Witch, demon, or mortal blood and death doesn't change it."

"You're valued." Branna looked from Meara to Boyle. "Sister and brother, for the choice you've made for love and loyalty, for right, and for light. We've always known your worth, but it's clear now so the fates do as well."

A thought wound through her head. Branna drew it back as Connor leaned over to kiss Meara and make her laugh. She kept it there, twirling it like a ribbon as her circle finished the meal.

OVER THE NEXT FEW DAYS SHE STUDIED AND TWIRLED THAT ribbon over and over. She saw how it could be done, but had to be certain it should be done. And in the end, whatever her own decision, it had to be a choice for all.

She slipped out of bed, on impulse taking her violin with her. Leaving Fin sleeping, she went down to her workshop where she kept her ball of crystal on a stand. After carrying it to the table, she lit the fire, and three candles. Then she sat, quietly playing while she watched Cabhan sleep in a sumptuous bed of gold in a dark chamber of his cave.

His own fire burned low and red, and she wondered what images he saw in the flames. Blood and death, as had been foretold? Or did he see only his own desires?

She could have sent her music to him, disturbed his sleep as thoughts of him too often disturbed hers. But she wanted to leave no trace for him to follow back to what she loved.

So she played for her own comfort and pleasure as she kept vigil.

She sensed him before he spoke, looked over as Fin came to sit beside her.

"You don't sleep enough, or rest well enough when you do."

"I'll be doing both when this is finished. See how well he sleeps. Is that a saying? The guilty lose little sleep? Something of the kind, I think."

"But he dreams, I know it."

"Put it away, Finbar. There are five who stand against you there, so the one must bend to the five. I know the wish of it. I thought, well, I could give him a troubled night, by only sending my music into his dreams. But why? What we do, what we send, it can be turned back on us. And we know what we will do, when March winds down."

"What will we do? There's something in here." He tapped her temple. "Something you're not saying to the rest of us. One not bending to five, Branna?"

"Not that at all. I haven't worked it all through yet. I promise you I'll tell you, and all—however I find I stand on it at the end. I only want to be sure where that is first."

"Then come back to bed. He'll give you no name tonight, and cause no harm. He sleeps, and so should you."

"All right." She laid her violin carefully in its case, took Fin's hand. "Kathel goes out again tomorrow. He's been out with Connor, with Meara, Iona, Boyle, and with you as well. You've all seen the wolf. I see it through Kathel. But all he—or I find—in the mind is a rage and a . . . caginess," she added as they moved through the kitchen, toward the stairs. "That's a different thing than active thought, that caginess, that rage. But it knows its name, as creatures do."

"I'll join Connor tomorrow, with the hawks, and with Kathel. It may be having me with your hound, and Connor to add more power, we'll find what we need."

"It should be you and I," she realized. "He confuses me with Sorcha from time to time, and covets her still—covets you. The two of us, with Kathel. And the two of us who can join with the hound. I should've thought of it."

"You think enough. We'll deal with it tomorrow." He drew her into bed, wrapped around her. "You'll sleep now."

Before she could understand and block, he kissed her forehead, and sent her into slumber.

For a time he lay beside her in a stream of pale moonlight, then he, too, began to drift into sleep.

And from sleep into dreams.

Baru's hooves rang against the hard dirt of the road not yet thawed. He didn't know this land, Fin thought, yet he did. Ireland. He could smell Ireland, but not his home. Not his own place in it.

The dark night, with a few pricks of stars and the wavering light of a moon that flowed in and out of clouds all closed around him.

And the moon showed a haze of red like blood. Like death.

He could smell smoke on the wind, and in the distance thought he saw the flicker of a fire. Campfire.

He wore a cloak. He could hear it snapping in the wind as they galloped—a dead run—along the ringing ground. The urgency consumed him; though he didn't know where he rode, he knew he must ride.

Blood and death follow. The words echoed in his head so he urged more speed out of the horse, took Baru up, into flight under the red-hazed moon.

The wind rushed through his hair, whipped at his cape so the song of it filled his ears. And still, beneath it, came the bright ring of hoofbeats.

He looked down, saw the rider—bright hair streaming—covering the ground swiftly, and well ahead of those who raced behind him.

And he saw the fog swirl and rise and blanket that rider, closing him off from the rest.

Without hesitation, Fin dived down, taking his horse straight into the dirty blanket of fog. It all but choked him, so thick it spread, closing off the wind, the air. The light from the scatter of stars and swimming bloody moon extinguished like candlewicks under the squeeze of fingers.

He heard the shout, the scream of a horse—sensed the horse's fear and panic and pain. Throwing up his hand, Fin caught the sword he brought to him, and set it to flame.

He charged forward, striking, slicing at the fog, cutting through its bitter cold, slashing a path with his flame and his will.

He saw the rider, for a moment saw him, the bright hair, the dark cape, the faintest glint from a copper brooch, from the sword he wielded at the attacking wolf.

Then the fog closed again.

Rushing forward blindly, Fin hacked at the fog, called out in hopes of drawing the wolf off the man and to him. He brought the wind, a torrent of it to tear and tatter the thick and filthy blanket that closed him in. Through the frayed ribbons of it, he saw the horse stumble, the wolf again gather to leap, and threw out power to block the attack as he charged into the battle.

The wolf turned, red stone, red eyes gleaming bright fire. It flew at Fin's throat, so fast, so fleet, Fin only had time to pivot Baru. Claws scored his left arm, shoulder to wrist, the force of it nearly unseating him, the pain a tidal wave that burned like hellfire. Swinging out with his sword arm, he lashed out with blade and flame, seared a line along the wolf's flank—and felt the quick pain of it stab ice through the mark on his shoulder.

He pivoted again, hacking, slicing as the fog once again closed in to blind him. Fighting free, he saw the maneuver had cost him distance. Another charge, another burst of power, but the wolf was already airborne, and though the wounded warrior swung his sword, the wolf streaked over the flash of the blade, and clamped his snapping jaws on the warrior's throat.

On a cry of rage, Fin spurred Baru forward, through the shifting curtains of fog.

Both horse and rider fell, and with a triumphant howl the wolf and fog vanished.

Even as Baru ran, Fin jumped down, fell to his knees beside the man with bright hair and glazed blue eyes.

"Stay with me," Fin told him, and laid his hand over the gaping, jagged wound. "Look at me. Look in me. I can help you. Stay with me."

But he knew the words were hollow. He had no power to heal death, and death lay under his hands.

He felt it—the last beat of heart, the last breath.

"You bled for him."

With rage, pain, grief all swirling a tempest inside him, Fin looked up, saw the woman. Branna, was his first thought, but he knew almost as soon as that thought formed, he was wrong.

"Sorcha."

"I am Sorcha. I am the Dark Witch of Mayo. It is my husband, dead on the ground. Daithi, the brave and bright."

Her dress, gray as the fog, swayed over the ground as she walked closer, and her dark eyes held Fin's.

"I watch him die, night after night, year after year, century by century. This is my punishment for betraying my gift, my oath. But tonight, you bled for him."

"I was too late. I didn't stop it. Saving him might have saved all, but I was too late."

"We cannot change what was, and still your blood, my love's, Cabhan's lay on this ground tonight. Not to change what was, but to show what can be."

She, too, knelt, then laid her lips on Daithi's. "He died for me, for his children. He died brave and true, as he ever was. It is I who failed. It is I who out of rage harmed you, who cursed you, an innocent, and so many others who came before you."

"Out of grief," Fin said. "Out of grief and torment."

"Grief and torment?" Her dark eyes flashed at him. "These can't balance the scales. I cursed you, and all who came between you and Cabhan, and as it is written, what I sent out into the world, has come back to me threefold. I burdened my children, and all the children who came after them."

"You saved them. Gave your own life for them. Your life and your power."

She smiled now, and though grief lived in the smile, he saw Branna in her eyes. "I held fast to that grief, as if it were a lover or a beloved child. I think it fed me through all the time. I wouldn't believe even what I was allowed to see. Of you or in you. Even knowing not just Cabhan's blood ran in you, I couldn't accept truth."

"What truth?"

She looked down at Daithi. "You are his as well. More his, I know now, than Cabhan's."

With a hand red with Daithi's blood and his own, Fin gripped her arm. Power shimmered at the contact. "What are you saying?"

"Cabhan healed—what's in him helped him come out of the ashes I'd made him. And healed, he sought vengeance. He couldn't reach my children—they were beyond him. But Daithi had sisters, and one so fair, so fresh, so sweet. He chose her, and he took her, and against her will planted his seed in her. She took her last breath when the child took his first. You are of that child. You are of her. You are of Daithi. You are his, and so, Finbar of the Burkes, you are mine. I've wronged you."

Carefully, she unpinned Daithi's brooch, one she'd made him for protection that held the image of horse, hound, hawk to represent their three children. "This is yours, as you are his. Forgive me."

"She has your face, and I hear her in every word you speak." He looked down at the brooch. "I still carry Cabhan's blood."

With a shake of her head, Sorcha closed Fin's fingers around the copper. "Light covers the dark. I swear to you by all I ever was, if I could break the curse I put on you, I would. But it is not for me."

She rose, keeping his hand in hers so they stood together over Daithi's body. "Blood and death here, blood and death to follow. It is beyond me to change it. I give my faith as I gave my power to my children, to the three who came from them, to the two who would stand with them, and to you, Finbar from Daithi, who carries both the light and the dark. Cabhan's time must end, what joined with him must end."

"Do you know its name?"

"That is beyond me as well. End it, but not to avenge, for there only leads to more blood, more death as I have learned too well. End it, for the light, for love, and for all who come from you."

She kissed his cheek, stepped back. "Remember, love has powers beyond all magicks. Go back to her."

He woke unsteady, disoriented, and with Branna desperately saying his name.

She crouched over him in the thin light of dawn, pressing her hands to his wounded arm. She wept as she spoke, as she pumped warmth into the wound. Some part of him stared at her, puzzled.

Branna never wept.

"Come back, come back. I can't heal this wound. I can't stop the bleeding. Come back."

"I'm here."

She let out a sobbing breath, looked from the wound to his face with tears running down her cheeks. "Stay with me. I couldn't reach you. I can't stop the bleeding. I can't— Oh, thank God, thank all the gods. It's healing now. Just stay, stay. Look at me. Fin, look at me. Look in me."

"I couldn't heal him. He died with my hands on him. It's his blood on my hands. His blood on me, in me."

"Hush, hush. Just let me work. These are deep and vicious. You've lost blood, too much already."

"You're crying."

"I'm not." But her tears fell on the wound, and closed it more cleanly than her hands. "Quiet, just be quiet and let me finish. It's healing well now. You'll need a potion, but it's healing well."

"I won't need one." He felt steadier, stronger, and altogether clearer. "I'm fine now. It's you who's shaking." He shifted up to sit, brushed his fingers over her damp cheeks. "It may be you who needs a potion."

"Is there pain now? Test your arm. Move it, flex it, so we see if it's as it should be."

He did as she asked. "It's all fine, and no, there's no more pain." But he glanced down, saw the sheets covered in blood. "Is all that mine?"

Though she trembled still, she rose, changed the sheets to fresh with a thought. But she went into the bath to wash her own hands, needed the time and distance to smooth out her nerves.

She came back, put on a robe.

"Here." Fin held out one of two glasses of whiskey. "I think you need this more than I."

She only shook her head, sat carefully on the side of the bed. "What happened?"

"You tell yours first."

She closed her eyes for a moment. "All right then. You began to thrash in your sleep. Violently. I tried to wake you, but I couldn't. I tried to find a way into the dream, to pull you out, but I couldn't. It was like a wall that couldn't be scaled, no matter what I did. Then the gashes on your arm, the blood flowing from them."

She had to pause a moment, press her hands to her face, gathered back her calm.

"I knew you were beyond where I could reach. I tried to pull you back. Tried to heal the wounds, but nothing I did stopped the blood. I thought you would die in your sleep, trapped in some dream he dragged you into, blocked me out of. You'd die because I couldn't reach you. He'd taken you from me when it seems I've only gotten you back. You'd die because I wasn't strong enough to heal you."

"But you did just that, and I didn't die, did I?" He slid up behind her, pressed a kiss to her shoulder. "You cried for me."

"Tears of panic and frustration."

But when he kissed her shoulder again, she spun around, wrapped around him, rocked. "Where did you go? Where did he take you?"

"He didn't take me, that I'm sure of. I went back to the night Cabhan killed Daithi. I saw Sorcha. I spoke with her."

Branna jerked back. "You spoke with her."

"As I'm speaking to you. You look so like her." He brushed her hair behind her back. "So very like her, though her eyes are dark, they have the same look as yours. It's the strength in them. And the power."

"What did she say to you?"

"I'll tell you, but I think it's best to tell all of us. And the truth is I could use some time to sort through it all myself."

"Then I'll tell them to come."

She dressed, asked him no more questions. In truth, she needed the time herself, to settle, to put on her armor. Not since the day she'd seen the mark on him had she felt the level of fear, of grief she'd known that dawn. She asked herself if feeling so much had blocked her powers to heal him, to bring him out of the dream. And didn't know the answers.

When she went down, she noted he'd put the kettle on, and already had coffee waiting for her.

"You'll think you need to cook up breakfast for the lot of us," he began. "We can fend for ourselves."

"It keeps my hands busy. If you want to fend, scrub and chip up some potatoes. You've skill enough for that."

They worked in silence until the others began to straggle in.

"Looks like a full fry's coming," Connor commented. "But a damned early hour for it. Had an adventure, did you?" he said to Fin.

"You could say it was."

"But you're okay." Iona touched his arm as if checking for herself.

"I am, and also clever enough to turn over the duty dropped on me here to Boyle, who has a better hand with it."

"Nearly all do." Boyle shoved up his sleeves and joined Branna.

With the air of anticipation hanging, they set the table, brewed tea, made the coffee, sliced the bread.

When all were settled at the table, all eyes turned to Fin.

"It's a strange tale, though some of it we know from the books. I found myself riding Baru at a hard gallop on a dirt road still hard from winter."

He wound his way through it, doing his best to leave out no details.

"Wait now." Boyle held up a hand. "How can you be so sure Cabhan didn't reel you into this? The wolf attacked you, went for your throat, and our Branna couldn't get through to help you, or to bring you back. It sounds like Cabhan's doing."

"I took him by surprise, I can swear to that. The wolf came at me only because I was there, and might interfere with the murder. If Cabhan had wanted to do me harm, why not lie in wait, and come at me? No, his aim was Daithi, and my coming into it something unexpected.

"I couldn't save him, and thinking over it all, was never meant to save him."

"He was a sacrifice," Iona said quietly. "His death, like Sorcha's, gave birth to the three."

"He had eyes like yours, bright and blue. I could see, when I could see, how brave and fierce he fought. But no matter that, no matter what I could bring to help, nothing could change what was done. Cabhan's power was great, more than he has now. Sorcha dimmed that power, though he healed. I think now some of the hunger that drives him is to gain it all back again. And to gain it, he must take it from the three."

"He never will," Branna said. "Tell them the rest. I only know a little of it."

"Daithi fell. I thought I could heal his wound, but it was too late for that. He drew his last breath almost as soon as I put my hands on him. And then she came. Sorcha."

"Sorcha?" Meara set down the coffee she'd started to drink. "She was there with you?"

"We spoke. It seemed a long time there on the bloody road, but I think it wasn't."

He went over it, word by word, her grief, her remorse, her strength. And then the words that changed so much inside him.

"Daithi? You come from him, your blood is mixed with his and Cabhan's?" Shaken, Branna got slowly to her feet. "How could I have not known? How could none of us have known? It's him you carry, it's him and what's in you that beats back Cabhan at every turn. But I didn't see it. Or wouldn't. Because I saw the mark."

"How could you see what I myself couldn't see in me? I saw the mark and let that weigh as heavy as you did. Heavier, I think. She knew, as she said, she knew, but didn't believe or trust. So I think she brought me there, to see what I would do. That last test of what burned strongest in me."

He reached in his pocket. "And in the end, she gave me this." He opened his hand, showed the brooch. "What she made for him, she gave to me."

"Daithi's brooch. Some have searched for it." Branna sat again, studied the copper brooch. "We thought it lost."

"The three guides as one." When Connor held out his hand, Fin gave him the brooch. "As you're the only among us who can speak with all three. It was always yours. Waiting for you, for her to give it to you."

"She sees Daithi die every night, she told me. Her punishment for the curse. I think the gods are harsh indeed to so condemn a grieving woman. Blood and death, she said, as you did, Branna. Blood and death follow, and so she gives us—all of us here, and her children—her faith. We must end him, but not for revenge, and I confess revenge rode high in me before this. We must end him for the light, for love, and all who will come from us. She said love had powers beyond all magicks, then sent me back. She said, 'Go back to her,' and I woke with you weeping over me."

Saying nothing, Branna held out a hand to Connor, then studied the brooch. "She made this for love, as she did what the three wear. It's strong magick here. And as we do, you must never be without it now that it's given to you."

"We can make him a chain for it," Iona suggested, "like ours."

"Yes, we'll do that. That's a fine idea. This all tells me why I've always needed so much of your blood to make a poison. It's never had enough of Cabhan in it."

With a half laugh, Fin decided to eat the eggs that had gone cold on his plate. "Ever practical."

"You're one of us," Iona realized. "I mean, you're a cousin. A really, really distant one, but you're a cousin."

"Welcome to the family then." Connor lifted his tea, toasted. "So it may be written, at some point, that the Cousins O'Dwyer, and their friends and lovers, sent Cabhan the black to hell."

"I'll raise a glass to that."

As Fin did, Boyle gave Iona's hand a squeeze. "I say we all raise them tonight, at the pub, and the new cousin stands the first round."

"I'm fine with that, and the second's on you." Fin lifted his own glass, then drank the coffee that had gone cold as his eggs.

And still he felt a warmth in him.

19

FIN WORE THE BROOCH ON A CHAIN, FELT THE WEIGHT of it. But when he looked in the mirror, he saw the same man. He was what he ever was.

And while the brooch lay near his heart, the mark still rode on his shoulder. Knowing his blood held both dark and light didn't change that, didn't change him.

It wouldn't change what would be in only a few weeks' time.

He ran his businesses, worked the stables, the school, spent time in his own workshop trying to perfect spells that could be useful to his circle.

He walked or rode with Branna, along with the dogs, hoping to lure out Cabhan, hoping they would find the way to dig out that last piece.

But the demon's name eluded them as February waned and March bloomed.

"Going back to the cave may be the only way left." Fin said it casually as he and Connor watched a pair of young hawks circle above a field.

"There's time yet."

"Time's passing, and he waits as we wait."

"And you're weary of the waiting, that's clear enough. But going back's not the answer, and you can't know you'll learn the name if you did."

Connor drew the white stone out of his pocket, the one Eamon of the first three had given him. "We all wait, Fin. Three and three and three, for I can't find Eamon in dreams now. I can't find him, and still I know he's there. Waiting as we are."

Fin could admire Connor's equanimity—and curse it. "Without the name, what do we wait for?"

"For what comes, and that's always been an easier matter for me than you. Tell me this, when it's done, when we finish it, and I believe we will, what then for you?"

"There are places in the world I haven't been."

Temper flashed, and Connor was a man slow to temper. "Your place is here, with Branna, with us."

"My home is here, and I can't deny it. But Branna and I can't have the life we wished for, so we take what we can while we can. We can't have the life you'll have with Meara, or Boyle with Iona. It's not meant."

"Ah, bollocks. She thinks too much for her own good, and you blame yourself for things beyond your doing. The past may be written, but the future isn't, and two such clever people should be able to suss out how to make one together."

"Having Daithi's blood in me doesn't change having Cabhan's, or bearing his mark. If we win this, and destroy him, the demon, his lair, what's to say I won't be pulled as he was, a year from now, or ten? I know just how dark and sweet that pull can be, and Branna knows it's in me. We could never have children who would carry that same burden."

"If, can't, doesn't." Connor dismissed all with a wave of his hand. "More bollocks. The pair of you stare into the hard side of things."

"A witch's dying curse may be regretted now, but its power holds.

It may be one of the places I haven't been holds the key to breaking it. I won't stop looking."

"Then when this is done, we'll all of us look. Think of all the free time on our hands once we dispatch Cabhan."

Fin smiled, but thought there were lives to be lived. "Let's keep our minds on dispatching him. And tell me, what sort of house are you thinking of building for yourself and your bride. Something such as . . ."

With a twirl of his finger, Fin floated an image of a glittery faerie palace over a silver lake.

With a laugh, Connor twirled his own. "To start, perhaps more this." And turned the palace into a thatched-roof cottage in a field of green.

"Likely suits you better. And what does Meara have to say about it?"

"That she doesn't want to think about it until Iona and Boyle are wed, and their house finished. At that time, as she's giving up her flat on the first of the month in any case, we thought it might be with Boyle and Iona tucked in their new place, we might give Branna her quiet and tuck ourselves into the flat over your garage."

"You could, indeed. As long as you like, but I think your fingers will be itching to make your own."

"Well, it may be I've drawn up a few ideas on it. I think—"

He broke off as his phone signaled a text.

"It's Branna. No, no, nothing's wrong," he said as Fin lunged to his feet. "She'd like us to come back is all, has something she wants to talk to us and Iona about. Hmm." Connor sent back a quick response. "Witches only, it seems, and I wonder what that's about."

"She's been brewing on something—in her head," Fin added. "She may be finished on the brewing of it."

And with Connor, he called the hawks.

Branna continued to work as she waited. She had indeed finished brewing on it, and felt the time had come to ask if the others were willing or thought the idea had merit.

She'd studied the means to do it, had gone over the ritual needed more times than she cared to count—as it was a great deal to ask, of all.

Was it another answer? she wondered. Another step needed for what they all hoped was the end?

Not an impulse, she assured herself as she filled the last bottles with fragrant oils for the shop. She'd given it far too much thought, considered it from every side and angle for it to be deemed an impulse.

No, it was a decision, a choice, and must be fully agreed to by all.

She washed her hands, wiped her counter, then went over to look into her crystal.

The cave was empty, but for the red glow of the fire, the dark smoke rising from the cauldron. So Cabhan wandered where he willed. And if he watched, would see nothing that offered him aid or insight. She'd seen to that.

She rose as Iona came in, and did what she always did. Put the kettle on.

"You said no worries, but—"

"There aren't," Branna assured her. "It's just a matter I need to talk over with you and Connor and Fin."

"But not Boyle or Meara."

"Not as yet. It's nothing we would do without them, I promise, only it needs to be discussed among us first. So, have you settled it all then on the wedding flowers?"

"Yes." Iona hung up her jacket and scarf, tried to shift topics as Branna wanted. "You were right about the florist, she's wonderful. We've nailed that all down, and I'm nearly done—I tell myself—changing the menu for the reception. And I'm glad I've left the music in your hands and Meara's or I'd drive myself crazy."

"We're happy to help, and Meara's making notes on what you're doing she might want to turn a bit for herself. Though she claims she's barely thinking of it all yet, she thinks of it quite a bit."

Branna started the tea. "And here come Fin and Connor now. Let's use the little table so we're all settled in one place."

"It's serious, isn't it?"

"That's for each to decide. Would you get the cups?"

Branna brought the teapot to the table, the sugar, the cream, the biscuits her brother particularly would expect.

And Connor's eyebrows lifted as he came in. "A tea party, is it?"

"A party, no, but there's tea. If we could all sit, I'm more than ready to say what's on my mind."

"And been on your mind for some time." Fin came over, sat.

"I had to be sure of my own thoughts and feelings on it before I asked for yours."

"But not the full circle," Connor pointed out.

"Not yet, you'll see why it's for us first."

"Okay." Iona blew out a breath. "You're killing me now. Spill it."

"I thought of what came through me the day Fin and I made the poison for the demon. What I said, all the words, at the moment all the work we'd done there came to fruition. We have the means to destroy Cabhan, and what's in him, or will when we have the name. And the means to destroy the stone, and close the portal."

"I love that one," Iona commented. "All the light and heat of it."

"It'll take all to close the dark. But there was more that came through me than poisons, than weapons. It's all risk, all duty, and the blood and death may be ours, any of us. And still, even fully myself again, one thing continued to echo in me. Three and three and three."

"And so we are," Connor agreed. "If you've found a way to connect us again with Sorcha's three, I'd like to hear it, for I feel, and all through me feel, they must be a part of it. They must be there."

"And I believe they will, as the shadows of them came on Samhain. To bring them full, it may be another thing. Three and three and three," Branna repeated. "But there are two armed with only courage and sword or fist. They have no magicks. Sorcha's three, we three, and Fin—part of us, part of Cabhan. Then Boyle and Meara. It doesn't truly balance."

"You said we wouldn't leave them out," Iona began.

"And I gave my word I'd never lock her or Boyle away, whatever my wish to protect them." Connor ignored the biscuits, frowned at his sister. "If you think to appeal to others of our blood, to our father or—"

"No. We are a circle, and nothing changes that. We go, three by three by three, as is meant. But that balance can be met, if we're willing. And in turn if Boyle and Meara are willing."

"You'd give them power." Fin sat back as he began to understand. "You would give them, as Sorcha did her children, what we have."

"I would—not near to all as she did, never that. We need what we are, and I would never burden two we loved with so much. But some, from all of us, to them. It can be done. I've studied how Sorcha did it, I've worked on how to pass—gently as we can—some of what we are. It's a risk if I've got any of it wrong, and it must be a choice for all."

"Sorcha's children already had power, through her," Iona pointed out, "through the blood. I'm newer at this than all of you, but I've never heard of transferring magicks into, well, let's say laypeople."

"They're connected. Not just to us, but also through their bloodline. With or without power, that connection is real. And it's that connection that would allow this to work, if it's meant to work."

"They'd have more protection," Connor considered.

"They would, though as much as I love them, my purpose here is balance. It's the fulfillment of what prophecy came through me. But it must be *our* purpose. Ours and theirs. And we can't know, not for certain, what the powers would be for them."

"But in having them," Fin began, "they, with me, become truly another three."

As that was exactly her thought, Branna let out a pent-up breath. "Yes, another three. I've come to believe that. Now each of you must think it through, and decide if you're willing to give them what is both gift and burden. I can show you how it can be done, how I believe it can be done, without draining any of us, or giving them more than they can hold. If any of us aren't sure, aren't willing, then we set it aside. If we are, but they aren't, again it's set aside. A gift like this must be given freely and with a full heart, and taken the same."

"Should any come from me? If there's willing on all sides," Fin continued, "should any come from me, as what I have is tainted?"

"I don't like hearing you say that," Iona replied.

"This is too large a step not to speak plain truth, *deirfiúr bheag*."

"I'll speak plain truth when I say I asked myself the same while I worked this through my head." After scanning the table, Branna looked directly at Fin. "Even before we learned you come from Daithi, I had come to believe—again with a full heart—that yes, also from you. They're yours," Branna told him, "as they're ours. And you are of the three. What you have in you isn't pure, but that—to my mind—makes the light in it all the stronger."

"I'll agree to it, if they do. They must be sure they can accept what comes from me."

"You need to take time to think it through," Branna said, and Connor snorted, grabbed a biscuit.

"And didn't I tell you this one thinks too much? Haven't you taxed your brain on this enough for all of us?" he asked Branna. "Fiddled and figured all the little steps, the ways and means, the pros and cons and the good Christ knows what else? If they'll take it, it's theirs." He looked to Iona.

"Absolutely. I'm not sure how Boyle will react to the idea. He accepts all this—we all know. And he'll fight and stand with us. But at the core . . ."

"He's a man with feet planted firm on the ground," Fin said. "That's true enough. We can only ask, as Branna's asked, and leave the rest to him, and to Meara."

"Well, I can see I wasted time making copious notes for the three of you."

Connor grinned at his sister. "Too much thinking," he said, and ate the biscuit.

"When do we ask?" Iona wondered.

"Sooner's better than later," Fin decided. "When the day's work's done?"

"Then I'm cooking for six." Branna shoved at her hair.

"Happens I've the fat chicken you put on the list for me," Fin told her. "And the makings for colcannon."

"As well. Dinner at Fin's then. I'll go over and start on that, but I think it best and fair we tell them what we're thinking before a meal. They'll need time to . . . digest it all, we'll say."

"Let's say they go for it. When would we try it?"

Branna nodded at Iona, finally picked up her own tea. "Sooner's better there as well. You know more than the rest of us, there's a bit of a learning curve."

SHE DID THE CHICKEN UP WITH GARLIC AND SAGE AND lemon, put the colcannon together, peeled carrots for baking in butter while the bird roasted. As she'd come up with the scheme, the others had decided she would broach it with Boyle and Meara.

As she worked she considered various ways of putting it all out to them, and finally concluded direct and frank the best possible route. It settled her down, until Meara came in.

"It smells a treat in here. And looks as though you've already done the work when I came soon as I could to give you some help with it."

"No worries."

"Well, I can set the table at least."

"Don't bother with it now." She didn't want plates and such

cluttering up the table when they talked. "Just keep me company. Sure let's break into Fin's vast store of wine."

"I'm for that. I tell you it's scraping my nerves raw seeing Cabhan lurking about every time I take a guided through. It must be doing the same with Iona," she added as she pulled a bottle of white from Fin's kitchen cooler. "She was nervy today, at least toward the end of it. She and Boyle will be around soon."

"So he shows himself to you, to Iona, even Connor now and then, but when Fin and I go out, he avoids us. We'll keep at it," Branna decided. "He won't be able to resist trying to bully or taunt for long."

"He doesn't have long, and that's my way of thinking." Meara drew the cork. "It's good we're getting together, all of us, so regular like this. You never know when another idea might spark."

Oh, I've an idea for you, Branna thought, but only smiled. "You'd be right. But let's put that aside for now. Tell me how your mother's doing."

"Happier than I ever thought she could be. And don't you know she's started taking piano lessons from a woman at the church? All the time on her hands, she tells me, and she can put it to use with the lessons, as she's always wanted to play. As if she didn't have a world of time before she moved in with Maureen, and—"

Meara held up both hands as if calling herself to a halt. "No, I'll say nothing negative about it. She's there, not here, happy not unhappy and flustered, and Maureen herself tells me it's lovely to have her."

"Nothing but good news there then."

"Well, she's marking some of the world of time she now has by sending me a lorry-load of suggestions for the wedding. Photos of gowns that would make me look like a giant princess wearing a wedding cake, and require so much tulle and lace there'd be none left in the whole of Mayo. Here." Meara reached in her pocket, pulled out her phone. "Have a look at her last vision for me."

Branna studied once Meara had scrolled to the image, a dress with an enormous skirt fashioned of stacked layers of tulle, and that decked with lace and beads and ribbons.

"I'd say you're a fortunate woman to be able to choose your own wedding dress."

"I am, and she'll be disappointed when she's learned I've something more like this in mind."

She scrolled to another picture of a fluid column, simple and unadorned.

"It's lovely, just lovely, and couldn't be more Meara Quinn. Worn with a little tiara, I'd see, as you're not the flowers-in-the-hair as Iona is. Just that touch of fancy and sparkle. She won't be disappointed when she sees you."

"A tiara . . . that might suit me, and would give her a bit of the princess she wants."

"You could find three—any of which you'd be happy to wear. Send her pictures, let her choose for you."

Meara picked up her wine. "You're a canny one."

"Oh, that I am."

As Boyle and Iona came in, Branna hoped Meara would think canny a compliment when she'd laid out the choice.

She waited while Meara passed out wine, while Fin and Connor came in, then asked everyone to sit around the table as there was something to discuss.

"Did something happen today?" Meara asked.

"Not today. You could say it happened a little while ago, and I've been working it out since." Straight and direct, Branna reminded herself. "I've told you all the words I spoke on the day Fin and I completed the second poison," she began.

And when she finished with, "It can be done, and the four of us are willing. But the choice of it is for you," there was a long, stunned silence.

Boyle broke it. "You're having us on."

"We're not." Iona rubbed a hand over his. "We think we can do it, but it's a big decision for you and for Meara."

"Are you saying you can make witches out of me and Boyle, if only we agree to it?"

"Not exactly that. I believe seeds of power are in us all," Branna continued. "In some, they sprout more than in others. The instincts, the feelings, the sensation of having done something before, of having been somewhere before. What we'd give would feed those seeds."

"Like manure?" Boyle said. "As it sounds like a barrow-load of it."

"You'd be the same people." Connor spread his hands. "The same people but with some traces of magicks that could be nurtured and honed."

"If you think to add protection for us—"

"There's the benefit of that." Fin interrupted Boyle in calm tones. "But the purpose is as Branna said. The balance, the interpretation of the prophecy."

"I need to walk around with this." Boyle did just that, rising and pacing. "You want to give us something we lack."

"To my mind, you lack nothing. Nothing," Branna repeated. "And to my mind, this was always meant. Always meant, just not seen or known until now. I may be wrong, but even if right, we'll find another way if it feels wrong for you."

"It feels wrong you'd give up something you have, to add to what we have," he said. "Sorcha left herself near to empty by doing the same."

"This is a worry for me as well," Meara put in. "Giving up power is part of what cost her life."

"She was one giving all she had to three. We're four, giving a small part of what we have to two." Connor smiled at her. "It's arithmetic."

"There's another choice, should you accept the first. It may be three into two," Fin added. "What I would give has some of Cabhan in it, so it's another piece to consider."

"It's all or it's none," Boyle snapped back. "Don't insult us."

"Agreed." Meara took a long drink. "All or none."

"Take whatever time you need to think on it." Branna rose. "Ask whatever comes to mind, and we'll try to answer. And know whatever your choice, we value you. We'll eat, if that suits everyone, and put this aside unless you have those questions."

"Eat." Boyle muttered to himself, continued to pace as food was brought to the table. Then Iona simply walked over, put her arms around him.

He heaved a sigh, met Meara's eyes over Iona's head. Meara's response was a simple lifting of shoulders.

"If we agree, how would it be done?" he wanted to know.

"In much the same way Sorcha did with her children," Branna told him. "At the base of it in any case. With some adjustments, of course, to fit our own needs."

"If we agreed," Meara added, "when would it be done?"

"Tonight." Connor waved off his sister's protest. "The ifs they're putting out are smoke. They've both of them decided to agree, because they see, as we do, it's another answer. So it's tonight, a clean, quick step, and giving them time to adjust to what's new in them." He took a heap of colcannon for his plate, before passing the dish to Meara. "Am I wrong?"

"You're a cocky one, Connor, but not wrong. Let's eat, Boyle, and eat hearty, for it's our last meal as we are."

"It doesn't change who you are, even what you are." Iona rubbed a hand on Boyle's arm. "It's . . . Think of it like gaining a new skill or talent."

"Like piano lessons," Meara said, and made Branna laugh and laugh.

So they ate, and talked, they cleared and talked more.

Then all six stood together in Fin's workshop.

"Cabhan mustn't see what we do here," Branna told Fin.

"He won't. I've cloaked my windows and doors to him long since, but another layer wouldn't hurt. Add your own. I have what we'll need. I read your notes," he added. "I'll lay out what's needed, and we'll leave it to you to use them."

"He'll feel something though, won't he?" Iona glanced toward the windows. "Power feels power."

"He may feel, but he won't know." Connor took Meara's hand. "You are the love of my life, before and after."

"That may be, but I'm hoping I get enough of whatever it is to give you a jolt whenever you might need one."

"You give me that already." He swept her back for a dramatic kiss.

"You're easy with it all," Boyle commented.

"I'm nervous as a cat in a dog kennel." Meara pressed her hand to her stomach. "But let's be honest, Boyle, we've seen our lives long what this is, what it means. We've four here who've shown us what this is must be respected and honored, so we will. And the more I think of it, the more I'm liking the idea of having a bit more to turn on Cabhan and his master."

"There is that, for certain, and I can't claim not to consider it. Even if I'd rather just use my fists."

"You're the man you are, so you don't see it's you who's giving tonight, not us." Iona took his face in her hands. "It's you." Then stepped back. "Is there something you need from us, Branna?"

"Three drops of blood from each who gives power. Three only. But first, we cast a circle, we light the fire to ring it. It's your home, Fin. You begin."

"Here and now the circle cast protecting all within, so inside its ring the ritual begin. Flames arise but not to burn, through the light our powers turn. Close the door and seal the locks. Turn away whatever knocks."

Fire flashed to ring them, cool and white.

"We are connected," Branna began. "Are now, have been, will be. If not by blood and bone, but heart and spirit. We seal that connection here with a gift, given and taken willingly.

"So say we all?" Branna asked.

"So say we all," the others answered.

So she began.

"Wine and honey, sweet and dark." She poured both into a bowl. "To help the light within you spark. Oil of herbs and joy-shed tears stirred within to ease your fears. From my heart a drop of blood times three." She pricked her wrist at the pulse, added the three drops to the cup. "Sister, brother, unto me, I share my light with both of thee."

She passed the bowl to Fin. "From heart, from spirit I shed for thee, a drop of blood times three. Sister, brother, unto me, I share my light with both of thee."

When he finished, he handed the bowl to Connor. "And now on a new journey you embark, I give three drops from my heart. Lover, brother, unto me, I share my light with both of thee."

And to Iona.

"You are my heart, you are my light, so that holds fast upon this night. From the beat of my heart, for sister, for love, one, two, and three. I share my light with both of thee."

"Sealed with fire, pure and white, the gift we give upon this night." Branna took the bowl, held it high as white fire flashed within. "Bless this gift and those who take what's given, know by right all here are driven. From bowl to cup for one, for two, pour forth this consecrated brew."

The liquid in the bowl fountained up, split into two with each arch spilling into a waiting cup.

Branna gestured to Connor, to Iona. "Those closest should make the final offering."

"Okay." Iona picked up a cup, turned to Boyle. She touched his cheek, then held out the cup. "In this place and in this hour, we offer you this taste of power. If your choice to take is free, say these words back to me. 'This I take into my body, into my heart, into my spirit willingly. As we will, so mote it be.' "

He repeated the words, hesitated briefly, then looked into her eyes. And drank.

Connor turned to Meara, gave her his words, her own.

She grinned at him, couldn't quite help it, and drank.

"Is that it?" she asked. "Did it work? I don't feel any different." She looked at Boyle.

"No, no different."

"How do we know it worked?" Meara demanded.

The circling fire flashed up in spears to the ceiling. The air quivered with light and heat. A shining beam of it showered over Boyle, over Meara like a welcome.

"That," Connor concluded, "would be an indicator."

"What can we do? What should we do?"

"We give thanks, close the circle." Branna smiled at her lifelong friend. "Then we'll see."

20

THEY PROVED NIMBLE STUDENTS AND WITHIN A WEEK could both spark a candlewick. Branna moved them on from that most basic skill to test them with other elements.

It didn't surprise her that Meara showed more aptitude with air and Boyle with fire. That connection again, she concluded. Meara to Connor, Boyle to Iona.

They put in a great deal of time training, discovering, and the progress pleased Branna. Meara could create tough little cyclones and found her affinity with horses enhanced. When goaded, Boyle conjured golf-ball-sized fireballs.

Frustrated, he slumped into a chair at Fin's. "What good does it all do? When he comes around, I'm bound by our agreement not to show our hand and left to give him nothing stronger than a hard look. And if I could give a taste of what I have now, he could smack it away like a tennis player returning a lob."

"The player's more likely to end up getting beaned," Connor

pointed out, "if the lob comes from an unexpected direction. You've done considerable, you and Meara, with the little you were given, and done considerable in a short time."

"Time's the trouble, isn't it?" Boyle pointed out.

"It is, and that's a hard fact." Fin contemplated his beer. "We thought as he wouldn't know we were looking, we'd find a way into the demon's name. Now I wonder if Cabhan's forgotten it, as the demon's been part of him for so long."

"That's a troubling thought." Connor considered it. "If it's true we can't end it without the demon's name, and if there's no longer a name to find, it may be it's Cabhan's name we have to speak as we poison them."

"Are such matters ever that simple?" Fin asked.

"They haven't proved to be. Still, maybe this will be. Only the name. The rest is complicated enough."

"And only days left to us now," Boyle put in. "Only a few weeks left till our wedding, and Iona isn't able to think of it the way women do. Not with this between."

"You might be grateful for that," Connor commented. "In my experience, from mates who've been through it, some women can go right mad."

"It's outside," Fin said quietly, and Connor came to attention.

"I don't sense him."

"He's shadowed, but I can just feel him out there, trying to watch, trying to get into my thoughts. Biding time, that's what he's doing. The taunting and shadowing, but biding all the same. He has, as he's proved, all the time in all the worlds."

"He's not looking for another fight." Boyle leaned forward now. "Not that he wouldn't take us all on, given the opportunity, but he's waiting us out now. That makes sense to me. Wear down our spirits, wait for the moment when we're careless. We've the wrong strategy, I think, on luring him back to Sorcha's cabin, for then he'll know we're ready for the battle."

"We have to get him there," Connor pointed out. "Everything depends on it."

"But he doesn't have to know we want him to come. What if he thinks we're hiding the fact that we're going from him—but he's so bloody smart and powerful, he got through the shields and sees us?"

"Why would we be going there if not for battle?" Connor argued.

"To pay our respects." Seeing Boyle's point, Fin nodded. "To honor Sorcha on the day of her death, to hold a ritual of respect—and perhaps try to appeal to her for help. Going under cover of our own fog so he won't stop us from paying those respects or making that appeal."

"And what we're doing is taking the high ground for the battle," Boyle finished, eager now that he could see the fight. "And instead of being taken by surprise, we give the surprise."

"Oh, I'm liking this idea." Connor took a long drink. "This is what comes of talking war with men. And if either of you should repeat that to any of the women, I'll be shocked and amazed at what liars you are."

"Since I want them fully behind this, they won't hear that from me. We set the trap," Fin said, "by letting him think he's set it."

BRANNA LISTENED TO THE NEW PLAN OVER PIZZA IN FIN'S living room. There had been some talk of an evening out, but no one understood priorities more than Branna O'Dwyer.

"It's clever, sure it's clever," she agreed. "And it annoys me I never thought of it on my own. We don't have much time to change from the plan we've settled on."

"And that one has the benefit of being simple," Meara added. "We transport ourselves there—or you transport the lot of us, along with horses, hawks, and hound, and we call him out. He'd come, as his pride wouldn't allow otherwise. But . . . this is more devious, and I can't help but like it."

“He’d like that we’re trying to hide from him,” Iona agreed. “That would appeal to his arrogance. And if he thinks we’re trying to call on Sorcha, he’d have to come—on the slim chance we could reach her, bring her to us, open her to him again.”

“You’d be giving up your own shadow spell,” Branna said to Fin. “Something he doesn’t know you have. It won’t be as useful to you when he does come.”

“It will have served. It changes little of what we do once he’s there, only the approach.”

“We’ll gather flowers, wine, bread, honey.” Thinking it through, Branna made mental notes. “All the things we’d take to a visit of respect for the dead. We’re somber and unsettled, and about to attempt raising the spirit of the witch who cursed one of us. He’d see many advantages to a strike then.”

“Could we start the ritual for it?” Iona wondered. “But when it’s too late for him, call the first three?”

Boyle laughed, reached over to kiss her soundly. “Who said women can’t plan wars?”

Meara angled her head. “Who did?”

“Rhetorical,” Connor said with a careless wave. “Well then, let’s plan a war.”

ON THE DAY, BRANNA GATHERED ALL SHE NEEDED. WHITE roses, wine, honey, bread she made herself, the herbs, all the offerings. In another pouch she placed the poisons, each carefully wrapped.

And separate, to risk no contamination, the bottle of light the three had created.

She’d bathed and anointed herself, had woven charms in her hair, added them to Kathel’s collar. Made more for Aine’s mane.

Alone, she lit the candles, cast a circle, and knelt inside it to offer her acceptance to what the fates deemed. There was a certainty to her that tonight would end Cabhan or end the three. A sharper certainty that whatever the fates deemed, her life would not be as it had been.

But still her life, and still her choices. She was, and would always be a servant and a child of the light. But she was also a woman.

She rose, certain in purpose. She gathered her things and with her hound, flew to Fin's.

She came to him in his workshop as he chose weapons from his case.

"You're early."

"I wanted time with you before the others, before we start. I've given myself to the fates, accept whatever comes. I'll fight more fiercely for the acceptance."

"I can only accept his end."

"I hope that's not true." She crossed to him. "Will you accept me, Fin?"

"I do. Of course."

My life, she thought again, my choice. Witch and woman.

"I give myself to you. Will you take me? Will you let me belong to you, and belong to me in turn?"

He touched her cheek, twined a lock of her hair around his finger. "I could never belong to another."

"I never will. Belong to me, and stay with me, for this is home for both of us. I want to live with you here, in this house you built from our young dreams. I want to be married to you, as that's a promise given and taken as well. I want to make my life with you."

As the words squeezed his heart, he laid the sword he'd chosen down. And stepped back from her. "You know we can't. Until I break the curse—"

"I don't know it." She rushed in now—no more thinking. Only feeling. "I know we let what was put on you by light and dark stop us. No more, Fin. We can make no children who would carry it as you do, and this is a grief for us both. But we'd have each other. We can't have the life we once dreamed of, planned for, but we can dream and plan another. I gave myself to the powers greater. I may die this night, and I can accept that. But when I gave myself, the powers didn't say to me—let him go—so I won't."

"Branna." He cupped her face, kissed her cheeks. "I have to find the way to break the curse. I don't know where the search will take me. I don't know, can't know, how long it might take me, if I ever find the answer."

"Then I'll follow you, wherever you go. I'll search with you, wherever it takes us. You can't hide or run from me. I'll follow you, Finbar, track you like a hound, I swear it on my life. I won't go back to living without what I love. I love you."

Overcome, he rested his brow to hers. "You take my breath away. A dozen years you haven't said those words to me. Three words that hold all the power of heaven and earth."

"I would bind you to me with them. We're meant, I know that with all I am. If you can't stay with me, I'll go with you. We can go or stay, but marry me, Fin. Make that vow to me, take that vow from me. Before we face what we have to face, take my love, promise your own."

"Can you live with this, every day?" He rubbed his arm. "Can you live with this, and what we know we can't have?"

She'd given herself to the light, she remembered, and the answer had come. So simple, so clear.

"You do, you live with it every day, and I'm yours. I'll give my life for duty if my life is needed, but I'll no longer close off my heart. Not to myself, not to you. Not to love."

"To have your love is everything to me. We can take it a day at a time, until—"

"No. No more just today. I need this from you." She laid her hands on his chest, on his heart. "I ask this of you. Take my love, and its promise, give yours to me. Whatever comes."

"In my life," he said, his voice quiet as a kiss, "you are all I've wanted. Above all else."

He kissed her lightly, then released her to go to a shelf, opened a puzzle box, took out a ring that flashed light from the fire.

"A circle," he said. "A symbol, a stone of heat and light. I found it in the sea, a warm blue sea where I swam and thought of you. I went to forget you, far away from here, from all. On an island where no one lived, and I swam away from even that, and saw this glint through the water. I knew it for yours, though I never thought to give it to you, never thought you'd take it."

She held out her hand. "Give me the promise, and take mine. If there's tomorrow, Fin, we'll take it as ours."

"I swear to you, I'll find a way to give you all your heart wishes."

"But don't you see, you already have. This is love, and love accepts all."

When he slipped the ring on her finger, the flames in the hearth roared up. Somewhere in the night behind the windows, lightning flashed.

"We'll take it," she said again, and clung to him, clung to the kiss.

Whatever comes, she thought, be it blood and death, they had this.

THEY GATHERED, A CIRCLE FORMED FROM HEART AND SPIRIT, loyalty and duty, and sealed by magicks. As night grew deep, they took up weapons.

"We don't have the name," Branna began. "Until we do we must keep Cabhan from escaping, keep him within our borders, prevent him from shifting time."

"We build the walls strong, lock the gate," Connor agreed. "And use all we have to draw the demon out, to draw out the name."

"Or thrash it out of him," Boyle countered.

"We each know what's to be done tonight, and how we'll do it," Fin continued. "We're stronger for what's shared among us, and if right's meant to triumph, Cabhan ends tonight. There are none I would rather go into battle with than those in this room. No man ever had truer friends."

"I say we go burn this bastard, then come back here for a full fry." Connor hugged Meara to his side.

"I'm for it." Meara laid a hand on the hilt of her sword. "And more than ready for the first."

"You've given me family, given me home. This has been the best year of my life," Iona continued. "And in this year, I'm going to marry the love of my life, and no demon from hell is going to stop me. So yeah, let's go burn the bastard."

With a laugh, Boyle plucked her off her feet, kissed her. "How can we lose with such as you?"

"We can't." Iona scanned the faces around her. "We won't."

"We have to prepare for—"

"Wait." Iona wiggled away from Boyle, pointed at Branna. "What's this? What *is* this?" She grabbed Branna's hand, gave a tearful laugh. "Oh boy, oh boy!" And launching herself at Branna, squeezed hard. "This is what I've been wishing for. Exactly what I've been wishing for."

"You'd think you'd have said something to the rest of us." Meara grabbed Branna's hand in turn as Iona swung around to wrap around Fin. "This shows right's meant to win. Right here." She pressed her cheek to Branna's, swayed. "It shows it."

"Far past time." Boyle gave Fin a light punch in the chest. "But well done."

Connor waited until Fin met his eyes. "So, you finally listened to me, and all my wisdom."

"I listened to your sister."

"As now you'll have no choice but to do for the rest of your life. And you owe me a hundred."

"What? Ah," Fin said as he remembered the wager. "So I do."

Connor gave Fin a full-on hug, then turned to take Branna's face, to kiss her cheeks. “Now the scales are truly balanced. Love feeds the light.”

Branna closed her hands around Connor’s wrists, kissed his cheeks in turn. “Well then, let’s go burn the bastard.”

“Are we ready then?” Fin waited for assents, and for the circle to form.

“Our place, our time as the hour strikes three,” Branna said and drew a breath. “This dawn brings our destiny.”

“With fist and light we bring the fight,” Boyle continued.

“To end demon-witch on this night,” Meara finished.

“Three by three by three we’ll ride.” Connor took Meara’s hand, looked to Iona.

“With horse and hawk and hound our guides,” Iona said.

“And while these mists flow from me, Cabhan sees only what we will him see.”

Fin spread his arms, circled them, spread them. Branna felt the mists wrap around her—warm and soft. No, she thought, this wasn’t Cabhan’s cold, bitter cloak.

They went down and out, and into the stables. While Branna braided charms into Aine’s mane, Iona stepped over. “She’s coming into season.”

“Aine?”

“Another day or two. She’ll be ready for Alastar if it’s what you want.”

“It is.”

“She isn’t afraid; none of the horses are afraid, but they know they’ll fly tonight, and why.”

“As does the hound. They’re ready.” Branna looked to Connor.

“And the hawks as well.”

“Mind your thoughts and words now,” Fin told them, “for I have to let him in, let him see enough to make him believe we go to honor Sorcha and try to raise her.”

With a nod Branna crouched to press her head to Kathel’s, then she mounted. And with the others, she flew through the dark heart of the night.

"Can we be sure we're cloaked?" she called to Fin.

"I've never done so wide a mist, but it's covered all, hasn't it? And what would Cabhan be doing watching us at this time of the night?"

Though Fin opened, blood calling to blood. As they flew through the trees, with the whisk of the wind rending small gaps in that cloak, he felt the stirring.

And told Branna with no more than a glance.

"It has to hold, give us time to block him out of the clearing, give us the time to pay our respects to Sorcha and work the spell to bring her spirit to us."

"I'd rather fight than try to converse with ghosts," Boyle muttered.

"She nearly defeated him," Iona pointed out. "She must know something that will help. We've tried everything. We have to try this. If it works . . ."

"It has to work," Meara put in. "It's driving me next to mad having him stalking us day by day."

"She's ours," Connor told her. "We'll reach her, and tonight, on the anniversary of her death, her sacrifice, her curse is our best hope for it."

"We can't wait another year." Branna brought Aine down as they flew through the vines, into the clearing. "We won't."

As agreed, Fin and the three went to the edges of the clearing, each taking a point of the compass. She would begin, with hopes that rather than holding Cabhan out, the ritual would give him time to slip through—and be closed in.

She lifted her arms, called to the north, poured the salt. Iona took the west. It was Connor, at the east, who whispered softly in Branna's head.

He's coming. Nearly here.

As her brother called on the east Branna's heart tripped.

The first step, luring him, had worked.

Fin called on the south, then all four walked the wide circle, salting the ground while Boyle and Meara set out the tools for the next part of the plan.

She felt the change, the lightest of chills as Cabhan's fog mixed with Fin's.

As they closed the barrier that would keep all out, keep all in, she prayed he wouldn't use the swirls and shadows to attack before they were ready.

Struggling not to rush, she lifted the roses, offered the bouquet to each so they could take a bloom. Fin hesitated.

"I can't see she'd want tribute from me, or accept it."

"You'll show her respect, and give her the tribute. She must understand you've fought and bled with us, and we can't defeat Cabhan without you. We have to try, Fin. Can you offer forgiveness to her for the mark you carry, with the tribute?"

"I have to try," was all he said.

Together, all six approached Sorcha's grave.

"We place upon your grave these pure white blooms to mark the anniversary of your doom. Bring wine and honey and bread, a tribute of life given to the dead."

It grew colder. Branna swore she could all but feel the rise of Cabhan's excitement, his greed. But she found no name in the undulating fog.

"These herbs we scatter on the ground to release your spirit from its bounds. With respect we kneel and make to you this appeal. Sealed with our blood, three and three, fire burn in through the night and meet our need most dire, grant us what we ask of thee."

One by one they scored their palms, let the blood drip onto the ground by the stone.

"In this place, at this hour, through your love and by our power, send to us your children three so all may meet their destiny."

A howl came through the fog, a sound of wild fury. Fin dropped the cloak as he drew his sword, leaped to his feet beside Branna and the others.

"Send them here and send them now," Branna shouted, and Fin

and Connor moved to block her from any attack. Iona, Boyle, and Meara worked quickly to cast a circle while she finished the ritual.

"Those with your powers you did endow. Three by three by three we fight." She shot out fire of her own to block Cabhan from pivoting into an attack as her friends hurried to cast the circle, and open a portal for the first three.

"Three by three by three we take the night. Mother, grant this boon, let them fly across the moon and set your spirit free. As we will, so mote it be."

The ground shook. She nearly lost her footing as she spun around to race toward the circle, glanced back quickly to see Cabhan hurl what looked like a wall of black fire toward Fin and Connor. Even as she reached for Iona's hand, to join what they had, the wind picked her up like a cold hand, threw her across the clearing.

Though she landed hard enough to rattle bones, she saw Fin battling back with flaming sword and heaving ground, Connor lashing the air like a whip. Light and dark clashed, and the sound was huge, like worlds toppling.

Meara charged forward, sword slashing, and Boyle released a volley of small fireballs that slashed and burned the snaking fog. With no choice but to attack, defend, it left Iona alone to complete the circle.

He's stronger, Branna realized, somehow stronger than he'd been on Samhain. Whatever was inside him had drawn on more, drawn out more. The last battle, she thought; they knew it, and so did Cabhan.

He called the rats so they vomited out of the ground. He called the bats, so they spilled like vengeance from the sky. And Iona, cut off, fought to hold them back as hawk, hound, horse trampled and tore.

Duty, loyalty. Love. Branna sprang to her feet, rushed through the boiling rats to leap onto Aine's back. And with a ball of fire in one hand, a shining wand in the other, flew toward her cousin and the incomplete circle.

She lashed out with fire, with light, carving a path. She called on her gift, brought down a hot rain to drown Cabhan's feral weapons. When she reached Iona, she released a torrent that drove all away from Sorcha's cabin.

"Finish it!" she shouted. "You can finish it."

Then came the snakes, boiling along the ground. She heard—felt—Kathel's pain as fangs tore at him. The fury that burst through her turned them to ash.

Branna wheeled her horse to guard Iona, but her cousin shouted, "I've got this! I've got it. Go help the others."

Fearing the worst, Branna charged through the wall of black fire.

It choked her, the stench of sulfur. She pulled rain, warm and pure, out of the air to wash it away. The fire snapped and sizzled as she fought her way through it.

They bled, her family, as they battled.

Once more she wheeled the horse, pulled her power up, up, up.

Now the rain, and the wind, now the quake and the fire. Now all at once in a maelstrom that crashed against Cabhan's wrath. Smoke swirled, a sting to the eyes, a burn in the throat, but she saw fear, just one wild flicker of it, in the sorcerer's eyes before he hunched and became the wolf.

"It's done!" Iona called out. "It's done. The light. It's growing."

"I see them," Meara, her face wet with sweat and blood, shouted. "I can see them, the shadows of them. Go," she said to Connor. "Go."

"We'll hold him." Boyle punched out, fire and fist.

"By God we will. Go." Fin met Branna's eyes. "Or it's for nothing."

No choice, she thought, holding out a hand for Connor so he could grip it, swing onto Aine with her.

"She's hurt. Meara's hurt."

"We have to pull them through, Connor. It's the three who bring the three. Without them, we may not be able to heal her."

Kathel, she thought, bleeding from the muzzle, from the flank,

Alastar slashing hooves in the air, hawks screaming as they dived with flashing talons.

And for nothing if they couldn't bring Sorcha's three fully into the now.

She rode straight into the circle, slid off the horse with her brother. She took Iona's hand, Connor's, and felt the power rise, felt the light burn.

"Three by three by three," she shouted. "This is magick's prophecy. Join with us no matter the cost, come through now or all is lost. Stand with us on this night and by our blood we finish this fight."

They came, Sorcha's three. Brannaugh with bow, Eamon with sword, Teagan with wand and great with child. Without a word they joined hands, so three became six.

Light exploded, all white, all brilliance. The heat of power poured into her, staggering, breathless, beyond any she'd known.

"Draw him away from them!" Branna heard her voice echo over the shaking air. "We have what will take him down, but they're too close."

"For me." Sorcha's Brannaugh held out the hand joined with her brother's. Arrows flew from her quill, flame white, to strike the ground between the wolf and the remaining three.

Crazed, the wolf turned, charged.

Branna broke the link; Connor closed it behind her.

"Hurry," he told her.

"A bit closer yet, just a bit." But she reached in the pouch, drew out the poison. The bottle throbbed in her hand, like a living thing. As the wolf leaped toward the circle, she sent the bottle flying.

Its screams rent the air, slammed her so she staggered back. All he'd called from the bowels of the dark flamed, and their screams joined the wolf's.

"It's not done." Iona gripped Teagan's hand. "Until we kill what lives in him, it can't be done."

"The name." Branna staggered, but Eamon caught her before she fell. "The demon's name. Do you know it?"

"No. We'll burn what's left of him, salt the ground."

"It's not enough. We must have its name. Fin!"

Even as she started forward, he waved her off, dropped to the ground with the bloody body of the wolf. "Start the ritual."

"You're bleeding—and Meara, Boyle. You'll be stronger if we take time to heal you."

"Start the ritual," he said between his teeth as he closed his hands around the wolf's throat. "That's for you. This is for me."

"Start it." Meara sprawled to the ground with Boyle. "And finish it."

So they rang the bell, opened the book, lit the candle.

And began the words.

Blood in the cauldron, of the light, of the dark. Shadows shifting like dancers.

On the ground, Fin dug his fingers into the torn ruff of the wolf.

"I know you," he murmured, staring into the red eyes. "You're mine, but I'm not yours." He tore the stone away, held it high. "And will never be. I am of Daithi." The brooch fell out of Fin's shirt, and the wolf's eyes wheeled in terror. "And I am your death. I know you. I have stood at your altar, and heard the damned call your name. I know you."

What was in the wolf pushed its dark until Fin's hands burned, until his own blood ran.

"In Sorcha's name I rebuke you. In Daithi's name, I rebuke you. In my name, I rebuke you, for I am Finbar Burke, and I know you."

When it came into him, it all but shattered his soul. The dark pulled, so strong, tore so deep. But he held on, held on, and looked toward Branna. Looked to her light.

"Its name is Cernunnos." He heaved the stone to Connor. "Cernunnos. Destroy it. Now. I can't hold much longer, much more. Get her clear." His breath heaved as he called to Boyle, "Get Meara clear."

"You have to let it go!" Tears streaming, Branna shouted, "Fin, let it go, come to us."

"I can't. He'll go into the earth, into the belly of it, and be lost to us again. I can hold him here, but not much longer. Do what must be done for all, for me. As you love me, Branna, free me. By all we are, free me."

To be sure of it, he threw out what he had so the stone ripped out of Connor's hand and into the cauldron. And as the light, blinding white, towered up, he called out the name himself.

"End it!"

"He suffers," Teagan murmured. "No more. Give him peace."

Sobbing, Branna called out the demon's name, and heaved the poison.

Blacker than black, thicker than tar. Through the whip of it rose wild, ululant cries; deep, throaty screams. And with it thousands of voices shrieking in tongues never heard.

She felt it, an instant before the light bloomed again, before the cauldron itself burned a pure white. The clearing, the sky, she thought the entire world flamed white.

She felt the stone crack, heard the destruction of it like great trees snapped by a giant's hand so the ground rocked like a stormy sea.

She felt the demon's death, and swore she felt her own.

It all drained out of her, breath, power, light, as she fell to her knees.

Blood and death follow, she thought. Blood and death.

Then she was up and running as she saw Fin, still, white, bloody, facedown on the blackened ash of what had been Cabhan, of what had birthed him.

"Hecate, Brighid, Morrigan, all the goddesses, show mercy. Don't take him." She pulled Fin's head into her lap. "Take what I am, take what I have, but don't take his life. I beg you, don't take his life."

She lifted her face to the sky still lit by white fire, threw her power to any who could hear. "Take what you will, what you must, but not his life."

Her tears ran warm, dropped onto his burned skin. "Sorcha," she prayed. "Mother. Right your wrong. Spare his life."

"Shh." Fin's fingers curled in hers. "I'm not gone. I'm here."

"You survived."

And the world righted again, the ground settled, the flames softened in the sky.

"How did you— I don't care. You survived." She pressed her lips to his face, to his hair. "Ah, God, you're bleeding, everywhere. Rest easy, easy, my love. Help me." She looked to Sorcha's Brannaugh. "Please."

"I will, of course. You're all she told me." She knelt down, laid hands on Fin's side where his shirt and flesh were rent and scorched. "He is my own Eoghan to the life."

"What?"

She squeezed Branna's hand. "His face is my own love's face, his heart, my own love's heart. He was never Cabhan's, not where it mattered." She looked down at Fin, and touched her lips to his brow. "You are mine as you are hers. Healing will hurt a bit."

"A bit," Fin said through gritted teeth as pain seared him.

"Look at me. Look into me," Branna crooned.

"I won't. You won't take this. It's mine. The others?"

"Being tended right now. Damn you to bloody hell, Finbar, for making me think I'd killed you. It's too much blood, and your shirt's still smoldering." She whipped it away with a flash of her hand. "Ah, God, some of these are deep. Connor!"

"I'm coming." Limping a little, Connor swiped bloodied sweat from his face. "Meara and Boyle are healing well, though Christ, she took a blow or two. Still . . . Well, Jesus, Fin, look at the mess you've made of yourself."

To solve things, he gripped Fin's head in his hands, and pushed his way into Fin's mind, and the pain.

"Ah fuck me," Connor hissed.

Minutes dragged on for centuries, even when the others joined them. Before it was done, both Connor and Fin were covered in sweat, breathless, quivering.

"He'll do." Teagan brushed a hand down Branna's arm. "You and my sister are very skilled healers. Some rest, some tonic, and he'll be fine."

"Yes, thank you. Thank you." Branna pressed her face into Connor's shoulder. "Thank you."

"He's mine as well."

"Ours," Eamon corrected. "We came home, and we had a part in destroying Cabhan. But he played the larger role in it. So you're ours, Finbar Burke, though you bear Cabhan's mark."

"No longer," Teagan murmured. "I put the mark on Cabhan, and our mother put it on his blood, all who followed. And I think now that she and the light have taken it. For this is not Cabhan's mark."

"What do you mean? It's—" Fin twisted to look, and on his shoulder, where he'd worn the mark of Cabhan since his eighteenth year, he now wore a Celtic trinity knot, the triquetra.

A sign of three.

It stunned him, more than the fire of the poison, more than the blinding flames of the white.

"It's gone." He touched his fingers to it, felt no pain, no dark, no stealthy pull. "I'm free of it. Free."

"You would have given your life. Your blood," Branna realized, as her eyes stung with pure joy. "Its death from your willing sacrifice. You broke the curse, Fin."

She laid her hand over his, over the sign of three. "You saved yourself and, I think, Sorcha's spirit. You saved us all."

"Some of us did a bit as well," Connor reminded her. But grinned at Fin. "It's a fine mark. I'm thinking the rest of us should get tattoos for matching."

"I like it," Meara declared, and swiped at tears.

"We've more than tattoos to think of." Boyle held down a hand.

"On your feet now." He gripped Fin's arms hard, then embraced him. "Welcome back."

"It's good to be here," he said as Iona just wrapped around him and wept a little. "But Christ, I'd like to be home. We need to finish altogether." He kissed the top of Iona's head. "We need to be done, and live."

"So we will." Eamon held out a hand, took Fin's in a strong grip. "When I get a son, he will carry your name, cousin."

They set the ashes on fire, more white flame, turned the earth, scattered them, salted all.

Then stood in the clearing, in peace.

"It's done. We're done with it." Sorcha's Brannaugh walked to her mother's grave. "And she's free. I'm sure of it."

"We honored her sacrifice, fulfilled our destiny. And I feel home calling." Eamon reached for Teagan's hand. "But I think we'll see you again, cousins."

Connor took the white stone out of his pocket, watched it glow. "I believe it."

"We're the three," Branna said, "as you are, and as they are." She gestured to Fin, Boyle, Meara. "We'll meet again. Bright blessings to you, cousins."

"And to you." Teagan looked over at their mother's grave as she started to fade. "She favored bluebells. Thank you."

"It's finished." Meara looked around the clearing. "I want to dance, and yet I'm shaky inside. What do we do now that it's finished?"

"Have a full fry. Dawn's breaking." Connor pointed east, and to a ribbon of soft pink light.

"We go home," Iona agreed, laughed when Boyle swung her around. "And we stay together for a while. Just together."

"We'll be along. I want a moment more. A moment more," Fin said to Branna.

"If you're much longer, I'll be making the eggs, and she'll be complaining." But Connor kissed Meara's hand, then mounted.

Iona cast one glance back, laid a hand to her heart, then swung it out toward Fin and Branna, forming a pretty little rainbow.

"She has the sweetest heart," Fin said quietly. "And now." He turned Branna toward him. "Here, where you first gave yourself to me. Here, where it all began, and where we've finally ended it, I have a question to ask."

"Haven't I answered them all?"

"Not this one. Will you, Branna, have the life with me we once dreamed? The life, the family, the all of it, we once imagined?"

"Oh, I will, Fin. I'll have all of it, and more. I'll have all the new dreams we make. And the new promises."

She stepped into his arms. "I love you. I have always, I will always. I'll live with you in your fine house, and we'll have all the children we want, and none of them to bear a mark. I'll travel with you, have you show me some of the world."

"We'll make magick."

"Today and always."

She kissed him by Sorcha's cabin where the wall of vines had fallen away, where bluebells bloomed and a little rainbow lingered on the air.

Then they flew, with horse, hound, hawk, into tomorrow.

Keep reading for an excerpt from

THE COLLECTOR

by Nora Roberts

Now available from G. P. Putnam's Sons

SHE THOUGHT THEY'D NEVER LEAVE. CLIENTS, ESPECIALLY new ones, tended to fuss and delay, revolving on the same loop of instructions, contacts, comments before finally heading out the door. She sympathized because when they walked out the door they left their home, their belongings, and in this case their cat, in someone else's hands.

As their house sitter, Lila Emerson did everything she could to send them off relaxed, and confident those hands were competent ones.

For the next three weeks, while Jason and Macey Kilderbrand enjoyed the south of France with friends and family, Lila would live in their most excellent apartment in Chelsea, water their plants, feed, water and play with their cat, collect their mail—and forward anything of import.

She'd tend Macey's pretty terrace garden, pamper the cat, take messages and act as a burglary deterrent simply by her presence.

While she did, she'd enjoy living in New York's tony London Terrace just as she'd enjoyed living in the charming flat in Rome—where for an additional fee she'd painted the kitchen—and the sprawling house in Brooklyn—with its frisky golden retriever, sweet and aging Boston terrier and aquarium of colorful tropical fish.

She'd seen a lot of New York in her six years as a professional house sitter, and in the last four had expanded to see quite a bit of the world as well.

Nice work if you can get it, she thought—and she could get it.

"Come on, Thomas." She gave the cat's long, sleek body one head-to-tail stroke. "Let's go unpack."

She liked the settling in, and since the spacious apartment boasted a second bedroom, unpacked the first of her two suitcases, tucking her clothes in the mirrored bureau or hanging them in the tidy walk-in closet. She'd been warned Thomas would likely insist on sharing the bed with her, and she'd deal with that. And she appreciated that the clients—likely Macey—had arranged a pretty bouquet of freesia on the nightstand.

Lila was big on little personal touches, the giving and the getting.

She'd already decided to make use of the master bath with its roomy steam shower and deep jet tub.

"Never waste or abuse the amenities," she told Thomas as she put her toiletries away.

As the two suitcases held nearly everything she owned, she took some care in distributing them where it suited her best.

After some consideration she set up her office in the dining area, arranging her laptop so she could look up and out at the view of New York. In a smaller space she'd have happily worked where she slept, but since she had room, she'd make use of it.

She'd been given instructions on all the kitchen appliances, the remotes, the security system—the place boasted an array of gadgets that appealed to her nerdy soul.

In the kitchen she found a bottle of wine, a pretty bowl of fresh fruit, an array of fancy cheeses with a note handwritten on Macey's monogrammed stationery.

Enjoy our home!

—Jason, Macey and Thomas

Sweet, Lila thought, and she absolutely would enjoy it.

She opened the wine, poured a glass, sipped and approved. Grabbing her binoculars, she carried the glass out on the terrace to admire the view.

The clients made good use of the space, she thought, with a couple of cushy chairs, a rough stone bench, a glass table—and the pots of thriving flowers, the pretty drops of cherry tomatoes, the fragrant herbs, all of which she'd been encouraged to harvest and use.

She sat, with Thomas in her lap, sipping wine, stroking his silky fur.

"I bet they sit out here a lot, having a drink, or coffee. They look happy together. And their place has a good feel to it. You can tell." She tickled Thomas under the chin and had his bright green eyes going dreamy. "She's going to call and e-mail a lot in the first couple days, so we're going to take some pictures of you, baby, and send them to her so she can see you're just fine."

Setting the wine aside, she lifted the binoculars, scanned the buildings. The apartment complex hugged an entire city block, and that offered little glimpses into other lives.

Other lives just fascinated her.

A woman about her age wore a little black dress that fit her tall, model-thin body like a second skin. She paced as she talked on her cell phone. She didn't look happy, Lila thought. Broken date. He has to work late—he says, Lila added, winding the plot in her head. She's fed up with that.

A couple floors above, two couples sat in a living room—art-covered walls, sleek, contemporary furnishings—and laughed over what looked like martinis.

Obviously they didn't like the summer heat as much as she and Thomas or they'd have sat outside on their little terrace.

Old friends, she decided, who get together often, sometimes take vacations together.

Another window opened the world to a little boy rolling around on the floor with a white puppy. The absolute joy of both zinged right through the air and had Lila laughing.

"He's wanted a puppy forever—forever being probably a few months at that age—and today his parents surprised him. He'll remember today his whole life, and one day he'll surprise his little boy or girl the same way."

Pleased to end on that note, Lila lowered the glasses. "Okay, Thomas, we're going to get a couple hours of work in. I know, I know," she continued, setting him down, picking up the half glass of wine. "Most people are done with work for the day. They're going out to dinner, meeting friends—or in the case of the killer blonde in the black dress, bitching about not going out. But the thing is . . ." She waited until he strolled into the apartment ahead of her. "I set my own hours. It's one of the perks."

She chose a ball—motion-activated—from the basket of cat toys in the kitchen closet, gave it a roll across the floor.

Thomas immediately pounced, wrestled, batted, chased.

"If I were a cat," she speculated, "I'd go crazy for that, too."

With Thomas happily occupied, she picked up the remote, ordered music. She made a note of which station played so she could be sure she returned it to their house music before the Kilderbrands came home. She moved away from the jazz to contemporary pop.

House-sitting provided lodging, interest, even adventure. But writing paid the freight. Freelance writing—and waiting tables—had kept her head just above water her first two years in New York. After she'd fallen into house-sitting, initially doing favors for friends, and friends of friends, she'd had the real time and opportunity to work on her novel.

Then the luck or serendipity of house-sitting for an editor who'd taken an interest. Her first, *Moon Rise*, had sold decently. No bust-out bestseller, but steady, and with a nice little following in the fourteen-to-eighteen set she'd aimed for. The second would hit the stores in October, so her fingers were crossed.

But more to the moment, she needed to focus on book three of the series.

She bundled up her long brown hair with a quick twist, scoop and the clamp of a chunky tortoiseshell hinge clip. While Thomas gleefully chased the ball, she settled in with her half glass of wine, a tall glass of iced water and the music she imagined her central character, Kaylee, listened to.

As a junior in high school, Kaylee dealt with all the ups and downs—the romance, the homework, the mean girls, the bullies, the politics, the heartbreaks and triumphs that crowded into the short, intense high school years.

A sticky road, especially for the new girl—as she'd been in the first book. And more, of course, as Kaylee's family were lycans.

It wasn't easy to finish a school assignment or go to the prom with a full moon rising when a girl was a werewolf.

Now, in book three, Kaylee and her family were at war with a rival pack, a pack that preyed on humans. Maybe a little bloodthirsty for some of the younger readers, she thought, but this was where the path of the story led. Where it had to go.

She picked it up where Kaylee dealt with the betrayal of the boy she thought she loved, an overdue assignment on the Napoleonic Wars and the fact that her beautiful blond nemesis had locked her in the science lab.

The moon would rise in twenty minutes—just about the same time the Science Club would arrive for their meeting.

She had to find a way out before the change.

Lila dived in, happily sliding into Kaylee, into the fear of exposure, the pain of a broken heart, the fury with the cheerleading, homecoming queening, man-eating (literally) Sasha.

By the time she'd gotten Kaylee out, and in the nick, courtesy of a smoke bomb that brought the vice principal—another thorn in Kaylee's side—dealt with the lecture, the detention, the streaking home as the change came on her heroine, Lila had put in three solid hours.

Pleased with herself, she surfaced from the story, glanced around.

Thomas, exhausted from play, lay curled on the chair beside her, and the lights of the city glittered and gleamed out the window.

She fixed Thomas's dinner precisely as instructed. While he ate she got her Leatherman, used the screwdriver of the multi-tool to tighten some screws in the pantry.

Loose screws, to her thinking, were a gateway to disaster. In people and in things.

She noticed a couple of wire baskets on runners, still in their boxes. Probably for potatoes or onions. Crouching, she read the description, the assurance of easy install. She made a mental note to e-mail Macey, ask if she wanted them put in.

It would be a quick, satisfying little project.

She poured a second glass of wine and made a late dinner out of the fruit, cheese and crackers. Sitting cross-legged in the dining room, Thomas in her lap, she ate while she checked e-mail, sent e-mail, scanned her blog—made a note for a new entry.

"Getting on to bedtime, Thomas."

He just yawned when she picked up the remote to shut off the music, then lifted him up and away so she could deal with her dishes and bask in the quiet of her first night in a new space.

After changing into cotton pants and a tank, she checked the security, then revisited her neighbors through the binoculars.

It looked like Blondie had gone out after all, leaving the living room light on low. The pair of couples had gone out as well. Maybe to dinner, or a show, Lila thought.

The little boy would be fast asleep, hopefully with the puppy curled up with him. She could see the shimmer of a television, imagined Mom and Dad relaxing together.

Another window showed a party going on. A crowd of people—

well-dressed, cocktail attire—mixed and mingled, drinks or small plates in hand.

She watched for a while, imagined conversations, including a whispered one between the brunette in the short red dress and the bronzed god in the pearl gray suit who, in Lila's imagination, were having a hot affair under the noses of his long-suffering wife and her clueless husband.

She scanned over, stopped, lowered the glasses a moment, then looked again.

No, the really built guy on the . . . twelfth floor wasn't completely naked. He wore a thong as he did an impressive bump and grind, a spin, drop.

He was working up a nice sweat, she noted, as he repeated moves or added to them.

Obviously an actor/dancer moonlighting as a stripper until he caught his big Broadway break.

She enjoyed him. A lot.

The window show kept her entertained for a half hour before she made herself a nest in the bed—and was indeed joined by Thomas. She switched on the TV for company, settled on an *NCIS* rerun where she could literally recite the dialogue before the characters. Comforted by that, she picked up her iPad, found the thriller she'd started on the plane from Rome, and snuggled in.

OVER THE NEXT WEEK, SHE DEVELOPED A ROUTINE. THOMAS would wake her more accurately than any alarm clock at seven precisely when he begged, vocally, for his breakfast.

She'd feed the cat, make coffee, water the plants indoors and out, have a little breakfast while she visited the neighbors.

Blondie and her live-in lover—they didn't have the married vibe—argued a lot. Blondie tended to throw breakables. Mr. Slick, and he was great to look at, had good reflexes, and a whole basket of charm. Fights, pretty much daily, ended in seduction or wild bursts of passion.

They suited each other, in her estimation. For the moment. Neither of them struck Lila as long-haul people with her throwing dishes or articles of clothing, him ducking, smiling and seducing.

Game players, she thought. Hot, sexy game players, and if he didn't have something going on, on the side, she'd be very surprised.

The little boy and the puppy continued their love affair, with Mom, Dad or nanny patiently cleaning up little accidents. Mom and Dad left together most mornings, garbed in a way that said high-powered careers to Lila.

The Martinis, as she thought of them, rarely used their little terrace. She was definitely one of the ladies-who-lunch, leaving the apartment every day, late morning, returning late afternoon usually with a shopping bag.

The Partiers rarely spent an evening at home, seemed to revel in a frantic sort of lifestyle.

And the Body practiced his bump and grind regularly—to her unabashed pleasure.

She treated herself to the show, and the stories she created every morning. She'd work into the afternoon, break to amuse the cat before she dressed and went out to buy what she thought she might like for dinner, to see the neighborhood.

She sent pictures of a happy Thomas to her clients, picked tomatoes, sorted mail, composed a vicious lycan battle, updated her blog. And installed the two baskets in the pantry.

On the first day of week two, she bought a good bottle of Barolo, filled in the fancy cheese selections, added some mini cupcakes from an amazing neighborhood bakery.

Just after seven in the evening, she opened the door to the party pack that was her closest friend.

"There you are." Julie, wine bottle in one hand, a fragrant bouquet of star lilies in the other, still managed to enfold her.

Six feet of curves and tumbled red hair, Julie Bryant struck the opposite end of Lila's average height, slim build, straight brown hair.

"You brought a tan back from Rome. God, I'd be wearing 500 SPF and still end up going lobster in the Italian sun. You look just great."

"Who wouldn't after two weeks in Rome? The pasta alone. I told you I'd get the wine," Lila added when Julie shoved the bottle into her hand.

"Now we have two. And welcome home."

"Thanks." Lila took the flowers.

"Wow, some place. It's huge, and the view's a killer. What do these people do?"

"Start with family money."

"Oh, don't I wish I had."

"Let's detour to the kitchen so I can fix the flowers, then I'll give you a tour. He works in finance, and I don't understand any of it. He loves his work and prefers tennis to golf. She does some interior design, and you can see she's good at it from the way the apartment looks. She's thinking about going pro, but they're talking about starting a family, so she's not sure it's the right time to start her own business."

"They're new clients, right? And they still tell you that kind of personal detail?"

"What can I say? I have a face that says tell me all about it. Say hello to Thomas."

Julie crouched to greet the cat. "What a handsome face he has."

"He's a sweetheart." Lila's deep brown eyes went soft as Julie and Thomas made friends. "Pets aren't always a plus on the jobs, but Thomas is."

She selected a motorized mouse out of Thomas's toy basket, enjoyed Julie's easy laugh as the cat pounced.

"Oh, he's a killer." Straightening, Julie leaned back on the stone-gray counter while Lila fussed the lilies into a clear glass vase.

"Rome was fabulous?"

"It really was."

"And did you find a gorgeous Italian to have mad sex with?"

"Sadly no, but I think the proprietor of the local market fell for me. He was about eighty, give or take. He called me *una bella donna* and gave me the most beautiful peaches."

"Not as good as sex, but something. I can't believe I missed you when you got back."

"I appreciate the overnight at your place between jobs."

"Anytime, you know that. I only wish I'd been there."

"How was the wedding?"

"I definitely need wine before I get started on Cousin Melly's Hamptons Wedding Week From Hell, and why I've officially retired as a bridesmaid."

"Your texts were fun for me. I especially liked the one . . . 'Crazy Bride Bitch says rose petals wrong shade of pink. Hysteria ensues. Must destroy CBB for the good of womankind.'"

"It almost came to that. Oh no! Sobs, tremors, despair. 'The petals are pink-pink! They have to be rose-pink. Julie! Fix it, Julie!' I came close to fixing her."

"Did she really have a half-ton truckload of petals?"

"Just about."

"You should have buried her in them. Bride smothered by rose petals. Everyone would think it was an ironic, if tragic, mishap."

"If only I'd thought of it. I really missed you. I like it better when you're working in New York, and I can come see your digs and hang out with you."

Lila studied her friend as she opened the wine. "You should come with me sometime—when it's someplace fabulous."

"I know, you keep saying." Julie wandered as she spoke. "I'm just not sure I wouldn't feel weird, actually staying in— Oh my God, look at this china. It has to be antique, and just amazing."

"Her great-grandmother's. And you don't feel weird coming over and spending an evening with me wherever, you wouldn't feel weird staying. You stay in hotels."

"People don't live there."

"Some people do. Eloise and Nanny did."

Julie gave Lila's long tail of hair a tug. "Eloise and Nanny are fictional."

"Fictional people are people, too, otherwise why would we care what happens to them? Here, let's have this on the little terrace. Wait until you see Macey's container garden. Her family started in France—vineyards."

Lila scooped up the tray with the ease of the waitress she'd once been. "They met five years ago when she was over there visiting her grandparents—like they are now—and he was on vacation and came to their winery. Love at first sight, they both claim."

"It's the best. First sight."

"I'd say fictional, but I just made a case for fictional." She led the way to the terrace. "Turned out they both lived in New York. He called her, they went out. And were exchanging 'I dos' about eighteen months later."

"Like a fairy tale."

"Which I'd also say fictional, except I love fairy tales. And they look really happy together. And as you'll see, she's got a seriously green thumb."

Julie tapped the binoculars as they started out. "Still spying?"

Lila's wide, top-heavy mouth moved into a pout. "It's not spying. It's observing. If people don't want you looking in, they should close the curtains, pull down the shades."

"Uh-huh. Wow." Julie set her hands on her hips as she scanned the terrace. "You're right about the green thumb."

Everything lush and colorful and thriving in simple terra-cotta pots made the urban space a creative oasis. "She's growing tomatoes?"

"They're wonderful, and the herbs? She started them from seeds."

"Can you do that?"

"Macey can. I—as they told me I could and should—harvested

some. I had a big, beautiful salad for dinner last night. Ate it out here, with a glass of wine, and watched the window show."

"You have the oddest life. Tell me about the window people."

Lila poured wine, then reached inside for the binoculars—just in case.

"We have the family on the tenth floor—they just got the little boy a puppy. The kid and the pup are both incredibly pretty and adorable. It's true love, and fun to watch. There's a sexy blonde on fourteen who lives with a very hot guy—both could be models. He comes and goes, and they have very intense conversations, bitter arguments with flying crockery, followed by major sex."

"You watch them have sex? Lila, give me those binoculars."

"No!" Laughing, Lila shook her head. "I don't watch them have sex. But I can tell that's what's going on. They talk, fight, pace around with lots of arm waving from her, then grab each other and start pulling off clothes. In the bedroom, in the living room. They don't have a terrace like this, but that little balcony deal off the bedroom. They barely made it back in once before they were both naked.

"And speaking of naked, there's a guy on twelve. Wait, maybe he's around."

Now she did get the glasses, checked. "Oh yeah, baby. Check this out. Twelfth floor, three windows from the left."

Curious enough, Julie took the binoculars, finally found the window. "Oh my. Mmmm, mmmm. He does have some moves. We should call him, invite him over."

"I don't think we're his type."

"Between us we're every man's type."

"Gay, Julie."

"You can't tell from here." Julie lowered the glasses, frowned, then lifted them again for another look. "Your gaydar can't leap over buildings in a single bound like Superman."

"He's wearing a thong. Enough said."

"It's for ease of movement."

"Thong," Lila repeated.

"Does he dance nightly?"

"Pretty much. I figure he's a struggling actor, working part-time in a strip club until he gets his break."

"He's got a great body. David had a great body."

"Had?"

Julie set down the glasses, mimed breaking a twig in half.

"When?"

"Right after the Hamptons Wedding Week From Hell. It had to be done, but I didn't want to do it at the wedding, which was bad enough."

"Sorry, honey."

"Thanks, but you didn't like David anyway."

"I didn't not like him."

"Amounts to the same. And though he was so nice to look at, he'd just gotten too clingy. Where are you going, how long will you be, blah blah. Always texting me, or leaving messages on my machine. If I had work stuff, or made plans with you and other friends, he'd get upset or sulky. God, it was like having a wife—in the worst way. No dis meant to wives, as I used to be one. I'd only been seeing him for a couple months, and he was pushing to move in. I don't want a live-in."

"You don't want the wrong live-in," Lila corrected.

"I'm not ready for the right live-in yet. It's too soon after Maxim."

"It's been five years."

Julie shook her head, patted Lila's hand. "Too soon. Cheating bastard still pisses me off. I have to get that down to mild amusement, I think. I hate breakups," she added. "They either make you feel sad—you've been dumped; or mean—you've done the dumping."

"I don't think I've ever dumped anyone, but I'll take your word."

"That's because you make them think it's their idea—plus you really don't let it get serious enough to earn the term 'dump.'"

Lila just smiled. "It's too soon after Maxim," she said, and made

Julie laugh. "We can order in. There's a Greek place the clients recommended. I haven't tried it yet."

"As long as there's baklava for after."

"I have cupcakes."

"Even better. I now have it all. Swank apartment, good wine, Greek food coming, my best pal. And a sexy . . . oh, and sweaty," she added as she lifted the glasses again. "Sexy, sweating dancing man—sexual orientation not confirmed."

"Gay," Lila repeated, and rose to get the takeout menu.

THEY POLISHED OFF MOST OF THE WINE WITH LAMB KABOBS—then dug into the cupcakes around midnight. Maybe not the best combination, Lila decided, considering her mildly queasy stomach, but just the right thing for a friend who was more upset about a breakup than she admitted.

Not the guy, Lila thought as she did the rounds to check security, but the act itself, and all the questions that dogged the mind and heart after it was done.

Is it me? Why couldn't I make it work? Who will I have dinner with?

When you lived in a culture of couples, it could make you feel less when you were flying solo.

"I don't," Lila assured the cat, who'd curled up in his own little bed sometime between the last kabob and the first cupcake. "I'm okay being single. It means I can go where I want, when I want, take any job that works for me. I'm seeing the world, Thomas, and okay, talking to cats, but I'm okay with that, too."

Still, she wished she'd been able to talk Julie into staying over. Not just for the company, but to help deal with the hangover her friend was bound to have come morning.

Mini cupcakes were Satan, she decided as she readied for bed. So cute and tiny, oh, they're like eating nothing, that's what you tell yourself, until you've eaten half a dozen.

Now she was wired up on alcohol and sugar, and she'd never get to sleep.

She picked up the binoculars. Still some lights on, she noted. She wasn't the only one still up at . . . Jesus, one forty in the morning.

Sweaty Naked Guy was still up, and in the company of an equally hot-looking guy. Smug, Lila made a mental note to tell Julie her gaydar was like Superman.

Party couple hadn't made it to bed yet; in fact it looked as though they'd just gotten in. Another swank deal from their attire. Lila admired the woman's shimmery orange dress, and wished she could see the shoes. Then was rewarded when the woman reached down, balancing a hand on the man's shoulder, and removed one strappy, sky-high gold sandal with a red sole.

Mmm, Louboutins.

Lila scanned down.

Blondie hadn't turned in yet either. She wore black again—snug and short—with her hair tumbling out of an updo. Been out on the town, Lila speculated, and it didn't go very well.

She's crying, Lila realized, catching the way the woman swiped at her face as she spoke. Talking fast. Urgently. Big fight with the boyfriend.

And where is he?

But even changing angles she couldn't bring him into view.

Dump him, Lila advised. Nobody should be allowed to make you so unhappy. You're gorgeous, and I bet you're smart, and certainly worth more than—

Lila jerked as the woman's head snapped back from a blow.

"Oh my God. He hit her. You bastard. Don't—"

She cried out herself as the woman tried to cover her face, cringed back as she was struck again.

And the woman wept, begged.

Lila made one leap to the bedside table and her phone, grabbed it, leaped back.

She couldn't see him, just couldn't see him in the dim light, but now the woman was plastered back against the window.

"That's enough, that's enough," Lila murmured, preparing to call 911.

Then everything froze.

The glass shattered. The woman exploded out. Arms spread wide, legs kicking, hair flying like golden wings, she dropped fourteen stories to the brutal sidewalk.

"Oh God, God, God." Shaking, Lila fumbled with the phone.

"Nine-one-one, what is your emergency?"

"He pushed her. He pushed her, and she fell out the window."

"Ma'am—"

"Wait. Wait." She closed her eyes a moment, forced herself to breathe in and out three times. Be clear, she ordered herself, give the details.

"This is Lila Emerson. I just witnessed a murder. A woman was pushed out a fourteenth-story window. I'm staying at . . ." It took her a moment to remember before she came to the Kilderbrands' address. "It's the building across from me. Ah, to the, to the west of me. I think. I'm sorry, I can't think. She's dead. She has to be dead."

"I'm dispatching a unit now. Will you hold the line?"

"Yes. Yes. I'll stay here."

Shuddering, she looked out again, but now the room beyond the broken window was dark.

#1 *NEW YORK TIMES* BESTSELLING AUTHOR

NORA ROBERTS

"You can't bottle wish fulfillment, but Ms. Roberts certainly knows how to put it on the page."

—The New York Times

ABOUT THE AUTHOR

Nora Roberts is the #1 *New York Times* bestselling author of more than two hundred novels. She is also the author of the bestselling In Death series written under the pen name J. D. Robb. There are more than five hundred million copies of her books in print.

CONNECT ONLINE

NoraRoberts.com

NoraRoberts